LITTLE WOMEN

LOUISA MAY ALCOTT

LITTLE WOMEN

AN ANNOTATED EDITION

EDITED BY *Daniel Shealy*

THE BELKNAP PRESS OF HARVARD UNIVERSITY PRESS

Cambridge, Massachusetts, and London, England   2013

DESIGN BY ANNAMARIE MCMAHON WHY

Frontispiece: Laurie spies on the Busy Bee Society. Clara M. Burd, *Little Women,* 1926.

Library of Congress Cataloging-in-Publication Data

Alcott, Louisa May, 1832-1888.

    Little women : an annotated edition / Louisa May Alcott ; edited by Daniel Shealy.

       p. cm.

    Includes bibliographical references.

    ISBN 978-0-674-05971-9 (alk. paper)

    1. March family (Fictitious characters)—Fiction.   2. Mothers and daughters—Fiction.   3. Young women—Fiction.   4. Sisters—Fiction.   5. New England—Fiction.   6. Domestic fiction.   7. Autobiographical fiction.   8. Bildungsromans.   I. Shealy, Daniel.   II. Title.

    PS1017.L5 2012b

    813′.4—dc23   2012036745

FOR MY CHILDREN,
LUKE SHEALY
AND
HANNAH SHEALY

Contents

Advertisement for the two-volume set of *Little Women* (1870).

Advertisement for *Little Women: Illustrated* (1880), with drawings by Frank Merrill. This was the first time the two parts of the novel were brought together in one volume.

Note on the Text

The textual history of *Little Women* provides valuable insight into the publishing world in the second half of the nineteenth century. Roberts Brothers, a Boston publisher, issued *Little Women or, Meg, Jo, Beth and Amy* in October 1868. The success of the novel motivated the composition of Part II, which Alcott's publisher brought out in April 1869. The sequel was also successful. Both volumes went through subsequent printings until 1870, when Roberts Brothers re-issued the books as a two-volume set. Over the next ten years, this *Little Women* two-volume set was reprinted several times. These various reprintings corrected obvious typographical, spelling, grammatical, and punctuation errors.

Finally, in 1880, with an eye toward Christmas sales, the publisher repackaged the books in a one-volume edition containing almost two hundred illustrations by Frank T. Merrill. In 1881, Roberts Brothers then re-issued the one-volume edition with only four illustrations. This edition, often referred to as the regular edition, went through a number of reprintings by Roberts Brothers and then Little, Brown and Company, which purchased Roberts Brothers in 1898. It is the text of this edition that was widely circulated throughout the twentieth century when the novel went out of copyright.

The 1880–1881 edition of *Little Women* greatly altered Alcott's writing. Roberts Brothers modernized punctuation and spelling, but most significantly, the publishing house attempted to "correct" Alcott's language, especially her use of slang. For example, the editors changed *ain't* to a proper contraction, *guess* to *think* or *fancy*, *pa* to *papa or father*, *ma* to *mamma* or *mother*, *grub* and *peg* to *work*, *lots* to *many*, *plenty*, *quantities*, or *heaps*. They also often substituted *won't* for *don't* and insisted on subject-verb agreement, especially wherever *don't* was used as a singular verb. Although these changes are important, I have not noted them in the Textual Variants, as they are too numerous. Alcott's involvement in these revisions remains unknown; however, the unpublished correspondence between the author and her editor at Roberts Brothers, Thomas Niles, suggests that she had little or no input, since she makes no reference to any changes. Alcott was otherwise actively engaged in the production of the new *Little Women*. For example, she offered comments on Merrill's illustrations, commending his work. But by 1880, Alcott's health was in decline. Perhaps a dwindling reserve of energy would have been used only for new writing projects. Other, more personal considerations may also have interfered with any plans to attend to revisions of her novel. In late December 1879, Alcott's sister May Alcott Neiriker had died in France soon after giving birth to a daughter, Louisa May, whom she named for her literary sibling. As 1880 dawned, Alcott was grieving over the loss of her artistic sister while trying to complete *Jack and Jill*, which was being serialized in *St. Nicholas* before its publication as a book in October. The new year also saw her preparing for the arrival of her niece that fall, as it was May's wish that the child be brought up by Louisa in America.

Another possible explanation for Alcott's apparent lack of involvement in the new *Little Women* is that she simply didn't care. She did not regard *Little Women* as the "great book" she yet aspired to write. Given her involvement in the revision of her first novel, *Moods* (1864), just a few years later in January 1882, Alcott, who changed that novel's ending drastically and omitted entire scenes, seemed to hold that first book more dear to her heart. Of course, the revision of *Moods* was also her chance to redeem a book that had been altered at her publisher's demands. In any case, whatever the reason for her apparent lack of involvement, Roberts Brothers seems to have exercised a free hand.

Why did Roberts Brothers make these changes to *Little Women*? Alcott's reviewers, especially those for religious and school publications, had often criticized her grammar and slang, not only in *Little Women*, but also in other works such as *An Old-Fashioned Girl* (1870), as a poor example for young readers. The revisions, then, were a response to the novel's critics and an attempt to broaden its appeal. In addition, the publisher may have feared that Alcott's writing was already beginning to look old fashioned to a new generation of young readers. These commercial motivations do not explain away but sit alongside other, deeper, cultural and political forces at play in Roberts Brothers' decisions.

The last half of the nineteenth century saw dramatic shifts in American life. Industrialism spawned great wealth for a few as well as poverty for many others. After the Civil War, immigration increased, especially in the northeastern cities, creating new social problems in health care, employment, and education. *Little Women* itself demonstrates these issues in its portrayal of the Irish and German immigrants. Immigrants, of course, were also bringing their own languages to America, a fact that many of the social elite saw as a problem. By the time Alcott was writing *Little Women* in

1868–1869, a war over a proper American language was already brewing. Gavin Jones, in *Strange Talk: The Politics of Dialect Literature in Gilded Age America* (Berkeley: University of California Press, 1999), observes: "Debate over language in the Gilded Age was dominated by the concern that the meaning of national identity was culturally shifting, away from its familiar Anglo-Saxon traditions. American nervousness about the stability and correctness of spoken standards stemmed from the deep fear of linguistic contamination, the fear that subaltern forms were radiating upward, affecting the language of the elite" (p. 10). William Dwight Whitney, one of America's foremost linguists and first president of the American Philological Association (1869), as well as the editor of *The Century Dictionary and Cyclopedia* (1889–1891), argued in *Language and the Study of Language: Twelve Lectures on the Principles of Linguistic Science* (New York: Charles Scribner, 1867), the year before *Little Women*'s original publication, that the "tendency to slang, to colloquial inelegancies, and even vulgarities" was to be avoided as it was "the besetting sin against which we, as Americans, have especially to guard and struggle" (p. 151). With the rise of regional and local-color fiction, much of which used dialect to portray realism, Jones notes, "[L]iterature was part of a crucial cultural debate in which ideological attempts to forge an ideal America—a nation conceived in linguistic unity—were constantly undermined by new and strange ways of talking" (*Strange Talk,* p. 12). In altering Alcott's language, Roberts Brothers was ultimately making political decisions about what constituted appropriate language for children.

Little Women: An Annotated Edition reproduces the 1868–1869 texts since later changes made by Roberts Brothers clearly work against the spirit of the novel: the 1868–1869 texts reveal a writer attempting to capture the realistic speech and language of nineteenth-century American youth. After examining several printings of the first editions of Parts I and II of *Little Women*, along with those of the 1870 two-volume set, I collated them with the 1880–1881 editions. I have retained Alcott's original, sometimes variable spelling and punctuation, with the exception of obvious errors, committed either by the printer or by Alcott. Significant changes between the editions are indicated by superscript letters in the text of the novel and are recorded in Textual Variants at the end of the book, so curious readers may see for themselves what Roberts Brothers considered important and necessary improvements. For a more complete list of textual variants, I encourage readers to examine the excellent work of Anne K. Phillips and Gregory Eiselein, the editors of the Norton Critical Edition of *Little Women* (New York and London: W. W. Norton, 2004), pp. 381–408.

Abbreviations

Her Own Time. Daniel Shealy, ed. *Alcott in Her Own Time: A Biographical Chronicle of Her Life, Drawn from Recollections, Interviews, and Memoirs by Family, Friends, and Associates.* Iowa City: University of Iowa Press, 2005.

Journals. Louisa May Alcott. *The Journals of Louisa May Alcott.* Ed. Joel Myerson and Daniel Shealy, assoc. ed. Madeleine B. Stern. Boston: Little, Brown, 1989; Athens: University of Georgia Press, 1997.

Journals of BA. Bronson Alcott. *The Journals of Bronson Alcott.* Ed. Odell Shepard. Boston: Little, Brown, 1938.

The Lady's Guide. Emily Thornwell, *The Lady's Guide to Perfect Gentility, in Manners, Dress, and Conversation, in the Family, in Company, at the Piano Forte, the Table, in the Street, and in Gentlemen's Society.* New York: Derby and Jackson, 1857.

Letters of ABA. A. Bronson Alcott. *The Letters of A. Bronson Alcott.* Ed. Richard Herrnstadt. Ames: Iowa State University Press, 1969.

LMA. Louisa May Alcott

LW Abroad. Louisa May Alcott and May Alcott. *Little Women Abroad: The Alcott Sisters' Letters from Europe, 1870–1871.* Ed. Daniel Shealy. Athens: University of Georgia Press, 2008.

OED. Oxford English Dictionary, online third edition, 2003 (http://dictionary.oed.com).

Selected Letters. Louisa May Alcott. *The Selected Letters of Louisa May Alcott.* Ed. Joel Myerson and Daniel Shealy, assoc. ed. Madeleine B. Stern. Boston: Little, Brown, 1987; Athens: University of Georgia Press, 1995.

LITTLE WOMEN

Introduction

IN MAY 1868, when beginning *Little Women,* Louisa May Alcott wrote in her journal a now-famous passage: "Never liked girls or knew many, except my sisters; but our queer plays and experiences may prove interesting, though I doubt it." By the time proofs of the novel arrived in August, she felt differently: "It reads better than I expected. Not a bit sensational, but simple and true, for we really lived most of it, and if it succeeds that will be the reason of it."[1] Written during the advent of the golden age of children's literature, a period ushered in by Lewis Carroll's *Alice's Adventures in Wonderland* (1865) in England and Mary Mapes Dodge's *Hans Brinker; or, The Silver Skates* (1865) in America, *Little Women* was almost instantly cherished by its readers, who returned to its pages time and again, passing the novel on to their own children and grandchildren. What did Louisa May Alcott create that transformed this novel about an impoverished family into one of the classic imaginative works of children's literature? What is its everlasting appeal? Why is it still relevant today—almost 150 years after it was first published?

Little Women was written as a girls' book—Alcott and her editor, Thomas Niles, were clear about that—but its reading audience is not limited to young women. From its publication, boys were among Alcott's devoted readers; even the Rough Rider, Theodore Roosevelt, who was ten when *Little Women* was published, declared that he "worshipped" the novel.[2] After all, Jo March much prefers the company of boys to that of girls. In its depiction of four very different sisters growing up in mid-nineteenth-century New England, *Little Women* especially captured the imagination of its female readers around the world by depicting the universal struggles of adolescent girls learning to become young women. In 1868, children's literature had yet to explore the lives of older teens preparing for adulthood. Alcott, who was thirty-five when the book was written, understood this struggle all too well: how to cope with little when others had more, how to learn to adjust to the sleights of others, how to resist social snobbery, how to be satisfied with hand-me-downs. She successfully depicts this period when

Thomas Niles, LMA's editor at Roberts Brothers Publishers. Hoping to emulate the success of gender-targeted books like the Oliver Optic books for boys, Niles encouraged LMA to write a novel for girls.

emotions collide with societal expectations, when melodramas that adults might find trivial loom large, when the body itself is changing rapidly, when the end of childhood is fast approaching.

What makes *Little Women* a landmark book in children's literature is that Alcott realistically captures all of that teenage pathos and sentiment. As she herself noted, Meg, Jo, Beth, and Amy *were* real. Meg yearns for nicer clothes and wealthy society; Amy desires popularity, good looks, and admiration; Beth wishes for a voice and self-confidence; and Jo burns for fame and literary success. Their hopes and dreams are largely those shared by adolescents then and now. The Marches do indeed often behave like real sisters—ones who quarrel, snip, correct one another, and, at times, fight bitterly—but who eventually support and confide in one another. They commit wrongs—knowingly even—but eventually see their own shortcomings. Their language is lively and realistic, full of slang and ungrammatical sentences. Their mother, who allows them the opportunity for self-discovery and failure, remains their steadfast, loving guide. For many readers, the Marches are the family they never had or the family to which they wished to belong.

At the center of *Little Women* is Mrs. March, the sisters' beloved Marmee, who provides the girls with a moral guidepost. When she presents them with copies of the New Testament on Christmas morning, she is their moral instructress, emphasizing not religion but love and compassion for others. Mr. March, of course, also does the same from afar, as his letters encourage his daughters to fight their bosom enemies and become little women. Marmee remains a continual presence in the sisters' lives, even after Mr. March returns from the Civil War. *Little Women* appeared at the height of the nineteenth-century cult of true motherhood, when the mother was responsible for the moral and spiritual nurturance of her children. Marmee advises her girls on proper etiquette, on the value of work, on giving to others who are more needy than they, on overcoming their own personal flaws.

Alcott once called her children's works "moral pap for the young."[3] As Catharine R. Stimpson observes, "Pap may be soft or semi-liquid food. However pap is also a nip-

INTRODUCTION

LMA's bedroom at Orchard House today. Her writing desk is in the corner. It was in this room that she wrote *Little Women* in 1868.

ple, the fount of maternal nourishment."[4] Mrs. March counsels Meg about modesty, Jo about temper, Beth about shyness, and Amy about affectation. However, her maternal advice in *Little Women* is most remembered in her conversations about marriage with Jo and Meg. In the nineteenth century, marriage was important to a young woman, especially as opportunities for work and financial support were certainly limited, and, after the carnage of the Civil War, eligible females outnumbered prospective husbands. Alcott preferred that Jo remain unmarried, like herself, but she also knew the realities for women of her day. Eventually she has Jo marry Professor Bhaer, a man more like her than Laurie was. However, the adolescent Jo, in Chapter 20 of Part I, confesses to her mother: "'Mercy me! I don't know anything about love, and such nonsense.'" Her simple comment betrays her innocence, confusion, and fear. But Mrs. March guides Jo and, in turn, the reader, when she declares that she would rather her daughters marry a man who possesses "love and virtue" than a man with money.

Louisa May Alcott, circa 1870, by E. L. Allen of
Boston.

Readers in the nineteenth and twentieth centuries, both children and parents, found in the novel a moral sustenance, a guide for how to live their own lives. The novel's morality remains more common sense than religious, and readers today can still find relevance in these same virtues of love, honesty, patience, duty, self-worth, charity, and compassion.

Another reason for the endurance of *Little Women* remains its afterglow of nostalgia. With the Civil War ended, readers reveled in the remembrance of a more simple time when family would gather around the hearth at day's end, content in the haven of their own home. Life in New England was relived and reimagined, from the lithographs of Currier and Ives to John Greenleaf Whittier's poem *Snow-Bound* (1866). In *Little Women,* readers experience life in a close-knit family of four sisters and their mother, set in a past that was quickly disappearing, even for Alcott's contemporary readers, as the Industrial Revolution took firm hold. Alcott, in a way, doubles the nostalgia as she looks back upon her own childhood. Even Louisa herself claimed that her "Concord days were the happiest of my life."[5] Here in *Little Women,* we see the simple joys of young people's creative entertainment, which is encouraged by adults: the sisters' play on Christmas Day, their family newspaper and Pickwick Club, the bird-house post office, croquet, cricket, ice skating, boating, picnicking, storytelling. It's as if Alcott is reminding readers: "Remember, childhood is fun!"

Perhaps the most important fact is that this nostalgic look at New England revolves around family. In the nineteenth century, family stood at the center of American civilization. Through the family, especially the examples of parents, children received nurture from the secure environment of home life. A forerunner emphasizing the importance of family was Horace Bushnell, a Massachusetts theologian, one whom Louisa's father, Bronson Alcott, had read. In one of his most famous works, *Christian Nurture* (1847), Bushnell observes how important family is to the development of children: "[The child] is not as yet a complete individual; he has only powers and capacities that prepare him to be, when they are unfolded. . . . Meantime, he is open to *impressions* from every thing he sees. His character is forming, under a principle, not of choice, but of nurture. The spirit of the house is breathed into his nature, day by day. The anger and gentleness, the fretfulness and patience—the appetites, passions,

"Louise Alcott"
The Children's Friend.

Lizbeth B. Comins

and manners—all the variant moods of feeling exhibited round him, pass into him as impressions, and become seeds of character in him. . . . The spirit of the house is in the members by nurture, not by teaching, not by any attempt to communicate the same, but because it is the air the children breathe."[6] Little has changed. A nurturing family, though not always the conventional one conceived by Alcott, remains at the heart of American life. In *Little Women,* seldom are enjoyable activities performed alone. From the bedtime chorus, accompanied by Beth's piano, at the end of Chapter 1 to the harvesting of apples at the conclusion of the novel, the happiness of family is celebrated. Sadness, even death, intrudes, but family prevails. In Part I, Jo bemoans the engagement of Meg and John because she fears it will break apart the family she loves so dearly, but by the novel's final chapter, "Harvest Time," Jo, knowing that she, too, needs love, declares: "'I do think that families are the most beautiful things in all the world.'" Later in that chapter, Jo, now "Mother Bhaer," creates her own new family (an unconventional one for its time) with her husband, her two boys, and all the

Frontispiece by Lizabeth B. Comins for Ednah Dow Cheney's book *Louisa May Alcott: The Children's Friend*, a keepsake volume for Alcott's young readers, published soon after the author's death in March 1888. The book was offered to "the children of America [as] a memorial to Louisa May Alcott, to whom a whole generation looks up with honor and affection as their benefactor and friend."

Concord center (circa 1865). During the Civil War, Concord was still a rural village with a population of approximately 2,000 people.

students of Plumfield. However, it is Mrs. March, the sixty-year-old matriarch, not Jo, who gives the final benediction in the novel. With her entire family about her, children and grandchildren, she reaches out her arms, crying, "'Oh, my girls, however long you may live, I never can wish you a greater happiness than this!'"

Within the March family, the four sisters are given almost equal attention by Alcott, but rebellious Jo remains forever fixed in readers' memories. With the creation of Jo March, Alcott spins a character out of her own life experiences that soon looms large on the American literary landscape. Impetuous, hot-tempered, fearless, tomboyish Jo immediately captivated readers, and she continues to touch them today. J. K. Rowling (who also goes by Jo) says: "I know I read *Little Women* when I was eight. . . . Naturally, I whole-heartedly identified with Jo March, she of the burning literary ambition and short temper."[7] "You see," she explains, "I was a plain—and that is relevant!

You know that is relevant, that isn't a trivial thing, especially when you're a kid—I was a very plain, bookish, freckly, bright little girl. I was a massive bookworm and I spent a significant part of my reading looking for people like me."[8] She found herself in Jo March. Like the author of the Harry Potter series, many female readers connect with Jo, a young, independent woman who cares little for the conventions of society, but who listens to her own creative voice within. Jo is a disturber of the peace—her own and those around her. In many ways, Jo March is an American success story. She becomes the writer she dreamed of becoming. Yes, she gives this up eventually, but Alcott provides her with another dream, one with a social conscience: a school for poor boys. As Jo says in the final chapter, "'I've always longed for lots of boys, and never had enough.'" She may not be the proper female character one would expect from a girls' book in 1868, but then again Alcott came reluctantly at first into the creative vortex that would result in an American classic that speaks as loudly to its readers now as it did then, and *Little Women*'s genesis remains a fascinating tale.

In September 1867, Louisa May Alcott recorded in her journal: "Niles, partner of Roberts, asked me to write a girls book. Said I'd try" (*Journals* 158). Although Alcott had tasted a small success with *Hospital Sketches* (1863), she was yet unprepared for the fame and fortune that Roberts Brothers Publishers of Boston was about to bring her. In May 1868, Louisa, who was hard at work on fantasy tales, confided that "Father saw Mr. Niles about a fairy book. Mr. N. wants a *girls' story*, and I begin 'Little Women.' Marmee, Anna, and May all approve my plan. So I plod away, though I don't enjoy this sort of thing" (*Journals* 165). Seeking approval from her mother and sisters, Louisa devised a "plan" to recreate the life of the Alcott sisters in the guise of the Marches: Anna, her older sister, became the beautiful Meg; Louisa (who was often called Lu by her family), the tomboy Jo; Lizzie, the shy, doomed Beth; and Abby May, the artistic Amy.

The Alcott sisters did indeed live "most of it," but their lives were far from the genteel poverty found in *Little Women*. In the novel Alcott would gloss over the hard times by having Mr. March lose his money in a financial misfortune. The reality for her own family was far worse. Raised by parents who were so different from each other—Bronson Alcott, teacher, Transcendentalist, the son of a poor Connecticut farmer, and Abigail May Alcott, the daughter of a wealthy Boston merchant, descendant of John Hancock and the Puritan Samuel Sewall—the sisters shared a childhood marked by hardship.

Four years after his marriage to Abigail May, Bronson Alcott, in 1834, founded his Temple School in Boston, where it operated successfully for several years before closing in 1838, ending his teaching career forever. With daughters Anna, Louisa, and

Early daguerreotype of Anna Alcott, circa late 1850s. Frederick Willis, a childhood friend of the Alcott sisters, writes in *Alcott Memoirs* (1915): "Anna . . . had a clematis and wild rose complexion, [and] wide open blue eyes . . . She had the calm poise of her father, a more amiable disposition than any of her sisters, was possessed of a quiet, keen sense of humor, and while taking full part in our play enjoyed the fun and frolic with a certain dignified zest that was in no sense a pose but rather a part of her" (181).

Elizabeth, the Alcotts moved to Concord, Massachusetts, in 1840, where within a few months their fourth girl, Abby May, was born. In June 1843, Bronson and his British friend Charles Lane established a Utopian community, ironically named Fruitlands, in nearby rural Harvard, Massachusetts. It failed by the end of the year, and its collapse thrust Bronson into depression, almost tearing apart the family. Years of hardship and poverty followed, with Abigail struggling to provide for her daughters. The rest of the decade and that of the 1850s saw the family move numerous times, often living on the meager salary earned by Abigail and on the charity of her father, brother, and friends, notably Ralph Waldo Emerson, their neighbor. In autumn 1848, as the family planned to move from Concord to Boston, where Abigail would run an employment office for the poor, Louisa sought out her favorite spot—an old cartwheel in

(left) Abigail May Alcott, circa late 1860s. Ednah Dow Cheney observed that LMA "early believed herself to be her mother's favorite child, knew she was close to her heart, her every struggle watched, her every fault rebuked, every aspiration encouraged, every effort after good recognized" (*Louisa May Alcott: Her Life, Letters and Journals* [1889], p. 390). (right) Amos Bronson Alcott, circa 1870. Frederick Willis, who as a boy was close friends with the Alcott family in the 1840s and 1850s, observes in *Alcott Memoirs* (1915): "Even in my youth Mr. Alcott seemed to me always strangely out of place in the midst of the practical utilitarianism of the 19th century, and out of place, too, clad in modern broadcloth. He should have been of the days of Socrates or Seneca and worn the flowing robes of classic Greece or the toga of ancient Rome. He was possessed of a captivating yet almost childlike simplicity of manner and bore about with him an air of serene repose, contrasting sharply with the bustling, business-like manner of most of the literary men of those days" (173).

the grass—to contemplate her future. Staring into the dull November sky, with its threat of the coming winter, the fifteen-year-old "shook [her] fist at fate" and promised: "I will do something by-and-by. Don't care what, teach, sew, act, write, anything to help the family; I'll be rich and famous and happy before I die, see if I won't."[9] Louisa performed all of those jobs and more, but it proved a burden for many years. Only when she tapped into the imaginative wellspring of creativity to portray her own experiences and those of her sisters would she find fame and fortune.

As spring 1868 began to drift into summer in Concord, the Alcott sisters' private lives were beginning to be lived out on the printed page. Falling to work at the small

The only known image of Elizabeth Sewall Alcott, a crayon drawing by Caroline Negus Hildreth (1814–1867), completed in 1857, a year before Lizzie's death. Ednah Dow Cheney, a friend of the Alcott family, noted in *Louisa May Alcott: Her Life, Letters and Journals* (1889): "Elizabeth was unlike the other sisters. Retiring in disposition, she would gladly have ever lived in the privacy of home, her only desire being for the music that she loved" (p. 392).

desk in her upstairs bedroom in Orchard House, Louisa May Alcott returned to the past, bringing back the escapades of her youth and those of her sisters. She recalled old childhood friends and recast them as fictional characters. Mingling fact and fiction, she created a wartime book set, not amid the battlefields or army hospitals, but in a humble New England home. As Bronson once had advised her to do, she inserted her morals gently as she framed a new type of *Pilgrim's Progress,* one that followed real girls as they fought their personal shortcomings. John Bunyan's famous work, one that her father often read aloud to the family, pervades the book, providing an allegorical backdrop to the sisters' trials and tribulations. Readers, even young ones, in Alcott's day would have been familiar with *The Pilgrim's Progress,* as it was one of the most commonly found books in American homes, especially in New England. Unlike the heavily didactic works of her own youth, Alcott's novel treads lightly on the spiritual journey of the allegory, emphasizing instead the earthly quest to become a better person.

INTRODUCTION

In June, she mailed twelve chapters to Niles, who, like Alcott herself, considered it dull. But she firmly resolved "to try the experiment; for lively, simple books are very much needed for girls, and perhaps I can supply the need" (*Journals* 166). Despite what Alcott had written about Niles thinking the novel "dull," his letter to her on June 16 indicated otherwise: "I have read the 12 chapters & am pleased—I ought to be more emphatic & say delighted so please to consider 'judgement' as favorable." Niles, who had first suggested the book, also offered Alcott a title that would soon become a household phrase: "What do you say to this . . . *Little Women*. Meg, Jo, Beth, and Amy. The story of their lives by Louisa M. Alcott. First Series."[10] With Niles's title, there would be no mistaking that Alcott's work was intended for girls. Acknowledging the suggestion that the novel *might* have a sequel, Alcott responded, telling her editor that "'Little Women' had better be the title for No 1. 'Young Women,' or something of that sort, for No. 2, *if* there is a No. 2."[11]

Side view of Fruitlands farmhouse, where the Alcotts lived during the last half of 1843. Bronson Alcott and co-founder Charles Lane sought to establish at Fruitlands "a Family in harmony with the primitive instincts in man." LMA satirized the Utopian community in "Transcendental Wild Oats" (1873).

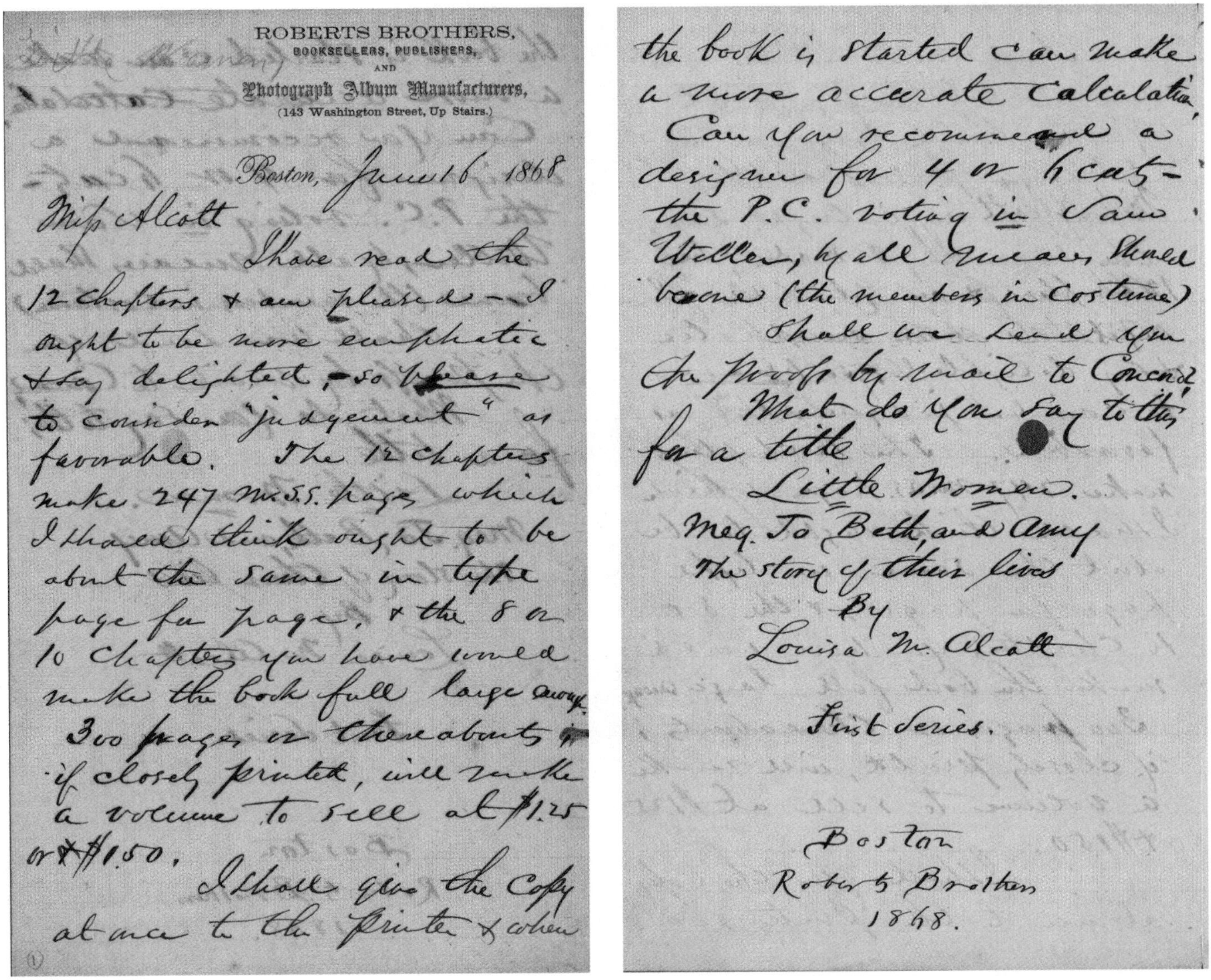

ROBERTS BROTHERS,
BOOKSELLERS, PUBLISHERS,
AND
Photograph Album Manufacturers,
(143 Washington Street, Up Stairs.)

Boston, June 16 1868

Miss Alcott

I have read the
12 chapters & am pleased — I
ought to be more emphatic
& say delighted, so please
to consider "judgement" as
favorable. The 12 chapters
make 247 m.s.s. pages which
I should think ought to be
about the same in type
page for page, & the 8 or
10 chapters you have would
make the book full large any
300 pages or thereabouts
if closely printed, will make
a volume to sell at $1.25
or $1.50.

I shall give the Copy
at once to the Printer & when
the book is started can make
a more accurate Calculation.

Can you recommend a
designer for 4 or 6 cuts —
the P.C. voting in Sam
Weller, by all means should
become (the members in Costume)

Shall we send you
the proofs by mail to Concord

What do you say to this
for a title

Little Women.
Meg, Jo, Beth, and Amy
The story of their lives
By
Louisa M. Alcott

First Series.

Boston
Roberts Brothers
1868.

And now while we are about business, wont You be kind enough to set Your price on this story, in an outright sale, the succeeding Volumes, if this one prospers, to be furnished at the same.

Yr Vy truly

T. Niles Jr

Thomas Niles of Roberts Brothers to Louisa May Alcott, June 16, 1868, in which he writes, "I have read the 12 chapters & am pleased—I ought to be more emphatic & say delighted—so *please* to consider 'judgement' as favorable." On page two, Niles offers Alcott a title for the novel: "What do you say to this for a title *Little Women*. Meg, Jo, Beth, and Amy. The story of their lives."

LITTLE WOMEN

OR,

MEG, JO, BETH AND AMY

BY LOUISA M. ALCOTT

ILLUSTRATED BY MAY ALCOTT

BOSTON
ROBERTS BROTHERS
1868

Title page for the first edition of *Little Women or, Meg, Jo, Beth and Amy* (1868).

On July 15, 1868, Louisa noted in her journal that she had completed the 402-page manuscript of the novel. With her ten new chapters, she sent the publisher more corrected page proofs. Since she did not have the first half of the book at hand to reread, she felt at "rather a disadvantage, as I dont remember it very well, so may have missed some of the threads." Alcott told her editor that she did not want a preface. Instead she suggested appropriate lines from Bunyan's *Pilgrim's Progress* "as a sort of motto . . . as they give some clue to the plan of the story" (*Selected Letters* 117). *Little Women* was now complete.

May Alcott, Louisa's youngest sister and a budding artist, had drawn illustrations for the book, which Louisa liked, though she thought "the engraver may see faults." She wrote to Niles that she hoped the engraver would not "spoil the pictures & make Meg cross-eyed, Beth with no nose or Jo with a double chin" (*Selected Letters* 117). It would not be the engraver's fault, however, that the illustrations were amateurish attempts. Even though May Alcott had studied anatomical drawing with the well-known artist William Rimmer, she still had far to go before she could professionally draw the human form. The drawings would catch the scornful eye of critics, and May Alcott would never again illustrate one of Louisa's works.

Niles knew that if the novel was successful, it would be profitable for both parties to continue the story of the Marches, and despite Alcott's uncertainty, he wanted her to prepare for that possibility. On July 25, 1868, he wrote to ask if she could add another chapter "in which allusions might be made to something in the future." He told her, "I have read the whole of it & I am sure it will 'hit', which means I think it will sell well."

The following month, Roberts Brothers offered Alcott $1,000 for the copyright to *Little Women*, a common practice in nineteenth-century publishing. Roberts Brothers would take a financial hit if the book did not sell well, but it also stood to profit greatly if the work proved successful, as all rights would belong to the publisher and Alcott would receive no royalties. If she accepted the offer, Alcott would not gamble on copies sold but pocket a reasonable sum for the work. After all, in 1867, she had

May Alcott, circa 1870. Ednah Dow Cheney noted: "bright, sparkling, capricious May,—quick in temper, quick in repentance, affectionate and generous, but full of her own plans, and quite inclined to have the world go on according to her fancies . . . she was like a nymph of Nature, full of friendly sportiveness, and disposed to live out her own life, since it might be only a brief summer day" (in *Louisa May Alcott: Her Life, Letters and Journals* [1889], pp. 392–393).

written twenty-five stories and earned $1,000 for the year. Here, she was offered the same amount of money for ten weeks' work. Alcott noted that although the publisher offered her $1,000, Niles had suggested that she retain the copyright. In 1885, she inserted the following passage into her journal entry of August 1868: "An honest publisher and a lucky author, for the copyright made her fortune, and the 'dull book' was the first golden egg of the ugly duckling" (*Journals* 166).

Alcott received page proofs of the complete novel on August 26, 1868. Rereading it, she liked it better than she had originally thought, as did her editor: "Mr. N. likes it better now, and says some girls who have read the manuscripts say it is 'splendid!' As it is for them, they are the best critics, so I should be satisfied" (*Journals* 166). Niles, a bachelor, was unsure of how to judge a successful girls' book, so he first gave it to his twenty-year-old niece Lily Almy, who devoured it. Niles, still unsure, then gave it to other young girls, who all declared it wonderful.[12]

Roberts Brothers advertised the forthcoming novel under Niles's proposed title *Lit-*

ROBERTS BROTHERS,
BOOKSELLERS, PUBLISHERS,
AND
Photograph Album Manufacturers,
(143 Washington Street, Up Stairs.)

Boston, July 25 1868

Miss Alcott

I am not sure that it would not be best to add another chapter to "Little Women". I have read the whole of it & I am sure it will "hit", which means I think it will sell well.

A chapter could well be added, in which allusions might be made to something in the future.

The M. S. S. is some 12 or more pages less than your number, by mistake in the paging & I am afraid we have not quite matter enough, but we will wait till the whole is in type & then decide.

The printers query of some of your "girl's talk" is quite amusing — pray what does he know, or what should he know about it.

Yours &c
T. Niles

Thomas Niles to Louisa May Alcott, July 25, 1868.
Niles writes to Alcott: "I have read the whole of it & I am sure it will 'hit', which means I think it will sell well."

tle Women; Meg, Jo, Beth and Amy, the Story of their Lives on September 1 in the American Literary Gazette, declaring: "This delightful book is destined to have a great run this fall."[13] The novel, its title slightly shortened, was published in early October 1868 in an edition of 2,000 copies. A short advertisement in the American Literary Gazette that month indicated little of the success to come, Niles perhaps still uncertain of how it would sell: "There is plenty of incident and sprightly conversation in this story, and it cannot fail to please the young people, especially the little girls."[14] The first edition sold out in October, with another 1,000 sold in November. By the end of the year approximately 4,500 copies of Little Women or, Meg, Jo, Beth and Amy had been printed.[15] Alcott and Niles were off to a promising beginning.

Reviews were positive and encouraging for the most part. "The book is fresh, sparkling, natural and full of soul," proclaimed the *Boston Daily Evening Transcript*. It also noted that the "illustrations, by Miss May Alcott, are very vigorous and impressive."[16] The *Providence Daily Journal* wrote that the book's "characterization is very clever, the girls talk and act like real girls (*American* girls, we must add, however, for English children would scarcely use so frequently the word 'guess' as a substitute for 'think' or 'suppose'). The tone of the book is healthy and the moral, without being obtrusive, sufficiently well marked to suit, we think, the most rigid of parents and guardians."[17] A review in the *Springfield Daily Republican* focused on the fact that the book was aimed not at children but at teenagers on the verge of adulthood: "The restless and confused period which divides the child from the woman is here represented under four different aspects, and with a great variety of domestic incident. The four sisters are natural in their sayings and strivings, because they are drawn from life." The reviewer also echoes an earlier apprehension of Louisa's when he notes that May Alcott's illustrations "have not had full justice done them by the engraver."[18]

The Nation, one of the country's leading magazines, published in New York City, would not be so kind to the budding artist, claiming that "Miss May Alcott betrays not only a want of anatomical knowledge, and that indifference to or non-recognition of the subtle beauty of the lines of the female figure which so generally marks women artists, but also the fact that she has not closely studied the text she illustrates." The periodical was not so harsh on the author, but it still noted flaws: "The girls depicted all belong to healthy types, and are drawn with a certain cleverness, although there is in the book a lack of what painters call atmosphere—things and people being painted too much in 'local colors,' and remaining, under all circumstances, somewhat too persistently themselves."[19]

Many readers, however, were like the one portrayed in *Putnam's Magazine*. The New York–based periodical noted, "Most Sunday-school books were stories of unnaturally good and pious boys and girls, who, however, were not attractive enough to rouse a desire of imitation in the youthful breast. But now we have a different order of things." It called *Little Women* "a thoroughly natural and charming book, fresh and full of life." Similar to Niles's test to judge the novel's possible popularity by giving it to his niece to read, *Putnam's* claimed: "We gave it to a little girl of twelve to read, for whose opinion we have great respect, and she pronounced it just the *nicest* book. 'I could read it right through three times, and it would be nicer and funnier every time.' And to our certain knowledge, she read it twice in one week, and would have read it again, had not the book been carried off."[20]

While most reviews praised the book, others condemned it. On October 22, 1868, *Zion's Herald,* a Methodist newspaper published by the Boston Wesleyan Association,

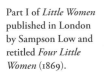

Part I of *Little Women* published in London by Sampson Low and retitled *Four Little Women* (1869).

would weigh in with a much more negative review. The book, the writer observed, "is a vivacious story of four girls and their hardly older mother, judging from the picture. What she should know of poverty is hard to conceive." But that was not their main concern: "We dislike the despiritualizing in it of Bunyon's [*sic*] great Allegory. . . . The fight with Apollyon is reduced to a conflict with an evil temper, and the Palace Beautiful and Vanity Fair are made to be only ordinary virtues or temptations." The paper's judgment was harsh: "We cannot commend the book as its quality merits. It is without Christ, and hence perilous in proportion to its assimilation to Christian forms. Don't put in the Sunday School library."[21] A few days later, on October 26, Niles wrote to Alcott, asking if she had corrections to make for a new printing and pointing out that the book had stirred up some controversy: "Some very good & pious people object to the theatrical part of the Merry Christmas chapter and on that acc[ount] object to its introduction into their Sunday School Libraries." Niles wondered if she was willing to replace part of it, even though he thought the episode "about the best part of the whole book." He added, "Why will people be so *very good.*" Obviously readers objected to the birth of Christ being celebrated with a play about a witch, villains, and a princess in distress. Alcott refused, and the episode remained unchanged.

By the end of October 1868, Louisa had moved to Boston and rented a room on Brookline Street, where she could have quiet solitude as she readied herself for undertaking what Niles had been encouraging: *Little Women, Part Second.* Before beginning, she had time one evening to hear Emerson lecture about Brook Farm and an opportunity to visit her sister Anna and her husband, John Pratt, with their two sons at their new home in Malden, a suburb of Boston. On October 30, she met with Thomas Niles, who informed her that Sampson Low, a London publishing firm, wanted to print *Little Women* in England (it appeared in early December) and that the novel was selling well, but that reading audiences wanted the story to continue: "Pleasant notices and letters arrive, and much interest in my little women, who seem to find friends by their truth to life, as I hoped" (*Journals* 167).

She recorded in her journal that she began work on the second part of *Little Women* on November 1. Her plan was to "do a chapter a day, and in a month I mean to be done." She prepared, like Jo March, to enter the vortex of creativity. While she had been reluctant to write a girls' book just months earlier, Alcott, with good reviews appearing and royalties forthcoming, now was determined not to waste opportunity or time: "A little success is so inspiring that I now find my 'Marches' sober, nice people, and as I can launch into the future, my fancy has more play." Of course, while she could now create imagined lives for the March sisters on her lined blue paper, she still had to relive Anna's wedding, the birth of her nephews, and most important—Lizzie

Alcott's death. With Part II set three years after the closing of Part I, she could now begin the new work with Meg's marriage to John Brooke. She was, however, irritated: "Girls write to ask who the little women marry, as if that was the only end and aim of a woman's life." Many readers wanted Jo to marry Laurie, but Alcott had other plans. She vowed: "I *won't* marry Jo to Laurie to please any one" (*Journals* 167). She would keep her promise.

On Monday, November 16, she took a break from her writing "for a change, as I have written like a steam engine since the 1st" (*Journals* 167). After hearing the minister John Weiss present his lecture on "Woman" at the Radical Club, held at 13 Chestnut Street, she lunched with the writers Kate Field and Celia Thaxter, along with the British wood-engraver, author, and reformer William James Linton, who had recently immigrated to America. In the evening she attended the New England Women's Club. But the next day, Alcott was back at work and almost on schedule. She finished her thirteenth chapter in seventeen days: "I am so full of my work, I can't stop to eat or sleep, or for anything but a daily run." On November 29, her thirty-sixth birthday, Louisa spent the day alone, "writing hard." The only present was a copy of her father's book *Tablets,* which Roberts Brothers had published in September: "I never seem to have many presents, as some do, though I give a good many. That is best perhaps, and makes a gift very precious when it does come" (*Journals* 167).

In December 1868, she and her sister May, who was now giving art lessons in the city, rented a room in the new Bellevue Hotel at 17 Beacon Street in Boston: "[May] does n't enjoy quiet corners as I do, so we took a sky-parlor, and had a queer time whisking up and down in the elevator, eating in a marble café, and sleeping on a sofa bed, that we might be genteel." However, the experience did not prove restful for

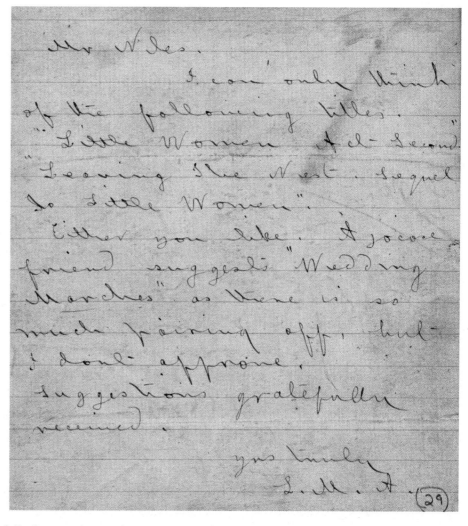

Louisa May Alcott to Thomas Niles, circa early 1869. Here LMA offers suggestions for the title to Part II of *Little Women*: "I can only think of the following titles 'Little Women Act Second' 'Leaving The Nest Sequel to Little Women.'"

Louisa, for she still felt overworked "with no rest for the brains that earn the money" (*Journals* 168). On Christmas Day, Roberts Brothers paid Alcott $300 in royalties for the first part of *Little Women.* In addition, throughout 1868, she had received $423 for her magazine stories and $500 for editing *Merry's Museum,* a children's periodical. It had been a profitable but hardworking year.

Alcott sent the second part of *Little Women* to Roberts Brothers on New Year's Day, 1869. In early January, she wrote Thomas Niles about a possible title for the new volume, suggesting "Little Women Act Second" and "Leaving the Nest. Sequel to Little Women." She mentioned that a friend jokingly offered "'Wedding *Marches*'" because there were several marriages, but Alcott was not amused. She ended by saying: "Suggestions gratefully received" (*Selected Letters* 119).

As the new year began, Louisa and May moved from Beacon Street to a boarding-house on Chauncey Street, where on January 6 she wrote to Alf Whitman, who had served as the partial inspiration for the character of Laurie: "All my little girl-friends are madly in love with Laurie & insist on a sequel, so I've written one which will make you laugh, especially the pairing off part." She confessed to Alf that she "didn't know how to settle my family any other way & I wanted to disappoint the young gossips [LMA first wrote "little dears" before striking it out and inserting "young gossips"] who vowed that Laurie & Jo *should* marry. Authors take dreadful liberties" (*Selected Letters* 120).

Although Alcott had yet to tell any of her correspondents how she had paired off couples or whom Laurie actually marries in the sequel, she already knew that many readers would not like the outcome. While marrying Amy to Laurie might disappoint young readers, marrying Jo to the older Germanic Professor Bhaer might cause them to toss up the book in disgust. Perhaps her most explicit remarks about the marriages of the March sisters appear in a letter to Elizabeth Powell, whom Louisa had known in Concord. She wrote to Powell, now a calisthenics instructor at Vassar College, on March 20, 1869, just several weeks before the second part was published, warning that it would probably be disliked because "publishers wont let authors finish up as they like but insist on having people married off in a wholesale manner which much afflicts me." Louisa declared, "'Jo' should have remained a literary spinster but so many enthusiastic young ladies wrote to me clamorously demanding that she should marry Laurie, *or* somebody, that I didn't dare to refuse & out of perversity went & made a funny match for her. I expect vials of wrath to be poured out upon my head, but rather enjoy the prospect" (*Selected Letters* 125).

On April 1, Roberts Brothers advertised that the large first printing of the second part of *Little Women* was almost all sold in advance orders, and sellers wanting the

Dust jacket for a Dutch edition of Part II of *Little Women* (translated as *On Their Own Wings*), promoting the 1949 film.

First editions of *Little Women*, Parts I (1868) and II (1869).

work upon publication needed to act at once.[22] *Little Women or, Meg, Jo, Beth and Amy, Part Second* appeared in bookshops on April 15, 1869. Niles already had written to Alcott on April 4, telling her that 3,000 copies of Part II had been presold and another thousand were now being printed. The first part of *Little Women* was also receiving good reviews in London, and Niles sent her a short notice from *The Spectator:* "The writer's strength is principally given to the portraiture of Jo, alias Josephine, a boy, we may call her, who by some misadventure finds himself or herself in the shape of a girl. She is indeed a person to be remembered. The character is not an easy one to draw, but it is managed without a shade of vulgarity or rudeness. Jo is always a young lady."[23] Sampson Low would also publish Part II later that spring as *Little Women Wedded* (a number of British editions over the years would publish Part II as *Good Wives*).

Niles also encouraged Alcott to give him a new book. But the author was overworked. She had completed both volumes of *Little Women* in less than eight months,

Account sheet of Sampson Low from 1872, detailing the costs of publishing *Little Women Wedded*, the British edition of Part II of *Little Women*.

in addition to writing thrillers for Frank Leslie and children's stories for Daniel Ford's *Youth's Companion* and Horace B. Fuller's *Merry's Museum*. She complained in her April journal: "Very poorly. Feel quite used up. Don't care much for myself, as rest is heavenly even in pain, but the family seem so panic-stricken and helpless when I break down, that I try to keep the mill going . . . Roberts wants a new book, but am afraid to get into a vortex lest I fall ill" (*Journals* 171). Surely, however, the reaction to the second part of *Little Women,* combined with excellent sales, lifted her spirits.

Reviews for the sequel were almost uniformly positive, better even than those for Part I. The *Boston Daily Evening Transcript* pointed out that the "little women who read the book are somewhat disappointed, at first, that Jo and Laurie do not marry, but older ones say, with a smile of calm superiority that they knew this would not be six months ago. . . . The volumes are good for girls, because they are free from cant and sham morality. They teach the religion of good works and teach wholesome truths."[24] The *Springfield Daily Union* especially liked Marmee's advice to the sisters: "The confidential intercourse between the mother and her daughters, in which the

INTRODUCTION

former makes herself as much the companion and friend as the guide of the latter, is just what should exist in every family, though we fear it does in too few."[25] Mrs. Henry Ward Beecher, wife of the famous minister and sister-in-law to Harriet Beecher Stowe, declared in *The Mother at Home and Household Magazine:* "It is amusing to see with how much spirit this simple little book is discussed by elderly people who generally look upon young folks' story-books as foolish things."[26] Frank Preston Stearns, son of the abolitionist Major George Luther Stearns and friend of the Alcott family, wrote in his *Sketches from Concord and Appledore* (1895) about the success of the second part of *Little Women:* "First the young people read it; then their fathers and mothers; and then the grandparents read it. Grave merchants and lawyers meeting on their way down town in the morning said to each other, 'Have you read "Little Women"'; and laughed as they said it. The clerks in my office read it, so also did the civil engineer, and the boy in the elevator. It was the rage in '69."[27]

Niles wrote to Louisa on April 29 that the novel "continues to sell well & win praises from all—I have not seen the person yet who does not like the second as well or better than the first." He also warned her of what fame would do: "If you don't send some pictures of Jo March, Concord will be infested with deputations of 'little women' & their *'Lauries'*; you have your choice." But "the deputations" had already begun. Alcott confessed in late April: "People begin to come and stare at the Alcotts. Reporters haunt the place to look at the authoress, who dodges into the woods *á la* Hawthorne, and won't be even a very small lion" (*Journals* 171). As her books sold briskly, so too grew her fame. People—young and old, male and female—wanted to know more about the author of *Little Women,* to meet her, to hug her, to see where she lived and wrote, to take away some token of their pilgrimage, to get just a glimmer of the real Jo March. The lion-hunters, autograph fiends, and Jo-worshippers, as Louisa would grow to call the celebrity-seekers, became such a bother that Alcott wrote a satiric letter on April 29, 1869, to the *Springfield Republican.* While her letter also referred to the other famous Concord authors, she clearly was the one who was currently under public scrutiny and made a veiled reference to herself: "It is whispered that one irascible spinster, driven to frenzy by twenty-eight visitors in a week, proposed to get a garden engine [a water hose] and 'play away' whenever a suspicious stranger was seen entering her gates" (*Selected Letters* 128). Louisa May Alcott's fame, and the burdens that came with it, would only increase as the years went by and her books continued to be popular.

While the first part of *Little Women* sold well, Part II was a runaway success. By the middle of May, the novel was in its seventh printing of 1,000, and by August, the eleventh 1,000 were in print and at booksellers.[28] Sales of Part I also continued at a steady pace. Roberts Brothers declared in the *American Literary Gazette* on September 1, 1869, that the "great literary hit of the season is undoubtedly Miss Alcott's *Little Women,* the orders for which continue to flow in upon us to such an extent as to make it impossible to answer them with promptness. We are now printing the twenty-third thousand."[29] As the Roberts Brothers' ledgers reveal, the ad refers to the total printing of both volumes combined, not just Part II.[30]

On Christmas Day 1869, Roberts Brothers sent Alcott a check for $2,500, her royalties for six months. Along with the check, the firm sent a congratulatory note: "At this 'Merry Christmas' time, when the inspiration of your mind is gladdening the hearts and homes of so many thousands, we would not forget the author; and we feel that we are but the factors of a public, who quick to recognize the genius displayed in 'Little Women,' where by a 'touch of nature,' you have made the whole world kin, generously enable to silver line your pocket." Three days later, Alcott thanked them, writing, "After toiling so many years along the up-hill road, always a hard one to women writers, it is peculiarly grateful to me to find the way growing easier at last . . . and the rough places made smooth by the courtesy and kindness of those who proved themselves 'friends' as well as 'publishers'" (*Selected Letters* 129).

Thomas Niles indeed proved to be a true friend to Louisa May Alcott. He not only helped guide her literary career but also offered business advice about how to invest her money. He would constantly request new works from her pen to keep her name before the reading public and devise marketing strategies to help sales. Novel after novel followed: *An Old-Fashioned Girl* (1870), *Eight Cousins* (1875), *Rose in Bloom* (1876), *Under the Lilacs* (1877), *Jack and Jill: A Village Story* (1880), all works in the vein of *Little Women*. Thirteen short-story volumes also appeared, including the multivolume collections *Aunt Jo's Scrap-Bag* (1872–1882) and *Lulu's Library* (1885–1889). Alcott would continue her story of the March family in *Little Men: Life at Plumfield with Jo's Boys* (1871). Written in Rome after Alcott had read newspaper reports of the sudden death of Anna's husband, John Bridge Pratt, the book, dedicated to her two nephews, John and Fred, allowed her to highlight the educational theories of her father. In 1886, she published the final volume in the trilogy, *Jo's Boys, and How They Turned Out: A Sequel to "Little Men,"* finally bringing a close to her story of the March family. But the adventures of the March sisters would live on in other forms as *Little Women* would be adapted for the stage and eventually the screen, ensuring the novel's enduring popularity.

Stage adaptations began soon after the novel was published, most of them informal plays, much like the March girls performed in the novel. In Bex, Switzerland, Louisa wrote to Anna on July 27, 1870, that "[Thomas Wentworth] Higginson and a little girl friend had written out the Operatic Tragedy in 'Little Women' and set the songs to music."[31] When William Henry Venable wrote to Alcott on November 21, 1872, for permission to use scenes from *Little Women* for dramatization of two short plays to include in his volume *The School Stage: A Collection of Juvenile Acting Plays* (1873), she agreed and replied: "Some of them have already been dramatized & acted here, & went very well. I esteem it an honor that my little stories are considered worthy to be used for the instruction as well as the amusement of young people" (*Selected Letters* 172). Florence Hilton, president of the Philocalian Society in Chicago, played Jo in several scene adaptations from the novel, including "The Witch's Curse," in late winter 1874 at Standard Hall. She wrote to Alcott, sending information about the play, and the author replied: "*Did* the bed actually shut up? If not, you missed one of the finest stage effects ever seen. When the play was acted here [Concord] by some Sunday-school children, that crash brought down the house, and I felt myself covered with glory, as the author of this superb idea" (*Selected Letters* 182).

The first Broadway production of the work appeared in 1912 as *Little Women: A Comedy in Four Parts,* produced in New York by William A. Brady and staged by Jessie Bonstelle and Bertram Harrison, with Marian De Forest adapting the novel to script. John S. Pratt Alcott recalled that he and his family were reluctant to grant the rights, not because his aunt would have disapproved, but because the book was the story of their family and they felt a play might cheapen it. What he discovered, however, was that more people would come to see a play than would read the novel.[32] Seven years later the production was successfully performed in London. Countless amateur productions have been staged through the years across the United States. In Louisa's hometown, the Concord Players, an acting troupe that credits its origins to Louisa's founding of the Concord Dramatic Union in 1856, have given performances of *Little Women* every ten years, beginning in 1932, with the exception of 1942, during World War Two.

The first musical adaption, *Little Women, an Operetta in Three Acts,* appeared in 1940 with John Ravold's dramatic treatment, Frederick Howard's lyrics, and Geoffrey O'Hara's music. In 1998, American composer Mark Adamo wrote the libretto for a new opera *Little Women,* which received critical acclaim. The March sisters found themselves again on the Great White Way in 2005, when *Little Women: The Musical*

Playbill for the Concord Players' first production of *Little Women* in 1932. The play, based on the Broadway dramatization by Marian deForest, featured LMA's great-nephew, Bronson Alcott Pratt, as Mr. March and her great-niece, Louisa Alcott Kussin, as Meg.

was first performed in New York. The advertising poster for this production read: "Six generations have read this story. This one will sing it."

Of all the adaptations of *Little Women,* however, it was film that brought the novel to life and captured a larger audience than ever read Alcott's classic. A British silent film version produced by G. B. Samuelson and directed by Alexander Butler first portrayed the Marches on the screen in 1917, and in January 1919 an American adaptation produced by William A. Brady and directed by Harley Knoles appeared, with Dorothy Bernard playing Jo. However, it was director George Cukor's 1933 RKO production that forever associated Jo with its star, Katherine Hepburn. Praised by the critics for her performance, she won the Venice Film Festival's Best Actress award in 1934 for the role. Nominated for Best Picture and Best Director, *Little Women* won an Academy Award for Best Screenplay Adaption for Sarah Y. Mason and Victor Heeman, a well-deserved honor as the screenplay borrowed heavily from Alcott's own words.

In 1949, Hollywood returned to the award-winning script of the 1933 adaptation (with the addition of Sally Benson's and Andrew Solt's contributions) for a remake of *Little Women* with an all-star cast directed by Mervyn LeRoy. June Allyson played Jo, with Janet Leigh as Meg, Margaret O'Brien as Beth, and Elizabeth Taylor as Amy. A visual treat, the film was *Little Women*'s debut in Technicolor, and it received an Academy Award nomination for Best Color Cinematography and won the award for Best Color Art Direction–Set Decoration. Premiering at Radio City Music Hall, *Little Women* became one of the highest-grossing films of the year.

Forty-five years later, *Little Women* would again be adapted to film, introducing a new generation to the March sisters. Opening nationwide on December 25, 1994, the film, directed by the Australian Gillian Armstrong, the first female to direct *Little Women,* proved to be a critical and commercial success. Robin Swicord's screenplay, unlike the previous adaptations, incorporated biographical details of Alcott's life. The film received Academy Award nominations for Best Costume Design and Best Original Score. Winona Ryder portrayed Jo, earning an Academy Award nomination for Best Actress for her performance. The cast, another all-star ensemble, included Trini Alvarado (Meg), Claire Danes (Beth), Kristin Dunst (the younger Amy), Samantha Mathis (the older Amy), Susan Sarandon (Marmee), and Christian Bale (Laurie). The film inspired a number of tie-ins, including several adaptations of the novel for young children, complete with scenes from the film.

Alcott's girls' book also found its way to the small screen in the 1970s. The BBC's version in 1970 ran approximately four hours and featured British actresses in the roles of the March sisters. In 1978, NBC offered American audiences another four-hour adaptation. With well-known television actresses such as Susan Dey (Jo), Meredith Baxter (Meg), and Eve Plumb (Beth) in the roles of the sisters, this version cast Hollywood veterans in the adult roles, with Dorothy McGuire as Marmee, Robert Young as Mr. Laurence, and Greer Garson as Aunt March. *Little Women* received two Emmy Awards: Outstanding Art Direction for a Series and Outstanding Cinematography for a Series.

The spin-offs of *Little Women* remain numerous, from the Madame Alexander dolls to the *Little Women* cartoons found in the magazine pages of 1988's feminist publication *Ms.,* from the postal stamps honoring Louisa May Alcott (1940) and *Little Women* (1993) to Geraldine Brooks' Pulitzer–Prize winning novel *March* (2005), a fictional account of Mr. March's wartime experiences. *Little Women* has appeared on numerous lists of classic books since the late nineteenth century. Thousands of admirers still make a pilgrimage every year to Orchard House, which has been open as a museum since 1911.

In the past twenty years, Alcott's status has become increasingly elevated; the popular author of juvenile fiction during the second part of the nineteenth century has now become the subject of probing critical examination, a writer who is securely fixed in the American literary canon. Alcott and *Little Women* have become the focus of numerous critical articles, books, and PhD dissertations. In 2006, the scholarly journal *Children's Literature* (volume 34), the annual publication of the Children's Literature Association, devoted its entire issue, guest-edited by Anne K. Phillips and Christine Doyle, to Louisa May Alcott. In 2009, the award-winning PBS documentary *Louisa May Alcott: The Woman behind Little Women,* produced by Nancy Porter and written by Harriet Reisen, aired on the network's *American Masters* series. Alcott has clearly secured, as her father hoped at her birth, a "place in the estimation of society."[33]

Despite the popularity of her other books, Alcott never repeated the success of *Little Women.* During her lifetime alone, Roberts Brothers printed 67,000 copies of the trade edition of Part I and 65,000 of Part II. Once the two volumes were combined into one, the press printed 60,350 copies of *Little Women* from 1881 through 1887, including printings of the deluxe *Little Women: Illustrated.* Over thirty years, from the publication of Part I of *Little Women* in 1868 until their sale of the firm to Little, Brown in 1898, Roberts Brothers printed 1,727,551 copies of Louisa May Alcott's books.[34] Little, Brown and Company would continue to publish Alcott's books after buying out Roberts Brother. In 1909, they celebrated the fortieth anniversary of *Little Women* by publishing a new edition. Demonstrating the enduring demand of the classic, the firm printed 100,000 copies. The *New York Times Book Review* wrote: "As a rule the classics of youth scarcely live beyond the immediate generation that welcomed their birth. It is a unique distinction of 'Little Women,' however, that it has never grown old, never appeared antiquated to the youngsters of today, who are rather prone, as a rule, to demand somewhat different literary fare from that which satisfied their elders."[35] By 1947, *Little Women* had sold over two million copies.[36] The novel has never been out of print and has been published in more than thirty countries around the world.[37] These accomplishments are not bad for an aspiring Alcott, who was told by the publisher James T. Fields in 1862, "'Stick to your teaching; you can't write'" (*Journals* 109). As Louisa May Alcott wrote to her cousin in an unpublished letter of May 16, 1869: "I never dreamed when we [the Alcott sisters] four Sanchos were cutting up capers years ago that we were to become the fashion & be regarded as 'dear, sweet funny things' by enthusiastic little parties then unborn. Such is life!"[38]

NOTES

1. *Journals,* pp. 165–166.

2. Theodore Roosevelt, *An Autobiography* (New York: Macmillan, 1913), p. 20.

3. Louisa May Alcott, *Jo's Boys, and How They Turned Out* (Boston: Roberts Brothers, 1886), p. 50.

4. Catharine R. Stimpson, "Reading for Love: Canons, Paragons, and Whistling Jo March," *New Literary History* 21.4 (Autumn 1990), pp. 957–976. Reprinted in *"Little Women" and the Feminist Imagination,* ed. Janice M. Alberghene and Beverly Lyon Clark (New York: Garland, 1999), p. 77.

5. Louisa May Alcott, "Recollections of My Childhood," *The Youth's Companion* 61 (May 24, 1888), p. 261.

6. Horace Bushnell, *Christian Nurture* (New York: Charles Scribner, 1861 [1847]), pp. 100–101.

7. J. J. Marsh, "Tea and Cake with JK Rowling," *Words with Jam* (June/July 2011), p. 7.

8. *Harry Potter and the Deathly Hallows—Part 2.* DVD Extras, "The Women of *Harry Potter,*" 2011.

9. Louisa May Alcott, "Recollections." Quoted in *Her Own Time,* p. 37.

10. Thomas Niles to Louisa May Alcott, June 16, 1868. Manuscript letter, Houghton Library, Harvard University (bMS Am 1130.8 [1–144]). All subsequent quotes from Niles's correspondence are from this manuscript collection.

11. *Selected Letters,* p. 116.

12. Cornelia Meigs, *Invincible Louisa* (Boston: Little, Brown, 1934), p. 206.

13. *American Literary Gazette* 11 (1868), p. 214.

14. *American Literary Gazette* 12 (1868), p. 16.

15. Joel Myerson and Daniel Shealy, "The Sales of Louisa May Alcott's Books," *Harvard Library Bulletin,* n.s. 1:1 (Spring 1990), p. 69.

16. Review of *Little Women,* in *Boston Daily Evening Transcript* (September 30, 1868), p. 2, quoted in *Louisa May Alcott: The Contemporary Reviews,* ed. Beverly Lyon Clark (Cambridge, England: Cambridge University Press, 2005), p. 61.

17. Review of *Little Women,* in *Providence Daily Journal* (October 15, 1868), p. 4, quoted in *Louisa May Alcott: The Contemporary Reviews,* p. 62.

18. Review of *Little Women,* in *Springfield Daily Republican* (October 21, 1868), pp. 3–5, quoted in *Louisa May Alcott: The Contemporary Reviews,* p. 62.

19. Review of *Little Women,* in *The Nation* (October 22, 1868), p. 335, quoted in *Louisa May Alcott: The Contemporary Reviews,* p. 63.

20. Review of *Little Women,* in *Putnam's Magazine* (December 1868), p. 760, quoted in *Louisa May Alcott: The Contemporary Reviews,* p. 67.

21. Review of *Little Women,* in *Zion's Herald* (October 22, 1868), p. 3, quoted in *Louisa May Alcott: The Contemporary Reviews,* pp. 63–64.

22. Raymond L. Kilgour, *Messrs. Roberts Brothers Publishers* (Ann Arbor: University of Michigan Press, 1952), p. 72.

23. Review of *Little Women,* in *The Spectator* (March 13, 1869), p. 332.

24. Review of *Little Women,* in *Boston Daily Evening Transcript* (April 21, 1869), p. 4, quoted in *Louisa May Alcott: The Contemporary Reviews,* p. 70.

25. Review of *Little Women,* in *Springfield Daily Union* (April 24, 1869), p. 6, quoted in *Louisa May Alcott: The Contemporary Reviews,* p. 71.

26. Review of *Little Women,* in *The Mother at Home and Household Magazine* 7 (July 1869), p. 221, quoted in *Louisa May Alcott: The Contemporary Reviews,* p. 77.

27. Frank Preston Stearns, *Sketches from Concord and Appledore* (New York: Putnam's, 1895), pp. 69–88. Quoted in *Her Own Time,* p. 85.

28. Myerson and Shealy, "The Sales of Louisa May Alcott's Books," p. 69.

29. *American Literary Gazette* 13 (1869), p. 275.

30. Myerson and Shealy, "The Sales of Louisa May Alcott's Books," p. 69.

31. *LW Abroad,* p. 158.

32. John S. P. Alcott, "The 'Little Women' of Long Ago," quoted in *Her Own Time,* pp. 154–155.

33. *Journals of BA,* p. 33.

34. Myerson and Shealy, "The Sales of Louisa May Alcott's Books," pp. 68–69.

35. *New York Times Book Review* (August 8, 1908).

36. Frank Luther Mott, *Golden Multitudes: The Story of Best Sellers in the United States* (New York: Macmillan, 1947), p. 102.

37. Gloria T. Delamar, *Louisa May Alcott and "Little Women": Biography, Critique, Publications, Poems, Songs and Contemporary Relevance* (Jefferson, N.C.: McFarland and Company, 1990), p. 192.

38. Louisa May Alcott to Elizabeth Sewall Willis Wells, May 16, 1869, manuscript letter, New York University, Fales Library.

LITTLE WOMEN

OR,

MEG, JO, BETH AND AMY

LOUISA M. ALCOTT

PART I

Contents

Preface

Go then, my little Book, and show to all
That entertain, and bid thee welcome shall,
What thou dost keep close shut up in thy breast;
And wish what thou dost show them may be blest
To them for good, may make them choose to be
Pilgrims better, by far, than thee or me.
Tell them of Mercy; she is one
Who early hath her pilgrimage begun.
Yea, let young damsels learn of her to prize
The world which is to come, and so be wise;
For little tripping maids may follow God
Along the ways which saintly feet have trod.

Adapted from John Bunyan[1]

1. John Bunyan (1628–1688) was a nonconformist English preacher and author of numerous Christian works. Imprisoned several times from 1660 to 1672 for preaching without a license, Bunyan, a Reformed Baptist, conceived his great allegory of Christian life, *The Pilgrim's Progress* (1678, 1684), while in jail. Significantly, LMA adapts as her preface to *Little Women* a passage from book two of *The Pilgrim's Progress*, instead of the better-known book one. In book one, Christian makes his spiritual journey to the Celestial City alone, leaving his family behind. In book two, Christiana, his wife, travels with her sons Matthew, Samuel, James, and Joseph, as well as Mercy, their young neighbor, on the same arduous journey to the Celestial City, facing hardship and trouble just as Christian had before them. Book two must have greatly appealed to LMA and her sisters, as it is a woman's journey. LMA knowingly selects as her preface a passage that focuses specifically on the hardships endured by young girls as they seek moral reform. In the character of young Mercy, the March sisters, as well as readers, see that the trials of the journey begin at a young age: "Tell them of Mercy, she is the one who early hath her pilgrimage begun." While the temptations and difficulties Christiana and Mercy face are not always the same as those of Christian, book two demonstrates the spiritual equality of both men and women. During the nineteenth century, this idea inspired individuals and groups to promote social change, from antislavery and abolitionism, to woman's rights and temperance reform.

Chapter 1

Playing Pilgrims

CHRISTMAS won't be Christmas without any presents," grumbled Jo, lying on the rug.

"It's so dreadful to be poor!" sighed Meg, looking down at her old dress.

"I don't think it's fair for some girls to have lots of pretty things, and other girls nothing at all," added little Amy, with an injured sniff.

"We've got father and mother, and each other, anyhow," said Beth, contentedly, from her corner.[1]

The four young faces on which the firelight shone brightened at the cheerful words, but darkened again as Jo said sadly,—

"We haven't got father, and shall not have him for a long time." She didn't say "perhaps never," but each silently added it, thinking of father far away, where the fighting was.[2]

Nobody spoke for a minute; then Meg said in an altered tone,—

"You know the reason mother proposed not having any presents this Christmas, was because it's going to be a hard winter for every one; and she thinks we ought not to spend money for pleasure, when our men are suffering so in the army. We can't do much, but we can make our little sacrifices, and ought to do it gladly. But I am afraid I don't;" and Meg shook her head, as she thought regretfully of all the pretty things she wanted.

"But I don't think the little we should spend would do any good. We've each got a dollar, and the army wouldn't be much helped by our giving that. I agree not to expect anything from mother or you, but I do want to buy Undine and Sintram[3] for myself; I've wanted it *so* long," said Jo, who was a bookworm.

1. In *"Little Women": A Family Romance* (New York: Twayne, 1999), Elizabeth Lennox Keyser observes, "The opening chapter, 'Playing Pilgrims,' begins to establish . . . the narrative method for much of the book. It opens with each of the four March sisters making a characteristic remark. Jo, who eventually emerges as the heroine of the book, speaks first; Beth, who dies before the end of the book, speaks last. . . . Thus we have on the very first page the technique that Alcott will employ throughout the first part of *Little Women*—the narrator's shift in focus from one girl to another (episode by episode or many times within the same episode) followed by a scene or sentence that includes and unites all four. This narrative method is perfectly adapted to Alcott's subject—the development of each girl's individuality, a process sometimes fraught with tension and conflict, within a cohesive family unit" (37–38).

2. The novel is set during the American Civil War and opens in December 1861. In *Little Women,* LMA never portrays the battlefield or army camp, but instead gives readers an alternative Civil War novel, one that depicts the family on the home front. Running throughout Part I of the novel is an undercurrent of tension, anxiety, and fear for Mr. March. Alcott well understood the often unspoken emotions that wartime families felt for absent loved ones.

As a daughter of parents who were fervent antislavery supporters, LMA longed to be involved in the war effort. As the Concord Artillery of the State Regiment, Massachusetts Volunteer Militia, departed Concord for Washington on April 19, 1861, Louisa noted: "A busy time getting them ready, and a sad day seeing them off, for in a little town like this we all seem like one family in times like these . . . I've often longed to see a war, and now I have my wish. I long to be a man, but as I can't fight, I will content myself with working for those who can" (*Journals* 105). Two weeks later, LMA recorded: "Spent our May-day working for our men . . . three hundred women all sewing together at the hall for two days" (*Journals* 105). In summer 1861, the United States Sanitary Commission was created to help promote healthy conditions at military hospitals, and Dorothea Dix, the country's first Supervisor of Nurses, set out to recruit nurses. LMA applied for a position and served as a nurse at the Union Hotel Hospital in Georgetown, D.C., from mid-December 1862 until she contracted typhoid fever in mid-January 1863. Her nursing experience led to her first real success as an author with the publication of *Hospital Sketches,* an early account of a military hospital. Originally written as letters to her family at home, LMA's hospital sketches were adapted into story form at the encouragement of her friend and fellow Concordian Franklin B. Sanborn, one of the "Secret Six" who had financially supported John Brown's raid on

Harper's Ferry in 1859. Published in installments in the *Boston Commonwealth* between May 22 and June 26, 1863, the sketches proved so successful that the abolitionist James Redpath gathered and reprinted them in book form in August 1863. Several months later, in December 1863, three of LMA's Civil War stories, along with an excerpt from *Hospital Sketches,* would be published as *On Picket Duty, and Other Tales* by Redpath, who rushed the book to press, hoping to capitalize on the popularity of *Hospital Sketches.*

3. *Undine, and Sintram and His Companions,* published by Wiley and Putnam in 1845, was a popular translation of the two novellas of the German Romantic author Friedrich de la Motte Fouqué (1777–1843). *Undine* (1811) tells the story of a water spirit who marries a human to receive a soul. *Sintram and His Companions* (1815) was, according to its author, inspired by Albrecht Dürer's woodcut *The Knight, Death and Satan* (1513). In this tale Sintram, a Christian knight, is tempted by the Devil and undergoes a quest of eventual self-discovery. The two works are also mentioned in *Jo's Boys* (1886). Alcott loved fairy tales, penning some thirty-eight fantasy works throughout her career, beginning with her first book in 1854, *Flower Fables.* See *Louisa May Alcott's Fairy Tales and Fantasy Stories,* ed. Daniel Shealy (Knoxville: University of Tennessee Press, 1992).

4. Kasper Faber began producing pencils in 1761 in Germany, and his son Anton Wilhelm took over in 1784, giving the company its famous brand name: A. W. Faber Co. Lothar Faber expanded the business and began manufacturing a more high-quality pencil. By 1843, Faber pencils were being imported to America, and in 1849, Faber operated an office in New York City. The company built a factory in Manhattan in 1861.

5. The *OED* defines *grub* as to work at a "grovellingly laborious occupation." In the 1880–1881 edition of *Little Women,* work is substituted for *grub* throughout the novel. For that new revised edition, the publisher modernized punctuation and spelling but, most significantly, altered LMA's language at times, especially her use of slang, in order to make her a more polished, "safe" author for juvenile readers.

6. Play the piano.

7. All of the March sisters work at their various jobs: Meg teaches in a private home, Jo serves as a companion to Aunt March, Beth helps keep house, and Amy attends school. Abigail Alcott believed in a cooperative family in which everyone worked for the good of all, an ideal instilled in LMA and her sisters at a young age. For example, in 1852, when LMA was twenty, she noted that her mother was operating an employment office for the poor, while the other family members also had their duties: "Anna and I taught [at home

"I planned to spend mine in new music," said Beth, with a little sigh, which no one heard but the hearth-brush and kettle-holder.

"I shall get a nice box of Faber's drawing pencils;[4] I really need them," said Amy, decidedly.

"Mother didn't say anything about our money, and she won't wish us to give up everything. Let's each buy what we want, and have a little fun; I'm sure we grub[5] hard enough to earn it," cried Jo, examining the heels of her boots in a gentlemanly manner.

"I know *I* do,—teaching those dreadful children[a] nearly all day, when I'm longing to enjoy myself at home," began Meg, in the complaining tone again.

"You don't have half such a hard time as I do," said Jo. "How would you like to be shut up for hours with a nervous, fussy old lady, who keeps you trotting, is never satisfied, and worries you till you're ready to fly out of the window or box her ears?"[b]

"It's naughty to fret,—but I do think washing dishes and keeping things tidy is the worst work in the world. It makes me cross; and my hands get so stiff, I can't practise[6] good a bit." And Beth looked at her rough hands with a sigh that any one could hear that time.

"I don't believe any of you suffer as I do," cried Amy; "for you don't have to go to school with impertinent girls, who plague you if you don't know your lessons, and laugh at your dresses, and label your father if he isn't rich, and insult you when your nose isn't nice."[7]

"If you mean *libel* I'd say so, and not talk about *labels,* as if pa was a pickle-bottle," advised Jo, laughing.

"I know what I mean, and you needn't be 'statirical' about it. It's proper to use good words, and improve your *vocabilary*," returned Amy, with dignity.

"Don't peck[8] at one another, children. Don't you wish we had the money papa lost when we were little, Jo?[9] Dear me, how happy and good we'd be, if we had no worries," said Meg, who could remember better times.

"You said the other day you thought we were a deal happier than the King children, for they were fighting and fretting all the time, in spite of their money."

"So I did, Beth. Well, I guess we are; for though we do have to

A delegation of suffragettes speaks before the House of Representatives, January 1871.

work, we make fun for ourselves, and are a pretty jolly set, as Jo would say."

"Jo does use such slang words," observed Amy, with a reproving look at the long figure stretched on the rug. Jo immediately sat up, put her hands in her apron pockets,[c] and began to whistle.

"Don't, Jo; it's so boyish."[10]

"That's why I do it."

"I detest rude, unlady-like girls."

"I hate affected, niminy piminy chits."[11]

"Birds in their little nests agree,"[12] sang Beth, the peace-maker, with such a funny face that both sharp voices softened to a laugh, and the "pecking" ended for that time.

"Really, girls, you are both to be blamed," said Meg, beginning to lecture in her elder sisterly fashion. "You are old enough to leave off boyish tricks, and behave better, Josephine. It didn't matter so much when you were a little girl; but now you are so tall, and turn up your hair,[13] you should remember that you are a young lady."

"I ain't! and if turning up my hair makes me one, I'll wear it in two tails till I'm twenty," cried Jo, pulling off her net, and shaking down a chestnut mane. "I hate to think I've got to grow up and be Miss March, and wear long gowns, and look as prim as a China-aster.[14] It's bad enough to be a girl, any-way, when I like boys' games, and work, and manners. I can't get over my disappoint-

in what was called a "parlor school"], Lizzie was our little house-keeper . . . May went to school, father wrote and talked when he could get classes or conversations" (*Journals* 67). However, the jobs of the Alcott sisters—as well as those of the March sisters—stand in contrast to those of the young women and girls who, by 1861, were working in New England factories. The nearby Lowell mills employed large numbers of young women, aged fifteen to twenty, as textile workers, who often toiled twelve hours a day, six days a week. LMA firmly endorsed the power of work, believing it to be a way for a woman to achieve independence. Throughout her early life, until the success of *Little Women*, LMA held a variety of jobs: teacher, governess, writer, seamstress, nurse, domestic helper, companion. From the knowledge acquired in these real-life positions, she wrote *Work: A Story of Experience* (1873), a chronicle of Christie Devon, who explores the employment options available to women in the nineteenth century.

8. According to the *OED*, a figurative expression, meaning "to pick on."

9. LMA attributes the Marches' poverty to bad investments made by Mr. March. In reality, the Alcott family struggled financially until LMA's success with *Little Women*. Abigail Alcott supported the family during the 1840s and 1850s, with the girls also earning money by sewing, teaching, and serving as governesses once they were in their teens. Ann Douglas notes in her "Introduction" to *Little Women*: "Mr. March's poverty, like Bronson Alcott's, protects his family from the psychological consequences of living in a profit-oriented society. If he acquires nothing, he learns and passes on none of the ugly lessons of acquisition" ([New York: Signet, 1983], pp. vii–xxvii; reprinted in *"Little Women" and the Feminist Imagination,* ed. Janice M. Alberghene and Beverly Lyon Clark [New York: Garland, 1999], pp. 43–62; quote p. 67). Unlike her impecunious husband, Abigail Alcott's well-to-do father, Col. Joseph May, did suffer a financial set-back after his business failed due to his partner's dishonest dealings. Friends, however, helped him obtain a position at an insurance company, thus securing a genteel lifestyle.

10. In *Tomboys: A Literary and Cultural History* (Philadelphia: Temple University Press, 2008), Michelle Ann Abate notes, "The invaluable work that adolescent girls and young women performed during the Civil War had a profound effect on the popularity of tomboyism. Whereas this code of conduct had been a relatively small societal practice during the antebellum era, it morphed into a widespread cultural phenomenon. During the 1860s and 1870s, Americans witnessed the benefits of creating physically strong, intellectually capable and emotionally resilient young women" (25).

However, as Abate also notes, many people still frowned on tom-boyism, as such masculine qualities would produce a more independent woman, ready to abandon the feminine private sphere. But is *Little Women* really about tomboyism? Critics, of course, are as much embedded in their historical moments as the writers they study. Today we might observe that if Jo behaves like a boy it has less to do with tomboyism than it does with the strong expression of a young, intelligent girl's desire to enjoy all the privileges of the male sex. Why not wish to be a boy if you are prevented from the full range of human activities as a girl? In "Beneath the Surface: Power and Passion in *Little Women*" (*Critical Essays on Louisa May Alcott*, ed. Madeleine B. Stern [Boston: G. K. Hall, 1984]), Madelon Bedell observes: "*Little Women* is not about 'being good,' nor even about growing up, but about the complexities of female power and the struggle to maintain it in a male-dominated society" (p. 147).

Along with her parents, LMA had long been a supporter of woman's rights. Growing up in the home of a Transcendentalist, LMA read Margaret Fuller's *Woman in the Nineteenth Century* (1845), which clearly inspired her to achieve self-development and self-reliance. In 1868, the same year LMA was composing *Little Women*, Susan B. Anthony and Elizabeth Cady Stanton were publishing a suffrage newspaper, *The Revolution,* and by the time Part II of *Little Women* appeared, the two had started to organize the National Woman Suffrage Association (NWSA). Many in the public, including LMA, saw their platform as too strident. With the support of the New England Woman Suffrage Association (NEWSA), Lucy Stone and other women formed a more moderate wing of the movement—the American Woman Suffrage Association (AWSA). They also published *The Woman's Journal,* viewed by many as the organization's forum. In July 1870, Alcott wrote to her family that the NWSA had attempted to garner her support: "Did I tell you that [Theodore] Tilton sent me a gushing letter asking me to write for 'The Revolution?' I shall not: for it is not our party unless the Boston and New York squabblers have joined forces. Have they?" She declared her allegiance to NEWSA: "If I wrote for any Woman's thing it would be for [Mary] Livermore's paper [Livermore's paper *The Agitator* merged with *The Woman's Journal* in 1870; Livermore then served as associate editor]. I would rather keep to my own work and lecture the public in a story, than hold forth . . . in the papers" (*Selected Letters* 144). LMA did, however, support Stone's paper by publishing eighteen pieces in *The Woman's Journal* between 1874 and 1887. She also lent her support to the National Congress of the Women in the United States, held in Syracuse, New York, in 1876. After promoting suffrage in Concord so women could vote in the

Illustration of the suffragist Victoria Woodhull attempting to vote in 1871. LMA was among the first women to vote in Concord, Mass., when she cast her vote for the school committee.

ment in not being a boy,[15] and it's worse than ever now, for I'm dying to go and fight with papa,[16] and I can only stay at home and knit like a poky old woman;" and Jo shook the blue army-sock till the needles rattled like castanets, and her ball[17] bounded across the room.

"Poor Jo; it's too bad! But it can't be helped, so you must try to be contented with making your name boyish, and playing brother to us girls," said Beth, stroking the rough head at her knee with a hand that all the dish-washing and dusting in the world could not make ungentle in its touch.

"As for you, Amy," continued Meg, "you are altogether too particular and prim. Your airs[18] are funny now, but you'll grow up an affected little goose[19] if you don't take care. I like your nice manners, and refined ways of speaking, when you don't try to be elegant[20]; but your absurd words are as bad as Jo's slang."

"If Jo is a tom-boy, and Amy a goose, what am I, please?" asked Beth, ready to share the lecture.

"You're a dear, and nothing else," answered Meg, warmly; and no one contradicted her, for the "Mouse"[21] was the pet of the family.

As young readers[22] like to know "how people look," we will

Hillside, home of the Alcotts in Concord, Mass., from 1845 to 1848. Many of the events recounted in Part I of *Little Women* took place here. Nathaniel Hawthorne renamed it Wayside when he purchased it from the Alcotts in 1852.

take this moment to give them a little sketch of the four sisters, who sat knitting away in the twilight, while the December snow fell quietly without, and the fire crackled cheerfully within.[23] It was a comfortable old room, though the carpet was faded and the furniture very plain, for a good picture or two hung on the walls, books filled the recesses, chrysanthemums and Christmas roses[24] bloomed in the windows, and a pleasant atmosphere of home-peace pervaded it.[25]

Margaret, the eldest of the four, was sixteen, and very pretty, being plump and fair, with large eyes, plenty of soft brown hair, a sweet mouth, and white hands, of which she was rather vain.[26] Fifteen-year-old Jo was very tall, thin and brown, and reminded one of a colt; for she never seemed to know what to do with her long limbs, which were very much in her way. She had a decided[27] mouth, a comical nose, and sharp gray eyes, which appeared to see everything, and were by turns fierce, funny, or thoughtful.[28] Her long, thick hair was her one beauty; but it was usually bundled into a net, to be out of her way. Round shoulders had Jo, big hands and feet, a fly-away look to her clothes,[29] and the uncomfortable appearance of a girl who was rapidly shooting up into a

elections for the school committee, she was among the first women to cast a vote there in 1879. Not only in *Little Women* but also in other novels, such as *An Old-Fashioned Girl* (1870), *Work: A Story of Experience* (1873), and *Jo's Boys* (1886), LMA addressed the issue of woman's rights.

11. The *OED* defines *niminy-piminy* as "mincing ['affectedly dainty, elegant, or mannered']; affected." It gives its etymology as "imitative of affected speech" and cites its first usage as 1786. A *chit* is "a very young child; a brat."

12. Beth quotes from Isaac Watts's *Divine Songs for Children* (1715), a pioneering collection of poems and songs especially composed to teach young people morals and good behavior. Though a British work, the collection became extremely popular in America. Beth recites from verse 2 of Song 17, known as "Love between brothers and sisters": "Birds in their little nests agree; / And 'tis a shameful sight, / When children of one family / Fall out, and chide, and fight."

13. In the nineteenth century, young girls wore their hair braided or long until they reached puberty, when wearing it up signified that they were mature and were coming out in society. Jo's protest here is another indication that she does not wish to grow up and become a young lady.

14. *Callistephus chinensis,* an annual flowering plant in the daisy family. Native to China, the plant was and often still is used as an ornamental in gardens and for cut flowers.

15. In 1860, LMA confessed to her good friend Alfred Whitman (1842–1907), who served as partial inspiration for the character of Laurie: "I was born with a boys nature & always had more sympathy for & interest in them than in girls, & have fought my fight for nearly fifteen [years] with a boys spirit under my 'bib and tucker' & a boys wrath when I get 'floored'" (*Selected Letters* 50–51). Frederick Willis reported in *Alcott Memoirs* (1915) that "Louisa always lamented she was not born a boy. With the exception of rope skipping, at which she excelled all of us in power of endurance, she preferred boys' games to those of her sex" (quoted in *Her Own Time* 178).

16. LMA, on May 19, 1861, wrote to Alf Whitman in Iowa: "Are you going to have a dab at the saucy Southerners? I long to fly at some body & free my mind on several points, but there is no opening for me at present so I study Dr Home on 'Gun shot wounds,' & get my highly connected self ready to go as a nurse when the slow coaches at Washington begin to lay about them & get their fellow men into a comfortably smashed condition" (*Selected Letters* 65). Over a year later, in autumn 1862, after several Union defeats, LMA confided: "I like the stir in the air, and long for battle like a warhorse when he smells powder. The blood of the Mays is up!" (*Journals* 109).

17. Jo's ball of yarn.

18. The *OED* defines airs as an "assumed manner, affected appearance, show."

19. A foolish or silly person.

20. Emily Thornwell, author of a popular nineteenth-century etiquette guide for girls, writes: "More particularly, young ladies should guard themselves against affectation. This is very easily acquired, and is so common a fault that the absence of it is always remarked as a great excellence. Some persons of many amiable qualities, and considerable intelligence, have been absolutely spoiled for society by attempting to assume in their manners what did not belong to them. Wherever anything of this kind exists, it requires but little sagacity to detect it; and even those who are not exactly sensible where the evil lies, are still aware that there is something which needs to be corrected" (*The Lady's Guide* 74).

21. The nickname comes from the phrase "as quiet as a mouse" and suits Beth because she is so shy.

22. LMA's direct address clearly indicates that she is keeping her targeted audience in mind as she writes her first "girl's book."

23. Today, most people associate *Little Women* with Orchard House, the home the Alcotts bought on Lexington Road in Concord, Massachusetts, and refurbished in 1858, and where they lived until 1877. Less than a mile from the center of Concord and even closer to Emerson's home, Orchard House is where LMA wrote *Little Women* at the small desk Bronson Alcott built for her in her front, second-story bedroom. Most of the popular film versions of the novel have also patterned the Marches' home on Orchard House, further establishing the house as the setting of the novel in the cultural imagination. However, many of the events that LMA fictionalizes in *Little Women* actually occurred at Hillside, next door to Orchard House, where the Alcotts lived from January 1845 to November 1848, when LMA and her older sister Anna were teenagers. In 1852, the Alcotts sold Hillside to Nathaniel Hawthorne, who renamed it Wayside and lived there, except for his time as U.S. consul in England, until his death in 1864. For *Little Women*, LMA, of course, also drew on her family memories of when the Alcotts lived in the Hosmer Cottage in Concord from 1840 to 1843 and also in various locations in Boston in the late 1840s. In 1912 Orchard House was opened as a museum. The house was restored to the way it looked when the Alcotts lived there, including much of the original furniture and furnishings. Overseen by the Louisa May Alcott Memorial Association, Orchard House, Home of the Alcotts, is open daily year-round. Wayside, owned and operated by the National Park Service, is also open as a museum documenting the lives of the Alcotts and Hawthorne. For more on the history of the two houses, see Patricia West, "Gender Politics and the Orchard House Museum," *Domesticating History: The Political Origins of America's House Museums* (Washington: Smithsonian Institution Press, 1999), pp. 39–91; Margaret M. Lothrop, *The Wayside: Home of Authors* (New York: American Book Company, 1968).

24. *Helleborus niger*, a perennial flowering plant that blooms in winter, producing large white flowers. Legend has it that a small girl who had no gift for the Christ child in the manger of Bethlehem cried tears that dropped in the snow and caused the Christmas rose to sprout.

25. In "'A Power in the House': *Little Women* and the Architecture of Individual Expression," in *"Little Women" and the Feminist Imagination*, pp. 185–212, David H. Watters writes: "When we come upon the March girls gathered in the parlor to await the homecoming of Marmee, we are initiated into the elaborate parlor game of the nineteenth century which uses the furnishings as gestures to signify the family's class, aesthetic, and moral values . . . Despite reduced circumstances, this family values the comfortable intimacy of the hearth, appreciates art, values literacy, and has the where-withal to keep a room warm enough for houseplants. Home peace counters national war" (186).

26. Anna Alcott Pratt wrote to an inquisitive admirer of the novel in 1871, while LMA was away in Europe: "'Meg' was never the pretty vain little maiden, who coquetted and made herself so charming. But 'Jo' always admired poor, plain 'Meg,' and when she came to put her in the story, she beautified her to suit the occasion, saying 'Dear me, girls, we must have one beauty in the book!'" (quoted in *Her Own Time* 18). Anna, LMA's closest companion and confidant growing up, became her protector in adulthood, as fame became a burden.

27. Determined.

28. Frederick L. H. Willis, a childhood friend of the Alcott girls, wrote in *Alcott Memoirs* (1915): "Louisa May . . . had a clear olive-brown complexion with brown hair and eyes. She answered perfectly an ideal of the 'Nut Brown Maid'; she was full of spirit and life; impulsive and moody, and at times irritable and nervous" (quoted in *Her Own Time* 177).

29. Streaming or loose clothes, here indicating that Jo gives little concern to dress. The phrase could also imply that Jo did not wear a corset. LMA was a longtime supporter of dress reform. In 1874, LMA's publisher, Roberts Brothers, published Abba Goold Woolson's *Dress-Reform: A Series of Lectures Delivered in Boston on Dress as It Affects the Health of Women*. The following year, LMA took up the cause of dress reform in Chapter 18 of her new novel *Eight Cousins* (1875), when Uncle Alec offers Rose Campbell, his guardian and the book's main character, an alternative dress style for the over-tight corset. The sequel, *Rose in Bloom* (1876), demonstrates the success of Uncle Alec's influence on Rose.

30. On January 18, 1868, LMA used this term to refer to her nephew, John Pratt: "Little Tranquility played alone all day and made a pretty picture sit-

LMA's writings on dress reform suggested that a young woman should not wear a tightly corseted dress such as the one shown here because it was unhealthy.

ting in 'marmar's lap' in his night-gown" (*Journals* 163). Willis, in *Alcott Memoirs* (1915), describes Elizabeth Alcott: "Elizabeth . . . was aptly named by her father 'Little Tranquility.' Pages would not better describe her. She was possessed of an even, lovable disposition, a temperament akin to Mr. Alcott, indeed more than akin, since it was a very counterpart. Under any and all conditions she was sunny and serene as a morning in June. Her appearance was that of a typical Puritan maid" (quoted in *Her Own Time* 181).

31. A character in Russian folk tales, the Snow Maiden is often depicted as a beautiful girl with long blonde hair.

woman, and didn't like it. Elizabeth,—or Beth, as every one called her,—was a rosy, smooth-haired, bright-eyed girl of thirteen, with a shy manner, a timid voice, and a peaceful expression, which was seldom disturbed. Her father called her "Little Tranquillity,"[30] and the name suited her excellently; for she seemed to live in a happy world of her own, only venturing out to meet the few whom she trusted and loved. Amy, though the youngest, was a most important person, in her own opinion at least. A regular snow maiden, with blue eyes, and yellow hair curling on her shoulders;[31] pale and slender, and always carrying herself like a young lady mindful

32. The Alcott family always made birthdays special with family ceremonies. Frank Sanborn, who conducted a private academy in Concord during the 1860s, quoted from Anna Alcott's 1843 diary written at Fruitlands, in his "Reminiscences of Louisa May Alcott" (1912): "'This was Lizzie's birthday. I rose before 5 o'clock, and went with Louisa and Willy Lane to the Grove, where we fixed a little pine tree in the ground, and hung all our presents on it. Mother gave her a silk thread case, Louisa a pincushion, I a fan, Willy a book, and Abby [May] a little pitcher. I made for each of us an oak-leaf wreath. After breakfast, we all . . . marched to the wood. Mr. Lane carried his violin and played, and we all sung first. Then father read a parable and an ode which he wrote himself.'" Sanborn noted: "These festivals were common and natural in this family, where in many simple ways imagination and generosity were cultivated or quickened" (quoted in *Her Own Time* 150–151).

of her manners. What the characters of the four sisters were, we will leave to be found out.

The clock struck six; and, having swept up the hearth, Beth put a pair of slippers down to warm. Somehow the sight of the old shoes had a good effect upon the girls, for mother was coming, and every one brightened to welcome her. Meg stopped lecturing, and lit the lamp, Amy got out of the easy-chair without being asked, and Jo forgot how tired she was as she sat up to hold the slippers nearer to the blaze.

"They are quite worn out; Marmee must have a new pair."

"I thought I'd get her some with my dollar," said Beth.

"No, I shall!" cried Amy.

"I'm the oldest," began Meg, but Jo cut in with a decided—

"I'm the man of the family now papa is away, and *I* shall provide the slippers, for he told me to take special care of mother while he was gone."

"I'll tell you what we'll do," said Beth; "let's each get her something for Christmas, and not get anything for ourselves."

"That's like you, dear! What will we get?" exclaimed Jo.

Every one thought soberly for a minute; then Meg announced, as if the idea was suggested by the sight of her own pretty hands, "I shall give her a nice pair of gloves."

"Army shoes, best to be had," cried Jo.

"Some handkerchiefs, all hemmed," said Beth.

"I'll get a little bottle of Cologne; she likes it, and it won't cost much, so I'll have some left to buy something for me," added Amy.

"How will we give the things?" asked Meg.

"Put 'em on the table, and bring her in and see her open the bundles. Don't you remember how we used to do on our birthdays?" answered Jo.

"I used to be *so* frightened when it was my turn to sit in the big chair with a crown on, and see you all come marching round to give the presents, with a kiss. I liked the things and the kisses, but it was dreadful to have you sit looking at me while I opened the bundles," said Beth, who was toasting her face and the bread for tea, at the same time.[32]

...ooney, *Little Women* (1955).

33. Anna Alcott was always interested in acting. She had parts in the plays she co-authored and performed with Louisa in the family's Hillside barn on Lexington Road in Concord in the 1840s. By 1850, Louisa confessed to her journal: "Anna wants to be an actress, and so do I. We could make plenty of money perhaps, and it is a very gay life. Mother says we are too young, and must wait. A. acts splendidly. I like tragic plays . . . We get up fine ones, and make harps, castles, armor, dresses, water-falls, and thunder, and have great fun" (*Journals* 63–64). In 1855, the Alcotts moved to Walpole, New Hampshire, where both girls joined in the comedies and farces of the Amateur Dramatic Company. In 1857, when they returned to Concord, Louisa helped Frank Sanborn, who had recently graduated from Harvard and established a private academy in the village, form the Concord Dramatic Union. Here, both Louisa and Anna took to the stage, along with Anna's future husband, John Bridge Pratt. For more on Alcott's interest in the theater, see Madeleine B. Stern, "Louisa Alcott, Trouper: Experiments in Theatricals, 1848–1880," in *Louisa May Alcott: From Blood & Thunder to Hearth and Home* (Boston: Northeastern University Press, 1998), pp. 13–38.

34. Stage boards. The *OED* lists the earliest use of the term as 1831 by Charles Lamb in *Ellistoniana* in *Englishman's Magazine:* "That harmonious fusion of the manners of the player into those of every day life, which brought the stage boards into streets, and dining-parlours." The second example of the use of the term appears in E. Bulwer-Lytton's 1858 play *What will he do with It?:* "She had never then trod the boards."

ngs for ourselves, and
to-morrow afternoon,
Christmas night," said
s behind her back, and

s time; I'm getting too
was as much a child as

u can trail round in a
ar gold-paper jewelry.
e'll be an end of every-
e ought to rehearse to-

35. Stern points out that "The Witches Curse" is based on several of the plays the Alcott girls wrote and performed between 1847 and 1849: "When she sat down to write the story for girls that was to make her fortune, Louisa was quick to include in it an account of the Hillside troupe, and, taking Hagar from 'The Unloved Wife,' Hugo from 'Norna; or, The Witch's Curse,' Zara from 'The Captive of Castile,' and miraculous potions from 'Bianca,' evolved a composite melodrama entitled 'The Witch's Curse, an Operatic Tragedy'" ("Louisa Alcott, Trouper" 17). These plays were later collected by Anna Alcott Pratt in *Comic Tragedies Written by "Jo" and "Meg" and Acted by the "Little Women"* (Boston: Roberts Brothers, 1893).

36. A trap door was sometimes used in stage productions of *Macbeth* for the appearance of Banquo's ghost at the banquet scene (3.4). The lines Jo quotes are Macbeth's famous words as he contemplates murdering Duncan, the king of Scotland (2.1.33). LMA perhaps is referring to Edwin Forrest (1806–1872), an American Shakespearean actor. During 1855, he had been engaged in a number of Shakespeare plays at the Boston Theater. She wrote to her father on November 28, 1855: "[T]ho Forrest does not act Shakespere well the beauty of the play shines thro the badly represented parts, & imagining what I should like to see, I can make up a better Macbeth & Hamlet for myself than Forrest with his gaspings & shoutings can give me" (*Selected Letters* 14).

night; come here, Amy, and do the fainting scene, for you are as stiff as a poker in that."

"I can't help it; I never saw any one faint, and I don't choose to make myself all black and blue, tumbling flat as you do. If I can go down easily, I'll drop; if I can't, I shall fall into a chair and be graceful; I don't care if Hugo does come at me with a pistol," returned Amy, who was not gifted with dramatic power, but was chosen because she was small enough to be borne out shrieking by the hero of the piece.[d]

"Do it this way; clasp your hands so, and stagger across the room, crying frantically, 'Roderigo! save me! save me!'" and away went Jo, with a melodramatic scream which was truly thrilling.

Amy followed, but she poked her hands out stiffly before her, and jerked herself along as if she went by machinery; and her "Ow!" was more suggestive of pins being run into her than of fear and anguish. Jo gave a despairing groan, and Meg laughed outright, while Beth let her bread burn as she watched the fun, with interest.

"It's no use! do the best you can when the time comes, and if the audience shout,[e] don't blame me. Come on, Meg."

Then things went smoothly, for Don Pedro defied the world in a speech of two pages without a single break; Hagar, the witch, chanted an awful incantation over her kettleful of simmering toads, with weird effect; Roderigo rent his chains asunder manfully, and Hugo died in agonies of remorse and arsenic, with a wild "Ha! ha!"

"It's the best we've had yet," said Meg, as the dead villain sat up and rubbed his elbows.

"I don't see how you can write and act such splendid things, Jo. You're a regular Shakespeare!" exclaimed Beth, who firmly believed that her sisters were gifted with wonderful genius in all things.

"Not quite," replied Jo, modestly. "I do think 'The Witch's Curse, an Operatic Tragedy,'[35] is rather a nice thing; but I'd like to try Macbeth, if we only had a trap-door for Banquo. I always wanted to do the killing part. 'Is that a dagger that I see before me?'" muttered Jo, rolling her eyes and clutching at the air, as she had seen a famous tragedian do.[36]

"No, it's the toasting fork, with ma's shoe on it instead of the bread. Beth's stage struck!" cried Meg, and the rehearsal ended in a general burst of laughter.

"Glad to find you so merry, my girls," said a cheery voice at the door, and actors and audience turned to welcome a stout,[f] motherly lady, with a "can-I-help-you" look about her which was truly delightful. She wasn't a particularly handsome person, but mothers are always lovely to their children,[g] and the girls thought the gray cloak and unfashionable bonnet[37] covered the most splendid woman in the world.

"Well, dearies, how have you got on to-day? There was so much to do, getting the boxes ready to go to-morrow, that I didn't come home to dinner. Has any one called,[38] Beth? How is your cold, Meg? Jo, you look tired to death. Come and kiss me, baby."

While making these maternal inquiries Mrs. March got her wet things off, her hot slippers on, and sitting down in the easy-chair, drew Amy to her lap, preparing to enjoy the happiest hour of her busy day. The girls flew about, trying to make things comfortable, each in her own way. Meg arranged the tea-table; Jo brought wood and set chairs, dropping, overturning, and clattering everything she touched; Beth trotted to and fro between parlor and kitchen, quiet and busy; while Amy gave directions to every one, as she sat with her hands folded.

As they gathered about the table, Mrs. March said, with a particularly happy face, "I've got a treat for you after supper."

A quick, bright smile went round like a streak of sunshine. Beth clapped her hands, regardless of the hot biscuit she held, and Jo tossed up her napkin, crying, "A letter! a letter! Three cheers for father!"

"Yes, a nice long letter.[39] He is well, and thinks he shall get through the cold season better than we feared. He sends all sorts of loving wishes for Christmas, and an especial message to you girls," said Mrs. March, patting her pocket as if she had got a treasure there.

"Hurry up, and get done. Don't stop to quirk[40] your little finger, and prink[41] over your plate,[h] Amy," cried Jo, choking in her tea, and dropping her bread, butter side down, on the carpet, in her haste to get at the treat.

37. Mrs. March's plain and "unfashionable" dress indicates that she cares more about other people's needs than about fashion.

38. Visited.

39. During the Civil War, postal delivery for the Union army was far better than for the Confederacy. A mail service usually followed the Union forces, selling them stamps and gathering mail. Often the U.S. Sanitary Commission provided free envelopes and paper for the troops. By 1864, stamps were no longer required if "Soldier's Letter" appeared on the envelope. With Union roads, waterways, and railroads basically unchallenged by the enemy, mail was able to travel quickly, even from armies on the move.

40. The *OED* defines *quirk:* "To jerk or twitch (something, esp. a part of the body); to bend or curve . . . suddenly and briefly," and it cites this passage in *Little Women* as its first usage.

41. To primp. The 1880–1881 edition changed the word to *simper,* which the *OED* defines as "to smile in a silly, self-conscious way."

Gillian Armstrong's film adaptation of *Little Women* (1994) casts a warm glow over the now-famous tableau of Marmee (Susan Sarandon) reading Mr. March's letter to the four sisters.

42. When the Civil War began in 1861, Bronson Alcott was too old to enlist in active service. A pacifist, he brooded about the fighting, following the daily accounts in the papers. When he visited an ill LMA in the Union Hotel Hospital in December 1862, he saw for himself the carnage wrought by the Battle of Fredericksburg: "Horrid war; and one sees its horrors in hospitals if any where" (*Journals of BA* 353).

43. A vivandière was a woman who provided meals to the French or continental armies.

44. A kind of hovering spiritual presence in the novel, Mr. March does not actually appear until Chapter 22 of Part I. While he serves to provide inspiration and advice to the girls through his letter, Mrs. March is their guide. Mr. March is based upon Bronson Alcott, a complex individual and surely a complex father. John Matteson provides an excellent description of Bronson Alcott in his Pulitzer Prize–winning book *Eden's Outcasts: The Story of Louisa May Alcott and Her Father* (New York: W. W. Norton, 2007): "So long as Alcott could move within the sphere of the ethereal and evanescent, he

Beth ate no more, but crept away, to sit in her shadowy corner and brood over the delight to come, till the others were ready.

"I think it was so splendid in father to go as a chaplain when he was too old to be draughted, and not strong enough for a soldier," said Meg, warmly.[42]

"Don't I wish I could go as a drummer, a *vivan*[43]—what's its name? or a nurse, so I could be near him and help him," exclaimed Jo, with a groan.

"It must be very disagreeable to sleep in a tent, and eat all sorts of bad-tasting things, and drink out of a tin mug," sighed Amy.

"When will he come home, Marmee?" asked Beth, with a little quiver in her voice.

"Not for many months, dear, unless he is sick. He will stay and do his work faithfully as long as he can, and we won't ask for him back a minute sooner than he can be spared.[44] Now come and hear the letter."

LITTLE WOMEN

Reading Father's letter. Jessie Willcox Smith, *Little Women* (1915).

moved with radiance and grace. As soon as he stepped into the world of things and actions or tried to project a durable image of himself, he began to lose his balance. When he attempted to astonish the world by performing a truly great task—and he found such tasks almost fatally irresistible—his ease, common sense, and good fortune deserted him entirely, and he fell to earth with a thud" (p. 7).

45. In "The Prophets and the Martyrs: Pilgrims and Missionaries in *Little Women* and *Jack and Jill*," in *"Little Women" and the Feminist Imagination*, pp. 213–236, Anne K. Phillips argues: "Many critics have noted Mr. March's absence and minor influence through much of the novel; nonetheless, he is a far more important character than many critics have acknowledged. Mr. March embodies many of the characteristics of Evangelist in Bunyan's work. Although Evangelist appears only three times during the pilgrimage, he is a significant influence on—and an evident supporter —of Christian. As Mr. March indirectly inspires the March daughters to begin their pilgrimage, so Evangelist provides Christian with his inspiration" (221).

46. In *A Hunger for Home: Louisa May Alcott's Place in American Culture* (New Brunswick: Rutgers University Press, 1987), Sarah Elbert argues that LMA took the phrase "little woman," and hence the book's title, from Charles Dickens's *Bleak House* (1852–1853), which she had read while serving as a nurse in Georgetown, D.C., in late 1862: "In this novel [*Bleak House*], the term 'little women' makes a prominent appearance when Esther, ward of the generous, sweethearted Mr. Jarndyce, is told by her guardian, 'You have wrought changes in me, little woman,' indicating that she has widened and deepened his sensibilities and hence his philanthropy . . . When Louisa May Alcott employed the term 'little women,' she infused it with this Dickensian meaning. *Little Women* portrays just such a complex overlapping of stages from childhood to elder child, little woman to young woman, that appears in *Bleak House.* Like Esther, each of Alcott's heroines has a scarring experience that jars her into painful awareness of vanished childhood innocence and the inescapable woman problem" (196). As with so many of Dickens's novels, *Bleak House* portrays the harsh treatment and injustices of poor children. It also serves as an indictment against the injustices of the British judiciary. Esther Summerson, Dickens's only female narrator, is brought up as a poor orphan because the identity of her parents is unknown. Her way is hard, yet Esther remains an unselfish character, often helping those more unfortunate than she. When her guardian, Mr. Jarndyce, calls her "little woman," he does so out of

They all drew to the fire, mother in the big chair with Beth at her feet, Meg and Amy perched on either arm of the chair, and Jo leaning on the back, where no one would see any sign of emotion if the letter should happen to be touching.

Very few letters were written in those hard times that were not touching, especially those which fathers sent home. In this one little was said of the hardships endured, the dangers faced, or the homesickness conquered; it was a cheerful, hopeful letter, full of lively descriptions of camp life, marches, and military news; and only at the end did the writer's heart overflow with fatherly love and longing for the little girls at home.

"Give them all my dear love and a kiss. Tell them I think of them by day, pray for them by night, and find my best comfort in their affection at all times. A year seems very long to wait before I see them, but remind them that while we wait we may all work, so that these hard days need not be wasted. I know they will remember all I said to them, that they will be loving children to you, will do their duty faithfully, fight their bosom enemies bravely, and conquer themselves so beautifully, that when I come back to them I may be fonder and prouder than ever of my little women."[45]

Everybody sniffed when they came to that part; Jo wasn't ashamed of the great tear that dropped off the end of her nose, and Amy never minded the rumpling of her curls as she hid her face on her mother's shoulder and sobbed out, "I *am* a selfish pig![i] but I'll truly try to be better, so he mayn't be disappointed in me by and by."

"We all will!" cried Meg. "I think too much of my looks, and hate to work, but won't any more, if I can help it."

"I'll try and be what he loves to call me, 'a little woman,'[46] and not be rough and wild; but do my duty here instead of wanting to be somewhere else," said Jo, thinking that keeping her temper at home was a much harder task than facing a rebel or two down South.

Beth said nothing, but wiped away her tears with the blue army-sock, and began to knit with all her might, losing no time in doing the duty that lay nearest her, while she resolved in her

Frontispiece for *The Pilgrim's Progress,* "Bunyan's Dream."

respect for how she has endured. Esther's life is indeed a "pilgrim's progress." In chapter 35 of *Bleak House,* Esther, now twenty-one and ill with scarlet fever, contemplates her own life: "I had never known before how short life really was and into how small a space the mind could put it."

"While I was very ill, the way in which these divisions of time became confused with one another distressed my mind exceedingly. At once a child, an elder girl, and the little woman I had been so happy as, I was not only oppressed by cares and difficulties adapted to each station, but by the great perplexity of endlessly trying to reconcile them. I suppose that few who have not been in such a condition can quite understand what I mean or what painful unrest arose from this source." Like Esther, LMA knows the stage between youth and adulthood is all-important; no journey is necessarily safe. Each stage has its unique burdens. The lessons learned and the guidance offered, however, may make the difference as a "little woman" transforms into an adult. Like *The Pilgrim's Progress, Bleak House,* though never mentioned in *Little Women,* serves as another model for the March sisters.

47. *The Pilgrim's Progress from This World to That Which Is to Come* (1678) by John Bunyan is a recurring presence in *Little Women.* It tells the allegorical story of Christian's journey from his home in the City of Destruction to the Celestial City. Leaving his wife and sons behind, he carries with him the burden of sin as he encounters obstacles along his way, such as the Hill of Difficulty, the Valley of Humiliation, and the Valley of the Shadow of Death. Often helped by allegorical figures such as Good Will, Faithful, and the Shining Ones, Christian eventually reaches heaven, the Celestial City. Part two of *The Pilgrim's Progress* (1684) recounts the journey of his wife, Christiana, and his four sons, who visit the same locations. This second part of the tale may have resonated greatly with the four Alcott girls when Bronson read them the book: one of its lessons is that females can also be pilgrims who overcome their burdens. In 1839, Bronson wrote: "The *Pilgrim's Progress* is a work of pure genius . . . This book is one of the few that gave me to myself. It is associated with reality. It unites me with childhood, and seems to chronicle my Identity. How I was rapt in it! How gladly did I seat myself, after the day's labours on the farm, in the chimney niche, with the tallow candle in my hand, and pore over its enchanting pages until late in the night! That book was incorporated into the very substance of my youthful being. I thought and spoke through it. It was my most efficient teacher" (*Journals of BA* 111). In 1843, while at Fruitlands,

quiet little soul to be all that father hoped to find her when the year brought round the happy coming home.

Mrs. March broke the silence that followed Jo's words, by saying in her cheery voice, "Do you remember how you used to play Pilgrim's Progress⁴⁷ when you were little things? Nothing delighted eleven-year-old Louisa copied some of her favorite passages from *The Pilgrim's Progress* into her journal (*Journals* 48–50). The game of *Pilgrim's Progress* that the Alcott girls played at Hillside was passed on to the next generation. John Sewall Pratt Alcott, Louisa's nephew (whom she legally adopted late in her life to ensure that her copyrights could be passed on), wrote in "The 'Little Women' of Long Ago" (1913): "We played 'Pilgrim's Progress' just as they did in 'Little Women'" (quoted in *Her Own Time* 160).

48. Bags that held patches of cloth, which were often used to make quilts.

49. Apollyon, the lord of the City of Destruction, in *The Pilgrim's Progress*. In the form of a dragon creature, he battles Christian in the Valley of Humiliation, hoping to force the pilgrim to serve him. Before his encounter with Apollyon, Christian had stopped overnight at the Palace Beautiful. Near the gates of the Palace Beautiful are two lions, which at first stop fearful Christian from continuing. However, Watchful, the porter of the Palace, assures him that the lions are chained, and Christian enters the palace. After battling Apollyon, Christian must go through the Valley of the Shadow of Death, where he meets two men who warn him that they saw hobgoblins, dragons, and satyrs in the darkness.

you more than to have me tie my piece-bags[48] on your backs for burdens, give you hats and sticks, and rolls of paper, and let you travel through the house from the cellar, which was the City of Destruction, up, up, to the house-top, where you had all the lovely things you could collect to make a Celestial City."

"What fun it was, especially going by the lions, fighting Apollyon, and passing through the Valley where the hobgoblins were," said Jo.[49]

"I liked the place where the bundles fell off and tumbled down stairs," said Meg.

"My favorite part was when we came out on the flat roof where our flowers and arbors, and pretty things were, and all stood and sung for joy up there in the sunshine," said Beth, smiling, as if that pleasant moment had come back to her.

"I don't remember much about it, except that I was afraid of the cellar and the dark entry, and always liked the cake and milk we had up at the top. If I wasn't too old for such things, I'd rather like to play it over again," said Amy, who began to talk of renouncing childish things at the mature age of twelve.

"We never are too old for this, my dear, because it is a play we are playing all the time in one way or another. Our burdens are here, our road is before us, and the longing for goodness and happiness is the guide that leads us through many troubles and mistakes to the peace which is a true Celestial City. Now, my little pilgrims, suppose you begin again, not in play, but in earnest, and see how far on you can get before father comes home."

"Really, mother? where are our bundles?" asked Amy, who was a very literal young lady.

"Each of you told what your burden was just now, except Beth; I rather think she hasn't got any," said her mother.

"Yes, I have; mine is dishes and dusters, and envying girls with nice pianos, and being afraid of people."

Beth's bundle was such a funny one that everybody wanted to laugh; but nobody did, for it would have hurt her feelings very much.

"Let us do it," said Meg, thoughtfully. "It is only another name for trying to be good, and the story may help us; for though we

As the sisters and Marmee gather round the piano on Christmas Eve night, Jo (Katherine Hepburn) stands off to the side in George Cukor's 1933 film *Little Women*.

do want to be good, it's hard work, and we forget, and don't do our best."

"We were in the Slough of Despond to-night, and mother came and pulled us out as Help did in the book.[50] We ought to have our roll of directions, like Christian. What shall we do about that?" asked Jo, delighted with the fancy which lent a little romance to the very dull task of doing her duty.

"Look under your pillows, Christmas morning, and you will find your guide-book," replied Mrs. March.

They talked over the new plan while old Hannah cleared the table; then out came the four little work-baskets, and the needles flew as the girls made sheets for Aunt March.[51] It was uninteresting sewing, but to-night no one grumbled. They adopted Jo's plan of dividing the long seams into four parts, and calling the quarters Europe, Asia, Africa and America, and in that way got on capitally, especially when they talked about the different countries as they stitched their way through them.

At nine they stopped work, and sung, as usual, before they went to bed. No one but Beth could get much music out of the old piano;[52] but she had a way of softly touching the yellow keys,

50. A boggy swamp Christian encounters on the way to the Wicket Gate; he falls into it and begins to sink with his burdens upon his back, but Help pulls him out. Bronson wrote in 1838: "Walking one day, I remember, with a cousin of mine . . . he carelessly slipped into a puddle of water in the way. So full of Bunyan's images was my fancy, that I said to him, . . . 'there you have fallen into the "Sloth of Despond."' I had read the book as without words; things and images had been before my mind's eye; *Sloth* was a word with whose meaning I was acquainted, *Slough* I had never heard, and had no dictionary . . . so I inferred the meanings from the connexion of the words in sentences. The book was, indeed, my dictionary. By it I learned the English tongue" (*Journals of BA* III).

51. Although LMA never claimed that she based Aunt March on a particular person, Cornelia Meigs, in her biography *Invincible Louisa* (Boston: Little, Brown, 1934), writes: "She [LMA] has declared that 'Aunt March is no one', but her family say otherwise. They all see in that autocratically generous lady the reflection of no other than the great Aunt Hancock [wife of John Hancock], with her connections in high places, her family tyranny and her good heart. Louisa could not remember her; but the family legend was enough" (209).

52. Elizabeth Alcott played the piano. Willis recalled in *Alcott Memoirs* (1915): "She loved music, played at the piano with more

ease than any of her sisters and with something of real appreciation" (quoted in *Her Own Time* 181). Elizabeth Alcott's melodeum, a small keyboard organ, is located in the front hall of Orchard House today.

53. "Twinkle, Twinkle, Little Star," first published as "The Star" and written by Jane Taylor for *Rhymes for the Nursery* (1806) by Ann and Jane Taylor.

and making a pleasant accompaniment to the simple songs they sung. Meg had a voice like a flute, and she and her mother led the little choir. Amy chirped like a cricket, and Jo wandered through the airs at her own sweet will, always coming out at the wrong place with a croak or a quaver that spoilt the most pensive tune. They had always done this from the time they could lisp

"Crinkle, crinkle, 'ittle 'tar,"[53]

and it had become a household custom, for the mother was a born singer. The first sound in the morning was her voice, as she went about the house singing like a lark; and the last sound at night was the same cheery sound, for the girls never grew too old for that familiar lullaby.

Chapter 2

A Merry Christmas

J O WAS the first to wake in the gray dawn of Christmas morning. No stockings hung at the fireplace, and for a moment she felt as much disappointed as she did long ago, when her little sock fell down because it was so crammed with goodies.[1] Then she remembered her mother's promise, and slipping her hand under her pillow, drew out a little crimson-covered book. She knew it very well, for it was that beautiful old story of the best life ever lived, and Jo felt that it was a true guide-book for any pilgrim going the long journey.[2] She woke Meg with a "Merry Christmas," and bade her see what was under her pillow. A green-covered book appeared, with the same picture inside, and a few words written by their mother, which made their one present very precious in their eyes. Presently Beth and Amy woke, to rummage and find their little books also,—one dove-colored,[3] the other blue; and all sat looking at and talking about them, while the East grew rosy with the coming day.

In spite of her small vanities, Margaret had a sweet and pious nature, which unconsciously influenced her sisters, especially Jo, who loved her very tenderly, and obeyed her because her advice was so gently given.

"Girls," said Meg, seriously, looking from the tumbled head[4] beside her to the two little night-capped ones in the room beyond, "mother wants us to read and love and mind these books, and we must begin at once. We used to be faithful about it; but since father went away, and all this war trouble unsettled us, we have neglected many things. You can do as you please; but *I* shall keep my book on the table here, and read a little every morning as

1. The Alcott sisters did celebrate Christmas with stockings and presents. Thirteen-year-old May Alcott wrote in her journal on December 24, 1853: "I went to bed early and . . . I hung up our stockings and asked Santa Claus to please fill them." On Christmas Day, she noted: "This morning as soon as we waked we pulled down our stockings, and found them brimmed full." She wrote that later that day she "had some beautifull presants from Mr Wheeler of a book named Elizabeth or the exile of Siberia and a box of Fabers pencils. Mother gave me a series of drawing books to copy from and a nice pair of warm leging to wear in the snow beside candy and such things" (Manuscript journal, Houghton Library, Harvard University, bMS Am 1817[56]).

2. In "The Prophets and the Martyrs: Pilgrims and Missionaries in *Little Women* and *Jack and Jill*," Anne K. Phillips argues that the little book is the New Testament, pointing out that in *The Pilgrim's Progress*, Christian is given the New Testament as a guide by the Interpreter and noting that in Chapter 19 of *Little Women*, "Amy's Will," Amy lays "her little Testament and hymn-book" on her chapel table. In *Little Women and the Feminist Imagination: Criticism, Controversy, Personal Essays,* ed. Janice M. Alberghene and Beverly Lyon Clark (New York and London: Garland, 1999), pp. 213–236, quotation 223.

3. Gray with a pink or purple tone.

4. Jo's tousled hair.

5. Blue was May Alcott's favorite color. She painted her room at Orchard House sky blue.

6. Abigail Alcott was greatly involved in helping the poor and in various reform movements of the time. From 1848 to 1850, she was employed as Boston's City Missionary—a social worker—a job in which she aided the poor, many of them Irish and German immigrants. She saw firsthand the inequalities in access to health care and education; she recognized, especially in children and women, the results of poverty, crime, alcoholism, physical abuse, and prostitution. As part of her official reports, Abigail wrote: "'My heart has always been pledged to the cause of the destitute and oppressed. Now my time shall be sacredly devoted to their relief'" (quoted in Cynthia Barton, *Transcendental Wife: The Life of Abigail May Alcott* [Lanham, MD: University Press of America, 1996], p. 143). She also advocated for unions, what she called "'labor associations . . . to protect the masses from the cupidity of the speculator and capitalist'" (quoted in Barton, p. 143). After resigning the position, Abigail Alcott operated an Intelligence Office for the poor, a type of employment service for women desiring domestic help. As she learned in her prior position, unemployment often led to poverty, crime, and vice: "'We do a good work when we clothe the poor, but a better one when we make the way easy for them to clothe themselves, the best when we so arrange society as to have no poor'" (quoted in Barton, p. 143). Abigail was also an active member of the Female Anti-Slavery Society in Philadelphia, when the Alcotts lived in Germantown, and then also in Boston and Concord. Nothing other than immediate emancipation, the Alcotts believed, would answer the evils of slavery. The Alcotts also sheltered runaway slaves in the 1840s. Clearly, LMA learned much about the reform of the individual and society from her mother, an idea she would bring to the forefront in her fiction.

7. Although the family occasionally hired a girl to help with work, especially if Mrs. Alcott was ill or away, no evidence has been found that the Alcotts had domestic servants on a regular basis until after the success of *Little Women*. Lydia Hosmer Wood asserted in "Beth Alcott's Playmate: A Glimpse of Concord Town in the Days of *Little Women*" (1913) that "the Hannah of the March household was a myth in the Alcott home" (quoted in *Her Own Time* 164). Hannah Mullet, the Marches' housekeeper, may be of English descent, as the name has its origins in Anglo-Saxon language. It is the diminutive of *mule*. Despite her nationality, Hannah, LMA clearly points out, is treated more like family than like a servant.

soon as I wake, for I know it will do me good, and help me through the day."

Then she opened her new book and began to read. Jo put her arm round her, and, leaning cheek to cheek, read also, with the quiet expression so seldom seen on her restless face.

"How good Meg is! Come, Amy, let's do as they do. I'll help you with the hard words, and they'll explain things if we don't understand," whispered Beth, very much impressed by the pretty books and her sisters' example.

"I'm glad mine is blue,"[5] said Amy; and then the rooms were very still while the pages were softly turned, and the winter sunshine crept in to touch the bright heads and serious faces with a Christmas greeting.

"Where is mother?" asked Meg, as she and Jo ran down to thank her for their gifts, half an hour later.

"Goodness only knows. Some poor creeter come a-beggin', and your ma went straight off to see what was needed.[6] There never *was* such a woman for givin' away vittles and drink, clothes and firin'," replied Hannah, who had lived with the family since Meg was born, and was considered by them all more as a friend than a servant.[7]

"She will be back soon, I guess; so do your cakes,[a] and have everything ready," said Meg, looking over the presents which were collected in a basket and kept under the sofa, ready to be produced at the proper time. "Why, where is Amy's bottle of Cologne?" she added, as the little flask did not appear.

"She took it out a minute ago, and went off with it to put a ribbon on it, or some such notion,"[8] replied Jo, dancing about the room to take the first stiffness off the new army-slippers.

"How nice my handkerchiefs look, don't they? Hannah washed and ironed them for me, and I marked them all myself," said Beth, looking proudly at the somewhat uneven letters which had cost her such labor.

"Bless the child, she's gone and put 'Mother' on them instead of 'M. March;' how funny!" cried Jo, taking up one.

"Isn't it right? I thought it was better to do it so, because Meg's initials are 'M. M.,' and I don't want any one to use these but Marmee," said Beth, looking troubled.

LITTLE WOMEN

"It's all right, dear, and a very pretty idea; quite sensible, too, for no one can ever mistake now. It will please her very much, I know," said Meg, with a frown for Jo, and a smile for Beth.

"There's mother; hide the basket, quick!" cried Jo, as a door slammed, and steps sounded in the hall.

Amy came in hastily, and looked rather abashed when she saw her sisters all waiting for her.

"Where have you been, and what are you hiding behind you?" asked Meg, surprised to see, by her hood and cloak, that lazy Amy had been out so early.

"Don't laugh at me, Jo, I didn't mean any one should know till the time came. I only meant to change the little bottle for a big one, and I gave *all* my money to get it, and I'm truly trying not to be selfish any more."

As she spoke, Amy showed the handsome flask which replaced the cheap one; and looked so earnest and humble in her little effort to forget herself, that Meg hugged her on the spot, and Jo pronounced her "a trump,"[9] while Beth ran to the window, and picked her finest rose to ornament the stately bottle.

"You see I felt ashamed of my present, after reading and talking about being good this morning, so I ran round the corner and changed it the minute I was up; and I'm *so* glad, for mine is the handsomest now."

Another bang of the street-door sent the basket under the sofa, and the girls to the table eager for breakfast.

"Merry Christmas, Marmee! Lots of them! Thank you for our books; we read some, and mean to every day," they cried, in chorus.

"Merry Christmas, little daughters! I'm glad you began at once, and hope you will keep on. But I want to say one word before we sit down. Not far away from here lies a poor woman with a little new-born baby. Six children are huddled into one bed to keep from freezing, for they have no fire. There is nothing to eat over there; and the oldest boy came to tell me they were suffering hunger and cold. My girls, will you give them your breakfast as a Christmas present?"[10]

They were all unusually hungry, having waited nearly an hour, and for a minute no one spoke; only a minute, for Jo exclaimed impetuously,—

8. By "notion," Jo means some cheap article found around the house, such as ribbon or thread.

9. A colloquial British expression for an excellent or first-rate person. Alcott may have picked up this term from Charles Dickens's *Pickwick Papers* (1836–1837), one of her favorite books as a young woman.

10. In January 1868, LMA's inaugural issue as editor of *Merry's Museum,* a children's magazine published by Horace B. Fuller, appeared, and in "Merry's Monthly Chat With His Friends," under the pseudonym "Cousin Tribulation," LMA recounts how four sisters, realistically named Nan, Lu, Beth, and May, give their New Year's breakfast to a poor, needy family. With slight changes it would form this episode in *Little Women.*

11. *Polygonum fagopyrum,* a plant that originated in China but spread to Europe. Introduced into North America by early European settlers, it was used to make a flour. Buckwheat cakes are similar to pancakes.

12. Nina Auerbach points out in *Communities of Women: An Idea in Fiction* (Cambridge, MA: Harvard University Press, 1978) that the March sisters' "pilgrimage to the poor quarter is significant only because they themselves are hungry, and the food that Marmee gently requests they renounce is vividly appetizing" (58).

13. German for "Oh, my God!"

Carrying breakfast to the Hummels. Frank Merrill, *Little Women: Illustrated* (1880).

"I'm so glad you came before we began!"

"May I go and help carry the things to the poor little children?" asked Beth, eagerly.

"*I* shall take the cream and the muffins," added Amy, heroically giving up the articles she most liked.

Meg was already covering the buckwheats,[11] and piling the bread into one big plate.

"I thought you'd do it," said Mrs. March, smiling as if satisfied. "You shall all go and help me, and when we come back we will have bread and milk for breakfast, and make it up at dinner-time."

They were soon ready, and the procession set out.[12] Fortunately it was early, and they went through back streets, so few people saw them, and no one laughed at the funny party.[b]

A poor, bare, miserable room it was, with broken windows, no fire, ragged bed-clothes, a sick mother, wailing baby, and a group of pale, hungry children cuddled under one old quilt, trying to keep warm. How the big eyes stared, and the blue lips smiled, as the girls went in!

"Ach, mein Gott![13] it is good angels come to us!" cried the poor woman,[c] crying for joy.

"Funny angels in hoods and mittens," said Jo, and set them laughing.

LITTLE WOMEN

In a few minutes it really did seem as if kind spirits had been at work there. Hannah, who had carried wood, made a fire, and stopped up the broken panes with old hats, and her own shawl.[d] Mrs. March gave the mother tea and gruel,[14] and comforted her with promises of help, while she dressed the little baby as tenderly as if it had been her own. The girls, meantime, spread the table, set the children round the fire, and fed them like so many hungry birds; laughing, talking, and trying to understand the funny broken English.

"Das ist gute!"[15] "Der angel-kinder!" cried the poor things, as they ate, and warmed their purple hands at the comfortable blaze. The girls had never been called angel children before, and thought it very agreeable, especially Jo, who had been considered "a Sancho"[16] ever since she was born. That was a very happy breakfast, though they didn't get any of it; and when they went away, leaving comfort behind, I think there were not in all the city four merrier people than the hungry little girls who gave away their breakfasts, and contented themselves with bread and milk on Christmas morning.

"That's loving our neighbor better than ourselves,[17] and I like it," said Meg, as they set out their presents, while their mother was up stairs collecting clothes for the poor Hummels.[18]

Not a very splendid show, but there was a great deal of love done up in the few little bundles; and the tall vase of red roses, white chrysanthemums, and trailing vines, which stood in the middle, gave quite an elegant air to the table.

"She's coming! strike up, Beth, open the door, Amy. Three cheers for Marmee!" cried Jo, prancing about, while Meg went to conduct mother to the seat of honor.

Beth played her gayest march, Amy threw open the door, and Meg enacted escort with great dignity. Mrs. March was both surprised and touched; and smiled with her eyes full as she examined her presents, and read the little notes which accompanied them. The slippers went on at once, a new handkerchief was slipped into her pocket, well scented with Amy's Cologne, the rose was fastened in her bosom, and the nice gloves were pronounced "a perfect fit."

14. A light porridge of boiled oatmeal, sometimes with meat or spices added, often given to invalids to soothe the stomach and aid digestion. It was also a staple of prisons and child workhouses in the nineteenth century.

15. German for "That is good!"

16. Sancho Panza is the skeptical, humorous, witty, and faithful "squire" or companion to Don Quixote in Don Miguel de Cervantes's *Don Quixote* (1604, 1616).

17. "And [Jesus] answering said, Thou shalt love the Lord thy God with all thy heart, and with all thy soul, and with all thy strength, and with all thy mind; and thy neighbour as thyself" (Luke 10:27).

18. Germans made up the largest group of immigrants in the United States after 1840. By 1860, well over a million German immigrants lived in America. Opposition to immigrants, especially the German and Irish, grew during the 1850s with the formation of Nativist political parties, such as the Know Nothing or American Party, which sought to curtail immigration and enforce stricter U.S. citizenship requirements. In *Little Women* LMA presents two opposing pictures of German immigrants: the poor Hummels and later, in Part II, the well-educated Professor Bhaer. LMA probably took the name Hummel from one of Abigail Alcott's clients in 1850, when her mother served as a social worker in Boston. Abigail wrote in her diary about a Mrs. Hummel who sewed a dozen coats but remained unpaid because her employer unfairly insisted that the work was not properly completed. LMA likely remembered her mother's outcry over the poor woman's treatment (Barton, *Transcendental Wife*, p. 143).

19. Many scholars attribute this saying to Plato's *Republic;* however, it may well predate Plato. It means, of course, that when people truly need something they will invent a solution.

20. A dish made to hold butter.

21. In a confused or disordered state; the furniture has been appropriated in some clever way by the girls for use as stage props.

22. Anna Alcott Pratt writes in "A Foreword by Meg" in *Comic Tragedies* (1893): "Jo, of course, played the villains, ghosts, bandits, and disdainful queens; for her tragedy-loving soul delighted in the lurid parts, and no drama was perfect in her eyes without a touch of the demonic or supernatural. Meg loved the sentimental roles, the tender maiden with the airy robes and flowing locks, who made impossible sacrifices for ideal lovers, or the cavalier, singing soft serenades and performing lofty acts of gallantry and prowess" (quoted in *Her Own Time* 74–75).

23. LMA's russet boots, which she used in the family dramatics, are on display at Orchard House.

24. A foil, invented in France in the eighteenth century as a training sword, is a slender, flexible sword used in fencing. A doublet, worn typically by men from the Middle Ages to the Renaissance, is a close-fitted buttoned or laced jacket. Usually quilted, a doublet is most often waist-length and worn over a shirt. LMA's doublet is on display today at Orchard House.

25. Anna, in "A Foreword by Meg," notes the ingenuity of such a small acting company: "But the most surprising part of the performances was the length of the cast and the size of the company; for Jo and Meg usually acted the whole play, each often assuming five or six characters, and with rapid change of dress becoming, in one scene, a witch, a soldier, a beauteous lady, and a haughty noble. This peculiar arrangement accounts for many queer devices, and the somewhat singular fact that each scene offers but two actors, who vanish and reappear at most inopportune moments, and in a great variety of costume. Long speeches were introduced to allow a ruffian to become a priest, or a lovely damsel to disguise herself in the garb of a sorceress; while great skill was required to preserve the illusion, and astonish the audience by these wonderful transformations" (quoted in *Her Own Time* 75).

26. In "Fun Forever? Toys, Games, and Play in Louisa May Alcott's *Little Women,*" *American Journal of Play* 2:4 (Spring 2010), pp. 401–418, Anne K. Phillips notes: "Although there are vestiges of play and amusement in novels for girls prior to the appearance of *Little Women,* Alcott's novel is really the first to show play that is

There was a good deal of laughing, and kissing, and explaining, in the simple, loving fashion which makes these home-festivals so pleasant at the time, so sweet to remember long afterward, and then all fell to work.

The morning charities and ceremonies took so much time, that the rest of the day was devoted to preparations for the evening festivities. Being still too young to go often to the theatre, and not rich enough to afford any great outlay for private performances, the girls put their wits to work, and, necessity being the mother of invention,[19] made whatever they needed. Very clever were some of their productions; paste-board guitars, antique lamps made of old-fashioned butter-boats,[20] covered with silver paper, gorgeous robes of old cotton, glittering with tin spangles from a pickle factory, and armor covered with the same useful diamond-shaped bits, left in sheets when the lids of tin preserve-pots were cut out. The furniture was used to being turned topsy-turvy,[21] and the big chamber was the scene of many innocent revels.

No gentlemen were admitted; so Jo played male parts to her heart's content,[22] and took immense satisfaction in a pair of russet-leather boots[23] given her by a friend, who knew a lady who knew an actor. These boots, an old foil, and a slashed doublet[24] once used by an artist for some picture, were Jo's chief treasures, and appeared on all occasions. The smallness of the company made it necessary for the two principal actors to take several parts apiece; and they certainly deserved some credit for the hard work they did in learning three or four different parts, whisking in and out of various costumes, and managing the stage besides.[25] It was excellent drill for their memories, a harmless amusement, and employed many hours which otherwise would have been idle, lonely, or spent in less profitable society.[26]

On Christmas night, a dozen girls piled on to the bed, which was the dress circle,[27] and sat before the blue and yellow chintz[28] curtains, in a most flattering state of expectancy. There was a good deal of rustling and whispering behind the curtain, a trifle of lamp-smoke,[29] and an occasional giggle from Amy, who was apt to get hysterical in the excitement of the moment. Presently a bell sounded, the curtains flew apart, and the Operatic Tragedy began.

"A gloomy wood," according to the one play-bill, was represented by a few shrubs in pots, a green baize[30] on the floor, and a cave in the distance. This cave was made with a clothes-horse[31] for a roof, bureaus for walls; and in it was a small furnace in full blast, with a black pot on it, and an old witch bending over it. The stage was dark, and the glow of the furnace had a fine effect, especially as real steam issued from the kettle when the witch took off the cover. A moment was allowed for the first thrill to subside; then Hugo, the villain, stalked in with a clanking sword at his side, a slouched hat, black beard, mysterious cloak, and the boots. After pacing to and fro in much agitation, he struck his forehead, and burst out in a wild strain, singing of his hatred to Roderigo, his love for Zara, and his pleasing resolution to kill the one and win the other. The gruff tones of Hugo's voice, with an occasional shout when his feelings overcame him, were very impressive, and the audience applauded the moment he paused for breath. Bowing with the air of one accustomed to public praise, he stole to the cavern and ordered Hagar to come forth with a commanding "What ho! minion! I need thee!"

Out came Meg, with gray horse-hair hanging about her face, a red and black robe, a staff, and cabalistic[32] signs upon her cloak. Hugo demanded a potion to make Zara adore him, and one to destroy Roderigo. Hagar, in a fine dramatic melody, promised both, and proceeded to call up the spirit who would bring the love philter:—[33]

> "Hither, hither, from thy home,
> Airy sprite, I bid thee come!
> Born of roses, fed on dew,
> Charms and potions canst thou brew?
> Bring me here, with elfin speed,
> The fragrant philter which I need;
> Make it sweet, and swift and strong;
> Spirit, answer now my song!"

A soft strain of music sounded, and then at the back of the cave appeared a little figure in cloudy white, with glittering wings, golden hair, and a garland of roses on its head. Waving a wand, it sung:—

celebrated and valued for its own sake . . . It accurately reflects multiple aspects of nineteenth-century American child culture, and it insists that play is not only desirable but a necessary component of a well-rounded life" (402).

27. In a theater, the dress circle contains the lowest tier of seats, closest to the stage.

28. A calico (unbleached cotton) cloth originally stained or painted, now printed, with various floral designs and patterns in different colors.

29. By the mid-nineteenth century, kerosene lamps were common in homes. A lamp would often give off smoke if its wick was not properly trimmed.

30. A course woolen cloth, similar in appearance to felt.

31. A wooden frame on which washed clothes were placed to dry.

32. Mysterious; having a secret or hidden meaning.

33. A love potion.

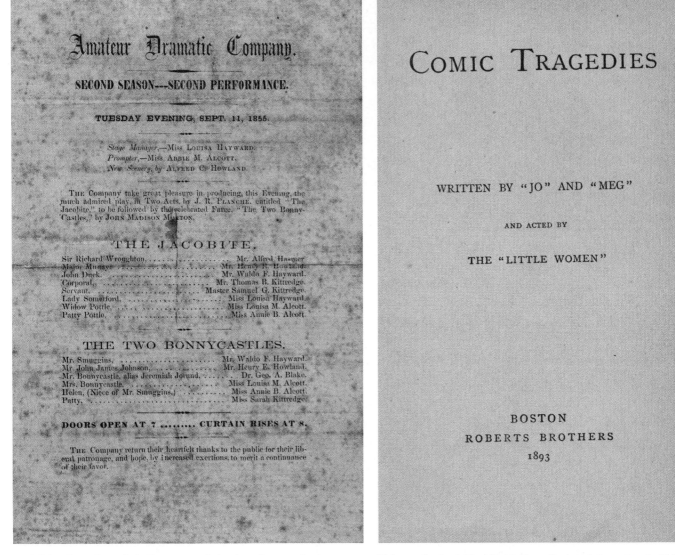

Playbill for *The Jacobite* and *The Two Bonnycastles* (1856), performances by the Walpole, New Hampshire, Amateur Dramatic Company that featured LMA and Anna Alcott.

Title page for *Comic Tragedies* (1893), a collection of plays written by LMA and Anna Alcott during their teens. Anna Alcott Pratt collected and published the plays five years after LMA's death.

Winona Ryder as the villain Hugo in Armstrong's *Little Women* (1994). Ryder received a Best Actress Academy Award nomination for her performance.

"Hither I come,
    From my airy home,
Afar in the silver moon;
    Take the magic spell,
        Oh, use it well!
Or its power will vanish soon!"

and dropping a small gilded bottle at the witch's feet, the spirit vanished. Another chant from Hagar produced another apparition,—not a lovely one, for, with a bang, an ugly, black imp appeared, and having croaked a reply, tossed a dark bottle at Hugo, and disappeared with a mocking laugh. Having warbled his thanks, and put the potions in his boots, Hugo departed; and Hagar informed the audience that, as he had killed a few of her friends in times past, she has cursed him, and intends to thwart his plans, and be revenged on him. Then the curtain fell, and the audience reposed and ate candy while discussing the merits of the play.

A good deal of hammering went on before the curtain rose again; but when it became evident what a masterpiece of stage carpentering had been got up, no one murmured at the delay. It was truly superb! A tower rose to the ceiling; half-way up appeared

Hagar with cabalistic signs on her cloak. Frank Merrill, *Little Women: Illustrated* (1880).

a window with a lamp burning at it, and behind the white curtain appeared Zara in a lovely blue and silver dress, waiting for Roderigo. He came, in gorgeous array, with plumed cap, red cloak, chestnut love-locks,[34] a guitar, and the boots, of course. Kneeling at the foot of the tower, he sung a serenade in melting tones. Zara replied, and after a musical dialogue, consented to fly. Then came the grand effect of the play. Roderigo produced a rope-ladder with five steps to it, threw up one end, and invited Zara to descend. Timidly she crept from her lattice, put her hand on Roderigo's shoulder, and was about to leap gracefully down, when, "alas, alas for Zara!" she forgot her train,[35]—it caught in the window; the tower tottered, leaned forward, fell with a crash, and buried the unhappy lovers in the ruins!

A universal shriek arose as the russet boots waved wildly from the wreck, and a golden head emerged, exclaiming, "I told you so! I told you so!" With wonderful presence of mind Don Pedro, the cruel sire,[36] rushed in, dragged out his daughter with a hasty aside,—

"Don't laugh, act as if it was all right!" and ordering Roderigo up, banished him from the kingdom with wrath and scorn. Though decidedly shaken by the fall of the tower upon him, Roderigo defied the old gentleman, and refused to stir. This dauntless example fired Zara; she also defied her sire, and he ordered them both to the deepest dungeons of the castle. A stout little retainer[37] came in with chains, and led them away, looking very much frightened, and evidently forgetting the speech he ought to have made.

Act third was the castle hall; and here Hagar appeared, having come to free the lovers and finish Hugo. She hears him coming, and hides; sees him put the potions into two cups of wine, and bid the timid little servant "Bear them to the captives in their cells, and tell them I shall come anon." The servant takes Hugo aside to tell him something, and Hagar changes the cups for two others which are harmless. Ferdinando, the "minion," carries them away, and Hagar puts back the cup which holds the poison meant for Roderigo. Hugo, getting thirsty after a long warble, drinks it, loses his wits, and after a good deal of clutching and

34. The *OED* defines *lovelock:* "Originally: a lock of hair worn longer than the rest and arranged so as to hang forward over one shoulder, often being tied with a ribbon (the style was popular among male courtiers in the late 16th and early 17th centuries). Later: any curl or lock of hair of an unusual or striking appearance."

35. The long portion of the dress that would trail the ground. Trains often denoted royalty or a woman of high standing.

36. Father.

37. Servant.

stamping, falls flat and dies; while Hagar informs him what she has done in a song of exquisite power and melody.

This was a truly thrilling scene; though some persons might have thought that the sudden tumbling down of a quantity of long hair rather marred the effect of the villain's death. He was called before the curtain, and with great propriety appeared leading Hagar, whose singing was considered more wonderful than all the rest of the performance put together.

Act fourth displayed the despairing Roderigo on the point of stabbing himself, because he has been told that Zara has deserted him. Just as the dagger is at his heart, a lovely song is sung under his window, informing him that Zara is true, but in danger, and he can save her if he will. A key is thrown in, which unlocks the door, and in a spasm of rapture he tears off his chains, and rushes away to find and rescue his lady-love.

Act fifth opened with a stormy scene between Zara and Don Pedro. He wishes her to go into a convent, but she won't hear of it; and, after a touching appeal, is about to faint, when Roderigo dashes in and demands her hand. Don Pedro refuses, because he is not rich. They shout and gesticulate tremendously, but cannot agree, and Roderigo is about to bear away the exhausted Zara, when the timid servant enters with a letter and a bag from Hagar, who has mysteriously disappeared. The latter informs the party that she bequeaths untold wealth to the young pair, and an awful doom to Don Pedro if he doesn't make them happy. The bag is opened, and several quarts of tin money shower down upon the stage, till it is quite glorified[38] with the glitter. This entirely softens the "stern sire;" he consents without a murmur, all join in a joyful chorus, and the curtain falls upon the lovers kneeling to receive Don Pedro's blessing, in attitudes of the most romantic grace.

Tumultuous applause followed, but received an unexpected check; for the cot-bed on which the "dress circle" was built, suddenly shut up, and extinguished the enthusiastic audience. Roderigo and Don Pedro flew to the rescue, and all were taken out unhurt, though many were speechless with laughter. The excitement had hardly subsided when Hannah appeared, with

38. Beautified.

39. Derived from the French word *bon* (good), a bonbon is a small sweet made from sugar or chocolate with a fruit or nut at its center.

40. While Santa Claus is found in various incarnations around the world, the American conception of Santa Claus as we know it today developed in the nineteenth century. "Old Santeclaus," an 1821 anonymous poem published in *A New-year's present, to the little ones from five to twelve,* presents an old man who carries toys to children on a reindeer sleigh. Clement Moore's December 1823 poem "A Visit from St. Nicholas" ("The Night before Christmas") establishes the modern-day vision of a heavyset, jolly Santa coming down the chimney with a bag of toys and even names the reindeer. Thomas Nast, a cartoonist, would illustrate the more modern Santa. Nast's 1863 *Harper's Weekly* cover illustration depicts Santa bringing cheer to the Union troops, while the December 29, 1866, *Harper's Weekly* has several illustrations, one of which is called "Santa Clausville, N. P." By the publication of *Little Women,* American children would have much the same idea of Santa Claus as do children today.

41. An out-of-the-ordinary impulse or sudden humor.

42. Maude Appleton McDowell, who served as the model for "Goldilocks," the daughter of Amy and Laurie in *Little Men* (1871), claimed in "Louisa May Alcott: By the Original 'Goldilocks'" (1936) that "Mr. Lawrence [*sic*] was the girls' grandfather, Colonel May" (quoted in *Her Own Time* 221). Col. Joseph May (1760–1841), Abigail Alcott's father, was a wealthy Boston merchant who had served as commander of Boston's Cadet Corps during the American Revolution, thus obtaining the honorary title of "colonel." LMA herself never stated who served as the model for Mr. Laurence. Although Col. May provided support for the Alcott family, he died before LMA was ten years old. Abigail Alcott's relationship with her father was strained because of Bronson's inability to support his family adequately. Upon Col. May's death in 1841, his will specified that Abigail's inheritance of just over $1,150 "'be secured by my executors to her sole and separate use, without the control of her husband or liability for his debts in such manner as they judge best'" (quoted in Sarah Elbert, *A Hunger for Home: Louisa May Alcott's Place in American Culture* [New Brunswick: Rutgers University Press, 1987], p. 48). It is perhaps more likely that the model was Abigail's brother, Samuel Joseph May, who, although not as wealthy as Mr. Laurence in *Little Women,* remained a longtime financial supporter of the family and with whom the Alcotts lived in the summer of 1850 in his "large house . . . with many comforts about us" at 88 Atkinson Street in Boston (*Journals* 60).

"Mrs. March's compliments, and would the ladies walk down to supper."

This was a surprise, even to the actors; and when they saw the table they looked at one another in rapturous amazement. It was like "Marmee" to get up a little treat for them, but anything so fine as this was unheard of since the departed days of plenty. There was ice cream, actually two dishes of it—pink and white,—and cake, and fruit, and distracting French bonbons,[39] and in the middle of the table four great bouquets of hot-house flowers!

It quite took their breath away; and they stared first at the table and then at their mother, who looked as if she enjoyed it immensely.

"Is it fairies?" asked Amy.

"It's Santa Claus,"[40] said Beth.

"Mother did it;" and Meg smiled her sweetest, in spite of her gray beard and white eyebrows.

"Aunt March had a good fit,[41] and sent the supper," cried Jo, with a sudden inspiration.

"All wrong; old Mr. Laurence[42] sent it," replied Mrs. March.

"The Laurence boy's grandfather! What in the world put such a thing into his head? We don't know him," exclaimed Meg.

"Hannah told one of his servants about your breakfast party; he is an odd old gentleman, but that pleased him. He knew my father, years ago, and he sent me a polite note this afternoon, saying he hoped I would allow him to express his friendly feeling toward my children by sending them a few trifles in honor of the day. I could not refuse, and so you have a little feast at night to make up for the bread and milk breakfast."[43]

"That boy put it into his head, I know he did! He's a capital fellow, and I wish we could get acquainted. He looks as if he'd like to know us; but he's bashful, and Meg is so prim she won't let me speak to him when we pass,"[44] said Jo, as the plates went round, and the ice began to melt out of sight, with ohs! and ahs! of satisfaction.

"You mean the people who live in the big house next door, don't you?" asked one of the girls. "My mother knows old Mr. Laurence, but says he's very proud, and don't like to mix with his neighbors. He keeps his grandson shut up when he isn't riding or walking with his tutor, and makes him study dreadful hard.[e] We invited him to our party, but he didn't come. Mother says he's very nice, though he never speaks to us girls."

"Our cat ran away once, and he brought her back, and we talked over the fence, and were getting on capitally, all about cricket,[45] and so on, when he saw Meg coming, and walked off. I mean to know him some day, for he needs fun, I'm sure he does," said Jo, decidedly.

"I like his manners, and he looks like a little gentleman, so I've no objection to your knowing him if a proper opportunity comes. He brought the flowers himself, and I should have asked him in if I had been sure what was going on up stairs. He looked so wistful as he went away, hearing the frolic, and evidently having none of his own."

"It's a mercy you didn't, mother," laughed Jo, looking at her boots. "But we'll have another play some time, that he *can* see. Maybe he'll help act; wouldn't that be jolly?"

"I never had a bouquet before; how pretty it is,"[46] and Meg examined her flowers with great interest.

"They *are* lovely, but Beth's roses are sweeter to me," said Mrs. March, sniffing at the half dead posy[f] in her belt.

Beth nestled up to her, and whispered, softly, "I wish I could send my bunch to father. I'm afraid he isn't having such a merry Christmas as we are."

43. Another LMA story from the January 1868 *Merry's Museum,* "Tilly's Christmas," found its theme incorporated into this chapter of *Little Women.* In the tale, three girls find a freezing robin in the snow. Tilly, practicing the Golden Rule taught to her by her mother, takes the bird home on Christmas Eve, not aware that the wealthy Mr. King has observed the children's conversation and actions. Knowing that there will be no presents on Christmas morning because they barely have any money for food or fuel, Tilly, the next day, is surprised to find wood, food, shoes, a shawl for her mother, and a warm blanket before the door. She never learns that Mr. King has rewarded her for thinking of others instead of herself. Alcott reshaped this into the March sisters' Christmas episodes, and Mr. King transformed into their neighbor Mr. Laurence.

44. In the nineteenth century, well-mannered young ladies did not speak to a male to whom they had not been formally introduced unless they were addressed first.

45. Cricket, a team sport played with ball and bat and two wickets on a grass field, originated in England during the sixteenth and seventeenth century.

46. The 1880–1881 edition changes Meg's statement: "I never had such a fine bouquet before!" Such a revision completely alters our reading. The original wording implies that Meg has never received flowers before, making her more innocent or less socially engaged with boys, while the 1880–1881 wording implies that boys have given her flowers before, just not as nice as Laurie's.

1. The attic. Jo, as a writer, has her own private space in which to create. In "'A power in the house': *Little Women* and the Architecture of Individual Expression," David H. Watters writes: "The third-floor garret is the repository of New England's past, a place of imagination removed from the public demands of patriarchal authority and performed rituals, an attic for child's play, memory, and the production of new books." In *Little Women and the Feminist Imagination,* ed. Janice M. Alberghene and Beverly Lyon Clark (New York: Garland, 1999), pp. 185–212, quotation 188.

2. Charlotte M. Yonge's book *The Heir of Redclyffe* (1853) was one of the best-selling romantic novels of the mid-nineteenth century. By 1878, it had gone through twenty-three editions. The novel revolves around Guy Morville, the heir of Redclyffe and a somewhat Byronic hero. As a result of rumors spread by his cousin Philip, Morville's impending marriage is stopped. After finally restoring his good name, Guy marries his true love. While on honeymoon in Italy, the two discover Philip suffering from a horrible fever. Guy, in nursing his cousin, contracts the fever and dies. For an excellent discussion of how LMA may have patterned Laurie on Yonge's Guy Morville, see Karen Sands-O'Connor, "Why Jo Didn't Marry Laurie: Louisa May Alcott and *The Heir of Redclyffe,*" *American Transcendental Quarterly* New Series 15.1 (March 2001), pp. 23–41.

3. LMA did write in the attic of the Alcott's home on 20 Pinckney Street in Boston. In April 1855, she noted: "I am in the garret with my papers round me, and a pile of apples to eat while I write my journal, plan stories, and enjoy the patter of rain on the roof, in peace and quiet." At a later date, upon rereading her journal, LMA inserted in brackets: "Jo in the garret" (*Journals* 71). As LMA recognized and as Virginia Woolf later advocated in her essay "A Room of One's Own" (1929), a woman writer needs to have her own private space in which to create. When she was thirteen, LMA, at Hillside in Concord, proudly declared: "I have at last got the little room I have wanted so long, and am very happy about it. It does me good to be alone, and Mother has made it very pretty and neat for me. My work-basket and desk are by the window" (*Journals* 59).

4. Russet apples have a mildly rough skin and a greenish-brown or yellowish-brown color, which is called russeting. In the nineteenth century, they were considered a very sweet, desired fruit. Bronson Alcott planted a number of apple trees on his property, hence the name Orchard House. He wrote in his journals: "Apples have other virtues than those that nourish merely. They refresh the spirits by their taste and perfume" (*Journals of BA* 344).

Chapter 3

The Laurence Boy

J o! Jo! where are you?" cried Meg, at the foot of the garret[1] stairs.

"Here," answered a husky voice from above; and running up, Meg found her sister eating apples and crying over the "Heir of Redcliffe,"[2] wrapped up in a comforter on an old three-legged sofa by the sunny window. This was Jo's favorite refuge;[3] and here she loved to retire with half a dozen russets[4] and a nice book, to enjoy the quiet and the society of a pet rat who lived near by, and didn't mind her a particle. As Meg appeared, Scrabble whisked into his hole. Jo shook the tears off her cheeks, and waited to hear the news.

"Such fun! only see! a regular note of invitation from Mrs. Gardiner for to-morrow night!" cried Meg, waving the precious paper, and then proceeding to read it, with girlish delight.

"'Mrs. Gardiner would be happy to see Miss March and Miss Josephine at a little dance on New-Year's-Eve.' Marmee is willing we should go; now what *shall* we wear?"

"What's the use of asking that, when you know we shall wear our poplins,[5] because we haven't got anything else," answered Jo, with her mouth full.

"If I only had a silk!" sighed Meg; "mother says I may when I'm eighteen, perhaps; but two years is an everlasting time to wait."

"I'm sure our pops look like silk, and they are nice enough for us. Yours is as good as new, but I forgot the burn and the tear in mine; whatever shall I do? the burn shows horridly,[a] and I can't take any out."

"You must sit still all you can, and keep your back out of sight; the front is all right. I shall have a new ribbon for my hair, and

Marmee will lend me her little pearl pin, and my new slippers are lovely, and my gloves will do, though they aren't as nice as I'd like."

"Mine are spoilt with lemonade, and I can't get any new ones, so I shall have to go without," said Jo, who never troubled herself much about dress.

"You *must* have gloves, or I won't go," cried Meg, decidedly. "Gloves are more important than anything else; you can't dance without them, and if you don't I should be *so* mortified."[6]

"Then I'll stay still; I don't care much for company dancing;[7] it's no fun to go sailing round, I like to fly about and cut capers."[8]

"You can't ask mother for new ones, they are so expensive, and you are so careless. She said, when you spoilt the others, that she shouldn't get you any more this winter. Can't you fix them any way?" asked Meg, anxiously.

"I can hold them crunched up in my hand, so no one will know how stained they are; that's all I can do. No! I'll tell you how we can manage—each wear one good one and carry a bad one; don't you see?"

"Your hands are bigger than mine, and you will stretch my glove dreadfully," began Meg, whose gloves were a tender point with her.

"Then I'll go without. I don't care what people say," cried Jo, taking up her book.

"You may have it, you may! only don't stain it, and do behave nicely; don't put your hands behind you, or stare, or say 'Christopher Columbus!' will you?"[9]

"Don't worry about me; I'll be as prim as a dish,[b] and not get into any scrapes, if I can help it. Now go and answer your note, and let me finish this splendid story."

So Meg went away to "accept with thanks,"[10] look over her dress, and sing blithely as she did up her one real lace frill;[11] while Jo finished her story, her four apples, and had a game of romps[12] with Scrabble.

On New-Year's-Eve the parlor was deserted, for the two younger girls played dressing maids, and the two elder were absorbed in the all-important business of "getting ready for the party." Simple as the toilets[13] were, there was a great deal of running up and

5. Poplin refers to the weave of a dress rather than to the material. It was a plain weave with crosswise ribs, making the fabric corded. Since poplin was a strong fabric, often cotton or wool, it was desirable for winter dresses.

6. In the mid-nineteenth century, it was considered improper for women without gloves to dance with men, as they would be holding hands. Emily Thornwell writes: "Gloves should harmonize with your dress; and must always be clean. Nothing can be more improper than high colored gloves: the primrose (and the white for evening parties) are the most elegant if your dress will admit of their being worn" (*The Lady's Guide* 124).

7. Jo means formal dancing, such a quadrille or waltz, where certain movements and steps are required.

8. To frolic or to skip or spring playfully.

9. Clara Gowing, who grew up in Concord in the 1840s and 1850s, recalled in *The Alcotts as I Knew Them* (1909) that "Louisa, though younger than Anna, was the controlling spirit, and often shocked her sensitive sister by some daring speech or deed" (quoted in *Her Own Time* 156).

10. Proper etiquette required a young lady to respond by writing a note thanking the person and accepting the invitation.

11. The *OED* defines "frill" as an "ornamental edging made of a strip of any woven material, of which one edge is gathered and the other left loose so as to give it a wavy or fluted appearance."

12. High-spirited play.

13. *Toilet* used in this manner means *dresses* or *attire*.

14. Before the advent of the modern curling iron, women would wrap their hair around cloth or paper and use a hot hair tong or hair iron to crimp it, thus creating a curl when the paper was removed. Often this procedure resulted in burned or scorched hair.

15. A tightly woven plain-weave wool suitable for winter dresses.

16. A ribbon or band to hold back a woman's hair.

17. During the mid-nineteenth century, small feet were considered desirable for a lady; thus many women would squeeze into smaller shoes even though uncomfortable. Emily Thornwell suggests: "The slippers should be small, wafer-like, yet strong, fitting exquisitely; and French silk stockings; all the taste you or your friends possess must be exerted to perfect your appearance in these particulars when dressing for an evening party" (*The Lady's Guide* 125).

18. Emily Thornwell writes: "Your handkerchief should be as fine as a 'snowy cobweb;' it should be bordered with deep, rich lace, and delicately perfumed" (*The Lady's Guide* 124).

19. Very nice.

down, laughing and talking, and at one time a strong smell of burnt hair pervaded the house. Meg wanted a few curls about her face, and Jo undertook to pinch the papered locks with a pair of hot tongs.[14]

"Ought they to smoke like that?" asked Beth, from her perch on the bed.

"It's the dampness drying," replied Jo.

"What a queer smell! it's like burnt feathers," observed Amy, smoothing her own pretty curls with a superior air.

"There, now I'll take off the papers and you'll see a cloud of little ringlets," said Jo, putting down the tongs.

She did take off the papers, but no cloud of ringlets appeared, for the hair came with the papers, and the horrified hair-dresser laid a row of little scorched bundles on the bureau before her victim.

"Oh, oh, oh! what *have* you done? I'm spoilt! I can't go! my hair, oh my hair!" wailed Meg, looking with despair at the uneven frizzle on her forehead.

"Just my luck! you shouldn't have asked me to do it; I always spoil everything. I'm no end sorry, but the tongs were too hot, and so I've made a mess," groaned poor Jo, regarding the black pancakes with tears of regret.

"It isn't spoilt; just frizzle it, and tie your ribbon so the ends come on your forehead a bit, and it will look like the last fashion. I've seen lots of girls do it so," said Amy, consolingly.

"Serves me right for trying to be fine. I wish I'd let my hair alone," cried Meg, petulantly.

"So do I, it was so smooth and pretty. But it will soon grow out again," said Beth, coming to kiss and comfort the shorn sheep.

After various lesser mishaps, Meg was finished at last, and by the united exertions of the family Jo's hair was got up, and her dress on. They looked very well in their simple suits, Meg in silvery drab,[15] with a blue velvet snood,[16] lace frills, and the pearl pin; Jo in maroon, with a stiff, gentlemanly linen collar, and a white chrysanthemum or two for her only ornament. Each put on one nice light glove, and carried one soiled one, and all pronounced the effect "quite easy and nice." Meg's high-heeled slippers were dreadfully tight, and hurt her, though she would not own it,[17] and Jo's nineteen hair-pins all seemed stuck straight into her head, which was not exactly comfortable; but, dear me, let us be elegant or die.

"Have a good time, dearies," said Mrs. March, as the sisters went daintily down the walk. "Don't eat much supper, and come away at eleven, when I send Hannah for you." As the gate clashed behind them, a voice cried from a window,—

"Girls, girls! *have* you both got nice pocket-handkerchiefs?"[18]

"Yes, yes, spandy nice,[19] and Meg has Cologne on hers," cried Jo, adding, with a laugh, as they went on, "I do believe Marmee would ask that if we were all running away from an earthquake."

"It is one of her aristocratic tastes, and quite proper, for a real lady is always known by neat boots, gloves, and handkerchief," replied Meg, who had a good many little "aristocratic tastes" of her own.

"Now don't forget to keep the bad breadth out of sight, Jo. Is my sash right; and does my hair look *very* bad?" said Meg, as she turned from the glass in Mrs. Gardiner's dressing-room, after a prolonged prink.

"I know I shall forget. If you see me doing anything wrong, you just remind me by a wink, will you?" returned Jo, giving her collar a twitch and her head a hasty brush.

"No, winking isn't lady-like; I'll lift my eyebrows if anything is wrong, and nod if you are all right. Now hold your shoulders straight, and take short steps, and don't shake hands if you are introduced to any one, it isn't the thing."

"How *do* you learn all the proper quirks?[c] I never can. Isn't that music gay?"

Down they went, feeling a trifle timid, for they seldom went to parties, and, informal as this little gathering was, it was an event to them. Mrs. Gardiner, a stately old lady, greeted them kindly, and handed them over to the eldest of her six daughters. Meg knew Sallie, and was at her ease very soon; but Jo, who didn't care much for girls or girlish gossip, stood about with her back carefully against the wall, and felt as much out of place as a colt in a flower-garden. Half a dozen jovial lads were talking about skates in another part of the room, and she longed to go and join them, for skating was one of the joys of her life. She telegraphed her

Jo curls Meg's hair. Thomas Fogarty, *Louisa Alcott's People* (1936).

Alfred Whitman (1842–1907), who served as a model for Laurie.

20. Emily Thornwell advises: "A lady cannot refuse the invitation of a gentleman to dance, unless she has already accepted that of another, for she would be guilty of an incivility which might occasion trouble; she would moreover seem to show contempt for him whom she refused, and would expose herself to receive an ill compliment from him" (*The Lady's Guide* 96).

21. Laurie is following proper etiquette by not addressing Jo by her first name, just as Jo should not address him as "Laurie." Thornwell warns ladies: "Do not be tempted to indulge in another proof of feminine indecorum, which may be countenanced, but can never be sanctioned by example; that of addressing young gentlemen of your acquaintance, who are unconnected with you, by their Christian names. It opens the way to unpleasant familiarities on their part" (*The Lady's Guide* 147). Jo's quick dismissal of these proper manners demonstrates how little she cares for formal society.

22. Although several boys who grew up with the Alcotts claimed to be the basis for the character of Laurie, LMA wrote to her friend Alfred Whitman, who lived in Concord in the late 1850s, on January 6, 1869: "'Laurie' is you & my Polish boy 'jintly' [Ladislas Wisniewski]. You are the sober half & my Ladislas (whom I met abroad)

wish to Meg, but the eyebrows went up so alarmingly that she dared not stir. No one came to talk to her, and one by one the group near her dwindled away, till she was left alone. She could not roam about and amuse herself, for the burnt breadth would show, so she stared at people rather forlornly till the dancing began. Meg was asked at once, and the tight slippers tripped about so briskly that none would have guessed the pain their wearer suffered smilingly. Jo saw a big red-headed youth approaching her corner, and fearing he meant to engage her,[20] she slipped into a curtained recess, intending to peep and enjoy herself in peace. Unfortunately, another bashful person had chosen the same refuge; for, as the curtain fell behind her, she found herself face to face with the "Laurence boy."

"Dear me, I didn't know any one was here!" stammered Jo, preparing to back out as speedily as she had bounced in.

But the boy laughed, and said, pleasantly, though he looked a little startled,—

"Don't mind me; stay, if you like."

"Shan't I disturb you?"

"Not a bit; I only came here because I don't know many people, and felt rather strange at first, you know."

"So did I. Don't go away, please, unless you'd rather."

The boy sat down again and looked at his boots, till Jo said, trying to be polite and easy,—

"I think I've had the pleasure of seeing you before; you live near us, don't you?"

"Next door;" and he looked up and laughed out right, for Jo's prim manner was rather funny when he remembered how they had chatted about cricket when he brought the cat home.

That put Jo at her ease; and she laughed too, as she said, in her heartiest way,—

"We did have such a good time over your nice Christmas present."

"Grandpa sent it."

"But you put it into his head, didn't you, now?"

"How is your cat, Miss March?"[21] asked the boy, trying to look sober, while his black eyes shone with fun.

"Nicely, thank you, Mr. Laurence; but I ain't Miss March, I'm only Jo," returned the young lady.

"I'm not Mr. Laurence, I'm only Laurie."[22]

"Laurie Laurence; what an odd name."

"My first name is Theodore, but I don't like it, for the fellows called me Dora, so I made them say Laurie instead."

"I hate my name, too—so sentimental! I wish every one would say Jo, instead of Josephine. How did you make the boys stop calling you Dora?"

"I thrashed 'em."

"I can't thrash Aunt March, so I suppose I shall have to bear it;" and Jo resigned herself with a sigh.

"Don't you like to dance, Miss Jo?" asked Laurie, looking as if he thought the name suited her.

"I like it well enough if there is plenty of room, and every one is lively. In a place like this I'm sure to upset something, tread on people's toes, or do something dreadful, so I keep out of mischief, and let Meg do the pretty.[23, d] Don't you dance?"

"Sometimes; you see I've been abroad a good many years, and haven't been about enough[e] yet to know how you do things here."

"Abroad!" cried Jo, "oh, tell me about it! I love dearly to hear people describe their travels."

is the gay whirligig half, he was a perfect dear . . . I can only think of you as sober Alf who used to come & have confidences on the couch, a la Laurie, & be very fascinating without knowing it" (*Selected Letters* 120). Whitman, who attended Sanborn's Academy and lived with Minot Pratt, father of John Bridge Pratt, while in Concord, moved to Lawrence, Kansas, in fall 1858, thus perhaps inspiring Laurie's surname. LMA met Ladislas Wisniewski in November 1865 at the Pension Victoria in Vevey, Switzerland. She confided: "L. very interesting & good. Pleasant walks & talks with him in the chateau garden & about Vevey" (*Journals* 145). In May 1866, she left her position as a companion for the invalid Anna Weld and went to Paris alone, where she again met Laddie, as she called him: "A very charming fortnight here, the days spent in seeing sights with Laddie, the evenings in reading, writing, hearing 'my boy' play, or resting" (*Journals* 151). She wrote about Alf and Laddie in "My Boys" in *Aunt Jo's Scrap Bag, Volume 1: My Boys Etc.* (1871). Frederick Willis, in *Alcott Memoirs* (1915), writes that just after Part I of *Little Women* was published, he met Bronson Alcott in the train station in Boston: "He came up to me, beaming, and rubbing his hands together . . . saying 'Well, my boy, did you recognize yourself as Laurie in Louisa's book?'" (quoted in *Her Own Time* 179). Julian Hawthorne, in "The Woman Who Wrote *Little Women*" (1922), claimed Louisa read him and her sisters parts of *Little Women*: "Abby was the heroine, and probably for that reason she felt obliged to select me for Laurie—an amiable idealization of course, she being Jo" (quoted in *Her Own*

Time 199). In a newspaper account of Bronson Alcott's lectures in Iowa in 1872, he was recorded as saying: "When she set about to write *Little Women* her sisters supplied the female characters, but they had no brother, and there must be a boy in the story. So four boys were called in who sometimes came to see them. However, since none of them alone would suit, Louisa took the best characteristics of each of the boys and out of these constructed the ideal boy of the story with whom the young ladies fell in love" (Herbert Hoeltje, "Some Iowa Lectures and Conversations of Amos Bronson Alcott," *Iowa Journal of History and Politics* 29 [July 1931]: 397).

23. Jo means she will let Meg be sociable and be seen. The 1880–1881 edition changes the expression to "let Meg sail about."

24. Vevey, Switzerland, is located on the bank of the Veveyse River, near its influx into Lake Geneva. LMA had visited Vevey in 1865. She was probably thinking of Edoward Sillig's Bellerive School in Vevey, a private academy for boys, which operated from 1836 to 1892. Karl Baedeker's *Switzerland and the Adjacent Portions of Italy, Savoy, and the Tyrol. Handbook for Travellers* (London, 1871) notes: "The little fleet belonging to the pupils is visible from the Hôtel Monnet, lying at anchor or cruising about on the lake" (201). The school attracted wealthy American and British families.

25. The *OED* defines "peg away" as a colloquial expression meaning "to toil laboriously over a long period of time; to work or go at persistently." Its first usage appeared in England in 1805, but the *OED* also gives an 1837 usage from Dickens's *Pickwick Papers,* where LMA may have acquired the expression.

Laurie didn't seem to know where to begin; but Jo's eager questions soon set him going, and he told her how he had been at school in Vevey, where the boys never wore hats, and had a fleet of boats on the lake, and for holiday fun went walking trips about Switzerland with their teachers.[24]

"Don't I wish I'd been there!" cried Jo. "Did you go to Paris?"

"We spent last winter there."

"Can you talk French?"

"We were not allowed to speak anything else at Vevey."

"Do say some. I can read it, but can't pronounce."

"Quel nom à cette jeune demoiselle en les pantoufles jolis?" said Laurie, good-naturedly.

"How nicely you do it! Let me see—you said, 'Who is the young lady in the pretty slippers,' didn't you?"

"Oui, mademoiselle."

"It's my sister Margaret, and you knew it was! Do you think she is pretty?"

"Yes; she makes me think of the German girls, she looks so fresh and quiet, and dances like a lady."

Jo quite glowed with pleasure at this boyish praise of her sister, and stored it up to repeat to Meg. Both peeped, and criticised, and chatted, till they felt like old acquaintances. Laurie's bashfulness soon wore off, for Jo's gentlemanly demeanor amused and set him at his ease, and Jo was her merry self again, because her dress was forgotten, and nobody lifted their eyebrows at her. She liked the "Laurence boy" better than ever, and took several good looks at him, so that she might describe him to the girls; for they had no brothers, very few male cousins, and boys were almost unknown creatures to them.

"Curly black hair, brown skin, big black eyes, long nose, nice teeth, little hands and feet, tall as I am;[f] very polite for a boy, and altogether jolly. Wonder how old he is?"

It was on the tip of Jo's tongue to ask; but she checked herself in time, and, with unusual tact, tried to find out in a roundabout way.

"I suppose you are going to college soon? I see you pegging away[25] at your books—no, I mean studying hard;" and Jo blushed at the dreadful "pegging"[f] which had escaped her.

Laurie smiled, but didn't seem shocked, and answered, with a shrug,—

"Not for two or three years yet;[g] I won't go before seventeen, any-way."

"Aren't you but fifteen?" asked Jo, looking at the tall lad, whom she had imagined seventeen already.

"Sixteen, next month."

"How I wish I was going to college; you don't look as if you liked it."

"I hate it! nothing but grinding or sky-larking;[26] and I don't like the way fellows do either, in this country."

"What do you like?"

"To live in Italy, and to enjoy myself in my own way."

Jo wanted very much to ask what his own way was; but his black brows looked rather threatening as he knit them, so she changed the subject by saying, as her foot kept time, "That's a splendid polka;[27] why don't you go and try it?"

"If you will come too," he answered, with a queer little French bow.[h]

"I can't; for I told Meg I wouldn't, because—" there Jo stopped, and looked undecided whether to tell or to laugh.

"Because what?" asked Laurie, curiously.

"You won't tell?"

"Never!"

"Well, I have a bad trick of standing before the fire, and so I burn my frocks, and I scorched this one; and, though it's nicely mended, it shows, and Meg told me to keep still, so no one would see it. You may laugh if you want to; it is funny, I know."

But Laurie didn't laugh; he only looked down a minute, and the expression of his face puzzled Jo, when he said very gently,—

"Never mind that; I'll tell you how we can manage: there's a long hall out there, and we can dance grandly, and no one will see us. Please come."

Jo thanked him, and gladly went, wishing she had two neat gloves, when she saw the nice pearl-colored ones her partner put on. The hall was empty, and they had a grand polk, for Laurie danced well, and taught her the German step,[28] which delighted Jo, being full of swing and spring. When the music stopped they

26. *Grinding* is studying hard; *sky-larking* is playing or frolicking.

27. The polka, which originated in Bohemia during the early nineteenth century, is a dance in 2/4 time. During the second half of the century, it became very popular in Europe and America.

28. The German cotillion, first introduced in the United States in the mid-nineteenth century, is a patterned dance with complex dance figures, a type of quadrille or square dance. The dance allowed participants to introduce themselves to others as they exchanged partners, thus giving them the opportunity to flirt.

29. Heidelberg, located in southwest Germany, has long been known for its academic life, most notably the University of Heidelberg, founded in 1386.

30. Meg is alluding to Exodus 10:21: "And the Lord said to Moses, 'Stretch out your hand toward heaven, that there may be darkness over the land of Egypt, even darkness which may be felt.'"

31. Rubber overshoes used to protect shoes or boots from water and mud.

32. LMA perhaps implies that Mr. Gardiner is having an alcoholic beverage.

33. A clumsy person.

sat down on the stairs to get their breath, and Laurie was in the midst of an account of a student's festival at Heidelberg,[29] when Meg appeared in search of her sister. She beckoned, and Jo reluctantly followed her into a side-room, where she found her on a sofa holding her foot, and looking pale.

"I've sprained my ankle. That stupid high heel turned, and gave me a horrid wrench.[i] It aches so, I can hardly stand, and I don't know how I'm ever going to get home," she said, rocking to and fro in pain.

"I knew you'd hurt your feet with those silly things.[j] I'm sorry; but I don't see what you can do, except get a carriage, or stay here all night," answered Jo, softly rubbing the poor ankle, as she spoke.

"I can't have a carriage without its costing ever so much; I dare say I can't get one at all, for most people come in their own, and it's a long way to the stable, and no one to send."

"I'll go."

"No, indeed; it's past ten,[k] and dark as Egypt.[30] I can't stop here, for the house is full; Sallie has some girls staying with her. I'll rest till Hannah comes, and then do the best I can."

"I'll ask Laurie; he will go," said Jo, looking relieved as the idea occurred to her.

"Mercy, no! don't ask or tell any one. Get me my rubbers,[31] and put these slippers with our things. I can't dance any more; but as soon as supper is over, watch for Hannah, and tell me the minute she comes."

"They are going out to supper now. I'll stay with you; I'd rather."

"No, dear; run along, and bring me some coffee. I'm so tired, I can't stir."

So Meg reclined, with the rubbers well hidden, and Jo went blundering away to the dining-room, which she found after going into a china-closet and opening the door of a room where old Mr. Gardiner was taking a little private refreshment.[32] Making a dive[l] at the table, she secured the coffee, which she immediately spilt, thereby making the front of her dress as bad as the back.

"Oh dear! what a blunderbuss[33] I am!" exclaimed Jo, finishing Meg's glove by scrubbing her gown with it.

　　　　　　　　　　　　　　　　　　　LITTLE WOMEN

"Can I help you?" said a friendly voice; and there was Laurie, with a full cup in one hand and a plate of ice[34] in the other.

"I was trying to get something for Meg, who is very tired, and some one shook me, and here I am, in a nice state," answered Jo, glancing, dismally, from the stained skirt to the coffee-colored glove.

"Too bad! I was looking for some one to give this to; may I take it to your sister?"

"Oh, thank you; I'll show you where she is. I don't offer to take it myself, for I should only get into another scrape if I did."

Jo led the way; and, as if used to waiting on ladies, Laurie drew up a little table, brought a second instalment of coffee and ice for Jo, and was so obliging that even particular Meg pronounced him a "nice boy." They had a merry time over the bonbons and mottos,[35] and were in the midst of a quiet game of "buzz"[36] with two or three other young people who had strayed in, when Hannah appeared. Meg forgot her foot, and rose so quickly that she was forced to catch hold of Jo, with an exclamation of pain.

"Hush! don't say anything," she whispered; adding aloud, "It's nothing; I turned my foot a little,—that's all," and limped up stairs to put her things on.

Hannah scolded, Meg cried, and Jo was at her wits' end, till she decided to take things into her own hands. Slipping out, she ran down, and finding a servant, asked if he could get her a carriage. It happened to be a hired waiter, who knew nothing about the neighborhood; and Jo was looking round for help, when Laurie, who had heard what she said, came up and offered his grandfather's carriage,[37] which had just come for him, he said.

"It's so early,—you can't mean to go yet," began Jo, looking relieved, but hesitating to accept the offer.

"I always go early,—I do, truly. Please let me take you home; it's all on my way, you know, and it rains, they say."

That settled it; and telling him of Meg's mishap, Jo gratefully accepted, and rushed up to bring down the rest of the party. Hannah hated rain as much as a cat does; so she made no trouble, and they rolled away in the luxurious close carriage, feeling very festive and elegant. Laurie went on the box, so Meg could keep her foot up, and the girls talked over their party in freedom.

34. A frozen confection.

35. A confection that contains a verse or saying on a piece of paper.

36. A game where people sit in a circle and go from person to person and count, starting with the number 1. For the number 7, multiples of 7, or numbers that contain 7, the word "buzz" is substituted. Variations of the game exist, and it is also often called Bizz Buzz.

37. In the nineteenth century, owning a carriage and horses was a sign of wealth. The Marches would have had to hire one.

38. A dance in 3/4 or 3/8 time, which originated as a Bohemian folk dance.

39. The phrase actually comes from Plato's Socratic Dialogue "Georgias" (ca. 380 BC), in which the philosopher attempts to find the true meaning of rhetoric. Polus, a student, says: "The truth is, that there is a great want of manners in bringing the argument to such a pass."

40. Arnica is a member of the Asteraceae family (sunflower) and has been used as a medicine for hundreds of years. Made into a liniment, it is useful for treating sprains.

"I had a capital time; did you?" asked Jo, rumpling up her hair, and making herself comfortable.

"Yes, till I hurt myself. Sallie's friend, Annie Moffat, took a fancy to me, and asked me to come and spend a week with her when Sallie does. She is going in the spring, when the opera comes, and it will be perfectly splendid if mother only lets me go," answered Meg, cheering up at the thought.

"I saw you dancing with the red-headed man I ran away from; was he nice?"

"Oh, very! his hair is auburn, not red; and he was very polite, and I had a delicious redowa[38] with him!"

"He looked like a grasshopper in a fit, when he did the new step. Laurie and I couldn't help laughing; did you hear us?"

"No, but it was very rude. What *were* you about all that time, hidden away there?"

Jo told her adventures, and by the time she had finished they were at home. With many thanks, they said "Good-night," and crept in, hoping to disturb no one; but the instant their door creaked, two little night-caps bobbed up, and two sleepy but eager voices cried out,—

"Tell about the party! tell about the party!"

With what Meg called "a great want of manners,"[39] Jo had saved some bonbons for the little girls, and they soon subsided, after hearing the most thrilling events of the evening.

"I declare, it really seems like being a fine young lady, to come home from my party in my carriage,[m] and sit in my dressing-gown with a maid to wait on me," said Meg, as Jo bound up her foot with arnica,[40] and brushed her hair.

"I don't believe fine young ladies enjoy themselves a bit more than we do, in spite of our burnt hair, old gowns, one glove apiece, and tight slippers, that sprain our ankles when we are silly enough to wear them." And I think Jo was quite right.

LITTLE WOMEN

Chapter 4

Burdens

O H DEAR, how hard it does seem to take up our packs[1] and go on," sighed Meg, the morning after the party; for now the holidays were over, the week of merry-making did not fit her for going on easily with the task she never liked.

"I wish it was Christmas or New-Year all the time; wouldn't it be fun?" answered Jo, yawning dismally.

"We shouldn't enjoy ourselves half so much as we do now. But it does seem so nice to have little suppers and bouquets, and go to parties, and drive home in a carriage,[a] and read and rest, and not grub. It's like other people, you know, and I always envy girls who do such things; I'm so fond of luxury," said Meg, trying to decide which of two shabby gowns was the least shabby.

"Well, we can't have it, so don't let's grumble, but shoulder our bundles and trudge along as cheerfully as Marmee does. I'm sure Aunt March is a regular Old Man of the Sea[2] to me, but I suppose when I've learned to carry her without complaining, she will tumble off, or get so light that I shan't mind her."

This idea tickled Jo's fancy, and put her in good spirits; but Meg didn't brighten, for her burden, consisting of four spoilt children, seemed heavier than ever. She hadn't heart enough even to make herself pretty, as usual, by putting on a blue neck-ribbon, and dressing her hair in the most becoming way.

"Where's the use of looking nice, when no one sees me but those cross midgets, and no one cares whether I'm pretty or not," she muttered, shutting her drawer with a jerk. "I shall have to toil and moil all my days, with only little bits of fun now and then,

1. Meg is referring to their own spiritual progress. Early in part two of *The Pilgrim's Progress,* Christiana says, "Come, my children, let us pack up, and be gone to the Gate that leads to the Celestial Country, that we may see your father and be with him and his companions in peace." As they are about to depart, Mercy joins them. As in Christiana's and Mercy's journey in part two of *The Pilgrim's Progress,* the March sisters must undertake the young woman's journey without their father, emphasizing that female burdens, in the nineteenth century, are different from male burdens. Like Christiana, Marmee will guide the children.

2. The Old Man of the Sea appears in both Greek mythology and Homer's *Odyssey;* however, here Jo alludes to a tale of "Sinbad the Sailor," from *The Thousand and One Nights (Arabian Nights).* On his fifth voyage, Sinbad meets the Old Man of the Sea, who has Sinbad carry him on his shoulders across the stream. Only after he gets the Old Man drunk is Sinbad able to remove the burden from his shoulders and kill him.

3. To speak despondingly.

4. The *OED* defines *grumps* as "the sulks; a fit of ill humour," noting the first use of the word in 1844. As its second example, the *OED* gives this sentence from *Little Women*.

5. The *OED* defines *bounce:* "to burst unceremoniously into, out of." The 1880–1881 edition changes the phrase to "Hannah, who stalked in . . . and stalked out again."

6. The *OED* defines *muff* as a "covering, often of fur and usually of cylindrical shape with open ends, into which both hands may be placed for warmth." LMA means that the turn-overs were used to warm the sisters' hands.

and get old and ugly and sour, because I'm poor, and can't enjoy my life as other girls do. It's a shame!"

So Meg went down, wearing an injured look, and wasn't at all agreeable at breakfast-time. Every one seemed rather out of sorts, and inclined to croak.[3] Beth had a headache, and lay on the sofa trying to comfort herself with the cat and three kittens; Amy was fretting because her lessons were not learned, and she couldn't find her rubbers; Jo *would* whistle, and make a great racket getting ready; Mrs. March was very busy trying to finish a letter, which must go at once; and Hannah had the grumps,[4] for being up late didn't suit her.

"There never *was* such a cross family!" cried Jo, losing her temper when she had upset an inkstand, broken both boot-lacings, and sat down upon her hat.

"You're the crossest person in it!" returned Amy, washing out the sum, that was all wrong, with the tears that had fallen on her slate.

"Beth, if you don't keep these horrid cats down cellar I'll have them drowned," exclaimed Meg, angrily, as she tried to get rid of the kitten, who had swarmed[b] up her back, and stuck like a burr just out of reach.

Jo laughed, Meg scolded, Beth implored, and Amy wailed, because she couldn't remember how much nine times twelve was.

"Girls! girls! do be quiet one minute. I *must* get this off by the early mail, and you drive me distracted with your worry," cried Mrs. March, crossing out the third spoilt sentence in her letter.

There was a momentary lull, broken by Hannah, who bounced[5] in,[c] laid two hot turn-overs on the table, and bounced out again.[d] These turn-overs were an institution; and the girls called them "muffs,"[6] for they had no others, and found the hot pies very comforting to their hands on cold mornings. Hannah never forgot to make them, no matter how busy or grumpy she might be, for the walk was long and bleak; the poor things got no other lunch, and were seldom home before three.[e]

"Cuddle your cats, and get over your headache, Bethy. Goodby, Marmee; we are a set of rascals this morning, but we'll come home regular angels. Now then, Meg," and Jo tramped away, feeling that the pilgrims were not setting out as they ought to do.

They always looked back before turning the corner, for their mother was always at the window, to nod, and smile, and wave her hand to them. Somehow it seemed as if they couldn't have got through the day without that, for whatever their mood might be, the last glimpse of that motherly face was sure to affect them like sunshine.

"If Marmee shook her fist instead of kissing her hand to us, it would serve us right, for more ungrateful minxes[7] than we are were never seen," cried Jo, taking a remorseful satisfaction in the slushy road[f] and bitter wind.

"Don't use such dreadful expressions," said Meg, from the depths of the veil in which she had shrouded herself like a nun sick of the world.

"I like good, strong words, that mean something," replied Jo, catching her hat as it took a leap off her head, preparatory to flying away altogether.

"Call yourself any names you like; but *I* am neither a rascal nor a minx,[g] and I don't choose to be called so."

"You're a blighted being, and decidedly cross to-day, because you can't sit in the lap of luxury[8] all the time. Poor dear! just wait till I make my fortune, and you shall revel in carriages, and ice-cream, and high-heeled slippers, and posies, and red-headed boys to dance with."

"How ridiculous you are, Jo!" but Meg laughed at the nonsense, and felt better in spite of herself.

"Lucky for you I am; for if I put on crushed airs, and tried to be dismal, as you do, we should be in a nice state. Thank goodness, I can always find something funny to keep me up. Don't croak any more, but come home jolly, there's a dear."

Jo gave her sister an encouraging pat on the shoulder as they parted for the day, each going a different way, each hugging her little warm turn-over, and each trying to be cheerful in spite of wintry weather, hard work, and the unsatisfied desires of pleasure-loving youth.

When Mr. March lost his property in trying to help an unfortunate friend, the two oldest girls begged to be allowed to do something toward their own support, at least. Believing that they could not begin too early to cultivate energy, industry, and inde-

7. Sly, bold young women or girls. Meg perhaps objects to the word because it carries sexual connotations as being pert or saucy. The 1880–1881 edition changes the word to *wretch*, which carries no sexual connotation.

8. The *OED* marks the first use of this phrase by Maria Edgeworth, one of Alcott's favorite authors, in her 1801 *Moral Tales*. *Lap* connotes comfort, as a child sitting in a mother's lap.

9. The sisters had made a formal entry or debut into society, meaning they were now available for social calls by young men.

10. The *OED* defines *companion* as a "person who lives with another in need of society, and who, though receiving remuneration, is treated rather as a friend and equal than as an inferior or servant."

11. *Peppery* can mean irritable, but another connotation suggests that Jo admires Aunt March because the old woman is spirited.

pendence, their parents consented, and both fell to work with the hearty good-will which, in spite of all obstacles, is sure to succeed at last. Margaret found a place as nursery governness, and felt rich with her small salary. As she said, she *was* "fond of luxury," and her chief trouble was poverty. She found it harder to bear than the others, because she could remember a time when home was beautiful, life full of ease and pleasure, and want of any kind unknown. She tried not to be envious or discontented, but it was very natural that the young girl should long for pretty things, gay friends, accomplishments, and a happy life. At the Kings she daily saw all she wanted, for the children's older sisters were just out,[9] and Meg caught frequent glimpses of dainty ball-dresses and bouquets, heard lively gossip about theatres, concerts, sleighing parties and merry-makings of all kinds, and saw money lavished on trifles which would have been so precious to her. Poor Meg seldom complained, but a sense of injustice made her feel bitter toward every one sometimes, for she had not yet learned to know how rich she was in the blessings which alone can make life happy.

Jo happened to suit Aunt March, who was lame, and needed an active person to wait upon her. The childless old lady had offered to adopt one of the girls when the troubles came, and was much offended because her offer was declined. Other friends told the Marches that they had lost all chance of being remembered in the rich old lady's will; but the unworldly Marches only said,—

"We can't give up our girls for a dozen fortunes. Rich or poor, we will keep together and be happy in one another."

The old lady wouldn't speak to them for a time, but, happening to meet Jo at a friend's, something in her comical face and blunt manners struck the old lady's fancy, and she proposed to take her for a companion.[10] This did not suit Jo at all; but she accepted the place, since nothing better appeared, and, to every one's surprise, got on remarkably well with her irascible relative. There was an occasional tempest, and once Jo had marched home, declaring she couldn't bear it any longer; but Aunt March always cleared up quickly, and sent for her back again with such urgency that she could not refuse, for in her heart she rather liked the peppery[11] old lady.

I suspect that the real attraction was a large library of fine books, which was left to dust and spiders since Uncle March died. Jo remembered the kind old gentleman who used to let her build railroads and bridges with his big dictionaries,[12] tell her stories about the queer pictures in his Latin books, and buy her cards of gingerbread[13] whenever he met her in the street. The dim, dusty room, with the busts staring down from the tall book-cases, the cosy chairs, the globes, and, best of all, the wilderness of books, in which she could wander where she liked, made the library a region of bliss to her. The moment Aunt March took her nap, or was busy with company, Jo hurried to this quiet place, and, curling herself up in the big chair, devoured poetry, romance, history, travels, and pictures, like a regular book-worm. But, like all happiness, it did not last long; for as sure as she had just reached the heart of the story, the sweetest verse of the song, or the most perilous adventure of her traveller, a shrill voice called, "Josy-phine! Josy-phine!" and she had to leave her paradise to wind yarn,[14] wash the poodle, or read Belsham's Essays,[15] by the hour together.

Jo's ambition was to do something very splendid; what it was she had no idea, but left it for time to tell her; and, meanwhile, found her greatest affliction in the fact that she couldn't read, run, and ride as much as she liked. A quick temper, sharp tongue, and restless spirit were always getting her into scrapes, and her life was a series of ups and downs, which were both comic and pathetic. But the training she received at Aunt March's was just what she needed; and the thought that she was doing something to support herself made her happy, in spite of the perpetual "Josy-phine!"

Beth was too bashful to go to school; it had been tried, but she suffered so much that it was given up, and she did her lessons at home, with her father. Even when he went away, and her mother was called to devote her skill and energy to Soldiers' Aid Societies,[16] Beth went faithfully on by herself, and did the best she could. She was a housewifely little creature, and helped Hannah keep home neat and comfortable for the workers, never thinking of any reward but to be loved.[17] Long, quiet days she spent, not lonely nor idle, for her little world was peopled with imaginary friends, and she was by nature a busy bee. There were six dolls to

12. LMA noted in her 1888 "Recollections of My Childhood": "One of my earliest memories is of playing with books in my father's study. Building towers and bridges of the big dictionaries, looking at pictures" (quoted in *Her Own Time* 33).

13. A popular term in the nineteenth century meaning a flat piece of gingerbread shaped like a card.

14. To roll spun fiber, most likely wool since it is winter, onto a wheel so it can be used for sewing.

15. William Belsham's *Essays, Philosophical, Historical, and Literary* (1789, 1791).

16. In order to supply the Concord Artillery with food, clothes, blankets, bandages, and other items that helped make army life more comfortable, the Concord Soldiers' Aid Society was formed in 1861. The first Soldiers' Aid Society had been organized a few months earlier on April 15, 1861, in Bridgeport, Connecticut. In Concord, approximately 150 women and men worked throughout the war to bring relief and help to the soldiers. In 1862, as the war entered its second year, the Concord Soldiers' Aid Society, with the help of the U.S. Sanitary Commission, expanded its outreach to supply not just Concord soldiers but all Union soldiers. Many of Concord's prominent families, including the Emersons, took part. The Soldiers' Aid Society also became part of the town's social life, as it raised money, not only by donations and dues, but also by holding picnics, theatricals, fairs, and dances. Both Abigail Alcott and LMA participated in the Concord Soldiers' Aid Society. In October 1861, LMA, with an allusion to the disappointing Union losses, especially at the Battle of Bull Run the previous July, noted: "Sewing and knitting for 'our boys' all the time. It seems as if a few energetic women could carry on the war better than the men do it so far" (*Journals* 106). See also the records of the Soldiers' Aid Society, including Alice Reynolds Keyes's "Soldiers' Aid Society 1861–1865, Concord, Mass." (typescript 1907), Special Collections, Concord Free Public Library; Jeanie Attie, *Patriotic Toil: Northern Women and the American Civil War* (Ithaca, NY: Cornell University Press, 1998).

17. Willis's *Alcott Memoirs* (1915) recalls Elizabeth Alcott: "She was possessed of her mother's practicality and housewifely qualities, and at a very early age aided in the preparation of the simple family repasts; later . . . taking full charge of the family kitchen" (quoted in *Her Own Time* 181).

18. Her specially cherished dolls. In *Made to Play House: Dolls and the Commercialization of American Girlhood, 1830–1930* (New Haven: Yale University Press, 1993), Miriam Formanek-Burnell observes: "Though the number of toys had increased since the colonial period, there were still few dolls around in the average middle-class household in the 1850s, a fact of doll demography that would change dramatically only after the Civil War" (14). Several of the Alcott sisters' dolls are on display at Orchard House.

19. LMA coins this word by putting *doll* and *humanity* together, which emphasizes that Beth treated her dolls as humans.

20. A bag in which scraps of cloth are saved.

21. The first poorhouse in America was constructed in 1662 in Boston. In the early 1800s, poorhouses, often called almshouses or poor farms, increased across the country as a way to provide relief to those unable or unfit to care for themselves. In 1821, the Massachusetts State Legislature appointed Josiah Quincy, a well-respected politician and later president of Harvard College, to lead an investigation into how poorhouses operated in the Commonwealth. Their report, now known as the Quincy Report, incited a reform and an expansion of the poorhouse system in Massachusetts and other states. Concord's poorhouse, funded by the town, and in operation for most of the nineteenth century, was located on Walden Street.

22. Foreshadowing the silence that falls on the March household, LMA alludes to Charles Dickens's *The Cricket on the Hearth. A Fairy Tale of Home* (1845), a sentimental novella about the Peerybingle family. The third of Dickens's five Christmas books, the tale features a cricket that serves as a guardian angel for the family, chirping on the hearth. *The Cricket on the Hearth* was more popular at the time than *A Christmas Carol* (1843). Within just a month of its publication, the novel saw seventeen different stage productions in London. In March 1865, LMA, along with Anna and her husband, John Bridge Pratt, acted in a public play of *The Cricket on the Hearth* for the New England Hospital for Women and Children (see *Journals* 139). The March 18, 1865, edition of *Boston Commonwealth* praised the "two daughters and a son-in-law of Mr. A. Bronson Alcott," noting their "superior histrionic ability" (2). She again performed an extract of the work as part of *Mrs. Jarley's Waxworks* twice in the winter of 1879 (see *Journals* 213).

be taken up and dressed every morning, for Beth was a child still, and loved her pets[18] as well as ever; not one whole or handsome one among them; all were outcasts till Beth took them in; for, when her sisters outgrew these idols, they passed to her, because Amy would have nothing old or ugly. Beth cherished them all the more tenderly for that very reason, and set up a hospital for infirm dolls. No pins were ever stuck into their cotton vitals; no harsh words or blows were ever given them; no neglect ever saddened the heart of the most repulsive, but all were fed and clothed, nursed and caressed, with an affection which never failed. One forlorn fragment of *dollanity*[19] had belonged to Jo; and, having led a tempestuous life, was left a wreck in the rag-bag,[20] from which dreary poor-house[21] it was rescued by Beth, and taken to her refuge. Having no top to its head, she tied on a neat little cap, and, as both arms and legs were gone, she hid these deficiencies by folding it in a blanket, and devoting her best bed to this chronic invalid. If any one had known the care lavished on that dolly, I think it would have touched their hearts, even while they laughed. She brought it bits of bouquets; she read to it, took it out to breathe the air, hidden under her coat; she sung it lullabys, and never went to bed without kissing its dirty face, and whispering tenderly, "I hope you'll have a good night, my poor dear."

Beth had her troubles as well as the others; and not being an angel, but a very human little girl, she often "wept a little weep," as Jo said, because she couldn't take music lessons and have a fine piano. She loved music so dearly, tried so hard to learn, and practised away so patiently at the jingling old instrument, that it did seem as if some one (not to hint Aunt March) ought to help her. Nobody did, however, and nobody saw Beth wipe the tears off the yellow keys, that wouldn't keep in tune, when she was all alone. She sung like a little lark about her work, never was too tired to play for Marmee and the girls, and day after day said hopefully to herself, "I know I'll get my music some time, if I'm good."

There are many Beths in the world, shy and quiet, sitting in corners till needed, and living for others so cheerfully, that no one sees the sacrifices till the little cricket on the hearth[22] stops chirping, and the sweet, sunshiny presence vanishes, leaving silence and shadow behind.

If anybody had asked Amy what the greatest trial of her life was, she would have answered at once, "My nose."[23] When she was a baby, Jo had accidentally dropped her into the coal-hod,[24] and Amy insisted that the fall had ruined her nose forever. It was not big, nor red, like poor "Petrea's;"[25] it was only rather flat, and all the pinching in the world could not give it an aristocratic point. No one minded it but herself, and it was doing its best to grow, but Amy felt deeply the want of a Grecian nose,[26] and drew whole sheets of handsome ones to console herself.

"Little Raphael,"[27] as her sisters called her, had a decided talent for drawing, and was never so happy as when copying flowers, designing fairies, or illustrating stories with queer specimens of art. Her teachers complained that instead of doing her sums, she covered her slate with animals; the blank pages of her atlas were used to copy maps on, and caricatures of the most ludicrous description came fluttering out of all her books at unlucky moments. She got through her lessons as well as she could, and managed to escape reprimands by being a model of deportment. She was a great favorite with her mates, being good-tempered, and possessing the happy art of pleasing without effort. Her little airs and graces were much admired, so were her accomplishments; for beside her drawing, she could play twelve tunes, crochet, and read French without mispronouncing more than two-thirds of the words. She had a plaintive way of saying, "When papa was rich we did so-and-so," which was very touching; and her long words were considered "perfectly elegant" by the girls.

Amy was in a fair way[28] to be spoilt; for every one petted her, and her small vanities and selfishnesses were growing nicely. One thing, however, rather quenched the vanities; she had to wear her cousin's clothes. Now Florence's mamma hadn't a particle of taste, and Amy suffered deeply at having to wear a red instead of a blue bonnet, unbecoming gowns, and fussy[29] aprons that did not fit. Everything was good, well made, and little worn; but Amy's artistic eyes were much afflicted, especially this winter, when her school dress was a dull purple, with yellow dots, and no trimming.

"My only comfort," she said to Meg, with tears in her eyes, "is, that mother don't take tucks[30] in my dresses whenever I'm

23. May Alcott did indeed worry about the shape of her nose. Bessie Holyoke wrote to a friend after visiting Anna Alcott Pratt in 1878, soon after May married Ernest Nieriker in Europe: "Mrs. Pratt showed me a picture of [Ernest] and called my attention to his nose which was a very handsome one. Her sister's on the contrary is very homely and has always been a trial to her, as the story says; so it is a great gratification to her that her husband's nose is beyond criticism" (quoted in *Her Own Time* 25).

24. A kettle or container for carrying coals, often called a coal-scuttle.

25. Petrea, who possesses a "large and somewhat clumsy" nose, is one of the main characters in Fredrika Bremer's *The Home, or Family Cares and Family Joys* (1839). In her Fruitlands diary of 1843, Alcott notes that in the evenings she is reading the Swedish author's *Home,* which was translated into English that year (*Journals* 51).

26. A Grecian nose does not have a dip between the line of the nose and the forehead.

27. Raffaello Sanzio da Urbino (1483–1520), commonly known as Raphael, the Italian painter during the High Renaissance period. In 1857, seventeen-year-old May Alcott was studying art in Boston and had just completed a drawing of Abigail Alcott's head, which Louisa proclaimed "a very good likeness. All of us proud as peacocks of our 'little Raphael'" (*Journals* 84). Ironically, when May toured Florence, Italy, in 1870, she wrote to her father: "But dreadful to relate the few Raphael Madonnas I have seen disappoint me and I am even so depraved as to prefer the fine steel engravings of them to the original paintings; they are charming in a way, but do not impress and interest me much" (*Little Women Abroad* 245).

28. To have a good chance of being spoiled.

29. Having many pleats or puffs.

30. A fold that is sewn in order to shorten.

31. Pockets.

32. Ednah Dow Cheney, friend of the Alcott family and LMA's first biographer, wrote in 1889: "[May] was Anna's special child, and Louisa was not always so patient with her as her older sister" (quoted in *Her Own Time* 57).

33. Careless or reckless.

34. Jo means she gained the most advantage.

35. Disrespectful.

36. A perennial plant, native to Mexico and Central America. Known for its large colorful flowers, a dahlia grows rather tall (1 ft. to 8 ft.), and the weight of the flowers can cause the plant to bend.

37. *The Vicar of Wakefield* (1766), the popular sentimental novel by the Irish author Oliver Goldsmith, tells the story of Dr. Primrose, his wife, and their six children as they attempt to overcome hard times after losing their fortune. In September 1843, ten-year-old LMA reports reading the novel at Fruitlands (*Journals* 45).

naughty, as Maria Parks' mother does. My dear, it's really dreadful; for sometimes she is so bad, her frock is up to her knees, and she can't come to school. When I think of this *deggerredation,* I feel that I can bear even my flat nose and purple gown, with yellow sky-rockets[31] on it."

Meg was Amy's confidant and monitor,[32] and, by some strange attraction of opposites, Jo was gentle Beth's. To Jo alone did the shy child tell her thoughts; and over her big, harum-scarum[33] sister, Beth unconsciously exercised more influence than any one in the family. The two older girls were a great deal to each other, but both took one of the younger into their keeping, and watched over them in their own way; "playing mother" they called it, and put their sisters in the places of discarded dolls, with the maternal instinct of little women.

"Has anybody got anything to tell? It's been such a dismal day I'm really dying for some amusement," said Meg, as they sat sewing together that evening.

"I had a queer time with aunt to-day, and, as I got the best of it,[34] I'll tell you about it," began Jo, who dearly loved to tell stories. "I was reading that everlasting Belsham, and droning away as I always do, for aunt soon drops off, and then I take out some nice book, and read like fury, till she wakes up. I actually made myself sleepy; and, before she began to nod, I gave such a gape that she asked me what I meant by opening my mouth wide enough to take the whole book in at once.

"I wish I could, and be done with it," said I, trying not to be saucy.[35]

"Then she gave me a long lecture on my sins, and told me to sit and think them over while she just 'lost' herself for a moment. She never finds herself very soon; so the minute her cap began to bob, like a top-heavy dahlia,[36] I whipped the 'Vicar of Wakefield'[37] out of my pocket, and read away, with one eye on him, and one on aunt. I'd just got to where they all tumbled into the water, when I forgot, and laughed out loud. Aunt woke up; and, being more good-natured after her nap, told me to read a bit, and show what frivolous work I preferred to the worthy and instructive Belsham. I did my very best, and she liked it, though she only said,—

Jo (Katherine Hepburn) reading to Aunt March (Edna May Oliver) in 1933's *Little Women*.

"'I don't understand what it's all about; go back and begin it, child.'

"Back I went, and made the Primroses as interesting as ever I could. Once I was wicked enough to stop in a thrilling place, and say meekly, 'I'm afraid it tires you, ma'am; shan't I stop now?'

"She caught up her knitting which had dropped out of her hands, gave me a sharp look through her specs, and said, in her short way,—

"'Finish the chapter, and don't be impertinent, miss.'"

"Did she own she liked it?" asked Meg.

"Oh, bless you, no! but she let old Belsham rest; and, when I ran back after my gloves this afternoon, there she was, so hard at the Vicar, that she didn't hear me laugh as I danced a jig in the hall, because of the good time coming. What a pleasant life she might have, if she only chose. I don't envy her much, in spite of her money, for after all rich people have about as many worries as poor ones, I guess," added Jo.

"That reminds me," said Meg, "that I've got something to tell. It isn't funny, like Jo's story, but I thought about it a good deal as I

Dahlia.

38. A ring made from a semi-precious gemstone.

came home. At the Kings to-day I found everybody in a flurry, and one of the children said that her oldest brother had done something dreadful, and papa had sent him away. I heard Mrs. King crying, and Mr. King talking very loud, and Grace and Ellen turned away their faces when they passed me, so I shouldn't see how red their eyes were. I didn't ask any questions, of course; but I felt so sorry for them, and was rather glad I hadn't any wild brothers to do wicked things, and disgrace the family."

"I think being disgraced in school is a great deal try*inger* than anything bad boys can do," said Amy, shaking her head, as if her experience of life had been a deep one. "Susie Perkins came to school to-day with a lovely red carnelian ring;[38] I wanted it dreadfully, and wished I was her with all my might. Well, she drew a picture of Mr. Davis, with a monstrous nose and a hump, and the words, 'Young ladies, my eye is upon you!' coming out of his mouth in a balloon thing. We were laughing over it, when all of a sudden his eye *was* on us, and he ordered Susie to bring up her slate. She was *parry*lized with fright, but she went, and oh, what *do* you think he did? He took her by the ear, the ear! just fancy how horrid! and led her to the recitation platform, and made her stand there half an hour, holding that slate so every one could see."

"Didn't the girls shout[h] at the picture?" asked Jo, who relished the scrape.

"Laugh! not a one; they sat as still as mice, and Susie cried quarts, I know she did. I didn't envy her then, for I felt that millions of carnelian rings wouldn't have made me happy after that. I never, never should have got over such a agonizing mortification;" and Amy went on with her work, in the proud consciousness of virtue, and the successful utterance of two long words in a breath.

"I saw something that I liked this morning, and I meant to tell it at dinner, but I forgot," said Beth, putting Jo's topsy-turvy basket in order as she talked. "When I went to get some oysters for Hannah, Mr. Laurence was in the first shop, but he didn't see me, for I kept behind a barrel, and he was busy with Mr. Cutter, the fish-man. A poor woman came in with a pail and a mop, and

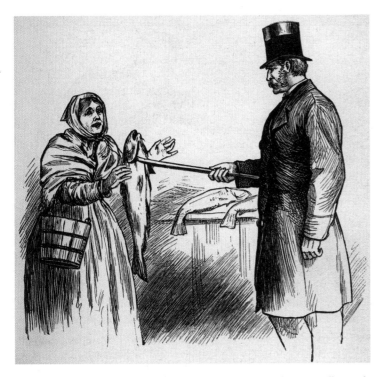

Mr. Laurence buys a fish for the poor woman. Frank Merrill, *Little Women: Illustrated* (1880).

asked Mr. Cutter if he would let her do some scrubbing for a bit of fish, because she hadn't any dinner for her children, and had been disappointed of a day's work. Mr. Cutter was in a hurry, and said 'No' rather crossly; so she was going away, looking hungry and sorry, when Mr. Laurence hooked up a big fish with the crooked end of his cane, and held it out to her. She was so glad and surprised she took it right in her arms, and thanked him over and over. He told her to 'go along and cook it,' and she hurried off, so happy! wasn't it nice of him? Oh, she did look so funny, hugging the big, slippery fish, and hoping Mr. Laurence's bed in heaven would be 'aisy.'"

When they had laughed at Beth's story, they asked their mother for one; and, after a moment's thought, she said soberly,—

"As I sat cutting out blue flannel jackets[39] to-day, at the rooms, I felt very anxious about father, and thought how lonely and help-less we should be if anything happened to him. It was not a wise

39. Blue jackets for the Union army.

40. Though of necessity the primary breadwinner of the family during the 1840s and 1850s, Abigail Alcott was foremost a home-maker who took an active role in raising her daughters. She was by all accounts a caring, giving mother. In December 1860, LMA confided: "All of the philosophy in our house is not in the study; a good deal is in the kitchen, where a fine old lady thinks high thoughts and does good deeds while she cooks and scrubs" (*Journals* 101).

thing to do, but I kept on worrying, till an old man came in with an order for some things. He sat down near me, and I began to talk to him, for he looked poor, and tired, and anxious.

"'Have you sons in the army?' I asked, for the note he brought was not to me.

"'Yes, ma'am; I had four, but two were killed; one is a prisoner, and I'm going to the other, who is very sick in a Washington hospital,' he answered, quietly.

"'You have done a great deal for your country, sir,' I said, feeling respect now, instead of pity.

"'Not a mite more than I ought, ma'am. I'd go myself, if I was any use; as I ain't, I give my boys, and give 'em free.'

"He spoke so cheerfully, looked so sincere, and seemed so glad to give his all, that I was ashamed of myself. I'd given one man, and thought it too much, while he gave four, without grudging them; I had all my girls to comfort me at home, and his last son was waiting, miles away, to say 'good-by' to him, perhaps. I felt so rich, so happy, thinking of my blessings, that I made him a nice bundle, gave him some money, and thanked him heartily for the lesson he had taught me."

"Tell another story, mother; one with a moral to it, like this. I like to think about them afterwards, if they are real, and not too preachy," said Jo, after a minute's silence.

Mrs. March smiled, and began at once; for she had told stories to this little audience for many years, and knew how to please them.[40]

"Once upon a time there were four girls, who had enough to eat, and drink, and wear; a good many comforts and pleasures, kind friends and parents, who loved them dearly, and yet they were not contented." (Here the listeners stole sly looks at one another, and began to sew diligently.) "These girls were anxious to be good, and made many excellent resolutions, but somehow they did not keep them very well, and were constantly saying, 'If we only had this,' or 'if we could only do that,' quite forgetting how much they already had, and how many pleasant things they actually could do; so they asked an old woman what spell they could use to make them happy, and she said, 'When you feel dis-

LITTLE WOMEN

contented, think over your blessings, and be grateful.'" (Here Jo looked up quickly, as if about to speak, but changed her mind, seeing that the story was not done yet.)

"Being sensible girls, they decided to try her advice, and soon were surprised to see how well off they were. One discovered that money couldn't keep shame and sorrow out of rich people's houses; another that though she was poor, she was a great deal happier with her youth, health, and good spirits, than a certain fretful, feeble old lady, who couldn't enjoy her comforts; a third, that, disagreeable as it was to help get dinner, it was harder still to have to go begging for it; and the fourth, that even carnelian rings were not so valuable as good behavior. So they agreed to stop complaining, to enjoy the blessings already possessed, and try to deserve them, lest they should be taken away entirely, instead of increased; and I believe they were never disappointed, or sorry that they took the old woman's advice."

"Now, Marmee, that is very cunning of you to turn our own stories against us, and give us a sermon instead of a 'spin'"[41] cried Meg.

"I like that kind of sermon; it's the sort father used to tell us," said Beth, thoughtfully, putting the needles straight on Jo's cushion.

"I don't complain near as much as the others do, and I shall be more careful than ever now, for I've had warning from Susie's downfall," said Amy, morally.

"We needed that lesson, and we won't forget it. If we do, you just say to us as Old Chloe did in Uncle Tom,—'Tink ob yer marcies, chillen, tink ob yer marcies,'"[42] added Jo, who could not for the life of her help getting a morsel of fun out of the little sermon, though she took it to heart as much as any of them.

41. A story—as in "to spin a yarn." The 1880–1881 edition changed *spin* to *romance*.

42. Uncle Tom is married to Chloe in Harriet Beecher Stowe's *Uncle Tom's Cabin; or Life Among the Lowly* (1852), one of the most successful novels of the nineteenth century. LMA, however, confuses the characters. In chapter 11, "The Property is Carried Off," Uncle Tom, who is about to be sold, attempts to comfort his wife: "'Let's think on our marcies!'" Chloe indignantly responds: "'Marcies! . . . don't see no marcy in 't! 't an't right!'" In 1852, the twenty-year-old Alcott listed her favorite books; among them was the recently published *Uncle Tom's Cabin* (*Journals* 68). A few years after the appearance of *Little Women*, Stowe herself would publish several books with Roberts Brothers.

1. A coat cut to fit loosely, with the back hanging straight from the shoulders.

2. Sir Walter Scott's historical novel *Ivanhoe* (1820), set in twelfth-century England. LMA read Scott as a young girl, and he remained a favorite of hers throughout her life.

3. Most readers believe that *Little Women* is set in Concord, Massachusetts, because LMA lived there as a young girl and an adult. However, the town is never mentioned in the book, and LMA never claimed Concord was the setting. In the nineteenth century, Concord, still a rural village, could not be considered a suburb of Boston. Geographically, Concord is sixteen miles from Boston, though longer by road. Frank Sanborn, a family friend, noted in "Reminiscences of Louisa M. Alcott" (1912): "The scene of the action is not exactly Concord, on the Lexington road, a quarter mile east of Emerson's corner, but an imaginary place, now here, now there, yet never far from Boston, from which the Orchard House is eighteen miles distant" (quoted in *Her Own Time* 149).

4. Greenhouse. Nicolette Scourse writes in *The Victorians and Their Flowers* (London: Croom Helm; Portland, OR: Timber Press, 1983): "By the 1850s the social desirability of a conservatory extended down the social scale well below the status of a gentleman with wealth . . . The conservatory gave enjoyment, and above all, it bestowed 'a certain claim to distinction on its possessor' . . . At the height of the social scale it was linked to a mansion by spacious glass doors" (95–96).

Chapter 5

Being Neighborly

WHAT IN THE WORLD are you going to do now, Jo?" asked Meg, one snowy afternoon, as her sister came clumping[a] through the hall, in rubber boots, old sack[1] and hood, with a broom in one hand and a shovel in the other.

"Going out for exercise," answered Jo, with a mischievous twinkle in her eyes.

"I should think two long walks, this morning, would have been enough. It's cold and dull out, and I advise you to stay, warm and dry, by the fire, as I do," said Meg, with a shiver.

"Never take advice; can't keep still all day, and not being a pussy-cat, I don't like to doze by the fire. I like adventures, and I'm going to find some."

Meg went back to toast her feet, and read "Ivanhoe,"[2] and Jo began to dig paths with great energy. The snow was light; and with her broom she soon swept a path all round the garden, for Beth to walk in when the sun came out; and the invalid dolls needed air. Now the garden separated the Marches' house from that of Mr. Laurence; both stood in a suburb of the city,[3] which was still country-like, with groves and lawns, large gardens, and quiet streets. A low hedge parted the two estates. On one side was an old brown house, looking rather bare and shabby, robbed of the vines that in summer covered its walls, and the flowers which then surrounded it. On the other side was a stately stone mansion, plainly betokening every sort of comfort and luxury, from the big coach-house and well-kept grounds to the conservatory,[4] and the glimpses of lovely things one caught between the rich curtains. Yet it seemed a lonely, lifeless sort of house; for no children frolicked on the lawn, no motherly face ever smiled at the windows, and few people went in and out, except the old gentleman and his grandson.

To Jo's lively fancy this fine house seemed a kind of enchanted palace,[5] full of splendors and delights, which no one enjoyed. She had long wanted to behold these hidden glories, and to know the "Laurence boy," who looked as if he would like to be known, if he only knew how to begin. Since the party she had been more eager than ever, and had planned many ways of making friends with him; but he had not been lately seen, and Jo began to think he had gone away, when she one day spied a brown face at an upper window, looking wistfully down into their garden, where Beth and Amy were snow-balling one another.

"That boy is suffering for society and fun," she said to herself. "His grandpa don't know what's good for him, and keeps him shut up all alone. He needs a lot of jolly boys to play with, or somebody young and lively. I've a great mind to go over and tell the old gentleman so."

The idea amused Jo, who liked to do daring things, and was always scandalizing Meg by her queer performances. The plan of "going over" was not forgotten; and, when the snowy afternoon came, Jo resolved to try what could be done. She saw Mr. Laurence drive off, and then sallied out to dig her way down to the hedge, where she paused, and took a survey. All quiet; curtains down at the lower windows; servants out of sight, and nothing human visible but a curly black head leaning on a thin hand, at the upper window.

"There he is," thought Jo; "poor boy! all alone, and sick, this dismal day! It's a shame! I'll toss up a snow-ball, and make him look out, and then say a kind word to him."

Up went a handful of soft snow, and the head turned at once, showing a face which lost its listless look in a minute, as the big eyes brightened, and the mouth began to smile. Jo nodded, and laughed, and flourished her broom as she called out,—

"How do you do? Are you sick?"

Laurie opened the window and croaked out as hoarsely as a raven,—

5. In *Whispers in the Dark: The Fiction of Louisa May Alcott* (Knoxville: University of Tennessee Press, 1993), Elizabeth Lennox Keyser argues: "Confined, almost imprisoned, in the big house next door, Laurie is freed by Jo in a reversal of the Sleeping Beauty tale. In boldly entering the house . . . and by confronting gruff old Mr. Laurence, Jo seems to be appropriating male power and freeing a part of her own nature" (66).

Jo calls to Laurie. Frank Merrill, original artwork for *Little Women: Illustrated* (1880).

"Better, thank you. I've had a horrid cold, and been shut up a week."

"I'm sorry. What do you amuse yourself with?"

"Nothing; it's as dull as tombs up here."

"Don't you read?"

"Not much; they won't let me."

"Can't somebody read to you?"

"Grandpa does, sometimes; but my books don't interest him, and I hate to ask Brooke[6] all the time."

"Have some one come and see you, then."

"There isn't any one I'd like to see. Boys make such a row,[7] and my head is weak."

"Isn't there some nice girl who'd read and amuse you? Girls are quiet, and like to play nurse."

"Don't know any."

"You know me,"[b] began Jo, then laughed, and stopped.

"So I do! Will you come, please?" cried Laurie.

"I'm not quiet and nice; but I'll come, if mother will let me. I'll go ask her. Shut that window, like a good boy, and wait till I come."

With that, Jo shouldered her broom and marched into the house, wondering what they would all say to her. Laurie was in a little flutter of excitement at the idea of having company, and flew about to get ready; for, as Mrs. March said, he was "a little gentleman," and did honor to the coming guest by brushing his curly pate, putting on a fresh collar,[8] and trying to tidy up the room, which, in spite of half a dozen servants, was anything but neat. Presently, there came a loud ring, then a decided voice, asking for "Mr. Laurie," and a surprised-looking servant came running up to announce a young lady.

"All right, show her up, it's Miss Jo," said Laurie, going to the door of his little parlor to meet Jo, who appeared, looking rosy and kind, and quite at her ease, with a covered dish in one hand, and Beth's three kittens in the other.

"Here I am, bag and baggage,"[9] she said, briskly. "Mother sent her love, and was glad if I could do anything for you. Meg wanted me to bring some of her blanc-mange;[10] she makes it very nice, and Beth thought her cats would be comforting. I knew you'd shout[11] at them,[c] but I couldn't refuse, she was so anxious to do something."

It so happened that Beth's funny loan was just the thing; for, in laughing over the kits, Laurie forgot his bashfulness, and grew sociable at once.

"That looks too pretty to eat," he said, smiling with pleasure, as Jo uncovered the dish, and showed the blanc-mange, surrounded by a garland of green leaves, and the scarlet flowers of Amy's pet[12] geranium.

"It isn't anything, only they all felt kindly, and wanted to show it. Tell the girl to put it away for your tea; it's so simple, you can eat it; and, being soft, it will slip down without hurting your sore throat. What a cosy room this is."

"It might be, if it was kept nice; but the maids are lazy, and I don't know how to make them mind. It worries me, though."

"I'll right it up in two minutes; for it only needs to have the hearth brushed, so,—and the things stood[d] straight on the mantelpiece, so,—and the books put here, and the bottles there, and your sofa turned from the light, and the pillows plumped up a bit. Now, then, you're fixed."

And so he was; for, as she laughed and talked, Jo had whisked things into place, and given quite a different air to the room. Laurie watched her in respectful silence; and, when she beckoned him to his sofa, he sat down with a sigh of satisfaction, saying, gratefully,—

"How kind you are! Yes, that's what it wanted. Now please take the big chair, and let me do something to amuse my company."

"No; I came to amuse you. Shall I read aloud?" and, Jo looked affectionately toward some inviting books near by.

"Thank you; I've read all those, and if you don't mind, I'd rather talk," answered Laurie.

"Not a bit; I'll talk all day if you'll only set me going. Beth says I never know when to stop."

"Is Beth the rosy one, who stays at home a good deal, and sometimes goes out with a little basket?" asked Laurie, with interest.

"Yes, that's Beth; she's my girl, and a regular good one she is, too."

6. LMA based John Brooke on her brother-in-law John Bridge Pratt, son of Minot Pratt, the Concord farmer praised by Thoreau in *Walden* (1854). The tutor's surname probably derives from the fact that the Pratt family lived for a time at Brook Farm, the Transcendentalist Utopian community in Roxbury, MA. Before his marriage to Sophia Peabody, Nathanial Hawthorne, who bought the Alcott's Hillside home in 1852, also lived at Brook Farm from April to November 1841.

7. Noise.

8. Detachable collars were extremely popular as part of a male's attire during the nineteenth century. These removable collars were often made of starched linen or cotton. Hannah Montague invented the detachable collar in 1827 in Troy, New York, because she wanted to be able to better clean the dirty rings around her husband's collar. The style became fashionable and the production of detachable collars became a significant industry in Troy. By 1860, the collar factories employed over 3,000 female workers, many Irish immigrants. Women worked as sewers, often stitching collars by hand, and others were laundresses, who washed, starched, and ironed the collars. Facing low wages and unsafe working conditions, the women decided to unionize. Led by Kate Mullaney and Esther Keegan, the Collar Laundry Union was organized in 1864, becoming the first women's union in the United States. Members immediately went on strike and within days had their demands met by the factory owners. The Troy Iron Molder's Union, composed of many of the fathers and brothers of the female workers, publicly showed their support for the women workers. See Carole Turbin, *Working Women of Collar City: Gender, Class, and Community in Troy, New York, 1864–86* (Champaign: University of Illinois Press, 1992).

9. The *OED* notes that *bag and baggage* was originally "a military phrase denoting all the property of an army collectively, and of soldiers individually." Here Jo is indicating that she has brought all the items she was given by the others.

10. A sweetmeat made from gelatin boiled with milk.

11. Laugh.

12. Favorite or cherished.

"The pretty one is Meg, and the curly-haired one is Amy, I believe?"

"How did you find that out?"

Laurie colored up,[13] but answered, frankly, "Why, you see, I often hear you calling to one another, and when I'm alone up here, I can't help looking over at your house, you always seem to be having such good times. I beg your pardon for being so rude, but sometimes you forget to put down the curtain at the window where the flowers are; and, when the lamps are lighted, it's like looking at a picture to see the fire, and you all round the table with your mother; her face is right opposite, and it looks so sweet behind the flowers, I can't help watching it. I haven't got any mother, you know;" and Laurie poked the fire to hide a little twitching of the lips that he could not control.

The solitary, hungry look in his eyes went straight to Jo's warm heart. She had been so simply taught that there was no nonsense in her head, and at fifteen she was as innocent and frank as any child. Laurie was sick and lonely; and, feeling how rich she was in home-love and happiness, she gladly tried to share it with him. Her brown face᷎ was very friendly, and her sharp voice unusually gentle, as she said,—

"We'll never draw that curtain any more, and I give you leave to look as much as you like. I just wish, though, instead of peeping, you'd come over and see us. Mother is so splendid, she'd do you heaps of good, and Beth would sing to you if *I* begged her to, and Amy would dance; Meg and I would make you laugh over our funny stage properties, and we'd have jolly times. Wouldn't your grandpa let you?"

"I think he would, if your mother asked him. He's very kind, though he don't look it; and he lets me do what I like, pretty much, only he's afraid I might be a bother to strangers," began Laurie, brightening more and more.

"We ain't strangers, we are neighbors, and you needn't think you'd be a bother. We *want* to know you, and I've been trying to do it this ever so long. We haven't been here a great while, you know, but we have got acquainted with all our neighbors but you."

"You see grandpa lives among his books, and don't mind much

what happens outside. Mr. Brooke, my tutor, don't stay here, you know, and I have no one to go round with me, so I just stop at home and get on as I can."

"That's bad; you ought to make a dive,[14] and go visiting everywhere you are asked; then you'll have lots of friends, and pleasant places to go to. Never mind being bashful, it won't last long if you keep going."

Laurie turned red again, but wasn't offended at being accused of bashfulness; for there was so much good-will in Jo, it was impossible not to take her blunt speeches as kindly as they were meant.

"Do you like your school?" asked the boy, changing the subject, after a little pause, during which he stared at the fire, and Jo looked about her well pleased.

"Don't go to school; I'm a business man—girl, I mean. I go to wait on my aunt, and a dear, cross old soul she is, too," answered Jo.

Laurie opened his mouth to ask another question; but remembering just in time that it wasn't manners to make too many inquiries into people's affairs, he shut it again, and looked uncomfortable. Jo liked his good breeding, and didn't mind having a laugh at Aunt March, so she gave him a lively description of the fidgety old lady, her fat poodle, the parrot that talked Spanish, and the library where she revelled. Laurie enjoyed that immensely; and when she told about the prim old gentleman who came once to woo Aunt March, and, in the middle of a fine speech, how Poll had tweaked his wig off to his great dismay, the boy lay back and laughed till the tears ran down his cheeks, and a maid popped her head in to see what was the matter.

"Oh! that does me lots of good; tell on, please," he said, taking his face out of the sofa-cushion, red and shining with merriment.

Much elated with her success, Jo did "tell on," all about their plays and plans, their hopes and fears for father, and the most interesting events of the little world in which the sisters lived. Then they got to talking about books; and to Jo's delight she found that Laurie loved them as well as she did, and had read even more than herself.

14. A plunge. The 1880–1881 edition changed the sentence: *You ought to make an effort.*

15. Comfortable upholstered armchairs with concave seats and high backs that were developed in the mid-nineteenth century and named after Sleepy Hollow, New York.

16. Works of art, usually statues, made from bronze.

17. Mischievous.

"If you like them so much, come down and see ours. Grandpa is out, so you needn't be afraid," said Laurie, getting up.

"I'm not afraid of anything," returned Jo, with a toss of the head.

"I don't believe you are!" exclaimed the boy, looking at her with much admiration, though he privately thought she would have good reason to be a trifle afraid of the old gentleman, if she met him in some of his moods.

The atmosphere of the whole house being summer-like, Laurie led the way from room to room, letting Jo stop to examine whatever struck her fancy; and so at last they came to the library, where she clapped her hands, and pranced, as she always did when especially delighted. It was lined with books, and there were pictures and statues, and distracting little cabinets full of coins and curiosities, and Sleepy-Hollow chairs,[15] and queer tables, and bronzes;[16] and, best of all, a great, open fireplace, with quaint tiles all round it.

"What richness!" sighed Jo, sinking into the depths of a velvet chair, and gazing about her with an air of intense satisfaction. "Theodore Laurence, you ought to be the happiest boy in the world," she added, impressively.

"A fellow can't live on books," said Laurie, shaking his head, as he perched on a table opposite.

Before he could say more, a bell rung, and Jo flew up, exclaiming with alarm, "Mercy me! it's your grandpa!"

"Well, what if it is? You are not afraid of anything, you know," returned the boy, looking wicked.[17]

"I think I am a little bit afraid of him, but I don't know why I should be. Marmee said I might come, and I don't think you're any the worse for it," said Jo, composing herself, though she kept her eyes on the door.

"I'm a great deal better for it, and ever so much obliged. I'm only afraid you are very tired talking to me; it was *so* pleasant, I couldn't bear to stop," said Laurie, gratefully.

"The doctor to see you, sir," and the maid beckoned as she spoke.

"Would you mind if I left you for a minute? I suppose I must see him," said Laurie.

"Don't mind me. I'm as happy as a cricket here," answered Jo.

Laurie went away, and his guest amused herself in her own way. She was standing before a fine portrait of the old gentleman, when the door opened again, and, without turning, she said decidedly, "I'm sure now that I shouldn't be afraid of him, for he's got kind eyes, though his mouth is grim, and he looks as if he had a tremendous will of his own. He isn't as handsome as *my* grandfather, but I like him."

"Thank you, ma'am," said a gruff voice behind her; and there, to her great dismay, stood old Mr. Laurence.

Poor Jo blushed till she couldn't blush any redder, and her heart began to beat uncomfortably fast as she thought what she had said. For a minute a wild desire to run away possessed her; but that was cowardly, and the girls would laugh at her; so she resolved to stay, and get out of the scrape as she could. A second look showed her that the living eyes, under the bushy gray eyebrows, were kinder even than the painted ones; and there was a sly twinkle in them, which lessened her fear a good deal. The gruff voice was gruffer than ever, as the old gentleman said abruptly, after that dreadful pause, "So, you're not afraid of me, hey?"

"Not much, sir."

"And you don't think me as handsome as your grandfather?"

"Not quite, sir."

"And I've got a tremendous will, have I?"

"I only said I thought so."

"But you like me, in spite of it?"

"Yes, I do, sir."

That answer pleased the old gentleman; he gave a short laugh, shook hands with her, and putting his finger under her chin, turned up her face, examined it gravely, and let it go, saying, with a nod, "You've got your grandfather's spirit, if you haven't his face. He *was* a fine man, my dear; but, what is better, he was a brave and an honest one, and I was proud to be his friend."

"Thank you, sir;" and Jo was quite comfortable after that, for it suited her exactly.

"What have you been doing to this boy of mine, hey?" was the next question, sharply put.

Jo (Katherine Hepburn) meets Mr. Laurence (Henry Stephenson) in *Little Women*. The RKO film was the fourth most popular film in America for 1933.

18. The bell that announces a light afternoon meal.

"Only trying to be neighborly, sir;" and Jo told how her visit came about.

"You think he needs cheering up a bit, do you?"

"Yes, sir; he seems a little lonely, and young folks would do him good, perhaps. We are only girls, but we should be glad to help if we could, for we don't forget the splendid Christmas present you sent us," said Jo, eagerly.

"Tut, tut, tut; that was the boy's affair. How is the poor woman?"

"Doing nicely, sir;" and off went Jo, talking very fast, as she told all about the Hummels, in whom her mother had interested richer friends than they were.

"Just her father's way of doing good. I shall come and see your mother some fine day. Tell her so. There's the tea-bell;[18] we have it early, on the boy's account. Come down, and go on being neighborly."

"If you'd like to have me, sir."

"Shouldn't ask you, if I didn't;" and Mr. Laurence offered her his arm with old-fashioned courtesy.

"What *would* Meg say to this?" thought Jo, as she was marched away, while her eyes danced with fun as she imagined herself telling the story at home.

"Hey! why what the dickens[19] has come to the fellow?" said the old gentleman, as Laurie came running down stairs, and brought up with a start of surprise at the astonishing sight of Jo arm in arm with his redoubtable[20] grandfather.

"I didn't know you'd come, sir," he began, as Jo gave him a triumphant little glance.

"That's evident, by the way you racket[21] down stairs. Come to your tea, sir, and behave like a gentleman;" and having pulled the boy's hair by way of a caress, Mr. Laurence walked on, while Laurie went through a series of comic evolutions behind their backs, which nearly produced an explosion of laughter from Jo.

The old gentleman did not say much as he drank his four cups of tea, but he watched the young people, who soon chatted away like old friends, and the change in his grandson did not escape him. There was color, light and life in the boy's face now, vivacity in his manner, and genuine merriment in his laugh.

"She's right; the lad *is* lonely. I'll see what these little girls can do for him," thought Mr. Laurence, as he looked and listened. He liked Jo, for her odd, blunt ways suited him; and she seemed to understand the boy almost as well as if she had been one herself.

If the Laurences had been what Jo called "prim and poky,"[22] she would not have got on at all, for such people always made her shy and awkward; but finding them free and easy, she was so herself, and made a good impression. When they rose she proposed to go, but Laurie said he had something more to show her, and took her away to the conservatory, which had been lighted for her benefit. It seemed quite fairy-like to Jo, as she went up and down the walks, enjoying the blooming walls on either side,—the soft light, the damp, sweet air, and the wonderful vines and trees that hung above her,—while her new friend cut the finest flowers till his hands were full; then he tied them up, saying, with the happy look Jo liked to see, "Please give these to your mother, and tell her I like the medicine she sent me very much."

They found Mr. Laurence standing before the fire in the great drawing-room,[23] but Jo's attention was entirely absorbed by a grand piano which stood open.

"Do you play?" she asked, turning to Laurie with a respectful expression.

19. The *OED* defines *the dickens* as "an interjectional exclamation expressing astonishment, impatience, irritation," dating back to the late sixteenth century. It is also slang for "the deuce, the devil."
20. Formidable.
21. Walk noisily.
22. Too formal and dull.
23. A room designated for receiving visitors.

24. Heliotropiums, also called heliotropes, are plants whose flowers turn to the sun during the day. Introduced into Europe from the Orient in the early nineteenth century, tea roses are so named because their fragrance resembles that of Chinese black tea.

25. Compliments, rewards.

26. Mr. Laurence shows his respect for Jo by addressing her as "Dr. Jo," a title usually reserved for males during this time. Perhaps more important is the fact that Jo maintains her gentle feminine manner as she listens to Laurie play the piano while burying her nose in the flowers, yet she still deserves and earns the respect accorded her by Mr. Laurence.

27. It was proper courtesy in the nineteenth century for a gentleman to escort a lady home after dark. Emily Thornwell advises: "After twilight, a young lady would not be conducting herself in a becoming manner, by walking alone; and if she passes the evening with anyone, she ought, beforehand, to provide some one to come for her at a stated hour; but if this is not practicable, she should politely ask the person whom she is visiting, to permit a servant to accompany her" (*The Lady's Guide* 78).

28. Jo's choice of words is important here because she sees a difference between a lady and a woman. Just over a decade before *Little Women*, LMA, in "The Lady and the Woman," offered a contrast between the stereotypical lady of the era and her vision of the ideal woman. Early in the tale, the elder Mr. Windsor claims that the "style of woman" he most admires can be found in those women "such as claim our protection and support, giving us in return affection and obedience. Beautiful and tender creatures, submissive to our will, confident in our judgement; and lenient to our faults—to be cherished in sunshine and sheltered in storms." Kate Loring, a young woman "with no pretensions to beauty," who had raised her four orphaned brothers, replies: "You have given your idol a heart, but no head. An affectionate or accomplished idiot is not my ideal of a woman. I would have her strong enough to stand alone, and give, not ask, support. Brave enough to think and act, as well as feel. Keen-eyed enough to see her own and other's faults, and wise enough to find a cure for them. I would have her humble, though self-reliant, gentle, though strong; man's companion, not his plaything; able and willing to face storms, as well as sunshines, and share life's burdens, as they come" (October 4, 1856, *Saturday Evening Gazette;* rpt. in *Louisa May Alcott: Selected Fiction,* ed. Daniel Shealy, Madeleine B. Stern, and Joel Myerson [Boston: Little, Brown and Company, 1990], p. 35). A few years later, LMA expanded upon this theme in her first novel, *Moods* (1864), as the protagonist Sylvia Yule,

"Sometimes," he answered, modestly.

"Please do now; I want to hear it, so I can tell Beth."

"Won't you first?"

"Don't know how; too stupid to learn, but I love music dearly."

So Laurie played, and Jo listened, with her nose luxuriously buried in heliotrope and tea roses.[24] Her respect and regard for the "Laurence boy" increased very much, for he played remarkably well, and didn't put on any airs. She wished Beth could hear him, but she did not say so; only praised him till he was quite abashed, and his grandfather came to the rescue. "That will do, that will do, young lady; too many sugar-plums[25] are not good for him. His music isn't bad, but I hope he will do as well in more important things. Going? Well, I'm much obliged to you, and I hope you'll come again. My respects to your mother; good-night, Doctor Jo."[26]

He shook hands kindly, but looked as if something did not please him. When they got into the hall, Jo asked Laurie if she had said anything amiss; he shook his head.

"No, it was me; he don't like to hear me play."

"Why not?"

"I'll tell you some day. John is going home with you, as I can't."[27]

"No need of that; I ain't a young lady,[28] and it's only a step. Take care of yourself, won't you?"

"Yes, but you will come again, I hope?"

"If you promise to come and see us after you are well."

"I will."

"Good-night, Laurie."

"Good-night, Jo, good-night."

When all the afternoon's adventures had been told, the family felt inclined to go visiting in a body, for each found something very attractive in the big house on the other side of the hedge. Mrs. March wanted to talk of her father with the old man who had not forgotten him; Meg longed to walk in the conservatory; Beth sighed for the grand piano, and Amy was eager to see the fine pictures and statues.

"Mother, why didn't Mr. Laurence like to have Laurie play?" asked Jo, who was of an inquiring disposition.

"I am not sure, but I think it was because his son, Laurie's father, married an Italian lady, a musician, which displeased the old man, who is very proud. The lady was good and lovely and accomplished, but he did not like her, and never saw his son after he married. They both died when Laurie was a little child, and then his grandfather took him home. I fancy the boy, who was born in Italy, is not very strong, and the old man is afraid of losing him, which makes him so careful. Laurie comes naturally by his love of music, for he is like his mother, and I dare say his grandfather fears that he may want to be a musician; at any rate, his skill reminds him of the woman he did not like, and so he 'glowered,'[29] as Jo said."

"Dear me, how romantic!" exclaimed Meg.

"How silly," said Jo; "let him be a musician, if he wants to, and not plague his life out sending him to college, when he hates to go."

"That's why he has such handsome black eyes and pretty manners, I suppose; Italians are always nice," said Meg, who was a little sentimental.

"What do you know about his eyes and his manners? you never spoke to him, hardly;" cried Jo, who was *not* sentimental.

"I saw him at the party, and what you tell shows that he knows how to behave. That was a nice little speech about the medicine mother sent him."

"He meant the blanc-mange, I suppose."

"How stupid you are, child; he meant you, of course."

"Did he?" and Jo opened her eyes as if it had never occurred to her before.

"I never saw such a girl! You don't know a compliment when you get it," said Meg, with the air of a young lady who knew all about the matter.

"I think they are great nonsense, and I'll thank you not to be silly, and spoil my fun. Laurie's a nice boy, and I like him, and I won't have any sentimental stuff about compliments and such rubbish. We'll all be good to him, because he hasn't got any mother, and he *may* come over and see us, mayn't he, Marmee?"

"Yes, Jo, your little friend is very welcome, and I hope Meg will remember that children should be children as long as they can."

ill equipped in life experiences and lacking the guidance of a mother, struggles to cope with a failing marriage based upon dependency (LMA felt so strongly about *Moods* that she drastically revised the novel in 1882, after having Roberts Brothers buy the copyright back from the publisher A. K. Loring). Sylvia Yule is a forerunner to Jo March, who eventually becomes the ideal woman who Kate Loring espouses here. LMA continued to explore this idea in many of her books, especially her adult novel *Work: A Story of Experience* (1873). For excellent discussions of the changing ideas of womanhood during LMA's time, see Jean V. Matthews, *The Rise of the New Woman: The Women's Movement in America, 1875–1930* (Chicago: Dee, 2003); and Frances B. Cogan, *All-American Girl: The Ideal of Real Womanhood in Mid-Nineteenth-Century America* (Athens: University of Georgia Press, 1989).

29. Stared intently or scowled.

30. In *The Pilgrim's Progress* the Wicket Gate is the location where pilgrims must enter the straight and narrow way to the Celestial City. The steep hill is the Hill of Difficulty that Christian must climb. At the top of the hill stands the Palace Beautiful, a way station for those pilgrims on the path to the Celestial City.

31. Jo alludes to the two chained lions guarding the way to the Palace Beautiful, from which Christian nearly turns back in fear.

"I don't call myself a child, and I'm not in my teens yet," observed Amy. "What do you say, Beth?"

"I was thinking about our 'Pilgrim's Progress,'" answered Beth, who had not heard a word. "How we got out of the Slough and through the Wicket Gate by resolving to be good, and up the steep hill, by trying; and that maybe the house over there, full of splendid things, is going to be our Palace Beautiful."[30]

"We have got to get by the lions, first,"[31] said Jo, as if she rather liked the prospect.

Chapter 6

Beth Finds the Palace Beautiful

1. Anne Brown Adams, daughter of the abolitionist John Brown, boarded with the Alcotts for a time in 1861, and late in her life she penned her recollections of those days. She claimed: "Mrs. Alcott was very fond of gathering the young people about her in the evening and playing games with them. She had a theory, and she practiced it too, that it is the duty of every mother in the land to invite a few young men to spend their evenings at their home, and so fill them with quiet rational amusements that it would draw the young men away from bad places" (quoted in *Her Own Time* 8).

THE BIG HOUSE did prove a Palace Beautiful, though it took some time for all to get in, and Beth found it very hard to pass the lions. Old Mr. Laurence was the biggest one; but, after he had called, said something funny or kind to each one of the girls, and talked over old times with their mother, nobody felt much afraid of him, except timid Beth. The other lion was the fact that they were poor and Laurie rich; for this made them shy of accepting favors which they could not return. But after a while they found that he considered them the benefactors, and could not do enough to show how grateful he was for Mrs. March's motherly welcome, their cheerful society, and the comfort he took in that humble home of theirs; so they soon forgot their pride, and interchanged kindnesses without stopping to think which was the greater.

All sorts of pleasant things happened about that time, for the new friendship flourished like grass in spring. Every one liked Laurie, and he privately informed his tutor that "the Marches were regularly splendid girls." With the delightful enthusiasm of youth, they took the solitary boy into their midst, and made much of him, and he found something very charming in the innocent companionship of these simple-hearted girls.[1] Never having known mother or sisters, he was quick to feel the influences they brought about him; and their busy, lively ways made him ashamed of the indolent life he led. He was tired of books, and found people so interesting now, that Mr. Brooke was obliged to make very unsatisfactory reports; for Laurie was always playing truant, and running over to the Marches.

2. Tableaux vivant, a form of entertainment in which a person or people in costume pose silently and motionless to portray a well-known painting or scene. LMA also employed the tableau vivant in her fiction. In "Behind a Mask; or, A Woman's Power" (1866), the actress Jean Muir depicts a Roundhead damsel hiding her lover with her mantle, his head buried in her bosom. In chapter 5 of the revised *Moods* (1882), Sylvia Yule, on a boat trip with her brother and his two male friends, portrays characters from Shakespeare: Ophelia, Lady Macbeth, Rosalind, and Juliet.

3. In his *Alcott Memoirs* (1915), Willis recalled the Alcotts' parlor: "Afternoons we usually gathered in the quaint, simple, charming, old-fashioned parlor at Hillside . . . To this day, over all the years, that simple Concord room with its pretty chintz curtains, its cool matting, its few fine engravings, its Parian busts of Clytie and Pestalozzi, and of Una and the Lion . . . its books and cut flowers, and its indescribable atmosphere of refinement, is deeply engraved within my memory as an expression of inherent simplicity and charm" (quoted in *Her Own Time* 172).

4. Meg may be playing off the title "The Mansion of Bliss," a popular British board game that was invented by Thomas Newton and produced by William Darton in 1822. Players used a spinning teetotum to move along the board. Spaces offered either a reward or a forfeit, each representing good or bad behavior. The goal of the game was to improve children and keep them away from vice or crime. The first player to enter "The Mansion of Bliss" won the game.

"Never mind, let him take a holiday, and make it up afterward," said the old gentleman. "The good lady next door says he is studying too hard, and needs young society, amusement, and exercise. I suspect she is right, and that I've been coddling the fellow as if I'd been his grandmother. Let him do what he likes, as long as he is happy; he can't get into mischief in that little nunnery over there, and Mrs. March is doing more for him than we can."

What good times they had, to be sure! Such plays and tableaux;[2] such sleigh-rides and skating frolics; such pleasant evenings in the old parlor,[3] and now and then such gay little parties at the great house. Meg could walk in the conservatory whenever she liked, and revel in bouquets; Jo browsed over the new library voraciously, and convulsed the old gentleman with her criticisms; Amy copied pictures and enjoyed beauty to her heart's content, and Laurie played lord of the manor in the most delightful style.

But Beth, though yearning for the grand piano, could not pluck up courage to go to the "mansion of bliss,"[4] as Meg called it. She went once with Jo, but the old gentleman, not being aware of her infirmity, stared at her so hard from under his heavy eyebrows, and said "hey!" so loud, that he frightened her so much her "feet chattered on the floor," she told her mother; and she ran away, declaring she would never go there any more, not even for the dear piano. No persuasions or enticements could overcome her fear, till the fact coming to Mr. Laurence's ear in some mysterious way, he set about mending matters. During one of the brief calls he made, he artfully led the conversation to music, and talked away about great singers whom he had seen, fine organs he had heard, and told such charming anecdotes, that Beth found it impossible to stay in her distant corner, but crept nearer and nearer, as if fascinated. At the back of his chair she stopped, and stood listening with her great eyes wide open, and her cheeks red with the excitement of this unusual performance. Taking no more notice of her than if she had been a fly, Mr. Laurence talked on about Laurie's lessons and teachers; and presently, as if the idea had just occurred to him, he said to Mrs. March,—

"The boy neglects his music now, and I'm glad of it, for he was getting too fond of it. But the piano suffers for want of use; wouldn't some of your girls like to run over, and practise on it now and then, just to keep it in tune, you know, ma'am?"

Beth took a step forward, and pressed her hands tightly together, to keep from clapping them, for this was an irresistible temptation; and the thought of practising on that splendid instrument quite took her breath away. Before Mrs. March could reply, Mr. Laurence went on with an odd little nod and smile,—

"They needn't see or speak to any one, but run in at any time, for I'm shut up in my study at the other end of the house. Laurie is out a great deal, and the servants are never near the drawing-room after nine o'clock." Here he rose, as if going, and Beth made up her mind to speak, for that last arrangement left nothing to be desired. "Please tell the young ladies what I say, and if they don't care to come, why, never mind;" here a little hand slipped into his, and Beth looked up at him with a face full of gratitude, as she said, in her earnest, yet timid way,—

"Oh, sir! they do care, very, very much!"

"Are you the musical girl?" he asked, without any startling "hey!" as he looked down at her very kindly.

"I'm Beth; I love it dearly, and I'll come if you are quite sure nobody will hear me—and be disturbed," she added, fearing to be rude, and trembling at her own boldness as she spoke.

"Not a soul, my dear; the house is empty half the day, so come and drum away as much as you like, and I shall be obliged to you."

"How kind you are, sir."

Beth blushed like a rose under the friendly look he wore, but she was not frightened now, and gave the big hand a grateful squeeze, because she had no words to thank him for the precious gift he had given her. The old gentleman softly stroked the hair off her forehead, and, stooping down, he kissed her, saying, in a tone few people ever heard,—

"I had a little girl once with eyes like these; God bless you, my dear; good-day, madam," and away he went, in a great hurry.

Beth had a rapture[5] with her mother, and then rushed up to

5. A feeling of intense happiness.

6. Her dolls.

7. Happiness.

8. Tunes or melodies.

9. To make with needlework. Although ready-made clothing was available by the 1860s, sewing by hand was still popular, and almost every young girl learned to sew by the age of twelve if not younger. Girls not only learned how to sew and mend useful items like clothing and linens but also mastered decorative arts like sewing samplers. Many household guides and etiquette books, such as Catherine Beecher and Harriet Beecher Stowe's *American Woman's Home* (1869), contained chapters on sewing. By 1860, Isaac Singer's mass-produced sewing machines were already extremely popular, and by the end of the nineteenth century the art of sewing by hand was waning. During the late 1840s and 1850s, LMA often sewed to supplement the family's income. In "Recollections of My Childhood" (1888), LMA wrote: "Needle-work began early, and at ten my skilful sister made a linen shirt beautifully" (quoted in *Her Own Time* 34).

impart the glorious news to her family of invalids,[6] as the girls were not at home. How blithely she sung that evening, and how they all laughed at her, because she woke Amy in the night, by playing the piano on her face in her sleep. Next day, having seen both the old and young gentleman out of the house, Beth, after two or three retreats, fairly got in at the side-door, and made her way as noiselessly as any mouse to the drawing-room, where her idol stood. Quite by accident, of course, some pretty, easy music lay on the piano; and, with trembling fingers, and frequent stops to listen and look about, Beth at last touched the great instrument, and straightway forgot her fear, herself, and everything else but the unspeakable delight which the music gave her, for it was like the voice of a beloved friend.

She stayed till Hannah came to take her home to dinner; but she had no appetite, and could only sit and smile upon every one in a general state of beatitude.[7]

After that, the little brown hood slipped through the hedge nearly every day, and the great drawing-room was haunted by a tuneful spirit that came and went unseen. She never knew that Mr. Laurence often opened his study door to hear the old-fashioned airs[8] he liked; she never saw Laurie mount guard in the hall, to warn the servants away; she never suspected that the exercise-books and new songs which she found in the rack were put there for her especial benefit; and when he talked to her about music at home, she only thought how kind he was to tell things that helped her so much. So she enjoyed herself heartily, and found, what isn't always the case, that her granted wish was all she had hoped. Perhaps it was because she was so grateful for this blessing that a greater was given her; at any rate, she deserved both.

"Mother, I'm going to work[9] Mr. Laurence a pair of slippers. He is so kind to me I must thank him, and I don't know any other way. Can I do it?" asked Beth, a few weeks after that eventful call of his.

"Yes, dear; it will please him very much, and be a nice way of thanking him. The girls will help you about them, and I will pay for the making up," replied Mrs. March, who took peculiar pleasure in granting Beth's requests, because she so seldom asked anything for herself.

After many serious discussions with Meg and Jo, the pattern was chosen, the materials bought, and the slippers begun. A cluster of grave yet cheerful pansies,[10] on a deeper purple ground, was pronounced very appropriate and pretty, and Beth worked away early and late, with occasional lifts[11] over hard parts. She was a nimble little needle-woman, and they were finished before any one got tired of them. Then she wrote a very short, simple note, and, with Laurie's help, got them smuggled on to the study-table one morning before the old gentleman was up.

When this excitement was over, Beth waited to see what would happen. All that day passed, and a part of the next, before any acknowledgment arrived, and she was beginning to fear she had offended her crotchety friend. On the afternoon of the second day she went out to do an errand, and give poor Joanna, the invalid doll, her daily exercise. As she came up the street on her return she saw three—yes, four heads popping in and out of the parlor windows; and the moment they saw her several hands were waved, and several joyful voices screamed,—

"Here's a letter from the old gentleman; come quick, and read it!"

"Oh, Beth! he's sent you—" began Amy, gesticulating with unseemly energy; but she got no further, for Jo quenched her by slamming down the window.

Beth hurried on in a twitter of suspense; at the door her sisters seized and bore her to the parlor in a triumphal procession, all pointing, and all saying at once, "Look there! look there!" Beth did look, and turned pale with delight and surprise; for there stood a little cabinet piano,[12] with a letter lying on the glossy lid, directed like a sign-board, to "Miss Elizabeth March."

"For me?" gasped Beth, holding on to Jo, and feeling as if she should tumble down, it was such an overwhelming thing altogether.

"Yes; all for you, my precious! Isn't it splendid of him? Don't

Illustration of a typical cabinet piano.

10. Pansies, the *Viola* genus, were extremely popular by the early nineteenth century as gardeners began to crossbreed the flower, developing over 300 different types by 1833.

11. Assistance or help.

12. Produced from about 1807 to 1840, cabinet pianos were tall with the strings arranged vertically behind the keyboard, the lower end of the strings almost level with the keys. The name derived from the cabinet shelves in the upper part of the case to the right of the strings.

13. A key to unlock the cabinet piano.

14. Common name for pansy.

15. Extremely beautiful. The 1880–1881 edition changed this slang expression to "They'll think it's splendid."

16. The *OED* indicates that "the motivation for [this] expression is unclear" and defines it as meaning "perfect order or neatness."

you think he's the dearest old man in the world? Here's the key[13] in the letter; we didn't open it, but we are dying to know what he says," cried Jo, hugging her sister, and offering the note.

"You read it; I can't, I feel so queer. Oh, it is too lovely!" and Beth hid her face in Jo's apron, quite upset by her present.

Jo opened the paper, and began to laugh, for the first words she saw were:—

"MISS MARCH:
 "Dear Madam—"

"How nice it sounds! I wish some one would write to me so!" said Amy, who thought the old-fashioned address very elegant.

"'I have had many pairs of slippers in my life, but I never had any that suited me so well as yours,'" continued Jo. "'Heart's-ease[14] is my favorite flower, and these will always remind me of the gentle giver. I like to pay my debts, so I know you will allow "the old gentleman" to send you something which once belonged to the little granddaughter he lost. With hearty thanks, and best wishes, I remain,

  "'Your grateful friend and humble servant,
   "'JAMES LAURENCE.'"

"There, Beth, that's an honor to be proud of, I'm sure! Laurie told me how fond Mr. Laurence used to be of the child who died, and how he kept all her little things carefully. Just think; he's given you her piano! That comes of having big blue eyes and loving music," said Jo, trying to soothe Beth, who trembled, and looked more excited than she had ever been before.

"See the cunning brackets to hold candles, and the nice green silk, puckered up with a gold rose in the middle, and the pretty rack and stool, all complete," added Meg, opening the instrument, and displaying its beauties.

"'Your humble servant, James Laurence;' only think of his writing that to you. I'll tell the girls; they'll think it's killing,"[15] said Amy, much impressed by the note.

"Try it, honey; let's hear the sound of the baby pianny," said Hannah, who always took a share in the family joys and sorrows.

So Beth tried it, and every one pronounced it the most remark-

Beth (Margaret O'Brien) thanks Mr. Laurence (C. Aubrey Smith) in Mervyn LeRoy's 1949 film adaptation of *Little Women*. In the film, Beth is portrayed as several years younger than Amy.

able piano ever heard. It had evidently been newly tuned, and put in apple-pie order;[16] but, perfect as it was, I think the real charm of it lay in the happiest of all happy faces which leaned over it, as Beth lovingly touched the beautiful black and white keys, and pressed the shiny[a] pedals.

"You'll have to go and thank him," said Jo, by way of a joke; for the idea of the child's really going, never entered her head.

"Yes, I mean to; I guess I'll go now, before I get frightened thinking about it;" and, to the utter amazement of the assembled family, Beth walked deliberately down the garden, through the hedge, and in at the Laurences' door.

"Well, I wish I may die, if it ain't the queerest thing I ever see! The pianny has turned her head; she'd never have gone, in her right mind," cried Hannah, staring after her, while the girls were rendered quite speechless by the miracle.

They would have been still more amazed, if they had seen what Beth did afterward. If you will believe me, she went and knocked at the study door before she gave herself time to think; and when a gruff voice called out, "Come in!" she did go in, right up to Mr. Laurence, who looked quite taken aback, and held out her hand, saying, with only a small quaver in her voice, "I came to thank you, sir, for—" but she didn't finish, for he looked so friendly that she forgot her speech; and, only remembering that he had lost the little girl he loved, she put both arms round his neck, and kissed him.

If the roof of the house had suddenly flown off, the old gentleman wouldn't have been more astonished; but he liked it—oh dear, yes! he liked it amazingly; and was so touched and pleased by that confiding little kiss, that all his crustiness vanished; and he just set her on his knee, and laid his wrinkled cheek against her rosy one, feeling as if he had got his own little granddaughter back again. Beth ceased to fear him from that moment, and sat there talking to him as cosily as if she had known him all her life; for love casts out fear, and gratitude can conquer pride. When she went home, he walked with her to her own gate, shook hands cordially, and touched his hat as he marched back again, looking very stately and erect, like a handsome, soldierly old gentleman, as he was.

When the girls saw that performance, Jo began to dance a jig, by way of expressing her satisfaction; Amy nearly fell out of the window in her surprise, and Meg exclaimed, with uplifted hands, "Well, I do believe the world is coming to an end!"

Chapter 7

Amy's Valley of Humiliation

T HAT BOY is a perfect Cyclops,[1] isn't he?" said Amy, one day, as Laurie clattered by on horseback, with a flourish of his whip as he passed.

"How dare you say so, when he's got both his eyes? and very handsome ones they are, too;" cried Jo, who resented any slighting remarks about her friend.

"I didn't say anything about his eyes, and I don't see why you need fire up when I admire his riding."

"Oh, my goodness! that little goose means a centaur,[2] and she called him a Cyclops," exclaimed Jo, with a burst of laughter.

"You needn't be so rude, it's only a 'lapse of lingy;'[3] as Mr. Davis says," retorted Amy, finishing Jo with her Latin. "I just wish I had a little of the money Laurie spends on that horse," she added, as if to herself, yet hoping her sisters would hear.

"Why?" asked Meg, kindly, for Jo had gone off in another laugh at Amy's second blunder.

"I need it so much; I'm dreadfully in debt, and it won't be my turn to have the rag-money[4] for a month."

"In debt, Amy; what do you mean?" and Meg looked sober.

"Why, I owe at least a dozen pickled limes,[5] and I can't pay them, you know, till I have money, for Marmee forbid my having anything charged at the shop."

"Tell me all about it. Are limes the fashion now? It used to be pricking bits of rubber to make balls;" and Meg tried to keep her countenance, Amy looked so grave and important.

"Why, you see, the girls are always buying them, and unless you want to be thought mean, you must do it, too. It's nothing

1. A cyclops, a giant with one eye in the middle of its forehead, appears in several accounts of ancient Greek and Roman writers, from Hesiod to Virgil; however, the most famous account is in Homer's *Odyssey*, where Odysseus meets the cyclops Polyphemus.

2. A half-human, half-horse creature in Greek mythology.

3. Amy is referring to the Latin term *apsus lingua*, meaning "slip of the tongue."

4. Money obtained from selling rags or old clothes to a rag dealer. Usually this would be a small sum; thus, Mrs. March allows the sisters to have the money for their personal use, what Amy calls "pocket money."

5. Pickled limes were popular in the nineteenth century, with many cookbooks providing recipes. Usually the lime peel was pierced and then the fruit was placed in a brine solution for several days. In *The Joy of Pickling* (Cambridge: Harvard Common Press, 1999), Linda Ziedrich observes: "In the West Indies, in the nineteenth and early twentieth centuries, ripe limes were packed whole in sea water or fresh-made brine and shipped to northeastern U.S. ports in barrels. In 1838, according to the Royal Horticultural Society of Great Britain, there was 'a fair demand in the New York market for pickled limes,' but by the late nineteenth century pickled limes were invariably sent to Boston. There they were sold from glass jars on top of candy-store counters, and some families even bought them by the barrel. Because the import tariff for pickled limes was quite low—importers fought to keep them classed as neither fresh fruit nor pickle—children could buy them cheaply, often for a penny apiece. Kids chewed, sucked, and traded pickled limes at school (and not just at recess) for decades, making the limes the perennial bane of New England schoolteachers. Doctors tended to disapprove of the limes, too; in 1869 a Boston physician wrote that pickled limes were among the 'unnatural and abominable' substances consumed by children with nutritional deficiencies. Parents, however, seemed generally content for children to indulge themselves in the pickled-lime habit" (p. 77). The following recipe appeared in the August 7, 1881, edition of the *New York Times*: "Pickled Limes.—Make a brine strong enough to float an egg; stick your limes on two sides with a silver fork; then put them in the brine with a weight on the limes to keep them well under the brine; let them stand in a warm place for a week; they are then fit to eat. You can add some red peppers to the brine.—West India Woman" (p. 9).

6. Bead-rings were rings made with small glass beads. Paper dolls, both homemade and commercially produced, were popular in nineteenth-century America. McLoughlin Brothers, a New York publishing firm founded in 1828, was the country's largest manufacturer of paper dolls.

7. A debt that is not binding but from a moral perspective should be paid.

8. Aching.

9. Like Amy in *Little Women*, Abby May Alcott was the only sister to attend school; the other three girls were taught at home. May began her education in Boston while the Alcotts were living on High Street. Bronson, highlighting his own failures, noted in his October 1851 journal: "Abby begins her studies today, and with hope and courage. The child has fair talents, and good disposition. She opens life with prospects somewhat fairer than fell to her elder sisters, who, with gifts no less promising, have yet been defrauded of deserved opportunities for study and culture, by social disabilities under which we have been struggling since the close of my Temple School. It was my hope in that, and afterwards in the Fruitlands endeavor, to provide the means of an improved culture in which my children might participate with others to the extent of an enthusiast's dream; but these plans were frustrated, and at the greatest personal hazard and domestic cost" (*Journals of BA* 254).

10. Meanly taunted.

11. Amy's earlier inability to return the favors of limes to her friends demonstrates the problem of both the genteel poor and those truly in poverty. She feels humiliated that she has taken but not returned the favor. Amy, however, needs to learn to give freely, as shown earlier with Marmee's Christmas gift, to think less of her self and more for others. LMA espouses here Christian charity, as when Paul says, "I have shewed you all things, how that so labouring ye ought to support the weak, and to remember the words of the Lord Jesus, how he said, It is more blessed to give than to receive" (Acts 20: 35).

12. "Bury the hatchet" is a commonly used phrase that comes from Native Americans. Warring Iroquois tribes would literally bury their weapons as a symbol of peace. The phrase first appears in English in the writings of Samuel Sewall, the Alcotts' infamous ancestor best known as a judge in the Salem witchcraft trial of 1692. In 1680, Sewall wrote: "'Meeting with ye Sachem the[y] came to an agreement and buried two Axes in ye Ground, which ceremony to them is more significant & binding than all Articles of Peace the Hatchet being a principal weapon'" (quoted in *The New England Historical & Genealogical Register* 1870).

but limes now, for every one is sucking them in their desks in school-time, and trading them off for pencils, bead-rings, paper dolls,[6] or something else, at recess. If one girl likes another, she gives her a lime; if she's mad with her, she eats one before her face, and don't offer even a suck. They treat by turns; and I've had ever so many, but haven't returned them, and I ought, for they are debts of honor,[7] you know."

"How much will pay them off, and restore your credit?" asked Meg, taking out her purse.

"A quarter would more than do it, and leave a few cents over for a treat for you. Don't you like limes?"

"Not much; you may have my share. Here's the money,—make it last as long as you can, for it isn't very plenty, you know."

"Oh, thank you! it must be so nice to have pocket-money. I'll have a grand feast, for I haven't tasted a lime this week. I felt delicate about taking any, as I couldn't return them, and I'm actually suffering[8] for one."

Next day Amy was rather late at school[9]; but could not resist the temptation of displaying, with pardonable pride, a moist brown paper parcel, before she consigned it to the inmost recesses of her desk. During the next few minutes the rumor that Amy March had got twenty-four delicious limes (she ate one on the way), and was going to treat, circulated through her "set," and the attentions of her friends became quite overwhelming. Katy Brown invited her to her next party on the spot; Mary Kingsley insisted on lending her her watch till recess, and Jenny Snow, a satirical young lady who had basely twitted[10] Amy upon her limeless state,[11] promptly buried the hatchet,[12] and offered to furnish answers to certain appalling[13] sums. But Amy had not forgotten Miss Snow's cutting remarks about "some persons whose noses were not too flat to smell other people's limes, and stuck-up people, who were not too proud to ask for them;" and she instantly crushed "that Snow girl's" hopes by the withering telegram, "You needn't be so polite all of a sudden, for you won't get any."

A distinguished personage happened to visit the school that morning, and Amy's beautifully drawn maps received praise, which honor to her foe rankled in the soul of Miss Snow, and caused Miss March to assume the airs of a studious young pea-cock.[14] But, alas, alas! pride goes before a fall, and the revengeful Snow turned the tables with disastrous success. No sooner had the guest paid the usual stale compliments, and bowed himself out, than Jenny, under pretence of asking an important question, informed Mr. Davis, the teacher, that Amy March had pickled limes in her desk.

Now Mr. Davis had declared limes a contraband article, and solemnly vowed to publicly ferule[15] the first person who was found breaking the law. This much-enduring man had succeeded in banishing gum[16] after a long and stormy war, had made a bonfire of the confiscated novels and newspapers, had suppressed a pri-vate post-office, had forbidden distortions of the face, nicknames, and caricatures, and done all that one man could do to keep half a hundred rebellious girls in order. Boys are trying enough to hu-man patience, goodness knows! but girls are infinitely more so, especially to nervous gentlemen with tyrannical tempers, and no more talent for teaching than "Dr. Blimber."[17] Mr. Davis knew any quantity of Greek, Latin, Algebra, and ologies[18] of all sorts, so he was called a fine teacher; and manners, morals, feelings, and examples were not considered of any particular importance.[19] It was a most unfortunate moment for denouncing Amy, and Jenny knew it. Mr. Davis had evidently taken his coffee too strong that morning; there was an east wind, which always affected his neu-ralgia,[20] and his pupils had not done him the credit which he felt he deserved; therefore, to use the expressive, if not elegant, lan-guage of a school-girl, "he was as nervous as a witch and as cross as a bear."[21] The word "limes" was like fire to powder; his yellow face flushed, and he rapped on his desk with an energy which made Jenny skip to her seat with unusual rapidity.

"Young ladies, attention, if you please!"

At the stern order the buzz ceased, and fifty pairs of blue, black, gray, and brown eyes were obediently fixed upon his awful[22] coun-tenance.

"Miss March, come to the desk."

Amy rose to comply, with outward composure, but a secret fear oppressed her, for the limes weighed upon her conscience.

Elizabeth Palmer Peabody (1804–1894).

13. Overwhelming.

14. A proud person.

15. To whip. An instrument used to switch or paddle students was called a ferule rod.

16. The State of Maine Pure Spruce Gum, developed by John B. Curtis (1827–1897) in 1848, was the first commercial chewing gum in America. In 1860, chicle, latex derived from trees, was imported from Mexico, and chewing gum grew in popularity during the 1860s and 1870s.

17. Dr. Blimber was the head of a boy's school in Charles Dick-ens's *Dombey and Son* (1848) but not a good teacher: "The Doctor only undertook the charge of ten young gentlemen, but he had, al-ways ready a supply of learning for a hundred, on the lowest esti-mate; and it was at once the business and delight of his life to gorge the unhappy ten with it" (chapter 11).

18. Academic fields of knowledge, especially those of the sciences.

19. LMA uses Mr. Davis to criticize American education, a topic she would have known much about since her father was at the fore-front of education reform in the nineteenth century. Never having attended formal school, LMA, like her sisters Anna and Beth, had been taught by Bronson Alcott. Bronson's most important ideas about education came out of his experiences at the Temple School

(so named because it was held in the Masonic Temple in Boston), which he operated from 1834 to 1838, with the help of Elizabeth Palmer Peabody and later Margaret Fuller. These experiences can be found in Peabody's *Record of a School* (1835) and Bronson's own *Conversations with the Children on the Gospel* (1836–1837). At the Temple School, he taught by the Socratic method, insisting, in accordance with his Transcendentalist beliefs, that all possessed the divinity within, even children. LMA's own ideas on education are seen most notably in *An Old-Fashioned Girl* (1870), *Little Men* (1871), and *Jo's Boys* (1886), although the theme appears in short stories as well. When *Little Men* was published, Roberts Brothers, in response to readers' questions about Plumfield, revised and reissued *Record of a School*. It would be 1874 before the revised edition finally appeared, retitled *Record of Mr. Alcott's School* (Boston: Roberts Brothers, 1874). Peabody, in her preface, quotes from LMA: "'The methods of education so successfully tried at the Temple long ago, are so kindly welcomed now, even the very imperfect hints in the story, that I cannot consent to receive the thanks and commendations due to another'" (p. 3). Whereas her father was often philosophical and idealistic, LMA is more practical, insisting on the importance of getting outdoors into the world of nature as well as studying various disciplines, such as math and history. Everyone, LMA believed, should be successfully prepared to achieve economic independence by being educated for suitable employment. Most of all, LMA wished to see education, for both males and females, encompass a person's whole being: physical, spiritual, and moral.

20. A sharp burning pain near a nerve. By 1870, LMA greatly complained of this ailment herself.

21. Ill-humored and annoyed. The origin of the phrase is unknown.

22. Dreadful.

23. Over a million Irish immigrated to America during and after the Great Irish Potato Famine of 1845–1852, many settling near the port cities of Boston and New York. By 1853, almost 40 percent of Boston's population was Irish. Most of the immigrants were Catholic, poverty-stricken, illiterate, and unskilled, and thus were often the object of discrimination, especially in New England, which was largely populated by Protestants of English descent. Alcott herself held the common prejudices of the time about the Irish. Here the Irish children are unable to attend school because they are poor; Amy's school is a private one.

"Bring with you the limes you have in your desk," was the unexpected command which arrested her before she got out of her seat.

"Don't take all," whispered her neighbor, a young lady of great presence of mind.

Amy hastily shook out half a dozen, and laid the rest down before Mr. Davis, feeling that any man possessing a human heart would relent when that delicious perfume met his nose. Unfortunately, Mr. Davis particularly detested the odor of the fashionable pickle, and disgust added to his wrath.

"Is that all?"

"Not quite," stammered Amy.

"Bring the rest, immediately."

With a despairing glance at her set she obeyed.

"You are sure there are no more?"

"I never lie, sir."

"So I see. Now take these disgusting things, two by two, and throw them out of the window."

There was a simultaneous sigh, which created quite a little gust as the last hope fled, and the treat was ravished from their longing lips. Scarlet with shame and anger, Amy went to and fro twelve mortal times;[a] and as each doomed couple, looking, oh, so plump and juicy! fell from her reluctant hands, a shout from the street completed the anguish of the girls, for it told them that their feast was being exulted over by the little Irish children, who were their sworn foes.[23] This—this was too much; all flashed indignant or appealing glances at the inexorable Davis, and one passionate lime-lover burst into tears.

As Amy returned from her last trip, Mr. Davis gave a portentous "hem," and said, in his most impressive manner,—

"Young ladies, you remember what I said to you a week ago. I am sorry this has happened; but I never allow my rules to be infringed, and I *never* break my word. Miss March, hold out your hand."

Amy started, and put both hands behind her, turning on him an imploring look, which pleaded for her better than the words

Amy (Joan Bennett) is punished in Cukor's 1933 *Little Women*. Shame replaces the novel's physical punishment. Bennett, who was twenty-one at the time, plays a teenage Amy.

she could not utter. She was rather a favorite with "old Davis," as, of course, he was called, and it's my private belief that he *would* have broken his word if the indignation of one irrepressible young lady had not found vent in a hiss. That hiss, faint as it was, irritated the irascible gentleman, and sealed the culprit's fate.

"Your hand, Miss March!" was the only answer her mute appeal received; and, too proud to cry or beseech, Amy set her teeth, threw back her head defiantly, and bore without flinching several tingling blows on her little palm. They were neither many nor heavy, but that made no difference to her. For the first time in her life she had been struck; and the disgrace, in her eyes, was as deep as if he had knocked her down.

"You will now stand on the platform till recess," said Mr. Davis, resolved to do the thing thoroughly, since he had begun.

That was dreadful; it would have been bad enough to go to her seat and see the pitying faces of her friends, or the satisfied ones of her few enemies; but to face the whole school, with that shame fresh upon her, seemed impossible, and for a second she felt as if she could only drop down where she stood, and break her heart with crying. A bitter sense of wrong, and the thought of Jenny Snow, helped her to bear it; and, taking the ignominious place,

24. The metal stove-funnel or stove-pipe connected the iron wood- or coal-burning stove to the chimney.

25. The room before the main classroom, which served as a coat-room in Amy's school.

26. A type of alcohol, derived from vegetable and animal fats and oils, that was used as an ointment.

27. Young girls.

28. Kindly.

she fixed her eyes on the stove-funnel[24] above what now seemed a sea of faces, and stood there so motionless and white, that the girls found it very hard to study, with that pathetic little[b] figure before them.

During the fifteen minutes that followed, the proud and sensitive little girl suffered a shame and pain which she never forgot. To others it might seem a ludicrous or trivial affair, but to her it was a hard experience; for during the twelve years of her life she had been governed by love alone, and a blow of that sort had never touched her before. The smart of her hand, and the ache of her heart, were forgotten in the sting of the thought,—

"I shall have to tell at home, and they will be so disappointed in me!"

The fifteen minutes seemed an hour; but they came to an end at last, and the word "recess!" had never seemed so welcome to her before.

"You can go, Miss March," said Mr. Davis, looking, as he felt, uncomfortable.

He did not soon forget the reproachful look[c] Amy gave him, as she went, without a word to any one, straight into the anteroom,[25] snatched her things, and left the place "forever," as she passionately declared to herself. She was in a sad state when she got home; and when the older girls arrived, some time later, an indignation meeting was held at once. Mrs. March did not say much, but looked disturbed, and comforted her afflicted little daughter in her tenderest manner. Meg bathed the insulted hand with glycerine[26] and tears; Beth felt that even her beloved kittens would fail as a balm for griefs like this, and Jo wrathfully proposed that Mr. Davis be arrested without delay, while Hannah shook her fist at the "villain," and pounded potatoes for dinner as if she had him under her pestle.

No notice was taken of Amy's flight, except by her mates; but the sharp-eyed demoiselles[27] discovered that Mr. Davis was quite benignant[28] in the afternoon, also unusually nervous. Just before school closed, Jo appeared, wearing a grim expression, as she stalked up to the desk, and delivered a letter from her mother; then collected Amy's property, and departed, carefully scraping the mud from her boots on the door-mat, as if she shook the dust of the place off her feet.[29]

"Yes, you can have a vacation from school, but I want you to study a little every day, with Beth," said Mrs. March, that evening. "I don't approve of corporal punishment, especially for girls.[30] I dislike Mr. Davis' manner of teaching, and don't think the girls you associate with are doing you any good, so I shall ask your father's advice before I send you anywhere else."

"That's good! I wish all the girls would leave, and spoil his old school. It's perfectly maddening to think of those lovely limes," sighed Amy, with the air of a martyr.

"I am not sorry you lost them, for you broke the rules, and deserved some punishment for disobedience," was the severe reply, which rather disappointed the young lady, who expected nothing but sympathy.

"Do you mean you are glad I was disgraced before the whole school?" cried Amy.

"I should not have chosen that way of mending a fault," replied her mother; "but I'm not sure that it won't do you more good than a milder method. You are getting to be altogether too conceited and important,[d] my dear, and it is quite time you set about correcting it. You have a good many little gifts and virtues, but there is no need of parading them, for conceit spoils the finest genius. There is not much danger that real talent or goodness will be overlooked long; even if it is, the consciousness of possessing and using it well should satisfy one, and the great charm of all power is modesty."

"So it is," cried Laurie, who was playing chess in a corner with Jo. "I knew a girl, once, who had a really remarkable talent for music, and she didn't know it; never guessed what sweet little things she composed when she was alone, and wouldn't have believed it if any one had told her."

"I wish I'd known that nice girl, maybe she would have helped me, I'm so stupid," said Beth, who stood beside him, listening eagerly.

"You do know her, and she helps you better than any one else could," answered Laurie, looking at her with such mischievous

29. LMA alludes to Jesus's command to his disciples to preach the word of God and how to react to those who will not hear it: "And whosoever shall not receive you, nor hear your words, when ye depart out of that house or city, shake off the dust of your feet" (Matthew 10:14).

30. Bronson Alcott's method of punishment in the schoolroom was described by Frances Bellows Sanborn in his reminiscence "The Alcotts" (1888): "Punishment, he said, should never be inflicted except as a reminder. Taken in any other way, punishment was coarse and brutal." He recalled that "one of the boys [in Alcott's school] was found guilty of some misdemeanor. Mr. Alcott called him up, and after talking gently with the offender, gave him a ruler and bade him apply it to his teacher. The boy hesitated, and drew back, but Mr. Alcott was firm; and the boy after administering one or two faint blows with a burst of tears begged Mr. Alcott to beat *him*,— 'anything, indeed, rather than that'" (quoted in *Her Own Time* 50). According to Anna's son John Pratt Alcott, in "The 'Little Women' of Long Ago" (1933), Bronson and Abigail also had a unique way to reprimand their daughters: "For example, they never admonished the child openly or reproved them in one another's presence. If one of them did anything reprehensible, she wouldn't know that it had displeased her parents until she went to bed and found under her pillow a little note from mother or father, discussing the fault committed and hinting at more desirable methods of behavior. The children thought these things over at leisure and then sent back their replies and conclusions in the same quiet, unobserved way. There was no chance for a flare of temper here, no opportunity to answer back; only a little silent contemplation of one's wrongdoings and then an endeavor to express contriteness and apology in writing. What a chastening of the spirit!" (quoted in *Her Own Time* 156–157).

meaning in his merry black eyes, that Beth suddenly turned very red, and hid her face in the sofa-cushion, quite overcome by such an unexpected discovery.

Jo let Laurie win the game, to pay for that praise of her Beth, who could not be prevailed upon to play for them after her compliment. So Laurie did his best, and sung delightfully, being in a particularly lively humor, for to the Marches he seldom showed the moody side of his character. When he was gone, Amy, who had been pensive all the evening, said, suddenly, as if busy over some new idea,—

"Is Laurie an accomplished boy?"

"Yes; he has had an excellent education, and has much talent; he will make a fine man, if not spoilt by petting,"[31] replied her mother.

"And he isn't conceited, is he?" asked Amy.

"Not in the least; that is why he is so charming, and we all like him so much."

"I see; it's nice to have accomplishments, and be elegant; but not to show off, or get perked up,"[32] said Amy, thoughtfully.

"These things are always seen and felt in a person's manner and conversation, if modestly used; but it is not necessary to display them," said Mrs. March.

"Any more than it's proper to wear all your bonnets, and gowns, and ribbons, at once, that folks may know you've got 'em," added Jo; and the lecture ended in a laugh.

Chapter 8

Jo Meets Apollyon

Apollyon is the lord of the City of Destruction in *The Pilgrim's Progress*. In the form of a dragon creature, he battles Christian in the Valley of Humiliation, hoping to force the pilgrim to serve him. After being wounded by Christian's sword, Apollyon flies away. In book two, Christiana and her sons, led by Mr. Great-heart, visit the site of the battle.

"GIRLS, where are you going?" asked Amy, coming into their room one Saturday afternoon, and finding them getting ready to go out, with an air of secrecy which excited her curiosity.

"Never mind; little girls shouldn't ask questions," returned Jo, sharply.

Now if there is anything mortifying to our feelings, when we are young, it is to be told that; and to be bidden to "run away, dear," is still more trying to us. Amy bridled up at this insult, and determined to find out the secret, if she teased for an hour. Turning to Meg, who never refused her anything very long, she said, coaxingly, "Do tell me! I should think you might let me go, too; for Beth is fussing over her dolls,ª and I haven't got anything to do, and am *so* lonely."

"I can't, dear, because you aren't invited," began Meg; but Jo broke in impatiently, "Now, Meg, be quiet, or you will spoil it all. You can't go, Amy; so don't be a baby, and whine about it."

"You are going somewhere with Laurie, I know you are; you were whispering and laughing together, on the sofa, last night, and you stopped when I came in. Aren't you going with him?"

"Yes, we are; now do be still, and stop bothering."

Amy held her tongue, but used her eyes, and saw Meg slip a fan into her pocket.

"I know! I know! you're going to the theatre to see the 'Seven Castles!' she cried; adding, resolutely, "and I *shall* go, for mother said I might see it; and I've got my rag-money, and it was mean not to tell me in time."

1. May Alcott suffered from eye weakness from her teen years onward.

2. In the nineteenth century, it was improper for a lady, even a young one, to sit alone at a theater.

3. No play entitled *The Seven Castles of the Diamond Lake* has been located. Anne K. Phillips and Gregory Eiselein suggest that Alcott may be alluding to Edward Stirling's 1844 play *The Seven Castles of the Passions: A Drama of Enchantment in Two-Acts* (Louisa May Alcott, *Little Women,* ed. Anne K. Phillips and Gregory Eiselein. A Norton Critical Edition [New York: W. W. Norton, 2004], 62n1).

"Just listen to me a minute, and be a good child," said Meg, soothingly. "Mother doesn't wish you to go this week, because your eyes[1] are not well enough yet to bear the light of this fairy piece. Next week you can go with Beth and Hannah, and have a nice time."

"I don't like that half as well as going with you and Laurie. Please let me; I've been sick with this cold so long, and shut up, I'm dying for some fun. Do, Meg! I'll be ever so good," pleaded Amy, looking as pathetic as she could.

"Suppose we take her. I don't believe mother would mind, if we bundle her up well," began Meg.

"If she goes *I* shan't; and if I don't, Laurie won't like it; and it will be very rude, after he invited only us, to go and drag in Amy. I should think she'd hate to poke herself where she isn't wanted," said Jo, crossly, for she disliked the trouble of overseeing a fidgety child, when she wanted to enjoy herself.

Her tone and manner angered Amy, who began to put her boots on, saying, in her most aggravating way, "I *shall* go; Meg says I may; and if I pay for myself, Laurie hasn't anything to do with it."

"You can't sit with us, for our seats are reserved, and you mustn't sit alone;[2] so Laurie will give you his place, and that will spoil our pleasure; or he'll get another seat for you, and that isn't proper, when you weren't asked. You shan't stir a step; so you may just stay where you are," scolded Jo, crosser than ever, having just pricked her finger in her hurry.

Sitting on the floor, with one boot on, Amy began to cry, and Meg to reason with her, when Laurie called from below, and the two girls hurried down, leaving their sister wailing; for now and then she forgot her grown-up ways, and acted like a spoilt child. Just as the party was setting out, Amy called over the banisters, in a threatening tone, "You'll be sorry for this, Jo March! see if you ain't."

"Fiddlesticks!" returned Jo, slamming the door.

They had a charming time, for "The Seven Castles of the Diamond Lake"[3] were as brilliant and wonderful as a heart could wish. But, in spite of the comical red imps, sparkling elves, and

LITTLE WOMEN

gorgeous princes and princesses, Jo's pleasure had a drop of bitterness in it; the fairy queen's yellow curls reminded her of Amy; and between the acts she amused herself with wondering what her sister would do to make her "sorry for it." She and Amy had had many lively skirmishes in the course of their lives, for both had quick tempers, and were apt to be violent when fairly roused. Amy teased Jo, and Jo irritated Amy, and semi-occasional explosions occurred, of which both were much ashamed afterward. Although the oldest, Jo had the least self-control, and had hard times trying to curb the fiery spirit which was continually getting her into trouble; her anger never lasted long, and, having humbly confessed her fault, she sincerely repented, and tried to do better. Her sisters used to say, that they rather liked to get Jo into a fury, because she was such an angel afterward. Poor Jo tried desperately to be good, but her bosom enemy was always ready to flame up and defeat her; and it took years of patient effort to subdue it.

When they got home, they found Amy reading in the parlor. She assumed an injured air as they came in; never lifted her eyes from her book, or asked a single question. Perhaps curiosity might have conquered resentment, if Beth had not been there to inquire, and receive a glowing description of the play. On going up to put away her best hat, Jo's first look was toward the bureau; for, in their last quarrel, Amy had soothed her feelings by turning Jo's top drawer upside down, on the floor. Everything was in its place, however; and after a hasty glance into her various closets, bags and boxes, Jo decided that Amy had forgiven and forgotten her wrongs.

There Jo was mistaken; for next day she made a discovery which produced a tempest. Meg, Beth and Amy were sitting together, late in the afternoon, when Jo burst into the room, looking excited, and demanding, breathlessly, "Has any one taken my story?"[b]

Meg and Beth said "No," at once, and looked surprised; Amy poked the fire, and said nothing. Jo saw her color rise, and was down upon her in a minute.

"Amy, you've got it!"

"No, I haven't."

Portrait of Louisa May Alcott by George Peter Alexander Healy (1813–1894), a Boston-born artist whose subjects included the most prominent people of the time, including Abraham Lincoln, Ulysses S. Grant, Daniel Webster, Nathaniel Hawthorne, and Henry Wadsworth Longfellow. LMA sat for Healy in spring 1871, while she and her sister May were in Rome, Italy. Today, the portrait hangs in the dining room of Orchard House.

"You know where it is, then!"

"No, I don't."

"That's a fib!" cried Jo, taking her by the shoulders, and looking fierce enough to frighten a much braver child than Amy.

"It isn't. I haven't got it, don't know where it is now, and don't care."

"You know something about it, and you'd better tell at once, or I'll make you," and Jo gave her a slight shake.

"Scold as much as you like, you'll never get your silly old story[c] again," cried Amy, getting excited in her turn.

"Why not?"

"I burnt it up."

"What! my little book I was so fond of, and worked over, and meant to finish before father got home? Have you really burnt it?" said Jo, turning very pale, while her eyes kindled and her hands clutched Amy nervously.

"Yes, I did! I told you I'd make you pay for being so cross yesterday, and I have, so—"

Amy got no farther, for Jo's hot temper mastered her, and she shook Amy till her teeth chattered in her head; crying, in a passion of grief and anger,—

"You wicked, wicked girl! I never can write it again, and I'll never forgive you as long as I live."

Meg flew to rescue Amy, and Beth to pacify Jo, but Jo was quite beside herself; and, with a parting box on her sister's ear, she rushed out of the room up to the old sofa in the garret, and finished her fight alone.

The storm cleared up below, for Mrs. March came home, and, having heard the story, soon brought Amy to a sense of the wrong she had done her sister. Jo's book was the pride of her heart, and was regarded by her family as a literary sprout of great promise. It was only half a dozen little fairy tales, but Jo had worked over them patiently, putting her whole heart into her work, hoping to make something good enough to print. She had just copied them with great care, and had destroyed the old manuscript, so that Amy's bonfire had consumed the loving work of several years. It seemed a small loss to others, but to Jo it was a dreadful calamity, and she felt that it never could be made up to her.[4] Beth mourned as for a departed kitten, and Meg refused to defend her pet; Mrs. March looked grave and grieved, and Amy felt that no one would love her till she had asked pardon for the act which she now regretted more than any of them.

When the tea-bell rung, Jo appeared, looking so grim and unapproachable, that it took all Amy's courage to say, meekly,—

"Please forgive me, Jo; I'm very, very sorry."

"I never shall forgive you," was Jo's stern answer; and, from that moment, she ignored Amy entirely.

No one spoke of the great trouble,—not even Mrs. March,—for all had learned by experience that when Jo was in that mood words were wasted; and the wisest course was to wait till some little accident, or her own generous nature, softened Jo's resentment, and healed the breach. It was not a happy evening; for, though they sewed as usual, while their mother read aloud from Bremer, Scott, or Edgeworth,[5] something was wanting, and the sweet home-peace was disturbed. They felt this most when singing-time came; for Beth could only play, Jo stood dumb as a stone, and Amy broke down, so Meg and mother sung alone. But, in spite of their efforts to be as cheery as larks, the flute-like voices did not seem to chord[6] as well as usual, and all felt out of tune.

As Jo received her good-night kiss, Mrs. March whispered, gently,—

"My dear, don't let the sun go down upon your anger; forgive each other, help each other, and begin again to-morrow."

Jo wanted to lay her head down on that motherly bosom, and cry her grief and anger all away; but tears were an unmanly weakness, and she felt so deeply injured that she really *couldn't* quite forgive yet. So she winked hard, shook her head, and said, gruffly, because Amy was listening,—

"It was an abominable thing, and she don't deserve to be forgiven."

With that she marched off to bed, and there was no merry or confidential gossip that night.

Amy was much offended that her overtures of peace had been repulsed, and began to wish she had not humbled herself, to feel

4. No biographical information has been located to suggest that this event actually happened. Alcott's first book was *Flower Fables* (1854), a collection of peaceful nature fairy tales that were originally told to Ellen Emerson, the first daughter of Ralph Waldo Emerson. The publisher Ticknor and Fields did misplace "Jamie's Wonder Book," a fantasy book LMA had written in 1864. She rewrote the work, but the publisher again lost the book, along with illustrations that had been completed by the artist Elizabeth B. Greene. Ticknor and Fields eventually paid LMA $150 for the manuscript in June 1867. It resurfaced in 1874, and LMA, on January 28, wrote to James R. Osgood, whose firm had succeeded Ticknor and Fields: "Even in my day of small things I fancy $150 would not be considered sufficient remuneration for a book, & not an unduly large compensation for the labor, loss & disappointment of the affair" (*Selected Letters* 181).

5. Frederika Bremer, Sir Walter Scott, and Maria Edgeworth (1767–1849), British author of numerous sentimental novels and stories for children. Clara Gowing, Louisa's childhood friend in Concord, recalled in *The Alcotts as I Knew Them* (1909): "Their library contained all Miss Edgeworth's novels, Scott's, Miss Bremer's and Dickens' works" (quoted in *Her Own Time* 137).

6. To harmonize.

7. To congratulate.

8. An ill-tempered person.

9. Investigating.

more injured than ever, and to plume[7] herself on her superior virtue in a way which was particularly exasperating. Jo still looked like a thunder-cloud, and nothing went well all day. It was bitter cold in the morning; she dropped her precious turn-over in the gutter, Aunt March had an attack of fidgets, Meg was pensive, Beth *would* look grieved and wistful when she got home, and Amy kept making remarks about people who were always talking about being good, and yet wouldn't try, when other people set them a virtuous example.

"Everybody is so hateful, I'll ask Laurie to go skating. He is always kind and jolly, and will put me to rights, I know," said Jo to herself, and off she went.

Amy heard the clash of skates, and looked out with an impatient exclamation,—

"There! she promised I should go next time, for this is the last ice we shall have. But it's no use to ask such a cross patch[8] to take me."

"Don't say that; you *were* very naughty, and it is hard to forgive the loss of her precious little book; but I think she might do it now, and I guess she will, if you try her at the right minute," said Meg. "Go after them; don't say anything till Jo has got good-natured with Laurie, then take a quiet minute, and just kiss her, or do some kind thing, and I'm sure she'll be friends, again, with all her heart."

"I'll try," said Amy, for the advice suited her; and, after a flurry to get ready, she ran after the friends, who were just disappearing over the hill.

It was not far to the river, but both were ready before Amy reached them. Jo saw her coming, and turned her back; Laurie did not see, for he was carefully skating along the shore, sounding[9] the ice, for a warm spell had preceded the cold snap.

"I'll go on to the first bend, and see if it's all right, before we begin to race," Amy heard him say, as he shot away, looking like a young Russian, in his fur-trimmed coat and cap.

Jo heard Amy panting after her run, stamping her feet, and blowing her fingers, as she tried to put her skates on; but Jo never turned, and went slowly zigzagging down the river, taking a bitter, unhappy sort of satisfaction in her sister's troubles. She had cherished her anger till it grew strong, and took possession of her, as evil thoughts and feelings always do, unless cast out at once. As Laurie turned the bend, he shouted back,—

"Keep near the shore; it isn't safe in the middle."

Jo heard, but Amy was just struggling to her feet, and did not catch a word. Jo glanced over her shoulder, and the little demon she was harboring said in her ear,—

"No matter whether she heard or not, let her take care of herself."

Laurie had vanished round the bend; Jo was just at the turn, and Amy, far behind, striking out toward the smoother ice in the middle of the river. For a minute Jo stood still, with a strange feeling at her heart; then she resolved to go on, but something held and turned her round, just in time to see Amy throw up her hands and go down, with the sudden crash of rotten ice, the splash of water, and a cry that made Jo's heart stand still with fear. She tried to call Laurie, but her voice was gone; she tried to rush forward, but her feet seemed to have no strength in them; and, for a second, she could only stand motionless, staring, with a terror-stricken face, at the little blue hood above the black water. Something rushed swiftly by her, and Laurie's voice cried out,—

"Bring a rail; quick, quick!"

How she did it, she never knew; but for the next few minutes she worked as if possessed, blindly obeying Laurie, who was quite self-possessed; and, lying flat, held Amy up by his arm and hockey,[10] till Jo dragged a rail from the fence, and together they got the child out, more frightened than hurt.

"Now then, we must walk her home as fast as we can; pile our things on her, while I get off these confounded skates," cried Laurie, wrapping his coat round Amy, and tugging away at the straps, which never seemed so intricate before.

Shivering, dripping, and crying, they got Amy home; and, after an exciting time of it, she fell asleep, rolled in blankets, before a hot fire. During the bustle Jo had scarcely spoken; but flown about, looking pale and wild, with her things half off, her dress torn, and her hands cut and bruised by ice and rails, and re-

May Alcott's illustration for the first edition of *Little Women* (1868).

10. The wooden stick used to play ice hockey.

Laurie saves Amy. Frank Merrill, *Little Women: Illustrated* (1880).

11. Stubborn.

fractory[11] buckles. When Amy was comfortably asleep, the house quiet, and Mrs. March sitting by the bed, she called Jo to her, and began to bind up the hurt hands.

"Are you sure she is safe?" whispered Jo, looking remorsefully at the golden head, which might have been swept away from her sight forever, under the treacherous ice.

"Quite safe, dear; she is not hurt, and won't even take cold, I think, you were so sensible in covering and getting her home quickly," replied her mother, cheerfully.

"Laurie did it all; I only let her go. Mother, if she *should* die, it would be my fault;" and Jo dropped down beside the bed, in a passion of penitent tears, telling all that had happened, bitterly condemning her hardness of heart, and sobbing out her gratitude for being spared the heavy punishment which might have come upon her.

"It's my dreadful temper! I try to cure it; I think I have, and then it breaks out worse than ever. Oh, mother! what shall I do! what shall I do ?" cried poor Jo, in despair.

"Watch and pray, dear; never get tired of trying; and never think it is impossible to conquer your fault," said Mrs. March,

LITTLE WOMEN

drawing the blowzy[12] head to her shoulder, and kissing the wet cheek so tenderly, that Jo cried harder than ever.

"You don't know; you can't guess how bad it is! It seems as if I could do anything when I'm in a passion; I get so savage, I could hurt any one, and enjoy it. I'm afraid I *shall* do something dreadful some day, and spoil my life, and make everybody hate me. Oh, mother! help me, do help me!"

"I will, my child; I will. Don't cry so bitterly, but remember this day, and resolve, with all your soul, that you will never know another like it. Jo, dear, we all have our temptations, some far greater than yours, and it often takes us all our lives to conquer them. You think your temper is the worst in the world; but mine used to be just like it."

"Yours, mother? Why, you are never angry!" and, for the moment, Jo forgot remorse in surprise.

"I've been trying to cure it for forty years, and have only succeeded in controlling it. I am angry nearly every day of my life, Jo; but I have learned not to show it; and I still hope to learn not to feel it, though it may take me another forty years to do so."

The patience and the humility of the face she loved so well, was a better lesson to Jo than the wisest lecture, the sharpest reproof. She felt comforted at once by the sympathy and confidence given her; the knowledge that her mother had a fault like hers, and tried to mend it, made her own easier to bear, and strengthened her resolution to cure it; though forty years seemed rather a long time to watch and pray, to a girl of fifteen.

"Mother, are you angry when you fold your lips tight together, and go out of the room sometimes, when Aunt March scolds, or people worry you?" asked Jo, feeling nearer and dearer to her mother than ever before.

"Yes, I've learned to check the hasty words that rise to my lips; and when I feel that they mean to break out against my will, I just go away a minute, and give myself a little shake, for being so weak and wicked," answered Mrs. March, with a sigh and a smile, as she smoothed and fastened up Jo's dishevelled hair.

"How did you learn to keep still? That is what troubles me—

12. Red-faced or flushed from crying.

13. Abigail Alcott's mother, Dorothy Sewall May, died in October 1825, the month Abigail turned twenty-five.

for the sharp words fly out before I know what I'm about; and the more I say the worse I get, till it's a pleasure to hurt people's feelings, and say dreadful things. Tell me how you do it, Marmee dear."

"My good mother used to help me—"

"As you do us—" interrupted Jo, with a grateful kiss.

"But I lost her when I was a little older than you are,[13] and for years had to struggle on alone, for I was too proud to confess my weakness to any one else. I had a hard time, Jo, and shed a good many bitter tears over my failures; for, in spite of my efforts, I never seemed to get on. Then your father came, and I was so happy that I found it easy to be good. But by and by, when I had four little daughters round me, and we were poor, then the old trouble began again; for I am not patient by nature, and it tried me very much to see my children wanting anything."

"Poor mother! what helped you then?"

"Your father, Jo. He never loses patience,—never doubts or complains,—but always hopes, and works, and waits so cheerfully, that one is ashamed to do otherwise before him. He helped and comforted me, and showed me that I must try to practise all the virtues I would have my little girls possess, for I was their example. It was easier to try for your sakes than for my own; a startled or surprised look from one of you, when I spoke sharply, rebuked me more than any words could have done; and the love, respect, and confidence of my children was the sweetest reward I could receive for my efforts to be the woman I would have them copy."

"Oh, mother! if I'm ever half as good as you, I shall be satisfied," cried Jo, much touched.

"I hope you will be a great deal better, dear; but you must keep watch over your 'bosom enemy,' as father calls it, or it may sadden, if not spoil your life. You have had a warning; remember it, and try with heart and soul to master this quick temper, before it brings you greater sorrow and regret than you have known to-day."

"I will try, mother; I truly will. But you must help me, remind me, and keep me from flying out. I used to see father sometimes put his finger on his lips, and look at you with a very kind, but sober face; and you always folded your lips tight, or went away; was he reminding you then?" asked Jo, softly.

"Yes; I asked him to help me so, and he never forgot it, but saved me from many a sharp word by that little gesture and kind look."

Jo saw that her mother's eyes filled, and her lips trembled, as she spoke; and, fearing that she had said too much, she whispered anxiously, "Was it wrong to watch you, and to speak of it? I didn't mean to be rude, but it's so comfortable to say all I think to you, and feel so safe and happy here."

"My Jo, you may say anything to your mother, for it is my greatest happiness and pride to feel that my girls confide in me, and know how much I love them."

"I thought I'd grieved you."

"No, dear; but speaking of father reminded me how much I miss him, how much I owe him, and how faithfully I should watch and work to keep his little daughters safe and good for him."

"Yet you told him to go, mother, and didn't cry when he went, and never complain now, or seem as if you needed any help," said Jo, wondering.

"I gave my best to the country I love, and kept my tears till he was gone. Why should I complain, when we both have merely done our duty, and will surely be the happier for it in the end? If I don't seem to need help, it is because I have a better friend, even than father, to comfort and sustain me. My child, the troubles and temptations of your life are beginning, and may be many; but you can overcome and outlive them all, if you learn to feel the strength and tenderness of your Heavenly Father as you do that of your earthly one. The more you love and trust Him, the nearer you will feel to Him, and the less you will depend on human power and wisdom. His love and care never tire or change, can never be taken from you, but may become the source of life-long peace, happiness, and strength. Believe this heartily, and go to God with all your little cares, and hopes, and sins, and sorrows, as freely and confidingly as you come to your mother."[14]

14. Mrs. March's speech is similar to a letter that Bronson wrote to Anna, Louisa, and Elizabeth (May was only one year old) on Christmas Eve 1841, in which he told them about Jesus: "He did not give himself to the indulgence of his appetites or passions, but governed himself in all things. He ruled his own spirit: he obeyed his Conscience . . . you may read [Jesus's words] and be made better by them yourselves. I have his Life you know, and you can read nothing better than this to help you in all resolutions of being good. Read it—think of it—strive to be good—and to make others good also" (*Letters of ABA* 58).

15. In January 1850, when she was seventeen and living in Boston, LMA confessed: "My quick tongue is always getting me into trouble, and my moodiness makes it hard to be cheerful when I think how poor we are . . . I can't talk to any one but mother about my troubles, and she has so many now to bear I try not to add any more. I know God is always ready to hear, but heaven's so far away in the city, and I so heavy I can't fly up to find Him" (*Journals* 61–62).

Jo's only answer was to hold her mother close, and, in the silence which followed, the sincerest prayer she had ever prayed left her heart, without words; for in that sad, yet happy hour, she had learned not only the bitterness of remorse and despair, but the sweetness of self-denial and self-control; and, led by her mother's hand, she had drawn nearer to the Friend who welcomes every child with a love stronger than that of any father, tenderer than that of any mother.[15]

Amy stirred, and sighed in her sleep; and, as if eager to begin at once to mend her fault, Jo looked up with an expression on her face which it had never worn before.

"I let the sun go down on my anger; I wouldn't forgive her, and today, if it hadn't been for Laurie, it might have been too late! How could I be so wicked?" said Jo, half aloud, as she leaned over her sister, softly stroking the wet hair scattered on the pillow.

As if she heard, Amy opened her eyes, and held out her arms, with a smile that went straight to Jo's heart. Neither said a word, but they hugged one another close, in spite of the blankets, and everything was forgiven and forgotten in one hearty kiss.

LITTLE WOMEN

Chapter 9

Meg Goes to Vanity Fair

DO THINK it was the most fortunate thing in the world, that those children[1] should have the measles just now," said Meg, one April day, as she stood packing the "go abroady" trunk[2] in her room, surrounded by her sisters.

"And so nice of Annie Moffat, not to forget her promise. A whole fortnight of fun will be regularly splendid," replied Jo, looking like a windmill, as she folded skirts with her long arms.

"And such lovely weather; I'm so glad of that," added Beth, tidily sorting neck and hair ribbons in her best box, lent for the great occasion.

"I wish I was going to have a fine time, and wear all these nice things," said Amy, with her mouth full of pins, as she artistically replenished her sister's cushion.

"I wish you were all going; but, as you can't, I shall keep my adventures to tell you when I come back. I'm sure it's the least I can do, when you have been so kind, lending me things, and helping me get ready," said Meg, glancing round the room at the very simple outfit, which seemed nearly perfect in their eyes.

"What did mother give you out of the treasure-box?" asked Amy, who had not been present at the opening of a certain cedar chest, in which Mrs. March kept a few relics of past splendor, as gifts for her girls when the proper time came.

"A pair of silk stockings, that pretty carved fan, and a lovely blue sash.[3] I wanted the violet silk; but there isn't time to make it over, so I must be contented with my old tarlatan."[4]

"It will look nicely over my new muslin skirt, and the sash will set it off beautifully. I wish I hadn't smashed my coral bracelet,

In *The Pilgrim's Progress,* Christian and his companion Faithful enter the city of Vanity, noted for its yearlong festival, Vanity Fair, a place where worthless material possessions are traded. Here the two are made fun of, covered with dirt, and eventually imprisoned. Faithful is burned at the stake but Christian manages to escape. In part two of *The Pilgrim's Progress,* Christiana, her sons, and Mercy, led by Mr. Great-Heart, also visit Vanity, staying with Mr. Mnason. The townspeople appear to regret how Faithful had been tortured, and the new pilgrims are now treated well. While there, Samuel and Joseph, Christiana's sons, marry Mr. Mnason's daughters, and Mercy performs many acts of charity for the poor. Mercy would have been a model for the Alcott sisters as they read part two of Bunyan's allegory. In practice, they would learn the idea of Christian love as they watched Mrs. Alcott devote herself tirelessly to those in need.

1. The King children, for whom Meg serves as governess.

2. Alcott refers to a steamer trunk, a large trunk with levels of trays to pack clothing, that travelers used to go abroad on steamships. Since Meg is going to be away for two weeks, she will need lots of space to pack, especially as she has to prepare for formal and informal occasions.

3. A scarf worn around the waist.

4. Thin muslin (plainweave, lightweight cotton fabric) frequently used in ball dresses during the nineteenth century.

5. Formal ball gowns during the 1860s were usually low-cut and short-sleeved.

6. *Turned* in this context could have two meanings. It could mean that the dress was turned inside-out and reworked or that it was simply shaped or formed. In *Our Own Snug Fireside: Images of the New England Home, 1760–1860* (New York: Alfred A. Knopf, 1993), Jane C. Nylander writes: "Thrifty New Englanders kept their clothing in good repair and extended its longevity with finely sewn seams and durable fabrics. It was not at all unusual to cut apart garments that had outlived their usefulness and to restyle them or make them over for another family member. This was, of course, most commonly done when adult clothing was cut down for children, but both silk or woolen garments could be carefully taken apart, cleaned, and the pieces turned over and stitched back together again. With the unfaded side turned out and worn spots concealed, a dress . . . would be good for many more years" (161).

7. Decorated or adorned.

8. A loose gown.

9. Umbrellas or parasols were popular accessories during the 1860s, used chiefly to shield ladies from the sun when outside.

10. Ordinary, everyday use.

11. Stylish.

12. Dress up in formal clothes.

for you might have had it," said Jo, who loved to give and lend, but whose possessions were usually too dilapidated to be of much use.

"There is a lovely old-fashioned pearl set in the treasure-box; but mother said real flowers were the prettiest ornament for a young girl, and Laurie promised to send me all I want," replied Meg. "Now, let me see; there's my new gray walking-suit,—just curl up the feather in my hat, Beth,—then my poplin, for Sunday, and the small party,—it looks heavy for spring, don't it? the violet silk would be so nice; oh, dear!"

"Never mind; you've got the tarlatan for the big party, and you always look like an angel in white," said Amy, brooding over the little store of finery in which her soul delighted.

"It isn't low-necked,[5] and it don't sweep enough, but it will have to do. My blue house-dress looks so well, turned[6] and freshly trimmed,[7] that I feel as if I'd got a new one. My silk sacque[8] isn't a bit the fashion, and my bonnet don't look like Sallie's; I didn't like to say anything, but I was dreadfully disappointed in my umbrella.[9] I told mother black, with a white handle, but she forgot, and bought a green one, with an ugly yellowish handle. It's strong and neat, so I ought not to complain, but I know I shall feel ashamed of it beside Annie's silk one, with a gold top," sighed Meg, surveying the little umbrella with great disfavor.

"Change it," advised Jo.

"I won't be so silly, or hurt Marmee's feelings, when she took so much pains to get my things. It's a nonsensical notion of mine, and I'm not going to give up to it. My silk stockings and two pairs of spandy gloves are my comfort. You are a dear, to lend me yours, Jo; I feel so rich, and sort of elegant, with two new pairs, and the old ones cleaned up for common;"[10] and Meg took a refreshing peep at her glove-box.

"Annie Moffat has blue and pink bows on her night-caps; would you put some on mine?" she asked, as Beth brought up a pile of snowy muslins, fresh from Hannah's hands.

"No, I wouldn't; for the smart[11] caps won't match the plain gowns, without any trimming on them. Poor folks shouldn't rig,"[12] said Jo, decidedly.

"I wonder if I shall *ever* be happy enough to have real lace on my clothes, and bows on my caps?" said Meg, impatiently.

"You said the other day that you'd be perfectly happy if you could only go to Annie Moffat's," observed Beth, in her quiet way.

"So I did! Well, I *am* happy, and I *won't* fret; but it does seem as if the more one gets the more one wants, don't it? There, now, the trays are ready, and everything in but my ball-dress, which I shall leave for mother," said Meg, cheering up, as she glanced from the half-filled trunk to the many-times pressed and mended white tarlatan, which she called her "ball-dress," with an important air.

The next day was fine, and Meg departed, in style, for a fortnight of novelty and pleasure. Mrs. March had consented to the visit rather reluctantly, fearing that Margaret would come back more discontented than she went. But she had begged so hard, and Sallie had promised to take good care of her, and a little pleasure seemed so delightful after a winter of hard[a] work, that the mother yielded, and the daughter went to take her first taste of fashionable life.[13]

The Moffats *were* very fashionable, and simple Meg was rather daunted, at first, by the splendor of the house, and the elegance of its occupants. But they were kindly people, in spite of the frivolous life they led, and soon put their guest at her ease. Perhaps Meg felt, without understanding why, that they were not particularly cultivated or intelligent people, and that all their gilding[14] could not quite conceal the ordinary material of which they were made. It certainly was agreeable to fare sumptuously, drive in a fine carriage, wear her best frock every day, and do nothing but enjoy herself. It suited her exactly; and soon she began to imitate the manners and conversation of those about her; to put on little airs and graces,[15] use French phrases,[16] crimp[17] her hair, take in her dresses, and talk about the fashions, as well as she could. The more she saw of Annie Moffat's pretty things, the more she envied her, and sighed to be rich. Home now looked bare and dismal as she thought of it, work grew harder than ever, and she felt that she was a very destitute and much injured girl, in spite of the new gloves and silk stockings.

13. LMA most likely did not base Meg's experiences at the Moffats on her sister Anna because in Anna's journal of January 30, 1861, she confessed: "I have but few such recollections connected with *my* childhood tho' it was a *very* happy one full of enjoyment & fun, and now at the age of 29 I can say I never danced at a ball" (Manuscript journal, Houghton Library, Harvard University, bMS Am 1130.14). It is likely that LMA was thinking of Major James Mansfield and his wife, Fanny Hildreth Mansfield, who invited May and Louisa, in August 1863, to spend a month at Clark's Island, near Plymouth, Mass. LMA declined as she was too busy preparing *Hospital Sketches*. She reported: "[May] had a riotously good time boating, singing, dancing, croqueting & captivating. The Island seems to be a most romantic place & she was quite carried away with her admiration of everything about it" (*Journals* 119). The following August, 1864, LMA accompanied May: "Went to Gloucester for a fortnight with May at the Mansfield's. Found a family of six pretty daughters, a pleasant mother, & a father who was an image of one of the Cheeryble Brothers [two kind, generous merchants in Dickens's *Nicholas Nickleby* (1838–1839)]. Had a jolly time boating, driving, charading dancing & picnicing . . . While at the M's Fanny was engaged & there being a house full of girls, it made a great stir" (*Journals* 131).

14. Made attractive by money.

15. The *OED* defines *airs* and *graces* as "affectations of elegance of manners."

16. In nineteenth-century America, France represented a culture of looser morals, especially in sexual relationships.

17. To make waves or curls, usually with the use of a crimping or curling iron.

18. A nickname for Margaret. In French, the name is *Marguerite,* which is also the French word for the oxeye daisy. Daisy was a popular name in the second half of the nineteenth century.

19. Alcott means that all the flattery will keep Meg from acting in a sensible manner.

20. Lacking firmness.

21. Stiff or firm.

22. Unblemished white skin was fashionable during this time. Tanned skin was frowned upon by ladies, as it was usually a sign of the working class; thus, ladies often avoided the sun.

23. The 1868 first edition of *Little Women* places a quotation mark here. Such punctuation would imply two people speaking—the man bringing the flowers and the maid handing Meg a note. This is likely an error since a male would not intrude on the group of girls preparing for the party. In fact, the maid, two paragraphs earlier, brings in the box of flowers; no mention is made of a man accompanying her. Once the man was at the Moffits' house, he would have delivered the flowers and note to the maid. Anne K. Phillips and Gregory Eiselein were the first to point out and correct this error in their Norton Critical Edition of *Little Women* (New York: W. W. Norton, 2004), p. 384.

She had not much time for repining, however, for the three young girls were busily employed in "having a good time." They shopped, walked, rode, and called all day; went to theatres and operas, or frolicked at home in the evening; for Annie had many friends, and knew how to entertain them. Her older sisters were very fine young ladies, and one was engaged, which was extremely interesting and romantic, Meg thought. Mr. Moffat was a fat, jolly old gentleman, who knew her father; and Mrs. Moffat, a fat, jolly old lady, who took as great a fancy to Meg as her daughter had done. Every one petted her; and "Daisy,"[18] as they called her, was in a fair way to have her head turned.[19]

When the evening for the "small party" came, she found that the poplin wouldn't do at all, for the other girls were putting on thin dresses, and making themselves very fine indeed; so out came the tarlatan, looking older, limper,[20] and shabbier than ever, beside Sallie's crisp[21] new one. Meg saw the girls glance at it, and then at one another, and her cheeks began to burn; for, with all her gentleness, she was very proud. No one said a word about it, but Sallie offered to do[b] her hair, and Annie to tie her sash, and Belle, the engaged sister, praised her white arms;[22] but, in their kindness, Meg saw only pity for her poverty, and her heart felt very heavy as she stood by herself, while the others laughed and chattered, prinked,[c] and flew about like gauzy butterflies. The hard, bitter feeling was getting pretty bad, when the maid brought in a box of flowers. Before she could speak, Annie had the cover off, and all were exclaiming at the lovely roses, heath, and ferns within.

"It's for Belle, of course; George always sends her some, but these are altogether ravishing," cried Annie, with a great sniff.

"They are for Miss March,[23] the man said. And here's a note," put in the maid, holding it to Meg.

"What fun! Who are they from? Didn't know you had a lover," cried the girls, fluttering about Meg in a high state of curiosity and surprise.

"The note is from mother, and the flowers from Laurie," said Meg, simply, yet much gratified that he had not forgotten her.

"Oh, indeed!" said Annie, with a funny look, as Meg slipped the note into her pocket, as a sort of talisman against envy, vanity, and false pride; for the few loving words had done her good, and the flowers cheered her up by their beauty.

Feeling almost happy again, she laid by a few ferns and roses for herself, and quickly made up the rest in dainty bouquets for the breasts, hair, or skirts of her friends, offering them so prettily, that Clara, the elder sister, told her she was "the sweetest little thing she ever saw;" and they looked quite charmed with her small attention. Somehow the kind act finished her despondency; and, when all the rest went to show themselves to Mrs. Moffat, she saw a happy, bright-eyed face in the mirror, as she laid her ferns against her rippling hair, and fastened the roses in the dress that didn't strike her as so *very* shabby now.

She enjoyed herself very much that evening, for she danced to her heart's content; every one was very kind, and she had three compliments. Annie made her sing, and some one said she had a remarkably fine voice; Major Lincoln asked who "the fresh little girl, with the beautiful eyes, was;" and Mr. Moffat insisted on dancing with her, because she "didn't dawdle, but had some spring in her," as he gracefully expressed it. So, altogether, she had a very nice time, till she overheard a bit of a conversation, which disturbed her extremely. She was sitting just inside the conservatory, waiting for her partner to bring her an ice, when she heard a voice ask, on the other side of the flowery wall,—

"How old is he?"

"Sixteen or seventeen, I should say," replied another voice.

"It would be a grand thing for one of those girls, wouldn't it? Sallie says they are very intimate now, and the old man quite dotes on them."

"Mrs. M. has laid her plans, I dare say, and will play her cards well, early as it is.[24] The girl evidently doesn't think of it yet," said Mrs. Moffat.

"She told that fib about her mamma, as if she did know, and colored up when the flowers came, quite prettily. Poor thing! she'd be so nice if she was only got up in style. Do you think she'd be offended if we offered to lend her a dress for Thursday?" asked another voice.

"She's proud, but I don't believe she'd mind, for that dowdy

24. Mrs. Moffat suggests that Mrs. March intends Meg to marry Laurie because of his grandfather's wealth.

tarlatan is all she has got. She may tear it to-night, and that will be a good excuse for offering a decent one."

"We'll see; I shall ask that[d] Laurence, as a compliment to her, and we'll have fun about it afterward."

Here Meg's partner appeared, to find her looking much flushed, and rather agitated. She was proud, and her pride was useful just then, for it helped her hide her mortification, anger, and disgust, at what she had just heard; for, innocent and unsuspicious as she was, she could not help understanding the gossip of her friends. She tried to forget it, but could not, and kept repeating to herself, "Mrs. M. has her plans," "that fib about her mamma," and "dowdy tarlatan," till she was ready to cry, and rush home to tell her troubles, and ask for advice. As that was impossible, she did her best to seem gay; and, being rather excited, she succeeded so well, that no one dreamed what an effort she was making. She was very glad when it was all over, and she was quiet in her bed, where she could think and wonder and fume till her head ached, and her hot cheeks were cooled by a few natural tears. Those foolish, yet well-meant words, had opened a new world to Meg, and much disturbed the peace of the old one, in which, till now, she had lived as happily as a child. Her innocent friendship with Laurie was spoilt by the silly speeches she had overheard; her faith in her mother was a little shaken by the worldly plans attributed to her by Mrs. Moffat, who judged others by herself; and the sensible resolution to be contented with the simple wardrobe which suited a poor man's daughter, was weakened by the unnecessary pity of girls, who thought a shabby dress one of the greatest calamities under heaven.

Poor Meg had a restless night, and got up heavy-eyed, unhappy, half resentful toward her friends, and half ashamed of herself for not speaking out frankly, and setting everything right. Everybody dawdled that morning, and it was noon before the girls found energy enough even to take up their worsted[25] work. Something in the manner of her friends struck Meg at once; they treated her with more respect, she thought; took quite a tender interest in what she said, and looked at her with eyes that plainly betrayed curiosity. All this surprised and flattered her, though she did not understand it till Miss Belle looked up from her writing, and said, with a sentimental air,—

"Daisy, dear, I've sent an invitation to your friend, Mr. Laurence, for Thursday. We should like to know him, and it's only a proper compliment to you."

Meg colored, but a mischievous fancy to tease the girls made her reply, demurely,—

"You are very kind, but I'm afraid he won't come."

"Why not, cherie?" asked Miss Belle.

"He's too old."

"My child, what do you mean? What is his age, I beg to know!" cried Miss Clara.

"Nearly seventy, I believe," answered Meg, counting stitches, to hide the merriment in her eyes.

"You sly creature! of course, we meant the young man," exclaimed Miss Belle, laughing.

"There isn't any; Laurie is only a little boy," and Meg laughed also at the queer look which the sisters exchanged, as she thus described her supposed lover.

"About your age," Nan said.

"Nearer my sister Jo's; *I* am seventeen in August," returned Meg, tossing her head.

"It's very nice of him to send you flowers, isn't it?" said Annie, looking wise about nothing.

"Yes, he often does, to all of us; for their house is full, and we are so fond of them. My mother and old Mr. Laurence are friends, you know, so it is quite natural that we children should play together;" and Meg hoped they would say no more.

"It's evident Daisy isn't out yet," said Miss Clara to Belle, with a nod.

"Quite a pastoral state of innocence all round," returned Miss Belle, with a shrug.

"I'm going out to get some little matters[26] for my girls; can I do anything for you, young ladies?" asked Mrs. Moffat, lumbering in, like an elephant, in silk and lace.

"No, thank you, ma'am," replied Sallie; "I've got my new pink silk for Thursday, and don't want a thing."

26. The *OED* defines *matters* as "physical objects, vaguely characterized" and gives this sentence as its seventh example.

27. Belle implies she will be the fairy godmother who magically adorns the poor Cinderella (Meg) in a fashionable ball gown.

28. The color of red coral.

29. French for *a hint* of rouge.

30. Delicate jewelry made with threads and beads.

"Nor I—" began Meg, but stopped, because it occurred to her that she *did* want several things, and could not have them.

"What shall you wear?" asked Sallie.

"My old white one again, if I can mend it fit to be seen; it got sadly torn last night," said Meg, trying to speak quite easily, but feeling very uncomfortable.

"Why don't you send home for another?" said Sallie, who was not an observing young lady.

"I haven't got any other." It cost Meg an effort to say that, but Sallie did not see it, and exclaimed, in amiable surprise,—

"Only that? how funny—," She did not finish her speech, for Belle shook her head at her, and broke in, saying, kindly,—

"Not at all; where is the use of having a lot of dresses when she isn't out? There's no need of sending home, Daisy, even if you had a dozen, for I've got a sweet blue silk laid away, which I've outgrown, and you shall wear it, to please me; won't you, dear?"

"You are very kind, but I don't mind my old dress, if you don't; it does well enough for a little girl like me," said Meg.

"Now do let me please myself by dressing you up in style. I admire to do it, and you'd be a regular little beauty, with a touch here and there. I shan't let any one see you till you are done, and then we'll burst upon them like Cinderella and her godmother, going to the ball,"[27] said Belle, in her persuasive tone.

Meg couldn't refuse the offer so kindly made, for a desire to see if she would be "a little beauty" after touching up caused her to accept, and forget all her former uncomfortable feelings towards the Moffats.

On the Thursday evening, Belle shut herself up with her maid; and, between them, they turned Meg into a fine lady. They crimped and curled her hair, they polished her neck and arms with some fragrant powder, touched her lips with coralline salve,[28] to make them redder, and Hortense would have added "a *soupçon*[29] of rouge," if Meg had not rebelled. They laced her into a sky-blue dress, which was so tight she could hardly breathe, and so low in the neck that modest Meg blushed at herself in the mirror. A set of silver filagree[30] was added, bracelets, necklace, brooch, and even ear-rings, for Hortense tied them on, with a bit of pink

Dressing up Meg. Harvé Stein, *Little Women* (1932).

silk, which did not show. A cluster of tea rose-buds at the bosom, and a *ruche*,[31] reconciled Meg to the display of her pretty white shoulders, and a pair of high-heeled blue silk boots satisfied the last wish of her heart. A laced handkerchief, a plumy fan, and a bouquet in a silver holder, finished her off; and Miss Belle surveyed her with the satisfaction of a little girl with a newly dressed doll.

"Mademoiselle is chamante, tres jolie,[32] is she not?" cried Hortense, clasping her hands in an affected rapture.

31. A frill or ruffle.
32. French for "Miss is lovely, very pretty."

33. Aesop's tale of the vain Jackdaw (a kind of crow), who, recognizing his ugliness, disguises himself in the brightest, most colorful feathers discarded by the other birds in order to be crowned king of birds. When the Jackdaw is nearly appointed king, the other, now indignant birds strip him of his borrowed plumes.

34. Magpies, also of the crow family, are intelligent birds. Interestingly, in folklore the appearance of a magpie was considered an ill omen. An English children's rhyme, usually called "One for Sorrow," declares one's luck good or bad depending on the number of magpies one sees.

35. A small scarf of lace worn around the head.

"Come and show yourself," said Miss Belle, leading the way to the room where the others were waiting.

As Meg went rustling after, with her long skirts trailing, her ear-rings tinkling, her curls waving, and her heart beating, she felt as if her "fun" had really begun at last, for the mirror had plainly told her that she *was* "a little beauty." Her friends repeated the pleasing phrase enthusiastically; and, for several minutes, she stood, like the jackdaw in the fable,[33] enjoying her borrowed plumes, while the rest chattered like a party of magpies.[34]

"While I dress, do you drill her, Nan, in the management of her skirt, and those French heels, or she will trip herself up. Put your silver butterfly in the middle of that white barbe,[35] and catch up that long curl on the left side of her head, Clara, and don't any of you disturb the charming work of my hands," said Belle, as she hurried away, looking well pleased with her success.

"I'm afraid to go down, I feel so queer and stiff, and half-dressed," said Meg to Sallie, as the bell rang, and Mrs. Moffat sent to ask the young ladies to appear at once.

"You don't look a bit like yourself, but you are very nice. I'm nowhere beside you, for Belle has heaps of taste, and you're quite French, I assure you. Let your flowers hang; don't be so careful of them, and be sure you don't trip," returned Sallie, trying not to care that Meg was prettier than herself.

Keeping that warning carefully in mind, Margaret got safely down stairs, and sailed into the drawing-rooms, where the Moffats and a few early guests were assembled. She very soon discovered that there is a charm about fine clothes which attracts a certain class of people, and secures their respect. Several young ladies, who had taken no notice of her before, were very affectionate all of a sudden; several young gentlemen, who had only stared at her at the other party, now not only stared, but asked to be introduced, and said all manner of foolish, but agreeable things to her; and several old ladies, who sat on sofas, and criticised the rest of the party, inquired who she was, with an air of interest. She heard Mrs. Moffat reply to one of them,—

"Daisy March—father a colonel in the army—one of our first families, but reverses of fortune, you know; intimate friends of the Laurences; sweet creature, I assure you; my Ned is quite wild about her."

"Dear me!" said the old lady, putting up her glass for another observation of Meg, who tried to look as if she had not heard, and been rather shocked at Mrs. Moffat's fibs.

The "queer feeling" did not pass away, but she imagined herself acting the new part of fine lady, and so got on pretty well, though the tight dress gave her a side-ache, the train kept getting under her feet, and she was in constant fear lest her ear-rings should fly off, and get lost or broken. She was flirting her fan,[36] and laughing at the feeble jokes of a young gentleman who tried to be witty, when she suddenly stopped laughing, and looked confused; for, just opposite, she saw Laurie. He was staring at her with undisguised surprise, and disapproval also, she thought; for, though he bowed and smiled, yet something in his honest eyes made her blush, and wish she had her old dress on. To complete her confusion, she saw Belle nudge Annie, and both glance from her to Laurie, who, she was happy to see, looked unusually boyish and shy.

"Silly creatures, to put such thoughts into my head! I won't care for it, or let it change me a bit," thought Meg, and rustled across the room to shake hands with her friend.

"I'm glad you came, for I was afraid you wouldn't," she said, with her most grown-up air.

"Jo wanted me to come, and tell her how you looked, so I did;" answered Laurie, without turning his eyes upon her, though he half smiled at her maternal tone.

"What shall you tell her?" asked Meg, full of curiosity to know his opinion of her, yet feeling ill at ease with him, for the first time.

"I shall say I didn't know you; for you look so grown-up, and unlike yourself, I'm quite afraid of you," he said, fumbling at his glove-button.

"How absurd of you! the girls dressed me up for fun, and I rather like it. Wouldn't Jo stare if she saw me?" said Meg, bent on making him say whether he thought her improved or not.

"Yes, I think she would," returned Laurie, gravely.

36. The *OED* defines *flirt a fan* as "to open and close it with a jerk, to wave it smartly."

37. The *OED* defines *fuss and feathers* as "bustle and display," and gives the first use of the term as 1866, just two years before the publication of *Little Women*.

38. Laurie suggests that it will cover up the immodestly low-cut bodice.

"Don't you like me so?" asked Meg.

"No, I don't," was the blunt reply.

"Why not?" in an anxious tone.

He glanced at her frizzled head, bare shoulders, and fantastically trimmed dress, with an expression that abashed her more than his answer, which had not a particle of his usual politeness about it.

"I don't like fuss and feathers."[37]

That was altogether too much from a lad younger than herself; and Meg walked away, saying, petulantly,—

"You are the rudest boy I ever saw."

Feeling very much ruffled, she went and stood at a quiet window, to cool her cheeks, for the tight dress gave her an uncomfortably brilliant color. As she stood there, Major Lincoln passed by; and, a minute after, she heard him saying to his mother,—

"They are making a fool of that little girl; I wanted you to see her, but they have spoilt her entirely; she's nothing but a doll, to-night."

"Oh, dear!" sighed Meg; "I wish I'd been sensible, and worn my own things; then I should not have disgusted other people, or felt so uncomfortable and ashamed myself."

She leaned her forehead on the cool pane, and stood half hidden by the curtains, never minding that her favorite waltz had begun, till some one touched her; and, turning, she saw Laurie looking penitent, as he said, with his very best bow, and his hand out,—

"Please forgive my rudeness, and come and dance with me."

"I'm afraid it will be too disagreeable to you," said Meg, trying to look offended, and failing entirely.

"Not a bit of it; I'm dying to do it. Come, I'll be good; I don't like your gown, but I do think you are—just splendid;" and he waved his hands, as if words failed to express his admiration.

Meg smiled, and relented, and whispered, as they stood waiting to catch the time,—

"Take care my skirt don't trip you up; it's the plague of my life, and I was a goose to wear it."

"Pin it round your neck, and then it will be useful,"[38] said Laurie, looking down at the little blue boots, which he evidently approved of.

Away they went, fleetly and gracefully; for, having practised at home, they were well matched, and the blithe young couple were a pleasant sight to see, as they twirled merrily round and round, feeling more friendly than ever after their small tiff.

"Laurie, I want you to do me a favor; will you?" said Meg, as he stood fanning her, when her breath gave out, which it did, very soon, though she would not own why.

"Won't I!" said Laurie, with alacrity.

"Please don't tell them at home about my dress to-night. They won't understand the joke, and it will worry mother."

"Then why did you do it?" said Laurie's eyes, so plainly, that Meg hastily added,—

"I shall tell them, myself, all about it, and ''fess' to mother how silly I've been. But I'd rather do it myself; so you'll not tell, will you?"

"I give you my word I won't; only what shall I say when they ask me?"

"Just say I looked nice,ᵉ and was having a good time."

"I'll say the first, with all my heart; but how about the other? You don't look as if you were having a good time; are you?" and Laurie looked at her with an expression which made her answer, in a whisper,—

"No; not just now. Don't think I'm horrid; I only wanted a little fun, but this sort don't pay, I find, and I'm getting tired of it."

"Here comes Ned Moffat; what does he want?" said Laurie, knitting his black brows, as if he did not regard his young host in the light of a pleasant addition to the party.

"He put his name down for three dances,³⁹ and I suppose he's coming for them; what a bore!" said Meg, assuming a languid air, which amused Laurie immensely.

He did not speak to her again till supper-time, when he saw her drinking champagne with Ned, and his friend Fisher, who were behaving "like a pair of fools," as Laurie said to himself, for he felt a brotherly sort of right to watch over the Marches, and fight their battles, whenever a defender was needed.

39. Meg means he is listed on her dance card, which prospective dance partners would sign to reserve dances with a young lady. A proper gentleman would always pledge himself to more than one dance.

40. The German cotillion.

41. A French phrase meaning "silence unto death." Laurie thus vows never to divulge Meg's secret.

"You'll have a splitting headache to-morrow, if you drink much of that. I wouldn't, Meg; your mother don't like it, you know," he whispered, leaning over her chair, as Ned turned to refill her glass, and Fisher stooped to pick up her fan.

"I'm not Meg, to-night; I'm 'a doll,' who does all sorts of crazy things. To-morrow I shall put away my 'fuss and feathers' and be desperately good again," she answered, with an affected little laugh.

"Wish to-morrow was here, then," muttered Laurie, walking off, ill-pleased at the change he saw in her.

Meg danced and flirted, chattered and giggled, as the other girls did; after supper she undertook the German,[40] and blundered through it, nearly upsetting her partner with her long skirt, and romping in a way that scandalized Laurie, who looked on and meditated a lecture. But he got no chance to deliver it, for Meg kept away from him till he came to say good-night.

"Remember!" she said, trying to smile, for the splitting headache had already begun.

"Silence à la mort,"[41] replied Laurie, with a melodramatic flourish, as he went away.

This little bit of by-play excited Annie's curiosity; but Meg was too tired for gossip, and went to bed, feeling as if she had been to a masquerade, and hadn't enjoyed herself as much as she expected. She was sick all the next day, and on Saturday went home, quite used up with her fortnight's fun, and feeling that she had sat in the lap of luxury long enough.

"It does seem pleasant to be quiet, and not have company manners on all the time. Home *is* a nice place, though it isn't splendid," said Meg, looking about her with a restful expression, as she sat with her mother and Jo on the Sunday evening.

"I'm glad to hear you say so, dear, for I was afraid home would seem dull and poor to you, after your fine quarters," replied her mother, who had given her many anxious looks that day; for motherly eyes are quick to see any change in children's faces.

Meg had told her adventures gayly, and said over and over what a charming time she had had; but something still seemed to weigh upon her spirits, and, when the younger girls were gone to bed, she sat thoughtfully staring at the fire, saying little, and looking worried. As the clock struck nine, and Jo proposed bed, Meg suddenly left her chair, and, taking Beth's stool, leaned her elbows on her mother's knee, saying, bravely,—

"Marmee, I want to ''fess.'"

"I thought so; what is it, dear?"

"Shall I go away?" asked Jo, discreetly.

"Of course not; don't I always tell you everything? I was ashamed to speak of it before the children, but I want you to know all the dreadful things I did at the Moffats."

"We are prepared," said Mrs. March, smiling, but looking a little anxious.

"I told you they rigged[42] me up, but I didn't tell you that they powdered, and squeezed, and frizzled, and made me look like a fashion-plate.[43] Laurie thought I wasn't proper; I know he did, though he didn't say so, and one man called me 'a doll.' I knew it was silly, but they flattered me, and said I was a beauty, and quantities of nonsense, so I let them make a fool of me."

"Is that all?" asked Jo, as Mrs. March looked silently at the downcast face of her pretty daughter, and could not find it in her heart to blame her little follies.

"No; I drank champagne, and romped, and tried to flirt, and was, altogether, abominable," said Meg, self-reproachfully.

"There is something more, I think;" and Mrs. March smoothed the soft cheek, which suddenly grew rosy, as Meg answered, slowly,—

"Yes; it's very silly, but I want to tell it, because I hate to have people say and think such things about us and Laurie."

Then she told the various bits of gossip she had heard at the Moffats; and, as she spoke, Jo saw her mother fold her lips tightly, as if ill pleased that such ideas[44] should be put into Meg's innocent mind.

"Well, if that isn't the greatest rubbish I ever heard," cried Jo, indignantly. "Why didn't you pop out and tell them so, on the spot?"

Laurie asks Meg to dance. Roberts Brothers engaged Hammatt Billings to illustrate Part II of the novel in 1869, and when they published *Little Women* as a two-volume set in 1870, the publisher added this and another new Billings drawing to Part I, while deleting two of May Alcott's original illustrations.

42. Dressed. The 1880–1881 edition changes *rigged* to *dressed*.

43. An illustration of the new fashionable dress style.

44. The idea that Mrs. March is trying to match Laurie with her girls only because he is wealthy.

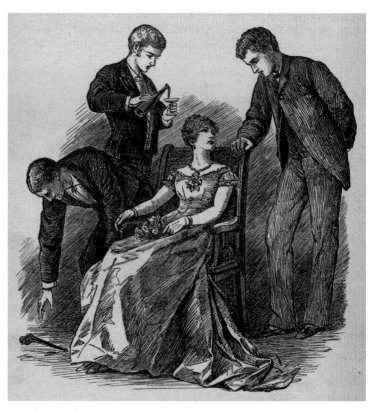

Meg's admirers. Frank Merrill, *Little Women: Illustrated* (1880).

"I couldn't, it was so embarrassing for me. I couldn't help hearing, at first, and then I was so angry and ashamed, I didn't remember that I ought to go away."

"Just wait till *I* see Annie Moffat, and I'll show you how to settle such ridiculous stuff. The idea of having 'plans,' and being kind to Laurie, because he's rich, and may marry us by and by! Won't he shout, when I tell him what those silly things say about us poor children?" and Jo laughed, as if, on second thoughts, the thing struck her as a good joke.

"If you tell Laurie, I'll never forgive you! She mustn't, must she, mother?" said Meg, looking distressed.

"No; never repeat that foolish gossip, and forget it as soon as you can," said Mrs. March, gravely. "I was very unwise to let you go among people of whom I know so little; kind, I dare say, but worldly, ill-bred, and full of these vulgar ideas about young people. I am more sorry than I can express, for the mischief this visit may have done you, Meg."

"Don't be sorry, I won't let it hurt me; I'll forget all the bad, and remember only the good; for I did enjoy a great deal, and thank you very much for letting me go. I'll not be sentimental or dissatisfied, mother; I know I'm a silly little girl, and I'll stay with you till I'm fit to take care of myself. But it *is* nice to be praised and admired, and I can't help saying I like it," said Meg, looking half ashamed of the confession.

"That is perfectly natural, and quite harmless, if the liking does not become a passion, and lead one to do foolish or unmaidenly things. Learn to know and value the praise which is worth having, and to excite the admiration of excellent people, by being modest[45] as well as pretty, Meg."

Margaret sat thinking a moment, while Jo stood with her hands behind her, looking both interested and a little perplexed; for it was a new thing to see Meg blushing and talking about admiration, lovers, and things of that sort, and Jo felt as if during that fortnight her sister had grown up amazingly, and was drifting away from her into a world where she could not follow.

"Mother, do you have 'plans' as Mrs. Moffat said?" asked Meg, bashfully.

"Yes, my dear, I have a great many; all mothers do, but mine differ somewhat from Mrs. Moffat's, I suspect. I will tell you some of them, for the time has come when a word may set this romantic little head and heart of yours right, on a very serious subject. You are young, Meg; but not too young to understand me, and mothers' lips are the fittest to speak of such things to girls like you. Jo, your turn will come in time, perhaps, so listen to my 'plans' and help me carry them out, if they are good."

Jo went and sat on one arm of the chair, looking as if she thought they were about to join in some very solemn affair. Holding a hand of each, and watching the two young faces wistfully, Mrs. March said, in her serious yet cheery way,—

"I want my daughters to be beautiful, accomplished, and good; to be admired, loved, and respected, to have a happy youth, to be well and wisely married, and to lead useful, pleasant lives, with as

45. Emily Thornwell agrees with Mrs. March: "The first great fundamental rule of good taste is *to be natural;* and it is from an infringement of this that many of our worst mistakes proceed. In manner or style, affectation is the source of the most flagrant offences against taste. Whether it be an affectation of fashion, or of learning, of ignorance, of wit, or of piety, it will be equally repugnant to the delicacy of a superior mind. Affectation is an offence against high moral feeling. It excites a suspicion of the truth of those who are guilty of it; and although it may have resolved itself into a mere habit, we cannot help feeling that it originates in artifice" (*The Lady's Guide* 68).

46. As she was beginning *Little Women,* LMA published "Happy Women" in the *New York Ledger* on April 11, 1868. In the sketch, she tells of four unnamed women (herself among them) who have found useful, productive lives without being married. She concludes: "It is not necessary to be a sour, spiteful spinster, with nothing to do but brew tea, talk scandal and tend a pocket-handkerchief. No, the world is full of work . . . Never was there so splendid an opportunity for women to enjoy their liberty and prove that they deserve it by using it wisely. If love comes as it should come, accept it in God's name and be worthy of His best blessing. If it never comes, then in God's name reject the shadow of it, for that can never satisfy a hungry heart" (reprinted in *Alternative Alcott,* ed. Elaine Showalter [New Brunswick: Rutgers University Press, 1988], p. 206). In chapter 14 of *Work: A Story of Experience* (1873), the laundress Cynthia Wilkins advises Christie Devon against marrying "for a livin'": "'Wal, now I'd rather one of my girls should grub the wust kind all their days than do that. Hows'ever, it may suit some folks ef they ain't got much heart, and is contented with fine clothes, nice vittles, and handsome furnitoor.'" LMA returned to the theme of marriage and spinsters in the final volume of the March family trilogy, *Jo's Boys* (1886), where in chapter 17, "Among the Maids," Meg and Jo advise the young female students at Plumfield. LMA herself never married. Her private writings seldom mention suitors or romantic interests. In April 1861, when she was twenty-eight, LMA confided: "Had a funny lover who met me in the cars, and said he lost his heart at once. Handsome man of forty. A Southerner, and very demonstrative and gushing, called and wished to pay his addresses, and being told I did n't wish to see him, retired, to write letters and haunt the road with his hat off, while the girls laughed and had great fun over Jo's lover. He went at last, and peace reigned. My adorers are all queer" (*Journals* 98). LMA also appears to have been romantically fascinated by

Ladislas Wisniewski, the partial inspiration for Laurie, whom she met in Vevey, Switzerland, in 1865 and with whom she spent two weeks in Paris in May 1866. When Louise Chandler Moulton wrote a sketch of LMA for *Our Famous Women* (Hartford, CT: A. D. Worthington, 1883), Alcott told her that she once thought she had been a horse in a former life because she loved to run so much. She then added: "'Now, I am more than half-persuaded that I am a man's soul, put by some freak of nature into a woman's body.'" When Moulton asked her why she thought that, LMA replied: "'Well, for one thing,' and the blue-gray eyes sparkled with laughter, 'because I have fallen in love in my life with so many pretty girls, and never the least bit with any man'" (p. 49). In the twenty-first century, from our modern perspectives, it is difficult to know how, exactly, to take LMA's remark. Many scholars have speculated about LMA's sexual orientation, but her private writings that do exist (some have been lost or destroyed by LMA and her family) provide no definitive evidence. For selected discussions of lesbian themes or ideas in LMA's work, see the following selections: Angela M. Estes and Kathleen Margaret Lant, "Dismembering the Text: The Horror of Louisa May Alcott's *Little Women*," *Children's Literature* 17 (1989): 98–123; Ann B. Murphy, "The Borders of Ethical, Erotic, and Artistic Possibilities in *Little Women*," *Signs* 15 (1990): 562–585; Gregory Eiselein, "Sentimental Discourse and the Bisexual Erotics of *Work*," *Texas Studies in Literature and Language* 41 (1999): 203–235; Roberta Seelinger Trites, "'Queer Performances': Lesbian Politics in *Little Women*," "*Little Women*" *and the Feminist Imagination*, ed. Janice M. Alberghene and Beverly Lyon Clark (New York: Garland, 1999), pp. 139–160; and Jessica Daigle Vidrine, "Notions on Marriage: Bisexual Desires and Spinsterhood as Intellectual and Artistic Genius in Louisa May Alcott's 'Happy Women' and *Diana and Persis*," *Women's Studies* 39 (2010): 136–154.

little care and sorrow to try them as God sees fit to send. To be loved and chosen by a good man is the best and sweetest thing which can happen to a woman; and I sincerely hope my girls may know this beautiful experience. It is natural to think of it, Meg; right to hope and wait for it, and wise to prepare for it; so that, when the happy time comes, you may feel ready for the duties, and worthy of the joy. My dear girls, I *am* ambitious for you, but not to have you make a dash in the world,—marry rich men merely because they are rich, or have splendid houses, which are not homes, because love is wanting. Money is a needful and precious thing,—and, when well used, a noble thing,—but I never want you to think it is the first or only prize to strive for. I'd rather see you poor men's wives, if you were happy, beloved, contented, than queens on thrones, without self-respect and peace."

"Poor girls don't stand any chance, Belle says, unless they put themselves forward," sighed Meg.

"Then we'll be old maids," said Jo, stoutly.

"Right, Jo; better be happy old maids than unhappy wives, or unmaidenly girls, running about to find husbands," said Mrs. March, decidedly.[46] "Don't be troubled, Meg; poverty seldom daunts a sincere lover. Some of the best and most honored women I know were poor girls, but so love-worthy that they were not allowed to be old maids. Leave these things to time; make this home happy, so that you may be fit for homes of your own, if they are offered you, and contented here if they are not. One thing remember, my girls, mother is always ready to be your confidant, father to be your friend; and both of us trust and hope that our daughters, whether married or single, will be the pride and comfort of our lives."

"We will, Marmee, we will!" cried both, with all their hearts, as she bade them good-night.

LITTLE WOMEN

Chapter 10

The P. C. and P. O.

A S SPRING CAME ON, a new set of amusements became the fashion, and the lengthening days gave long afternoons for work and play of all sorts. The garden had to be put in order, and each sister had a quarter of the little plot to do what she liked with.[1] Hannah used to say, "I'd know which each of them gardings belonged to, ef I see 'em in Chiny;" and so she might, for the girls' tastes differed as much as their characters. Meg's had roses and heliotrope, myrtle, and a little orange-tree in it. Jo's bed was never alike two seasons, for she was always trying experiments; this year it was to be a plantation of sun-flowers, the seeds of which cheerful and aspiring plant were to feed "Aunt Cockle-top" and her family of chicks. Beth had old-fashioned, fragrant flowers in her garden; sweet peas and mignonette, larkspur, pinks, pansies, and southernwood, with chickweed for the bird and catnip for the pussies.[2] Amy had a bower in hers,—rather small and earwiggy, but very pretty to look at,—with honeysuckles and morning-glories hanging their colored horns and bells in graceful wreaths all over it; tall white lilies, delicate ferns, and as many brilliant, picturesque plants as would consent to blossom there.

Gardening, walks, rows on the river, and flower-hunts employed the fine days; and for rainy ones, they had house diversions,—some old, some new,—all more or less original. One of these was the "P. C."; for, as secret societies were the fashion, it was thought proper to have one; and, as all of the girls admired Dickens,[3] they called themselves the Pickwick Club.[4] With a few interruptions, they had kept this up for a year, and met every Sat-

1. The phenomenon of the language of flowers, often called floriography, was a belief that flowers or their arrangement conveyed special, coded meanings. Although originating in Europe and England, it became extremely popular in America during the nineteenth century, peaking during the last half of the century. Hundreds of editions of books on the language of flowers were published in the United States, listing various types of flowers and their symbolic meaning. The topic became so popular, in fact, that even etiquette guides devoted space to the language of flowers. One of the more popular works on the subject in America was *Flora's Interpreter; or, the American Book of Flowers and Sentiments* (1832), published by Sara Josepha Hale, editor of the wide-selling periodical *Godey's Lady's Book*. The language of flowers would have been well known to LMA, and throughout *Little Women*, she specifically names numerous flowers and plants. Here, for instance, each sister's garden tells readers something about her. According to the 1840 edition of *Flora's Interpreter*, the flowers in Meg's garden show readers that she is preparing for love and courtship: roses (*love*), heliotropes (*devotion*), myrtle (*love in absence*), and orange blossoms (*woman's worth*). Jo's sunflowers symbolize *lofty or wise thoughts*. Beth's old-fashioned flowers indicate her special qualities and hint, perhaps, at her impending death: sweet peas (*departure*), mignone (*your qualities surpass your loveliness*), pinks (*woman's love*), pansies (*tender and pleasant thoughts*), and larkspur (*haughtiness*). Amy's white lilies symbolize *purity and beauty* while morning glories mean *coquetry*.

2. Sweet pea (*Lathyrus odoratus*) is a flowering annual that can climb over six feet if supported. By the late nineteenth century, the sweet pea was a highly favored plant for gardens. The mignonette, also called the reseda, is a flowering plant popular during the mid-nineteenth century because of its fragrance, and it is still used to make perfumes. Larkspur is the common name for the genus *Delphinium*, a perennial in the buttercup family that blooms from late spring to the end of summer. Pinks (*Dianthus plumarius*) are similar to carnations with white or pink flowers, often with a dark center. Southernwood (*Artemisia abrotanum*) is a shrub with gray-green leaves and small yellow flowers. Through the centuries, the plant was used for a number of medicinal purposes, including liver and stomach problems. Also known by Lover's Plant and Lad's Love, it was thought to increase virility. Chickenweed (*Stellaria media*) is an annual garden weed with small white flowers. It gets its name because chickens would eat it. Catnip (*Nepeta cataria*), also called catmint in England, was long used for medicinal purposes in teas and tinctures, for its soothing properties. The common name comes from the effects it has upon cats. When they smell the leaves or

stems, most cats will paw the plant, roll on it, and even eat it, causing a variety of symptoms from drowsiness to aggressive behavior.

3. LMA admired Dickens as much as the March sisters do. In *Alcott Memoirs* (1915), Willis noted that "Louisa was an enthusiastic admirer of Dickens. She reveled in his works and could recite many chapters from memory. His literary style made an indelible impression upon hers and the effect of his humor is very perceptible in all her works. His characters were living beings to her and she was on terms of remarkably close intimacy with all of them" (quoted in *Her Own Time* 178). In *Little Women*, Dickens's presence looms large, from the many allusions LMA makes to his works and characters to the British expressions she employs at times. Already regarded 'as one of the greatest novelists of the nineteenth century, Dickens was as popular in America as in England. When LMA visited England for the first time in 1865–1866, the writer and reformer Moses Coit Tyler guided her on a tour of streets and houses around London where Dickens had set his works. She published the account as "A Dickens Day" in the December 26, 1867, edition of *Independent*. LMA was disappointed, however, when she finally heard the inimitable Dickens give a public reading. The first time she saw him was in London in June 1866. In an untitled note in the September 21, 1867, issue of the *Boston Commonwealth*, LMA wrote that Dickens's "youth and comeliness were gone, but the foppishness remained, and the red-faced man, with false teeth, and the voice of a worn-out actor, had his scanty grey hair curled" (p. 1). She saw him again in December 1867 and noted: "Heard Dickens & was disappointed" (*Journals* 159). She later inserted: "An old dandy" (*Journals* 161n21).

4. Charles Dickens's *Pickwick Papers* (1837), also published serially as *The Posthumous Papers of the Pickwick Club* (1836–1837), was the author's first novel and quickly brought him literary acclaim. It remained a favorite for the Alcott sisters. The elderly Samuel Pickwick, Esquire, owner of Pickwick Hall, is the wealthy founder and president of the Pickwick Club, whose four members travel about the English countryside and describe their encounters and discoveries. The other three members are the middle-aged Tracy Tupman, who has a fondness for women; Augustus Snodgrass, a poet who has never written a poem; and Nathaniel Winkle, who thinks himself a sportsman. The Alcott sisters did indeed form their own Pickwick Club.

5. Orchard House possesses the only known Pickwick Club badge used by the Alcott sisters.

6. While the Alcott sisters may have formed the Pickwick Club in Concord, the creation of "The Pickwick Portfolio" occurred a few years later in Boston and assumed three forms. *The Olive Leaf,*

Sweet pea.

urday evening in the big garret, on which occasions the ceremonies were as follows: Three chairs were arranged in a row before a table, on which was a lamp, also four white badges, with a big "P. C." in different colors on each,[5] and the weekly newspaper, called "The Pickwick Portfolio,"[6] to which all contributed something; while Jo, who revelled in pens and ink, was the editor. At seven o'clock, the four members ascended to the club-room, tied their badges round their heads, and took their seats with great solemnity. Meg, as the eldest, was Samuel Pickwick; Jo, being of a literary turn, Augustus Snodgrass; Beth, because she was round and rosy, Tracy Tupman; and Amy, who was always trying to do what she couldn't, was Nathaniel Winkle. Pickwick, the President, read the paper, which was filled with original tales, poetry, local news, funny advertisements, and hints, in which they good-naturedly reminded each other of their faults and short-comings. On one occasion, Mr. Pickwick put on a pair of spectacles without any glasses, rapped upon the table, hemmed, and, having stared hard at Mr. Snodgrass, who was tilting back in his chair, till he arranged himself properly, began to read,—

"The Pickwick Portfolio"

MAY 20, 18–.

Poet's Corner.

ANNIVERSARY ODE.

Again we meet to celebrate
    With badge and solemn rite,
Our fifty-second anniversary,
    In Pickwick Hall, to-night.

We all are here in perfect health,
    None gone from our small band;
Again we see each well-known face,
    And press each friendly hand.

Our Pickwick, always at his post,
    With reverence we greet,
As, spectacles on nose, he reads
    Our well-filled weekly sheet.

Although he suffers from a cold,
    We joy to hear him speak,
For words of wisdom from him fall,
    In spite of croak or squeak.

Old six-foot Snodgrass looms on high.
    With elephantine[7] grace,
And beams upon the company,
    With brown and jovial face.

Poetic fire lights up his eye,
    He struggles 'gainst his lot;
Behold ambition on his brow,
    And on his nose a blot!

Next our peaceful Tupman comes,
    So rosy, plump and sweet,
Who chokes with laughter at the puns,
    And tumbles off his seat.

Prim little Winkle too is here,
    With every hair in place,
A model of propriety,
    Though he hates to wash his face.

The year is gone, we still unite
    To joke and laugh and read,
And tread the path of literature
    That doth to glory lead.

Long may our paper prosper well,
    Our club unbroken be,
And coming years their blessings pour
    On the useful, gay "P. C."
                A. SNODGRASS.

THE MASKED MARRIAGE.[8]

A TALE OF VENICE.

Gondola after gondola swept up to the marble steps, and left its lovely load to swell the brilliant throng that filled the stately halls of Count de Adelon. Knights and ladies, elves and pages, monks and flower-girls, all mingled gaily in the dance. Sweet voices and rich melody filled the air; and so with mirth and music the masquerade went on.

"Has your Highness seen the Lady Viola to-night?" asked a gallant troubadour of the fairy queen who floated down the hall upon his arm.

"Yes; is she not lovely, though so sad! Her dress is well chosen, too, for in a week she weds Count Antonio, whom she passionately hates."

"By my faith I envy him. Yonder he comes, arrayed like a bridegroom, except the black mask. When that is off we shall see how he regards the fair maid whose heart he cannot win, though her stern father bestows her hand," returned the troubadour.

produced on July 19, 1849, was the first issue of a family newspaper, the title perhaps having been inspired by *The Olive Branch,* a popular Boston periodical. Just several months later, in the fall of 1849, the paper was renamed *The Portfolio.* One of the earliest surviving manuscripts of this paper, dated October 24, 1849, tells of the paper's brief history: "Our paper was commenced last June under the name of the (Olive leaf) but owing to the absence of one of our valued members was dis-continued. We are now again together and hope to be able to continue it thru the coming winter under the name of The Portfolio—God give us success" (*Portfolio,* no. 4, Manuscript, Houghton Library, Harvard University, MS Am 1817.2[23]). Although the editor claims that the paper began in June 1849, the first issue is dated the middle of July, when Louisa was still sixteen. Perhaps it was conceived in June but took several weeks to produce. Anna Alcott, who accepted a governess position in Jamaica Plain, Mass., that late summer and early fall, was most likely the missing "valued" member. Of all the surviving forms of the family newspaper, *The Portfolio* demonstrates the progress of the young writers. A nearly successive run of seven issues, dating from October 24, 1849, to February 3, 1850, shows the development of the paper. Like its precursor, *The Portfolio* was produced weekly in a handwritten issue. No duplicate issues have been located, and the contributions are in different handwriting, suggesting that each sister penned her own literary work and only one copy was produced and read at the meeting of the Pickwick Club. Finally, a third variation of the paper appeared under the title *The Pickwick,* most likely dating from 1850 or 1851. The fifteen known manuscript issues of the family paper are located in the Alcott collection at the Houghton Library of Harvard University and the Louisa May Alcott collection in the Barrett Library of the University of Virginia. Like the example used here in the novel, the original Pickwick Portfolio contains notices, riddles, poetry, romances, fantasies, and autobiographical sketches.

7. Clumsy.

8. "The Masked Marriage" was published in the December 18, 1852, issue of *Dodge's Literary Museum,* but it actually originated in the family newspaper, where it was serialized over several issues. Set in Italy, "The Masked Marriage" is a tale of romantic love thwarted by a greedy parent. With its use of long-hidden secrets, disguises, and revenge, the story is a forerunner of the sensational tales Alcott would publish for Frank Leslie's periodicals in the early 1860s. The two known copies of the family newspaper that contain chapters of the story are dated only by the month: October and November 9. But several clues point to the composition of the tale. No chapters

Charles Dickens (1812–1870), circa 1867.

The Pickwick Club, illustrated by Robert Seymour in Charles Dickens's *Pickwick Papers* (1836–1837).

"'Tis whispered that she loves the young English artist who haunts her steps, and is spurned by the old count," said the lady, as they joined the dance.

The revel was at its height when a priest appeared, and, withdrawing the young pair to an alcove hung with purple velvet, he motioned them to kneel. Instant silence fell upon the gay throng; and not a sound, but the dash of fountains or the rustle of orange groves sleeping in the moonlight, broke the hush, as Count de Adelon spoke thus:—

"My lords and ladies; pardon the ruse by which I have gathered you here to witness the marriage of my daughter. Father, we wait your services."

All eyes turned toward the bridal party, and a low murmur of amazement went through the throng, for neither bride nor groom removed their masks. Curiosity and wonder possessed all hearts, but respect restrained all tongues till the holy rite was over. Then the eager spectators gathered round the count, demanding an explanation.

"Gladly would I give it if I could; but I only know that it was the whim of my timid Viola, and I yielded to it. Now, my children, let the play end. Unmask, and receive my blessing."

But neither bent the knee; for the young bridegroom replied, in a tone that startled all listeners, as the mask fell, disclosing the noble face of Ferdinand Devereux, the artist lover, and, leaning on the breast where now flashed the star of an English earl, was the lovely Viola, radiant with joy and beauty.

"My lord, you scornfully bade me claim your daughter when I could boast as high a name and vast a fortune as the Count Antonio. I can do more; for even your ambitious soul cannot refuse the Earl of Devereux and De Vere, when he gives his ancient name and boundless wealth in return for the beloved hand of this fair lady, now my wife."

The count stood like one changed to stone; and, turning to the bewildered crowd, Ferdinand added, with a gay smile of triumph, "To you, my gallant friends, I can only wish that your wooing may prosper as mine has done; and that you may all win as fair a bride as I have, by this masked marriage."

S. PICKWICK

Why is the P. C. like the Tower of Babel? It is full of unruly members.

THE HISTORY OF A SQUASH.

Once upon a time a farmer planted a little seed in his garden, and after a while it sprouted and became a vine, and bore many squashes. One day in October, when they were ripe, he picked one and took it to market. A grocer man bought and put it in his shop. That same morning, a little girl, in a brown hat and blue dress, with a round face and snubby nose, went and bought it for her mother. She lugged it home, cut it up, and boiled it in the big pot; mashed some of it, with salt and butter, for dinner; and to the rest she added a pint of milk, two eggs, four spoons of sugar, nutmeg, and some crackers; put it in a deep dish, and baked it till it was brown and nice; and next day it was eaten by a family named March.

T. TUPMAN.

Mr. Pickwick, *Sir:*—

I address you upon the subject of sin the sinner I mean is a man named Winkle who makes trouble in his club by laughing and sometimes won't write his piece in this fine paper I hope you will pardon his badness and let him send a French fable because he can't write out of his head as he has so many lessons to do and no brains in future I will try to take time by the fetlock[9] and prepare some work which will be all *commy la fo*—that means all right—I am in haste as it is nearly school time[10]

Yours respectably N. WINKLE.

Original manuscript of *The Pickwick* (circa 1850–1851), with LMA's story "The Masked Marriage."

appear in the original paper, *The Olive Leaf,* nor in *The Portfolio* when it recommenced in October 1849 after a brief hiatus and was produced through at least February 1850. The two known issues with the story have a new masthead: *The Pickwick.* Since the story was published in December 1852, the tale must have appeared in the fall issues of 1850 or 1851. A comparison of the two known chapters of the *Pickwick* manuscript with the published story in *Dodge's Literary Museum* reveals some changes but not significant ones; little revision has taken place. The version in *Little Women* has more significant changes in word choice, but it is still similar to the manuscript. Alcott does, however, change the bride's name from Alice to Lady Viola.

9. Amy confuses *fetlock,* the tuft of hair on the back of a horse's leg, with *forelock,* a lock of hair growing over the forehead. The quotation "Take Time by the forelock" is credited to the Greek philosopher Thales of Miletus (ca. 624–ca. 546 BC) and means "to act quickly and decisively." In early depictions of Father Time, he was shown as an old man with only a forelock on his head. LMA must have been fond of the phrase as she uses it in an August 11, 1870, letter to her mother, placing the phrase in quotation marks (See *Little Women Abroad* 188).

10. Amy once again confuses her language. The French *comme il faut* translates "as is respectable."

11. Soft soap is made with potash lye and is usually semi-liquid.

12. Under "the Poet's Corner" in *The Olive Leaf* of July 19, 1849, is a poem to "Pat Puss," the family's cat. Penned by Augustus Snodgrass (LMA), the poem resembles "A Lament for S. B. Pat Paw" (Manuscript, Houghton Library, Harvard University).

[The above is a manly and handsome acknowledgment of past misdemeanors. If our young friend studied punctuation, it would be well.]

A SAD ACCIDENT.

On Friday last, we were startled by a violent shock in our basement, followed by cries of distress. On rushing, in a body, to the cellar, we discovered our beloved President prostrate upon the floor, having tripped and fallen while getting wood for domestic purposes. A perfect scene of ruin met our eyes; for in his fall Mr. Pickwick had plunged his head and shoulders into a tub of water, upset a keg of soft soap[11] upon his manly form, and torn his garments badly. On being removed from this perilous situation, it was discovered that he had suffered no injury but several bruises; and, we are happy to add, is now doing well.

Ed.

THE PUBLIC BEREAVEMENT.

It is our painful duty to record the sudden and mysterious disappearance of our cherished friend, Mrs. Snowball Pat Paw. This lovely and beloved cat was the pet of a circle of warm and admiring friends; for her beauty attracted all eyes, her graces and virtues endeared her to all hearts, and her loss is deeply felt by the whole community.

When last seen, she was sitting at the gate, watching the butcher's cart; and it is feared that some villain, tempted by her charms, basely stole her. Weeks have passed, but no trace of her has been discovered; and we relinquish all hope, tie a black ribbon to her basket, set aside her dish, and weep for her as one lost to us forever.

A sympathizing friend sends the following gem:—

A LAMENT

FOR S. B. PAT PAW.[12]

We mourn the loss of our little pet,
    And sigh o'er her hapless fate,
For never more by the fire she'll sit,
    Nor play by the old green gate.

The little grave where her infant sleeps,
    Is 'neath the chestnut tree;
But o'er her grave we may not weep,
    We know not where it may be.

Her empty bed, her idle ball,
    Will never see her more;
No gentle tap, no loving purr
    Is heard at the parlor door.

Another cat comes after her mice,
    A cat with a dirty face;
But she does not hunt as our darling did,
    Nor play with her airy grace.

Her stealthy paws tread the very hall
    Where Snowball used to play,
But she only spits at the dogs our pet
    So gallantly drove away.

She is useful and mild, and does her best,
    But she is not fair to see;
And we cannot give her your place, dear,
    Nor worship her as we worship thee.

A.S.

13. In 1855, LMA noted that she "delivered my burlesque lecture on 'Woman, and Her Position; by Oronthy Bluggage'" (*Journals* 74). Her good friend Alfred Whitman noted in "Miss Alcott's Letters to Her 'Laurie'" (1901) that the "original monologue . . . was not given in public, but was given occasionally at home, to the intense enjoyment of the fortunate few who were permitted to hear her" (quoted in *Her Own Time* 102). Edward Emerson, son of Ralph Waldo Emerson, in "When Louisa Alcott Was a Girl" (1898), recalled that one evening while visiting the Alcotts, "Louisa was persuaded by her mother to do something for our amusement. She disappeared and soon came in transformed. Her hair, which girls in those days wore brushed low and braided, was twisted up into a little knob on her head so tight that she could hardly wink. The broad collar, white undersleeves and hoopskirt of the day were gone, and she appeared in an ugly, scant, brown calico dress, with bloomer trousers to match, blue stockings and coarse shoes. She had a manuscript in one hand, and a pen in the other, which she thrust behind her ear and began a harangue on the "'Rights of Woman'" (quoted in *Her Own Time* 95).

14. While Elizabeth Alcott was excellent with the sewing needle, LMA noted in "Recollections of My Childhood" (1888) that "at twelve I set up as a doll's dress-maker, with my sign out, and wonderful models in my window. All the children employed me, and my turbans were the rage at one time to the great dismay of the neighbors' hens, who were hotly hunted down, that I might tweak out their downiest feathers to adorn the dolls' head-gear" (quoted in *Her Own Time* 34).

15. "The Greek Slave" was one of the original plays written by LMA and Anna Alcott and compiled in *Comic Tragedies* (1893). The Alcott sisters usually performed their dramas in the barn at their home, Hillside, on Lexington Road in Concord.

16. Folds or pleats.

17. Average.

As the President finished reading the paper (which I beg leave to assure my readers is a *bona fide* copy of one written by *bona fide* girls[18] once upon a time), a round of applause followed, and then Mr. Snodgrass rose to make a proposition.

"Mr. President and gentlemen," he began, assuming a parliamentary attitude and tone, "I wish to propose the admission of a new member; one who highly deserves the honor, would be deeply grateful for it, and would add immensely to the spirit of the club, the literary value of the paper, and be no end jolly and nice. I propose Mr. Theodore Laurence as an honorary member of the P. C. Come now, do have him."

Jo's sudden change of tone made the girls laugh; but all looked rather anxious, and no one said a word, as Snodgrass took his seat.

"We'll put it to vote," said the President. "All in favor of this motion please to manifest it by saying 'Aye.'"

A loud response from Snodgrass, followed, to everybody's surprise, by a timid one from Beth.

"Contrary minded say 'No.'"

Meg and Amy were contrary minded; and Mr. Winkle rose to say, with great elegance, "We don't wish any boys; they only joke and bounce about. This is a ladies' club, and we wish to be private and proper."

"I'm afraid he'll laugh at our paper, and make fun of us afterward," observed Pickwick, pulling the little curl on her forehead, as she always did when doubtful.

Up bounced[a] Snodgrass, very much in earnest. "Sir! I give you my word as a gentleman, Laurie won't do anything of the sort. He likes to write, and he'll give a tone to our contributions, and keep us from being sentimental, don't you see? We can do so little for him, and he does so much for us, I think the least we can do is to offer him a place here, and make him welcome, if he comes."

This artful allusion to benefits conferred, brought Tupman to his feet, looking as if he had quite made up his mind.

"Yes; we ought to do it, even if we *are* afraid. I say he *may* come, and his grandpa too, if he likes."

This spirited burst from Beth electrified the club, and Jo left

18. LMA is not quite correct here. The fact that she changed the language of "A Masked Marriage" as well as the name of one of its characters suggests that she used various issues of the family newspaper to compile her version for the novel.

19. Samuel Weller is Mr. Pickwick's servant and traveling companion in *The Pickwick Papers*. When the comical Cockney character appeared in chapter 10 of the serial, sales increased and Weller became a favorite of the reading public, even inspiring Sam Weller joke books. He remains one of Dickens's most popular characters.

20. A long-handled covered pan used to hold hot coals and warm a bed's sheets during cold weather.

21. Sam Weller in *The Pickwick Papers* reverses his *v*'s and *w*'s.

22. Clara Gowing, who was the same age as Louisa, grew up in Concord during the 1840s. She described the creation of the P. O. in *The Alcotts as I Knew Them* (1909): "The three months of school being over, we could not of course be together every day, and the plan of having a postoffice was originated; so on the hillside about midway between our homes, a hollow stump was cleared out and a box duly installed to receive our missives, and much sentiment and much fun passed through this repository. It was visited daily or oftener, and cruelly abused did we feel if on going there we did not find something for ourselves. Each had a fictitious signature" (quoted in *Her Own Time* 136).

23. Bird house for the Purple Martin *(Progne subis),* a North American swallow noted for its aerial agility.

her seat to shake hands approvingly. "Now then, vote again. Everybody remember it's our Laurie, and say 'Aye!'" cried Snodgrass, excitedly.

"Aye! aye! aye!" replied three voices at once.

"Good! bless you! now, as there's nothing like taking 'time by the *fetlock*' as Winkle characteristically observes, allow me to present the new member;" and, to the dismay of the rest of the club, Jo threw open the door of the closet, and displayed Laurie sitting on a rag-bag, flushed and twinkling with suppressed laughter.

"You rogue! you traitor! Jo, how could you?" cried the three girls, as Snodgrass led her friend triumphantly forth; and, producing both a chair and a badge, installed him in a jiffy.

"The coolness of you two rascals is amazing," began Mr. Pickwick, trying to get up an awful frown, and only succeeding in producing an amiable smile. But the new member was equal to the occasion; and, rising with a grateful salutation to the Chair, said, in the most engaging manner,—"Mr. President and ladies,—I beg pardon, gentlemen—, allow me to introduce myself as Sam Weller,[19] the very humble servant of the club."

"Good, good!" cried Jo, pounding with the handle of the old warming-pan[20] on which she leaned.

"My faithful friend and noble patron," continued Laurie, with a wave of the hand, "who has so flatteringly presented me, is not to be blamed for the base stratagem of to-night. I planned it, and she only gave in after lots of teasing."

"Come now, don't lay it all on yourself; you know I proposed the cupboard," broke in Snodgrass, who was enjoying the joke amazingly.

"Never you mind what she says. I'm the wretch that did it, sir," said the new member, with a Welleresque nod to Mr. Pickwick. "But on my honor, I never will do so again, and henceforth *dewote*[21] myself to the interest of this immortal club."

"Hear! hear!" cried Jo, clashing the lid of the warming-pan like a cymbal.

"Go on, go on!" added Winkle and Tupman, while the President bowed benignly.

"I merely wish to say, that as a slight token of my gratitude for

Jo at the Pickwick Club. Frank Merrill, original artwork for *Little Women: Illustrated* (1880). LMA approved of Merrill's drawings.

the honor done me, and as a means of promoting friendly relations between adjoining nations, I have set up a post-office in the hedge in the lower corner of the garden;[22] a fine, spacious building, with padlocks on the doors, and every convenience for the mails,—also the females, if I may be allowed the expression. It's the old martin-house;[23] but I've stopped up the door, and made the roof open, so it will hold all sorts of things, and save our valuable time. Letters, manuscripts, books and bundles can be passed

24. Francis Bacon (1561–1626) was a British scientist, philosopher, lawyer, statesman, and author of numerous works. In 1852, LMA listed John Milton's epic *Paradise Lost* (1667) and *Comus* (1634) among her favorite literary works (*Journals* 67).

25. A cravat, best known as a scarf worn around the neck by men, could also be a long woolen scarf.

in there; and, as each nation has a key, it will be uncommonly nice, I fancy. Allow me to present the club key; and, with many thanks for your favor, take my seat."

Great applause as Mr. Weller deposited a little key on the table, and subsided; the warming-pan clashed and waved wildly, and it was some time before order could be restored. A long discussion followed, and every one came out surprising, for every one did her best; so it was an unusually lively meeting, and did not adjourn till a late hour, when it broke up with three shrill cheers for the new member.

No one ever regretted the admittance of Sam Weller, for a more devoted, well-behaved, and jovial member no club could have. He certainly did add "spirit" to the meetings, and "a tone" to the paper; for his orations convulsed his hearers, and his contributions were excellent, being patriotic, classical, comical, or dramatic, but never sentimental. Jo regarded them as worthy of Bacon, Milton,[24] or Shakespeare; and remodelled her own works with good effect, she thought.

The P. O. was a capital little institution, and flourished wonderfully, for nearly as many queer things passed through it as through the real office. Tragedies and cravats,[25] poetry and pickles, garden seeds and long letters, music and gingerbread, rubbers, invitations, scoldings and puppies. The old gentleman liked the fun, and amused himself by sending odd bundles, mysterious messages, and funny telegrams; and his gardener, who was smitten with Hannah's charms, actually sent a love-letter to Jo's care. How they laughed when the secret came out, never dreaming how many love-letters that little post-office would hold in the years to come!

Chapter 11

Experiments

THE FIRST OF JUNE; the Kings are off to the seashore to-morrow, and I'm free! Three months' vacation! how I shall enjoy it!" exclaimed Meg, coming home one warm day to find Jo laid upon the sofa in an unusual state of exhaustion, while Beth took off her dusty boots, and Amy made lemonade for the refreshment of the whole party.

"Aunt March went to-day, for which, oh be joyful!" said Jo. "I was mortally afraid she'd ask me to go with her; if she had, I should have felt as if I ought to do it; but Plumfield[1] is about as festive[a] as a churchyard, you know, and I'd rather be excused. We had a flurry getting the old lady off, and I had a scare every time she spoke to me, for I was in such a hurry to be through that I was uncommonly helpful and sweet, and feared she'd find it impossible to part from me. I quaked till she was fairly in the carriage, and had a final fright, for, as it drove off, she popped out her head, saying, 'Josy-phine, won't you—?' I didn't hear any more, for I basely turned and fled; I did actually run, and whisked round the corner, where I felt safe."

"Poor old Jo! she came in looking as if bears were after her," said Beth, as she cuddled her sister's feet with a motherly air.

"Aunt March is a regular samphire,[2] is she not?" observed Amy, tasting her mixture critically.

"She means *vampire,* not seaweed; but it don't matter; it's too warm to be particular about one's parts of speech," murmured Jo.

"What shall you do all your vacation?" asked Amy, changing the subject, with tact.

"I shall lie abed late, and do nothing," replied Meg, from the

1. Plumfield may be a play on Fruitlands, the Utopian community that Bronson Alcott and Charles Lane established on June 1, 1843. Located on ninety acres in Harvard, MA, approximately sixteen miles from Concord, Fruitlands originally had fourteen residents, including Bronson and Abigail Alcott, along with their four daughters. Abby May Alcott, not yet three, was the youngest; LMA celebrated her eleventh birthday there. Lane and Bronson Alcott's goal was to form a consociate family, one that believed in the same ideals. As their published letter in the *Liberator* declared: "The family, in its highest divinest sense, is therefore our true position, our sacred earthly destiny. It comprehends every divine, every humane relation consistent with universal good, and all others it rejects" (152). Their diet was vegan—no meat, no dairy products, no eggs. Their clothing consisted of linen garments and canvas shoes. Cotton was forbidden since it was the product of slavery. Wool came at the expense of animals. Of the ninety acres, fewer than ten were farmable. Alcott and Lane were often away, attempting to attract other members to this new Eden, thus leaving Abigail and the remaining seven adults with both the housework and the farming. As summer waned into autumn, members drifted away, the crops were not sufficient for the coming winter, and personalities collided. The experiment failed and both Lane and the Alcotts left Fruitlands in January 1844. Bronson's journals for the Fruitlands period were lost. However, ten-year-old LMA's fragments from those months exist, and they portray a troubled time: "Father and Mr L[ane]. had a talk, and father asked us if *we* saw any reason for us to separate. Mother wanted to, she is so tired. I like it, but not the school part or Mr L[ane]" (*Journals* 47). In the December 18, 1873, issue of *The Independent,* LMA satirized the experience in "Transcendental Wild Oats: A Chapter from an Unwritten Romance." Here, Sister Hope, based on Abigail Alcott, is the heroine of the failed Utopian attempt. See Richard Francis, *Fruitlands: The Alcott Family and Their Search for Utopia* (New Haven, CT: Yale University Press, 2010); and Sandra H. Petrulionis, "By the Light of Her Mother's Lamp: Woman's Work versus Man's Philosophy in Louisa May Alcott's 'Transcendental Wild Oats,'" *Studies in the American Renaissance* (1995): pp. 69–81.

2. Samphire is the common name given to many edible plants growing in coastal regions, often on rocks. One of the most common is the glasswort *(Salicornia).*

3. Jo means to make good use of her time. She alludes to verse 1 of Song 20, known as "Against Idleness and Mischief," in Isaac Watts's *Divine Songs for Children* (1715): "How doth the little busy bee / Improve each shining hour."

4. Jo is playing off the bird names here, alluding to the fact that Laurie is a singer. Interestingly, the North American warbler, a small, brightly colored bird, is not known for its song while the European warbler, a plain-colored bird, is.

5. In Dickens's *Life and Adventures of Martin Chuzzlewit,* serialized in 1843–1844, the comical Sairey Gamp, an alcoholic, serves as a nurse and a midwife. Gamp was one of Louisa's favorite characters, and in theatricals, she played Sairey to Anna's Betsey Prig, a nurse and friend of Gamp's in the novel. LMA often addressed herself as "Sairy" or "Sairey" in her letters, especially those to Anna. Willis recalls in *Alcott Memoirs* (1915): "[LMA] and her sister Anna often acted in costume, inimitably, the quarrel scene between Sairy Gamp and Betsey Prigg over the imaginary Mrs. Harris . . . I have rarely seen anything better in comedy by professionals and I recall many instances of Mrs. Alcott laughing until tears came to her eyes over the girls' performances" (quoted in *Her Own Time* 178).

6. LMA perhaps has in mind the Concord River, formed in Middlesex County in Massachusetts at the confluence of the Sudbury and Assabet rivers. During the mid-nineteenth century, the river was often the scene of social activities including rowing and picnicking by the Alcott sisters and their friends.

7. Published in 1850 under the pseudonym Elizabeth Wetherell, *The Wide, Wide World* by Susan Warner was a sentimental American novel about the life of young Ellen Montgomery. When her parents go to Europe in hopes that her ill mother will recover, Ellen is forced to live with Fortune Emerson, an aunt she hardly knows. Feeling alone in the world, Ellen seeks solace from others, especially John Humphreys, who guides Ellen in her growth as a person, notably her moral and spiritual development. The novel, a favorite for young girls, was one of the most popular books of the last half of the nineteenth century. For parallels in Warner's novel and LMA's story of the March sisters, see Donna Campbell, "Sentimental Conventions and Self-Protection: *Little Women* and *The Wide, Wide World*," *Legacy* 11 (1994): 118–129.

depths of the rocking-chair. "I've been routed up early all winter, and had to spend my days working for other people; so now I'm going to rest and revel to my heart's content."

"Hum!"[b] said Jo; "that dozy way wouldn't suit me. I've laid in a heap of books, and I'm going to improve my shining hours[3] reading on my perch in the old apple-tree, when I'm not having l—"

"Don't say 'larks!'" implored Amy, as a return snub for the "samphire" correction.

"I'll say 'nightingales,' then, with Laurie; that's proper and appropriate, since he's a warbler."[4]

"Don't let us do any lessons, Beth, for a while, but play all the time, and rest, as the girls mean to," proposed Amy.

"Well, I will, if mother don't mind. I want to learn some new songs, and my children need fixing[c] up for the summer; they are dreadfully out of order, and really suffering for clothes."

"May we, mother?" asked Meg, turning to Mrs. March, who sat sewing, in what they called "Marmee's corner."

"You may try your experiment for a week, and see how you like it. I think by Saturday night you will find that all play, and no work, is as bad as all work, and no play."

"Oh, dear, no! it will be delicious, I'm sure," said Meg, complacently.

"I now propose a toast, as my 'friend and pardner, Sairy Gamp,'[5] says. Fun forever, and no grubbage," cried Jo, rising, glass in hand, as the lemonade went round.

They all drank it merrily, and began the experiment by lounging for the rest of the day. Next morning, Meg did not appear till ten o'clock; her solitary breakfast did not taste good, and the room seemed lonely and untidy, for Jo had not filled the vases, Beth had not dusted, and Amy's books lay scattered about. Nothing was neat and pleasant but "Marmee's corner," which looked as usual; and there she sat, to "rest and read," which meant yawn, and imagine what pretty summer dresses she would get with her salary. Jo spent the morning on the river,[6] with Laurie, and the afternoon reading and crying over "The Wide, Wide World,"[7] up in the apple-tree. Beth began by rummaging everything out of the big closet, where her family resided; but, getting tired before half

LITTLE WOMEN

done, she left her establishment topsy-turvy, and went to her music, rejoicing that she had no dishes to wash. Amy arranged her bower, put on her best white frock, smoothed her curls, and sat down to draw, under the honeysuckles, hoping some one would see and inquire who the young artist was. As no one appeared but an inquisitive daddy-long-legs, who examined her work with interest, she went to walk, got caught in a shower, and came home dripping.

At tea-time they compared notes, and all agreed that it had been a delightful, though unusually long day. Meg, who went shopping in the afternoon, and got a "sweet blue muslin," had discovered, after she had cut the breadths off, that it wouldn't wash,[8] which mishap made her slightly cross. Jo had burnt the skin off her nose boating, and got a raging headache by reading too long. Beth was worried by the confusion of her closet, and the difficulty of learning three or four songs at once; and Amy deeply regretted the damage done her frock, for Katy Brown's party was to be the next day; and now, like Flora McFlimsy, she had "nothing to wear."[9] But these were mere trifles; and they assured their mother that the experiment was working finely. She smiled, said nothing, and, with Hannah's help, did their neglected work, keeping home pleasant, and the domestic machinery running smoothly. It was astonishing what a peculiar and uncomfortable state of things was produced by the "resting and revelling" process. The days kept getting longer and longer; the weather was unusually variable, and so were tempers; an unsettled feeling possessed every one, and Satan found plenty of mischief for the idle hands to do.[10] As the height of luxury, Meg put out some of her sewing, and then found time hang so heavily, that she fell to snipping and spoiling her clothes, in her attempts to furbish them up, à la Moffat. Jo read till her eyes gave out, and she was sick of books; got so fidgety that even good-natured Laurie had a quarrel with her, and so reduced in spirits that she desperately wished she had gone with Aunt March. Beth got on pretty well, for she was constantly forgetting that it was to be *all play, and no work,* and fell back into her old ways, now and then; but something in the air affected her, and, more than once, her tranquillity was much

8. Breadths are the finished, nonfraying edges of a length of woven fabric. By "wouldn't wash" Meg means that the dress was no longer acceptable. The *OED* notes the first usage of this definition of *wash* as 1849.

9. William Allen Butler's satirical poem "Nothing to Wear," published in the February 7, 1857, edition of *Harper's Weekly,* tells the story of Flora McFlimsey, who goes shopping in Paris for six weeks, buying every style of clothing and accessories she finds and shipping them home to New York: "And yet, though scarce three months have passed since the day / This merchandise went, on twelve carts, up Broadway, / This same Miss M'Flimsey, of Madison Square, / The last time we met, was in utter despair, / Because she had nothing whatever to wear!" May Alcott's copy of *Nothing to Wear: An Episode of City Life* (New York: Rudd & Carlton, 1857), inscribed "From Mother August 1857," is located in the Houghton Library, Harvard University, *AC85.Al191.Zz857b.

10. LMA once again alludes to Isaac Watts's famous poem "Against Idleness and Mischief" in *Divine Songs for Children* (1715): "In works of labour or of skill I would be busy too; For Satan finds some mischief still for idle hands to do."

11. Boaz was the husband of Ruth in the Old Testament's Book of Ruth. Amy confuses him with Job from the Book of Job, who endures many temptations from Satan and calamities in his life, but remains true to God.

12. Mrs. Malaprop, the comic character who confuses or misuses words in Richard Brinsley Sheridan's comedy of manners *The Rivals* (1775). Her name comes from *malapropos,* which means "inappropriate."

13. Housekeeping in the mid-nineteenth century was difficult, time-consuming physical labor performed largely by women. Fires had to be started and then tended throughout the day. Cooking on wood stoves was especially problematic as it was hard to keep the temperature even. Kerosene lamps had to be filled, wicks trimmed, and lamp chimneys cleaned. With the use of fires and woodstoves came soot and ash, which had to be cleaned almost daily. Floors had to be swept with a broom and then mopped and rugs beaten. Typically women were neither rewarded nor appreciated for this labor. As a servant, Hannah would have been compensated, but the wages would have been low, especially if they included room and board. Remembering all the hard work that Mrs. Alcott did to support the family and keep house for so many years, LMA dedicated her novel *Work: A Story of Experience* (1873) to "MY MOTHER, whose life has been a long labor of love." Among the main character's many jobs in the novel, Christie Devon works as a servant, a job that LMA held for almost two months in 1851. Based on her experience, LMA published the satirical story "How I Went Out to Service" in *The Independent* on June 4, 1874, a commentary on society's views that housekeeping is woman's work and of little value.

14. A pantry or room where food is stored.

disturbed; so much so, that, on one occasion, she actually shook poor dear Joanna, and told her she was "a fright." Amy fared worst of all, for her resources were small; and, when her sisters left her to amuse and care for herself, she soon found that accomplished and important little self a great burden. She didn't like dolls; fairy tales were childish, and one couldn't draw all the time. Tea-parties didn't amount to much, neither did picnics, unless very well conducted. "If one could have a fine house, full of nice girls, or go travelling, the summer would be delightful; but to stay at home with three selfish sisters, and a grown-up boy, was enough to try the patience of a Boaz,"[11] complained Miss Malaprop,[12] after several days devoted to pleasure, fretting, and *ennui.*

No one would own that they were tired of the experiment; but, by Friday night, each acknowledged to herself that they were glad the week was nearly done. Hoping to impress the lesson more deeply, Mrs. March, who had a good deal of humor, resolved to finish off the trial in an appropriate manner; so she gave Hannah a holiday, and let the girls enjoy the full effect of the play system.

When they got up on Saturday morning, there was no fire in the kitchen, no breakfast in the dining-room, and no mother anywhere to be seen.

"Mercy on us! what *has* happened?" cried Jo, staring about her in dismay.

Meg ran upstairs, and soon came back again, looking relieved, but rather bewildered, and a little ashamed.

"Mother isn't sick, only very tired, and she says she is going to stay quietly in her room all day, and let us do the best we can. It's a very queer thing for her to do, she don't act a bit like herself; but she says it *has* been a hard week for her, so we mustn't grumble, but take care of ourselves."

"That's easy enough, and I like the idea; I'm aching for something to do—that is, some new amusement, you know," added Jo, quickly.

In fact it *was* an immense relief to them all to have a little work, and they took hold with a will, but soon realized the truth of Hannah's saying, "Housekeeping ain't no joke."[13] There was plenty of food in the larder,[14] and, while Beth and Amy set the table,

LITTLE WOMEN

Meg and Jo got breakfast; wondering, as they did so, why servants ever talked about hard work.

"I shall take some up to mother, though she said we were not to think of her, for she'd take care of herself," said Meg, who presided, and felt quite matronly behind the teapot.

So a tray was fitted out before any one began, and taken up, with the cook's compliments. The boiled tea was very bitter, the omelette scorched, and the biscuits speckled with saleratus;[15] but Mrs. March received her repast with thanks, and laughed heartily over it after Jo was gone.

"Poor little souls, they will have a hard time, I'm afraid; but they won't suffer, and it will do them good," she said, producing the more palatable viands[16] with which she had provided herself, and disposing of the bad breakfast, so that their feelings might not be hurt;—a motherly little deception, for which they were grateful.

Many were the complaints below, and great the chagrin of the head cook, at her failures. "Never mind, I'll get the dinner, and be servant; you be missis, keep your hands nice, see company, and give orders," said Jo, who knew still less than Meg about culinary affairs.

This obliging offer was gladly accepted; and Margaret retired to the parlor, which she hastily put in order by whisking the litter under the sofa, and shutting the blinds, to save the trouble of dusting. Jo, with perfect faith in her own powers, and a friendly desire to make up the quarrel, immediately put a note in the office, inviting Laurie to dinner.

"You'd better see what you have got before you think of having company," said Meg, when informed of the hospitable, but rash act.

"Oh, there's corned beef, and plenty of potatoes; and I shall get some asparagus, and a lobster, 'for a relish' as Hannah says. We'll have lettuce, and make a salad; I don't know how, but the book tells. I'll have blanc-mange[17] and strawberries for dessert; and coffee, too, if you want to be elegant."

"Don't try too many messes,[18] Jo, for you can't make anything but gingerbread and molasses candy, fit to eat. I wash my hands of

15. A leavening of sodium bicarbonate; baking soda.
16. Provisions of food.
17. A sweetmeat dessert made from gelatin boiled with milk.
18. Courses of food.

19. Pudding is synonymous with dessert; Jo refers to the blancmange and strawberries.

20. The name perhaps comes from the main character, Pip, in Charles Dickens's *Great Expectations* (1860–1861).

21. Pip's death memorably brings home to readers, especially young readers, the consequences of neglected work. Charles Dickens, LMA's guide in matters of social conscience, often depicts cruelty toward animals in his works. In his essay "Frauds on the Fairies," which appeared in *Household Words* on October 1, 1853, Dickens wrote about the power of fairy tales to nourish in children "[f]orbearance, courtesy, consideration for the poor and aged, kind treatment of animals, the love of nature, abhorrence of tyranny and brute force."

22. Tart or sour strawberries.

23. Sooty.

24. Sourdough bread is made from fermenting dough, often left over from a previous baking, that is used as a leavening agent.

25. An aged complexion.

the dinner-party; and, since you have asked Laurie on your own responsibility, you may just take care of him."

"I don't want you to do anything but be clever[d] to him, and help to the pudding.[19] You'll give me your advice if I get stuck, won't you?" asked Jo, rather hurt.

"Yes; but I don't know much, except about bread, and a few trifles. You had better ask mother's leave, before you order anything," returned Meg, prudently.

"Of course I shall; I ain't a fool," and Jo went off in a huff at the doubts expressed of her powers.

"Get what you like, and don't disturb me; I'm going out to dinner, and can't worry about things at home," said Mrs. March, when Jo spoke to her. "I never enjoyed housekeeping, and I'm going to take a vacation today, and read, write, go visiting and amuse myself."

The unusual spectacle of her busy mother rocking comfortably, and reading early in the morning, made Jo feel as if some natural phenomenon had occurred; for an eclipse, an earthquake, or a volcanic eruption would hardly have seemed stranger.

"Everything is out of sorts, somehow," she said to herself, going down stairs. "There's Beth crying; that's a sure sign that something is wrong with this family. If Amy is bothering, I'll shake her."

Feeling very much out of sorts herself, Jo hurried into the parlor to find Beth sobbing over Pip,[20] the canary, who lay dead in the cage, with his little claws pathetically extended, as if imploring the food, for want of which he had died.

"It's all my fault—I forgot him—there isn't a seed or drop left—oh, Pip! oh, Pip! how could I be so cruel to you?" cried Beth, taking the poor thing in her hands, and trying to restore him.[21]

Jo peeped into his half-open eye, felt his little heart, and finding him stiff and cold, shook her head, and offered her domino-box for a coffin.

"Put him in the oven, and maybe he will get warm, and revive," said Amy, hopefully.

"He's been starved, and he shan't be baked, now he's dead. I'll make him a shroud, and he shall be buried in the grave;[e] and I'll never have another bird, never, my Pip! for I am too bad to own one," murmured Beth, sitting on the floor with her pet folded in her hands.

"The funeral shall be this afternoon, and we will all go. Now, don't cry, Bethy; it's a pity, but nothing goes right this week, and Pip has had the worst of the experiment. Make the shroud, and lay him in my box; and, after the dinner-party, we'll have a nice little funeral," said Jo, beginning to feel as if she had undertaken a good deal.

Leaving the others to console Beth, she departed to the kitchen, which was in a most discouraging state of confusion. Putting on a big apron, she fell to work, and got the dishes piled up ready for washing, when she discovered that the fire was out.

"Here's a sweet prospect!" muttered Jo, slamming the stove door open, and poking vigorously among the cinders.

Having rekindled it, she thought she would go to market while the water heated. The walk revived her spirits; and, flattering herself that she had made good bargains, she trudged home again, after buying a very young lobster, some very old asparagus, and two boxes of acid strawberries.[22] By the time she got cleared up, the dinner arrived, and the stove was red-hot. Hannah had left a pan of bread to rise, Meg had worked it up early, set it on the hearth for a second rising, and forgotten it. Meg was entertaining Sallie Gardiner, in the parlor, when the door flew open, and a floury, crocky,[23] flushed and dishevelled figure appeared, demanding, tartly,—

"I say, isn't bread 'riz' enough when it runs over the pans?"

Sallie began to laugh; but Meg nodded, and lifted her eyebrows as high as they would go, which caused the apparition to vanish, and put the sour bread[24] into the oven without further delay. Mrs. March went out, after peeping here and there to see how matters went, also saying a word of comfort to Beth, who sat making a winding-sheet, while the dear departed lay in state in the domino-box. A strange sense of helplessness fell upon the girls as the gray bonnet vanished round the corner; and despair seized them, when, a few minutes later, Miss Crocker appeared, and said she'd come to dinner. Now this lady was a thin, yellow[25] spinster, with

"'How could I be so cruel to you?' cried Beth." Barbara Cooney, *Little Women* (1955).

26. To deacon is to package fruit with the finest pieces on the top. The *OED* notes the first usage of this American slang in James Russell Lowell's *Biglow Papers* (1866) and its second usage as this line from *Little Women*.

a sharp nose, and inquisitive eyes, who saw everything, and gossiped about all she saw. They disliked her, but had been taught to be kind to her, simply because she was old and poor, and had few friends. So Meg gave her the easy-chair, and tried to entertain her, while she asked questions, criticised everything, and told stories of the people whom she knew.

Language cannot describe the anxieties, experiences, and exertions which Jo underwent that morning; and the dinner she served up became a standing joke. Fearing to ask any more advice, she did her best alone, and discovered that something more than energy and good-will is necessary to make a cook. She boiled the asparagus hard for an hour, and was grieved to find the heads cooked off, and the stalks harder than ever. The bread burnt black; for the salad dressing so aggravated her, that she let everything else go, till she had convinced herself that she could not make it fit to eat. The lobster was a scarlet mystery to her, but she hammered and poked, till it was unshelled, and its meagre proportions concealed in a grove of lettuce-leaves. The potatoes had to be hurried, not to keep the asparagus waiting, and were not done at last. The blanc-mange was lumpy, and the strawberries not as ripe as they looked, having been skilfully "deaconed."[26]

"Well, they can eat beef, and bread and butter, if they are hungry; only it's mortifying to have to spend your whole morning for nothing," thought Jo, as she rang the bell half an hour later than usual, and stood hot, tired, and dispirited, surveying the feast spread for Laurie, accustomed to all sorts of elegance, and Miss Crocker, whose curious eyes would mark all failures, and whose tattling tongue would report them far and wide.

Poor Jo would gladly have gone under the table, as one thing after another was tasted and left; while Amy giggled, Meg looked distressed, Miss Crocker pursed up her lips, and Laurie talked and laughed with all his might, to give a cheerful tone to the festive scene. Jo's one strong point was the fruit, for she had sugared it well, and had a pitcher of rich cream to eat with it. Her hot cheeks cooled a trifle, and she drew a long breath, as the pretty glass plates went round, and every one looked graciously at the little rosy islands floating in a sea of cream. Miss Crocker tasted first,

LITTLE WOMEN

made a wry face, and drank some water hastily. Jo, who had refused, thinking there might not be enough, for they dwindled
sadly after the picking over, glanced at Laurie, but he was eating
away manfully, though there was a slight pucker about his mouth,
and he kept his eye fixed on his plate. Amy, who was fond of delicate fare, took a heaping spoonful, choked, hid her face in her
napkin, and left the table precipitately.

"Oh, what is it?" exclaimed Jo, trembling.

"Salt instead of sugar, and the cream is sour," replied Meg, with
a tragic gesture.

Jo uttered a groan, and fell back in her chair; remembering that
she had given a last hasty powdering to the berries out of one of
the two boxes on the kitchen table, and had neglected to put the
milk in the refrigerator.[27] She turned scarlet, and was on the verge
of crying, when she met Laurie's eyes, which *would* look merry in
spite of his heroic efforts; the comical side of the affair suddenly
struck her, and she laughed till the tears ran down her cheeks. So
did every one else, even "Croaker," as the girls called the old lady;
and the unfortunate dinner ended gaily, with bread and butter,
olives and fun.

"I haven't strength of mind enough to clear up now, so we will
sober ourselves with a funeral," said Jo, as they rose; and Miss
Crocker made ready to go, being eager to tell the new story at
another friend's dinner-table.

They did sober themselves, for Beth's sake; Laurie dug a grave
under the ferns in the grove, little Pip was laid in, with many
tears, by his tender-hearted mistress, and covered with moss,
while a wreath of violets and chickweed was hung on the stone
which bore his epitaph, composed by Jo, while she struggled with
the dinner:—

> "Here lies Pip March,
>   Who died the 7th of June;
> Loved and lamented sore,[28]
>   And not forgotten soon."

At the conclusion of the ceremonies, Beth retired to her room,
overcome with emotion and lobster; but there was no place of re-

27. Refrigeration during the middle of the nineteenth century
was accomplished by using an icebox, a container with insulated
walls. A large block of ice was placed in a tray near the top of the
icebox; the cold air would drift down and keep food cool. By the
middle of the nineteenth century, ice harvesting was a profitable
business. Workers would cut large blocks of ice from frozen lakes or
rivers in the winter, and the ice would be hauled to an ice house,
where it would be insulated, thus ensuring that most of it would
survive until sold. The iceman would then deliver the blocks of ice
to homes. Henry David Thoreau, in Chapter 16, "The Pond in
Winter," in *Walden* (1854), describes the ice on Walden Pond being
harvested by 100 Irishmen from Cambridge.

28. Greatly.

John Brown (1800–1859), American abolitionist. The morning of his execution, Brown wrote: "I, John Brown, am now quite certain that the crimes of this guilty land will never be purged away but with blood."

29. Calling or formal visiting was popular among women in the nineteenth century. Often women of society would set certain days and times to accept calls. A calling card with the lady's name on it was often left if the person called upon was not available. The March sisters are obliged to properly receive their callers.

30. Marmee's admonition to her daughters anticipates a more enlightened era in which domestic chores are shared by both men and women. She suggests that domestic equality must be the model for true democratic society. In his essay "Domestic Life," Ralph Waldo Emerson writes: "[H]ousekeeping is not beautiful; it cheers and raises neither the husband, the wife, nor the child; neither the host, nor the guest; it oppresses women. A house kept to the end of prudence is laborious without joy; a house kept to the end of display is impossible to all but a few women, and their success is dearly bought" (*Society and Solitude: Twelve Chapters,* in *The Concord Edition of the Complete Works of Ralph Waldo Emerson* [Boston and New York: Houghton Mifflin, 1904], p. 111).

31. Once again Jo alludes to verse 1 of Song 20, known as "Against Idleness and Mischief" in Isaac Watts's *Divine Songs for Children* (1715): "How doth the little busy bee / Improve each shining hour."

32. Although Part I of *Little Women* is set during 1861–1862, the first years of the Civil War, LMA never directly addresses the issue of slavery. Each of the approximately six times that the word *slave* occurs in the text, it is used exclusively as a metaphor, with phrases such as "make a slave of yourself." The reason may be simple. By the time LMA was writing *Little Women,* the Civil War had been over for almost three years. LMA was not interested in persuading read-

pose, for the beds were not made, and she found her grief much assuaged by beating up pillows and putting things in order. Meg helped Jo clear away the remains of the feast, which took half the afternoon, and left them so tired that they agreed to be contented with tea and toast for supper. Laurie took Amy to drive, which was a deed of charity, for the sour cream seemed to have had a bad effect upon her temper. Mrs. March came home to find the three older girls hard at work in the middle of the afternoon; and a glance at the closet gave her an idea of the success of one part of the experiment.

Before the housewives could rest, several people called,[29] and there was a scramble to get ready to see them; then tea must be got, errands done; and one or two bits of sewing were necessary, but neglected till the last minute.[f] As twilight fell, dewy and still, one by one they gathered in the porch where the June roses were budding beautifully, and each groaned or sighed as she sat down, as if tired or troubled.

"What a dreadful day this has been!" begun Jo, usually the first to speak.

"It has seemed shorter than usual, but *so* uncomfortable," said Meg.

"Not a bit like home," added Amy.

"It can't seem so without Marmee and little Pip," sighed Beth, glancing, with full eyes, at the empty cage above her head.

"Here's mother, dear, and you shall have another bird to-morrow, if you want it."

As she spoke, Mrs. March came and took her place among them, looking as if her holiday had not been much pleasanter than theirs.

"Are you satisfied with your experiment, girls, or do you want another week of it?" she asked, as Beth nestled up to her, and the rest turned toward her with brightening faces, as flowers turn toward the sun.

"I don't!" cried Jo, decidedly.

"Nor I," echoed the others.

"You think, then, that it is better to have a few duties, and live a little for others, do you?"

"Lounging and larking don't pay," observed Jo, shaking her

head. "I'm tired of it, and mean to go to work at something right off."

"Suppose you learn plain cooking; that's a useful accomplishment, which no woman should be without," said Mrs. March, laughing audibly[g] at the recollection of Jo's dinner-party; for she had met Miss Crocker, and heard her account of it.

"Mother! did you go away and let everything be, just to see how we'd get on?" cried Meg, who had had suspicions all day.

"Yes; I wanted you to see how the comfort of all depends on each doing their share faithfully. While Hannah and I did your work, you got on pretty well, though I don't think you were very happy or amiable; so I thought, as a little lesson, I would show you what happens when every one thinks only of herself. Don't you feel that it is pleasanter to help one another, to have daily duties which make leisure sweet when it comes, and to bear or forbear, that home may be comfortable and lovely to us all?"[30]

"We do, mother, we do!" cried the girls.

"Then let me advise you to take up your little burdens again; for though they seem heavy sometimes, they are good for us, and lighten as we learn to carry them. Work is wholesome, and there is plenty for every one; it keeps us from *ennui* and mischief; is good for health and spirits, and gives us a sense of power and independence better than money or fashion."

"We'll work like bees,[31] and love it too; see if we don't!" said Jo. "I'll learn plain cooking for my holiday task; and the next dinner-party I have shall be a success."

"I'll make the set of shirts for father, instead of letting you do it, Marmee. I can and I will, though I'm not fond of sewing; that will be better than fussing over my own things, which are plenty nice enough as they are," said Meg.

"I'll do my lessons every day, and not spend so much time with my music and dolls. I am a stupid thing, and ought to be studying, not playing," was Beth's resolution; while Amy followed their example, by heroically declaring, "I shall learn to make buttonholes, and attend to my parts of speech."

"Very good! then I am quite satisfied with the experiment, and fancy that we shall not have to repeat it; only don't go to the other extreme, and delve like slaves.[32] Have regular hours for work and

ers of the evils of slavery; thousands of men had died in the recent past to accomplish that. While LMA does not address slavery in *Little Women,* her interest in reform, especially woman's rights, had begun with her involvement with the antislavery movement. Both of her parents, along with her mother's brother Rev. Samuel Joseph May, had long been participants. A friend to William Lloyd Garrison, leader of the American Anti-Slavery Society (1833–1870), Bronson joined the newly formed organization. Abigail Alcott was a member of the Boston Female Anti-Slavery Society (1833–1840) as well as the Concord Female Anti-Slavery Society, whose founding members in 1837 included Sophia and Helen Thoreau, sisters of Henry David Thoreau; Mary Merrick Brooks, wife of Concord lawyer Nathan Brooks; and Lidian Emerson, wife of Ralph Waldo Emerson. With its antislavery supporters, Concord was a station on the Underground Railroad, and the Alcotts themselves occasionally harbored runaway slaves. In her "Recollections of My Childhood" (1888), LMA wrote: "Fugitive slaves were sheltered under our roof, and my first pupil was a very black George Washington whom I taught to write on the hearth with charcoal, his big fingers finding pen and pencil unmanageable" (quoted in *Her Own Time,* p. 36). A number of antislavery leaders, many of whom LMA knew or at least met, came to Concord to speak and seek moral and financial support: Garrison, Wendell Phillips, Frederick Douglass, Angelina and Sarah Grimke, Harriet Tubman, William and Ellen Craft. John Brown came to Concord twice in the late 1850s, meeting with Emerson, Thoreau, Bronson Alcott, and others. Franklin Benjamin Sanborn, a Harvard graduate, reformer, and schoolmaster of a newly opened academy in Concord, was so inspired by Brown that he joined others as part of the "Secret Six" to finance John Brown's raid on Harper's Ferry. Helping Sanborn were two Alcott family friends: Theodore Parker and Thomas Wentworth Higginson. After Brown's defeat and imprisonment, LMA noted in November 1859: "The Harper's Ferry tragedy makes this a memorable month. Glad I lived to see the Antislavery movement and this last heroic act in it. Wish I could do my part in it" (*Journals* 95). The following month, after Brown was convicted and hanged, LMA observed: "The execution of Saint John the Just took place on the second. A meeting at the hall, and all Concord was there. Emerson, Father, and Sanborn spoke, and all were full of reverence and admiration for the martyr" (*Journals* 95). LMA, moved by the experience, wrote "With a Rose, That Bloomed on the Day of John Brown's Martyrdom," published in Garrison's newspaper, the *Liberator,* on January 20, 1860. Many years later, in February 1884, at the funeral for Wendell Phillips,

William Lloyd Garrison (1805–1879), the most prominent abolitionist leader in America. At Abigail Alcott's funeral in November 1877, Garrison shared his recollections of Mrs. Alcott's role in the antislavery movement.

LMA sat between Frederick Douglass and his wife: "A goodly gathering of all left of the old workers. Glad & proud to be among them" (*Journals* 243). From the antislavery movement, in which she had been both an observer and a participant, LMA's enthusiasm for reform of all kinds would blossom into her involvement in the suffrage movement, the temperance movement, and dress and education reform, among others. For an excellent study of abolition and antislavery in Concord, see Sandra Harbert Petrulionis, *To Set This World Right: The Antislavery Movement in Thoreau's Concord* (Ithaca, NY: Cornell University Press, 2006).

play; make each day both useful and pleasant, and prove that you understand the worth of time by employing it well. Then youth will be delightful, old age will bring few regrets, and life become a beautiful success, in spite of poverty."

"We'll remember, mother!" and they did.

Chapter 12

Camp Laurence

1. Penny posts were an early system of home mail delivery. In Britain, the first penny post appeared in 1680, and for a penny a letter up to one pound in weight would be delivered in the towns of Westminster and London. By 1840, England had set up the Uniform Penny Post, which led to the development of postage stamps. One of the earliest penny posts in America was Spauldings Penny Post, founded in 1847, which delivered mail between New York City and Buffalo.

2. The cuffs of sleeves.

BETH was post-mistress, for, being most at home, she could attend to it regularly, and dearly liked the daily task of unlocking the little door and distributing the mail. One July day she came in with her hands full, and went about the house leaving letters and parcels, like the penny post.[1]

"Here's your posy, mother! Laurie never forgets that," she said, putting the fresh nosegay in the vase that stood in "Marmee's corner," and was kept supplied by the affectionate boy.

"Miss Meg March, one letter, and a glove," continued Beth, delivering the articles to her sister, who sat near her mother, stitching wristbands.[2]

"Why, I left a pair over there, and here is only one," said Meg, looking at the gray cotton glove.

"Didn't you drop the other in the garden?"

"No, I'm sure I didn't; for there was only one in the office."

"I hate to have odd gloves! Never mind, the other may be found. My letter is only a translation of the German song I wanted; I guess Mr. Brooke did it, for this isn't Laurie's writing."

Mrs. March glanced at Meg, who was looking very pretty in her gingham morning-gown, with the little curls blowing about her forehead, and very womanly, as she sat sewing at her little work-table, full of tidy white rolls; so, unconscious of the thought in her mother's mind, she sewed and sung while her fingers flew, and her mind was busied with girlish fancies as innocent and fresh as the pansies in her belt, that Mrs. March smiled, and was satisfied.

"Two letters for Doctor Jo, a book, and a funny old hat, which covered the whole post-office, stuck outside," said Beth, laughing, as she went into the study, where Jo sat writing.

"What a sly fellow Laurie is! I said I wished bigger hats were the fashion, because I burn my face every hot day. He said, 'Why mind the fashion? wear a big hat, and be comfortable!' I said I would, if I had one, and he has sent me this, to try me; I'll wear it, for fun, and show him I *don't* care for the fashion;" and, hanging the antique broad-brim on a bust of Plato, Jo read her letters.

One from her mother made her cheeks glow, and her eyes fill, for it said to her,—

"MY DEAR:

"I write a little word to tell you with how much satisfaction I watch your efforts to control your temper. You say nothing about your trials, failures, or successes, and think, perhaps, that no one sees them but the Friend whose help you daily ask, if I may trust the well-worn cover of your guide-book.[3] *I*, too, have seen them all, and heartily believe in the sincerity of your resolution, since it begins to bear fruit. Go on, dear, patiently and bravely, and always believe that no one sympathizes more tenderly with you than your loving

MOTHER."

"That does me good! that's worth millions of money, and pecks of praise. Oh, Marmee, I do try! I will keep on trying, and not get tired, since I have you to help me."

Laying her head on her arms, Jo wet her little romance with a few happy tears, for she *had* thought that no one saw and appreciated her efforts to be good, and this assurance was doubly precious, doubly encouraging, because unexpected, and from the person whose commendation she most valued. Feeling stronger than ever to meet and subdue her Apollyon, she pinned the note inside her frock, as a shield and a reminder, lest she be taken unaware, and proceeded to open her other letter, quite ready for either good or bad news. In a big, dashing hand, Laurie wrote,—

"DEAR JO,

What ho!

Some English girls and boys are coming to see me to-morrow, and I want to have a jolly time. If it's fine, I'm going to pitch my tent in Longmeadow, and row up the whole crew to lunch and croquet;—have a fire, make messes, gypsy fashion, and all sorts of larks. They are nice people, and like such things. Brooke will go, to keep us boys steady, and Kate Vaughn will play propriety for the girls.[4] I want you all to come; can't let Beth off, at any price, and nobody shall worry her. Don't bother about rations,—I'll see to that, and everything else,—only do come, there's a good fellow!

"In a tearing hurry,[5]
Yours ever, LAURIE."

"Here's richness!" cried Jo, flying in to tell the news to Meg. "Of course we can go, mother! it will be such a help to Laurie, for I can row, and Meg see to the lunch, and the children be useful some way."

"I hope the Vaughn's are not fine, grown-up people. Do you know anything about them, Jo?" asked Meg.

"Only that there are four of them. Kate is older than you, Fred and Frank (twins) about my age, and a little girl (Grace), who is nine or ten. Laurie knew them abroad, and liked the boys; I fancied, from the way he primmed up his mouth in speaking of her, that he didn't admire Kate much."

"I'm so glad my French print is clean, it's just the thing, and so becoming!" observed Meg, complacently. "Have you anything decent, Jo?"

"Scarlet and gray boating suit, good enough for me; I shall row and tramp about, so I don't want any starch to think of. You'll come, Betty?"

"If you won't let any of the boys talk to me."

"Not a boy!"

"I like to please Laurie; and I'm not afraid of Mr. Brooke, he is so kind; but I don't want to play, or sing, or say anything. I'll

4. As the oldest female in the group, she will chaperone the girls.
5. Furious rush.

6. In "Louisa May Alcott: By the Original 'Goldilocks'" (1936), Maude Appleton McDowell wrote that May Alcott "was very like the pretty, young, artistic sister who said her greatest trial in life was her turn-up nose and who actually *did* put a clothespin on it to improve its shape" (quoted in *Her Own Time* 221). On January 5, 1869, May Alcott wrote to Alfred Whitman: "Did you recognize the Cyclops in Little Women & that horrid stupid Amy as something like me even to putting a cloths pin on her nose?" (Manuscript Letter, Houghton Library, Harvard University, bMS Am 1130[35]).

7. Leghorn hats were made with plaited dried and bleached straw. Originally they were imported from Leghorn in Tuscany. The *OED* lists the first usage of the term as an advertisement for the hat in the 1740 *Pennsylvania Gazette*.

work hard, and not trouble any one; and you'll take care of me, Jo, so I'll go."

"That's my good girl; you do try to fight off your shyness, and I love you for it; fighting faults isn't easy, as I know; and a cheery word kind of gives a lift. Thank you, mother," and Jo gave the thin cheek a grateful kiss, more precious to Mrs. March than if it had given her back the rosy roundness of her youth.

"I had a box of chocolate drops, and the picture I wanted to copy," said Amy, showing her mail.

"And I got a note from Mr. Laurence, asking me to come over and play to him to-night, before the lamps are lighted, and I shall go," added Beth, whose friendship with the old gentleman prospered finely.

"Now let's fly round, and do double duty today, so that we can play to-morrow with free minds," said Jo, preparing to replace her pen with a broom.

When the sun peeped into the girls' room early next morning, to promise them a fine day, he saw a comical sight. Each had made such preparation for the fête as seemed necessary and proper. Meg had an extra row of little curl papers across her forehead, Jo had copiously anointed her afflicted face with cold cream, Beth had taken Joanna to bed with her to atone for the approaching separation, and Amy had capped the climax by putting a clothes-pin on her nose, to uplift the offending feature.[6] It was one of the kind artists use to hold the paper on their drawing-boards; therefore, quite appropriate and effective for the purpose to which it was now put. This funny spectacle appeared to amuse the sun, for he burst out with such radiance that Jo woke up, and roused all her sisters by a hearty laugh at Amy's ornament.

Sunshine and laughter were good omens for a pleasure party, and soon a lively bustle began in both houses. Beth, who was ready first, kept reporting what went on next door, and enlivened her sisters' toilets by frequent telegrams from the window.

"There goes the man with the tent! I see Mrs. Barker doing up the lunch, in a hamper, and a great basket. Now Mr. Laurence is looking up at the sky, and the weathercock; I wish he would go, too! There's Laurie looking like a sailor,—nice boy! Oh, mercy

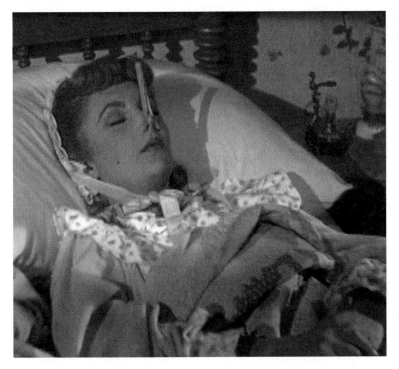

Amy (Elizabeth Taylor) with a clothespin on her nose in the 1949 film of *Little Women*.

me! here's a carriage full of people—a tall lady, a little girl, and two dreadful boys. One is lame; poor thing, he's got a crutch! Laurie didn't tell us that. Be quick, girls! it's getting late. Why, there is Ned Moffat, I do declare. Look, Meg! isn't that the man who bowed to you one day, when we were shopping?"

"So it is; how queer that he should come! I thought he was at the Mountains. There is Sallie; I'm glad she got back in time. Am I all right, Jo?" cried Meg, in a flutter.

"A regular daisy; hold up your dress, and put your hat straight; it looks sentimental tipped that way, and will fly off at the first puff. Now, then, come on!"

"Oh, oh, Jo! you ain't going to wear that awful hat? It's too absurd! You shall *not* make a guy of yourself," remonstrated Meg, as Jo tied down, with a red ribbon, the broad-brimmed, old-fashioned Leghorn[7] Laurie had sent for a joke.

"I just will, though! it's capital; so shady, light, and big. It will make fun; and I don't mind being a guy, if I'm comfortable." With that Jo marched straight away, and the rest followed; a bright little

8. Two possible definitions exist for how LMA uses *jaunty* here. According to the *OED,* it could mean "stylish," but it could also mean "affecting airy self-satisfaction or unconcern."

9. A light rowboat.

10. LMA may have chosen this exclamation for Jo to denote her spirit. As she writes in "Recollections of My Childhood" (1888): "Being born on the birthday of Columbus I seem to have something of my patron saint's spirit of adventure" (quoted in *Her Own Time* 33). Columbus's birthday is unknown, but is believed to be before October 31, 1451; LMA was born on November 29, 1832. The exclamation was an acceptable substitute that LMA could use instead of an expression like "For Christ's Sake" or "Holy Cow." In the 1933 film version of *Little Women,* Katherine Hepburn would make this expression effective and memorable.

11. Probably opera glasses or a small spyglass.

band of sisters, all looking their best, in summer suits, with happy faces, under the jaunty[8] hat-brims.

Laurie ran to meet, and present them to his friends, in the most cordial manner. The lawn was the reception room, and for several minutes a lively scene was enacted there. Meg was grateful to see that Miss Kate, though twenty, was dressed with a simplicity which American girls would do well to imitate; and she was much flattered by Mr. Ned's assurances that he came especially to see her. Jo understood why Laurie "primmed up his mouth" when speaking of Kate, for that young lady had a stand-off-don't-touch-me air, which contrasted strongly with the free and easy demeanor of the other girls. Beth took an observation of the new boys, and decided that the lame one was not "dreadful," but gentle and feeble, and she would be kind to him, on that account. Amy found Grace a well-mannered, merry little person; and, after staring dumbly at one another for a few minutes, they suddenly became very good friends.

Tents, lunch, and croquet utensils having been sent on beforehand, the party was soon embarked, and the two boats pushed off together, leaving Mr. Laurence waving his hat on the shore. Laurie and Jo rowed one boat; Mr. Brooke and Ned the other; while Fred Vaughn, the riotous twin, did his best to upset both, by paddling about in a wherry,[9] like a disturbed water-bug. Jo's funny hat deserved a vote of thanks, for it was of general utility; it broke the ice in the beginning, by producing a laugh; it created quite a refreshing breeze, flapping to and fro, as she rowed, and would make an excellent umbrella for the whole party, if a shower came up, she said. Kate looked rather amazed at Jo's proceedings, especially as she exclaimed "Christopher Columbus!"[10] when she lost her oar; and Laurie said, "My dear fellow, did I hurt you?" when he tripped over her feet in taking his place. But after putting up her glass[11] to examine the queer girl several times, Miss Kate decided that she was "odd, but rather clever," and smiled upon her from afar.

Meg, in the other boat, was delightfully situated, face to face with the rowers, who both admired the prospect, and feathered their oars with uncommon "skill and dexterity." Mr. Brooke was a

The Old North Bridge (a replica) crosses the Concord River. The Concord River, a tributary of the Merrimack River, is formed by the confluence of the Assabet and Sudbury rivers. On April 19, 1775, the bridge was the site of the Battle of Concord, the skirmish that ignited the Revolutionary War. With its calm, slow-moving water, the river was a favorite spot for picnics and boating in the nineteenth century.

grave, silent young man, with handsome brown eyes, and a pleasant voice. Meg liked his quiet manners, and considered him a walking encyclopædia of useful knowledge. He never talked to her much; but he looked at her a good deal, and she felt sure that he did not regard her with aversion. Ned being in college, of course put on all the airs which Freshmen think it their bounden duty to assume; he was not very wise, but very good-natured and merry,[a] and, altogether, an excellent person to carry on a picnic. Sallie Gardiner was absorbed in keeping her white piquè[12] dress clean, and chattering with the ubiquitous Fred, who kept Beth in constant terror by his pranks.

It was not far to Longmeadow; but the tent was pitched, and the wickets down, by the time they arrived. A pleasant green field, with three wide-spreading oaks in the middle, and a smooth strip of turf for croquet.[13]

"Welcome to Camp Laurence!" said the young host, as they landed, with exclamations of delight. "Brooke is commander-in-chief; I am commissary-general;[14] the other fellows are staff-officers; and you, ladies, are company. The tent is for your especial benefit, and that oak is your drawing-room; this is the mess-

12. A lightly woven fabric with a ribbed pattern.

13. Croquet is a lawn game played by hitting wooden balls through wickets with mallets. The sport of croquet, brought to England from France in the early seventeenth century, was originally known as pall mall. The first set of rules of the modern game called croquet was devised by Isaac Spratt in 1856 in London. During the 1860s, the game became extremely popular in England and in America. May Alcott especially enjoyed the game. In her journal for 1863, she first mentions playing croquet at the home of Edith Emerson (the second daughter of Ralph Waldo Emerson), and by the middle of May 1863, she notes that she has her own set. In June, she records that she "played Croquet from 9 A M to 9 P.M. Not a very useful day but I am considered a fine player which is very gratifying" (Houghton Library, Harvard University bMS Am 1817 [56]). While in Vevey, Switzerland, with LMA in 1870, she wrote to Anna: "We also have croquet from morning till night . . . and as I cannot use my eyes much I am glad to play at all hours. They call me Mlle Mitrailleuse after the famous French gun." (*Little Women Abroad* 194).

14. In military terms, one who is responsible for meals and supplies.

Croquet was a popular outdoor game during the last half of the nineteenth century and a favorite of May Alcott's.

15. Dining hall.

16. A popular phrase after the American Revolution with a number of newspapers adopting it for their masthead. It conveys the great enthusiasm that American colonists showed for the Declaration of Independence in 1776 and the Revolution. Concord was especially proud of its role in the fight. The Revolutionary War began when British troops and local militiamen clashed at Lexington and Concord on April 19, 1775. In Ralph Waldo Emerson's "Concord Hymn," a poem written for the dedication of the obelisk at the Old North Bridge on July 4, 1837, he memorialized the American War for Independence, the battles fought at Concord and Lexington, and especially the spirit of the Revolution. The first stanza contains Emerson's most famous lines: "By the rude bridge that arched the flood, / Their flag to April's breeze unfurled, / Here once the embattled farmers stood, / And fired the shot heard round the world." LMA was not quite four years old when James Madison, the last of the surviving Founders, died in 1836.

room,[15] and the third is the camp kitchen. Now let's have a game before it gets hot, and then we'll see about dinner."

Frank, Beth, Amy, and Grace, sat down to watch the game played by the other eight. Mr. Brooke chose Meg, Kate, and Fred; Laurie took Sallie, Jo, and Ned. The Englishers played well; but the Americans played better, and contested every inch of the ground as strongly as if the spirit of '76[16] inspired them. Jo and Fred had several skirmishes, and once narrowly escaped high words. Jo was through the last wicket, and had missed the stroke, which failure ruffled her a good deal. Fred was close behind her, and his turn came before hers; he gave a stroke, his ball hit the wicket, and stopped an inch on the wrong side. No one was very near; and, running up to examine, he gave it a sly nudge with his toe, which put it just an inch on the right side.

"I'm through! now, Miss Jo, I'll settle you, and get in first," cried the young gentleman, swinging his mallet for another blow.

"You pushed it; I saw you; it's my turn now," said Jo, sharply.

LITTLE WOMEN

"Upon my word I didn't move it! it rolled a bit, perhaps, but that is allowed; so stand off, please, and let me have a go at the stake."

"We don't cheat in America; but *you* can, if you choose," said Jo, angrily.

"Yankees[17] are a deal[18] the most tricky, everybody knows. There you go," returned Fred, croqueting her ball far away.

Jo opened her lips to say something rude; but checked herself in time, colored up to her forehead, and stood a minute, hammering down a wicket with all her might, while Fred hit the stake, and declared himself out, with much exultation. She went off to get her ball, and was a long time finding it, among the bushes; but she came back, looking cool and quiet, and waited her turn patiently. It took several strokes to regain the place she had lost; and, when she got there, the other side had nearly won, for Kate's ball was the last but one, and lay near the stake.

"By George, it's all up with us! Good-by, Kate; Miss Jo owes me one, so you are finished," cried Fred, excitedly, as they all drew near to see the finish.

"Yankees have a trick of being generous to their enemies," said Jo, with a look that made the lad redden, "especially when they beat them," she added, as, leaving Kate's ball untouched, she won the game by a clever stroke.

Laurie threw up his hat; then remembered that it wouldn't do to exult over the defeat of his guests, and stopped in the middle of a cheer to whisper to his friend,—

"Good for you, Jo! he did cheat, I saw him; we can't tell him so, but he won't do it again, take my word for it."

Meg drew her aside, under pretence of pinning up a loose braid, and said, approvingly—,

"It was dreadfully provoking; but you kept your temper, and I'm so glad, Jo."

"Don't praise me, Meg, for I could box his ears this minute. I should certainly have boiled over, if I hadn't stayed among the nettles till I got my rage under enough to hold my tongue. It's simmering now, so I hope he'll keep out of my way," returned Jo, biting her lips, as she glowered at Fred from under her big hat.

17. *Yankee* originally referred to a person from New England. The *OED* records the first use of the word in *Oppression, a poem by an American* (1765). The etymology of *Yankee* is unclear, but the OED notes: "Perhaps the most plausible conjecture is that it comes from Dutch *Janke,* diminutive of *Jan* John, applied as a derisive nickname by either Dutch or English in the New England states (J. N. A. Thierry, 1838, in *Life of Ticknor,* 1876, II. vii. 124)."

18. Very much.

19. Suffering from dyspepsia, a condition of indigestion, of feeling full before eating much.

20. A key reserve held back for use at an opportune time. The phrase comes from a card game in which a trump card outranks all others and is held back in order to win a trick.

"Time for lunch," said Mr. Brooke, looking at his watch. "Commissary-general, will you make the fire, and get water, while Miss March, Miss Sallie, and I spread the table. Who can make good coffee?"

"Jo can," said Meg, glad to recommend her sister. So Jo, feeling that her late lessons in cookery were to do her honor, went to preside over the coffee-pot, while the children collected dry sticks, and the boys made a fire, and got water from a spring near by. Miss Kate sketched, and Frank talked to Beth, who was making little mats of braided rushes, to serve as plates.

The commander-in-chief and his aids soon spread the table-cloth with an inviting array of eatables and drinkables, prettily decorated with green leaves. Jo announced that the coffee was ready, and every one settled themselves to a hearty meal; for youth is seldom dyspeptic,[19] and exercise develops wholesome appetites. A very merry lunch it was; for everything seemed fresh and funny, and frequent peals of laughter startled a venerable horse, who fed near by. There was a pleasing inequality in the table, which produced many mishaps to cups and plates; acorns dropped into the milk, little black ants partook of the refreshments without being invited, and fuzzy caterpillars swung down from the tree, to see what was going on. Three white-headed children peeped over the fence, and an objectionable dog barked at them from the other side of the river, with all his might and main.

"There's salt, here, if you prefer it," said Laurie, as he handed Jo a saucer of berries.

"Thank you; I prefer spiders," she replied, fishing up two unwary little ones, who had gone to a creamy death. "How dare you remind me of that horrid dinner-party, when yours is so nice in every way?" added Jo, as they both laughed, and ate out of one plate, the china having run short.

"I had an uncommonly good time that day, and haven't got over it yet. This is no credit to me, you know; I don't do anything; it's you, and Meg, and Brooke, who make it go, and I'm no end obliged to you. What shall we do when we can't eat any more?" asked Laurie, feeling that his trump card[20] had been played when lunch was over.

LITTLE WOMEN

"Have games, till it's cooler. I brought 'Authors,'[21] and I dare say Miss Kate knows something new and nice. Go and ask her; she's company, and you ought to stay with her more."

"Aren't you company, too? I thought she'd suit Brooke; but he keeps talking to Meg, and Kate just stares at them through that ridiculous glass of hers. I'm going, so you needn't try to preach propriety, for you can't do it, Jo."

Miss Kate did know several new games; and as the girls would not, and the boys could not, eat any more, they all adjourned to the drawing-room, to play "Rigmarole."[22]

"One person begins a story, any nonsense you like, and tells as long as they[b] please, only taking care to stop short at some exciting point, when the next takes it up, and does the same. It's very funny, when well done, and makes a perfect jumble of tragical comical stuff to laugh over. Please start it, Mr. Brooke," said Kate, with a commanding gesture,[c] which surprised Meg, who treated the tutor with as much respect as any other gentleman.

21. *Authors* was a card game first produced by G. M. Whipple and A. A. Smith of Salem, Mass., in 1861. This popular game, which still exists today, was created by Anne Abbott (1808–1908) of Beverly, Mass., who also created one of the earliest American board games, *The Mansion of Happiness,* in 1843. Similar to the British *Mansion of Bliss* (1822), Abbott's game depicts a spiral path on which players race as they spin a teetotum to move along spaces marked with vices and virtues on the journey to heaven. Abbott was a writer, reviewer, and, from 1851 to 1858, the editor of *The Children's Friend,* a periodical for young people. On May 11, 1863, May Alcott mentions in her journal that she played *Authors* (Houghton Library, Harvard University, bMS Am 1817 [56]). LMA herself was one of the first American women writers to be included in *Authors.*

22. The game is aptly named because *rigmarole* is a story that is considered incoherent or nonsensical. The word itself, according to the *OED,* comes from *Ragman Roll,* a term whose first usage was around 1393: "A game of chance in which players draw out an item in a roll of writing, by pulling a string to which it is attached."

Lying on the grass, at the feet of the two young ladies, Mr. Brooke obediently began the story, with the handsome brown eyes steadily fixed upon the sunshiny river.

"Once on a time, a knight went out into the world to seek his fortune, for he had nothing but his sword and his shield. He travelled a long while, nearly eight-and-twenty years, and had a hard time of it, till he came to the palace of a good old king, who had offered a reward to any one who would tame and train a fine, but unbroken colt, of which he was very fond. The knight agreed to try, and got on slowly, but surely; for the colt was a gallant fellow, and soon learned to love his new master, though he was freakish and wild. Every day, when he gave his lessons to this pet of the king's, the knight rode him through the city; and, as he rode, he looked everywhere for a certain beautiful face, which he had seen many times in his dreams, but never found. One day, as he went prancing down a quiet street, he saw at the window of a ruinous castle the lovely face. He was delighted, inquired who lived in this old castle, and was told that several captive princesses were kept there by a spell, and spun all day to lay up money to buy their liberty. The knight wished intensely that he could free them; but he was poor, and could only go by each day, watching for the sweet face, and longing to see it out in the sunshine. At last, he resolved to get into the castle, and ask how he could help them. He went and knocked; the great door flew open, and he beheld—"

"A ravishingly lovely lady, who exclaimed, with a cry of rapture, 'At last! at last!;" continued Kate, who had read French novels, and admired the style. "'Tis she!' cried Count Gustave, and fell at her feet in an ecstasy of joy. 'Oh, rise!' she said, extending a hand of marble fairness. 'Never! till you tell me how I may rescue you,' swore the knight, still kneeling. 'Alas, my cruel fate condemns me to remain here till my tyrant is destroyed.' 'Where is the villain?' 'In the mauve salon; go, brave heart, and save me from despair.' 'I obey, and return victorious or dead!' With these thrilling words he rushed away, and, flinging open the door of the mauve salon, was about to enter, when he received—"

"A stunning blow from the big Greek lexicon, which an old fellow in a black gown fired at him," said Ned. "Instantly Sir What's-his-name recovered himself, pitched the tyrant out of the window, and turned to join the lady, victorious, but with a bump on his brow; found the door locked, tore up the curtains, made a rope ladder, got half-way down when ladder broke, and he went head first into the moat, sixty feet below. Could swim like a duck, paddled round the castle till he came to a little door guarded by two stout fellows; knocked their heads together till they cracked like a couple of nuts, then, by a trifling exertion of his prodigious strength, he smashed in the door, went up a pair of stone steps covered with dust a foot thick, toads as big as your fist, and spiders that would frighten you into hysterics, Miss March. At the top of these steps he came plump upon a sight that took his breath away and chilled his blood—"

"A tall figure, all in white, with a veil over its face, and a lamp in its wasted hand," went on Meg. "It beckoned, gliding noiselessly before him down a corridor as dark and cold as any tomb. Shadowy effigies in armor stood on either side, a dead silence reigned, the lamp burned blue, and the ghostly figure ever and anon turned its face toward him, showing the glitter of awful eyes through its white veil. They reached a curtained door, behind which sounded lovely music; he sprang forward to enter, but the spectre plucked him back, and waved, threateningly, before him a—"

"Snuff-box,"[23] said Jo, in a sepulchral tone, which convulsed the audience. "'Thankee,' said the knight, politely, as he took a pinch, and sneezed seven times so violently that his head fell off. 'Ha! ha!' laughed the ghost; and, having peeped through the key-hole at the princesses spinning away for dear life, the evil spirit picked up her victim and put him in a large tin box, where there were eleven other knights packed together without their heads, like sardines, who all rose and began to—"

"Dance a hornpipe,"[24] cut in Fred, as Jo paused for breath; "and, as they danced, the rubbishy old castle turned to a man-of-war[25] in full sail. 'Up with the jib,[26] reef the tops'l halliards,[27] helm hard a lee,[28] and man the guns,' roared the captain, as a Portuguese pirate hove in sight, with a flag black as ink flying from her foremast. 'Go in and win my hearties,' says the captain; and a tre-

23. Snuff, pulverized tobacco that is inhaled or applied to the gums, was popular in the eighteenth and nineteenth century among both men and women.

24. A solo dance to a hornpipe (a reed instrument) performed by British sailors.

25. A warship.

26. A triangular sail that stretches from the foremast to the jib beam.

27. To reduce the size of the highest sail by pulling on the halyards, lines that lower or hoist the sail.

28. Steer the ship away from the direction the wind is blowing.

29. Opening on the side of a ship's deck that allows water—or in this case, blood—to drain. The *lee side* is the side away from the direction the wind is blowing.

30. A shortened form of boatswain's mate, an assistant to the officer in charge of the ship's rigging and deck crew.

31. Fred means for the mate to take a loop in one sheet of the dangling or loose jib sail's sheet, which is a rope that is attached to one or both of the lower corners of a sail, and to tie the hands of the pirate before he is forced to walk off a plank extending over the side of the ship.

32. Sailors.

33. To sink the ship by cutting a hole in its hull.

34. Fred is quoting a jump-rope rhyme: "Columbus went to sea, sea, sea / To see what he could see, see, see. / But all that he could see, see, see / Was the bottom on the sea, sea, sea."

mendous fight begun. Of course the British beat—they always do; and, having taken the pirate captain prisoner,[d] sailed slap over the schooner, whose decks were piled with dead, and whose lee-scuppers[29] ran blood, for the order had been 'Cutlasses, and die hard.' 'Bosen's mate,[30] take a bight of the flying jib sheet, and start this villain[31] if he don't confess his sins double quick,' said the British captain. The Portuguese held his tongue like a brick, and walked the plank, while the jolly tars[32] cheered like mad. But the sly dog dived, came up under the man-of-war, scuttled her,[33] and down she went, with all sail set, 'To the bottom of the sea, sea, sea,' where—"[34]

"Oh, gracious! what *shall* I say?" cried Sallie, as Fred ended his rigmarole, in which he had jumbled together, pell-mell, nautical phrases and facts, out of one of his favorite books. "Well, they went to the bottom, and a nice mermaid welcomed them, but was much grieved on finding the box of headless knights, and kindly pickled them in brine, hoping to discover the mystery about them; for, being a woman, she was curious. By and by a diver came down, and the mermaid said, 'I'll give you this box of pearls if you can take it up;' for she wanted to restore the poor things to life, and couldn't raise the heavy load herself. So the diver hoisted it up, and was much disappointed, on opening it, to find no pearls. He left it in a great lonely field, where it was found by a—"

"Little goose-girl, who kept a hundred fat geese in the field," said Amy, when Sallie's invention gave out. "The little girl was sorry for them, and asked an old woman what she should do to help them. 'Your geese will tell you, they know everything,' said the old woman. So she asked what she should use for new heads, since the old ones were lost, and all the geese opened their hundred mouths, and screamed—"

"'Cabbages!' continued Laurie, promptly. 'Just the thing,' said the girl, and ran to get twelve fine ones from her garden. She put them on, the knights revived at once, thanked her, and went on their way rejoicing, never knowing the difference, for there were so many other heads like them in the world, that no one thought anything of it. The knight in whom I'm interested went back to

LITTLE WOMEN

find the pretty face, and learned that the princesses had spun themselves free, and all gone to be married, but one. He was in a great state of mind at that; and, mounting the colt, who stood by him through thick and thin, rushed to the castle to see which was left. Peeping over the hedge, he saw the queen of his affections picking flowers in her garden. 'Will you give me a rose?' said he. 'You must come and get it; I can't come to you; it isn't proper,' said she, as sweet as honey. He tried to climb over the hedge, but it seemed to grow higher and higher; then he tried to push through, but it grew thicker and thicker, and he was in despair. So he patiently broke twig after twig, till he had made a little hole, through which he peeped, saying, imploringly, 'Let me in! let me in!' But the pretty princess did not seem to understand, for she picked her roses quietly, and left him to fight his way in. Whether he did or not, Frank will tell you."

"I can't; I'm not playing, I never do," said Frank, dismayed at the sentimental predicament out of which he was to rescue the absurd couple. Beth had disappeared behind Jo, and Grace was asleep.

"So the poor knight is to be left sticking in the hedge, is he?" asked Mr. Brooke, still watching the river, and playing with the wild rose in his button-hole.

"I guess the princess gave him a posy, and opened the gate, after awhile," said Laurie, smiling to himself, as he threw acorns at his tutor.

"What a piece of nonsense we have made! With practice we might do something quite clever. Do you know 'Truth?'"[35] asked Sallie, after they had laughed over their story.

"I hope so," said Meg, soberly.

"The game, I mean?"

"What is it?" said Fred.

"Why, you pile up your hands, choose a number, and draw out in turn, and the person who draws at the number has to answer truly any questions put by the rest. It's great fun."

"Let's try it," said Jo, who liked new experiments.

Miss Kate and Mr. Brooke, Meg and Ned, declined; but Fred, Sallie, Jo and Laurie piled and drew; and the lot fell to Laurie.

35. In her journal of August 11, 1863, May Alcott describes a game similar to Truth, called Candor, which she played with friends: "Had tea at ten & then played Candor on the wharf, which was the greatest fun as all had to answer with perfect truth all kinds of trying questions we played till very late, forming ourselves into the C. C. or Candor Club to meet regularly every evening in boats if possible so as to prevent any one hearing our confidential conversations" (Manuscript journal, Houghton Library, Harvard University, bMS Am1817 [57]).

36. *The Sea-Lion; or, The Privateer of Penobscot: A Story of the Ocean Life and the Heart's Love* (1853) by Sylvanus Cobb, Jr. (1823–1887). Cobb, a popular writer of sensational fiction, amassed great wealth from the hundreds of stories and novels that he published, including tales for *The Flag of Our Union,* a periodical for which LMA contributed a number of thrillers during the mid-1860s.

37. A typical Englishman. The term comes from John Arbuthnot (1667–1735), an English physician, writer, and mathematician, who in 1712 published a series of five satiric pamphlets featuring the character John Bull that collectively became *The History of John Bull.*

38. Disturb or inflict torment upon.

"Who are your heroes?" asked Jo.

"Grandfather and Napoleon."

"What lady do you think prettiest?" said Sallie.

"Margaret."

"Which do you like best?" from Fred.

"Jo, of course."

"What silly questions you ask!" and Jo gave a disdainful shrug as the rest laughed at Laurie's matter-of-fact tone.

"Try again; Truth isn't a bad game," said Fred.

"It's a very good one for you," retorted Jo, in a low voice.

Her turn came next.

"What is your greatest fault?" asked Fred, by way of testing in her the virtue he lacked himself.

"A quick temper."

"What do you most wish for?" said Laurie.

"A pair of boot-lacings," returned Jo, guessing and defeating his purpose.

"Not a true answer; you must say what you really do want most."

"Genius; don't you wish you could give it to me, Laurie?" and she slyly smiled in his disappointed face.

"What virtues do you most admire in a man?" asked Sallie.

"Courage and honesty."

"Now my turn," said Fred, as his hand came last.

"Let's give it to him," whispered Laurie to Jo, who nodded, and asked at once,

"Didn't you cheat at croquet?"

"Well, yes, a little bit."

"Good! Didn't you take your story out of 'The Sea Lion?'"[36] said Laurie.

"Rather."

"Don't you think the English nation perfect in every respect?" asked Sallie.

"I should be ashamed of myself if I didn't."

"He's a true John Bull.[37] Now, Miss Sallie, you shall have a chance without waiting to draw. I'll harrow up[38] your feelings first by asking if you don't think you are something of a flirt," said Laurie, as Jo nodded to Fred, as a sign that peace was declared.

"You impertinent boy! of course I'm not," exclaimed Sallie, with an air that proved the contrary.

"What do you hate most?" asked Fred.

"Spiders and rice pudding."

"What do you like best?" asked Jo.

"Dancing and French gloves."

"Well, *I* think Truth is a very silly play; let's have a sensible game of Authors, to refresh our minds," proposed Jo.

Ned, Frank, and the little girls joined in this, and, while it went on, the three elders sat apart, talking. Miss Kate took out her sketch again, and Margaret watched her, while Mr. Brooke lay on the grass, with a book, which he did not read.

"How beautifully you do it; I wish I could draw," said Meg, with mingled admiration and regret in her voice.

"Why don't you learn? I should think you had taste and talent for it," replied Miss Kate, graciously.

"I haven't time."

"Your mamma prefers other accomplishments, I fancy. So did mine; but I proved to her that I had talent, by taking a few lessons privately, and then she was quite willing I should go on. Can't you do the same with your governess?"

"I have none."

"I forgot; young ladies in America go to school more than with us. Very fine schools they are, too, papa says. You go to a private one, I suppose?"

"I don't go at all; I am a governess myself."

"Oh, indeed!" said Miss Kate; but she might as well have said, "Dear me, how dreadful!" for her tone implied it, and something in her face made Meg color, and wish she had not been so frank.

Mr. Brooke looked up, and said, quickly, "Young ladies in America love independence as much as their ancestors did, and are admired and respected for supporting themselves."

"Oh, yes; of course! it's very nice and proper in them to do so. We have many most respectable and worthy young women, who

39. *Mary Stuart* (1800), the five-act tragedy by the German writer Friedrich von Schiller. The drama depicts the final days of Mary Stuart, who is imprisoned in England by her cousin Queen Elizabeth I because Mary is a claimant to the British throne. In 1852, LMA listed Schiller's plays as among her favorite works (*Journals* 67). Schiller was one of Anna Alcott's favorite playwrights. She translated Schiller's play *The Maid of Orleans* (1801), and her handwritten manuscript, dated September 1, 1852, is located at Houghton Library, Harvard University (MS Am 1130.14[8]).

40. Meg, without knowing it, insults Kate's reading as unpoetical, a fact that amuses John.

do the same; and are employed by the nobility, because, being the daughters of gentlemen, they are both well-bred and accomplished, you know," said Miss Kate, in a patronizing tone, that hurt Meg's pride, and made her work seem not only more distasteful, but degrading.

"Did the German song suit, Miss March?" inquired Mr. Brooke, breaking an awkward pause.

"Oh, yes! it was very sweet, and I'm much obliged to whoever translated it for me;" and Meg's downcast face brightened as she spoke.

"Don't you read German?" asked Miss Kate, with a look of surprise.

"Not very well. My father, who taught me, is away, and I don't get on very fast alone, for I've no one to correct my pronunciation."

"Try a little now; here is Schiller's 'Mary Stuart,'[39] and a tutor who loves to teach," and Mr. Brooke laid his book on her lap, with an inviting smile.

"It's so hard, I'm afraid to try," said Meg, grateful, but bashful in the presence of the accomplished young lady beside her.

"I'll read a bit, to encourage you;" and Miss Kate read one of the most beautiful passages, in a perfectly correct, but perfectly expressionless, manner.

Mr. Brooke made no comment, as she returned the book to Meg, who said, innocently,—

"I thought it was poetry."[40]

"Some of it is; try this passage."

There was a queer smile about Mr. Brooke's mouth, as he opened at poor Mary's lament.

Meg, obediently following the long grass-blade which her new tutor used to point with, read, slowly and timidly, unconsciously making poetry of the hard words, by the soft intonation of her musical voice. Down the page went the green guide, and presently, forgetting her listener in the beauty of the sad scene, Meg read as if alone, giving a little touch of tragedy to the words of the unhappy queen. If she had seen the brown eyes then, she would have stopped short; but she never looked up, and the lesson was not spoilt for her.

"Very well, indeed!" said Mr. Brooke, as she paused, quite ignoring her many mistakes, and looking as if he did, indeed, "love to teach."

Miss Kate put up her glass, and, having taken a survey of the little tableau before her, shut her sketchbook, saying, with condescension,—

"You've a nice accent, and, in time, will be a clever reader. I advise you to learn, for German is a valuable accomplishment to teachers. I must look after Grace, she is romping;" and Miss Kate strolled away, adding to herself, with a shrug, "I didn't come to chaperone a governess, though she *is* young and pretty. What odd people these Yankees are! I'm afraid Laurie will be quite spoilt among them."

"I forgot that English people rather turn up their noses at governesses, and don't treat them as we do," said Meg, looking after the retreating figure with an annoyed expression.

"Tutors, also, have rather a hard time of it there, as I know to my sorrow. There's no place like America for us workers, Miss Margaret," and Mr. Brooke looked so contented and cheerful, that Meg was ashamed to lament her hard lot.

"I'm glad I live in it, then. I don't like my work, but I get a good deal of satisfaction out of it, after all, so I won't complain; I only wish I liked teaching as you do."

"I think you would, if you had Laurie for a pupil. I shall be very sorry to lose him next year," said Mr. Brooke, busily punching holes in the turf.

"Going to college, I suppose?" Meg's lips asked that question, but her eyes added, "And what becomes of you?"

"Yes; it's high time he went, for he is nearly ready, and as soon as he is off I shall turn soldier."ᵉ

"I'm glad of that!" exclaimed Meg; "I should think every young man would want to go; though it is hard for the mothers and sisters, who stay at home," she added, sorrowfully.

"I have neither, and very few friends, to care whether I live

41. Edward Emerson, in "When Louisa Alcott Was a Girl" (1898), recalled that May Alcott "was overflowing with spirits and energy, danced well, and rode recklessly whenever she could, by rare chance, come by a saddle-horse for an hour" (quoted in *Her Own Time* 95).

42. In *A Hunger for Home: Louisa May Alcott's Place in American Culture* (New Brunswick: Rutgers University Press, 1987), Sarah Elbert notes that Jo sits in an apple tree reading Susan B. Warner's popular book *The Wide Wide World* (1852), and that the "March sisters, in fact, name their apple tree 'Ellen-tree' after Ellen Montgomery, the orphaned heroine of that story. Amy and Jo . . . use the tree as a hobby horse, not being fortunate enough to get a real pony as Ellen does in Warner's novel" (197).

43. Grace is referring to Rotten Row, a broad roadway through Hyde Park in London. Created by William III in 1690, it was known originally as Route de Roi (King's Road in French) but became known popularly as Rotten Row.

or die," said Mr. Brooke, rather bitterly, as he absently put the dead rose in the hole he had made, and covered it up, like a little grave.

"Laurie and his grandfather would care a great deal, and we should all be very sorry to have any harm happen to you," said Meg, heartily.

"Thank you; that sounds pleasant," began Mr. Brooke, looking cheerful again; but, before he could finish his speech, Ned, mounted on the old horse, came lumbering up, to display his equestrian skill before the young ladies, and there was no more quiet that day.

"Don't you love to ride?" asked Grace of Amy, as they stood resting, after a race round the field with the others, led by Ned.

"I dote upon it;[41] my sister Meg used to ride, when papa was rich, but we don't keep any horses now,—except Ellen Tree,"[42] added Amy, laughing.

"Tell me about Ellen Tree; is it a donkey?" asked Grace, curiously.

"Why, you see, Jo is crazy about horses, and so am I, but we've only got an old side-saddle, and no horse. Out in our garden is an apple-tree, that has a nice low branch; so I[f] put the saddle on it, fixed some reins on the part that turns up, and we bounce away on Ellen Tree whenever we like."

"How funny!" laughed Grace. "I have a pony at home, and ride nearly every day in the park, with Fred and Kate; it's very nice, for my friends go too, and the Row[43] is full of ladies and gentlemen."

"Dear, how charming! I hope I shall go abroad, some day; but I'd rather go to Rome than the Row," said Amy, who had not the remotest idea what the Row was, and wouldn't have asked for the world.

Frank, sitting just behind the little girls, heard what they were saying, and pushed his crutch away from him with an impatient gesture, as he watched the active lads going through all sorts of comical gymnastics. Beth, who was collecting the scattered Author-cards, looked up, and said, in her shy yet friendly way,—

"I'm afraid you are tired; can I do anything for you?"

"Talk to me, please; it's dull, sitting by myself," answered Frank, who had evidently been used to being made much of at home.

If he had asked her to deliver a Latin oration, it would not have seemed a more impossible task to bashful Beth; but there was no place to run to, no Jo to hide behind now, and the poor boy looked so wistfully at her, that she bravely resolved to try.

"What do you like to talk about?" she asked, fumbling over the cards, and dropping half as she tried to tie them up.

"Well, I like to hear about cricket, and boating, and hunting," said Frank, who had not yet learned to suit his amusements to his strength.

"My heart! whatever shall I do! I don't know anything about them," thought Beth; and, forgetting the boy's misfortune in her flurry, she said, hoping to make him talk, "I never saw any hunting, but I suppose you know all about it."

"I did once; but I'll never hunt again, for I got hurt leaping a confounded five-barred gate;[44] so there's no more horses and hounds for me," said Frank, with a sigh that made Beth hate herself for her innocent blunder.

"Your deer are much prettier than our ugly buffaloes," she said, turning to the prairies for help, and feeling glad that she had read one of the boys' books in which Jo delighted.

Buffaloes proved soothing and satisfactory; and, in her eagerness to amuse another, Beth forgot herself, and was quite unconscious of her sister's surprise and delight at the unusual spectacle of Beth talking away to one of the dreadful boys, against whom she had begged protection.

"Bless her heart! She pities him, so she is good to him," said Jo, beaming at her from the croquet-ground.

"I always said she was a little saint," added Meg, as if there could be no further doubt of it.

"I haven't heard Frank laugh so much for ever so long," said Grace to Amy, as they sat discussing dolls, and making tea-sets out of the acorn-cups.

"My sister Beth is a very fastidious girl, when she likes to be," said Amy, well pleased at Beth's success. She meant "fascinating,"

45. They marched in a procession like a circus parade. Fox and goose is a game of chase or tag in which one person attempts to catch others as they run from one goal to another.

46. The lines are from the 1840 four-stanza poem "Serenade," by James Russell Lowell (1819–1891), American poet and the first editor of *The Atlantic Monthly*. Each stanza closes with the refrain: "Alone, alone! ah woe! alone!" The poem was set to music several times in the nineteenth century, beginning in 1855 by Elizabeth Philip. In 1864, George Boweryem set it to music again, making it a popular song titled "Alone! Alone!"

but, as Grace didn't know the exact meaning of either word, "fastidious" sounded well, and made a good impression.

An impromptu circus, fox and geese,[45] and an amicable game of croquet, finished the afternoon. At sunset the tent was struck, hampers packed, wickets pulled up, boats loaded, and the whole party floated down the river, singing at the tops of their voices. Ned, getting sentimental, warbled a serenade with the pensive refrain,—

"Alone, alone, ah! woe, alone,"

and at the lines—

"We each are young, we each have a heart,
Oh, why should we stand thus coldly apart?"[46]

he looked at Meg with such a lackadaisical expression, that she laughed outright, and spoilt his song.

"How can you be so cruel to me?" he whispered, under cover of a lively chorus; "you've kept close to that starched-up English woman all day, and now you snub me."

"I didn't mean to; but you looked so funny I really couldn't help it," replied Meg, passing over the first part of his reproach; for it was quite true that she *had* shunned him, remembering the Moffat party and the talk after it.

Ned was offended, and turned to Sallie for consolation, saying to her, rather pettishly, "There isn't a bit of flirt in that girl, is there?"

"Not a particle; but she's a dear," returned Sallie, defending her friend even while confessing her shortcomings.

"She's not a stricken deer, any-way," said Ned, trying to be witty, and succeeding as well as very young gentlemen usually do.

On the lawn where it had gathered, the little party separated with cordial good-nights and good-byes, for the Vaughns were going to Canada. As the four sisters went home through the garden, Miss Kate looked after them, saying, without the patronizing tone in her voice, "In spite of their demonstrative manners, American girls are very nice when one knows them."

"I quite agree with you," said Mr. Brooke.

Chapter 13

Castles in the Air

L AURIE lay luxuriously swinging to and fro in his hammock, one warm September afternoon, wondering what
his neighbors were about, but too lazy to go and find out. He was
in one of his moods; for the day had been both unprofitable and
unsatisfactory, and he was wishing he could live it over again. The
hot weather made him indolent; and he had shirked his studies,
tried Mr. Brooke's patience to the utmost, displeased his grandfather by practising half the afternoon, frightened the maid-servants
half out of their wits, by mischievously hinting that one of his
dogs was going mad, and, after high words with the stableman
about some fancied neglect of his horse, he had flung himself into
his hammock, to fume over the stupidity of the world in general,
till the peace of the lovely day quieted him in spite of himself.
Staring up into the green gloom of the horse-chestnut trees above
him, he dreamed dreams of all sorts, and was just imagining himself tossing on the ocean, in a voyage round the world, when the
sound of voices brought him ashore in a flash. Peeping through
the meshes of the hammock, he saw the Marches coming out, as
if bound on some expedition.

"What in the world are those girls about now?" thought Laurie, opening his sleepy eyes to take a good look, for there was
something rather peculiar in the appearance of his neighbors.
Each wore a large, flapping hat, a brown linen pouch slung over
one shoulder, and carried a long staff; Meg had a cushion, Jo a
book, Beth a dipper,[a] and Amy a portfolio. All walked quietly
through the garden, out at the little back gate, and began to climb
the hill that lay between the house and river.

1. Unfriendly.

2. Pinework was popular in nineteenth-century America. Nico-lette Scourse, in *The Victorians and Their Flowers* (London: Croom Helm; Portland, OR: Timber Press, 1983), writes that pinework "involved cutting off the scales of large pine cones and arranging them like fish scales to make items like baskets and even pincush-ions" (29).

"Well, that's cool!"[1] said Laurie to himself, "to have a picnic and never ask me. They can't be going in the boat, for they haven't got the key. Perhaps they forgot it; I'll take it to them, and see what's going on."

Though possessed of half a dozen hats, it took him some time to find one; then there was a hunt for the key, which was at last discovered in his pocket, so that the girls were quite out of sight when he leaped the fence and ran after them. Taking the shortest way to the boat-house, he waited for them to appear; but no one came, and he went up the hill to take an observation. A grove of pines covered one part of it, and from the heart of this green spot came a clearer sound than the soft sigh of the pines, or the drowsy chirp of the crickets.

"Here's a landscape!" thought Laurie, peeping through the bushes, and looking wide awake and good-natured already.

It *was* rather a pretty little picture; for the sisters sat together in the shady nook, with sun and shadow flickering over them,—the aromatic wind lifting their hair and cooling their hot cheeks,—and all the little wood-people going on with their affairs as if these were no strangers, but old friends. Meg sat upon her cushion, sewing daintily with her white hands, and looking as fresh and sweet as a rose, in her pink dress, among the green. Beth was sorting the cones that lay thick under the hemlock near by, for she made pretty things of them.[2] Amy was sketching a group of ferns, and Jo was knitting as she read aloud. A shadow passed over the boy's face as he watched them, feeling that he ought to go, be-cause uninvited; yet lingering, because home seemed very lonely, and this quiet party in the woods most attractive to his restless spirit. He stood so still, that a squirrel, busy with its harvesting, ran down a pine close beside him, saw him suddenly, and skipped back, scolding so shrilly that Beth looked up, espied the wistful face behind the birches, and beckoned with a reassuring smile.

"May I come in, please? or shall I be a bother?" he asked, ad-vancing slowly.

Meg lifted her eyebrows, but Jo scowled at her defiantly, and said, at once, "Of course you may. We should have asked you be-fore, only we thought you wouldn't care for such a girl's game as this."

LITTLE WOMEN

Laurie spies on the Busy Bee Society.
Clara M. Burd, *Little Women* (1926).

"I always like your games; but if Meg don't want me, I'll go away."

"I've no objection, if you do something; it's against the rule to be idle here," replied Meg, gravely, but graciously.

"Much obliged; I'll do anything if you'll let me stop a bit, for it's as dull as the desert of Sahara down there. Shall I sew, read, cone, draw, or do all at once? Bring on your bears;[3] I'm ready," and Laurie sat down with a submissive expression delightful to behold.

3. The *OED* defines this colloquial American phrase as "a defiant challenge to an adversary to do his worst."

The Busy Bee Society. Harvé Stein, *Little Women* (1932).

4. Sew the heel for her sock.

"Finish this story while I set my heel,"[4] said Jo, handing him the book.

"Yes'm," was the meek answer, as he began, doing his best to prove his gratitude for the favor of an admission into the "Busy Bee Society."

The story was not a long one, and, when it was finished, he ventured to ask a few questions as a reward of merit.

"Please, mum, could I inquire if this highly instructive and charming institution is a new one?"

"Would you tell him?" asked Meg of her sisters.

"He'll laugh," said Amy, warningly.

"Who cares?" said Jo.

"I guess he'll like it," added Beth.

"Of course I shall! I give you my word I won't laugh. Tell away, Jo, and don't be afraid."

"The idea of being afraid of you! Well, you see we used to play 'Pilgrim's Progress' and we have been going on with it in earnest, all winter and summer."

"Yes, I know," said Laurie, nodding wisely.

"Who told you?" demanded Jo.

"Spirits."

"No, it was me; I wanted to amuse him one night when you were all away, and he was rather dismal. He did like it, so don't scold, Jo," said Beth, meekly.

"You can't keep a secret. Never mind; it saves trouble now."

"Go on, please," said Laurie, as Jo became absorbed in her work, looking a trifle displeased.

"Oh, didn't she tell you about this new plan of ours? Well, we have tried not to waste our holiday, but each has had a task, and worked at it with a will. The vacation is nearly over, the stints are all done, and we are ever so glad that we didn't dawdle."

"Yes, I should think so;" and Laurie thought regretfully of his own idle days.[5]

"Mother likes to have us out of doors as much as possible; so we bring our work here, and have nice times. For the fun of it we bring our things in these bags, wear the old hats, use poles to climb the hill, and play pilgrims, as we used to do years ago. We call this hill the 'Delectable Mountain,'[6] for we can look far away and see the country where we hope to live some time."

Jo pointed, and Laurie sat up to examine; for through an opening in the wood one could look across the wide, blue river,—the meadows on the other side,—far over the outskirts of the great city,[7] to the green hills that rose to meet the sky. The sun was low, and the heavens glowed with the splendor of an autumn sunset. Gold and purple clouds lay on the hill-tops; and rising high into the ruddy light were silvery white peaks, that shone like the airy spires of some Celestial City.

5. Laurie's feelings recall Thomas Carlyle's "Labour," which LMA would use to provide an epigraph for the title page of *Work: A Story of Experience* (1873): "An endless significance lies in work; in idleness alone is there perpetual despair."

6. In *The Pilgrim's Progress,* the Delectable Mountains are beautiful mountains inhabited by shepherds and their sheep. Splendid sights can be viewed from them, and the Celestial City can be seen from Mount Clear.

7. Boston.

8. Beth is referring to the gates to the Celestial City.

9. The River of Death surrounds Mount Zion, atop which sits the Celestial City. One must cross the horrible river, which becomes deeper or shallower depending upon the pilgrim's faith. As Christian comes through the gate into the Celestial City, the "Desired Country," the Shining Ones (holy angels) welcome him.

10. Daydreams or aspirations for the future.

"How beautiful that is!" said Laurie, softly, for he was quick to see and feel beauty of any kind.

"It's often so; and we like to watch it, for it is never the same, but always splendid," replied Amy, wishing she could paint it.

"Jo talks about the country where we hope to live some time; the real country, she means, with pigs and chickens, and haymaking. It would be nice, but I wish the beautiful country up there was real, and we could ever go to it," said Beth, musingly.

"There is a lovelier country even than that, where we *shall* go, by and by, when we are good enough," answered Meg, with her sweet voice.

"It seems so long to wait, so hard to do; I want to fly away at once, as those swallows fly, and go in at that splendid gate."[8]

"You'll get there, Beth, sooner or later; no fear of that," said Jo; "I'm the one that will have to fight and work, and climb and wait, and maybe never get in after all."

"You'll have me for company, if that's any comfort. I shall have to do a deal of travelling before I come in sight of your Celestial City. If I arrive late, you'll say a good word for me, won't you, Beth?"

Something in the boy's face troubled his little friend; but she said cheerfully, with her quiet eyes on the changing clouds, "If people really want to go, and really try all their lives, I think they will get in; for I don't believe there are any locks on that door, or any guards at the gate. I always imagine it is as it is in the picture, where the shining ones stretch out their hands to welcome poor Christian as he comes up from the river."[9]

"Wouldn't it be fun if all the castles in the air[10] which we make could come true, and we could live in them?" said Jo, after a little pause.

"I've made such quantities it would be hard to choose which I'd have," said Laurie, lying flat, and throwing cones at the squirrel who had betrayed him.

"You'd have to take your favorite one. What is it?" asked Meg.

"If I tell mine, will you tell yours?"

"Yes, if the girls will too."

"We will. Now, Laurie!"

"After I'd seen as much of the world as I want to, I'd like to settle in Germany, and have just as much music as I choose. I'm to be a famous musician myself, and all creation is to rush to hear me; and I'm never to be bothered about money or business, but just enjoy myself, and live for what I like. That's my favorite castle. What's yours, Meg?"

Margaret seemed to find it a little hard to tell hers, and moved[b] a brake[11] before her face, as if to disperse imaginary gnats, while she said, slowly, "I should like a lovely house, full of all sorts of luxurious things; nice food, pretty clothes, handsome furniture, pleasant people, and heaps of money. I am to be mistress of it, and manage it as I like, with plenty of servants, so I never need work a bit. How I should enjoy it! for I wouldn't be idle, but do good, and make every one love me dearly."[12]

"Wouldn't you have a master for your castle in the air?" asked Laurie, slyly.

"I said 'pleasant people,' you know;" and Meg carefully tied up her shoe as she spoke, so that no one saw her face.

"Why don't you say you'd have a splendid, wise, good husband, and some angelic little children? you know your castle wouldn't be perfect without," said blunt Jo, who had no tender fancies yet, and rather scorned romance, except in books.

"You'd have nothing but horses, inkstands, and novels in yours," answered Meg, petulantly.

"Wouldn't I, though! I'd have a stable full of Arabian steeds, rooms piled with books, and I'd write out of a magic inkstand,[13] so that my works should be as famous as Laurie's music. I want to do something splendid before I go into my castle,—something heroic, or wonderful,—that won't be forgotten after I'm dead. I don't know what, but I'm on the watch for it, and mean to astonish you all, some day. I think I shall write books, and get rich and famous; that would suit me, so that is *my* favorite dream."[14]

"Mine is to stay at home safe with father and mother, and help take care of the family," said Beth, contentedly.

"Don't you wish for anything else?" asked Laurie.

"Since I had my little piano I am perfectly satisfied. I only wish we may all keep well, and be together; nothing else."[15]

11. A fern.

12. Anna Alcott (Meg) married John Bridge Pratt in 1860, and they had two sons, Frederick Alcott Pratt, born 1863, and John Sewall Pratt, born 1865. John B. Pratt worked as a bookkeeper, and Anna took care of the family. They lived modestly in various suburbs of Boston until John's sudden death in November 1870. After John's death, LMA supported her sister's family, most notably helping Anna to buy the old Thoreau house on Main Street in Concord in 1877. In turn, Anna did her best to protect LMA's privacy and time during the last decade of the writer's life. Anna died in 1893.

13. In *Twain, Alcott, and the Birth of the Adolescent Reform Novel* (Iowa City: University of Iowa Press, 2007), Roberta Seelinger Trites points out that "Amy, Laurie, and Jo, all long for artistic fame: Amy with painting, Laurie with music, and Jo with writing. But only Jo introduces a fantastic element to her castle in the air: she wants 'a magic inkstand.' While everyone else in the group expects to succeed by ordinary means, she expresses her own success as something that would be magical" (49).

14. LMA (Jo) did indeed become rich and famous. Before *Little Women,* she had published three books and numerous stories, but she still struggled financially. After the success of *Little Women* in 1868, LMA became one of the most famous authors in America. In *Jo's Boys* (1886), she would write about the burdens of fame an author must endure. At the time of her death in March 1888, she had published two dozen books and over three hundred short stories. Her income from Roberts Brothers for 1868–1888 was $103,375, a sum that is equal to approximately two million dollars today.

15. Elizabeth Alcott, usually called Lizzie by her family and friends, did remain at home. After contracting scarlet fever in 1856, Lizzie never fully recovered her strength. She died at home in Concord on March 14, 1858, several months shy of her twenty-third birthday.

16. May Alcott did become an artist. With LMA's financial support she studied in France and England for a year in 1873. She traveled to Europe again in September 1876, never to return to America. She settled in Paris, studying art with Edouard Krug. In April 1877, her still-life was selected for the Paris Salon exhibition, a great honor. In March 1878, she married Ernest Nieriker, a Swiss businessman, fourteen years her junior. In spring 1879, her painting *Negresse* was selected for the Paris Salon exhibition. That November, her daughter, Louisa May Nieriker (nicknamed Lulu), was born. May never recovered from childbirth; she died on December 29, 1879. Her daughter came to America the following autumn to be raised by her Aunt Louisa.

17. The *OED* dates the first use of *hang* as "an angry refusal" to about 1400.

18. Another way of saying "By God!" In Roman mythology, Jupiter was the king of the gods.

19. Laurie means his grandfather is contrary to his own dispositions or desires.

"I have lots of wishes; but the pet one is to be an artist, and go to Rome, and do fine pictures, and be the best artist in the whole world," was Amy's modest desire.[16]

"We're an ambitious set, aren't we? Every one of us but Beth, wants to be rich and famous, and gorgeous in every respect. I do wonder if any of us will ever get our wishes," said Laurie, chewing grass, like a meditative calf.

"I've got the key to my castle in the air; but whether I can unlock the door, remains to be seen," observed Jo, mysteriously.

"I've got the key to mine, but I'm not allowed to try it. Hang[17] college!" muttered Laurie, with an impatient sigh.

"Here's mine!" and Amy waved her pencil.

"I haven't got any," said Meg, forlornly.

"Yes you have," said Laurie, at once.

"Where?"

"In your face."

"Nonsense; that's of no use."

"Wait and see if it doesn't bring you something worth having," replied the boy, laughing at the thought of a charming little secret which he fancied he knew.

Meg colored behind the brake, but asked no questions, and looked across the river with the same expectant expression which Mr. Brooke had worn when he told the story of the knight.

"If we are all alive ten years hence, let's meet, and see how many of us have got our wishes, or how much nearer we are them than now," said Jo, always ready with a plan.

"Bless me! how old I shall be,—twenty-seven!" exclaimed Meg, who felt grown up already, having just reached seventeen.

"You and I shall be twenty-six, Teddy; Beth twenty-four, and Amy twenty-two; what a venerable party!" said Jo.

"I hope I shall have done something to be proud of by that time; but I'm such a lazy dog, I'm afraid I shall 'dawdle,' Jo."

"You need a motive, mother says; and when you get it, she is sure you'll work splendidly."

"Is she? By Jupiter[18] I will, if I only get the chance!" cried Laurie, sitting up with sudden energy. "I ought to be satisfied to please grandfather, and I do try, but it's working against the grain,[19] you see, and comes hard. He wants me to be an India merchant,[20] as he was, and I'd rather be shot; I hate tea, and silk, and spices, and every sort of rubbish his old ships bring, and I don't care how soon they go to the bottom when I own them. Going to college ought to satisfy him, for if I give him four years he ought to let me off from the business; but he's set, and I've got to do just as he did, unless I break away and please myself, as my father did. If there was any one left to stay with the old gentleman, I'd do it to-morrow."

Laurie spoke excitedly, and looked ready to carry his threat into execution on the slightest provocation; for he was growing up very fast, and, in spite of his indolent ways, had a young man's hatred of subjection,—a young man's restless longing to try the world for himself.

"I advise you to sail away in one of your ships, and never come home again till you have tried your own way," said Jo, whose imagination was fired by the thought of such a daring exploit, and whose sympathy was excited by what she called "Teddy's wrongs."

"That's not right, Jo; you mustn't talk in that way, and Laurie mustn't take your bad advice. You should do just what your grand-father wishes, my dear boy," said Meg, in her most maternal tone. "Do your best at college, and, when he sees that you try to please him, I'm sure he won't be hard or unjust to you. As you say, there is no one else to stay with and love him, and you'd never forgive yourself if you left him without his permission. Don't be dismal, or fret, but do your duty; and you'll get your reward, as good Mr. Brooke has, by being respected and loved."

"What do you know about him?" asked Laurie, grateful for the good advice, but objecting to the lecture, and glad to turn the conversation from himself, after his unusual outbreak.

"Only what your grandpa told mother[c] about him; how he took good care of his own mother till she died, and wouldn't go abroad as tutor to some nice person, because he wouldn't leave her; and how he provides now for an old woman who nursed his mother; and never tells any one, but is just as generous, and patient, and good as he can be."

20. Laurie's grandfather obviously engaged in shipping trade with the East Indies, which included South Asia, Southwestern Asia, and the Oceania islands, since Laurie mentions tea, silk, and spices—all items imported to America by the shipping merchants. Such trade to the East Indies or the West Indies or the Caribbean was often dangerous but extremely profitable as seen by the wealthy Mr. Laurence. Salem, Massachusetts, was one of the main seaports in America for the India trade. However, by the mid-nineteenth century, profits in the India trade had declined.

"So he is, dear old fellow!" said Laurie, heartily, as Meg paused, looking flushed and earnest, with her story. "It's like grandpa to find out all about him, without letting him know, and to tell all his goodness to others, so that they might like him. Brooke couldn't understand why your mother was so kind to him, asking him over with me, and treating him in her beautiful, friendly way. He thought she was just perfect, and talked about it for days and days, and went on about you all, in flaming[21] style. If ever I do get my wish, you see what I'll do for Brooke."

"Begin to do something now, by not plaguing his life out," said Meg, sharply.

"How do you know I do, miss?"

"I can always tell by his face, when he goes away. If you have been good, he looks satisfied, and walks briskly; if you have plagued him, he's sober, and walks slowly, as if he wanted to go back and do his work better."

"Well, I like that! So you keep an account of my good and bad marks in Brooke's face, do you? I see him bow and smile as he passes your window, but I didn't know you'd got up a telegraph."

"We haven't; don't be angry, and oh, don't tell him I said anything! It was only to show that I cared how you get on, and what is said here is said in confidence, you know," cried Meg, much alarmed at the thought of what might follow from her careless speech.

"*I* don't tell tales," replied Laurie, with his "high and mighty" air, as Jo called a certain expression which he occasionally wore. "Only if Brooke is going to be a thermometer, I must mind and have fair weather for him to report."

"Please don't be offended; I didn't mean to preach or tell tales, or be silly; I only thought Jo was encouraging you in a feeling which you'd be sorry for, by and by. You are so kind to us, we feel as if you were our brother, and say just what we think; forgive me, I meant it kindly!" and Meg offered her hand with a gesture both affectionate and timid.

Ashamed of his momentary pique, Laurie squeezed the kind little hand, and said, frankly, "I'm the one to be forgiven; I'm cross, and have been out of sorts all day. I like to have you tell me

my faults, and be sisterly; so don't mind if I am grumpy sometimes; I thank you all the same."

Bent on showing that he was not offended, he made himself
as agreeable as possible; wound cotton for Meg, recited poetry to
please Jo, shook down cones for Beth, and helped Amy with her
ferns, proving himself a fit person to belong to the "Busy Bee Society." In the midst of an animated discussion on the domestic
habits of turtles (one of which amiable creatures having strolled
up from the river), the faint sound of a bell warned them that
Hannah had put the tea "to draw,"[22] and they would just have
time to get home to supper.

"May I come again?" asked Laurie.

"Yes, if you are good, and love your book, as the boys in the
primer[23] are told to do," said Meg, smiling.

"I'll try."

"Then you may come, and I'll teach you to knit as the Scotch-
men[24] do; there's a demand for socks just now,"[25] added Jo, waving
hers, like a big blue worsted banner, as they parted at the gate.

That night, when Beth played to Mr. Laurence in the twilight,
Laurie, standing in the shadow of the curtain, listened to the little
David, whose simple music always quieted his moody spirit,[26] and
watched the old man, who sat with his gray head on his hand,
thinking tender thoughts of the dead child he had loved so much.
Remembering the conversation of the afternoon, the boy said to
himself, with the resolve to make the sacrifice cheerfully, "I'll let
my castle go, and stay with the dear old gentleman while he needs
me, for I am all he has."

22. The *OED* notes that the first use of the phrase "to draw" appeared about 1430. It means "to extract the essence from." Thus
Hannah is allowing the tea to steep in the hot water.

23. It is unclear to which reading instruction book Meg refers, as
numerous American primers were in use by the mid-nineteenth century. It is possible she means the well-known *New England Primer*,
which had been used by children since the late seventeenth century
and was still in use during the nineteenth century. In its alphabet,
which has a woodcut illustration and a short verse for each letter,
the *New England Primer* has the following quote for "H": "My Book
and Heart / Shall never part."

24. During the seventeenth and eighteenth centuries, Scotland
became noted for its knitting industry. A new knitting method, the
Fair Isle technique, named for an island in the North of Scotland,
was used to produce colorful patterns for the sweaters of fishermen.

25. Jo is referring to the great number of socks needed by the
Union soldiers at war. In October 1861, LMA reported: "Sewing and
knitting for 'our boys' all the time" (*Journals* 106).

26. LMA alludes to Saul being comforted by David's harp: "And
it came to pass, when the evil spirit from God was upon Saul, that
David took an harp, and played with his hand: so Saul was refreshed,
and was well, and the evil spirit departed" (1 Samuel 16:23).

1. Jo selected an appropriate name for the pet rat in her writing garret as *scrabble* means "to scribble."

2. A reflector oven made of polished metal. Placed before an open fire or stove, the metal reflects the heat and helps cook the food faster.

Chapter 14

Secrets

JO WAS VERY BUSY up in the garret, for the October days began to grow chilly, and the afternoons were short. For two or three hours the sun lay warmly in at the high window, showing Jo seated on the old sofa writing busily, with her papers spread out upon a trunk before her, while Scrabble,[1] the pet rat, promenaded the beams overhead, accompanied by his oldest son, a fine young fellow, who was evidently very proud of his whiskers. Quite absorbed in her work, Jo scribbled away till the last page was filled, when she signed her name with a flourish, and threw down her pen, exclaiming,—

"There, I've done my best! If this don't suit I shall have to wait till I can do better."

Lying back on the sofa, she read the manuscript carefully through, making dashes here and there, and putting in many exclamation points, which looked like little balloons; then she tied it up with a smart red ribbon, and sat a minute looking at it with a sober, wistful expression, which plainly showed how earnest her work had been. Jo's desk up here was an old tin kitchen,[2] which hung against the wall. In it she kept her papers, and a few books, safely shut away from Scrabble, who, being likewise of a literary turn, was fond of making a circulating library of such books as were left in his way, by eating the leaves. From this tin receptacle Jo produced another manuscript; and, putting both in her pocket, crept quietly down stairs, leaving her friends to nibble her pens and taste her ink.

She put on her hat and jacket as noiselessly as possible, and, go-

Norman Rockwell, *The Most Beloved American Writer* (1937). Along with this depiction of Jo in her garret, Rockwell executed a number of drawings and several oil paintings for Katharine Anthony's biographical piece "America's Most Beloved Author," which appeared in the *Ladies Home Companion* in 1937–1938.

3. Omnibus (*omni* meaning "for all" in Latin) was, during the first part of the nineteenth century, a popular form of transportation in cities. Larger than a conventional stage, the horse-drawn omnibus usually had lengthwise seats. During the mid-1800s, more than twenty companies provided omnibus service to Boston and its surroundings. By 1856, Boston started to install rails in the streets so the horses could pull larger vehicles.

4. The *OED* defines *stock still* as standing "[a]s still as a stock [a tree stump] or log; quite motionless."

ing to the back entry window, got out upon the roof of a low porch, swung herself down to the grassy bank, and took a round-about way to the road. Once there she composed herself, hailed a passing omnibus,[3] and rolled away to town, looking very merry and mysterious.

If any one had been watching her, he would have thought her movements decidedly peculiar; for, on alighting, she went off at a great pace till she reached a certain number in a certain busy street; having found the place with some difficulty, she went into the door-way, looked up the dirty stairs, and, after standing stock still[4] a minute, suddenly dived into the street, and walked away as rapidly as she came. This manœuvre she repeated several times, to the great amusement of a black-eyed young gentleman lounging in the window of a building opposite. On returning for the third time, Jo gave herself a shake, pulled her hat over her eyes, and walked up the stairs, looking as if she was going to have all her teeth out.

There was a dentist's sign, among others, which adorned the entrance, and, after staring a moment at the pair of artificial jaws which slowly opened and shut to draw attention to a fine set of teeth, the young gentleman put on his coat, took his hat, and went down to post himself in the opposite door-way, saying, with a smile and a shiver,—

"It's like her to come alone, but if she has a bad time she'll need some one to help her home."

In ten minutes Jo came running down stairs with a very red face, and the general appearance of a person who had just passed through a trying ordeal of some sort. When she saw the young gentleman she looked anything but pleased, and passed him with a nod; but he followed, asking with an air of sympathy,—

"Did you have a bad time?"

"Not very."

"You got through quick."

"Yes, thank goodness!"

"Why did you go alone?"

"Didn't want any one to know."

"You're the oddest fellow I ever saw. How many did you have out?"

Jo looked at her friend as if she did not understand him; then began to laugh, as if mightily amused at something.

"There are two which I want to have come out, but I must wait a week."

"What are you laughing at? You are up to some mischief, Jo," said Laurie, looking mystified.

"So are you. What were you doing, sir, up in that billiard saloon?"

"Begging your pardon, ma'am, it wasn't a billiard saloon, but a gymnasium, and I was taking a lesson in fencing."

"I'm glad of that!"

"Why?"

"You can teach me; and then, when we play Hamlet, you can be Laertes,[5] and we'll make a fine thing of the fencing scene."

Laurie burst out with a hearty boy's laugh, which made several passers-by smile in spite of themselves.

"I'll teach you, whether we play Hamlet or not; it's grand fun, and will straighten you up capitally. But I don't believe that was your only reason for saying 'I'm glad,' in that decided way; was it, now?"

"No, I was glad you were not in the saloon, because I hope you never go to such places. Do you?"

"Not often."

"I wish you wouldn't."

"It's no harm, Jo, I have billiards at home, but it's no fun unless you have good players; so, as I'm fond of it, I come sometimes and have a game with Ned Moffat or some of the other fellows."[6]

"Oh dear, I'm so sorry, for you'll get to liking it better and better, and will waste time and money, and grow like those dreadful boys. I did hope you'd stay respectable, and be a satisfaction to your friends," said Jo, shaking her head.

"Can't a fellow take a little innocent amusement now and then without losing his respectability?" asked Laurie, looking nettled.

"That depends upon how and where he takes it. I don't like

5. Laertes is Ophelia's brother in Shakespeare's tragedy *Hamlet.* In the play's final scene he avenges the deaths of his sister and his father, Polonius, by stabbing Hamlet with a poisoned sword during a climactic swordfight. LMA, in "Recollections of My Childhood" (1888), once wrote that of Shakespeare's plays, "Hamlet was my favorite hero." (quoted in *Her Own Time* 38).

6. Billiards originated in Europe in the fourteenth century and was a favorite sport of royalty. However, colonial America, especially New England with its Puritan heritage, associated billiards with taverns where men gambled, smoked, and drank alcohol. When John Quincy Adams placed a pool table in the White House in 1825, many people questioned his moral character. Michael Phelan (1817–1871), often called the father of American billiards, helped change the popular attitude toward the game when he opened an elegant pool hall in New York in 1850.

7. Mrs. March does not like people who follow the fashion of the day. The *OED* defines *fashionable:* "Of things, esp. dress: Conformable to fashion; in accordance with prevailing usage; of the kind in vogue among persons of the upper class. Of immaterial things: Approved by custom, generally accepted, current (now in depreciatory sense)."

8. Cardboard or wooden boxes, usually cylindrical, that were used to hold small clothing accessories or attire.

9. Laurie means he will be free of impurities. He may be playing on words here, as alcohol was also double distilled.

Ned and his set, and wish you'd keep out of it. Mother won't let us have him at our house, though he wants to come, and if you grow like him she won't be willing to have us frolic together as we do now."

"Won't she?" asked Laurie, anxiously.

"No, she can't bear fashionable[7] young men, and she'd shut us all up in bandboxes[8] rather than have us associate with them."

"Well, she needn't get out her bandboxes yet; I'm not a fashionable party, and don't mean to be; but I do like harmless larks now and then, don't you?"

"Yes, nobody minds them, so lark away, but don't get wild, will you? or there will be an end of all our good times."

"I'll be a double distilled[9] saint."

"I can't bear saints; just be a simple, honest, respectable boy, and we'll never desert you. I don't know what I *should* do if you acted like Mr. King's son; he had plenty of money, but didn't know how to spend it, and got tipsy, and gambled, and ran away, and forged his father's name, I believe, and was altogether horrid."

"You think I'm likely to do the same? Much obliged."

"No I don't—oh, *dear,* no!—but I hear people talking about money being such a temptation, and I sometimes wish you were poor; I shouldn't worry then."

"Do you worry about me, Jo?"

"A little, when you look moody or discontented, as you sometimes do, for you've got such a strong will if you once get started wrong, I'm afraid it would be hard to stop you."

Laurie walked in silence a few minutes, and Jo watched him, wishing she had held her tongue, for his eyes looked angry, though his lips still smiled as if at her warnings.

"Are you going to deliver lectures all the way home?" he asked, presently.

"Of course not; why?"

"Because if you are, I'll take a 'bus; if you are not, I'd like to walk with you, and tell you something very interesting."

"I won't preach any more, and I'd like to hear the news immensely."

LITTLE WOMEN

"Very well, then; come on. It's a secret, and if I tell you, you must tell me yours."

"I haven't got any," began Jo, but stopped suddenly, remembering that she had.

"You know you have; you can't hide anything, so up and 'fess, or I won't tell," cried Laurie.

"Is your secret a nice one?"

"Oh, isn't it! all about people you know, and such fun! You ought to hear it, and I've been aching to tell this long time. Come! you begin."

"You'll not say anything about it at home, will you?"

"Not a word."

"And you won't tease me in private?"

"I never tease."

"Yes, you do; you get everything you want out of people. I don't know how you do it, but you are a born wheedler."[10]

"Thank you; fire away!"

"Well, I've left two stories with a newspaper man, and he's to give his answer next week," whispered Jo, in her confidant's ear.

"Hurrah for Miss March, the celebrated American authoress!" cried Laurie, throwing up his hat and catching it again, to the great delight of two ducks, four cats, five hens, and half a dozen Irish children; for they were out of the city now.

"Hush! it won't come to anything, I dare say; but I couldn't rest till I had tried, and I said nothing about it, because I didn't want any one else to be disappointed."

"It won't fail! Why, Jo, your stories are works of Shakespeare compared to half the rubbish that's published every day. Won't it be fun to see them in print; and shan't we feel proud of our authoress?"

Jo's eyes sparkled, for it's always pleasant to be believed in; and a friend's praise is always sweeter than a dozen newspaper puffs.[11]

"Where's *your* secret? Play fair, Teddy, or I'll never believe you again," she said, trying to extinguish the brilliant hopes that blazed up at a word of encouragement.

"I may get into a scrape for telling; but I didn't promise not to,

10. A person who persuades or cajoles people, usually with flattery.

11. Short laudatory reviews or advertisements of literary works.

12. Laurie has told Jo that John Brooke has been keeping one of Meg's gloves in his pocket. Gloves have long been associated with love. During the Middle Ages a knight would often carry a lady's glove into battle as a token of his love. In the nineteenth century, paper valentines in the shape of gloves were popular, as was the following verse: "If that from Glove you take the letter G, / Then Glove is Love and that I send to thee."

so I will, for I never feel easy in my mind till I've told you any plummy bit of news I get. I know where Meg's glove is."

"Is that all?" said Jo, looking disappointed, as Laurie nodded and twinkled, with a face full of mysterious intelligence.

"It's quite enough for the present, as you'll agree when I tell you where it is."

"Tell, then."

Laurie bent and whispered three words in Jo's ear, which produced a comical change. She stood and stared at him for a minute, looking both surprised and displeased, then walked on, saying sharply, "How do you know?"

"Saw it."

"Where?"

"Pocket."[12]

"All this time?"

"Yes; isn't that romantic?"

"No, it's horrid."

"Don't you like it?"

"Of course I don't; it's ridiculous; it won't be allowed. My patience! what would Meg say?"

"You are not to tell any one; mind that."

"I didn't promise."

"That was understood, and I trusted you."

"Well, I won't for the present, any-way; but I'm disgusted, and wish you hadn't told me."

"I thought you'd be pleased."

"At the idea of anybody coming to take Meg away? No, thank you."

"You'll feel better about it when somebody comes to take you away."

"I'd like to see any one try it," cried Jo, fiercely.

"So should I!" and Laurie chuckled at the idea.

"I don't think secrets agree with me; I feel rumpled up in my mind since you told me that," said Jo, rather ungratefully.

"Race down this hill with me, and you'll be all right," suggested Laurie.

No one was in sight; the smooth road sloped invitingly before

LITTLE WOMEN

her, and, finding the temptation irresistible, Jo darted away, soon leaving hat and comb behind her, and scattering hair-pins as she ran. Laurie reached the goal first, and was quite satisfied with the success of his treatment; for his Atlanta[13] came panting up with flying hair, bright eyes, ruddy cheeks, and no signs of dissatisfaction in her face.

"I wish I was a horse; then I could run for miles in this splendid air, and not lose my breath.[14] It was capital; but see what a guy it's made me. Go, pick up my things, like a cherub as you are," said Jo, dropping down under a maple tree, which was carpeting the bank with crimson leaves.

Laurie leisurely departed to recover the lost property, and Jo bundled up her braids, hoping no one would pass by till she was tidy again. But some one did pass, and who should it be but Meg, looking particularly lady-like in her state and festival suit,[15] for she had been making calls.

"What in the world are you doing here?" she asked, regarding her dishevelled sister with well-bred surprise.

"Getting leaves," meekly answered Jo, sorting the rosy handful she had just swept up.

"And hair-pins," added Laurie, throwing half a dozen into Jo's lap. "They grow on this road, Meg; so do combs and brown straw hats."

"You have been running, Jo; how could you?[16] When *will* you stop such romping ways?" said Meg, reprovingly, as she settled her cuffs and smoothed her hair, with which the wind had taken liberties.

"Never till I'm stiff and old, and have to use a crutch. Don't try to make me grow up before my time, Meg; it's hard enough to have you change all of a sudden; let me be a little girl as long as I can."

As she spoke, Jo bent over her work[a] to hide the trembling of her lips; for lately she had felt that Margaret was fast getting to be a woman, and Laurie's secret made her dread the separation which must surely come some time, and now seemed very near. He saw the trouble in her face, and drew Meg's attention from it by asking, quickly, "Where have you been calling, all so fine?"

13. In Greek mythology Atalanta, the daughter of Iasus, was a renowned hunter. Although her father wanted her to marry, she desired to remain a virgin and declared she would only marry a suitor who could beat her in a footrace. Melanion fell under Atalanta's charm and sought help from Aphrodite, who gave him three golden apples and a plan to win the race. Each time that Atalanta ran ahead of him, Melanion would toss or roll one of the apples ahead of her. She could not resist, and each time she stopped to retrieve the apple. After the third apple was tossed, she failed to catch up and agreed to marry Melanion.

14. LMA, in "Recollections of My Childhood" (1888), wrote: "I always thought I must have been a deer or a horse in some former state, because it was such a joy to run. No boy could be my friend till I had beaten him in a race" (quoted in *Her Own Time* 34). Willis recalled in *Alcott Memoirs* (1915): "[LMA] could run like a gazelle. She was the most beautiful girl runner I ever saw" (quoted in *Her Own Time* 177).

15. Clothing that was appropriate for social or formal events.

16. Meg, aware of how a young lady should act in public, knows that running is improper conduct. Emily Thornwell advises: "A lady ought to adopt a modest and measured gait; too great hurry injures the grace which ought to characterize her" (*The Lady's Guide* 78).

17. Distressed or sorrowful.

18. Jo had submitted her two stories to "The Spread Eagle."

19. Once again, Amy incorrectly says the French phrase *comme il faut* ("as is respectable").

"At the Gardiners; and Sallie has been telling me all about Belle Moffat's wedding. It was very splendid, and they have gone to spend the winter in Paris; just think how delightful that must be!"

"Do you envy her, Meg?" said Laurie.

"I'm afraid I do."

"I'm glad of it!" muttered Jo, tying on her hat with a jerk.

"Why?" asked Meg, looking surprised.

"Because, if you care much about riches, you will never go and marry a poor man," said Jo, frowning at Laurie, who was mutely warning her to mind what she said.

"I shall never '*go* and marry' any one," observed Meg, walking on with great dignity, while the others followed, laughing, whispering, skipping stones, and "behaving like children," as Meg said to herself, though she might have been tempted to join them if she had not had her best dress on.

For a week or two Jo behaved so queerly, that her sisters got quite bewildered. She rushed to the door when the postman rang; was rude to Mr. Brooke whenever they met; would sit looking at Meg with a woe-begone[17] face, occasionally jumping up to shake, and then to kiss her, in a very mysterious manner; Laurie and she were always making signs to one another, and talking about "Spread Eagles,"[18] till the girls declared they had both lost their wits. On the second Saturday after Jo got out of the window, Meg, as she sat sewing at her window, was scandalized by the sight of Laurie chasing Jo all over the garden, and finally capturing her in Amy's bower. What went on there, Meg could not see, but shrieks of laughter were heard, followed by the murmur of voices, and a great flapping of newspapers.

"What shall we do with that girl? She never *will* behave like a young lady," sighed Meg, as she watched the race with a disapproving face.

"I hope she won't; she is so funny and dear as she is," said Beth, who had never betrayed that she was a little hurt at Jo's having secrets with any one but her.

"It's very trying, but we never can make her *comme la fo*"[19] added Amy, who sat making some new frills for herself, with her curls tied up in a very becoming way,—two agreeable things, which made her feel unusually elegant and lady-like.

In a few minutes Jo bounced in, laid herself on the sofa, and affected to read.

"Have you anything interesting there?" asked Meg, with condescension.

"Nothing but a story; don't amount to much, I guess," returned Jo, carefully keeping the name of the paper out of sight.

"You'd better read it loud; that will amuse us, and keep you out of mischief," said Amy, in her most grown-up tone.

"What's the name?" asked Beth, wondering why Jo kept her face behind the sheet.

"The Rival Painters."

"That sounds well; read it," said Meg.

With a loud "hem!" and a long breath, Jo began to read very fast. The girls listened with interest, for the tale was romantic, and somewhat pathetic, as most of the characters died in the end.

"I like that about the splendid picture," was Amy's approving remark, as Jo paused.

"I prefer the lovering[20] part. Viola and Angelo are two of our favorite names; isn't that queer?" said Meg, wiping her eyes, for the "lovering part" was tragical.

"Who wrote it?" asked Beth, who had caught a glimpse of Jo's face.

The reader suddenly sat up, cast away the paper, displaying a flushed countenance, and, with a funny mixture of solemnity and excitement, replied in a loud voice, "Your sister!"[21]

"You?" cried Meg, dropping her work.

"It's very good," said Amy, critically.

"I knew it! I knew it! oh, my Jo, I *am* so proud!" and Beth ran to hug her sister and exult over this splendid success.

Dear me, how delighted they all were, to be sure; how Meg wouldn't believe it till she saw the words, "Miss Josephine March," actually printed in the paper; how graciously Amy criticised the artistic parts of the story, and offered hints for a sequel, which unfortunately couldn't be carried out, as the hero and heroine were dead; how Beth got excited, and skipped and sung with

20. The romantic or courting behavior of the characters.

21. LMA anonymously published "The Rival Painters: A Tale of Rome" in *The Olive Branch* (May 8, 1852). She confessed in her journal: "My first story was printed, and $5 paid for it. It was written in Concord when I was sixteen. Great rubbish! Read it aloud to sisters, and when they praised it, not knowing the author, I proudly announced her name" (*Journals* 67). In the published tale, the main characters are Madeline and Guido, not Viola and Angelo as Meg indicates here.

22. A proud or vain person. A peacock is the raucous, colorful male sex of the pea fowl, famous for "showing off" its feathers (raising its tail in a brilliant display). The female of the species is smaller and a dull brown color.

23. The British author Frances Burney (1752–1840) published *Evelina or the History of a Young Lady's Entrance into the World* (1778). This popular sentimental, epistolary novel was published anonymously and without her father's permission because at the time it was considered unladylike to write for the public. However, the book received numerous positive reviews, including one by Samuel Johnson. When Burney was revealed as the author, her father, impressed by the favorable public reviews, approved, and she went on to write more popular novels and plays. LMA read or re-read the novel in June 1861, noting: "Dear old 'Evelina' as a change, was pleasant" (*Journals* 105).

joy; how Hannah came in to exclaim, "Sakes alive, well I never!" in great astonishment at "that Jo's doins;" how proud Mrs. March was when she knew it; how Jo laughed, with tears in her eyes, as she declared she might as well be a peacock[22] and done with it; and how the "Spread Eagle" might be said to flap his wings triumphantly over the house of March, as the paper passed from hand to hand.

"Tell us about it." "When did it come?" "How much did you get for it?" "What *will* father say" "Won't Laurie laugh?" cried the family, all in one breath, as they clustered about Jo; for these foolish, affectionate people made a jubilee of every little household joy.

"Stop jabbering, girls, and I'll tell you everything," said Jo, wondering if Miss Burney felt any grander over her "Evelina"[23] than she did over her "Rival Painters." Having told how she disposed of her tales, Jo added, "And when I went to get my answer the man said he liked them both, but didn't pay beginners, only let them print in his paper, and noticed the stories. It was good practice, he said; and, when the beginners improved, any one would pay. So I let him have the two stories, and today this was sent to me, and Laurie caught me with it, and insisted on seeing it, so I let him; and he said it was good, and I shall write more, and he's going to get the next paid for, and oh—I *am* so happy, for in time I may be able to support myself and help the girls."

Jo's breath gave out here; and, wrapping her head in the paper, she bedewed her little story with a few natural tears; for to be independent, and earn the praise of those she loved, were the dearest wishes of her heart, and this seemed to be the first step toward that happy end.

LITTLE WOMEN

Chapter 15

A Telegram

1. Both LMA and her father, Bronson, were born on November 29.

2. An ink blot.

3. The *OED* defines *tread-mill* as a "horizontal cylinder made to revolve by the weight of persons treading on boards arranged as equidistant steps around its periphery. Formerly in use as an instrument of prison discipline." The term was first used in 1822 in a pamphlet describing the invention by William Cubitt of Ipswich, England, and constructed at the House of Correction in Brixton, England.

4. Some of May's early clay models are displayed at Orchard House. She later gave fellow Concordian and famous sculptor Daniel Chester French (1850–1931), best known for his statue of Abraham Lincoln at the Lincoln Memorial, his first sculpting lessons.

NOVEMBER is the most disagreeable month in the whole year," said Margaret, standing at the window one dull afternoon, looking out at the frost-bitten garden.

"That's the reason I was born in it,"[1] observed Jo, pensively, quite unconscious of the blot[2] on her nose.

"If something very pleasant should happen now, we should think it a delightful month," said Beth, who took a hopeful view of everything, even November.

"I dare say; but nothing pleasant ever *does* happen in this family," said Meg, who was out of sorts. "We go grubbing along day after day, without a bit of change, and very little fun. We might as well be in a tread-mill."[3]

"My patience, how blue we are!" cried Jo. "I don't much wonder, poor dear, for you see other girls having splendid times, while you grind, grind, year in and year out. Oh, don't I wish I could fix[a] things for you as I do for my heroines! you're pretty enough and good enough already, so I'd have some rich relation leave you a fortune unexpectedly; then you'd dash out as an heiress, scorn every one who has slighted you, go abroad, and come home my Lady Something, in a blaze of splendor and elegance."

"People don't have fortunes left them in that style now-a-days; men have to work, and women to marry for money. It's a dreadfully unjust world," said Meg, bitterly.

"Jo and I are going to make fortunes for you all; just wait ten years, and see if we don't," said Amy, who sat in a corner making "mud pies," as Hannah called her little clay models of birds, fruit and faces.[4]

5. The post office.

6. The Samuel Morse electrical telegraph had been patented in 1837, and by the end of October 1861, it connected the West and East coasts of the United States. Since sending a telegraph cost more money than mailing a letter, Hannah knows it contains urgent news. Mrs. March fears the worst—that Mr. March has been killed in the war. She has every reason to be worried. The casualties during the Civil War were staggering. According to William E. Fox, *Regimental Losses in the American Civil War, 1861-65* (1889), the number of deaths on both sides totaled 623,026; the number of wounded was 471,427. In the Union army alone, the realities of the bloody war are appalling: 110,070 were killed in battle; 199,790 died from disease; 24,866 perished in Confederate prisons. This does not include the thousands of others who died from accidents, explosions, enemy execution, murder, and other causes.

7. LMA was well acquainted with death and illness in Civil War hospitals. In December 1862, she left Concord to report for duty as a nurse in Georgetown, D.C. She confided in her journal: "So I set forth in the December twilight, with May and Julian Hawthorne [Nathaniel and Sophia Hawthorne's son] as escort, feeling as if I was the son of the house going to war" (*Journals* 110). LMA would see firsthand the terrible carnage of the war as she dressed wounds, and washed, fed, and consoled the sick and wounded. Bronson had supported LMA's decision to go to Washington but feared for his daughter's health. He was right to do so, for LMA soon contracted typhoid pneumonia. On January 14, 1863, the Alcotts received a telegram informing them that LMA was ill; that same day Bronson left on the noon train to be beside his daughter. Father and daughter arrived home on January 24, accompanied by Nathaniel Hawthorne's daughter Una, who was returning from Boston. In a letter of February 20, 1863, to Annie Adams Fields, wife of the publisher James T. Fields, Sophia Hawthorne vividly describes LMA's homecoming and illness: "Una happened to come up on the same train, and Louisa lay upon her shoulder all the way, looking ghastly, and uprolling her eyes, while she was like a sheaf of flames in Una's arms. . . . She arrived on Saturday night[.] On Monday I saw her for a few moments, but she was quite unconscious and did not notice me. She was so changed I think I should not have known her. After that, no one saw her but the physician, for she was delirious almost uninterruptedly, and often very furious, and Mrs Alcott told me she was haunted by hospital scenes and men, as well as by the distress of the journey, and the fear that she should never get home . . . One day she sprang out of bed, when they left her for a moment, and

"Can't wait, and I'm afraid I haven't much faith in ink and dirt, though I'm grateful for your good intentions."

Meg sighed, and turned to the frost-bitten garden again; Jo groaned, and leaned both elbows on the table in a despondent attitude, but Amy spatted away energetically; and Beth, who sat at the other window, said, smiling, "Two pleasant things are going to happen right away; Marmee is coming down the street, and Laurie is tramping through the garden as if he had something nice to tell."

In they both came, Mrs. March with her usual question, "Any letter from father, girls?" and Laurie to say, in his persuasive way, "Won't some of you come for a drive? I've been pegging[b] away at mathematics till my head is in a muddle, and I'm going to freshen my wits by a brisk turn. It's a dull day, but the air isn't bad, and I'm going to take Brooke home, so it will be gay inside, if it isn't out. Come, Jo, you and Beth will go, won't you?"

"Of course we will."

"Much obliged, but I'm busy;" and Meg whisked out her workbasket, for she had agreed with her mother that it was best, for her at least, not to drive often with the young gentleman.

"We three will be ready in a minute," cried Amy, running away to wash her hands.

"Can I do anything for you, Madam Mother?" asked Laurie, leaning over Mrs. March's chair, with the affectionate look and tone he always gave her.

"No, thank you, except call at the office,[5] if you'll be so kind, dear. It's our day for a letter, and the penny[c] postman hasn't been. Father is as regular as the sun, but there's some delay on the way, perhaps."

A sharp ring interrupted her, and a minute after Hannah came in with a letter.

"It's one of them horrid telegraph[6] things, mum," she said, handing it as if she was afraid it would explode, and do some damage.

At the word "telegraph," Mrs. March snatched it, read the two lines it contained, and dropped back into her chair as white as if the little paper had sent a bullet to her heart. Laurie dashed down stairs for water, while Meg and Hannah supported her, and Jo read aloud, in a frightened voice,—

LITTLE WOMEN

"MRS. MARCH:

"Your husband is very ill. Come at once.

"S. HALE,

"Blank Hospital, Washington."

How still the room was as they listened breathlessly! how strangely the day darkened outside! and how suddenly the whole world seemed to change, as the girls gathered about their mother, feeling as if all the happiness and support of their lives was about to be taken from them. Mrs. March was herself again directly; read the message over, and stretched out her arms to her daughters, saying, in a tone they never forgot, "I shall go at once, but it may be too late; oh, children, children! help me to bear it!"[7]

For several minutes there was nothing but the sound of sobbing in the room, mingled with broken words of comfort, tender

beneath they heard a sudden step above, and then a heavy fall. Horror stricken they rushed up, and Louisa was stretched upon the floor. Mrs. Alcott immediately went into hysterics, and Abby [May] dragged up Louisa and laid her on the bed, where she exclaimed 'how could you leave me when the room was full of men!' She had an ulcerated throat and a terrible cough, and severe fever fits, where her whole face was nothing but mahogany color, with large black circles round her eyes, which looked wild and blood shot." It would be later that spring before LMA would have the strength to leave her room. On March 25, 1863, Bronson wrote to his mother about his daughter's near death: "That was our contribution to the war and one we should not have made willingly had we known the danger and the sacrifices" (*Letters of ABA* 336). One wonders if the experience made him think differently of the thousands of sacrifices other parents had made?

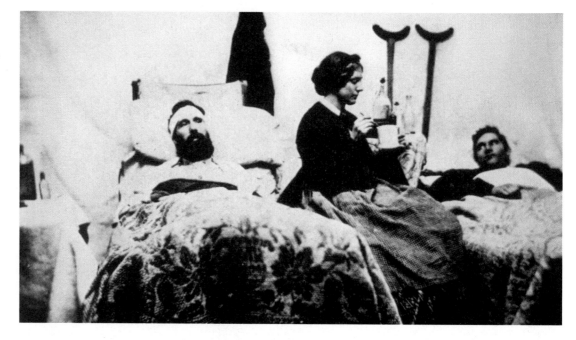

A typical Civil War nurse tending the wounded at a hospital in Tennessee.

assurances of help, and hopeful whispers, that died away in tears. Poor Hannah was the first to recover, and with unconscious wisdom she set all the rest a good example; for, with her, work was the panacea for most afflictions.

"The Lord keep the dear man! I won't waste no time a cryin', but git your things ready right away, mum," she said, heartily, as she wiped her face on her apron, gave her mistress a warm shake of the hand with her own hard one, and went away to work, like three women in one.

"She's right; there's no time for tears now. Be calm, girls, and let me think."

They tried to be calm, poor things, as their mother sat up looking pale, but steady, and put away her grief to think and plan for them.

"Where's Laurie?" she asked presently, when she had collected her thoughts, and decided on the first duties to be done.

"Here, ma'am; oh, let me do something!" cried the boy, hurrying from the next room, whither he had withdrawn, feeling that their first sorrow was too sacred for even his friendly eyes to see.

"Send a telegram saying I will come at once. The next train goes early in the morning; I'll take that."

"What else? The horses are ready; I can go anywhere,—do anything," he said, looking ready to fly to ends of the earth.

"Leave a note at Aunt March's. Jo, give me that pen and paper."

Tearing off the blank side of one of her newly-copied pages, Jo drew the table before her mother, well knowing that money for the long, sad journey, must be borrowed, and feeling as if she could do anything to add a little to the sum for her father.

"Now go, dear; but don't kill yourself driving at a desperate pace; there is no need of that."

Mrs. March's warning was evidently thrown away; for five minutes later Laurie tore by the window, on his own fleet horse, riding as if for his life.

"Jo, run to the rooms, and tell Mrs. King that I can't come. On the way get these things. I'll put them down; they'll be needed, and I must go prepared for nursing. Hospital stores are not always good. Beth, go and ask Mr. Laurence for a couple of bottles of old wine; I'm not too proud to beg for father; he shall have the best of everything. Amy, tell Hannah to get down the black trunk; and Meg, come and help me find my things, for I'm half bewildered."

Writing, thinking, and directing all at once, might well bewilder the poor lady, and Meg begged her to sit quietly in her room for a little while, and let them work. Every one scattered, like leaves before a gust of wind; and the quiet, happy household was broken up as suddenly as if the paper had been an evil spell.

Mr. Laurence came hurrying back with Beth, bringing every comfort the kind old gentleman could think of for the invalid, and friendliest promises of protection for the girls, during the mother's absence, which comforted her very much. There was nothing he didn't offer, from his own dressing-gown to himself as escort. But that last was impossible. Mrs. March would not hear of the old gentleman's undertaking the long journey; yet an expression of relief was visible when he spoke of it, for anxiety ill fits one for travelling. He saw the look, knit his heavy eyebrows, rubbed his hands, and marched abruptly away, saying he'd be

8. Given their earlier conversation about temper, Jo would have realized that Mrs. March was keeping her anger at Aunt March's note concealed.

9. The *OED* defines this expression as "with, or as with, a slap and a bang; without delay, immediately; without due consideration or regard to the consequences." According to *Brewer's Dictionary of Phrase and Fable,* 15th ed. (New York: Harper Collins, 1995), "The term was formerly applied to cheap eating houses, where one 'slapped' one's money down as the food was 'banged' on the table" (999).

10. Wild idea.

11. Maria S. Porter, a longtime friend of LMA, recounts in "Recollections of Louisa May Alcott" (1892) the following story that LMA told her one summer night as they floated on the Concord River: "'When I was a girl of eighteen or thereabouts,' she said, 'I had very fine dark brown hair, thick and long, almost touching the floor as I stood. At a time when the family needs were great, and discouragement weighed heavily upon us, I went to a barber, let down my hair, and asked him how much money he would give me for it. When he told me the sum, it seemed so large to me that I then and there determined I would part with my most precious possession if during the next week the clouds did not lift.' This costly gift, however, was not laid upon the family altar by the heroic girl. A friend . . . came to the rescue" (quoted in *Her Own Time* 61–62). While LMA did not sell her hair then, she probably found the inspiration for this scene in *Little Women* in her hospital illness in Georgetown, for in her February 1863 journal she wrote: "Had all my hair 1 ½ yard long cut off & went into caps like a grandma. Felt badly about losing my one beauty. Never mind, it might have been my head & a wig outside is better than a loss of wits inside" (*Journals* 117).

12. The New England name for a Spanish real, which was valued at twelve and a half cents. Spanish currency was the most popular form of money in colonial America and continued to be in use during the first part of the nineteenth century. The real was replaced by the Spanish escudo in 1864.

back directly. No one had time to think of him again till, as Meg ran through the entry, with a pair of rubbers in one hand and a cup of tea in the other, she came suddenly upon Mr. Brooke.

"I'm very sorry to hear of this, Miss March," he said, in the kind, quiet tone which sounded very pleasantly to her perturbed spirit. "I came to offer myself as escort to your mother. Mr. Laurence has commissions for me in Washington, and it will give me real satisfaction to be of service to her there."

Down dropped the rubbers, and the tea was very near following, as Meg put out her hand, with a face so full of gratitude, that Mr. Brooke would have felt repaid for a much greater sacrifice than the trifling one of time and comfort, which he was about to make.

"How kind you all are! Mother will accept, I'm sure; and it will be such a relief to know that she has some one to take care of her. Thank you very, very much!"

Meg spoke earnestly, and forgot herself entirely till something in the brown eyes looking down at her made her remember the cooling tea, and lead the way into the parlor, saying she would call her mother.

Everything was arranged by the time Laurie returned with a note from Aunt March, enclosing the desired sum, and a few lines repeating what she had often said before, that she had always told them it was absurd for March to go into the army, always predicted that no good would come of it, and she hoped they would take her advice next time. Mrs. March put the note in the fire, the money in her purse, and went on with her preparations, with her lips folded tightly, in a way which Jo would have understood if she had been there.[8]

The short afternoon wore away; all the other errands were done, and Meg and her mother busy at some necessary needlework, while Beth and Amy got tea, and Hannah finished her ironing with what she called a "slap and a bang,"[9] but still Jo did not come. They began to get anxious; and Laurie went off to find her, for no one ever knew what freak[10] Jo might take into her head. He missed her, however, and she came walking in with a very queer expression of countenance, for there was a mixture of fun and fear, satisfaction and regret in it, which puzzled the family as much as did the roll of bills she laid before her mother, saying, with a little choke in her voice, "That's my contribution towards making father comfortable, and bringing him home!"

"My dear, where did you get it! Twenty-five dollars! Jo, I hope you haven't done anything rash?"

"No, it's mine honestly; I didn't beg, borrow, nor steal it. I earned it; and I don't think you'll blame me, for I only sold what was my own."

As she spoke, Jo took off her bonnet, and a general outcry arose, for all her abundant hair was cut short.[11]

"Your hair! Your beautiful hair!" "Oh, Jo, how could you? Your one beauty." "My dear girl, there was no need of this." "She don't look like my Jo any more, but I love her dearly for it!"

As every one exclaimed, and Beth hugged the cropped head tenderly, Jo assumed an indifferent air, which did not deceive any one a particle, and said, rumpling up the brown bush, and trying to look as if she liked it, "It doesn't affect the fate of the nation, so don't wail, Beth. It will be good for my vanity; I was getting too proud of my wig. It will do my brains good to have that mop taken off; my head feels deliciously light and cool, and the barber said I could soon have a curly crop, which will be boyish, becoming, and easy to keep in order. I'm satisfied; so please take the money, and let's have supper."

"Tell me all about it, Jo; *I* am not quite satisfied, but I can't blame you, for I know how willingly you sacrificed your vanity, as you call it, to your love. But, my dear, it was not necessary, and I'm afraid you will regret it, one of these days," said Mrs. March.

"No I won't!" returned Jo, stoutly, feeling much relieved that her prank was not entirely condemned.

"What made you do it?" asked Amy, who would as soon have thought of cutting off her head as her pretty hair.

"Well, I was wild to do something for father," replied Jo, as they gathered about the table, for healthy young people can eat even in the midst of trouble. "I hate to borrow as much as mother does, and I knew Aunt March would croak; she always does, if you ask for a ninepence.[12] Meg gave all her quarterly salary toward

Jo's haircut. Betty Fraser, *Little Women* (1962).

the rent, and I only got some clothes with mine, so I felt wicked, and was bound to have some money, if I sold the nose off my face to get it."

"You needn't feel wicked, my child, you had no winter things, and got the simplest, with your own hard earnings," said Mrs. March, with a look that warmed Jo's heart.

"I hadn't the least idea of selling my hair at first, but as I went along I kept thinking *what* I could do, and feeling as if I'd like to dive into some of the rich stores and help myself. In a barber's window I saw tails of hair with the prices marked; and one black tail, longer, but not so thick[d] as mine, was forty dollars. It came over me all of a sudden that I had one thing to make money out of, and, without stopping to think, I walked in, asked if they bought hair, and what they would give for mine."

"I don't see how you dared to do it," said Beth, in a tone of awe.

"Oh, he was a little man who looked as if he merely lived to oil his hair. He rather stared, at first, as if he wasn't used to having girls bounce into his shop and ask him to buy their hair. He said he didn't care about mine, it wasn't the fashionable color, and he never paid much for it in the first place; the work put into it made it dear, and so on. It was getting late, and I was afraid, if it wasn't done right away, that I shouldn't have it done at all, and you know, when I start to do a thing, I hate to give it up; so I begged him to

LITTLE WOMEN

take it, and told him why I was in such a hurry. It was silly, I dare say, but it changed his mind, for I got rather excited, and told the story in my topsy-turvy way, and his wife heard, and said so kindly,"—

"'Take it, Thomas, and oblige the young lady; I'd do as much for our Jimmy any day if I had a spire of hair worth selling.'"

"Who was Jimmy?" asked Amy, who liked to have things explained as they went along.

"Her son, she said, who is in the army. How friendly such things make strangers feel, don't they? She talked away all the time the man clipped, and diverted my mind nicely."

"Didn't you feel dreadfully when the first cut came?" asked Meg, with a shiver.

"I took a last look at my hair while the man got his things, and that was the end of it. I never snivel over trifles like that; I will confess, though, I felt queer when I saw the dear old hair laid out on the table, and felt only the short, rough ends on my head. It almost seemed as if I'd an arm or a leg off. The woman saw me look at it, and picked out a long lock for me to keep. I'll give it to you, Marmee, just to remember past glories by; for a crop is so comfortable I don't think I shall ever have a mane again."

Mrs. March folded the wavy, chestnut lock, and laid it away with a short gray one[13] in her desk. She only said "Thank you, deary," but something in her face made the girls change the subject, and talk as cheerfully as they could about Mr. Brooke's kindness, the prospect of a fine day to-morrow, and the happy times they would have when father came home to be nursed.

No one wanted to go to bed, when, at ten o'clock, Mrs. March put by the last finished job, and said, "Come, girls." Beth went to the piano and played the father's favorite hymn; all began bravely, but broke down one by one till Beth was left alone, singing with all her heart, for to her music was always a sweet consoler.

"Go to bed, and don't talk, for we must be up early, and shall need all the sleep we can get. Good-night, my darlings," said Mrs. March, as the hymn ended, for no one cared to try another.

They kissed her quietly, and went to bed as silently as if the dear invalid lay in the next room. Beth and Amy soon fell asleep

13. A lock of Mr. March's hair, which he had most likely given her when he went off to war. Mr. March would likely have a keepsake as well from Marmee—a locket or tin-type, along with a snippet of hair.

14. A bed covering or bedspread.

in spite of the great trouble, but Meg lay awake thinking the most serious thoughts she had ever known in her short life. Jo lay motionless, and her sister fancied that she was asleep, till a stifled sob made her exclaim, as she touched a wet cheek,—

"Jo, dear, what is it? Are you crying about father?"

"No, not now."

"What then?"

"My—my hair," burst out poor Jo, trying vainly to smother her emotion in the pillow.

It did not sound at all comical to Meg, who kissed and caressed the afflicted heroine in the tenderest manner.

"I'm not sorry," protested Jo, with a choke. "I'd do it again to-morrow, if I could. It's only the vain, selfish part of me that goes and cries in this silly way. Don't tell any one, it's all over now. I thought you were asleep, so I just made a little private moan for my one beauty. How came you to be awake?"

"I can't sleep, I'm so anxious," said Meg.

"Think about something pleasant, and you'll soon drop off."

"I tried it, but felt wider awake than ever."

"What did you think of?"

"Handsome faces; eyes particularly," answered Meg smilingly, to herself, in the dark.

"What color do you like best?"

"Brown—that is sometimes—blue are lovely."

Jo laughed, and Meg sharply ordered her not to talk, then amiably promised to make her hair curl, and fell asleep to dream of living in her castle in the air.

The clocks were striking midnight, and the rooms were very still, as a figure glided quietly from bed to bed, smoothing a coverlid[14] here, setting a pillow there, and pausing to look long and tenderly at each unconscious face, to kiss each with lips that mutely blessed, and to pray the fervent prayers which only mothers utter. As she lifted the curtain to look out into the dreary night, the moon broke suddenly from behind the clouds, and shone upon her like a bright benignant face, which seemed to whisper in the silence, "Be comforted, dear heart! there is always light behind the clouds."[e]

Chapter 16

Letters

N THE cold gray dawn the sisters lit their lamp, and read their chapter with an earnestness never felt before, for now the shadow of a real trouble had come, showing them how rich in sunshine their lives had been. The little books[a] were full of help and comfort; and, as they dressed, they agreed to say good-by cheerfully, hopefully, and send their mother on her anxious journey unsaddened by tears or complaints from them. Everything seemed very strange when they went down; so dim and still outside, so full of light and bustle within. Breakfast at that early hour seemed odd, and even Hannah's familiar face looked unnatural as she flew about her kitchen with her night cap on. The big trunk stood ready in the hall, mother's cloak and bonnet lay on the sofa, and mother herself sat trying to eat, but looking so pale and worn with sleeplessness and anxiety, that the girls found it very hard to keep their resolution. Meg's eyes kept filling in spite of herself; Jo was obliged to hide her face in the kitchen roller[1] more than once, and the little girls' young faces wore a grave, troubled expression, as if sorrow was a new experience to them.

Nobody talked much, but, as the time drew very near, and they sat waiting for the carriage, Mrs. March said to the girls, who were all busied about her, one folding her shawl, another smoothing out the strings of her bonnet, a third putting on her overshoes, and a fourth fastening up her travelling bag,—

"Children, I leave you to Hannah's care, and Mr. Laurence's protection; Hannah is faithfulness itself, and our good neighbor will guard you as if you were his own. I have no fears for you, yet I

2. Abigail Alcott used this phrase to inspire Louisa as a child. She wrote the following note in LMA's 1845 journal: "MY DEAREST LOUY,—I often peep into your diary, hoping to see some record of more happy days. 'Hope, and keep busy,' dear daughter, and in all perplexity or trouble come freely to your MOTHER" (*Journals* 55).

3. In book two of *The Pilgrim's Progress,* the Interpreter offers his kind servant, Mr. Great-Heart, to serve as a guide and protector for Christiana, Christian's wife, as she and her companions travel from the Interpreter's house to the Celestial City. In many ways, *Little Women* resembles book two of *The Pilgrim's Progress.* Like Christiana, Marmee undertakes the journey alongside her children. Bunyan is entirely explicit in his belief in the spiritual equality of men and women, and LMA shows how that idea has taken root in nineteenth-century America, by motivating individual and cooperative actions for social change. LMA's pilgrims are themselves agents of change and fully deserving of the same rights and dignity as their male counterparts.

am anxious that you should take this trouble rightly. Don't grieve and fret when I am gone, or think that you can comfort yourselves by being idle, and trying to forget. Go on with your work as usual, for work is a blessed solace. Hope, and keep busy;[2] and, whatever happens, remember that you never can be fatherless."

"Yes, mother."

"Meg dear, be prudent, watch over your sisters, consult Hannah, and, in any perplexity, go to Mr. Laurence. Be patient, Jo, don't get despondent, or do rash things; write to me often, and be my brave girl, ready to help and cheer us all. Beth, comfort yourself with your music, and be faithful to the little home duties; and you, Amy, help all you can, be obedient, and keep happy safe at home."

"We will, mother! we will!"

The rattle of an approaching carriage made them all start and listen. That was the hard minute, but the girls stood it well; no one cried, no one ran away, or uttered a lamentation, though their hearts were very heavy as they sent loving messages to father, remembering, as they spoke, that it might be too late to deliver them. They kissed their mother quietly, clung about her tenderly, and tried to wave their hands cheerfully, when she drove away.

Laurie and his grandfather came over to see her off, and Mr. Brooke looked so strong, and sensible, and kind, that the girls christened him "Mr. Greatheart,"[3] on the spot.

"Good-by, my darlings! God bless and keep us all," whispered Mrs. March, as she kissed one dear little face after the other, and hurried into the carriage.

As she rolled away, the sun came out, and, looking back, she saw it shining on the group at the gate, like a good omen. They saw it also, and smiled and waved their hands; and the last thing she beheld, as she turned the corner, was the four bright faces, and behind them, like a body-guard, old Mr. Laurence, faithful Hannah, and devoted Laurie.

"How kind every one is to us," she said, turning to find fresh proof of it in the respectful sympathy of the young man's face.

"I don't see how they can help it," returned Mr. Brooke, laughing so infectiously that Mrs. March could not help smiling; and so the long journey began with the good omens of sunshine, smiles, and cheerful words.

"I feel as if there had been an earthquake," said Jo, as their neighbors went home to breakfast, leaving them to rest and refresh themselves.

"It seems as if half the house was gone," added Meg, forlornly.

Beth opened her lips to say something, but could only point to the pile of nicely-mended hose which lay on mother's table, showing that even in her last hurried moments she had thought and worked for them. It was a little thing, but it went straight to their hearts; and, in spite of their brave resolutions, they all broke down, and cried bitterly.

Hannah wisely allowed them to relieve their feelings; and, when the shower showed signs of clearing up, she came to the rescue, armed with a coffee-pot.

"Now, my dear young ladies, remember what your ma said, and don't fret; come and have a cup of coffee all round, and then let's fall to work, and be a credit to the family."

Coffee was a treat,[4] and Hannah showed great tact in making it that morning. No one could resist her persuasive nods, or the fragrant invitation issuing from the nose of the coffee-pot. They drew up to the table, exchanged their handkerchiefs for napkins, and, in ten minutes, were all right again.

"'Hope and keep busy;' that's the motto for us, so let's see who will remember it best. I shall go to Aunt March, as usual; oh, won't she lecture, though!" said Jo, as she sipped, with returning spirit.

"I shall go to my Kings, though I'd much rather stay at home and attend to things here," said Meg, wishing she hadn't made her eyes so red.

"No need of that; Beth and I can keep house perfectly well," put in Amy, with an important air.

"Hannah will tell us what to do; and we'll have everything nice when you come home," added Beth, getting out her mop and dish-tub without delay.

"I think anxiety is very interesting," observed Amy, eating sugar, pensively.

4. For the Marches, coffee would have been something special. Before and during the Civil War, coffee, being an import, was relatively expensive and was not served at most American tables. Most people drank hot tea. However, Union soldiers were given a ration of coffee and grew to enjoy it. Not willing to give up their caffeine addiction after the war, returning veterans made coffee popular, resulting in an increase in production and consumption.

5. The *OED* defines *mandarin* as an "ornament (typically made of porcelain) representing a seated figure in traditional Chinese costume, with a head which continues to nod for a long time after being shaken."

6. According to J. S. Farmer's *Americanisms* (1889), "New England girls use this term to denote acts of romping, or, to employ an English phrase, which seems its exact equivalent, *to train* is 'to carry on'" (quoted in *OED*).

The girls couldn't help laughing, and felt better for it, though Meg shook her head at the young lady who could find consolation in a sugar-bowl.

The sight of the turn-overs made Jo sober again; and, when the two went out to their daily tasks, they looked sorrowfully back at the window where they were accustomed to see their mother's face. It was gone; but Beth had remembered the little household ceremony, and there she was, nodding away at them like a rosy-faced mandarin.[5]

"That's so like my Beth!" said Jo, waving her hat, with a grateful face. "Good-by, Meggy; I hope the Kings won't train[6] to-day. Don't fret about father, dear," she added, as they parted.

"And I hope Aunt March won't croak. Your hair *is* becoming, and it looks very boyish and nice," returned Meg, trying not to smile at the curly head, which looked comically small on her tall sister's shoulders.

"That's my only comfort;" and, touching her hat à la Laurie, away went Jo, feeling like a shorn sheep on a wintry day.

News from their father comforted the girls very much; for, though dangerously ill, the presence of the best and tenderest of nurses had already done him good. Mr. Brooke sent a bulletin every day, and, as the head of the family, Meg insisted on reading the despatches, which grew more and more cheering as the week passed. At first, every one was eager to write, and plump envelopes were carefully poked into the letter-box, by one or other of the sisters, who felt rather important with their Washington correspondence. As one of these packets contained characteristic notes from the party, we will rob an imaginary mail, and read them:—

"MY DEAREST MOTHER,—

"It is impossible to tell you how happy your last letter made us, for the news was so good we couldn't help laughing and crying over it. How very kind Mr. Brooke is, and how fortunate that Mr. Laurence's business detains him near you so long, since he is so useful to you and father. The girls are all as good as gold. Jo helps me with the sewing, and insists on doing all sorts of hard jobs. I

LITTLE WOMEN

should be afraid she might overdo, if I didn't know that her 'moral fit' wouldn't last long. Beth is as regular about her tasks as a clock, and never forgets what you told her. She grieves about father, and looks sober, except when she is at her little piano. Amy minds me nicely, and I take great care of her. She does her own hair, and I am teaching her to make button-holes, and mend her stockings. She tries very hard, and I know you will be pleased with her improvement when you come. Mr. Laurence watches over us like a motherly old hen, as Jo says; and Laurie is very kind and neighborly. He and Jo keep us merry, for we get pretty blue sometimes, and feel like orphans, with you so far away. Hannah is a perfect saint; she does not scold at all, and always calls me 'Miss Margaret,' which is quite proper, you know, and treats me with respect. We are all well and busy; but we long, day and night, to have you back. Give my dearest love to father, and believe me, ever your own

MEG."

This note, prettily written on scented paper, was a great contrast to the next, which was scribbled on a big sheet of thin, foreign paper, ornamented with blots, and all manner of flourishes and curly-tailed letters:—

"MY PRECIOUS MARMEE,—

"Three cheers for dear old[b] father! Brooke was a trump to telegraph right off, and let us know the minute he was better. I rushed up garret when the letter came, and tried to thank God for being so good to us; but I could only cry and say, 'I'm glad! I'm glad!' Didn't that do as well as a regular prayer? for I felt a great many in my heart. We have such funny times; and now I can enjoy 'em, for every one is so desperately good, it's like living in a nest of turtle-doves. You'd laugh to see Meg head the table, and try to be motherish. She gets prettier every day, and I'm in love with her sometimes. The children are regular archangels,[7] and I-well, I'm Jo, and never shall be anything else. Oh, I must tell you that I came near having a quarrel with Laurie. I freed my mind about a silly little thing, and he was offended. I was right, but didn't speak as I ought, and he marched home, saying he wouldn't

7. The highest rank of all angels.

come again till I begged pardon. I declared I wouldn't, and got mad. It lasted all day; I felt bad, and wanted you very much. Laurie and I are both so proud, it's hard to beg pardon; but I thought he'd come to it, for I *was* in the right. He didn't come; and just at night I remembered what you said when Amy fell into the river. I read my little book, felt better, resolved not to let the sun set on *my* anger, and ran over to tell Laurie I was sorry. I met him at the gate, coming for the same thing. We both laughed, begged each other's pardon, and felt all good and comfortable again.

"I made a 'pome' yesterday, when I was helping Hannah wash; and, as father likes my silly little things, I put it in to amuse him. Give him the lovingest hug that ever was, and kiss yourself a dozen times, for your

"TOPSY-TURVY[8] JO.

"A SONG FROM THE SUDS.

"Queen of my tub, I merrily sing,
  While the white foam rises high;
And sturdily wash, and rinse, and wring,
  And fasten the clothes to dry;
Then out in the free fresh air they swing,
  Under the sunny sky.

"I wish we could wash from our hearts and souls
  The stains of the week away,
And let water and air by their magic make
  Ourselves as pure as they;
Then on the earth there would be indeed
  A glorious washing-day!

"Along the path of a useful life,
  Will heart's-ease ever bloom;
The busy mind has no time to think
  Of sorrow, or care, or gloom;
And anxious thoughts may be swept away,
  As we busily[c] wield a broom.

"I am glad a task to me is given,
    To labor at day by day;
For it brings me health, and strength, and hope,
    And I cheerfully learn to say,—
'Head you may think, Heart you may feel,
    But Hand you shall work alway!'"

"DEAR MOTHER:

"There is only room for me to send my love, and some pressed pansies from the root I have been keeping safe in the house, for father to see. I read every morning, try to be good all day, and sing myself to sleep with father's tune. I can't sing 'Land of the Leal'[9] now; it makes me cry. Every one is very kind, and we are as happy as we can be without you. Amy wants the rest of the page, so I must stop. I didn't forget to cover the holders,[10] and I wind the clock and air the rooms every day.

"Kiss dear father on the cheek he calls mine. Oh, do come soon to your loving

                    "LITTLE BETH."

"MA CHERE MAMMA:

"We are all well I do my lessons always and never corroberate the girls—Meg says I mean contradick so I put in both words and you can take the properest. Meg is a great comfort to me and lets me have jelly every night at tea its so good for me Jo says because it keeps me sweet tempered. Laurie is not as respeckful as he ought to be now I am almost in my teens, he calls me Chick and hurts my feelings by talking French to me very fast when I say Merci or Bon jour as Hattie King does. The sleeves of my blue dress were all worn out and Meg put in new ones but the full front came wrong and they are more blue than the dress. I felt bad but did not fret I bear my troubles well but I do wish Hannah would put more starch in my aprons and have buck wheats every day. Can't she? Didn't I make that interrigation point[11] nice. Meg says my punchtuation and spelling are disgraceful and I am mortyfied but dear me I have so many things to do I can't stop. Adieu, I send heaps of love to Papa.

9. "The Land o' the Leal" (1798) by Caroline Oliphant, Lady Nairne (1766–1845), a Scottish songwriter. Like Robert Burns, she collected a number of Scottish tunes to which she often contributed her original lyrics. In this lyric, the singer seeks a happier life in the land of the leal (the faithful, the honest, the true): "My saul langs to be free, John, / And angels beckon me / To the land o' the leal."

10. Beth is probably referring to a fire-starter holder, also called a fire starter pot, which had been in use since colonial days. The holder was usually a cast iron or brass pot that held a flammable liquid, most likely kerosene in the 1860s. A pumice wand was left to soak in the pot, and then when it was time to start a fire the pumice was lit and held to the kindling. It was a safer and more convenient way to light the fire than using small matches. Since the kerosene was highly flammable it was important that Beth remembered to keep the holders closed.

11. Amy means the *interrogation* point, now commonly called a question mark.

PART I   CHAPTER 16   235

12. Treated with a blue laundry powder, which leaves the clothing blue.

13. Prudent.

14. An American slang term for capers or pranks.

15. The Rappahannock River in eastern Virginia begins in the Blue Ridge Mountains and flows into the Chesapeake Bay. Because it had few bridges and fords, the river was difficult for the Union army to cross during the Civil War, and thus served as the war's eastern-theater boundary. It was the site of several significant battles during the war, including the battle of Fredericksburg (1862) and the battle of Rappahannock Station (1863).

16. In the army, the quartermaster is charged with laying out the camps and overseeing rations, supplies, and ammunition. Like her military counterpart, Hannah oversees the household duties. Laurie's military language reflects the patriotic interest in the Civil War by those on the home front.

"Your affectionate daughter,

"AMY CURTIS MARCH."

"DEAR MIS MARCH:

"I jes drop a line to say we git on fust rate. The girls is clever and fly round right smart. Miss Meg is goin to make a proper good housekeeper; she hes the liking for it, and gits the hang of things surprisin quick. Jo doos beat all for goin ahead, but she don't stop to cal'k'late fust, and you never know where she's like to bring up. She done out a tub of clothes on Monday, but she starched em afore they was wrenched, and blued[12] a pink calico dress till I thought I should a died a laughin. Beth is the best of little creeters, and a sight of help to me, bein so forehanded[13] and dependable. She tries to learn everything, and really goes to market beyond her years; likewise keeps accounts, with my help, quite wonderful. We have got on very economical so fur; I don't let the girls hev coffee only once a week, accordin to your wish, and keep em on plain wholesome vittles. Amy does well about frettin, wearin her best clothes and eatin sweet stuff. Mr. Laurie is as full of didoes[14] as usual, and turns the house upside down frequent; but he heartens up the girls, and so I let em hev full swing. The old man sends heaps of things, and is rather wearin, but means wal, and it aint my place to say nothin. My bread is riz, so no more at this time. I send my duty to Mr. March, and hope he's seen the last of his Pewmonia.

"Yours respectful,

"HANNAH MULLET."

"HEAD NURSE OF WARD II.:

"All serene on the Rappahannock,[15] troops in fine condition, commissary department well conducted, the Home Guard under Colonel Teddy always on duty, Commander-in-chief General Laurence reviews the army daily, Quartermaster[16] Mullett keeps order in camp, and Major Lion does picket duty at night. A salute of twenty-four guns was fired on receipt of good news from Washington, and a dress parade took place at head-quarters. Commander-in-chief sends best wishes, in which he is heartily joined by

COLONEL TEDDY."

LITTLE WOMEN

"DEAR MADAM:

"The little girls are all well; Beth and my boy report daily; Hannah is a model servant, guards pretty Meg like a dragon. Glad the fine weather holds; pray make Brooke useful, and draw on me for funds if expenses exceed your estimate. Don't let your husband want anything. Thank God he is mending.

"Your sincere friend and servant,

"JAMES LAURENCE."

1. *Arsenicum album*, popular in homeopathic medicine, is arsenic oxide and is used to treat a wide range of ailments.

2. The Kings' household. The 1880–1881 edition changed *kingdom* to *her pupils*.

3. Beth feels that time has stopped.

Chapter 17

Little Faithful

FOR A WEEK the amount of virtue in the old house would have supplied the neighborhood. It was really amazing, for every one seemed in a heavenly frame of mind, and self-denial was all the fashion. Relieved of their first anxiety about their father, the girls insensibly relaxed their praiseworthy efforts a little, and began to fall back into the old ways. They did not forget their motto, but hoping and keeping busy seemed to grow easier; and, after such tremendous exertions, they felt that Endeavor deserved a holiday, and gave it a good many.

Jo caught a bad cold through neglecting to cover the shorn head enough, and was ordered to stay at home till she was better, for Aunt March didn't like to hear people read with colds in their heads. Jo liked this, and after an energetic rummage from garret to cellar, subsided on to the sofa to nurse her cold with arsenicum[1] and books. Amy found that house-work and art did not go well together, and returned to her mud pies. Meg went daily to her kingdom,[2] and sewed, or thought she did, at home, but much time was spent in writing long letters to her mother, or reading the Washington despatches over and over. Beth kept on with only slight relapses into idleness or grieving. All the little duties were faithfully done each day, and many of her sisters' also, for they were forgetful, and the house seemed like a clock, whose pendulum was gone a-visiting.[3] When her heart got heavy with longings for mother, or fears for father, she went away into a certain closet, hid her face in the folds of a certain dear old gown, and made her little moan, and prayed her little prayer quietly by herself. Nobody knew what cheered her up after a sober fit, but every one felt how sweet and helpful Beth was, and fell into a way of going to her for comfort or advice in their small affairs.

All were unconscious that this experience was a test of character; and, when the first excitement was over, felt that they had done well, and deserved praise. So they did; but their mistake was in ceasing to do well, and they learned this lesson through much anxiety and regret.

"Meg, I wish you'd go and see the Hummels; you know mother told us not to forget them," said Beth, ten days after Mrs. March's departure.

"I'm too tired to go this afternoon," replied Meg, rocking comfortably, as she sewed.

"Can't you, Jo?" asked Beth.

"Too stormy for me, with my cold."

"I thought it was most[a] well."

"It's well enough for me to go out with Laurie, but not well enough to go the Hummels," said Jo laughing, but looking a little ashamed of her inconsistency.

"Why don't you go yourself?" asked Meg.

"I *have* been every day, but the baby is sick, and I don't know what to do for it. Mrs. Hummel goes away to work, and Lottchen takes care of it; but it gets sicker and sicker, and I think you or Hannah ought to go."

Beth spoke earnestly, and Meg promised she would go tomorrow.

"Ask Hannah for some nice little mess, and take it round, Beth, the air will do you good;" said Jo, adding apologetically, "I'd go, but I want to finish my story."[b]

"My head aches, and I'm tired, so I thought maybe some of you would go," said Beth.[4]

"Amy will be in presently, and she will run down for us," suggested Meg.

"Well, I'll rest a little, and wait for her."

So Beth lay down on the sofa, the others returned to their work, and the Hummels were forgotten. An hour passed, Amy did not come; Meg went to her room to try on a new dress; Jo was absorbed in her story, and Hannah was sound asleep before the

4. Beth's uncharacteristic slowness to come to the aid of others suggests she is already suffering symptoms of scarlet fever. Were her sisters less self-involved they might have taken notice that something is terribly wrong.

5. Camphor is a crystalline compound derived from the aromatic bark and wood of the camphor laurel and used in medicine as a mild analgesic.

6. In June 1856, LMA arrived home "to find dear Betty very ill with scarlet-fever caught from some poor children Mother nursed when they fell sick, living over a cellar where pigs had been kept. The landlord (a deacon) would not clean the place till Mother threatened to sue him for allowing a nuisance. Too late to save two of the poor babies or Lizzie and May from the fever" (*Journals* 79). Elizabeth Alcott would never fully recover from the lingering effects of scarlet fever; she died in Concord on March 14, 1858.

7. The use of *Atropa belladano,* or the deadly nightshade, helped form the basis for homeopathic medicine. The poisoning produced by the plant resembles the symptoms of scarlet fever. The leaves and the root of the plant are pulverized and the juice steeped in alcohol and eventually filtered and diluted to treat scarlet fever.

kitchen fire, when Beth quietly put on her hood, filled her basket with odds and ends for the poor children, and went out into the chilly air with a heavy head, and a grieved look in her patient eyes. It was late when she came back, and no one saw her creep upstairs and shut herself into her mother's room. Half an hour after Jo went to "mother's closet" for something, and there found Beth sitting on the medicine chest, looking very grave with red eyes, and a camphor[5] bottle in her hand.

"Christopher Columbus! what's the matter?" cried Jo, as Beth put out her hand as if to warn her off, and asked quickly,—

"You've had scarlet fever, haven't you?"

"Years ago, when Meg did. Why?"

"Then I'll tell you—oh, Jo, the baby's dead!"

"What baby?"

"Mrs. Hummel's; it died in my lap before she got home," cried Beth, with a sob.

"My poor dear, how dreadful for you! I ought to have gone," said Jo, taking her sister in her lap[c] as she sat down in her mother's big chair, with a remorseful face.

"It wasn't dreadful, Jo, only so sad! I saw in a minute that it was sicker, but Lottchen said her mother had gone for a doctor, so I took baby and let Lotty rest. It seemed asleep, but all of a sudden it gave a little cry, and trembled, and then lay very still. I tried to warm its feet, and Lotty gave it some milk, but it didn't stir, and I knew it was dead."[6]

"Don't cry, dear! what did you do?"

"I just sat and held it softly till Mrs. Hummel came with the doctor. He said it was dead, and looked at Heinrich and Minna, who have got sore throats. 'Scarlet fever, ma'am; ought to have called me before,' he said, crossly. Mrs. Hummel told him she was poor, and had tried to cure baby herself, but now it was too late, and she could only ask him to help the others, and trust to charity for his pay. He smiled then, and was kinder, but it was very sad, and I cried with them till he turned round all of a sudden, and told me to go home and take belladonna[7] right away, or I'd have the fever."

LITTLE WOMEN

"No you won't!" cried Jo, hugging her close, with a frightened look. "Oh, Beth, if you should be sick I never could forgive myself! What *shall* we do?"

"Don't be frightened, I guess I shan't have it badly; I looked in mother's book, and saw that it begins with headache, sore throat, and queer feelings like mine, so I did take some belladonna, and I feel better," said Beth, laying her cold hands on her hot forehead, and trying to look well.

"If mother was only at home!" exclaimed Jo, seizing the book, and feeling that Washington was an immense way off. She read a page, looked at Beth, felt her head, peeped into her throat, and then said, gravely, "You've been over the baby every day for more than a week, and among the others who are going to have it, so I'm afraid you're going to have it, Beth. I'll call Hannah; she knows all about sickness."

"Don't let Amy come; she never had it, and I should hate to give it to her. Can't you and Meg have it over again?" asked Beth, anxiously.

"I guess not; don't care if I do; serve me right, selfish pig, to let you go, and stay writing rubbish myself!" muttered Jo, as she went to consult Hannah.

The good soul was wide awake in a minute, and took the lead

at once, assuring Jo that there was no need to worry; every one had scarlet fever, and, if rightly treated, nobody died; all of which Jo believed, and felt much relieved as they went up to call Meg.

"Now I'll tell you what we'll do," said Hannah, when she had examined and questioned Beth; "we will have Dr. Bangs, just to take a look at you, dear, and see that we start right; then we'll send Amy off to Aunt March's, for a spell, to keep her out of harm's way, and one of you girls can stay at home and amuse Beth for a day or two."

"I shall stay, of course, I'm oldest;" began Meg, looking anxious and self-reproachful.

"*I* shall, because it's my fault she is sick; I told mother I'd do the errands, and I haven't," said Jo, decidedly.

"Which will you have, Beth? there ain't no need of but one," said Hannah.

"Jo, please;" and Beth leaned her head against her sister, with a contented look, which effectually settled that point.

"I'll go and tell Amy," said Meg, feeling a little hurt, yet rather relieved, on the whole, for she did not like nursing, and Jo did.

Amy rebelled outright, and passionately declared that she had rather have the fever than go to Aunt March. Meg reasoned, pleaded, and commanded, all in vain. Amy protested that she would *not* go; and Meg left her in despair, to ask Hannah what should be done. Before she came back, Laurie walked into the parlor to find Amy sobbing, with her head in the sofa cushions. She told her story, expecting to be consoled; but Laurie only put his hands in his pockets and walked about the room, whistling softly, as he knit his brows in deep thought. Presently he sat down beside her and said, in his most wheedlesome[8] tone, "Now be a sensible little woman, and do as they say. No, don't cry, but hear what a jolly plan I've got. You go to Aunt March's, and I'll come and take you out every day, driving or walking, and we'll have capital times. Won't that be better than moping here?"

"I don't wish to be sent off as if I was in the way," began Amy, in an injured voice.

"Bless your heart, child! it's to keep you well. You don't want to be sick, do you?"

"No, I'm sure I don't; but I dare say I shall be, for I've been with Beth all this time."

"That s the very reason you ought to go away at once, so that you may escape it. Change of air and care will keep you well, I dare say; or, if it don't entirely, you will have the fever more lightly. I advise you to be off as soon as you can, for scarlet fever is no joke, miss."[9]

"But it's dull at Aunt March's, and she is so cross," said Amy, looking rather frightened.

"It won't be dull with me popping in every day to tell you how Beth is, and take you out gallivanting. The old lady likes me, and I'll be as clever[d] as possible to her, so she won't peck at us, whatever we do."

"Will you take me out in the trotting wagon with Puck?"[10]

"On my honor as a gentleman."

"And come every single day?"

"See if I don't."

"And bring me back the minute Beth is well?"

"The identical minute."

"And go to the theatre, truly?"

"A dozen theatres, if we may."

"Well—I guess—I will," said Amy, slowly.

"Good girl! Sing out for Meg, and tell her you'll give in," said Laurie, with an approving pat, which annoyed Amy more than the "giving in."

Meg and Jo came running down to behold the miracle which had been wrought; and Amy, feeling very precious and self-sacrificing, promised to go, if the doctor said Beth was going to be ill.

"How is the little dear?" asked Laurie; for Beth was his especial pet, and he felt more anxious about her than he liked to show.

"She is lying down on mother's bed, and feels better. The baby's death troubled her, but I dare say she has only got cold. Hannah *says* she thinks so; but she *looks* worried, and that makes me fidgety," answered Meg.

"What a trying world it is!" said Jo, rumpling up her hair in a fretful sort of way. "No sooner do we get out of one trouble than

9. Scarlet fever, caused by the bacterium *Streptococcus,* was the scourge of the nineteenth century, killing many people, mostly children. The incubation period is one to four days. Its symptoms are high fever, sore throat, a bright red tongue, and, most telling, a red rash. A world pandemic of scarlet fever occurred between 1820 and 1880, mainly because it was easily spread and no real treatment was effective. It would be 1874 before a connection to streptococcus was discovered, and it wasn't until the development of penicillin in the mid-twentieth century that there was an effective and easy cure for scarlet fever. In the nineteenth century, the main treatments were to keep the patient resting in a cool room while trying to control the fever with frequent sponge baths. While various medicines were often given, they did more to ease the fever or pain than to stop the infectious bacteria. An epidemic of scarlet fever broke out in Massachusetts in 1858–1859, killing 2,089 people. Of that number, 95 percent were children under the age of sixteen. Another epidemic occurred in 1867–1868. See Alan C. Swedlund and Alison K. Dunta, "Scarlet Fever Epidemics of the Nineteenth-Century: A Case of Evolved Pathogenic Virulence?" *Human Biologists in the Archives: Demography, Health, Nutrition and Genetics,* ed. D. Ann Herring and Alan C. Swedlund (Cambridge University Press, 2003), pp. 159–177.

10. A trotting wagon is a lightweight, four-wheeled skeleton carriage used for racing. The horse, Puck, is named for the character in Shakespeare's *Midsummer Night's Dream* (written ca. 1594–1596). A mischievous elf, Puck serves as a jester to the fairy king Oberon.

down comes another. There don't seem to be anything to hold on to when mother's gone; so I'm all at sea."

"Well, don't make a porcupine of yourself, it isn't becoming. Settle your wig, Jo, and tell me if I shall telegraph to your mother, or do anything?" asked Laurie, who never had been reconciled to the loss of his friend's one beauty.

"That is what troubles me," said Meg. "I think we ought to tell her if Beth is really ill, but Hannah says we mustn't, for mother can't leave father, and it will only make them anxious. Beth won't be sick long, and Hannah knows just what to do, and mother said we were to mind her, so I suppose we must, but it don't seem quite right to me."

"Hum, well, I can't say; suppose you ask grandfather, after the doctor has been."

"We will; Jo, go and get Dr. Bangs at once," commanded Meg; "we can't decide anything till he has been."

"Stay where you are, Jo; I'm errand boy to this establishment," said Laurie, taking up his cap.

"I'm afraid you are busy," began Meg.

"No, I've done my lessons for the day."

"Do you study in vacation time?" asked Jo.

"I follow the good example my neighbors set me," was Laurie's answer, as he swung himself out of the room.

"I have great hopes of my boy," observed Jo, watching him fly over the fence with an approving smile.

"He does very well—for a boy," was Meg's somewhat ungracious answer, for the subject did not interest her.

Dr. Bangs came, said Beth had symptoms of the fever, but thought she would have it lightly, though he looked sober over the Hummel story. Amy was ordered off at once, and provided with something to ward off danger; she departed in great state, with Jo and Laurie as escort.

Aunt March received them with her usual hospitality.

"What do you want now?" she asked, looking sharply over her spectacles, while the parrot, sitting on the back of her chair, called out,—

"Go away; no boys allowed here."

Laurie retired to the window, and Jo told her story.

"No more than I expected, if you are allowed to go poking about among poor folks. Amy can stay and make herself useful if she isn't sick, which I've no doubt she will be,—looks like it now. Don't cry, child, it worries me to hear people sniff."

Amy *was* on the point of crying, but Laurie slyly pulled the parrot's tail, which caused Polly to utter an astonished croak, and call out,—

"Bless my boots!" in such a funny way, that she laughed instead.

"What do you hear from your mother?" asked the old lady, gruffly.

"Father is much better," replied Jo, trying to keep sober.

"Oh, is he? Well, that won't last long, I fancy; March never had any stamina," was the cheerful reply.

"Ha, ha! never say die, take a pinch of snuff, good-by, good-by!" squalled Polly, dancing on her perch, and clawing at the old lady's cap as Laurie tweaked him in the rear.

"Hold your tongue, you disrespectful old bird! and, Jo, you'd better go at once; it isn't proper to be gadding[11] about so late with a rattle-pated boy like—"

"Hold your tongue, you disrespectful old bird!" cried Polly, tumbling off the chair with a bounce, and running to peck the "rattle-pated"[12] boy, who was shaking with laughter at the last speech.

"I don't think I *can* bear it, but I'll try," thought Amy, as she was left alone with Aunt March.

"Get along, you're a fright!" screamed Polly, and at that rude speech Amy could not restrain a sniff.

11. Roaming about from place to place with no serious purpose.
12. Foolish or empty-headed.

1. LMA noted the effect of Elizabeth's illness on the family in June 1856: "An anxious time" (*Journals* 79). Like the quiet, shy Beth in the novel, Lizzie (sometimes Betty), as she was called by her family and friends, seemed very much a shadowy figure in Louisa's life. Born on June 24, 1835, in Boston, Elizabeth would always be the spiritual, ethereal child of the family. Called "Psyche" by her father, Lizzie affected all of the Alcotts' lives. She would be the Angel in the House, as Louisa calls her in *Little Women*. Almost eighteen years later, the family, now relocated to High Street in Boston, were all busy, with Anna and Louisa keeping school for five students in the family parlor. Lizzie, Louisa noted, "was our little housekeeper—our angel in a cellar kitchen" (*Journals* 67). The following year, "Betty was still the home bird" (*Journals* 69). At one point, Louisa called her, in 1854, "Cinderella," implying that she was the sister, like the fairy-tale character, continually performing housework while the others were out in the working world (*Journals* 72).

Chapter 18

Dark Days

BETH did have the fever, and was much sicker than any one but Hannah and the doctor suspected. The girls knew nothing about illness, and Mr. Laurence was not allowed to see her, so Hannah had everything all her own way, and busy Dr. Bangs did his best, but left a good deal to the excellent nurse. Meg stayed at home, lest she should infect the Kings, and kept house, feeling very anxious, and a little guilty, when she wrote letters in which no mention was made of Beth's illness. She could not think it right to deceive her mother, but she had been bidden to mind Hannah, and Hannah wouldn't hear of "Mrs. March bein' told, and worried just for sech a trifle." Jo devoted herself to Beth day and night; not a hard task, for Beth was very patient, and bore her pain uncomplainingly as long as she could control herself. But there came a time when during the fever fits she began to talk in a hoarse, broken voice, to play on the coverlet, as if on her beloved little piano, and try to sing with a throat so swollen, that there was no music left; a time when she did not know the familiar faces round her, but addressed them by wrong names, and called imploringly for her mother. Then Jo grew frightened, Meg begged to be allowed to write the truth, and even Hannah said she "would think of it, though there was no danger yet." A letter from Washington added to their trouble, for Mr. March had had a relapse, and could not think of coming home for a long while.

How dark the days seemed now, how sad and lonely the house, and how heavy were the hearts of the sisters as they worked and waited, while the shadow of death hovered over the once happy home![1] Then it was that Margaret, sitting alone with tears dropping often on her work, felt how rich she had been in things more precious than any luxuries money could buy; in love, protection, peace and health, the real blessings of life. Then it was that Jo, living in the darkened room with that suffering little sister always before her eyes, and that pathetic voice sounding in her ears, learned to see the beauty and the sweetness of Beth's nature, to feel how deep and tender a place she filled in all hearts, and to acknowledge the worth of Beth's unselfish ambition, to live for others, and make home happy by the exercise of those simple virtues which all may possess, and which all should love and value more than talent, wealth or beauty. And Amy, in her exile, longed eagerly to be at home, that she might work for Beth, feeling now that no service would be hard or irksome, and remembering, with regretful grief, how many neglected tasks those willing hands had done for her. Laurie haunted the house like a restless ghost, and Mr. Laurence locked the grand piano, because he could not bear to be reminded of the young neighbor who used to make the twilight pleasant for him. Every one missed Beth. The milk-man, baker, grocer and butcher inquired how she did; poor Mrs. Hummel came to beg pardon for her thoughtlessness, and to get a shroud for Minna; the neighbors sent all sorts of comforts and good wishes, and even those who knew her best, were surprised to find how many friends shy little Beth had made.

Meanwhile she lay on her bed with old Joanna at her side, for even in her wanderings she did not forget her forlorn *protégé.* She longed for her cats, but would not have them brought, lest they should get sick; and, in her quiet hours, she was full of anxiety about Jo. She sent loving messages to Amy, bade them tell her mother that she would write soon; and often begged for pencil and paper to try to say a word, that father might not think she had neglected him. But soon even these intervals of consciousness ended, and she lay hour after hour tossing to and fro with incoherent words on her lips, or sank into a heavy sleep which brought her no refreshment. Dr. Bangs came twice a day, Hannah sat up at night, Meg kept a telegram in her desk all ready to send off at any minute, and Jo never stirred from Beth's side.

The first of December was a wintry day indeed to them, for a

Louisa May Alcott, circa 1870s. After the success of *Little Women*, LMA posed for a number of professional photographs, which were then given as a *carte de visite* or a cabinet card to her admirers.

bitter wind blew, snow fell fast, and the year seemed getting ready for its death. When Dr. Bangs came that morning, he looked long at Beth, held the hot hand in both his own a minute, and laid it gently down, saying, in a low tone, to Hannah,—

"If Mrs. March can leave her husband, she'd better be sent for."

Hannah nodded without speaking, for her lips twitched nervously; Meg dropped down into a chair as the strength seemed to go out of her limbs at the sound of those words, and Jo, after standing with a pale face for a minute, ran to the parlor, snatched up the telegram, and, throwing on her things, rushed out into the storm. She was soon back, and, while noiselessly taking off her cloak, Laurie came in with a letter, saying that Mr. March was mending again. Jo read it thankfully, but the heavy weight did not seem lifted off her heart, and her face was so full of misery that Laurie asked, quickly,—

"What is it? is Beth worse?"

"I've sent for mother," said Jo, tugging at her rubber boots with a tragical expression.

"Good for you, Jo! Did you do it on your own responsibility?" asked Laurie, as he seated her in the hall chair, and took off the rebellious boots, seeing how her hands shook.

"No, the doctor told us to."

"Oh, Jo, it's not so bad as that?" cried Laurie, with a startled face.

"Yes, it is; she don't know us, she don't even talk about the flocks of green doves, as she calls the vine leaves on the wall; she don't look like my Beth, and there's nobody to help us bear it; mother and father both gone, and God seems so far away I can't find Him."

As the tears streamed fast down poor Jo's cheeks, she stretched out her hand in a helpless sort of way, as if groping in the dark, and Laurie took it in his, whispering, as well as he could, with a lump in his throat,—

"I'm here, hold on to me, Jo, dear!"

She could not speak, but she did "hold on," and the warm grasp of the friendly human hand comforted her sore heart, and seemed to lead her nearer to the Divine arm which alone could uphold her in her trouble. Laurie longed to say something tender and comfortable, but no fitting words came to him, so he stood silent, gently stroking her bent head as her mother used to do. It was the best thing he could have done; far more soothing than the most eloquent words, for Jo felt the unspoken sympathy, and, in the silence, learned the sweet solace which affection administers to sorrow. Soon she dried the tears which had relieved her, and looked up with a grateful face.

"Thank you, Teddy, I'm better now; I don't feel so forlorn, and will try to bear it if it comes."

"Keep hoping for the best; that will help you lots, Jo. Soon your mother will be here, and then everything will be right."

"I'm so glad father is better; now she won't feel so bad about leaving him. Oh, me! it does seem as if all the troubles came in a heap, and I got the heaviest part on my shoulders," sighed Jo, spreading her wet handkerchief over her knees, to dry.

"Don't Meg pull fair?"[2] asked Laurie, looking indignant.

"Oh, yes; she tries to, but she don't[a] love Bethy as I do; and she won't miss her as I shall. Beth is my conscience, and I *can't* give her up; I can't! I can't!"

Down went Jo's face into the wet handkerchief, and she cried despairingly; for she had kept up bravely till now, and never shed a tear. Laurie drew his hand across his eyes, but could not speak till he had subdued the choky feeling in his throat, and steadied his lips. It might be unmanly, but he couldn't help it, and I am glad of it. Presently, as Jo's sobs quieted, he said, hopefully, "I don't think she will die; she's so good, and we all love her so much, I don't believe God will take her away yet."

"The good and dear people always do die," groaned Jo, but she stopped crying, for her friend's words cheered her up, in spite of her own doubts and fears.

"Poor girl! you're worn out. It isn't like you to be forlorn. Stop a bit; I'll hearten you up in a jiffy."

Laurie went off two stairs at a time, and Jo laid her wearied head down on Beth's little brown hood, which no one had thought of moving from the table where she left it. It must have

2. To do her share of the housework or the nursing of Beth.

3. The phrase means to give one's inner-self deep pleasure or contentment. The *OED* indicates that the original phrase was "Rejoice the cockles of the heart" and gives its earliest use as 1669. The origin of the phrase is less clear, but it is most likely linked to the English name for a type of bivalve mollusk, the shape of which resembles a heart. The zoological name for the cockle is *Cardium,* which derives from the Greek word meaning *heart.*

possessed some magic, for the submissive spirit of its gentle owner seemed to enter into Jo; and, when Laurie came running down with a glass of wine, she took it with a smile, and said, bravely, "I drink—Health to my Beth! You are a good doctor, Teddy, and *such* a comfortable friend; how can I ever pay you?" she added, as the wine refreshed her body, as the kind words had done her troubled mind.

"I'll send in my bill, by and by; and to-night I'll give you something that will warm the cockles of your heart[3] better than quarts of wine," said Laurie, beaming at her with a face of suppressed satisfaction at something.

"What is it?" cried Jo, forgetting her woes for a minute, in her wonder.

"I telegraphed to your mother yesterday, and Brooke answered she'd come at once, and she'll be here to-night, and everything will be all right. Aren't you glad I did it?"

Laurie spoke very fast, and turned red and excited all in a minute, for he had kept his plot a secret, for fear of disappointing the girls or harming Beth. Jo grew quite white, flew out of her chair, and the moment he stopped speaking she electrified him by throwing her arms round his neck, and crying out, with a joyful cry, "Oh, Laurie! oh, mother! I *am* so glad!" She did not weep again, but laughed hysterically, and trembled and clung to her friend as if she was a little bewildered by the sudden news. Laurie, though decidedly amazed, behaved with great presence of mind; he patted her back soothingly, and, finding that she was recovering, followed it up by a bashful kiss or two, which brought Jo round at once. Holding on to the banisters, she put him gently away, saying, breathlessly, "Oh, don't! I didn't mean to; it was dreadful of me; but you were such a dear to go and do it in spite of Hannah, that I couldn't help flying at you. Tell me all about it, and don't give me wine again; it makes me act so."

"I don't mind!" laughed Laurie, as he settled his tie. "Why, you see I got fidgety, and so did grandpa. We thought Hannah was overdoing the authority business, and your mother ought to know. She'd never forgive us if Beth,—well, if anything happened, you know. So I got grandpa to say it was high time we did something, and off I pelted to the office yesterday, for the doctor looked sober, and Hannah most took my head off when I proposed a telegram. I never *can* bear to be 'marmed over;'[4] so that settled my mind, and I did it. Your mother will come, I know, and the late train is in at two, A.M. I shall go for her; and you've only got to bottle up your rapture, and keep Beth quiet, till that blessed lady gets here."

"Laurie, you're an angel! How shall I ever thank you?"

"Fly at me again; I rather like it," said Laurie, looking mischievous,—a thing he had not done for a fortnight.

"No, thank you. I'll do it by proxy, when your grandpa comes. Don't tease, but go home and rest, for you'll be up half the night. Bless you, Teddy; bless you!"

Jo had backed into a corner; and, as she finished her speech, she vanished precipitately into the kitchen, where she sat down upon a dresser, and told the assembled cats that she was "happy, oh, *so* happy!" while Laurie departed, feeling that he had made rather a neat thing of it.

"That's the interferingest chap I ever see; but I forgive him, and do hope Mrs. March is coming on right away," said Hannah, with an air of relief, when Jo told the good news.

Meg had a quiet rapture, and then brooded over the letter, while Jo set the sick-room in order, and Hannah "knocked up a couple of pies in case of company unexpected." A breath of fresh air seemed to blow through the house, and something better than sunshine brightened the quiet rooms; everything appeared to feel the hopeful change; Beth's bird began to chirp again, and a half-blown rose was discovered on Amy's bush in the window; the fires seemed to burn with unusual cheeriness, and every time the girls met their pale faces broke into smiles as they hugged one another, whispering, encouragingly, "Mother's coming, dear! mother's coming!" Every one rejoiced but Beth; she lay in that heavy stupor, alike unconscious of hope and joy, doubt and danger. It was a piteous sight,—the once rosy face so changed and vacant,—the once busy hands so weak and wasted,—the once smiling lips quite dumb,—and the once pretty, well-kept hair scattered rough and tangled on the pillow. All day she lay so, only rousing now

4. To be told how to do something or to be under the authority of a woman. *Marm,* which derives from *ma'am,* is also a schoolteacher. In the 1880–1881 edition, the verb is changed to *lorded over.*

5. Once again LMA reminds her readers that they inhabit a kind of alternative Civil War novel. Here the heartache and challenges faced by the girls and Marmee are specifically likened to the killing fields of the war.

6. The "pale shadow" foreshadows events in Part II. The Bible describes the Four Horsemen of the Apocalypse, the fourth one being Death: "And I looked, and behold a pale horse: and his name that sat on him was Death" (Revelation 6:6). It is interesting to note that Beth rhymes with *death*.

and then to mutter, "Water!" with lips so parched they could hardly shape the word; all day Jo and Meg hovered over her, watching, waiting, hoping, and trusting in God and mother; and all day the snow fell, the bitter wind raged, and the hours dragged slowly by. But night came at last; and every time the clock struck the sisters, still sitting on either side the bed, looked at each other with brightening eyes, for each hour brought help nearer. The doctor had been in to say that some change for better or worse would probably take place about midnight, at which time he would return.

Hannah, quite worn out, lay down on the sofa at the bed's foot, and fell fast asleep; Mr. Laurence marched to and fro in the parlor, feeling that he would rather face a rebel battery than Mrs. March's anxious countenance as she entered;[5] Laurie lay on the rug, pretending to rest, but staring into the fire with the thoughtful look which made his black eyes beautifully soft and clear.

The girls never forgot that night, for no sleep came to them as they kept their watch, with that dreadful sense of powerlessness which comes to us in hours like those.

"If God spares Beth I never will complain again," whispered Meg, earnestly.

"If God spares Beth I'll try to love and serve Him all my life," answered Jo, with equal fervor.

"I wish I had no heart, it aches so," sighed Meg, after a pause.

"If life is often as hard as this, I don't see how we ever shall get through it," added her sister, despondently.

Here the clock struck twelve, and both forgot themselves in watching Beth, for they fancied a change passed over her wan face. The house was still as death, and nothing but the wailing of the wind broke the deep hush. Weary Hannah slept on, and no one but the sisters saw the pale shadow[6] which seemed to fall upon the little bed. An hour went by, and nothing happened except Laurie's quiet departure for the station. Another hour,—still no one came; and anxious fears of delay in the storm, or accidents by the way, or, worst of all, a great grief at Washington, haunted the poor girls.

LITTLE WOMEN

It was past two, when Jo, who stood at the window thinking how dreary the world looked in its winding-sheet of snow, heard a movement by the bed, and, turning quickly, saw Meg kneeling before their mother's easy-chair, with her face hidden. A dreadful fear passed coldly over Jo, as she thought, "Beth is dead, and Meg is afraid to tell me."

She was back at her post in an instant, and to her excited eyes a great change seemed to have taken place. The fever flush, and the look of pain, were gone, and the beloved little face looked so pale and peaceful in its utter repose, that Jo felt no desire to weep or to lament. Leaning low over this dearest of her sisters, she kissed the damp forehead with her heart on her lips, and softly whispered, "Good-by, my Beth; good-by!"

As if waked by the stir, Hannah started out of her sleep, hurried to the bed, looked at Beth, felt her hands, listened at her lips, and then, throwing her apron over her head, sat down to rock to and fro, exclaiming, under her breath, "The fever's turned; she's sleepin nat'ral; her skin's damp, and she breathes easy. Praise be given! Oh, my goodness me!"

Before the girls could believe the happy truth, the doctor came to confirm it. He was a homely man, but they thought his face quite heavenly when he smiled, and said, with a fatherly look at them, "Yes, my dears; I think the little girl will pull through this time. Keep the house quiet; let her sleep, and when she wakes, give her—"

What they were to give, neither heard; for both crept into the dark hall, and, sitting on the stairs, held each other close, rejoicing with hearts too full for words. When they went back to be kissed and cuddled by faithful Hannah, they found Beth lying, as she used to do, with her cheek pillowed on her hand, the dreadful pallor gone, and breathing quietly, as if just fallen asleep.

"If mother would only come now!" said Jo, as the winter night began to wane.

"See," said Meg, coming up with a white, half-opened rose, "I thought this would hardly be ready to lay in Beth's hand to-morrow if she—went away from us. But it has blossomed in the night, and now I mean to put it in my vase here, so that when the darling wakes, the first thing she sees will be the little rose, and mother's face."

Never had the sun risen so beautifully, and never had the world seemed so lovely, as it did to the heavy eyes of Meg and Jo, as they looked out in the early morning, when their long, sad vigil was done.

"It looks like a fairy world," said Meg, smiling to herself, as she stood behind the curtain watching the dazzling sight.

"Hark!" cried Jo, starting to her feet.

Yes, there was a sound of bells at the door below, a cry from Hannah, and then Laurie's voice, saying, in a joyful whisper, "Girls! she's come! she's come!"

Chapter 19

Amy's Will

WHILE THESE things were happening at home, Amy was having hard times at Aunt March's. She felt her exile deeply, and, for the first time in her life, realized how much she was beloved and petted at home. Aunt March never petted any one; she did not approve of it; but she meant to be kind, for the well-behaved little girl pleased her very much, and Aunt March had a soft place in her old heart for her nephew's children, though she didn't think proper to confess it. She really did her best to make Amy happy, but, dear me, what mistakes she made! Some old people keep young at heart in spite of wrinkles and gray hairs, can sympathize with children's little cares and joys, make them feel at home, and can hide wise lessons under pleasant plays, giving and receiving friendship in the sweetest way. But Aunt March had not this gift, and she worried Amy most to death with her rules and orders, her prim ways, and long, prosy[1] talks. Finding the child more docile and amiable than her sister, the old lady felt it her duty to try and counteract, as far as possible, the bad effects of home freedom and indulgence. So she took Amy in hand, and taught her as she herself had been taught sixty years ago; a process which carried dismay to Amy's soul, and made her feel like a fly in the web of a very strict spider.

She had to wash the cups every morning, and polish up the old-fashioned spoons, the fat silver teapot, and the glasses, till they shone. Then she must dust the room, and what a trying job that was! Not a speck escaped Aunt March's eye, and all the furniture had claw legs, and much carving, which was never dusted to suit. Then Polly must be fed, the lap-dog combed, and a dozen

2. Groomed him.

3. While many immigrants to the United States in the nineteenth century Anglicized their names, employers did not regularly insist upon it. With anti-Catholic discrimination and prejudice high in Boston, perhaps Aunt March does not want her society friends to readily know her servant is Catholic. Aunt March herself does not seem to be anti-Catholic since she both hires Esther and does not ask her to abandon Catholicism. The name *Estelle* is of French and Latin origin, meaning *star*. To most readers in Alcott's day, the name Estelle would be almost immediately identified with the character Estelle Havisham in Charles Dickens's *Great Expectations* (1860–1861), the young orphan adopted by the eccentric Mrs. Havisham and brought up to be a lady. Esther, an old Hebrew name, recalls the character Esther Summerton in Dickens's *Bleak House* (1852–1853).

4. Organized.

5. A common bird of the crow family with a reputation for taking and hoarding objects.

6. Cabinet that has characteristic Chinese designs, usually imported in the nineteenth century by the East India Company.

trips upstairs and down, to get things or deliver orders, for the old lady was very lame, and seldom left her big chair. After these tiresome labors she must do her lessons, which was a daily trial of every virtue she possessed. Then she was allowed one hour for exercise or play, and didn't she enjoy it? Laurie came every day, and wheedled Aunt March till Amy was allowed to go out with him, when they walked and rode, and had capital times. After dinner she had to read aloud, and sit still while the old lady slept, which she usually did for an hour, as she dropped off over the first page. Then patch-work or towels appeared, and Amy sewed with outward meekness and inward rebellion till dusk, when she was allowed to amuse herself as she liked, till tea-time. The evenings were the worst of all, for Aunt March fell to telling long stories about her youth, which were so unutterably dull, that Amy was always ready to go to bed, intending to cry over her hard fate, but usually going to sleep before she had squeezed out more than a tear or two.

If it had not been for Laurie and old Esther, the maid, she felt that she never could have got through that dreadful time. The parrot alone was enough to drive her distracted, for he soon felt that she did not admire him, and revenged himself by being as mischievous as possible. He pulled her hair whenever she came near him, upset his bread and milk to plague her when she had newly cleaned his cage, made Mop bark by pecking at him while Madame dozed; called her names before company, and behaved in all respects like a reprehensible old bird. Then she could not endure the dog, a fat, cross beast, who snarled and yelped at her when she made his toilet,[2] and who laid on his back with all his legs in the air, and a most idiotic expression of countenance, when he wanted something to eat, which was about a dozen times a day. The cook was bad-tempered, the old coachman deaf, and Esther the only one who ever took any notice of the young lady.

Esther was a French woman, who had lived with "Madame," as she called her mistress, for many years, and who rather tyrannized over the old lady, who could not get along without her. Her real name was Estelle; but Aunt March ordered her to change it, and she obeyed, on condition that she was never asked to change her

Mourning locket with lock of hair.

religion.[3] She took a fancy to Mademoiselle, and amused her very much, with odd stories of her life in France, when Amy sat with her while she got up[4] Madame's laces. She also allowed her to roam about the great house, and examine the curious and pretty things stored away in the big wardrobes and the ancient chests; for Aunt March hoarded like a magpie.[5] Amy's chief delight was an Indian cabinet[6] full of queer drawers, little pigeon-holes, and secret places in which were kept all sorts of ornaments, some precious, some merely curious, all more or less antique. To examine and arrange these things gave Amy great satisfaction, especially the jewel cases; in which, on velvet cushions, reposed the ornaments which had adorned a belle forty years ago. There was the garnet set which Aunt March wore when she came out, the pearls

7. Mourning jewelry, worn as a memorial to a deceased person, was extremely fashionable in the nineteenth century and reached the height of its popularity during the Civil War. Many pieces were made from jet, a semi-precious fossilized coal that could be highly polished.

8. During the nineteenth century, the art of weaving a deceased loved one's locks of hair into an elaborate design and placing it in a locket or brooch was popular. Hair was often woven into the shape of a weeping willow tree *(Salix babylonica)*, which was a symbol of mourning, as its long, slender, hanging branches appeared to be weeping.

9. As a Protestant, Amy would not necessarily be familiar with this uniquely Catholic string of beads used to keep count of the recital of devotions. Small beads symbolized *Hail Marys* and large ones *Our Fathers* and *Glory Bes.*

10. Trinket or jewel. Aunt March clearly uses the beads not as a rosary but as a necklace since she keeps them with her other jewelry of forty years ago. Most likely she bought them in her travels or they were given to her because of their ornamental appearance.

11. It is important to note Esther's words here. Although she changed her name for Aunt March's sake, she does not give up her Catholic faith; but neither, on the other hand, does Esther expect Amy to subscribe to her Catholic beliefs. Christine Doyle observes: "Esther then helps Amy to set up a small chapel, complete with a picture of the Virgin Mary, for quiet meditation: Amy adds her New Testament and hymn-book to the decor, but draws the line at Esther's gift of a rosary, which she uses as a decoration for her chapel but not as an instrument of prayer. Unlike more vehemently negative depictions of Catholic behavior, Alcott's contains neither pressure for conversion nor criticism of Esther's or Amy's methods of devotion; instead, she projects an attitude of acceptance for whatever method brings the soul to God" (*Louisa May Alcott & Charlotte Brontë: Transatlantic Translations* [Knoxville: University of Tennessee Press, 2000], p. 89). LMA herself was never a member of a particular religion. On February 5, 1884, she wrote to young Maggie Lukens, who appeared to be struggling with her own faith: "My parents never bound us to any church but taught us that the love of goodness was the love of God, the cheerful doing of duty made life happy, & that the love of one's neighbor in its widest sense was the best help for oneself" (*Selected Letters* 276).

her father gave her on her wedding day, her lover's diamonds, the jet mourning rings and pins,[7] the queer lockets, with portraits of dead friends, and weeping willows made of hair inside,[8] the baby bracelets her one little daughter had worn; Uncle March's big watch, with the red seal so many childish hands had played with, and in a box, all by itself, lay Aunt March's wedding ring, too small now for her fat finger, but put carefully away, like the most precious jewel of them all.

"Which would Mademoiselle choose if she had her will?" asked Esther, who always sat near to watch over and lock up the valuables.

"I like the diamonds best, but there is no necklace among them, and I'm fond of necklaces, they are so becoming. I should choose this if I might," replied Amy, looking with great admiration at a string of gold and ebony beads, from which hung a heavy cross of the same.

"I, too, covet that, but not as a necklace; ah, no! to me it is a rosary,[9] and as such I should use it like a good Catholic," said Esther, eyeing the handsome thing wistfully.

"Is it meant to use as you use the string of good-smelling wooden beads hanging over your glass?" asked Amy.

"Truly, yes, to pray with. It would be pleasing to the saints if one used so fine a rosary as this, instead of wearing it as a vain bijou."[10]

"You seem to take a deal[a] of comfort in your prayers, Esther, and always come down looking quiet and satisfied. I wish I could."

"If Mademoiselle was a Catholic, she would find true comfort; but, as that is not to be,[11] it would be well if you went apart each day to meditate, and pray, as did the good mistress whom I served before Madame. She had a little chapel, and in it found solacement for much trouble."

"Would it be right for me to do so too?" asked Amy, who, in her loneliness, felt the need of help of some sort, and found that she was apt to forget her little book, now that Beth was not there to remind her of it.

"It would be excellent and charming; and I shall gladly arrange the little dressing-room for you, if you like it. Say nothing to Madame, but when she sleeps go you and sit alone a while to think good thoughts, and ask the dear God to preserve your sister."

Esther was truly pious, and quite sincere in her advice; for she had an affectionate heart, and felt much for the sisters in their anxiety. Amy liked the idea, and gave her leave to arrange the light closet[12] next her room, hoping it would do her good.

"I wish I knew where all these pretty things would go when Aunt March dies," she said, as she slowly replaced the shining rosary, and shut the jewel cases one by one.

"To you and your sisters. I know it; Madame confides in me; I witnessed her will, and it is to be so," whispered Esther, smiling.

"How nice! but I wish she'd let us have them now. Pro-cras-ti-nation is not agreeable," observed Amy, taking a last look at the diamonds.

"It is too soon yet for the young ladies to wear these things. The first one who is affianced[13] will have the pearls—Madame has said it; and I have a fancy that the little turquoise ring will be given to you when you go, for Madame approves your good behavior and charming manners."

"Do you think so? Oh, I'll be a lamb, if I can only have that lovely ring! It's ever so much prettier than Kitty Bryant's. I do like Aunt March, after all;" and Amy tried on the blue ring with a delighted face, and a firm resolve to earn it.

From that day she was a model of obedience, and the old lady complacently admired the success of her training. Esther fitted up the closet with a little table, placed a footstool before it, and over it a picture, taken from one of the shut-up rooms. She thought it was of no great value, but, being appropriate, she borrowed it, well knowing that Madame would never know it, nor care if she did. It was, however, a very valuable copy of one of the famous pictures of the world, and Amy's beauty-loving eyes were never tired of looking up at the sweet face of the divine mother,[14] while tender thoughts of her own were busy at her heart. On the table she laid her little Testament and hymn-book, kept a vase always full of the best flowers Laurie brought her, and came every day to "sit alone, thinking good thoughts, and praying the dear God to

12. LMA means that the closet is of little importance or that it is relatively empty.

13. Engaged.

14. The Virgin Mary.

15. On September 12, 1852, twelve-year-old May Alcott confessed in her journal: "Louisa helped me fix a little Alter, at which I am to say my devotions every day, I have got a little bust, of a boy kneeling with his eyes upwards and I have set that on the table, there is a curtain which hangs each side so it looks very pretyly. I have done my devotions for to day and think I feel happyer for it. The girls think it is nonsense but I think it with [will] teach me to be a good girl. This evening we sat round the large table in the parlar and read. Lizzie and I when we went to bed we said a prayer and we read in the Testament, then went to bed. I have been a good girl to day I think and it makes me feel happy. I love my Alter very much. I am trying to get rid of thouse bad feelings, and when I think of my Alter they go away." On September 16 she noted, "Mother got me a little cross for my Alter and it makes it look very pretty. I have not missed saying my devotions. I love to say them." But ten days later, she confided: "After breakfast, I did not say my devotions because I had just been cross to Anna and did not feel wright to say them . . . I read a good deal in the 'Testament', for I did not say my devotions this morning. I like to have Sunday come very much, but I used to dislike it because I was idle, & do not think I am very inderestus [industrious] now, but am better than I used to be" (Manuscript journal, Houghton Library, Harvard University, bMS Am 1817 [56]). May's misspellings, including *alter,* remind one of Amy.

16. Jesus.

17. A fabric woven with a raised pattern.

18. An undercoat, often padded for warmth, worn so that it would show beneath an open gown or dress. Quilted petticoats were popular in the eighteenth century.

preserve her sister." Esther had given her a rosary of black beads, with a silver cross, but Amy hung it up, and did not use it, feeling doubtful as to its fitness for Protestant prayers.[15]

The little girl was very sincere in all this, for, being left alone outside the safe home-nest, she felt the need of some kind hand to hold by so sorely, that she instinctively turned to the strong and tender Friend,[16] whose fatherly love most closely surrounds His little children. She missed her mother's help to understand and rule herself, but having been taught where to look, she did her best to find the way, and walk in it confidingly. But Amy was a young pilgrim, and just now her burden seemed very heavy. She tried to forget herself, to keep cheerful, and be satisfied with doing right, though no one saw or praised her for it. In her first effort at being very, very good, she decided to make her will, as Aunt March had done; so that if she *did* fall ill and die, her possessions might be justly and generously divided. It cost her a pang even to think of giving up the little treasures which in her eyes were as precious as the old lady's jewels.

During one of her play hours she wrote out the important document as well as she could, with some help from Esther as to certain legal terms; and, when the good-natured French woman had signed her name, Amy felt relieved, and laid it by to show Laurie, whom she wanted as a second witness. As it was a rainy day, she went upstairs to amuse herself in one of the large chambers, and took Polly with her for company. In this room there was a wardrobe full of old-fashioned costumes, with which Esther allowed her to play, and it was her favorite amusement to array herself in the faded brocades,[17] and parade up and down before the long mirror, making stately courtesies, and sweeping her train about, with a rustle which delighted her ears. So busy was she on this day, that she did not hear Laurie's ring, nor see his face peeping in at her, as she gravely promenaded to and fro, flirting her fan and tossing her head, on which she wore a great pink turban, contrasting oddly with her blue brocade dress and yellow quilted petticoat.[18] She was obliged to walk carefully, for she had on high-heeled shoes, and, as Laurie told Jo afterward, it was a comical sight to see her mince[19] along in her gay suit, with Polly sidling and bridling[20] just behind her, imitating her as well as he could, and occasionally stopping to laugh, or exclaim, "Ain't we fine? Get along you fright! Hold your tongue! Kiss me, dear; ha! ha!"

Having with difficulty restrained an explosion of merriment, lest it should offend her majesty, Laurie tapped, and was graciously received.

"Sit down and rest while I put these things away; then I want to consult you about a very serious matter," said Amy, when she had shown her splendor, and driven Polly into a corner. "That bird is the trial of my life," she continued, removing the pink mountain from her head, while Laurie seated himself astride of a chair. "Yesterday, when aunt was asleep, and I was trying to be as still as a mouse, Polly began to squall and flap about in his cage; so I went to let him out, and found a big spider there. I poked it out, and it ran under the book-case; Polly marched straight after it, stooped down and peeped under the book-case, saying, in his funny way, with a cock of his eye, 'Come out and take a walk, my dear.' I *couldn't* help laughing, which made Poll swear, and aunt woke up and scolded us both."

"Did the spider accept the old fellow's invitation?" asked Laurie, yawning.

"Yes; out it came, and away ran Polly, frightened to death, and scrambled up on aunt's chair, calling out, 'Catch her! catch her! catch her!' as I chased the spider."

"That's a lie! Oh lor!" cried the parrot, pecking at Laurie's toes.

"I'd wring your neck if you were mine, you old torment," cried Laurie, shaking his fist at the bird, who put his head on one side, and gravely croaked, "Allyluyer! bless your buttons, dear!"

"Now I'm ready," said Amy, shutting the wardrobe, and taking a paper out of her pocket. "I want you to read that, please, and tell me if it is legal and right. I felt that I ought to do it, for life is uncertain, and I don't want any ill-feeling over my tomb."

Laurie bit his lips, and turning a little from the pensive speaker, read the following document, with praiseworthy gravity, considering the spelling:—

19. The *OED* defines *mince* as "to walk with short steps and an affected preciseness or daintiness; to walk or move in an affected or effeminate manner." While the *OED* notes its first usage as 1562, it also lists this line from *Little Women* as one of its examples.

20. The *OED* defines *sidling* as making "a sidelong . . . movement" and *bridling* as "throw[ing] up the head and draw[ing] in the chin, (as a horse does when reined in), expressing pride, vanity, or resentment."

Laurie witnesses Amy's will. Frank Merrill, *Little Women: Illustrated* (1880).

"MY LAST WILL AND TESTIMENT.

"I, Amy Curtis March, being in my sane mind, do give and bequeethe all my earthly property—viz. to wit—: namely

"To my father, my best pictures, sketches, maps, and works of art, including frames. Also my $100, to do what he likes with.

"To my mother, all my clothes, except the blue apron with pockets,—also my likeness, and my medal, with much love.

"To my dear sister Margaret, I give my turkquoise ring (if I get it), also my green box with the doves on it, also my piece of real lace for her neck, and my sketch of her as a memorial of her 'little girl.'

"To Jo I leave my breast-pin, the one mended with sealing

wax, also my bronze inkstand—she lost the cover,—and my most precious plaster rabbit, because I am sorry I burnt up her story.

"To Beth (if she lives after me)[21] I give my dolls and the little bureau, my fan, my linen collars and my new slippers if she can wear them being thin when she gets well. And I herewith also leave her my regret that I ever made fun of old Joanna.

"To my friend and neighbor Theodore Laurence I bequeethe my paper marshay[22] portfolio, my clay model of a horse though he did say it hadn't any neck. Also in return for his great kindness in the hour of affliction any one of my artistic works he likes, Noter Dame is the best.

"To our venerable benefactor Mr. Laurence I leave my purple box with a looking glass in the cover which will be nice for his pens and remind him of the departed girl who thanks him for his favors to her family, specially Beth.

"I wish my favorite playmate Kitty Bryant to have the blue silk apron and my gold-bead ring with a kiss.

"To Hannah I give the band-box she wanted and all the patch work I leave hoping she 'will remember me, when it you see.'[23]

"And now having disposed of my most valuable property I hope all will be satisfied and not blame the dead. I forgive every one, and trust we may all meet when the trump shall sound. Amen.

"To this will and testament I set my hand and seal on this 20th day of Nov. Anni Domino 1861.[24]

"AMY CURTIS MARCH.
"*Witnesses:* {ESTELLE VALNOR,
{THEODORE LAURENCE.

The last name was written in pencil, and Amy explained that he was to rewrite it in ink, and seal it up for her properly.

"What put it into your head? Did any one tell you about Beth's

21. To the self-involved Amy, her own death appears more real and imminent than her seriously ill sister's. Laurie, amused, agrees to witness the will. The scene offers some comic relief to the tension created by Beth's illness, but death remains the topic, and by the end of the chapter, the possibility of Beth's dying becomes real for Amy.

22. Amy means papier-mâché (French for "chewed paper"), a mixture of paper and glue (sometimes paper, flour, and water) that hardens when dry and is used to make ornaments and other objects.

23. A popular phrase, often seen on samplers or tombstones, usually written as "When this you see, remember me."

24. Amy means *Anno Domini,* Latin for "In the year of the Lord." The novel opens in December 1861, so the correct date should be November 1862. It is uncertain whether this is Amy's error or LMA's. However, it remained unchanged over numerous printings and editions.

25. An inkstand that holds pens, ink, and writing materials. The taper, a small slender candle, would be used to melt the stick of sealing wax so it could seal a folded paper or an envelope.

26. Either Beth got a new bird (near the end of Chapter 11, Marmee tells her she may have another one if she wants) or LMA forgot that Beth's bird died in chapter 11. The 1880–1881 edition changed *bird* to *cats*.

27. This sentence cuts two ways. The selfish Amy is thinking of her sister Beth, but even her sister's life is measured in turquoise rings. In Chapter 20, she will ask Marmee for permission to wear the turquoise ring as a way to remind herself not to be selfish, to be more like Beth. Her mother agrees, but tells Amy that she has "more faith in the corner of the closet," meaning more faith in the power of prayer and reflection.

giving away her things?" asked Laurie, soberly, as Amy laid a bit of red tape, with sealing-wax, a taper, and a standish[25] before him.

She explained; and then asked, anxiously, "What about Beth?"

"I'm sorry I spoke; but as I did, I'll tell you. She felt so ill one day, that she told Jo she wanted to give her piano to Meg, her bird[26] to you, and the poor old doll to Jo, who would love it for her sake. She was sorry she had so little to give, and left locks of hair to the rest of us, and her best love to grandpa. *She* never thought of a will."

Laurie was signing and sealing as he spoke, and did not look up till a great tear dropped on the paper. Amy's face was full of trouble; but she only said, "Don't people put sort of postscrips to their wills, sometimes."

"Yes; 'codicils,' they call them."

"Put one in mine then—that I wish *all* my curls cut off, and given round to my friends. I forgot it; but I want it done, though it will spoil my looks."

Laurie added it, smiling at Amy's last and greatest sacrifice. Then he amused her for an hour, and was much interested in all her trials. But when he came to go, Amy held him back to whisper, with trembling lips, "Is there really any danger about Beth?"

"I'm afraid there is; but we must hope for the best, so don't cry, dear;" and Laurie put his arm about her with a brotherly gesture, which was very comforting.

When he had gone, she went to her little chapel, and, sitting in the twilight, prayed for Beth with streaming tears and an aching heart, feeling that a million turquoise rings would not console her for the loss of her gentle little sister.[27]

LITTLE WOMEN

Chapter 20

Confidential

I DON'T THINK I have any words in which to tell the meeting of the mother and daughters; such hours are beautiful to live, but very hard to describe, so I will leave it to the imagination of my readers; merely saying that the house was full of genuine happiness, and that Meg's tender hope was realized; for when Beth woke from that long, healing sleep, the first objects on which her eyes fell *were* the little rose and mother's face. Too weak to wonder at anything, she only smiled, and nestled close into the loving arms about her, feeling that the hungry longing was satisfied at last. Then she slept again, and the girls waited upon their mother, for she would not unclasp the thin hand which clung to hers, even in sleep. Hannah had "dished up" an astonishing breakfast for the traveller, finding it impossible to vent her excitement in any other way; and Meg and Jo fed their mother like dutiful young storks, while they listened to her whispered account of father's state, Mr. Brooke's promise to stay and nurse him, the delays which the storm occasioned on the homeward journey, and the unspeakable comfort Laurie's hopeful face had given her when she arrived, worn out with fatigue, anxiety and cold.

What a strange, yet pleasant day that was! so brilliant and gay without, for all the world seemed abroad to welcome the first snow; so quiet and reposeful within, for every one slept, spent with watching, and a Sabbath stillness reigned through the house, while nodding Hannah mounted guard at the door. With a blissful sense of burdens lifted off, Meg and Jo closed their weary eyes, and lay at rest like storm-beaten boats, safe at anchor in a quiet harbor. Mrs. March would not leave Beth's side, but rested in the

The March sisters. Jessie Willcox Smith, *Little Women* (1915).

big chair, waking often to look at, touch, and brood over her child, like a miser over some recovered treasure.

Laurie, meanwhile, posted off to comfort Amy, and told his story so well that Aunt March actually "sniffed" herself, and never once said, "I told you so." Amy came out so strong on this occasion, that I think the good thoughts in the little chapel really began to bear fruit. She dried her tears quickly, restrained her impatience to see her mother, and never even thought of the turquoise ring, when the old lady heartily agreed in Laurie's opinion, that she behaved "like a capital little woman." Even Polly seemed impressed, for he called her "good girl," blessed her buttons, and begged her to "come and take a walk, dear," in his most affable tone. She would very gladly have gone out to enjoy the bright wintry weather; but, discovering that Laurie was dropping with sleep in spite of manful efforts to conceal the fact, she persuaded him to rest on the sofa, while she wrote a note to her mother. She was a long time about it; and, when returned, he was stretched out with both arms under his head, sound asleep, while Aunt March had pulled down the curtains, and sat doing nothing in an unusual fit of benignity.

After a while, they began to think he was not going to wake till night, and I'm not sure that he would, had he not been effectually roused by Amy's cry of joy at sight of her mother. There probably were a good many happy little girls in and about the city that day, but it is my private opinion that Amy was the happiest of all, when she sat in her mother's lap and told her trials, receiving consolation and compensation in the shape of approving smiles and fond caresses. They were alone together in the chapel, to which her mother did not object when its purpose was explained to her.

"On the contrary, I like it very much, dear," she said, looking from the dusty rosary to the well-worn little book, and the lovely picture with its garland of evergreen. "It is an excellent plan to have some place where we can go to be quiet, when things vex or grieve us. There are a good many hard times in this life of ours, but we can always bear them if we ask help in the right way. I think my little girl is learning this?"

"Yes, mother; and when I go home I mean to have a corner in

the big closet to put my books, and the copy of that picture which I've tried to make. The woman's face is not good, it's too beautiful for me to draw, but the baby is done better, and I love it very much. I like to think He was a little child once, for then I don't seem so far away, and that helps me."

As Amy pointed to the smiling Christ-child on his mother's knee, Mrs. March saw something on the lifted hand that made her smile. She said nothing, but Amy understood the look, and, after a minute's pause, she added, gravely,—

"I wanted to speak to you about this, but I forgot it. Aunt gave me the ring today; she called me to her and kissed me, and put it on my finger, and said I was a credit to her, and she'd like to keep me always. She gave that funny guard to keep the torquoise on, as it's too big. I'd like to wear them, mother; can I?"

"They are very pretty, but I think you're rather too young for such ornaments, Amy," said Mrs. March, looking at the plump little hand, with the band of sky-blue stones on the forefinger, and the quaint guard, formed of two tiny, golden hands clasped together.

"I'll try not to be vain," said Amy; "I don't think I like it, only because it's so pretty; but I want to wear it as the girl in the story wore her bracelet, to remind me of something."

"Do you mean Aunt March?" asked her mother, laughing.

"No, to remind me not to be selfish." Amy looked so earnest and sincere about it, that her mother stopped laughing, and listened respectfully to the little plan.

"I've thought a great deal lately about 'my bundle of naughties,' and being selfish is the largest one in it; so I'm going to try hard to cure it, if I can. Beth isn't selfish, and that's the reason every one loves her, and feels so bad at the thoughts of losing her. People wouldn't feel half so bad about me if I was sick, and I don't deserve to have them; but I'd like to be loved and missed by a great many friends, so I'm going to try and be like Beth all I can. I'm apt to forget my resolutions; but, if I had something always about me to remind me, I guess I should do better. May I try this way?"[1]

"Yes; but I have more faith in the corner of the big closet. Wear

1. While Amy's speech may be motivated, in part, by her desire to wear the ring Aunt March gave her, it also marks a turning point in her character. She is learning to become less self-involved. Amy now fades into the background for the rest of Part I as John and Meg's relationship takes center stage. Three years later, in Part II of *Little Women,* Amy more fully emerges as a mature, gracious, and thoughtful character.

your ring, dear, and do your best; I think you will prosper, for the sincere wish to be good is half the battle. Now, I must go back to Beth. Keep up your heart, little daughter, and we will soon have you home again."

That evening, while Meg was writing to her father, to report the traveller's safe arrival, Jo slipped upstairs into Beth's room, and, finding her mother in her usual place, stood a minute twisting her fingers in her hair, with a worried gesture and an undecided look.

"What is it, deary?" asked Mrs. March, holding out her hand with a face which invited confidence.

"I want to tell you something, mother."

"About Meg?"

"How quick you guessed! Yes, it's about her, and though it's a little thing, it fidgets me."

"Beth is asleep; speak low, and tell me all about it. That Moffat hasn't been here, I hope?" asked Mrs. March, rather sharply.

"No; I should have shut the door in his face if he had," said Jo, settling herself on the floor at her mother's feet. "Last summer Meg left a pair of gloves over at the Laurences, and only one was returned. We forgot all about it, till Teddy told me that Mr. Brooke had it. He kept it in his waistcoat pocket, and once it fell out, and Teddy joked him about it, and Mr. Brooke owned that he liked Meg, but didn't dare say so, she was so young and he so poor. Now isn't it a *dreadful* state of things?"

"Do you think Meg cares for him?" asked Mrs. March, with an anxious look.

"Mercy me! I don't know anything about love, and such nonsense!" cried Jo, with a funny mixture of interest and contempt. "In novels, the girls show it by starting and blushing, fainting away, growing thin, and acting like fools. Now Meg don't do anything of the sort; she eats and drinks, and sleeps, like a sensible creature; she looks straight in my face when I talk about that man, and only blushes a little bit when Teddy jokes about lovers. I forbid him to do it, but he don't mind me as he ought."

"Then you fancy that Meg is *not* interested in John?"

"Who?" cried Jo, staring.

"Mr. Brooke; I call him 'John' now; we fell into the way of do-ing so at the hospital, and he likes it."

"Oh, dear! I know you'll take his part; he's been good to fa-ther, and you won't send him away, but let Meg marry him, if she wants to. Mean thing! to go petting pa and truckling[2] to you,[a] just to wheedle you into liking him;" and Jo pulled her hair again with a wrathful tweak.

"My dear, don't get angry about it, and I will tell you how it happened. John went with me at Mr. Laurence's request, and was so devoted to poor father, that we couldn't help getting fond of him. He was perfectly open and honorable about Meg, for he told us he loved her; but would earn a comfortable home before he asked her to marry him. He only wanted our leave to love her and work for her, and the right to make her love him if he could. He is a truly excellent young man, and we could not refuse to listen to him; but I will not consent to Meg's engaging herself so young."

"Of course not; it would be idiotic! I knew there was mischief brewing; I felt it; and now it's worse than I imagined. I just wish I could marry Meg myself, and keep her safe in the family."

This odd arrangement made Mrs. March smile; but she said, gravely, "Jo, I confide in you, and don't wish you to say anything to Meg yet. When John comes back, and I see them together, I can judge better of her feelings toward him."

"She'll see his in those handsome eyes that she talks about, and then it will be all up with her. She's got such a soft heart, it will melt like butter in the sun if any one looks sentimentally at her. She read the short reports he sent more than she did your letters, and pinched me when I spoke of it, and likes brown eyes, and don't think John an ugly name, and she'll go and fall in love, and there's an end of peace and fun, and cosy times, together. I see it all! they'll go lovering round the house, and we shall have to dodge; Meg will be absorbed, and no good to me any more; Brooke will scratch up a fortune somehow,—carry her off and make a hole in the family; and I shall break my heart, and every-thing will be abominably uncomfortable. Oh, deary me! why weren't we all boys?[b] then there wouldn't be any bother!"

Jo leaned her chin on her knees, in a disconsolate attitude, and

2. To be subservient. The *OED* notes that the verb derives from *truckle-bed* (also called a trundle bed), a low bed, usually on castors, which can be pushed under a higher bed when not in use.

3. LMA explores the subject of marriage in a number of her works. She firmly believed that in a truly democratic society husband and wife must be equals. Her first novel, *Moods* (1864), explores this idea in a way that unsettled many of the novel's early readers and reviewers; more particularly, LMA looks at what happens when a young woman is unprepared for marriage. John Brooke understands that Meg is too young for marriage, which is why he approaches Mr. and Mrs. March first. Almost twenty years after *Little Women,* in the September 1887 issue of *Ladies Home Journal,* LMA wrote "Early Marriages," in which she admonishes young women for marrying too young: "The fact that a youth and maiden love another is not sufficient reason for them to marry unless they are fitted to be and to do all that this sacred relation requires. Principle not passion should preside over the affair. Temperaments should harmonize, tastes and aims be not too different, and above all both parties should clearly understand the religious significance of the tie, and not lightly bind themselves while under the rosy glamour and romance of a first fancy.

"Few girls of eighteen are ready, either physically or mentally, to become wives and mothers. Twenty-five is a better age, since then she is mature and should be in her prime. Young men do not attain their full growth before twenty-eight, and few before that age have seriously taken up the work of life and are fit to become the heads of families" (p. 3).

shook her fist at the reprehensible John. Mrs. March sighed, and Jo looked up with an air of relief.

"You don't like it, mother? I'm glad of it; let's send him about his business, and not tell Meg a word of it, but all be jolly together as we always have been."

"I did wrong to sigh, Jo. It is natural and right you should all go to homes of your own, in time; but I do want to keep my girls as long as I can; and I am sorry that this happened so soon, for Meg is only seventeen, and it will be some years before John can make a home for her. Your father and I have agreed that she shall not bind herself in any way, nor be married, before twenty.³ If she and John love one another, they can wait, and test the love by doing so. She is conscientious, and I have no fear of her treating him unkindly. My pretty, tender-hearted girl! I hope things will go happily with her."

"Hadn't you rather have her marry a rich man?" asked Jo, as her mother's voice faltered a little over the last words.

"Money is a good and useful thing, Jo; and I hope my girls will never feel the need of it too bitterly, nor be tempted by too much. I should like to know that John was firmly established in some good business, which gave him an income large enough to keep free from debt, and make Meg comfortable. I'm not ambitious for a splendid fortune, a fashionable position, or a great name for my girls. If rank and money come with love and virtue, also, I should accept them gratefully, and enjoy your good fortune; but I know, by experience, how much genuine happiness can be had in a plain little house, where the daily bread is earned, and some privations give sweetness to the few pleasures; I am content to see Meg begin humbly, for, if I am not mistaken, she will be rich in the possession of a good man's heart, and that is better than a fortune."

"I understand, mother, and quite agree; but I'm disappointed about Meg, for I'd planned to have her marry Teddy by and by, and sit in the lap of luxury all her days. Wouldn't it be nice?" asked Jo, looking up with a brighter face.

"He is younger than she, you know," began Mrs. March; but Jo broke in,—

"Oh, that don't matter; he's old for his age, and tall; and can be quite grown-up in his manners, if he likes. Then he's rich, and generous, and good, and loves us all; and *I* say it's a pity my plan is spoilt."

"I'm afraid Laurie is hardly grown-up enough for Meg, and altogether too much of a weathercock,[4] just now, for any one to depend on. Don't make plans, Jo; but let time and their own hearts mate your friends. We can't meddle safely in such matters, and had better not get 'romantic rubbish,' as you call it, into our heads, lest it spoil our friendship."

"Well, I won't; but I hate to see things going all criss-cross, and getting snarled up, when a pull here, and a snip there, would straighten it out. I wish wearing flat-irons[5] on our heads would keep us from growing up. But buds will be roses, and kittens, cats,—more's the pity!"

"What's that about flat-irons and cats?" asked Meg, as she crept into the room, with the finished letter in her hand.

"Only one of my stupid speeches. I'm going to bed; come on, Peggy," said Jo, unfolding herself, like an animated puzzle.

"Quite right, and beautifully written. Please add that I send my love to John," said Mrs. March, as she glanced over the letter, and gave it back.

"Do you call him 'John'?" asked Meg, smiling, with her innocent eyes looking down into her mother's.

"Yes; he has been like a son to us, and we are very fond of him," replied Mrs. March, returning the look with a keen one.

"I'm glad of that; he is so lonely. Good-night, mother, dear. It is so inexpressibly comfortable to have you here," was Meg's quiet answer.

The kiss her mother gave her was a very tender one; and, as she went away, Mrs. March said, with a mixture of satisfaction and regret, "She does not love John yet, but will soon learn to."

4. Marmee means that Laurie is too inconstant, like a weather-vane (commonly made in the shape of a rooster or gamecock) that moves according to the direction of the wind.

5. A heavy metal iron with a flat face used for ironing clothes and linen.

1. Jo feels "important" because she knows what Meg does not: that John Brooke has spoken to her parents about his love for Meg.

2. Because of.

Chapter 21

Laurie Makes Mischief, and Jo Makes Peace

J O'S FACE was a study next day, for the secret rather weighed upon her, and she found it hard not to look mysterious and important.[1] Meg observed it, but did not trouble herself to make inquiries, for she had learned that the best way to manage Jo was by the law of contraries, so she felt sure of being told everything if she did not ask. She was rather surprised, therefore, when the silence remained unbroken, and Jo assumed a patronizing air, which decidedly aggravated Meg, who in her turn assumed an air of dignified reserve, and devoted herself to her mother. This left Jo to her own devices; for Mrs. March had taken her place as nurse, and bid her rest, exercise, and amuse herself after her long confinement. Amy being gone, Laurie was her only refuge; and, much as she enjoyed his society, she rather dreaded him just then, for he was an incorrigible tease, and she feared he would coax her secret from her.

She was quite right; for the mischief-loving lad no sooner suspected a mystery, than he set himself to finding it out, and led Jo a trying life of it. He wheedled, bribed, ridiculed, threatened and scolded; affected indifference, that he might surprise the truth from her; declared he knew, then that he didn't care; and, at last, by dint of[2] perseverance, he satisfied himself that it concerned Meg and Mr. Brooke. Feeling indignant that he was not taken into his tutor's confidence, he set his wits to work to devise some proper retaliation for the slight.

Meg meanwhile had apparently forgotten the matter, and was

absorbed in preparations for her father's return; but all of a sudden a change seemed to come over her, and, for a day or two, she was quite unlike herself. She started when spoken to, blushed when looked at, was very quiet, and sat over her sewing with a timid, troubled look on her face. To her mother's inquiries she answered that she was quite well, and Jo's she silenced by begging to be let alone.

"She feels it in the air—love, I mean—and she's going very fast. She's got most of the symptoms, is twittery and cross, don't eat, lies awake, and mopes in corners. I caught her singing that song about 'the silver-voiced brook,'[a] and once she said 'John,' as you do, and then turned as red as a poppy. Whatever shall we do?" said Jo, looking ready for any measures, however violent.

"Nothing but wait. Let her alone, be kind and patient, and father's coming will settle everything," replied her mother.

"Here's a note to you, Meg, all sealed up. How odd! Teddy never seals mine," said Jo, next day, as she distributed the contents of the little post-office.

Mrs. March and Jo were deep in their own affairs, when a sound from Meg made them look up to see her staring at her note, with a frightened face.

"My child, what is it?" cried her mother, running to her, while Jo tried to take the paper which had done the mischief.

"It's all a mistake—he didn't send it—oh, Jo, how could you do it?" and Meg hid her face in her hands, crying as if her heart was quite broken.

"Me! I've done nothing! What's she talking about?" cried Jo, bewildered.

Meg's mild eyes kindled with anger as she pulled a crumpled note from her pocket, and threw it at Jo, saying, reproachfully,—

"You wrote it, and that bad boy helped you. How could you be so rude, so mean, and cruel to us both?"

Jo hardly heard her, for she and her mother were reading the note, which was written in a peculiar hand.

"MY DEAREST MARGARET,—

"I can no longer restrain my passion, and must know my fate

Louisa May Alcott, circa 1860s.

before I return. I dare not tell your parents yet, but I think they would consent if they knew that we adored one another. Mr. Laurence will help me to some good place, and then, my sweet girl, you will make me happy. I implore you to say nothing to your family yet, but to send one word of hope through Laurie to

"Your devoted
"JOHN."

"Oh, the little villain! that's the way he meant to pay me for keeping my word to mother. I'll give him a hearty scolding, and bring him over to beg pardon," cried Jo, burning to execute immediate justice. But her mother held her back, saying, with a look she seldom wore,—

"Stop, Jo, you must clear yourself first. You have played so many pranks, that I am afraid you have had a hand in this."

"On my word, mother, I haven't! I never saw that note before, and don't know anything about it, as true as I live!" said Jo, so earnestly, that they believed her. "If I *had* taken a part in it I'd have done it better than this, and have written a sensible note. I should think you'd have known Mr. Brooke wouldn't write such stuff as that," she added, scornfully tossing down the paper.

"It's like his writing," faltered Meg, comparing it with the note in her hand.

"Oh, Meg, you didn't answer it?" cried Mrs. March, quickly.

"Yes, I did!" and Meg hid her face again, overcome with shame.

"Here's a scrape! *Do* let me bring that wicked boy over to explain, and be lectured. I can't rest till I get hold of him;" and Jo made for the door again.

"Hush! let me manage this, for it is worse than I thought. Margaret, tell me the whole story," commanded Mrs. March, sitting down by Meg, yet keeping hold of Jo, lest she should fly off.

"I received the first letter from Laurie, who didn't look as if he knew anything about it," began Meg, without looking up. "I was worried at first, and meant to tell you; then I remembered how you liked Mr. Brooke, so I thought you wouldn't mind if I kept my little secret for a few days. I'm so silly that I liked to think no one knew; and, while I was deciding what to say, I felt like the girls in books, who have such things to do. Forgive me, mother, I'm paid for my silliness now; I never can look him in the face again."

"What did you say to him?" asked Mrs. March.

"I only said I was too young to do anything about it yet; that I didn't wish to have secrets from you, and he must speak to father. I was very grateful for his kindness, and would be his friend, but nothing more, for a long while."

Mrs. March smiled, as if well pleased, and Jo clapped her hands, exclaiming, with a laugh,—

"You are almost equal to Caroline Percy,[3] who was a pattern of prudence! Tell on, Meg. What did he say to that?"

"He writes in a different way entirely; telling me that he never sent any love-letter at all, and is very sorry that my roguish[4] sister, Jo, should take such liberties with our names. It's very kind and respectful, but think how dreadful for me!"

Meg leaned against her mother, looking the image of despair, and Jo tramped about the room, calling Laurie names. All of a sudden she stopped, caught up the two notes, and, after looking at them closely, said, decidedly, "I don't believe Brooke ever saw either of these letters. Teddy wrote both, and keeps yours to crow over me with, because I wouldn't tell him my secret."

"Don't have any secrets, Jo; tell it to mother, and keep out of trouble, as I should have done," said Meg, warningly.

"Bless you, child! mother told me."

"That will do, Jo. I'll comfort Meg while you go and get Laurie. I shall sift the matter to the bottom,[5] and put a stop to such pranks at once."

Away ran Jo, and Mrs. March gently told Meg Mr. Brooke's real feelings. "Now, dear, what are your own? Do you love him enough to wait till he can make a home for you, or will you keep yourself quite free for the present?"

"I've been so scared and worried, I don't want to have anything to do with lovers for a long while,—perhaps never," answered Meg, petulantly. "If John *doesn't* know anything about this non-

3. Caroline Percy, one of the main characters in Maria Edgeworth's four-volume novel *Patronage* (1814): "Ingenuous, unaffected, and with all the simplicity of youth, there was a certain dignity and graceful self-possession in [Caroline's] manner, which gave the idea of a superior character," vol. 1, 3rd ed. (London: 1815), 21.

4. Mischievous.

5. Get to the bottom of it.

sense, don't tell him, and make Jo and Laurie hold their tongues. I won't be deceived and plagued, and made a fool of,—it's a shame!"

Seeing that Meg's usually gentle temper was roused, and her pride hurt by this mischievous joke, Mrs. March soothed her by promises of entire silence, and great discretion for the future. The instant Laurie's step was heard in the hall, Meg fled into the study, and Mrs. March received the culprit alone. Jo had not told him why he was wanted, fearing he wouldn't come; but he knew the minute he saw Mrs. March's face, and stood twirling his hat with a guilty air, which convicted him at once. Jo was dismissed, but chose to march up and down the hall like a sentinel, having some fear that the prisoner might bolt. The sound of voices in the parlor rose and fell for half an hour; but what happened during that interview the girls never knew.

When they were called in, Laurie was standing by their mother with such a penitent face, that Jo forgave him on the spot, but did not think it wise to betray the fact. Meg received his humble apology, and was much comforted by the assurance that Brooke knew nothing of the joke.

"I'll never tell him to my dying day,—wild horses shan't drag it out of me; so you'll forgive me, Meg, and I'll do anything to show how out-and-out sorry I am," he added, looking very much ashamed of himself.

"I'll try; but it was a very ungentlemanly thing to do. I didn't think you could be so sly and malicious, Laurie," replied Meg, trying to hide her maidenly confusion under a gravely reproachful air.

"It was altogether abominable, and I don't deserve to be spoken to for a month; but you will, though, won't you?" and Laurie folded his hands together, with such an imploring gesture, and rolled up his eyes in such a meekly repentant way,[b] as he spoke in his irresistibly persuasive tone, that it was impossible to frown upon him, in spite of his scandalous behavior. Meg pardoned him, and Mrs. March's grave face relaxed, in spite of her efforts to keep sober, when she heard him declare that he would atone for his sins by all sorts of penances, and abase himself like a worm before the injured damsel.

Jo stood aloof, meanwhile, trying to harden her heart against him, and succeeding only in primming up her face into an expression of entire disapprobation. Laurie looked at her once or twice, but, as she showed no sign of relenting, he felt injured, and turned his back on her till the others were done with him, when he made her a low bow, and walked off without a word.

As soon as he had gone, she wished she had been more forgiving; and, when Meg and her mother went upstairs, she felt lonely, and longed for Teddy. After resisting for some time, she yielded to the impulse, and, armed with a book to return, went over to the big house.

"Is Mr. Laurence in?" asked Jo, of a housemaid, who was coming down stairs.

"Yes, miss; but I don't believe he's seeable just yet."

"Why not; is he ill?"

"La, no, miss! but he's had a scene with Mr. Laurie, who is in one of his tantrums about something, which vexes the old gentleman, so I dursn't go nigh him."

"Where is Laurie?"

"Shut up in his room, and he won't answer, though I've been a-tapping. I don't know what's to become of the dinner, for it's ready, and there's no one to eat it."

"I'll go and see what the matter is. I'm not afraid of either of them."

Up went Jo, and knocked smartly on the door of Laurie's little study.

"Stop that, or I'll open the door and make you!" called out the young gentleman, in a threatening tone.

Jo immediately pounded^c again; the door flew open, and in she bounced, before Laurie could recover from his surprise. Seeing that he really *was* out of temper,[6] Jo, who knew how to manage him, assumed a contrite expression, and, going artistically down upon her knees, said, meekly, "Please forgive me for being so cross. I came to make it up, and can't go away till I have."

7. Laurie means his grandfather seized him and literally shook him as punishment.

8. Laurie partially quotes the oath given by witnesses under sworn testimony: "Do you swear to tell the truth, the whole truth, and nothing but the truth, so help you God?"

"It's all right; get up, and don't be a goose, Jo," was the cavalier reply to her petition.

"Thank you; I will. Could I ask what's the matter? You don't look exactly easy in your mind."

"I've been shaken,[7] and I won't bear it!" growled Laurie, indignantly.

"Who did it?" demanded Jo.

"Grandfather; if it had been any one else I'd have—" and the injured youth finished his sentence by an energetic gesture of the right arm.

"That's nothing; I often shake you, and you don't mind," said Jo, soothingly.

"Pooh! you're a girl, and it's fun; but I'll allow no man to shake *me*."

"I don't think any one would care to try it, if you looked as much like a thunder-cloud as you do now. Why were you treated so?"

"Just because I wouldn't say what your mother wanted me for. I'd promised not to tell, and of course I wasn't going to break my word."

"Couldn't you satisfy your grandpa in any other way?"

"No; he *would* have the truth, the whole truth, and nothing but the truth.[8] I'd have told my part of the scrape, if I could, without bringing Meg in. As I couldn't, I held my tongue, and bore the scolding till the old gentleman collared me. Then I got angry, and bolted, for fear I should forget myself."

"It wasn't nice, but he's sorry, I know; so go down and make up. I'll help you."

"Hanged if I do! I'm not going to be lectured and pummelled by every one, just for a bit of a frolic. I *was* sorry about Meg, and begged pardon like a man; but I won't do it again, when I wasn't in the wrong."

"He didn't know that."

"He ought to trust me, and not act as if I was a baby. It's no use, Jo; he's got to learn that I'm able to take care of myself, and don't need any one's apron-string to hold on by."

"What pepper-pots[9] you are!" sighed Jo. "How do you mean to settle this affair?"

"Well, he ought to beg pardon, and believe me when I say I can't tell him what the row's[d] about."

"Bless you! he won't do that."

"I won't go down till he does."

"Now, Teddy, be sensible; let it pass, and I'll explain what I can. You can't stay here, so what's the use of being melodramatic?"

"I don't intend to stay here long, any-way. I'll slip off and take a journey somewhere, and when grandpa misses me he'll come round fast enough."

"I dare say; but you ought not to go and worry him."

"Don't preach. I'll go to Washington and see Brooke; it's gay there, and I'll enjoy myself after the troubles."

"What fun you'd have! I wish I could run off too!" said Jo, forgetting her part of Mentor[10] in lively visions of martial life at the capital.

"Come on, then! Why not? You go and surprise your father, and I'll stir up old Brooke. It would be a glorious joke; let's do it, Jo! We'll leave a letter saying we are all right, and trot off at once. I've got money enough; it will do you good, and be no harm, as you go to your father."

For a moment Jo looked as if she would agree; for, wild as the plan was, it just suited her. She was tired of care and confinement, longed for change, and thoughts of her father blended temptingly with the novel charms of camps and hospitals, liberty and fun. Her eyes kindled as they turned wistfully toward the window, but they fell on the old house opposite, and she shook her head with sorrowful decision.

"If I was a boy, we'd run away together, and have a capital time; but as I'm a miserable girl, I must be proper, and stop at home. Don't tempt me, Teddy, it's a crazy plan."[11]

"That's the fun of it!" began Laurie, who had got a wilful fit on him, and was possessed to break out of bounds in some way.

"Hold your tongue!" cried Jo, covering her ears. "'Prunes and prisms'[12] are my doom, and I may as well make up my mind to it.

9. Hot-tempered people. On a more literal level, a pepper pot is a pepper shaker.

10. In Homer's *Odyssey,* Mentor, friend of Odysseus, looked after Odysseus's palace and his son, Telemachus, while Odysseus fought in the Trojan War. Athena also took the form of Mentor to advise Telemachus about his mother's many suitors, urging him to search for his father. The word *mentor* derives from this character and means one who provides wisdom and advice to one less experienced.

11. Jo is aware of the inequality of the sexes here. Laurie can travel alone but Jo cannot. A young woman or girl simply did not travel with a male who was not an appropriate chaperone: a father, a brother, or a guardian. If Jo were to run away with Laurie, she would bring shame and scandal to the March family.

12. The *OED* notes that *prunes-and-prisms* was originally "a phrase notionally or actually spoken aloud in order to form the lips into an attractive shape . . . designating a prim or affected facial expression or manner of speaking. In extended use: affected mannerism, superficial accomplishments." Jo means she must obey proper manners even though she does not want to.

Jo discusses Laurie's wrongdoings with Mr. Laurence. Frank Merrill, *Little Women: Illustrated* (1880).

I came here to moralize, not to hear about things that make me skip to think of."

"I knew Meg would wet-blanket[13] such a proposal, but I thought you had more spirit," began Laurie, insinuatingly.

"Bad boy, be quiet. Sit down and think of your own sins, don't go making me add to mine. If I get your grandpa to apologize for the shaking, will you give up running away?" asked Jo, seriously.

"Yes, but you won't do it," answered Laurie, who wished to "make up," but felt that his outraged dignity must be appeased first.

"If I can manage the young one I can the old one," muttered Jo, as she walked away, leaving Laurie bent over a railroad map,[14] with his head propped up on both hands.

"Come in!" and Mr. Laurence's gruff voice sounded gruffer than ever, as Jo tapped at his door.

"It's only me, sir, come to return a book," she said, blandly, as she entered.

"Want any more?" asked the old gentleman, looking grim and vexed, but trying not to show it.

"Yes, please, I like old Sam so well, I think I'll try the second volume," returned Jo, hoping to propitiate him by accepting a second dose of "Boswell's Johnson,"[15] as he had recommended that lively work.

The shaggy eyebrows unbent a little, as he rolled the steps toward the shelf where the Johnsonian literature was placed. Jo skipped up, and, sitting on the top step, affected to be searching for her book, but was really wondering how best to introduce the dangerous object of her visit. Mr. Laurence seemed to suspect that something was brewing in her mind; for, after taking several brisk turns about the room, he faced round on her, speaking so abruptly, that "Rasselas"[16] tumbled face downward on the floor.

"What has that boy been about? Don't try to shield him, now! I know he has been in mischief, by the way he acted when he came home. I can't get a word from him; and, when I threatened to shake the truth out of him, he bolted upstairs, and locked himself into his room."

LITTLE WOMEN

"He did do wrong, but we forgave him, and all promised not to say a word to any one," began Jo, reluctantly.

"That won't do; he shall not shelter himself behind a promise from you soft-hearted girls. If he's done anything amiss, he shall confess, beg pardon, and be punished. Out with it, Jo! I won't be kept in the dark."

Mr. Laurence looked so alarming, and spoke so sharply, that Jo would have gladly run away, if she could, but she was perched aloft on the steps, and he stood at the foot, a lion in the path,[17] so she had to stay and brave it out.

"Indeed, sir, I cannot tell, mother forbid it. Laurie has confessed, asked pardon, and been punished quite enough. We don't keep silence to shield him, but some one else, and it will make more trouble if you interfere. Please don't; it was partly my fault, but it's all right now, so let's forget it, and talk about the 'Rambler,'[18] or something pleasant."

"Hang the 'Rambler!' come down and give me your word that this harum-scarum[19] boy of mine hasn't done anything ungrateful or impertinent. If he has, after all your kindness to him, I'll thrash him with my own hands."

The threat sounded awful, but did not alarm Jo, for she knew the irascible old man would never lift a finger against his grandson, whatever he might say to the contrary. She obediently descended, and made as light of the prank as she could without betraying Meg, or forgetting the truth.

"Hum! ha! well, if the boy held his tongue because he'd promised, and not from obstinacy, I'll forgive him. He's a stubborn fellow, and hard to manage," said Mr. Laurence, rubbing up his hair till it looked as if he'd been out in a gale, and smoothing the frown from his brow with an air of relief.

"So am I; but a kind word will govern me when all the king's horses and all the king's men couldn't,"[20] said Jo, trying to say a kind word for her friend, who seemed to get out of one scrape only to fall into another.

"You think I'm not kind to him, hey?" was the sharp answer.

"Oh, dear, no, sir; you are rather too kind sometimes, and then

13. The *OED* notes that the use of *wet-blanket* as a verb, meaning to "throw a damper over," originated in 1866 and gives this quotation in *Little Women* as its second example.

14. Laurie is studying a schedule and map of trains to figure out how to get to Washington.

15. Samuel Johnson (1709–1784), the British poet, essayist, and lexicographer, is perhaps best known for his *Dictionary of the English Language* (1755), but he wrote in various genres and was one of the most important literary figures of his time. Dr. Johnson, as he was known, was Abigail Alcott's favorite author. In 1791, James Boswell (1740–1795), Johnson's friend since 1763, published his two-volume *Life of Samuel Johnson, LL.D.*

16. Johnson published *The Prince of Abissinia: A Tale* in 1759 (the book was retitled *The History of Rasselas, Prince of Abissinia*, in 1768). This philosophical story tells of Rasselas, son of the king of Abissinia, who is confined in a beautiful valley until it is time for him to assume the throne. Dissatisfied with his life, he, after much thought, flees with his sister and friends to search for happiness. However, after spending time in Egypt, they return home. Alcott most likely chose this title because the work mirrors Laurie's desires to see the world.

17. LMA may be alluding to *The Pilgrim's Progress*, where Christian, after climbing the Hill of Difficulty, finds two lions standing guard near the Palace Beautiful.

18. From 1750 to 1752 Samuel Johnson published, twice weekly, a series of essays called *The Rambler*, comprising over 200 articles on topics as varied as religion, literature, and politics.

19. Rash or reckless.

20. Jo quotes from the nursery rhyme "Humpty Dumpty," which was first published in *Gammer Gurton's Garland* (1810). In this version, "Threescore men and threescore more" replaces the now-famous "All the king's horses and all the king's men" (See *The Oxford Dictionary of Nursery Rhymes*. ed. Iona and Peter Opie [London: Oxford University Press, 1952], p. 215).

21. Patient.

22. Jo clearly intends this as a joke, which shows how relaxed she is now around Mr. Laurence. She is fully aware of the scandal she would cause if she and Laurie ran away together.

23. A mischievous or badly-behaved girl.

just a trifle hasty when he tries your patience. Don't you think you are?"

Jo was determined to have it out now, and tried to look quite placid, though she quaked a little after her bold speech. To her great relief and surprise, the old gentleman only threw his spectacles on to the table with a rattle, and exclaimed, frankly,—

"You're right, girl, I am! I love the boy, but he tries my patience past bearing, and I don't know how it will end, if we go on so."

"I'll tell you,—he'll run away." Jo was sorry for that speech the minute it was made; she meant to warn him that Laurie would not bear much restraint, and hoped he would be more forbearing[21] with the lad.

Mr. Laurence's ruddy face changed suddenly, and he sat down with a troubled glance at the picture of a handsome man, which hung over his table. It was Laurie's father, who *had* run away in his youth, and married against the imperious old man's will. Jo fancied he remembered and regretted the past, and she wished she had held her tongue.

"He won't do it, unless he is very much worried, and only threatens it sometimes, when he gets tired of studying. I often think I should like to, especially since my hair was cut; so, if you ever miss us, you may advertise for two boys, and look among the ships bound for India."[22]

She laughed as she spoke, and Mr. Laurence looked relieved, evidently taking the whole as a joke.

"You hussy,[23] how dare you talk in that way? where's your respect for me, and your proper bringing up? Bless the boys and girls! what torments they are; yet we can't do without them," he said, pinching her cheeks good-humoredly.

"Go and bring that boy down to his dinner, tell him it's all right, and advise him not to put on tragedy airs with his grandfather; I won't bear it."

"He won't come, sir; he feels badly because you didn't believe him when he said he couldn't tell. I think the shaking hurt his feelings very much."

Jo tried to look pathetic, but must have failed, for Mr. Laurence began to laugh, and she knew the day was won.

LITTLE WOMEN

"I'm sorry for that, and ought to thank him for not shaking *me,* I suppose. What the dickens does the fellow expect?" and the old gentleman looked a trifle ashamed of his own testiness.

"If I was you, I'd write him an apology, sir. He says he won't come down till he has one; and talks about Washington, and goes on in an absurd way. A formal apology will make him see how foolish he is, and bring him down quite amiable. Try it; he likes fun, and this way is better than talking. I'll carry it up, and teach him his duty."

Mr. Laurence gave her a sharp look, and put on his spectacles, saying, slowly, "You're a sly puss! but I don't mind being managed by you and Beth. Here, give me a bit of paper, and let us have done with this nonsense."

The note was written in the terms which one gentleman would use to another after offering some deep insult. Jo dropped a kiss on the top of Mr. Laurence's bald head, and ran up to slip the apology under Laurie's door, advising him, through the key-hole, to be submissive, decorous, and a few other agreeable impossibilities. Finding the door locked again, she left the note to do its work, and was going quietly away, when the young gentleman slid down the banisters, and waited for her at the bottom, saying, with his most virtuous expression of countenance, "What a good fellow you are, Jo! Did you get blown up?" he added, laughing.

"No; he was pretty clever,[24] on the whole."

"Ah! I got it all round! even you cast me off over there, and I felt just ready to go to the deuce,"[25] he began, apologetically.

"Don't talk in that way; turn over a new leaf and begin again, Teddy, my son."

"I keep turning over new leaves, and spoiling them, as I used to spoil my copy-books; and I make so many beginnings there never will be an end," he said, dolefully.

"Go and eat your dinner; you'll feel better after it. Men always croak when they are hungry," and Jo whisked out at the front door after that.

"That's a 'label' on my 'sect,'" answered Laurie, quoting Amy,[26] as he went to partake of humble-pie[27] dutifully with his grandfa-

24. The *OED* defines this use of *clever* as a colloquial American expression meaning "good-natured, well-disposed; amiable." The 1880–1881 edition changed *clever* to *mild.*

25. Go to the devil.

26. Amy means "a libel on my sex."

27. To apologize humbly.

ther, who was quite saintly in temper, and overwhelmingly respectful in manner, all the rest of the day.

Every one thought the matter ended, and the little cloud blown over; but the mischief was done, for, though others forgot it, Meg remembered. She never alluded to a certain person, but she thought of him a good deal, dreamed dreams more than ever; and, once, Jo, rummaging her sister's desk for stamps, found a bit of paper scribbled over with the words, "Mrs. John Brooke;" whereat she groaned tragically, and cast it into the fire, feeling that Laurie's prank had hastened the evil day for her.

Chapter 22

Pleasant Meadows

LIKE SUNSHINE after storm were the peaceful weeks which followed. The invalids improved rapidly, and Mr. March began to talk of returning early in the new year. Beth was soon able to lie on the study sofa all day, amusing herself with the well-beloved cats, at first, and, in time, with doll's sewing, which had fallen sadly behindhand. Her once active limbs were so stiff and feeble that Jo took her a daily airing about the house, in her strong arms. Meg cheerfully blackened and burnt her white hands cooking delicate messes for "the dear;" while Amy, a loyal slave of the ring, celebrated her return by giving away as many of her treasures as she could prevail on her sisters to accept.

As Christmas approached, the usual mysteries began to haunt the house, and Jo frequently convulsed the family by proposing utterly impossible, or magnificently absurd ceremonies, in honor of this unusually merry Christmas. Laurie was equally impracticable, and would have had bonfires, sky-rockets, and triumphal arches, if he had had his own way. After many skirmishes and snubbings, the ambitious pair were considered effectually quenched, and went about with forlorn faces, which were rather belied by explosions of laughter when the two got together.

Several days of unusually mild weather fitly ushered in a splendid Christmas-day. Hannah "felt in her bones that it was going to be an uncommonly plummy day,"[a] and she proved herself a true prophetess, for everybody and everything seemed bound to produce a grand success. To begin with: Mr. March wrote that he should soon be with them; then Beth felt uncommonly well that morning, and, being dressed in her mother's gift,—a soft crimson

1. A shawl made from the wool of a merino sheep, a breed that originated in Spain and is known for its fine wool. Later the term came to mean any fine wool.

2. In German, *jungfrau* is a virgin or maiden.

3. Jo and Laurie's carol is based upon the traditional British Christmas carol "God Rest You Merry, Gentlemen." Its author is unknown, but the carol is believed to have originated in the mid-eighteenth century.

4. Peg is a nickname of Margaret.

5. Mount Blanc, the highest mountain in the Alps, is situated between the Aosta Valley of Italy and the Haute-Savoie of France.

6. The exchange that follows between the sisters and Mrs. March recalls the novel's opening. Happy and thankful as the family is, Christmas won't be Christmas without Mr. March.

7. The Concord grape, a dark purple, fragrant grape, was developed by Ephraim Wales Bull in 1849 and began to be marketed by 1854; however, LMA does not indicate that these were Concord grapes. Whatever the variety, the grapes had to have been cultivated nearby as railroads and ships would not have traveled fast enough to prevent spoilage, and refrigerator cars had not yet appeared in the 1860s. Since Beth's fresh grapes are eaten in winter, they most likely would have been grown in a grapery or vinery—a large greenhouse specifically constructed for grape growing. Glass vineries were fairly prevalent in northeastern cities by 1862, as the grape culture experienced major growth during the 1850s and 1860s. Grapes in winter would have been an expensive treat, one that the Marches could not have afforded. See Erica Hannickel, *Imperial Vineland: Grape Culture in 19th Century America* (Philadelphia: University of Pennsylvania Press, 2013).

8. Jo had desired the book the previous Christmas but forwent it in order to buy a present for her mother.

9. Hair art in jewelry was extremely popular as a form of keepsake or remembrance in the nineteenth century. The sisters had made the brooch from their hair and Marmee's hair.

10. Laurie is joyful in his betrayal of trust in the secret that Mr. March has returned. Soldiers did not ordinarily return home for Christmas, but in Chapter 1, Mr. March seems to anticipate his arrival home about this time when he writes: "A year seems very long to wait before I see them [his daughters]." Perhaps he was not being precise. In any case, clearly he arrives home when he is not expected: Laurie indicates that Mr. March's arrival is "another present" for the family. Likely Mr. Laurence provided the money for Mr. March's train fare. Mrs. March herself had to borrow money from Aunt March earlier to travel to Washington to be with her husband.

merino wrapper,[1]—was borne in triumph to the window, to behold the offering of Jo and Laurie. The Unquenchables had done their best to be worthy of the name, for, like elves, they had worked by night, and conjured up a comical surprise. Out in the garden stood a stately snow-maiden, crowned with holly, bearing a basket of fruit and flowers in one hand, a great roll of new music in the other, a perfect rainbow of an Afghan round her chilly shoulders, and a Christmas carol issuing from her lips, on a pink paper streamer:—

"THE JUNGFRAU[2] TO BETH.

"God bless you, dear Queen Bess!
　　May nothing you dismay;
But health, and peace, and happiness,
　　Be yours, this Christmas-day.[3]

"Here's fruit to feed our busy bee,
　　And flowers for her nose;
Here's music for her pianee,—
　　An Afghan for her toes.

"A portrait of Joanna, see,
　　By Raphael No. 2,
Who labored with great industry,
　　To make it fair and true.

"Accept a ribbon red I beg,
　　For Madam Purrer's tail;
And ice cream made by lovely Peg,—[4]
　　A Mont Blanc[5] in a pail.

"Their dearest love my makers laid
　　Within my breast of snow,
Accept it, and the Alpine maid,
　　From Laurie and from Jo."

How Beth laughed when she saw it! how Laurie ran up and down to bring in the gifts, and what ridiculous speeches Jo made as she presented them![6]

"I'm so full of happiness, that, if father was only here, I couldn't hold one drop more," said Beth, quite sighing with contentment as Jo carried her off to the study to rest after the excitement, and to refresh herself with some of the delicious grapes[7] the "Jungfrau" had sent her.

"So am I," added Jo, slapping the pocket wherein reposed the long-desired Undine and Sintram.[8]

"I'm sure I am," echoed Amy, poring over the engraved copy of the Madonna and Child, which her mother had given her, in a pretty frame.

"Of course I am," cried Meg, smoothing the silvery folds of her first silk dress; for Mr. Laurence had insisted on giving it.

"How can *I* be otherwise!" said Mrs. March, gratefully, as her eyes went from her husband's letter to Beth's smiling face, and her hand caressed the brooch made of gray and golden, chestnut and dark brown hair,[9] which the girls had just fastened on her breast.

Now and then, in this work-a-day world, things do happen in the delightful story-book fashion, and what a comfort that is. Half an hour after every one had said they were so happy they could only hold one drop more, the drop came. Laurie opened the parlor door, and popped his head in very quietly. He might just as well have turned a somersault, and uttered an Indian war-whoop; for his face was so full of suppressed excitement, and his voice so treacherously[10] joyful, that every one jumped up, though he only said, in a queer, breathless voice, "Here's another Christmas present for the March family."

Before the words were well out of his mouth, he was whisked away somehow, and in his place appeared a tall man, muffled up to the eyes, leaning on the arm of another tall man, who tried to say something and couldn't. Of course there was a general stampede; and for several minutes everybody seemed to lose their wits, for the strangest things were done, and no one said a word. Mr. March became invisible in the embrace[11] of four pairs of loving arms; Jo disgraced herself by nearly fainting away, and had to be doctored by Laurie in the china closet; Mr. Brooke kissed Meg entirely by mistake, as he somewhat incoherently explained; and Amy, the dignified, tumbled over a stool, and, never stopping to get up, hugged and cried over her father's boots in the most

Orchard House in winter. A detachable doorway helped prevent the cold air from entering when the front door was opened.

11. Until now Mr. March has remained unseen in the novel, a kind of hovering spiritual presence urging the sisters forward in their journey. He no sooner returns home than he disappears again—"becomes invisible"—in the embrace of his daughters and wife. He will remain largely invisible after his return; we see the girls' love for him more clearly than we do Mr. March himself. *Little Women* is, after all, the March sisters' story.

Jo and Laurie's snowmaiden. Tasha Tudor, *Little Women* (1969).

12. With his look, Mr. March asks his wife if Meg knows Brooke's intentions, and she silently assures him that Meg does.

13. Beef tea, often given to invalids, was made from the juice of beef that had been simmering for a long time in a small amount of water.

14. Plum pudding, a traditional Christmas dessert, is a boiled pudding containing spices, raisins, and currants.

touching manner. Mrs. March was the first to recover herself, and held up her hand with a warning, "Hush! remember Beth!"

But it was too late; the study door flew open,—the little red wrapper appeared on the threshold,—joy put strength into the feeble limbs,—and Beth ran straight into her father's arms. Never mind what happened just after that; for the full hearts overflowed, washing away the bitterness of the past, and leaving only the sweetness of the present.

It was not at all romantic, but a hearty laugh set everybody straight again,—for Hannah was discovered behind the door, sobbing over the fat turkey, which she had forgotten to put down when she rushed up from the kitchen. As the laugh subsided, Mrs. March began to thank Mr. Brooke for his faithful care of her husband, at which Mr. Brooke suddenly remembered that Mr. March needed rest, and, seizing Laurie, he precipitately retired. Then the two invalids were ordered to repose, which they did, by both sitting in one big chair, and talking hard.

Mr. March told how he had longed to surprise them, and how, when the fine weather came, he had been allowed by his doctor to take advantage of it; how devoted Brooke had been, and how he was altogether a most estimable and upright young man. Why Mr. March paused a minute just there, and, after a glance at Meg, who was violently poking the fire, looked at his wife with an inquiring lift of the eyebrows, I leave you to imagine; also why Mrs. March gently nodded her head, and asked, rather abruptly, if he wouldn't have something to eat.[12] Jo saw and understood the look; and she stalked grimly away, to get wine and beef tea,[13] muttering to herself, as she slammed the door, "I hate estimable young men with brown eyes!"

There never *was* such a Christmas dinner as they had that day. The fat turkey was a sight to behold, when Hannah sent him up, stuffed, browned and decorated. So was the plum-pudding,[14] which quite melted in one's mouth; likewise the jellies, in which Amy revelled like a fly in a honey-pot. Everything turned out well; which was a mercy, Hannah said, "For my mind was that flustered, mum, that it's a merrycle I didn't roast the pudding and stuff the turkey with raisens, let alone bilin' of it in a cloth."

LITTLE WOMEN

Beth greets her father. May Alcott, *Little Women* (1868).

Mr. Laurence and his grandson dined with them; also Mr. Brooke,—at whom Jo glowered darkly, to Laurie's infinite amusement. Two easy-chairs stood side by side at the head of the table, in which sat Beth and her father, feasting, modestly, on chicken and a little fruit. They drank healths,[15] told stories, sung songs, "reminisced," as the old folks say, and had a thoroughly good time. A sleigh-ride had been planned, but the girls would not leave their father; so the guests departed early, and, as twilight gathered, the happy family sat together round the fire.

"Just a year ago we were groaning over the dismal Christmas we expected to have. Do you remember?" asked Jo, breaking a short pause, which had followed a long conversation about many things.

"Rather a pleasant year on the whole!" said Meg, smiling at

15. Toasts.

16. These are the first words Mr. March speaks in *Little Women*. Significantly, they are a reminder of his letter in Chapter 1, in which he admonishes the girls to remember his instructions, so "that when I come back to them I may be fonder and prouder than ever of my little women." Over the past year, the sisters have indeed made great strides forward in their spiritual journey. Meg, now on the threshold of womanhood, has, after her experience at the Moffats, become less vain. Beth, befriended by Mr. Laurence, has become less shy. Amy is less selfish, more mature. Though Mr. March notes otherwise, Jo, to many readers, seems less changed. Her exuberant spirit and unconventional manners remain intact, and her reluctance to accept Meg's courtship with John Brooke indicates there is more growth to come. Roberta Seelinger Trites observes: "Another reason that *Little Women* resonates with modern readers may be our perception that Jo—especially the vibrant Jo of the novel's first half—does not really need to change. Her aspirations, her goals, her interests, and her talent all seem admirable, as does her self-despised temper and inner strength" (*Twain, Alcott, and the Birth of the Adolescent Reform Novel* [Iowa City: University of Iowa Press, 2007], p. 47).

17. An old English proverb meaning that a small detail can reveal important information.

18. A cricket stool or footstool.

the fire, and congratulating herself on having treated Mr. Brooke with dignity.

"I think it's been a pretty hard one," observed Amy, watching the light shine on her ring, with thoughtful eyes.

"I'm glad it's over, because we've got you back," whispered Beth, who sat on her father's knee.

"Rather a rough road for you to travel, my little pilgrims, especially the latter part of it.[16] But you have got on bravely; and I think the burdens are in a fair way to tumble off very soon," said Mr. March, looking, with fatherly satisfaction, at the four young faces gathered round him.

"How do you know? Did mother tell you?" asked Jo.

"Not much; straws show which way the wind blows;[17] and I've made several discoveries today."

"Oh, tell us what they are!" cried Meg, who sat beside him.

"Here is one!" and, taking up the hand which lay on the arm of his chair, he pointed to the roughened forefinger, a burn on the back, and two or three little hard spots on the palm. "I remember a time when this hand was white and smooth, and your first care was to keep it so. It was very pretty then, but to me it is much prettier now,—for in these seeming blemishes I read a little history. A burnt offering has been made of vanity; this hardened palm has earned something better than blisters, and I'm sure the sewing done by these pricked fingers will last a long time, so much good-will went into the stitches. Meg, my dear, I value the womanly skill which keeps home happy, more than white hands or fashionable accomplishments; I'm proud to shake this good, industrious little hand, and hope I shall not soon be asked to give it away."

If Meg had wanted a reward for hours of patient labor, she received it in the hearty pressure of her father's hand, and the approving smile he gave her.

"What about Jo? Please say something nice; for she has tried so hard, and been so very, very good to me," said Beth, in her father's ear.

He laughed, and looked across at the tall girl who sat opposite, with an unusually mild expression in her brown face.

"In spite of the curly crop, I don't see the 'son Jo' whom I left a year ago," said Mr. March. "I see a young lady who pins her collar straight, laces her boots neatly, and neither whistles, talks slang, nor lies on the rug, as she used to do. Her face is rather thin and pale, just now, with watching and anxiety; but I like to look at it, for it has grown gentler, and her voice is lower; she doesn't bounce, but moves quietly, and takes care of a certain little person in a motherly way, which delights me. I rather miss my wild girl; but if I get a strong, helpful, tender-hearted woman in her place, I shall feel quite satisfied. I don't know whether the shearing sobered our black sheep, but I do know that in all Washington I couldn't find anything beautiful enough to be bought with the five-and-twenty dollars which my good girl sent me."

Jo's keen eyes were rather dim for a minute, and her thin face grew rosy in the firelight, as she received her father's praise, feeling that she did deserve a portion of it.

"Now Beth;" said Amy, longing for her turn, but ready to wait.

"There's so little of her I'm afraid to say much, for fear she will slip away altogether, though she is not so shy as she used to be," began their father, cheerfully; but, recollecting how nearly he *had* lost her, he held her close, saying, tenderly, with her cheek against his own, "I've got you safe, my Beth, and I'll keep you so, please God."

After a minute's silence, he looked down at Amy, who sat on the cricket[18] at his feet, and said, with a caress of the shining hair,—

"I observed that Amy took drumsticks at dinner, ran errands for her mother all the afternoon, gave Meg her place to-night, and has waited on every one with patience and good-humor. I also observe that she does not fret much, nor prink[b] at the glass, and has not even mentioned a very pretty ring which she wears; so I conclude that she has learned to think of other people more, and of herself less, and has decided to try and mould her character as carefully as she moulds her little clay figures. I am glad of this; for though I should be very proud of a graceful statue made by her, I shall be infinitely prouder of a lovable daughter, with a talent for making life beautiful to herself and others."

Amy (Elizabeth Taylor), with sketchbook, Beth (Margaret O'Brien), and Meg (Janet Leigh). This winter scene forms the opening sequence in LeRoy's 1949 film version of *Little Women*.

19. The Land of Beulah in part one of *The Pilgrim's Progress.* Christian and Hopeful rest in this garden-like area before crossing the River of Death, which encircles Mount Zion, the location of the Celestial City.

20. Beth's hymn is the shepherd boy's song in "The Valley of Humiliation" in *The Pilgrim's Progress,* part two. The hymn must have been a favorite of LMA's because, at age eleven, she copied the first two stanzas in her 1843 Fruitlands diary on Christmas Day. After the second stanza, LMA later inserted "Little Lu began early to feel the family cares and peculiar trials" (*Journals* 49–50).

"What are you thinking of, Beth?" asked Jo, when Amy had thanked her father, and told about her ring.

"I read in 'Pilgrim's Progress' today, how, after many troubles, Christian and Hopeful came to a pleasant green meadow, where lilies bloomed all the year round, and there they rested happily, as we do now, before they went on to their journey's end,"[19] answered Beth; adding, as she slipped out of her father's arms, and went slowly to the instrument, "It's singing time now, and I want to be in my old place. I'll try to sing the song of the shepherd boy which the Pilgrim's heard. I made the music for father, because he likes the verses."

So, sitting at the dear little piano, Beth softly touched the keys, and, in the sweet voice they had never thought to hear again, sung, to her own accompaniment, the quaint hymn, which was a singularly fitting song for her:—

> "He that is down need fear no fall;
>   He that is low no pride;
> He that is humble ever shall
>   Have God to be his guide.
>
> "I am content with what I have,
>   Little be it or much;
> And, Lord! contentment still I crave,
>   Because Thou savest such.
>
> "Fulness to them a burden is,
>   That go on Pilgrimage;
> Here little, and hereafter bliss,
>   Is best from age to age!"[20]

Chapter 23

Aunt March Settles the Question

1. *Brewer's Dictionary of Phrase and Fable* (15th ed.) notes that the phrase means "to overwhelm with benevolence. It is said that Draco, the Athenian legislator, was killed by his popularity, being smothered in the theatre of Aegina by the number of caps and cloaks showered on him by the spectators (590 BC)" (593).

2. Favor or blessing.

LIKE BEES swarming after their queen, mother and daughters hovered about Mr. March the next day, neglecting everything to look at, wait upon, and listen to, the new invalid, who was in a fair way to be killed by kindness.[1] As he sat propped up in the big chair by Beth's sofa, with the other three close by, and Hannah popping in her head now and then, "to peek at the dear man," nothing seemed needed to complete their happiness. But something *was* needed, and the elder ones felt it, though none confessed the fact. Mr. and Mrs. March looked at one another with an anxious expression, as their eyes followed Meg. Jo had sudden fits of sobriety, and was seen to shake her fist at Mr. Brooke's umbrella, which had been left in the hall; Meg was absent-minded, shy and silent, started when the bell rang, and colored when John's name was mentioned; Amy said "Every one seemed waiting for something, and couldn't settle down, which was queer, since father was safe at home," and Beth innocently wondered why their neighbors didn't run over as usual.

Laurie went by in the afternoon, and, seeing Meg at the window, seemed suddenly possessed with a melodramatic fit, for he fell down upon one knee in the snow, beat his breast, tore his hair, and clasped his hands imploringly, as if begging some boon;[2] and when Meg told him to behave himself, and go away, he wrung imaginary tears out of his handkerchief, and staggered round the corner as if in utter despair.

"What does the goose mean?" said Meg, laughing, and trying to look unconscious.

3. In a childish, ill-tempered way.

4. Jo wishes everything would remain unchanged, and she fears that John Brooke will break the family apart by taking Meg away. But things, of course, cannot remain the same, and Jo's desire that they do is a sign that she still has some growing up to do. Here LMA reminds the reader that Jo is only sixteen, a mark of maturity perhaps only in Meg's eyes.

5. Like so many writers, Jo is a watcher, an observer of others. LMA's Concord neighbor Nathaniel Hawthorne experienced as keenly as any writer what it is to feel like a mere observer of other people's lives. In chapter 9 of *The Blithedale Romance* (1852), Hawthorne's narrator, the minor poet Myles Coverdale, ponders the dangers of observing others' lives: "It is not, I apprehend, a healthy kind of mental occupation, to devote ourselves too exclusively to the study of individual men and women. If the person under examination be one's self, the result is pretty certain to be diseased action of the heart, almost before we can snatch a second glance. Or, if we take the freedom to put a friend under our microscope, we thereby insulate him from many of his true relations, magnify his peculiarities, inevitably tear him into parts, and, of course, patch him very clumsily together again."

6. Meg moves sideways so she will not have to turn her eyes away from John.

"He's showing you how your John will go on by and by. Touching, isn't it?" answered Jo, scornfully.

"Don't say *my John,* it isn't proper or true;" but Meg's voice lingered over the words as if they sounded pleasant to her. "Please don't plague me, Jo; I've told you I don't care *much* about him, and there isn't to be anything said, but we are all to be friendly, and go on as before."

"We can't, for something *has* been said, and Laurie's mischief has spoilt you for me. I see it, and so does mother; you are not like your old self a bit, and seem ever so far away from me. I don't mean to plague you, and will bear it like a man, but I do wish it was all settled. I hate to wait; so if you mean ever to do it, make haste, and have it over quick," said Jo, pettishly.[3]

"*I* can't say or do anything till he speaks, and he won't, because father said I was too young," began Meg, bending over her work with a queer little smile, which suggested that she did not quite agree with her father on that point.

"If he did speak, you wouldn't know what to say, but would cry or blush, or let him have his own way, instead of giving a good, decided, No."

"I'm not so silly and weak as you think. I know just what I should say, for I've planned it all, so I needn't be taken unawares; there's no knowing what may happen, and I wished to be prepared."

Jo couldn't help smiling at the important air which Meg had unconsciously assumed, and which was as becoming as the pretty color varying in her cheeks.

"Would you mind telling me what you'd say?" asked Jo, more respectfully.

"Not at all; you are sixteen now, quite old enough to be my confidant, and my experience will be useful to you by and by, perhaps, in your own affairs of this sort."[4]

"Don't mean to have any; it's fun to watch other people philander, but I should feel like a fool doing it myself," said Jo, looking alarmed at the thought.[5]

"I guess not, if you liked any one very much, and he liked you." Meg spoke as if to herself, and glanced out at the lane where she had often seen lovers walking together in the summer twilight.

"I thought you were going to tell your speech to that man," said Jo, rudely shortening her sister's little revery.

"Oh, I should merely say, quite calmly and decidedly, 'Thank you, Mr. Brooke, you are very kind, but I agree with father, that I am too young to enter into any engagement at present; so please say no more, but let us be friends as we were.'"

"Hum! that's stiff and cool enough. I don't believe you'll ever say it, and I know he won't be satisfied if you do. If he goes on like the rejected lovers in books, you'll give in, rather than hurt his feelings."

"No I won't! I shall tell him I've made up my mind, and shall walk out of the room with dignity."

Meg rose as she spoke, and was just going to rehearse the digni-fied exit, when a step in the hall made her fly into her seat, and begin to sew as if her life depended on finishing that particular seam in a given time. Jo smothered a laugh at the sudden change, and, when some one gave a modest tap, opened the door with a grim aspect, which was anything but hospitable.

"Good afternoon, I came to get my umbrella,—that is, to see how your father finds himself today," said Mr. Brooke, getting a trifle confused, as his eye went from one tell-tale face to the other.

"It's very well, he's in the rack, I'll get him, and tell it you are here," and having jumbled her father and the umbrella well to-gether in her reply, Jo slipped out of the room to give Meg a chance to make her speech, and air her dignity. But the instant she vanished, Meg began to sidle[6] toward the door, murmur-ing,—

"Mother will like to see you, pray sit down, I'll call her."

"Don't go; are you afraid of me, Margaret?" and Mr. Brooke looked so hurt, that Meg thought she must have done something very rude. She blushed up to the little curls on her forehead, for he had never called her Margaret before, and she was surprised to find how natural and sweet it seemed to hear him say it. Anxious to appear friendly and at her ease, she put out her hand with a confiding gesture, and said, gratefully,—

"How can I be afraid when you have been so kind to father? I only wish I could thank you for it."

Nathaniel Hawthorne (1804–1864) was the Alcott's next-door neighbor when he and his family lived at Wayside. Long an admirer of Hawthorne's fiction, LMA saw it as a triumph when the author finally allowed her into his writing study in the "tower" on the upper floor. Writing to her cousin in July 1860, when the Hawthornes arrived in Concord after almost five years abroad, LMA observed: "Mr. H. is as queer as ever and we catch glimpses of a dark mysterious looking man in a big hat and red slippers darting over the hills or skimming by as if he expected the house of Alcott were about to rush out and clutch him" (*Selected Letters* 57).

7. Rounded.

8. John alludes to the brief German lesson he gave Meg at Camp Laurence.

9. The *OED* defines *coquetry* as "the use of arts intended to excite the admiration or love of the opposite sex, without any intention of responding to the feelings awakened."

"Shall I tell you how?" asked Mr. Brooke, holding the small hand fast in both his big ones, and looking down at Meg with so much love in the brown eyes, that her heart began to flutter, and she both longed to run away and to stop and listen.

"Oh no, please don't—I'd rather not," she said, trying to withdraw her hand, and looking frightened in spite of her denial.

"I won't trouble you, I only want to know if you care for me a little, Meg, I love you so much, dear," added Mr. Brooke, tenderly.

This was the moment for the calm, proper speech, but Meg didn't make it, she forgot every word of it, hung her head, and answered, "I don't know," so softly, that John had to stoop down to catch the foolish little reply.

He seemed to think it was worth the trouble, for he smiled to himself as if quite satisfied, pressed the plump[7] hand gratefully, and said, in his most persuasive tone, "Will you try and find out? I want to know *so* much; for I can't go to work with any heart until I learn whether I am to have my reward in the end or not."

"I'm too young," faltered Meg, wondering why she was so fluttered, yet rather enjoying it.

"I'll wait; and, in the meantime, you could be learning to like me. Would it be a very hard lesson, dear?"

"Not if I chose to learn it, but—"

"Please choose to learn, Meg. I love to teach, and this is easier than German,"[8] broke in John, getting possession of the other hand, so that she had no way of hiding her face, as he bent to look into it.

His tone was properly beseeching; but, stealing a shy look at him, Meg saw that his eyes were merry as well as tender, and that he wore the satisfied smile of one who had no doubt of his success. This nettled her; Annie Moffat's foolish lessons in coquetry[9] came into her mind, and the love of power, which sleeps in the bosoms of the best of little women, woke up all of a sudden, and took possession of her. She felt excited and strange, and, not knowing what else to do, followed a capricious impulse, and, withdrawing her hands, said, petulantly, "I *don't* choose; please go away, and let me be!"

LITTLE WOMEN

Poor Mr. Brooke looked as if his lovely castle in the air was tumbling about his ears, for he had never seen Meg in such a mood before, and it rather bewildered him.

"Do you really mean that?" he asked, anxiously, following her as she walked away.

"Yes, I do; I don't want to be worried about such things. Father says I needn't; it's too soon, and I'd rather not."

"Mayn't I hope you'll change your mind by and by? I'll wait, and say nothing till you have had more time. Don't play with me, Meg. I didn't think that of you."

"Don't think of me at all. I'd rather you wouldn't," said Meg, taking a naughty satisfaction in trying her lover's patience and her own power.

He was grave and pale now, and looked decidedly more like the novel heroes whom she admired; but he neither slapped his forehead nor tramped about the room, as they did; he just stood looking at her so wistfully, so tenderly, that she found her heart relenting in spite of her. What would have happened next I cannot say, if Aunt March had not come hobbling in at this interesting minute.

The old lady couldn't resist her longing to see her nephew; for she had met Laurie as she took her airing,[10] and, hearing of Mr. March's arrival, drove straight out to see him. The family were all busy in the back part of the house, and she had made her way quietly in, hoping to surprise them. She did surprise two of them so much, that Meg started as if she had seen a ghost, and Mr. Brooke vanished into the study.

"Bless me! what's all this?" cried the old lady, with a rap of her cane, as she glanced from the pale young gentleman to the scarlet young lady.

"It's father's friend. I'm *so* surprised to see you!" stammered Meg, feeling that she was in for a lecture now.

"That's evident," returned Aunt March, sitting down. "But what is father's friend saying, to make you look like a peony?[11] There's mischief going on, and I insist upon knowing what it is!" with another rap.

"We were merely talking. Mr. Brooke came for his umbrella,"

10. Her carriage drive to be out in the fresh air.

11. Having the dark red color, especially the cheeks, of a peony flower.

12. A touch of contrariness. In his short story "The Imp of the Perverse" (1845), Edgar Allan Poe offers a memorable definition of the spirit of the perverse: "We perpetrate [perverse acts] merely because we feel that we should *not*. Beyond or behind this there is no intelligible principle; and we might, indeed, deem this perverseness a direct instigation of the arch-fiend, were it not occasionally known to operate in the furtherance of good."

13. Aunt March does not actually "settle" the question of whether Meg should marry John. Meg defies her aunt because she has real feelings for John, though she has not yet fully acknowledged them. This is Meg's first experience with love; she is confused and somewhat frightened.

14. A phrase showing contempt or anger.

began Meg, wishing that Mr. Brooke and the umbrella were safely out of the house.

"Brooke? That boy's tutor? Ah! I understand now. I know all about it. Jo blundered into a wrong message in one of your pa's letters, and I made her tell me. You haven't gone and accepted him, child?" cried Aunt March, looking scandalized.

"Hush! he'll hear! Shan't I call mother?" said Meg, much troubled.

"Not yet. I've something to say to you, and I must free my mind at once. Tell me, do you mean to marry this Cook? If you do, not one penny of my money ever goes to you. Remember that, and be a sensible girl," said the old lady, impressively.

Now Aunt March possessed, in perfection, the art of rousing the spirit of opposition in the gentlest people, and enjoyed doing it. The best of us have a spice of perversity[12] in us, especially when we are young, and in love. If Aunt March had begged Meg to accept John Brooke, she would probably have declared she couldn't think of it; but, as she was peremptorily ordered *not* to like him, she immediately made up her mind that she would. Inclination as well as perversity made the decision easy, and, being already much excited, Meg opposed the old lady with unusual spirit.

"I shall marry whom I please, Aunt March, and you can leave your money to any one you like," she said, nodding her head with a resolute air.[13]

"Highty tighty![14] Is that the way you take my advice, miss? You'll be sorry for it, by and by, when you've tried love in a cottage, and found it a failure."

"It can't be a worse one than some people find in big houses," retorted Meg.

Aunt March put on her glasses and took a look at the girl,—for she did not know her in this new mood. Meg hardly knew herself, she felt so brave and independent,—so glad to defend John, and assert her right to love him, if she liked. Aunt March saw that she had begun wrong, and, after a little pause, made a fresh start, saying, as mildly as she could, "Now, Meg, my dear, be reasonable, and take my advice. I mean it kindly, and don't want you to spoil your whole life by making a mistake at the beginning. You ought

LITTLE WOMEN

Aunt March (Lucile Watson) orders Meg (Janet Leigh) not to marry John Brooke in 1949's *Little Women*.

Meg stands up to Aunt March. Harvé Stein, *Little Women* (1932).

15. The *OED* defines this use of *meanness* as a "smallness of character or mind; pettiness."

to marry well, and help your family; it's your duty to make a rich match, and it ought to be impressed upon you."

"Father and mother don't think so; they like John, though he *is* poor."

"Your pa and ma, my dear, have no more worldly wisdom than two babies."

"I'm glad of it," cried Meg, stoutly.

Aunt March took no notice, but went on with her lecture. "This Rook is poor, and hasn't got any rich relations, has he?"

"No; but he has many warm friends."

"You can't live on friends; try it, and see how cool they'll grow. He hasn't any business, has he?"

"Not yet; Mr. Laurence is going to help him."

"That won't last long. James Laurence is a crotchety old fellow, and not to be depended on. So you intend to marry a man without money, position, or business, and go on working harder than you do now, when you might be comfortable all your days by minding me, and doing better? I thought you had more sense, Meg."

"I couldn't do better if I waited half my life! John is good and wise; he's got heaps of talent; he's willing to work, and sure to get on, he's so energetic and brave. Every one likes and respects him, and I'm proud to think he cares for me, though I'm so poor, and young, and silly," said Meg, looking prettier than ever in her earnestness.

"He knows *you* have got rich relations, child; that's the secret of his liking, I suspect."

"Aunt March, how dare you say such a thing? John is above such meanness,[15] and I won't listen to you a minute if you talk so," cried Meg, indignantly, forgetting everything but the injustice of the old lady's suspicions. "My John wouldn't marry for money, any more than I would. We are willing to work, and we mean to wait. I'm not afraid of being poor, for I've been happy so far, and I know I shall be with him, because he loves me, and I—"

Meg stopped there, remembering, all of a sudden, that she hadn't made up her mind; that she had told "her John" to go away, and that he might be overhearing her inconsistent remarks.

Aunt March was very angry, for she had set her heart on having her pretty niece make a fine match, and something in the girl's happy your face made the lonely old woman feel both sad and sour.

"Well; I wash my hands of the whole affair! You are a wilful child, and you've lost more than you know by this piece of folly. No, I won't stop; I'm disappointed in you, and haven't spirits to see your pa now. Don't expect anything from me when you are married; your Mr. Book's friends must take care of you. I'm done with you forever."

And, slamming the door in Meg's face, Aunt March drove off in high dudgeon.[16] She seemed to take all the girl's courage with her; for, when left alone, Meg stood a moment undecided whether to laugh or cry. Before she could make up her mind, she was taken possession of by Mr. Brooke, who said, all in one breath, "I couldn't help hearing, Meg. Thank you for defending me, and Aunt March for proving that you *do* care for me a little bit."

"I didn't know how much, till she abused you," began Meg.

"And I needn't go away, but may stay and be happy—may I, dear?"

Here was another fine chance to make the crushing speech and the stately exit, but Meg never thought of doing either, and disgraced herself forever in Jo's eyes, by meekly whispering, "Yes, John," and hiding her face on Mr. Brooke's waistcoat.

Fifteen minutes after Aunt March's departure, Jo came softly down stairs, paused an instant at the parlor door, and, hearing no sound within, nodded and smiled, with a satisfied expression, saying to herself, "She has sent him away as we planned, and that affair is settled. I'll go and hear the fun, and have a good laugh over it."

But poor Jo never got her laugh, for she was transfixed upon the threshold by a spectacle which held her there, staring with her mouth nearly as wide open as her eyes. Going in to exult over a fallen enemy, and to praise a strong-minded sister for the banishment of an objectionable lover, it certainly *was* a shock to behold the aforesaid enemy serenely sitting on the sofa, with the strong-

16. Anger.

minded sister enthroned upon his knee, and wearing an expression of the most abject submission. Jo gave a sort of gasp, as if a cold shower-bath had suddenly fallen upon her,—for such an unexpected turning of the tables actually took her breath away. At the odd sound, the lovers turned and saw her. Meg jumped up, looking both proud and shy; but "that man," as Jo called him, actually laughed, and said, coolly, as he kissed the astonished new comer, "Sister Jo, congratulate us!"

That was adding insult to injury! it was altogether too much! and, making some wild demonstration with her hands, Jo vanished without a word. Rushing upstairs, she startled the invalids by exclaiming, tragically, as she burst into the room, "Oh, *do* somebody go down quick! John Brooke is acting dreadfully, and Meg likes it!"

Mr. and Mrs. March left the room with speed; and, casting herself upon the bed, Jo cried and scolded tempestuously as she told the awful news to Beth and Amy. The little girls, however, considered it a most agreeable and interesting event, and Jo got little comfort from them; so she went up to her refuge in the garret, and confided her troubles to the rats.

Nobody ever knew what went on in the parlor that afternoon; but a great deal of talking was done, and quiet Mr. Brooke astonished his friends by the eloquence and spirit with which he pleaded his suit, told his plans, and persuaded them to arrange everything just as he wanted it.

The tea-bell rang before he had finished describing the paradise which he meant to earn for Meg, and he proudly took her into supper, both looking so happy, that Jo hadn't the heart to be jealous or dismal. Amy was very much impressed by John's devotion and Meg's dignity. Beth beamed at them from a distance, while Mr. and Mrs. March surveyed the young couple with such tender satisfaction, that it was perfectly evident Aunt March was right in calling them as "unworldly as a pair of babies." No one ate much, but every one looked very happy, and the old room seemed to brighten up amazingly when the first romance of the family began there.

"You can't say 'nothing pleasant ever happens now,' can you,

Meg?" said Amy, trying to decide how she would group the lovers in the sketch she was planning to take.

"No, I'm sure I can't. How much has happened since I said that! It seems a year ago," answered Meg, who was in a blissful dream, lifted far above such common things as bread and butter.

"The joys come close upon the sorrows this time, and I rather think the changes have begun," said Mrs. March. "In most families there comes, now and then, a year full of events; this has been such an one, but it ends well, after all."[17]

"Hope the next will end better," muttered Jo, who found it very hard to see Meg absorbed in a stranger before her face; for Jo loved a few persons very dearly, and dreaded to have their affection lost or lessened in any way.

"I hope the third year from this *will* end better; I mean it shall, if I live to work out my plans," said Mr. Brooke, smiling at Meg, as if everything had become possible to him now.

"Doesn't it seem very long to wait?" asked Amy, who was in a hurry for the wedding.

"I've got so much to learn before I shall be ready, it seems a short time to me," answered Meg, with a sweet gravity in her face, never seen there before.

"You have only to wait. *I* am to do the work," said John, beginning his labors by picking up Meg's napkin, with an expression which caused Jo to shake her head, and then say to herself, with an air of relief, as the front door banged, "Here comes Laurie; now we shall have a little sensible conversation."

But Jo was mistaken; for Laurie came prancing in, overflowing with spirits, bearing a great bridal-looking bouquet for "Mrs. John Brooke," and evidently laboring under the delusion that the whole affair had been brought about by his excellent management.

"I knew Brooke would have it all his own way,—he always does; for when he makes up his mind to accomplish anything, it's done, though the sky falls," said Laurie, when he had presented his offering and his congratulations.

"Much obliged for that recommendation. I take it as a good omen for the future, and invite you to my wedding on the spot,"

17. As Part I of *Little Women* draws to an end, exactly one year has passed. Just as the novel opens on Christmas Eve, it closes on the day after Christmas 1862. Meg is now seventeen, Jo sixteen, Beth fourteen, and Amy twelve.

answered Mr. Brooke who felt at peace with all mankind, even his mischievous pupil.

"I'll come if I'm at the ends of the earth; for the sight of Jo's face alone, on that occasion, would be worth a long journey. You don't look festive, ma'am; what's the matter?" asked Laurie, following her into a corner of the parlor, whither all had adjourned to greet Mr. Laurence.

"I don't approve of the match, but I've made up my mind to bear it, and shall not say a word against it," said Jo, solemnly. "You can't know how hard it is for me to give up Meg," she continued, with a little quiver in her voice.

"You don't give her up. You only go halves," said Laurie, consolingly.

"It never can be the same again. I've lost my dearest friend," sighed Jo.

"You've got me, anyhow. I'm not good for much, I know; but I'll stand by you, Jo, all the days of my life; upon my word I will!" and Laurie meant what he said.

"I know you will, and I'm ever so much obliged; you are always a great comfort to me, Teddy," returned Jo, gratefully shaking hands.

"Well, now, don't be dismal, there's a good fellow. It's all right, you see. Meg is happy; Brooke will fly round and get settled immediately; grandpa will attend to him, and it will be very jolly to see Meg in her own little house. We'll have capital times after she is gone, for I shall be through college before long, and then we'll go abroad, or some nice trip or other. Wouldn't that console you?"

"I rather think it would; but there's no knowing what may happen in three years," said Jo, thoughtfully.

"That's true! Don't you wish you could take a look forward, and see where we shall all be then? I do," returned Laurie.

"I think not, for I might see something sad; and every one looks so happy now, I don't believe they could be much improved," and Jo's eyes went slowly round the room, brightening as they looked, for the prospect was a pleasant one.

Father and mother sat together quietly re-living the first chapter of the romance which for them began some twenty years ago. Amy was drawing the lovers, who sat apart in a beautiful world of their own, the light of which touched their faces with a grace the little artist could not copy. Beth lay on her sofa talking cheerily with her old friend, who held her little hand as if he felt that it possessed the power to lead him along the peaceful ways she walked. Jo lounged in her favorite low seat, with the grave, quiet look which best became her; and Laurie, leaning on the back of her chair, his chin on a level with her curly head, smiled with his friendliest aspect, and nodded at her in the long glass which reflected them both.

So grouped the curtain falls upon Meg, Jo, Beth and Amy. Whether it ever rises again, depends upon the reception given to the first act of the domestic drama, called "LITTLE WOMEN."

LITTLE WOMEN

OR,

MEG, JO, BETH AND AMY

LOUISA M. ALCOTT

PART II

Contents

Chapter 1

Gossip

IN ORDER THAT we may start afresh and go to Meg's wedding with free minds, it will be well to begin with a little gossip about the Marches. And here let me premise, that if any of the elders think there is too much "lovering" in the story, as I fear they may (I'm not afraid the young folks will make that objection), I can only say with Mrs. March, "What *can* you expect when I have four gay girls in the house, and a dashing young neighbor over the way?"

The three years that have passed have brought but few changes to the quiet family.[1] The war is over, and Mr. March safely at home, busy with his books and the small parish which found in him a minister by nature as by grace.[2] A quiet, studious man, rich in the wisdom that is better than learning, the charity which calls all mankind "brother," the piety that blossoms into character, making it august and lovely.

These attributes, in spite of poverty and the strict integrity which shut him out from the more worldly successes, attracted to him many admirable persons, as naturally as sweet herbs draw bees, and as naturally he gave them the honey into which fifty years of hard experience had distilled no bitter drop. Earnest young men found the gray-headed scholar as earnest and as young at heart as they;[a] thoughtful or troubled women instinctively brought their doubts and sorrows to him, sure of finding the gentlest sympathy, the wisest counsel; sinners told their sins to the pure-hearted old man, and were both rebuked and saved; gifted men found a companion in him; ambitious men caught glimpses of nobler ambitions than their own; and even worldlings[3] con-

1. Part II of *Little Women* moves forward in time to June 1866, although the exact year is never mentioned. The older March sisters have grown into young adults: Meg is now twenty, Jo nineteen. Beth is seventeen and Amy fifteen. Much has happened in the country in the intervening three years. On April 9, 1865, General Robert E. Lee surrendered his Confederate forces to General Ulysses S. Grant at Appomattox Courthouse, Virginia, marking the end of the long and bloody Civil War. Less than a week later, John Wilkes Booth assassinated President Abraham Lincoln at Ford's Theater in Washington, D.C., on April 14—Good Friday. LMA confessed in her journal: "On the 15th in the midst of the rejoicing came the sad news of the President's assassination & the city went into mourning. I am glad to have seen such a strange & sudden change in a nation's feelings. Saw the great procession, & though colored men were in it one was walking arm in arm with a white gentleman & I exulted thereat" (*Journals* 140). Two weeks earlier, she had watched Booth's brother, Edwin, perform *Hamlet* at the Boston Theater.

2. Bronson Alcott was sixty-one years old when the Civil War began, too old to enlist in active duty. He could have served in the U.S. Sanitary Commission, but he decided to focus his time on education. In April 1859, he was appointed Superintendent of Schools in Concord, a position he held until spring 1864; it paid, however, only $100 a year. As Frederick C. Dahlstrand notes in *Amos Bronson Alcott: An Intellectual Biography* (East Brunswick, NJ: Associated University Presses, 1982), "[H]is appointment as superintendent meant acknowledgement as an authority in education, a status denied him since the failure of the Temple School. It was a kind of vindication, a sign to him that the dull and dense public was finally beginning to appreciate his true worth" (p. 255). As superintendent, Bronson visited all the Concord schools, held monthly meetings at Orchard House with the teachers, and he even held meetings with each school's pupils and parents to discuss the importance of a family's involvement in children's education.

During the Civil War years he published various articles and poems, mostly in his friend Frank Sanborn's Boston *Commonwealth*. He spoke occasionally, but these were not the extended engagements that he had undertaken before the war. The war years also saw happiness in Bronson's life as Anna Alcott Pratt gave birth to his first grandson, Frederick Alcott Pratt, on March 28, 1863. Most of 1865 was spent at home, working the grounds of Orchard House, constructing a fence of twisted tree boughs around the yard. The failure of the Temple School and Fruitlands and the dire poverty of the 1840s and 1850s seem to have receded into memory. Bronson was gaining a reputation as one of Concord's sages. On Independence

Day 1865, Emerson spent the evening with him, and Bronson was hopeful for the future: "The Republic now begins to look sweet and beautiful, as if honest patriotic citizens might walk upright without shame or apologies as in years before this rebellion" (*Journals of BA* 372).

3. People who are interested only in the actual world, not the spiritual or philosophical one.

4. Before the end of the Civil War, Soldiers' Homes began to appear in the Northeast, offering care and support for veterans and their widows and orphans. Female charitable organizations soon began working for a national or state system. The U.S. Sanitary Commission also helped establish temporary homes. With the approval of the Senate, the National Asylum for Disabled Volunteer Soldiers was incorporated on March 21, 1866, with eleven branches nationwide, aiding both Union and Confederate veterans.

5. John Bridge Pratt, the model for John Brooke, did not fight in the Civil War. Although he was drafted, his poor health prevented him from serving. The exact nature of Brooke's wound is not given. Although the war has ended as Part II of *Little Women* begins, its effects linger. The close of the Civil War saw approximately 2,400,000 soldiers, Union and Confederate, returning to their homes across the United States. The cost of the Civil War was immense. In government expenditures and property destruction, the war cost approximately 7 billion dollars, equivalent to about 75 billion dollars today. Human costs were even more horrific. In *This Republic of Suffering: Death and the American Civil War* (New York: Alfred A. Knopf, 2008), Drew Gilpin Faust writes: "The number of soldiers who died between 1861 and 1865, an estimated 620,000, is approximately equal to the total American fatalities in the Revolution, the War of 1812, the Mexican War, the Spanish-American War, World War I, World War II, and the Korean War combined. The Civil War's rate of death, its incidence in comparison with the size of the American population, was six times that of World War II. A similar rate, about 2 percent, in the United States today would mean six million fatalities" (p. xi). In addition to the large death toll, numerous veterans returned home disabled. Over 50,000 amputations were performed during the war, and many soldiers lost more than one limb. LMA, who had seen the results of horrific fighting on human bodies while serving as a nurse in Georgetown, D.C., wrote about amputations in a somewhat humorous but pathetic scene in *Hospital Sketches* (1863). In chapter 3, "A Day," the narrator meets a young sergeant lying in his bed, who tells her: "'Lord! What a scramble there'll be for arms and legs, when we old boys come out of our graves, on the Judgment Day: wonder if we shall get our own

fessed that his beliefs were beautiful and true, although "they wouldn't pay."

To outsiders, the five energetic women seemed to rule the house, and so they did in many things; but the quiet man sitting among his books was still the head of the family, the household conscience, anchor and comforter; for to him the busy, anxious women always turned in troublous times, finding him, in the truest sense of those sacred words, husband and father.

The girls gave their hearts into their mother's keeping—their souls into their father's; and to both parents, who lived and labored so faithfully for them, they gave a love that grew with their growth, and bound them tenderly together by the sweetest tie which blesses life and outlives death.

Mrs. March is as brisk and cheery, though rather grayer than when we saw her last, and just now so absorbed in Meg's affairs, that the hospitals and homes, still full of wounded "boys" and soldiers' widows, decidedly miss the motherly missionary's visits.[4]

John Brooke did his duty manfully for a year, got wounded, was sent home, and not allowed to return.[5] He received no stars or bars,[6] but he deserved them, for he cheerfully risked all he had; and life and love are very precious when both are in full bloom. Perfectly resigned to his discharge, he devoted himself to getting well, preparing for business, and earning a home for Meg. With the good sense and sturdy independence that characterized him, he refused Mr. Laurence's more generous offers, and accepted the place of under book-keeper, feeling better satisfied to begin with an honestly-earned salary, than by running any risks with borrowed money.

Meg had spent the time in working as well as waiting, growing womanly in character, wise in housewifery arts, and prettier than ever; for love is a great beautifier. She had her girlish ambitions and hopes, and felt some disappointment at the humble way in which the new life must begin. Ned Moffat had just married Sallie Gardiner, and Meg couldn't help contrasting their fine house and carriage, many gifts, and splendid outfit, with her own, and secretly wishing she could have the same. But somehow envy and discontent soon vanished when she thought of all the patient love and labor John had put into the little home awaiting her; and

LITTLE WOMEN

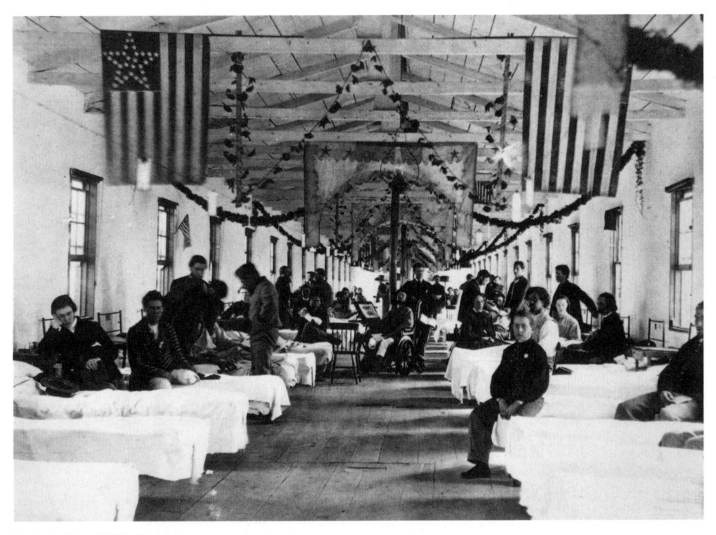

Interior of a Union Civil War Hospital.

when they sat together in the twilight, talking over their small plans, the future always grew so beautiful and bright, that she forgot Sallie's splendor, and felt herself the richest, happiest girl in Christendom.

Jo never went back to Aunt March, for the old lady took such a fancy to Amy, that she bribed her with the offer of drawing lessons from one of the best teachers going; and for the sake of this advantage, Amy would have served a far harder mistress. So she gave her mornings to duty, her afternoons to pleasure, and prospered finely. Jo, meantime, devoted herself to literature and Beth,

again? If we do, my leg will have to tramp from Fredericksburg, my arm from here, I suppose, and meet my body, wherever it may be.'" The town of Concord also saw its losses. Although no official records of enlistments were kept by Concord, William Shouler, in volume two of *A History of Massachusetts in the Civil War* (Boston: E. P. Dutton, 1868), indicates that Concord provided 229 men (p. 402). On April 19, 1867, Concord's Civil War monument was dedicated, with Ralph Waldo Emerson giving an address. The obelisk, designed by artist and architect Hammatt Billings (who had also illustrated the second part of *Little Women* in 1869), lists thirty-two Concordians who gave their lives for the Union. In chapter 6 of *Hospital*

Sketches, LMA paints a poignant and private scene of the loss so many endured: "To me, the saddest sight I saw . . . was the spectacle of a grey-haired father, sitting hour after hour by his son, dying from the poison of his wound . . . [W]hen the son slept, the father watched him . . . and though no feature of his grave countenance changed, the rough hand, smoothing the lock of hair upon the pillow, the bowed attitude of the grey head, were more pathetic than the loudest lamentations."

6. Medals or promotions to a higher rank.

7. The phrase comes from the narrative poem "The Angel in the House," by the British poet Coventry Patmore (1823–1896). Published in four parts from 1854 to 1862, the poem, which became extremely popular, details Patmore's courtship with his first wife, Emily, and sets up the feminine ideal of the mid- to late-nineteenth-century as a woman who selflessly devotes herself to her family.

8. The Boston *Saturday Evening Gazette,* in which LMA published a number of stories in the late 1850s and early 1860s, is likely the real-life antecedent for *The Spread Eagle.* Ranging from sentimental romances to sensational melodramas, from realistic to domestic fiction, the stories usually earned LMA ten to twenty dollars each and taught her how to tailor her stories to suit the paper's demands.

9. As we learn from a clue given in a later chapter, Laurie attends Harvard College. During Laurie's matriculation, Harvard was an all-male institution. In the 1870s, Radcliffe College began to develop informally as Harvard faculty tutored women. Within the circle of her parents' friends, LMA knew a number of Harvard graduates, most notably her neighbors Ralph Waldo Emerson, who entered the college at age fourteen in 1817 and graduated in the middle of his class in 1821, and Henry David Thoreau, who began at age sixteen in 1833 and graduated in 1837, the year Emerson delivered his famous "American Scholar" oration to Harvard's Phi Beta Kappa fraternity. LMA's father, Bronson Alcott, however, did not attend college. Coming from a poor farm family, he was self-educated. When LMA was writing *Little Women,* Harvard was in the middle of a prodigious fundraising campaign to construct Memorial Hall, an impressive gothic structure dedicated to the memory of Harvard graduates who had sacrificed their lives for the Union.

Drawing of Memorial Hall, Harvard College.

who remained delicate long after the fever was a thing of the past. Not an invalid exactly, but never again the rosy, healthy creature she had been; yet always hopeful, happy, and serene, busy with the quiet duties she loved, every one's friend, and an angel in the house,[7] long before those who loved her most had learned to know it.

As long as "The Spread Eagle" paid her a dollar a column for her "rubbish," as she called it, Jo felt herself a woman of means, and spun her little romances diligently.[8] But great plans fermented in her busy brain and ambitious mind, and the old tin kitchen in the garret held a slowly increasing pile of blotted manuscript, which was one day to place the name of March upon the roll of fame.

Laurie, having dutifully gone to college[9] to please his grandfather, was now getting through it in the easiest possible manner to please himself. A universal favorite, thanks to money, manners, much talent, and the kindest heart that ever got its owner into scrapes by trying to get other people out of them, he stood in great danger of being spoilt, and probably would have been, like many another promising boy, if he had not possessed a talisman against evil in the memory of the kind old man who was bound

Dove Cottage in Concord, Mass., where the Alcotts lived from 1840 to 1843.

up in his success, the motherly friend who watched over him as if he were her son, and last, but not least by any means, the knowledge that four innocent girls loved, admired, and believed in him with all their hearts.

Being only "a glorious human boy,"[10] of course he frolicked and flirted, grew dandified, aquatic, sentimental or gymnastic, as college fashions ordained; hazed and was hazed, talked slang, and more than once came perilously near suspension and expulsion. But as high spirits and the love of fun were the causes of these pranks, he always managed to save himself by frank confession, honorable atonement, or the irresistible power of persuasion which he possessed in perfection. In fact, he rather prided himself on his narrow escapes, and liked to thrill the girls with graphic accounts of his triumphs over wrathful tutors, dignified professors, and vanquished enemies. The "men of my class" were heroes in the eyes of the girls, who never wearied of the exploits of "our fellows," and were frequently allowed to bask in the smiles of these great creatures, when Laurie brought them home with him.

11. Meg's Dovecote was probably based on the Hosmer Cottage in Concord, which the Alcotts rented from Edmund Hosmer when they first moved to the village in April 1840. Bronson named it after Wordsworth's home in the Lake District of England. LMA also called the home in Chelsea, MA, that Anna and John lived in after marriage by the same name. In May 1861, LMA visited the dove-cot for the first time: "Saw Anna's honeymoon home at Chelsea,—a little cottage in a blooming apple-orchard. Pretty place, simple and sweet. God bless it!" (*Journals* 99). In October 1861, she wrote: "A week with Nan in the dove-cot. As happy as ever" (*Journals* 106). The turtle dove has long been a symbol of devoted love and appears a number of times in the Old Testament's Song of Solomon: "O my dove, *that art* in the clefts of the rock, in the secret *places* of the stairs, let me see thy countenance, let me hear thy voice; for sweet *is* thy voice, and thy countenance *is* comely" (2:14).

12. The *OED* defines *bill* as "to stroke bill with bill (as doves)," and the phrase to *bill and coo* means "to converse caressingly or amorously."

13. Undrunk cold tea was emptied into a slop bowl, part of a traditional tea set, before a cup was refilled with hot tea.

14. Larches are deciduous conifers, meaning that they have needles but lose them in the fall and winter.

15. A disorderly headlong rush.

Amy especially enjoyed this high honor, and became quite a belle among them; for her ladyship early felt and learned to use the gift of fascination with which she was endowed. Meg was too much absorbed in her private and particular John to care for any other lords of creation, and Beth too shy to do more than peep at them, and wonder how Amy dared to order them about so; but Jo felt quite in her element, and found it very difficult to refrain from imitating the gentlemanly attitudes, phrases, and feats which seemed more natural to her than the decorums prescribed for young ladies. They all liked Jo immensely, but never fell in love with her, though very few escaped without paying the tribute of a sentimental sigh or two at Amy's shrine. And speaking of sentiment brings us very naturally to the "Dove-cote."[11]

That was the name of the little brown house which Mr. Brooke had prepared for Meg's first home. Laurie had christened it, saying it was highly appropriate to the gentle lovers, who "went on together like a pair of turtle-doves, with first a bill[12] and then a coo." It was a tiny house, with a little garden behind, and a lawn about as big as a pocket-handkerchief in front. Here Meg meant to have a fountain, shrubbery, and a profusion of lovely flowers; though just at present the fountain was represented by a weather-beaten urn, very like a dilapidated slop-bowl;[13] the shrubbery consisted of several young larches,[14] who looked undecided whether to live or die, and the profusion of flowers was merely hinted by regiments of sticks, to show where seeds were planted. But inside, it was altogether charming, and the happy bride saw no fault from garret to cellar. To be sure, the hall was so narrow, it was fortunate that they had no piano, for one never could have been got in whole. The dining-room was so small, that six people were a tight fit, and the kitchen stairs seemed built for the express purpose of precipitating both servants and china pell-mell[15] into the coal-bin. But once get used to these slight blemishes, and nothing could be more complete, for good sense and good taste had presided over the furnishing, and the result was highly satisfactory. There were no marble-topped tables, long mirrors, or lace curtains in the little parlor, but simple furniture, plenty of books, a fine picture or two, a stand of flowers in the bay-window, and, scattered all about, the pretty gifts which came from friendly hands, and were the fairer for the loving messages they brought.

I don't think the Parian Psyche[16] Laurie gave, lost any of its beauty because Brooke put up the bracket it stood upon; that any upholsterer could have draped the plain muslin curtains more gracefully than Amy's artistic hand; or that any store-room was ever better provided with good wishes, merry words, and happy hopes, than that in which Jo and her mother put away Meg's few boxes, barrels, and bundles; and I am morally certain that the spandy-new kitchen never *could* have looked so cosy and neat, if Hannah had not arranged every pot and pan a dozen times over, and laid the fire all ready for lighting, the minute "Mis. Brooke came home." I also doubt if any young matron ever began life with so rich a supply of dusters, holders,[17] and piece-bags,—for Beth made enough to last till the silver wedding came round, and invented three different kinds of dishcloths for the express service of the bridal china.

People who hire all these things done for them, never know what they lose; for the homeliest tasks get beautified if loving hands do them, and Meg found so many proofs of this, that everything in her small nest, from the kitchen roller to the silver vase on her parlor table, was eloquent of home love and tender forethought.

What happy times they had planning together; what solemn shopping excursions, what funny mistakes they made, and what shouts of laughter arose over Laurie's ridiculous bargains! In his love of jokes, this young gentleman, though nearly through college, was as much of a boy as ever. His last whim had been to bring with him, on his weekly visits, some new, useful, and ingenious article for the young housekeeper. Now a bag of remarkable clothes-pins; next a wonderful nutmeg grater, which fell to pieces at the first trial; a knife-cleaner that spoilt all the knives; or a sweeper that picked the nap neatly off the carpet, and left the dirt; labor-saving soap that took the skin off one's hands; infallible cements[18] which stuck firmly to nothing but the fingers of the deluded buyer; and every kind of tin-ware, from a toy savings-bank for odd pennies, to a wonderful boiler which would wash articles in its own steam, with every prospect of exploding in the process.

16. Parian is a fine white porcelain used in the production of large statuettes. Resembling Parian marble, it was first created in England around 1840. In Greek mythology, Cupid falls in love with Psyche, a beautiful mortal. In works of art, Psyche is usually depicted with butterfly wings.

17. Probably a reference to pot holders.

18. A type of bonding glue.

19. Jo refers to a character in the comedy *The Toodles* (1848) by the British actor, publisher, playwright, and theater manager William Evans Burton (1804–1860), who moved to America in 1831 and worked primarily in New York, Philadelphia, and Baltimore. Burton himself played Timothy Toodle, who gets exasperated with his wife when she keeps buying unneeded items at auctions. Finally, he purchases a coffin at auction, telling his wife that he could use it if she dies before him. The play was one of Burton's most successful.

20. Mercury, a Roman god, was the messenger of the gods. The son of Jupiter, he is depicted in works of art wearing winged sandals or a winged hat.

21. A piece of furniture with open shelves, one above the other, that was used to display ornaments, figurines, pottery, or various pieces of artwork.

22. A type of apron that covered the entire front of a dress to protect it from dirt.

In vain Meg begged him to stop. John laughed at him, and Jo called him "Mr. Toodles."[19] He was possessed with a mania for patronizing Yankee ingenuity, and seeing his friends fitly furnished forth. So each week beheld some fresh absurdity.

Everything was done at last, even to Amy's arranging different colored soaps to match the different colored rooms, and Beth's setting the table for the first meal.

"Are you satisfied? Does it seem like home, and do you feel as if you should be happy here?" asked Mrs. March, as she and her daughter went through the new kingdom, arm-in-arm—for just then they seemed to cling together more tenderly than ever.

"Yes, mother, perfectly satisfied, thanks to you all, and *so* happy that I can't talk about it," answered Meg, with a look that was far better than words.

"If she only had a servant or two it would be all right," said Amy, coming out of the parlor, where she had been trying to decide whether the bronze Mercury[20] looked best on the whatnot[21] or the mantle-piece.

"Mother and I have talked that over, and I have made up my mind to try her way first. There will be so little to do, that, with Lotty to run my errands and help me here and there, I shall only have enough work to keep me from getting lazy or homesick," answered Meg, tranquilly.

"Sallie Moffat has four," began Amy.

"If Meg had four the house wouldn't hold them, and master and missis would have to camp in the garden," broke in Jo, who, enveloped in a big blue pinafore,[22] was giving the last polish to the door-handles.

"Sallie isn't a poor man's wife, and many maids are in keeping with her fine establishment. Meg and John begin humbly, but I have a feeling that there will be quite as much happiness in the little house as in the big one. It's a great mistake for young girls like Meg to leave themselves nothing to do but dress, give orders, and gossip. When I was first married, I used to long for my new clothes to wear out, or get torn, so that I might have the pleasure of mending them; for I got heartily sick of doing fancy work and tending my pocket handkerchief."

"Why didn't you go into the kitchen and make messes, as Sallie says she does, to amuse herself, though they never turn out well, and the servants laugh at her," said Meg.

"I did, after a while; not to 'mess,' but to learn of Hannah how things should be done, that my servants need *not* laugh at me. It was play then, but there came a time when I was truly grateful that I not only possessed the will, but the power to cook wholesome food for my little girls, and help myself when I could no longer afford to hire help. You begin at the other end, Meg, dear, but the lessons you learn now will be of use to you by and by, when John is a richer man, for the mistress of a house, however splendid, should know how work *ought* to be done, if she wishes to be well and honestly served."

"Yes, mother, I'm sure of that," said Meg, listening respectfully to the little lecture; for the best of women will hold forth upon the all-absorbing subject of housekeeping. "Do you know I like this room best of all in my baby-house," added Meg, a minute after, as they went upstairs, and she looked into her well-stored linen closet.

Beth was there, laying the snowy piles smoothly on the shelves, and exulting over the goodly array. All three laughed as Meg spoke; for that linen closet was a joke. You see, having said that if Meg married "that Brooke" she shouldn't have a cent of her money, Aunt March was rather in a quandary, when time had appeased her wrath, and made her repent her vow. She never broke her word, and was much exercised in her mind how to get round it, and at last devised a plan whereby she could satisfy herself. Mrs. Carrol, Florence's mamma, was ordered to buy, have made and marked a generous supply of house and table linen, and send it as *her* present. All of which was faithfully done, but the secret leaked out, and was greatly enjoyed by the family; for Aunt March tried to look utterly unconscious, and insisted that she could give nothing but the old-fashioned pearls, long promised to the first bride.

"That's a housewifely taste, which I am glad to see. I had a young friend who set up housekeeping with six sheets, but she had finger bowls[23] for company, and that satisfied her," said Mrs. March, patting the damask[24] table-cloths with a truly feminine appreciation of their fineness.

23. A small bowl, usually of glass, that holds water used to rinse one's fingers, especially after dessert.

24. A twilled linen fabric, with many designs and figures, used for table linen. True damask was originally made of silk.

25. A set of china.

26. A streaming or loose coat.

"I haven't a single finger bowl, but this is a 'set out'[25] that will last me all my days, Hannah says;" and Meg looked quite contented, as well she might.

"Toodles is coming," cried Jo from below, and they all went down to meet Laurie, whose weekly visit was an important event in their quiet lives.

A tall, broad-shouldered young fellow, with a cropped head, a felt-basin of a hat, and a fly-away coat,[26] came tramping down the road at a great pace, walked over the low fence, without stopping to open the gate, straight up to Mrs. March, with both hands out, and a hearty—

"Here I am, mother! Yes, it's all right."

The last words were in answer to the look the elder lady gave him; a kindly, questioning look, which the handsome eyes met so frankly that the little ceremony closed as usual, with a motherly kiss.

"For Mrs. John Brooke, with the maker's congratulations and compliments. Bless you, Beth! What a refreshing spectacle you are, Jo! Amy, you are getting altogether too handsome for a single lady."

As Laurie spoke, he delivered a brown paper parcel to Meg, pulled Beth's hair ribbon, stared at Jo's big pinafore, and fell into an attitude of mock rapture before Amy, then shook hands all round, and every one began to talk.

"Where is John?" asked Meg, anxiously.

"Stopped to get the license for to-morrow, ma'am."

"Which side won the last match, Teddy?" inquired Jo, who persisted in feeling an interest in manly sports, despite her nineteen years.

"Ours, of course. Wish you'd been there to see."

"How is the lovely Miss Randal?" asked Amy, with a significant smile.

"More cruel than ever; don't you see how I'm pining away?" and Laurie gave his broad chest a sounding slap, and heaved a melodramatic sigh.

"What's the last joke? Undo the bundle and see, Meg," said Beth, eyeing the knobby parcel with curiosity.

"It's a useful thing to have in the house in case of fire or thieves," observed Laurie, as a small watchman's rattle[27] appeared amid the laughter of the girls.

"Any time when John is away, and you get frightened, Mrs. Meg, just swing that out of the front window, and it will rouse the neighborhood in a jiffy. Nice thing, isn't it?" and Laurie gave them a sample of its powers that made them cover up their ears.

"There's gratitude for you! and, speaking of gratitude, reminds me to mention that you may thank Hannah for saving your wedding-cake from destruction. I saw it going into your house as I came by, and if she hadn't defended it manfully I'd have had a pick at it, for it looked like a remarkably plummy one."

"I wonder if you will ever grow up, Laurie," said Meg, in a matronly tone.

"I'm doing my best, ma'am, but can't get much higher, I'm afraid, as six feet is about all men can do in these degenerate days," responded the young gentleman, whose head was about level with the little chandelier. "I suppose it would be profanation to eat anything in this bran-new[28] bower, so, as I'm tremendously hungry, I propose an adjournment," he added, presently.

"Mother and I are going to wait for John. There are some last things to settle," said Meg, bustling away.

"Beth and I are going over to Kitty Bryant's to get more flowers for to-morrow," added Amy, tying a picturesque hat over her picturesque curls, and enjoying the effect as much as anybody.

"Come, Jo, don't desert a fellow. I'm in such a state of exhaustion I can't get home without help. Don't take off your apron, whatever you do; it's peculiarly becoming," said Laurie, as Jo bestowed his especial aversion in her capacious pocket, and offered her arm to support his feeble steps.

"Now, Teddy, I want to talk seriously to you about to-morrow," began Jo, as they strolled away together. "You *must* promise to behave well, and not cut up any pranks, and spoil our plans."

"Not a prank."

"And don't say funny things when we ought to be sober."

"I never do; you are the one for that."

27. The *OED* defines a *watchman's rattle* as "an instrument with a vibrating tongue fixed in a frame, which slips over the teeth of a ratchet wheel and produces a loud raucous sound when whirled around."

28. LMA uses a typical nineteenth-century spelling of *brand-new,* which, according to the *OED,* means "perfectly new." The etymology of the word comes from *brand* and *new* "as if fresh and glowing from the furnace." The 1880–1881 edition changed the adjective to *spick and span new bower.*

"And I implore you not to look at me during the ceremony; I shall certainly laugh if you do."

"You won't see me; you'll be crying so hard that the thick fog round you will obscure the prospect."

"I never cry unless for some great affliction."

"Such as old fellows[b] going to college, hey?" cut in Laurie, with suggestive laugh.

"Don't be a peacock. I only moaned a trifle to keep the girls company."

"Exactly. I say, Jo, how is grandpa this week? pretty amiable?"

"Very; why, have you got into a scrape, and want to know how he'll take it?" asked Jo, rather sharply.

"Now Jo, do you think I'd look your mother in the face, and say 'All right,' if it wasn't?"—and Laurie stopped short, with an injured air.

"No, I don't."

"Then don't go and be suspicious; I only want some money," said Laurie, walking on again, appeased by her hearty tone.

"You spend a great deal, Teddy."

"Bless you, I don't spend it; it spends itself, somehow, and is gone before I know it."

"You are so generous and kind-hearted, that you let people borrow, and can't say 'No' to any one. We heard about Henshaw, and all you did for him. If you always spent money in that way, no one would blame you," said Jo, warmly.

"Oh, he made a mountain out of a mole-hill. You wouldn't have me let that fine fellow work himself to death, just for the want of a little help, when he is worth a dozen of us lazy chaps, would you?"

"Of course not; but I don't see the use of your having seventeen waistcoats, endless neckties, and a new hat every time you come home. I thought you'd got over the dandy period; but every now and then it breaks out in a new spot. Just now it's the fashion to be hideous; to make your head look like a scrubbing brush, wear a strait-jacket, orange gloves, and clumping, square-toed boots. If it was cheap ugliness, I'd say nothing; but it costs as much as the other, and I don't get any satisfaction out of it."

LITTLE WOMEN

Laurie threw back his head, and laughed so heartily at this attack, that the felt-basin fell off, and Jo trampled on it, which insult only afforded him an opportunity for expatiating on the advantages of a rough-and-ready costume, as he folded up the maltreated hat, and stuffed it into his pocket.

"Don't lecture any more, there's a good soul; I have enough all through the week, and like to enjoy myself when I come home. I'll get myself up regardless of expense, to-morrow, and be a satisfaction to my friends."

"I'll leave you in peace if you'll *only* let your hair grow. I'm not aristocratic, but I do object to being seen with a person who looks like a young prize-fighter," observed Jo, severely.

"This unassuming style promotes study; that's why we adopt it," returned Laurie, who certainly could not be accused of vanity, having voluntarily sacrificed a handsome, curly crop, to the demand for quarter of an inch long stubble.[29]

"By the way, Jo, I think that little Parker is really getting desperate about Amy. He talks of her constantly, writes poetry, and moons[30] about in a most suspicious manner. He'd better nip his little passion in the bud, hadn't he?" added Laurie, in a confidential, elder-brotherly tone, after a minute's silence.

"Of course he had; we don't want any more marrying in this family for years to come. Mercy on us, what *are* the children thinking of!" and Jo looked as much scandalized as if Amy and little Parker were not yet in their teens.

"It's a fast[31] age, and I don't know what we are coming to, ma'am. You are a mere infant, but you'll go next, Jo, and we'll be left lamenting," said Laurie, shaking his head over the degeneracy of the times.

"Me! don't be alarmed;[c] I'm not one of the agreeable sort. Nobody will want me, and it's a mercy, for there should always be one old maid in a family."

"You won't give any one a chance," said Laurie, with a sidelong glance, and a little more color than before in his sunburnt face. "You won't show the soft side of your character; and if a fellow gets a look at it by accident, and can't help showing that he likes it, you treat him as Mrs. Gummidge did her sweetheart; throw

29. Laurie is a victim of fashion. During the first part of the nineteenth century, men wore their hair at mid-length, but by 1860, short hair had become popular.

30. To act listlessly.

31. The *OED* notes that *fast* "usually impl[ies] a greater or less degree of immorality."

32. Laurie is referring to the widow Mrs. Gummidge in Dickens's *David Copperfield* (1849–1850). Mr. Peggoty, when visiting David late in the novel, tells him that the widow had been proposed to by a ship's cook: "Missis Gummidge, 'stead of saying 'thank you, I'm much obleeged to you, I ain't a-going fur to change my condition at my time of life,' up'd with a bucket as was standing by, and laid it over that theer ship's cook's head 'till he sung out fur help, and I went in and reskied of him" (Chapter 63).

33. The *OED* identifies *raspy* in this usage as an American expression, meaning "easily exasperated; irritable; ill-tempered," and cites this sentence in Part II of *Little Women* as its first example. The 1880–1881 edition changed *raspy* to *cross*.

cold water over him, and get so thorny no one dares touch or look at you."[32]

"I don't like that sort of thing; I'm too busy to be worried with nonsense, and I think it's dreadful to break up families so. Now don't say any more about it; Meg's wedding has turned all our heads, and we talk of nothing but lovers and such absurdities. I don't wish to get raspy,[33] so let's change the subject;" and Jo looked quite ready to fling cold water on the slightest provocation.

Whatever his feelings might have been, Laurie found a vent for them in a long low whistle, and the fearful prediction, as they parted at the gate,—"Mark my words, Jo, you'll go next."

Chapter 2

The First Wedding

Lily of the valley.

THE JUNE ROSES over the porch were awake bright and early on that morning, rejoicing with all their hearts in the cloudless sunshine, like friendly little neighbors, as they were. Quite flushed with excitement were their ruddy faces, as they swung in the wind, whispering to one another what they had seen; for some peeped in at the dining-room windows, where the feast was spread, some climbed up to nod and smile at the sisters, as they dressed the bride, others waved a welcome to those who came and went on various errands in garden, porch and hall, and all, from the rosiest full-blown flower to the palest baby-bud, offered their tribute of beauty and fragrance to the gentle mistress who had loved and tended them so long.

Meg looked very like a rose herself; for all that was best and sweetest in heart and soul, seemed to bloom into her face that day, making it fair and tender, with a charm more beautiful than beauty. Neither silk, lace, nor orange flowers[1] would she have. "I don't want to look strange or fixed up, to-day," she said; "I don't want a fashionable wedding, but only those about me whom I love, and to them I wish to look and be my familiar self."

So she made her wedding gown herself, sewing into it the tender hopes and innocent romances of a girlish heart. Her sisters braided up her pretty hair, and the only ornaments she wore were the lilies of the valley,[2] which "her John" liked best of all the flowers that grew.

"You *do* look just like our own dear Meg, only so very sweet and lovely, that I should hug you if it wouldn't crumple your dress," cried Amy, surveying her with delight, when all was done.

"Then I am satisfied. But please hug and kiss me, every one,

1. The tradition of brides wearing orange blossoms originated in ancient China. Because the orange tree is one of the few plants that bloom and bear fruit at the same time, it became a symbol of fruitfulness and good fortune. During the Crusades the fashionable custom spread throughout Europe and eventually America in the early 1800s.

2. The lily of the valley *(convallaria majalis)* is a woodland flowering plant, noted for its scented flowers. In the language of flowers, it symbolizes sweetness, humility, and the return to happiness. Ironically, all parts of the plant are poisonous.

John Bridge Pratt, Anna's husband, circa 1860s. When John Pratt died suddenly in November 1870, LMA, who was in Rome, wrote to her grieving sister: "He did more to make us trust & respect men than any one I know" (*Selected Letters* 153).

and don't mind my dress; I want a great many crumples of this sort put into it to-day;" and Meg opened her arms to her sisters, who clung about her with April faces,[3] for a minute, feeling that the new love had not changed the old.

"Now I'm going to tie John's cravat[4] for him, and then to stay a few minutes with father, quietly in the study;" and Meg ran down to perform these little ceremonies, and then to follow her mother wherever she went, conscious that in spite of the smiles on the motherly face, there was a secret sorrow hidden in the motherly heart, at the flight of the first bird from the nest.

As the younger girls stand together, giving the last touches to their simple toilet, it may be a good time to tell of a few changes which three years have wrought in their appearance; for all are looking their best, just now.

Jo's angles are much softened; she has learned to carry herself with ease, if not grace. The curly crop has lengthened into a thick coil, more becoming to the small head atop of the tall figure. There is a fresh color in her brown cheeks, a soft shine in her eyes; only gentle words fall from her sharp tongue to-day.

Beth has grown slender, pale, and more quiet than ever; the beautiful, kind eyes, are larger, and in them lies an expression that saddens one, although it is not sad itself. It is the shadow of pain which touches the young face with such pathetic patience; but Beth seldom complains, and always speaks hopefully of "being better soon."

Amy is with truth considered "the flower of the family"; for at sixteen she has the air and bearing of a full-grown woman—not beautiful, but possessed of that indescribable charm called grace. One saw it in the lines of her figure, the make and motion of her hands, the flow of her dress, the droop of her hair—unconscious, yet harmonious, and as attractive to many as beauty itself. Amy's nose still afflicted her, for it never *would* grow Grecian; so did her mouth, being too wide, and having a decided underlip.[a] These offending features gave character to her whole face, but she never could see it, and consoled herself with her wonderfully fair complexion, keen blue eyes, and curls, more golden and abundant than ever.

All three wore suits of thin, silvery gray (their best gowns for

Rev. Samuel Joseph May (1797–1871), Abigail Alcott's brother.

the summer), with blush roses[5] in hair and bosom; and all three looked just what they were—fresh-faced, happy-hearted girls, pausing a moment in their busy lives to read with wistful eyes the sweetest chapter in the romance of womanhood.[6]

There were to be no ceremonious performances; everything was to be as natural and homelike as possible; so when Aunt March arrived, she was scandalized to see the bride come running to welcome and lead her in, to find the bridegroom fastening up a garland that had fallen down, and to catch a glimpse of the paternal minister marching upstairs with a grave countenance, and a wine bottle under each arm.

"Upon my word, here's a state of things!" cried the old lady, taking the seat of honor prepared for her, and settling the folds of her lavender *moire*[7] with a great rustle. "You oughtn't to be seen till the last minute, child."[8]

3. LMA may be alluding to the madrigal (a secular vocal music composition) "April is in my mistress' face," by Thomas Morley (1557?–1602), the British composer and organist of St. Paul's Cathedral: "April is in my mistress' face, / And July in her eyes hath place; / Within her bosom is September, / But in her heart a cold December." She may mean that while the happiness of spring shines on the sisters' faces, their hearts are sad at losing a sister.

4. The cravat, which originated in the 1630s from military dress, is a neckband or scarf that could be tied in a number of styles.

5. Delicate pink roses.

6. Anna Alcott and John Bridge Pratt were married in the parlor of Orchard House on May 23, 1860 (the same day as Bronson and Abigail's marriage in 1830), by Abigail Alcott's brother, the fervent abolitionist Rev. Samuel Joseph May. Among the small group in attendance were Lidian and Ralph Waldo Emerson, Henry David Thoreau, Frank Sanborn, and Elizabeth Palmer Peabody. Since Rev. May was not a licensed minister in Middlesex County, he was assisted by Ephraim Bull (developer of the Concord grape). Anna's simple wedding dress is on display today at Orchard House. LMA described Anna's wedding in her May 1860 journal: "The dear girl was married on the 23d, the same day as Mother's wedding. A lovely day; the house full of sunshine, flowers, friends, and happiness. Uncle S. J. May married them, with no fuss, but much love, and we all stood round her. She in her silver-gray silk, with lilies of the valley (John's flower) in her bosom and hair. We in gray thin stuff and roses,—sackcloth, I called it, and ashes of roses, for I mourn the loss of my Nan, and am not comforted. We have had a little feast . . . then the old folks danced round the bridal pair on the lawn in the German fashion, making a pretty picture to remember" (*Journals* 99).

7. A fabric, most often silk, that has a wavelike or watered effect.

8. Aunt March is referring to the tradition that the bride not appear, especially to the groom, until the wedding begins. Meg's not following this tradition clearly emphasizes the informality of the wedding she desired.

9. Twenty-nine-year-old Anna Alcott, on August 15, 1860, wrote about her wedding almost three months after the ceremony, recalling her feelings that special day: "Hoping to be married in the evening I had prepared a very simple white dress meaning to look like a bride, but on deciding it should be in the morning & knowing myself to be neither young nor pretty, I laid it aside as unsuitable & wore my riding dress of silvery grey & Louy placed in my hair & upon my bosom sprays of lilies of the valley.

"I *felt* very young and happy and when John came to me for a few moments alone & taking me in his arms looked down in my face saying with such an indescribable glance, 'Annie are you happy' it was almost impossible to answer I felt so very full of happiness. He told me how hopeful he felt, how tranquil and full of love and we went down among our friends at peace with one another & all the world feeling that no ceremony could make us more married than we already were" (Manuscript Journal, Houghton Library, Harvard University, bMS Am 1130.14[6]).

10. After the Roman conquest of Egypt, Jupiter, the king of the gods, was equated with the highest Egyptian deity, Amun, and known as Jupiter Ammon.

11. As one of his legendary labors, Hercules, the Roman demigod, son of Jupiter and the mortal Alcmena, killed the dragon that guarded the golden apples in the garden of Hesperides.

12. The *OED* defines this usage of *distract* as "to throw into a state of mind in which one knows not how to act."

13. Mischievous.

"I'm not a show, aunty, and no one is coming to stare at me, to criticise my dress, or count the cost of my luncheon. I'm too happy to care what any one says or thinks, and I'm going to have my little wedding just as I like it.[9] John, dear, here's your hammer," and away went Meg to help "that man" in his highly improper employment.

Mr. Brooke didn't even say "Thank you," but as he stooped for the unromantic tool, he kissed his little bride behind the folding-door, with a look that made Aunt March whisk out her pocket-handkerchief, with a sudden dew in her sharp old eyes.

A crash, a cry, and a laugh from Laurie, accompanied by the indecorous exclamation, "Jupiter Ammon![10] Jo's upset the cake again!" caused a momentary flurry, which was hardly over, when a flock of cousins arrived, and "the party came in," as Beth used to say when a child.

"Don't let that young giant come near me; he worries me worse than mosquitoes," whispered the old lady to Amy, as the rooms filled, and Laurie's black head towered above the rest.

"He has promised to be very good to-day, and he *can* be perfectly elegant if he likes," returned Amy, gliding away to warn Hercules to beware of the dragon,[11] which warning caused him to haunt the old lady with a devotion that nearly distracted[12] her.

There was no bridal procession, but a sudden silence fell upon the room as Mr. March and the young pair took their places under the green arch. Mother and sisters gathered close, as if loath to give Meg up; the fatherly voice broke more than once, which only seemed to make the service more beautiful and solemn; the bridegroom's hand trembled visibly, and no one heard his replies; but Meg looked straight up in her husband's eyes, and said, "I will!" with such tender trust in her own face and voice, that her mother's heart rejoiced, and Aunt March sniffed audibly.

Jo did *not* cry, though she was very near it once, and was only saved from a demonstration by the consciousness that Laurie was staring fixedly at her, with a comical mixture of merriment and emotion in his wicked[13] black eyes. Beth kept her face hidden on her mother's shoulder, but Amy stood like a graceful statue, with

LITTLE WOMEN

Meg's wedding in the 1933 film adaptation of *Little Women*. Unlike the scene in the novel, here Meg (Frances Dee) wears a traditional wedding dress and veil. John Davis Lodge portrayed John Brooke and Samuel S. Hinds played Mr. March.

a most becoming ray of sunshine touching her white forehead and the flower in her hair.

It wasn't at all the thing,[14] I'm afraid, but the minute she was fairly married, Meg cried, "The first kiss for Marmee!" and, turning, gave it with her heart on her lips. During the next fifteen minutes she looked more like a rose than ever, for every one availed themselves of their privileges to the fullest extent, from Mr. Laurence to old Hannah, who, adorned with a head-dress fearfully and wonderfully made, fell upon her in the hall, crying, with a sob and a chuckle, "Bless you, deary, a hundred times! The cake ain't hurt a mite, and everything looks lovely."

Everybody cleared up after that, and said something brilliant, or tried to, which did just as well, for laughter is ready when hearts are light. There was no display of gifts, for they were already in the little house, nor was there an elaborate breakfast, but a plentiful lunch of cake and fruit, dressed with flowers. Mr. Laurence and Aunt March shrugged and smiled at one another[15] when water, lemonade, and coffee were found to be the only sorts of nectar which the three Hebes[16] carried around. No one said anything,

14. LMA refers to the tradition that the first kiss goes to the groom. In "Men and *Little Women:* Notes of a Resisting (Male) Reader" (*"Little Women" and the Feminist Imagination,* pp. 162–172), Jan Susina argues that when Meg breaks tradition and gives the first kiss to Marmee, "she informs John that he remains on the margins of the March household" (p. 165). Another way of reading this action is that the kiss signals Meg's reassurance to her mother that she will remain a part of the March family.

15. The look means that Aunt March is wondering what happened to the wine she had sent for the wedding.

16. Hebe, in Greek mythology, was the goddess of youth. The daughter of Zeus and Hera, she was the cupbearer to the gods, pouring them nectar and ambrosia.

17. A flat metal serving tray, usually silver, for glasses or dishes.

18. The Soldiers' Home, established in Washington, D.C., in 1851 after the Mexican-American War, was a refuge for old and disabled veterans. President Lincoln lived in a cottage on the grounds of the Soldiers' Home from June 1862 to November 1864. LMA would have been aware of the Soldiers' Home during her short stay in Washington, D.C., in late 1862 and early 1863.

19. Here Laurie takes the temperance pledge to abstain from drinking alcohol. Temperance movements started in the United States in the late eighteenth century and increased during the first half of the nineteenth century. At first, the organizations advocated temperance, the use of alcohol in moderation, rather than abstinence. The temperance pledge was a promise, usually signed, that one would not drink alcohol. As an adult, LMA was not a teetotaler. While in Europe in 1870, she writes of drinking wine and champagne. In fact, Edward Emerson, son of Ralph Waldo Emerson, gave LMA and May Alcott a case of champagne as a departure gift before their grand European tour (See *Little Women Abroad* 9n6). Bronson Alcott, however, did abstain from alcohol. LMA does caution against drinking in *Rose in Bloom* (1876) and in her serial "Silver Pitchers" in the 1875 *Youth's Companion,* in which the girl characters start a small temperance organization. LMA herself served as secretary to Concord's temperance society in the 1880s. She wrote a public letter to the feminist paper the *Woman's Journal* on February 4, 1882: "While a bar room door stands open between two churches [in Concord], and men drink themselves to death before our eyes, it seems as if Christian men and women should better themselves to try at least to stop it . . . If women could vote on the license question I think the bar-room would be closed, but while those who own the place say, 'It would lessen the value of the property to make a temperance house of it,' and the license matter is left to the decision of those men who always grant it, the women can only wait and hope and pray for the good time when souls are counted of more value than dollars, and law and gospel can go hand in hand" (*Selected Letters* 256–257). In March 1882, she noted: "Helped start a Temperance Society. Much needed in C[oncord]. a great deal of drinking, not among the Irish but young Americans, gentlemen as well as farmers & mill hands. Women anxious to do something but find no interest beyond a few. Have meetings & try to learn how to work. I was secretary & wrote records, letters, & sent pledges &c" (*Journals* 233).

20. *Chasee,* originally a ballet term, is a dance step of many variants. All are triple-step: step, together, step.

however, till Laurie, who insisted on serving the bride, appeared before her with a loaded salver[17] in his hand, and a puzzled expression on his face.

"Has Jo smashed all the bottles by accident?" he whispered, "or am I merely laboring under a delusion that I saw some lying about loose this morning?"

"No; your grandfather kindly offered us his best, and Aunt March actually sent some, but father put away a little for Beth, and despatched the rest to the Soldier's Home.[18] You know he thinks that wine should only be used in illness, and mother says that neither she nor her daughters will ever offer it to any young man under her roof."

Meg spoke seriously, and expected to see Laurie frown or laugh; but he did neither,—for after a quick look at her, he said, in his impetuous way, "I like that; for I've seen enough harm done to wish other women would think as you do!"

"You are not made wise by experience, I hope?" and there was an anxious accent in Meg's voice.

"No; I give you my word for it. Don't think too well of me, either; this is not one of my temptations. Being brought up where wine is as common as water, and almost as harmless, I don't care for it; but when a pretty girl offers it, one don't like to refuse, you see."

"But you will, for the sake of others, if not for your own. Come, Laurie, promise, and give me one more reason to call this the happiest day of my life."

A demand so sudden and so serious, made the young man hesitate a moment, for ridicule is often harder to bear than self-denial. Meg knew that if he gave the promise he would keep it at all costs; and, feeling her power, used it as a woman may for her friend's good. She did not speak, but she looked up at him with a face made very eloquent by happiness, and a smile which said, "No one can refuse me anything to-day." Laurie, certainly, could not; and, with an answering smile, he gave her his hand, saying, heartily, "I promise, Mrs. Brooke!"

"I thank you, very, very much."

"And I drink 'Long life to your resolution,' Teddy," cried Jo, baptizing him with a splash of lemonade, as she waved her glass, and beamed approvingly upon him.

So the toast was drunk, the pledge made,[19] and loyally kept, in spite of many temptations; for, with instinctive wisdom, the girls had seized a happy moment to do their friend a service, for which he thanked them all his life.

After lunch, people strolled about, by twos and threes, through the house and garden, enjoying the sunshine without and within. Meg and John happened to be standing together in the middle of the grass-plot, when Laurie was seized with an inspiration which put the finishing touch to this unfashionable wedding.

"All the married people take hands and dance round the new-made husband and wife, as the Germans do, while we bachelors and spinsters prance in couples outside!" cried Laurie, galloping[b] down the path with Amy, with such infectious spirit and skill that every one else followed their example without a murmur. Mr. and Mrs. March, Aunt and Uncle Carrol, began it; others rapidly joined in; even Sallie Moffat, after a moment's hesitation, threw her train over her arm, and whisked Ned into the ring. But the crowning joke was Mr. Laurence and Aunt March; for when the stately old gentleman *chasséed*[20] solemnly up to the old lady, she just tucked her cane under her arm, and hopped briskly away to join hands with the rest, and dance about the bridal pair, while the young folks pervaded the garden, like butterflies on a mid-summer day.[21]

Want of breath brought the impromptu ball to a close, and then people began to go.

"I wish you well, my dear; I heartily wish you well; but I think you'll be sorry for it," said Aunt March to Meg, adding to the bridegroom, as he led her to the carriage, "You've got a treasure, young man,—see that you deserve it."

"That is the prettiest wedding I've been to for an age, Ned, and I don't see why, for there wasn't a bit of style about it," observed Mrs. Moffat to her husband, as they drove away.

"Laurie, my lad, if you ever want to indulge in this sort of thing, get one of those little girls to help you, and I shall be per-

Broadside advocating temperance reform.

21. On August 15, 1860, Anna recalled her wedding, which had taken place almost three months earlier: "I was in a dream . . . John looked like an angel, fair innocent, with such loving eyes that I could not look at them but only held his hand, and thought, He is my husband . . . My dear family all very red about the eyes and with such sadly happy faces that my heart felt uncomfortably big, hovered about me full of anxious affection. We danced on the lawn under the Elm we said lovely things in out of the way corners . . . and then the carriage came and I began to wake up, & think 'I am going away'" (Manuscript Journal, Houghton Library, Harvard University, bMS Am 1130.14[6]).

Women singing hymns in support of temperance reform.

22. Mr. Laurence means that he will be happy if Laurie marries one of the March sisters.

23. LMA indicates that there was no honeymoon.

24. Meg was dressed as simply as a Quaker woman in her plain gray dress and straw bonnet.

25. Historically, the grand tour, which could last from several months to years, was an extended trip across Europe undertaken by upper-class European men as part of their classical education. By the mid-nineteenth century, as steamships and railroads made the journey more affordable, wealthy Americans went on the grand tour, especially newlyweds on their honeymoon. LMA and her sister May toured Europe from April 1870 to autumn 1871, visiting France, Switzerland, Italy, Germany, and England. See *Little Women Abroad*.

26. Almost three months after becoming John Pratt's wife, Anna, on August, 15, 1860, wrote about her arrival at the Dove-cot on her wedding night: "Very quietly we came to our little married house, we two alone, and peacefully we sat thro' the summer evening with the moon looking down upon us, not more serene than were our hearts, for we felt that we belonged to one another, that henceforth thro' joy or sorrow life and death nothing would part us. A happier wedding day a woman c'd not ask (Manuscript Journal, Houghton Library, Harvard University, bMS Am 1130.14[6]).

fectly satisfied,"[22] said Mr. Laurence, settling himself in his easy-chair to rest, after the excitement of the morning.

"I'll do my best to gratify you, sir," was Laurie's unusually dutiful reply, as he carefully unpinned the posy Jo had put in his button-hole.

The little house was not far away, and the only bridal journey[23] Meg had was the quiet walk with John, from the old home to the new. When she came down, looking like a pretty Quakeress,[24] in her dove-colored suit and straw bonnet tied with white, they all gathered about her to say "good-by," as tenderly as if she had been going to make the grand tour.[25]

"Don't feel that I am separated from you, Marmee dear, or that I love you any the less for loving John so much," she said, clinging to her mother, with full eyes, for a moment. "I shall come every day, father, and expect to keep my old place in all your hearts, though I *am* married. Beth is going to be with me a great deal, and the other girls will drop in now and then to laugh at my housekeeping struggles. Thank you all for my happy wedding-day. Good-by, good-by!"

They stood watching her with faces full of love, and hope, and tender pride, as she walked away, leaning on her husband's arm, with her hands full of flowers, and the June sunshine brightening her happy face,—and so Meg's married life began.[26]

LITTLE WOMEN

Chapter 3

Artistic Attempts

I T TAKES PEOPLE a long time to learn the difference between talent and genius,[1] especially ambitious young men and women. Amy was learning this distinction through much tribulation, for, mistaking enthusiasm for inspiration, she attempted every branch of art with youthful audacity.[2] For a long time there was a lull in the "mud-pie" business, and she devoted herself to the finest pen-and-ink drawing, in which she showed such taste and skill, that her graceful handiwork proved both pleasant and profitable. But overstrained eyes caused pen and ink to be laid aside for a bold attempt at poker-sketching.[3] While this attack lasted, the family lived in constant fear of a conflagration, for the odor of burning wood pervaded the house at all hours; smoke issued from attic and shed with alarming frequency, red-hot pokers lay about promiscuously, and Hannah never went to bed without a pail of water and the dinner-bell at her door, in case of fire. Raphael's face was found boldly executed on the underside of the moulding board,[4] and Bacchus[5] on the head of a beer barrel; a chanting cherub adorned the cover of the sugar bucket, and attempts to portray "Garrick buying gloves of the grisette,"[6] supplied kindlings for some time.

From fire to oil was a natural transition for burned fingers, and Amy fell to painting with undiminished ardor. An artist friend fitted her out with his cast-off palettes, brushes, and colors, and she daubed away, producing pastoral and marine views, such as were never seen on land or sea. Her monstrosities in the way of cattle would have taken prizes at an agricultural fair; and the perilous pitching of her vessels would have produced sea-sickness in

1. In his essay "The Poet" (1844), Ralph Waldo Emerson writes: "Talent may frolic and juggle; genius realizes and adds" (*Essays: Second Series. The Concord Edition of Ralph Waldo Emerson* [Boston and New York: Houghton, Mifflin, 1904], p. 11). At the time of publication of *Little Women* (1868–1869), May Alcott had studied formally with several prominent artists in Boston, including William Rimmer and William Morris Hunt, but she had as yet no real accomplishments as an artist. A European trip with LMA in 1870–1871 inspired May to return to Europe in 1873 to rededicate herself to the study of art (a trip funded by LMA). At the National Gallery in London, May labored long, copying the watercolors of J. M. W. Turner. After a year's work abroad, May returned to Concord in March 1874 and once again took up her duties at home. Her literary sister, however, was pleased with her efforts: "May came home with a portfolio full . . . Must have worked like a busy bee to have done so much. Very happy in her success, for she has proved her talent, having copied Turner so well that [John] Ruskin (meeting her in the National Gallery at work) told her that she 'caught Turner's spirit wonderfully'" (*Journals* 192). May returned to Europe again in 1876, establishing a friendship with an American artist from Philadelphia, Mary Cassatt. By December 1876, May wrote home, claiming: "'I am getting on, and I feel as if it was not all a mistake; for I have some talent, and will prove it'" (*Journals* 201). Louisa would respond: "Modesty is a sign of genius, and I think our girl has both. The money I invest in her pays the sort of interest I like. I am proud to have her show what she can do, and have her depend upon no one but me. Success to little Raphael!" (*Journals* 201). In April 1877, when one of her paintings was selected for the Paris Salon exhibition, May wrote to her mother with a triumphant tone: "'Who would have imagined such good fortune, and so strong a proof that Lu does not monopolize all the Alcott talent.'" As an aside, she chided Louisa: "'Ha! ha! sister, this is the first feather plucked from your cap, and I shall endeavor to fill mine with so many waving in the breeze that you will be quite ready to lay down your pen and rest on your laurels already won'" (quoted in Caroline Ticknor, *May Alcott: A Memoir* [Boston: Little, Brown, 1928], p. 192). In March 1878, May married Ernest Nieriker, a Swiss businessman, and the two settled in Paris, where May focused on painting in oils. She confessed: "'I mean to combine painting and family, and show that it is a possibility if *let alone* . . . This blessed lot is mine, and from my purpose I never intend to be diverted'" (quoted in Ticknor, pp. 278–279). That same year, LMA began *Diana and Persis,* based upon May's life as an artist and her romance with Ernest Nieriker, a book that examines the question of whether a female artist can have a

May Alcott, *Lake Avernus: The Fates and the Golden Bough,* after J. M. W. Turner, watercolor on paper, circa 1873–1879. While in England in 1873, May Alcott was commended by the British critic John Ruskin for her copies of Turner.

successful professional career and also be a good wife and mother. May Alcott Nieriker died on December 29, 1879, less than two months after giving birth to her daughter. After May's death, LMA abandoned the four-chapter manuscript of *Diana and Persis* (See Sarah Elbert, ed., *Diana and Persis* [New York: Arno Press, 1978]). What May Alcott may have accomplished will never be known. The two oil paintings selected in the Paris Salon exhibitions of 1877 and 1878 were the only two she ever submitted. Today, Orchard House displays several of May's works; others are still owned by the Nieriker family in Europe.

2. Visitors to Orchard House today can see May Alcott's early artwork throughout the house. Her small blue bedroom was her canvas for the creation of artistic sensibilities. Outlined in pencil, pen, and paint on the walls and window frames are the figures from mythology, primarily figures she traced and copied from John Flaxman's illustrations for *The Illiad* and *The Odyssey,* such as "Neptune Rising." May also decorated doors, lettered mantels, and painted panels with nature scenes in color (what she called "potboilers" because they were easy to complete and sold well). Orchard House itself became a tangible expression of May's vitality and development.

3. Anne Brown Adams, daughter of the abolitionist John Brown, in her recollections of boarding with the Alcotts in 1861, wrote about May Alcott's poker sketches: "Miss May Alcott was absent, teaching while I boarded there, but for the benefit of the vast army of home decorators, I will de-

scribe some fire boards she made. She had a carpenter make a smooth board to fit into the front of the fireplace. I think plain unvarnished oak was the wood she used. First she traced an outline head of some goddess, or a pretty child, then she went over the tracings with a red hot poker, burning an etching on the board" (quoted in *Her Own Time* 10–11). May Alcott noted in her journal for August 28, 1863: "Drew on fathers fire board, copying an illumination of our coat of arms which he prefers to any thing else" (Manuscript journal, Houghton Library, Harvard University, bMS Am 1817[57]). Orchard House has on display two of May Alcott's fireboards: one with the Alcott coat of arms that May refers to above and one of Moses with the stone tablets of the Ten Commandments.

4. A board on which to knead dough. May Alcott's pyrography—the breadboard with Raphael's head—is on display in the kitchen of Orchard House today.

5. The Roman god of wine.

6. LMA—or perhaps Amy—appears to confuse characters here. The reference is to the 1830 watercolor by Gilbert Stuart Newton (1799–1835) entitled *Yorick and the Grisette,* which illustrated a scene from Laurence Sterne's *Sentimental Journey Through France and Italy* (1768). In the scene Yorick (widely thought to be Sterne himself) enters a shop where a grisette, a young French working woman, usually employed as a seamstress, convinces him to buy a pair of gloves. Traditionally, a grisette is also viewed as a flirt or coquette, which may explain how she convinces Yorick. Newton, born in Nova Scotia, was the nephew of the famous portrait painter Gilbert Stuart. He moved to Europe, where he studied in Florence and then entered the Royal Academy in England. The watercolor was later engraved by H. Bourne (1825–1907) and became popular. David Garrick (1717–1779) was a significant British actor, playwright, and manager during the eighteenth century. He was friends with Sterne (1713–1768), the Anglo-Irish clergyman and author.

May Alcott's painting of calla lilies. The oil on wood panel (1863) hangs today over the half-moon desk in LMA's bedroom at Orchard House. It is visible in the photograph on p. 3.

7. Bartolamé Esteban Murillo (1617–1682) was a Spanish Baroque painter who was known not only for his religious paintings but also for his depictions of women and children, such as the ragged boys and flower girls of Seville.

8. Rembrandt van Rijn (1606–1669), the famous Dutch painter and etcher. LMA may be referring to Amy's unsuccessful attempt to reproduce Rembrandt's well-known use of chiaroscuro, the employment of light and shadow.

9. Swollen.

10. Peter Paul Rubens (1577–1640), the Flemish Baroque painter noted for his depictions of religious and mythological scenes. His paintings of full-figured women inspired the term "Rubenesque."

11. J. M. W. Turner (1775–1851), British Romantic painter known for his watercolor landscapes. The washes of paint on a number of his paintings made his work unique. May Alcott, when studying art abroad in the 1870s, made a name for herself as a copier of Turner's works.

12. Plaster casts of a hand and a foot are displayed today in May's studio at Orchard House. May Alcott recorded one of her attempts at plaster casting in her journal for September 17, 1863: "I cast my head that I have worked over with so much care but great was my disappointment after getting up at six so as to have plenty of time to finish it nicely, to find that having used my precious English plaster, with great economy, yet it hadn't hardened & was still in the puddingy state & nothing was to be done but scrape it all carefully off and save the mould if possible, as it was a fine sharp one. Then feeling rather disheartened . . . but determined to persevere & accomplish something I took the *second-rate* plaster & run it into the mould soon beginning to chisel it out as it hardened quite well. At this exciting moment when at every blow I was in danger of breaking the nose mouth or perhaps the whole thing, Louisa and Annie [Anna] saw me from one of the windows & came to watch the process of bringing out a beautiful head from what seemed to be a plaster pie. I had nearly finished breaking off the mould when two fearful cracks developed themselves & my treasured cast was all in pieces, I could have cried & should if I had been alone, but as it was merely picked up the remains, as I found the profile quite perfect & then put away my tools for the day, a little sorrowfully" (Manuscript journal, Houghton Library, Harvard University, bMS Am 1817 [57]).

13. Any number of plants of the genus *Verbascum* (also known as velvet plants) in the figwort family. They have a tall flowering stem, which is easily broken.

the most nautical observer, if the utter disregard to all known rules of ship building and rigging had not convulsed him with laughter at the first glance. Swarthy boys and dark-eyed Madonnas staring at you from one corner of the studio, did *not* suggest[a] Murillo;[7] oily brown shadows of faces, with a lurid streak in the wrong place, meant Rembrandt;[8] buxom ladies and dropsical[9] infants, Rubens;[10] and Turner[11] appeared in tempests of blue thunder, orange lightning, brown rain, and purple clouds, with a tomato-colored splash in the middle, which might be the sun or a buoy, a sailor's shirt or a king's robe, as the spectator pleased.

Charcoal portraits came next; and the entire family hung in a row, looking as wild and crocky as if just evoked from a coal-bin. Softened into crayon sketches, they did better; for the likenesses were good, and Amy's hair, Jo's nose, Meg's mouth, and Laurie's eyes were pronounced "wonderfully fine." A return to clay and plaster followed, and ghostly casts of her acquaintances haunted corners of the house, or tumbled off closet shelves on to people's heads.[12] Children were enticed in as models, till their incoherent accounts of her mysterious doings caused Miss Amy to be regarded in the light of a young ogress. Her efforts in this line, however, were brought to an abrupt close by an untoward accident, which quenched her ardor. Other models failing her for a time, she undertook to cast her own pretty foot, and the family were one day alarmed by an unearthly bumping and screaming; and, running to the rescue, found the young enthusiast hopping wildly about the shed, with her foot held fast in a pan-full of plaster, which had hardened with unexpected rapidity. With much difficulty and some danger, she was dug out; for Jo was so overcome with laughter while she excavated, that her knife went too far, cut the poor foot, and left a lasting memorial of one artistic attempt, at least.

After this Amy subsided, till a mania for sketching from nature set her to haunting river, field, and wood, for picturesque studies, and sighing for ruins to copy. She caught endless colds sitting on damp grass to book "a delicious bit," composed of a stone, a stump, one mushroom, and a broken mullein[13] stalk, or "a heavenly mass of clouds," that looked like a choice display of feather-beds when done. She sacrificed her complexion floating on the river in the midsummer sun, to study light and shade, and got a wrinkle over her nose, trying after "points of sight,"[14] or whatever the squint-and-string performance is called.

If "genius is eternal patience," as Michael Angelo affirms,[15] Amy certainly had some claim to the divine attribute, for she persevered in spite of all obstacles, failures, and discouragements, firmly believing that in time she should do something worthy to be called "high art."[16]

She was learning, doing, and enjoying other things, meanwhile, for she had resolved to be an attractive and accomplished woman, even if she never became a great artist. Here she succeeded better; for she was one of those happily created beings who please without effort, make friends everywhere, and take life so gracefully and easily, that less fortunate souls are tempted to believe that such are born under a lucky star. Everybody liked her, for among her good gifts was tact. She had an instinctive sense of what was pleasing and proper, always said the right thing to the right person, did just what suited the time and place, and was so self-possessed that her sisters used to say, "If Amy went to court without any rehearsal beforehand, she'd know exactly what to do."

One of her weaknesses was a desire to move in "our best society," without being quite sure what the *best* really was. Money, position, fashionable accomplishments, and elegant manners, were most desirable things in her eyes, and she liked to associate with those who possessed them; often mistaking the false for the true, and admiring what was not admirable. Never forgetting that by birth she was a gentlewoman, she cultivated her aristocratic tastes and feelings, so that when the opportunity came, she might be ready to take the place from which poverty now excluded her.

"My lady," as her friends called her, sincerely desired to be a genuine lady, and was so, at heart, but had yet to learn that money cannot buy refinement of nature, that rank does not always confer nobility, and that true breeding makes itself felt in spite of external drawbacks.

"I want to ask a favor of you, mamma," Amy said, coming in with an important air, one day.

"Well, little girl, what is it?" replied her mother, in whose eyes the stately young lady still remained "the baby."

Amy's artistic mishap. Frank Merrill, *Little Women: Illustrated* (1880).

14. The *OED* defines this term in two ways: "*(Art)* the point in space that represents the eye of the observer; *(Perspective)* the point from which straight lines are drawn to the object being delineated, their intersections with the place of delineation forming the drawing."

15. This saying is attributed to Michelangelo (1475–1564), the noted Italian Renaissance sculptor, painter, poet, and architect.

16. May Alcott was twenty-nine when Part II of *Little Women* was published, and although she had yet to achieve any significant artistic success, she continued with her ambitions by both teaching and studying art. While LMA's words might sum up May's work so far, they also serve as encouragement for her younger sister not to give up her dream.

17. Maria Theresa (1717–1780), the powerful sovereign of Austria, Hungary, Bohemia, and the Austrian Netherlands. After her marriage she also became the Grand Duchess of Tuscany and Holy Roman Empress. Her reign of forty years, 1740–1780, greatly influenced Europe for the following century.

18. Amy alludes to the fairy tale "The Ugly Duckling" by the Danish author Hans Christian Andersen (1805–1875).

19. The tongue of a cow or ox. High in fat, this rich cut of meat was often boiled or roasted.

20. The *OED* defines *beach wagon* as a "light open wagon, with two or more seats," and cites this passage as its first usage.

21. A char-à-banc is a long vehicle with benches.

"Our drawing class breaks up next week, and before the girls separate for the summer, I want to ask them out here for a day. They are wild to see the river, sketch the broken bridge, and copy some of the things they admire in my book. They have been very kind to me in many ways, and I am grateful; for they are all rich, and know I am poor, yet they never made any difference."

"Why should they!" and Mrs. March put the question with what the girls called her "Maria Theresa[17] air."

"You know as well as I that it *does* make a difference with nearly every one, so don't ruffle up like a dear, motherly hen, when your chickens get pecked by smarter birds; the ugly duckling turned out a swan you know;"[18] and Amy smiled without bitterness, for she possessed a happy temper and hopeful spirit.

Mrs. March laughed, and smoothed down her maternal pride, as she asked,—

"Well, my swan, what is your plan?"

"I should like to ask the girls out to lunch next week, to take them a drive to the places they want to see,—a row on the river, perhaps,—and make a little artistic fête for them."

"That looks feasible. What do you want for lunch? Cake, sandwiches, fruit and coffee, will be all that is necessary, I suppose?"

"Oh dear, no! we must have cold tongue[19] and chicken, French chocolate and ice-cream besides. The girls are used to such things, and I want my lunch to be proper and elegant, though I *do* work for my living."

"How many young ladies are there?" asked her mother, beginning to look sober.

"Twelve or fourteen in the class, but I dare say they won't all come."

"Bless me, child, you will have to charter an omnibus to carry them about."

"Why, mother, how *can* you think of such a thing; not more than six or eight will probably come, so I shall hire a beach-wagon[20] and borrow Mr. Laurence's cherry-bounce." (Hannah's pronunciation of *char-a-banc.*[21])

"All of this will be expensive, Amy."

"Not very; I've calculated the cost, and I'll pay for it myself."

"Don't you think, dear, that as these girls are used to such

A typical nineteenth-century horse-drawn omnibus.

things, and the best we can do will be nothing new, that some simpler plan would be pleasanter to them, as a change, if nothing more, and much better for us than buying or borrowing what we don't need, and attempting a style not in keeping with our circumstances?"

"If I can't have it as I like I don't care to have it at all. I know that I can carry it out perfectly well, if you and the girls will help a little; and I don't see why I can't, if I'm willing to pay for it," said Amy, with the decision which opposition was apt to change into obstinacy.

Mrs. March knew that experience was an excellent teacher, and, when it was possible, she left her children to learn alone the lessons which she would gladly have made easier, if they had not objected to taking advice as much as they did salts and senna.[22]

"Very well, Amy; if your heart is set upon it, and you see your way through without too great an outlay of money, time, and temper, I'll say no more. Talk it over with the girls, and whichever way you decide, I'll do my best to help you."

"Thanks, mother; you are always *so* kind," and away went Amy to lay her plan before her sisters.

22. Epsom salts or salt that is derived from magnesium sulphate and used as a laxative. Senna is made from the dried leaves of the *Cassia* shrub and is used to induce vomiting.

23. During the nineteenth century, before the addition of magnesium carbonate, salt absorbed moisture and formed clumps. For meals, the clumps would be crushed and the salt placed in a bowl called a salt-cellar. Diners would use a salt-spoon, a small utensil approximately two or three inches long, to sprinkle the salt on their food. It wasn't until about 1930 that the process of using magnesium carbonate as a moisture-absorbing agent made it possible to use salt shakers.

24. To be submissive.

25. A short, four-wheeled closed carriage that held two passengers. The driver's seat was outside.

26. Stimulated.

27. Defeated.

28. Mrs. Grundy is a character in Thomas Morton's 1798 play *Speed of the Plough.* Although she never appears onstage, Mrs. Grundy is a bastion of respectability. Dame Ashfield, her neighbor, often wonders how Mrs. Grundy would react to certain events or situations.

Meg agreed at once, and promised her aid,—gladly offering anything she possessed, from her little house itself to her very best salt-spoons.[23] But Jo frowned upon the whole project, and would have nothing to do with it at first.

"Why in the world should you spend your money, worry your family, and turn the house upside down for a parcel of girls who don't care a sixpence for you? I thought you had too much pride and sense to truckle[24] to any mortal woman just because she wears French boots and rides in a *coupé*,"[25] said Jo, who, being called from the tragical climax of her novel, was not in the best mood for social enterprises.

"I *don't* truckle, and I hate being patronized as much as you do!" returned Amy, indignantly, for the two still jangled when such questions arose. "The girls do care for me, and I for them, and there's a great deal of kindness, and sense, and talent among them, in spite of what you call fashionable nonsense. You don't care to make people like you, to go into good society, and cultivate your manners and tastes. I do, and I mean to make the most of every chance that comes. *You* can go through the world with your elbows out and your nose in the air, and call it independence, if you like. That's not my way."

When Amy had whetted[26] her tongue and freed her mind she usually got the best of it, for she seldom failed to have common sense on her side, while Jo carried her love of liberty and hate of conventionalities to such an unlimited extent, that she naturally found herself worsted[27] in an argument. Amy's definition of Jo's idea of independence was such a good hit, that both burst out laughing, and the discussion took a more amiable turn. Much against her will, Jo at length consented to sacrifice a day to Mrs. Grundy,[28] and help her sister through what she regarded as "a nonsensical business."

The invitations were sent, most all accepted, and the following Monday was set apart for the grand event. Hannah was out of humor because her week's work was deranged, and prophesied that "ef the washin' and ironin' warn't done reg'lar nothin' would go well anywheres." This hitch in the main-spring of the domestic machinery had a bad effect upon the whole concern; but Amy's motto was *"Nil desperandum,"*[29] and having made up her mind what to do, she proceeded to do it in spite of all obstacles. To begin with: Hannah's cooking didn't turn out well; the chicken was tough, the tongue too salt, and the chocolate wouldn't froth properly. Then the cake and ice cost more than Amy expected, so did the wagon; and various other expenses, which seemed trifling at the outset, counted up rather alarmingly afterward. Beth got cold and took to her bed; Meg had an unusual number of callers to keep her at home, and Jo was in such a divided state of mind that her breakages, accidents, and mistakes were uncommonly numerous, serious, and trying.

"If it hadn't been for mother I never should have got through," as Amy declared afterward, and gratefully remembered, when "the best joke of the season" was entirely forgotten by everybody else.

If it was not fair on Monday, the young ladies were to come on Tuesday, an arrangement which aggravated Jo and Hannah to the last degree. On Monday morning the weather was in that undecided state which is more exasperating than a steady pour. It drizzled a little, shone a little, blew a little, and didn't make up its mind till it was too late for any one else to make up theirs. Amy was up at dawn, hustling people out of their beds and through their breakfasts, that the house might be got in order. The parlor struck her as looking uncommonly shabby, but without stopping to sigh for what she had not, she skillfully made the best of what she had, arranging chairs over the worn places in the carpet, covering stains on the walls with pictures framed in ivy, and filling up empty corners with home-made statuary, which gave an artistic air to the room, as did the lovely vases of flowers Jo scattered about.

The lunch looked charmingly; and, as she surveyed it, she sincerely hoped it would taste good, and that the borrowed glass, china, and silver would get safely home again. The carriages were promised, Meg and mother were all ready to do the honors, Beth was able to help Hannah behind the scenes, Jo had engaged to be as lively and amiable as an absent mind, an aching head, and a very decided disapproval of everybody and everything would allow, and, as she wearily dressed, Amy cheered herself with antici-

29. Latin phrase meaning "Never despair."

pations of the happy moment when, lunch safely over, she should drive away with her friends for an afternoon of artistic delights; for the "cherry-bounce" and the broken bridge were her strong points.

Then came the hours of suspense, during which she vibrated from parlor to porch, while public opinion varied like the weathercock. A smart[30] shower, at eleven, had evidently quenched the enthusiasm of the young ladies who were to arrive at twelve, for nobody came; and, at two, the exhausted family sat down in a blaze of sunshine to consume the perishable portions of the feast, that nothing might be lost.

"No doubt about the weather to-day; they will certainly come, so we must fly round and be ready for them," said Amy, as the sun woke her next morning. She spoke briskly, but in her secret soul she wished she had said nothing about Tuesday, for her interest, like her cake, was getting a little stale.

"I can't get any lobsters, so you will have to do without salad to-day," said Mr. March, coming in half an hour later, with an expression of placid despair.

"Use the chicken then, the toughness won't matter in a salad," advised his wife.

"Hannah left it on the kitchen table a minute, and the kittens got at it. I'm very sorry, Amy," added Beth, who was still a patroness of cats.

"Then, I *must* have a lobster, for tongue alone won't do," said Amy, decidedly.

"Shall I rush into town and demand one?" asked Jo, with the magnanimity of a martyr.

"You'd come bringing it home under your arm, without any paper, just to try me. I'll go myself," answered Amy, whose temper was beginning to fail.

Shrouded in a thick veil, and armed with a genteel travelling-basket, she departed, feeling that a cool drive would soothe her ruffled spirit, and fit her for the labors of the day. After some delay, the object of her desire was procured, likewise a bottle of dressing, to prevent further loss of time at home, and off she drove again, well pleased with her own forethought.

As the omnibus contained only one other passenger, a sleepy old lady, Amy pocketed her veil, and beguiled[31] the tedium of the way by trying to find out where all her money had gone to. So busy was she with her card full of refractory[32] figures that she did not observe a new-comer, who entered without stopping the vehicle, till a masculine voice said, "Good morning, Miss March," and looking up she beheld one of Laurie's most elegant college friends. Fervently hoping that he would get out before she did, Amy utterly ignored the basket at her feet, and congratulating herself that she had on her new travelling dress, returned the young man's greeting with her usual suavity and spirit.

They got on excellently; for Amy's chief care was soon set at rest, by learning that the gentleman would leave first, and she was chatting away in a peculiarly lofty strain, when the old lady got out. In stumbling to the door, she upset the basket, and oh, horror! the lobster, in all its vulgar size and brilliancy, was revealed to the high-born eyes of a Tudor![33]

"By Jove, she's forgotten her dinner!" cried the unconscious youth, poking the scarlet monster into its place with his cane, and preparing to hand out the basket after the old lady.

"Please don't—it's—it's mine," murmured Amy, with a face nearly as red as her fish.

"Oh, really, I beg pardon; it's an uncommonly fine one, isn't it?" said Tudor, with great presence of mind, and an air of sober interest that did credit to his breeding.

Amy recovered herself in a breath, set her basket boldly on the seat, and said, laughing,—

"Don't you wish you were to have some of the salad he's to make, and to see the charming young ladies who are to eat it?"

Now that was tact, for two of the ruling foibles of the masculine mind were touched; the lobster was instantly surrounded by a halo of pleasing reminiscences, and curiosity about "the charming young ladies" diverted his mind from the comical mishap.

"I suppose he'll laugh and joke over it with Laurie, but I shan't see them; that's a comfort," thought Amy, as Tudor bowed and departed.

31. The *OED* defines this use of *beguile* as "to elude the disagreeable sensation of, and so to cause to pass insensibly or pleasantly; to charm away, wile away."

32. Unmanageable.

33. The name conveys the idea of power and royalty, as the House of Tudor, beginning with Henry II, ruled England and its kingdoms from 1485 to 1603.

She did not mention this meeting at home (though she discovered that, thanks to the upset, her new dress was much damaged by the rivulets of dressing that meandered down the skirt), but went through with the preparations which now seemed more irksome than before; and at twelve o'clock all was ready again. Feeling that the neighbors were interested in her movements, she wished to efface the memory of yesterday's failure by a grand success to-day; so she ordered the "cherry-bounce," and drove away in state to meet and escort her guests to the banquet.

"There's the rumble, they're coming! I'll go into the porch to meet them; it looks hospitable, and I want the poor child to have a good time after all her trouble," said Mrs. March, suiting the action to the word. But after one glance, she retired with an indescribable expression, for, looking quite lost in the big carriage, sat Amy and one young lady.

"Run, Beth, and help Hannah clear half the things off the table; it will be too absurd to put a luncheon for twelve before a single girl," cried Jo, hurrying away to the lower regions, too excited to stop even for a laugh.

In came Amy, quite calm, and delightfully cordial to the one guest who had kept her promise; the rest of the family, being of a dramatic turn, played their parts equally well, and Miss Eliott found them a most hilarious set; for it was impossible to entirely control the merriment which possessed them. The remodelled lunch being gaily partaken of, the studio and garden visited, and art discussed with enthusiasm, Amy ordered a buggy (alas for the elegant cherry-bounce!) and drove her friend quietly about the neighborhood till sunset, when "the party went out."

As she came walking in, looking very tired, but as composed as ever, she observed that every vestige of the unfortunate fête had disappeared, except a suspicious pucker about the corners of Jo's mouth.

"You've had a lovely afternoon for your drive, dear," said her mother, as respectfully as if the whole twelve had come.

"Miss Eliott is a very sweet girl, and seemed to enjoy herself, I thought," observed Beth, with unusual warmth.

"Could you spare me some of your cake? I really need some, I have so much company, and I can't make such delicious stuff as yours," asked Meg, soberly.

"Take it all; I'm the only one here who likes sweet things, and it will mould before I can dispose of it," answered Amy, thinking with a sigh of the generous store she had laid in for such an end as this!

"It's a pity Laurie isn't here to help us," began Jo, as they sat down to ice-cream and salad for the fourth[b] time in two days.

A warning look from her mother checked any further remarks, and the whole family ate in heroic silence, till Mr. March mildly observed, "Salad was one of the favorite dishes of the ancients, and Evelyn"—here a general explosion of laughter cut short the "history of sallets," to the great surprise of the learned gentleman.[34]

"Bundle everything into a basket and send it to the Hummels—Germans like messes. I'm sick of the sight of this; and there's no reason you should all die of a surfeit[35] because I've been a fool," cried Amy, wiping her eyes.

"I thought I *should* have died when I saw you two girls rattling about in the what-you-call-it, like two little kernels in a very big nutshell, and mother waiting in state to receive the throng," sighed Jo, quite spent with laughter.

"I'm very sorry you were disappointed, dear, but we all did our best to satisfy you," said Mrs. March, in a tone full of motherly regret.

"I *am* satisfied; I've done what I undertook, and it's not my fault that it failed; I comfort myself with that," said Amy, with a little quiver in her voice. "I thank you all very much for helping me, and I'll thank you still more, if you won't allude to it for a month, at least."

No one did for several months; but the word "fête" always produced a general smile, and Laurie's birthday gift to Amy was a tiny coral lobster in the shape of a charm for her watch-guard.[36]

34. Mr. March alludes to John Evelyn's *Acetaria: A Discourse on Sallets* (1699), an early landmark work in the history of vegetarianism. Bronson Alcott, who espoused vegetarianism, would have been familiar with this book. Willis in his *Alcott Memoirs* (1915) recalled that "Mr. Alcott's table talks were constantly delightful. It was particularly at these times he took especial care to so discourse that the youngest listener might comprehend and fully understand. I have seen him take an apple upon his fork, and while preparing it for eating, give a fascinating little lecture as to its growth and development from germ to mature fruit, his language quaintly beautiful and charmingly poetical. . . . He rarely talked of else at table but nature's wonderful and benevolent processes in preparing food for the maintenance of man" (quoted in *Her Own Time* 172–173).

35. Excessive eating.

36. A chain or ribbon used to secure a pocket watch.

1. LMA often used the term *vortex* to describe the periods of intense inspiration and creativity when she devoted herself completely to writing. For example, she wrote to her sister Anna in August 1860, complaining that too much housework was stifling her literary output: "You ask what I am writing. Well, two books half done, nine stories simmering, and stacks of fairy stories moulding on the shelf. I can't do much, as I have no time to get into a real good vortex. It unfits me for work, worries Ma to see me look pale, eat nothing, and ply by night" (*Selected Letters* 59).

2. In February 1861, as LMA worked relentlessly on her first novel, *Moods* (1864), she noted, "Mother made me a green silk cap with a red bow, to match the old green and red party wrap, which I wore as a 'glory cloak.' Thus arrayed I sat in groves of manuscripts" (*Journals* 103).

3. The phrase "clear the decks" is a naval expression meaning leave the decks and get prepared for action below. Jo means she's ready to write.

4. Inspiration. LMA often used this term when describing her own creativity. For example, when "Mark Field's Success" was published in the April 16, 1859, edition of *Saturday Evening Gazette*, LMA wrote: "'Mark' was a success, and much praised. So I found the divine afflatus did descend" (*Journals* 94). In April 1861, she wrote: "Stories simmered in my brain, demanding to be writ; but I let them simmer, knowing that the longer the divine afflatus was bottled up the better it would be" (*Journals* 105).

5. LMA, working on *Moods* in 1861, described one of her vortexes: "Another turn at 'Moods,' which I remodeled. From the 2d to the 25th I sat writing, with a run at dusk; could not sleep, and for three days was so full of it I could not stop to get up. . . . Mother wandered in and out with cordial cups of tea, worried because I could n't eat. Father thought it fine, and brought his reddest apples and hardest cider for my Pegasus to feed upon. All sorts of fun was going on; but I did n't care if the world returned to chaos if I and my inkstand only 'lit' in the same place.

"It was very pleasant and queer while it lasted; but after three weeks of it I found that my mind was too rampant for my body, as my head was dizzy, legs shaky, and no sleep would come. So I dropped the pen, and took long walks, cold baths, and had Nan up to frolic with me" (*Journals* 103–104).

6. Likely LMA refers to courses offered by the Lowell Institute in Boston. In 1836, John Lowell, Jr., a wealthy Boston merchant, bequeathed half of his estate to fund free public lectures. According to Harriette Knight Smith, *The History of the Lowell Institute* (Boston: Lamson, Wolffe, 1898), the institute offered 427 courses from De-

Chapter 4

Literary Lessons

FORTUNE suddenly smiled upon Jo, and dropped a good-luck penny in her path. Not a golden penny, exactly, but I doubt if half a million would have given more real happiness than did the little sum that came to her in this wise.

Every few weeks she would shut herself up in her room, put on her scribbling suit, and "fall into a vortex,"[1] as she expressed it, writing away at her novel with all her heart and soul, for till that was finished she could find no peace. Her "scribbling suit" consisted of a black pinafore[a] on which she could wipe her pen at will, and a cap of the same material, adorned with a cheerful red bow,[2] into which she bundled her hair when the decks were cleared for action.[3] This cap was a beacon to the inquiring eyes of her family, who, during these periods, kept their distance, merely popping in their heads semi-occasionally, to ask, with interest, "Does genius burn, Jo?" They did not always venture even to ask this question, but took an observation of the cap, and judged accordingly. If this expressive article of dress was drawn low upon the forehead, it was a sign that hard work was going on; in exciting moments it was pushed rakishly askew, and when despair seized the author it was plucked wholly off, and cast upon the floor. At such times the intruder silently withdrew; and not until the red bow was seen gaily erect upon the gifted brow, did any one dare address Jo.

She did not think herself a genius by any means; but when the writing fit came on, she gave herself up to it with entire abandon, and led a blissful life, unconscious of want, care, or bad weather, while she sat safe and happy in an imaginary world, full of friends almost as real and dear to her as any in the flesh. Sleep forsook her eyes, meals stood untasted, day and night were all too short to enjoy the happiness which blessed her only at such times, and made these hours worth living, even if they bore no other fruit. The divine afflatus[4] usually lasted a week or two, and then she emerged from her "vortex" hungry, sleepy, cross, or despondent.[5]

She was just recovering from one of these attacks when she was prevailed upon to escort Miss Crocker to a lecture, and in return for her virtue was rewarded with a new idea. It was a People's Course,[6]—the lecture on the Pyramids,—and Jo rather wondered at the choice of such a subject for such an audience, but took it for granted that some great social evil would be remedied, or some great want supplied by unfolding the glories of the Pharaohs, to an audience whose thoughts were busy with the price of coal and flour, and whose lives were spent in trying to solve harder riddles than that of the Sphinx.[7]

They were early; and while Miss Crocker set the heel of her stocking, Jo amused herself by examining the faces of the people who occupied the seat with them. On her left were two matrons with massive foreheads, and bonnets to match, discussing Woman's Rights[8] and making tatting.[9] Beyond sat a pair of humble lovers artlessly[10] holding each other by the hand, a sombre spinster eating peppermints out of a paper bag, and an old gentleman taking his preparatory nap behind a yellow bandanna. On her right, her only neighbor was a studious-looking lad absorbed in a newspaper.

It was a pictorial sheet, and Jo examined the work of art nearest her, idly wondering what unfortuitous concatenation[11] of circumstances needed the melodramatic illustration of an Indian in full war costume, tumbling over a precipice with a wolf at his throat, while two infuriated young gentlemen, with unnaturally small feet and big eyes, were stabbing each other close by, and a dishevelled female was flying away in the background, with her mouth wide open. Pausing to turn a page, the lad saw her looking, and, with boyish good-nature, offered half his paper, saying, bluntly, "Want to read it? That's a first-rate story."

Jo accepted it with a smile, for she had never outgrown her liking for lads, and soon found herself involved in the usual labyrinth of love, mystery, and murder, for the story belonged to that

Margaret Fuller (1810–1850). The Transcendentalist author's life and work impressed on LMA the importance of the struggle for woman's rights.

cember 1839 to January 1898, or 4,325 "all absolutely free lectures, prepared by the best minds of the age, and representing the highest developments in all the various departments of science, literature, and art" (p. 29). The demand for tickets to the lectures was high. Crowds grew so large that people "crushed in the windows of the Old Corner Book Store, the place of distribution" (p. 22). Thereafter, tickets were given out by lottery with 8,000 to 10,000 applicants for the 2,000 available seats. The lectures were usually about an hour and featured speakers such as scientists Joseph Lovering, Louis Agassiz, and Benjamin Silliman and writers James Russell Lowell, William Dean Howells, and Edward Everett Hale. Topics were far-ranging: astronomy, botany, geology, political economy, ancient Egypt, Greek poetry, mental hygiene, and philosophy of religion, among many others. When asked about the importance of the Lowell Institute (which is still in existence today), Dr. Oliver Wendell Holmes replied: "'When you have said every enthusiastic thing that you may, you will not have half filled the measure of its importance to Boston—New England—the country at large'" (pp. ix–x).

7. The Sphinx is a mythical creature with a lion's body and a human head. LMA confuses the Egyptian sphinx with the Greek version. The Greek sphinx stood guard over the entrance to the city Thebes in Greece and asked travelers to solve a riddle before it allowed passage. The Egyptian sphinxes are also thought to be guardians as they often flank the entrance to temples.

8. The singular "woman's rights" was the term most commonly used by feminists in the nineteenth century to identify their movement. Not only does it give emphasis to the value of the individual and serve as a strategic and ideological expression of the commitment to unify women, but the term is also a nod in the direction of the British writer Mary Wollstonecraft's treatise *A Vindication of the Rights of Woman: With Strictures on Political and Moral Subjects* (1792), which argued that a woman deserves the same rights as a man, especially with regard to education. With the formation of the new republic in the United States and the emphasis on individual rights and democracy, the struggle for woman's rights began early in this country. By the beginning of the nineteenth century, the movement was under way, and both Bronson and Abigail Alcott were among its active supporters. Of the Transcendentalists, Margaret Fuller stood at the front lines. Her book *Woman in the Nineteenth Century* (1845) was an extremely influential text, one that inspired LMA. Alcott herself remained active in the Woman's Rights movement throughout her life. As she wrote in August 1885 to Lucy Stone, one of the early suffragist leaders: "[I]t is impossible for me ever to 'go back' on Womans Suffrage. I earnestly desire to go forward on that line as far & as fast as the prejudices, selfishness & blindness of the world will let us" (*Selected Letters* 291).

9. Tatting is handcrafted lace made by a series of knots and loops; it was often used for doilies or collars. LMA seems to highlight the contradiction that the women are performing such a domestic task while discussing woman's rights.

10. The *OED* defines this usage of *artlessly* as "with unaffected simplicity, guilelessly."

11. Series of events.

12. LMA alludes to E. D. E. N. Southworth (1819–1899), one of the most popular and successful authors of the nineteenth century. She wrote over sixty novels, and her sensational works, including her most well known—*The Hidden Hand* (1859)—appeared in Robert Bonner's *New York Ledger*.

13. Giovanni Battista Belzoni (1778–1823), a Venetian explorer and archaeologist, laid the groundwork for the excavation of Egyptian antiquities. Cheops, also called the Pyramid of Khufu, after the ruler for whom it was constructed, is the Great Pyramid of Giza. The largest of the seven wonders of the ancient world, the pyramid took approximately twenty years to build and was completed about 2560 B.C.E. Scarabei are images of beetles utilized by Egyptians in various decorations. Hieroglyphics was the ancient Egyptian writing system.

14. Sensational literature or thrillers contained shocking subject matter, such as murder, revenge, drug and alcohol abuse, sexual intrigue,

class of light literature in which the passions have a holiday, and when the author's invention fails, a grand catastrophe clears the stage of one-half the *dramatis personæ,* leaving the other half to exult over their downfall.

"Prime, isn't it?" asked the boy, as her eye went down the last paragraph of her portion.

"I guess you and I could do most as well as that if we tried," returned Jo, amused at his admiration of the trash.

"I should think I was a pretty lucky chap if I could. She makes a good living out of such stories, they say;" and he pointed to the name of Mrs. S. L. A. N. G. Northbury,[12] under the title of the tale.

"Do you know her?" asked Jo, with sudden interest.

"No; but I read all her pieces, and I know a fellow that works in the office where this paper is printed."

"Do you say she makes a good living out of stories like this?" and Jo looked more respectfully at the agitated group and thickly-sprinkled exclamation points that adorned the page.

"Guess she does! she knows just what folks like, and gets paid well for writing it."

Here the lecture began, but Jo heard very little of it, for while Professor Sands was prosing away about Belzoni, Cheops, scarabei, and hieroglyphics,[13] she was covertly taking down the address of the paper, and boldly resolving to try for the hundred dollar prize offered in its columns for a sensational story.[14] By the time the lecture ended, and the audience awoke, she had built up a splendid fortune for herself (not the first founded upon paper), and was already deep in the concoction of her story, being unable to decide whether the duel should come before the elopement or after the murder.

She said nothing of her plan at home, but fell to work next day, much to the disquiet of her mother, who always looked a little anxious when "genius took to burning." Jo had never tried this style before, contenting herself with very mild romances for the "Spread Eagle." Her theatrical experience and miscellaneous reading were of service now, for they gave her some idea of dramatic effect, and supplied plot, language, and costumes. Her story was as full of desperation and despair as her limited acquaintance with those uncomfortable emotions enabled her to make it, and, having located it in Lisbon, she wound up with an earthquake,[15] as a striking and appropriate *denouement*. The manuscript was privately despatched, accompanied by a note, modestly saying that if the tale didn't get the prize, which the writer hardly dared expect, she would be very glad to receive any sum it might be considered worth.

Six weeks is a long time to wait, and a still longer time for a girl to keep a secret; but Jo did both, and was just beginning to give up all hope of ever seeing her manuscript again, when a letter arrived which almost took her breath away; for, on opening it, a check for a hundred dollars fell into her lap. For a minute she stared at it as if it had been a snake, then she read her letter, and began to cry. If the amiable gentleman who wrote that kindly note could have known what intense happiness he was giving a fellow-creature, I think he would devote his leisure hours, if he has any, to that amusement; for Jo valued the letter more than the money, because it was encouraging; and after years of effort it was *so* pleasant to find that she had learned to do *something*, though it was only to write a sensation story.

A prouder young woman was seldom seen than she, when, having composed herself, she electrified the family by appearing before them with the letter in one hand, the check in the other, announcing that she had won the prize![16] Of course there was a great jubilee, and when the story came every one read and praised it; though after her father had told her that the language was good, the romance fresh and hearty, and the tragedy quite thrilling, he shook his head, and said in his unworldly way,—

"You can do better than this, Jo. Aim at the highest, and never mind the money."[17]

"*I* think the money is the best part of it. What *will* you do with such a fortune?" asked Amy, regarding the magic slip of paper with a reverential eye.

"Send Beth and mother to the sea-side for a month or two," answered Jo promptly.

"Oh, how splendid! No, I can't do it, dear, it would be so selfish," cried Beth, who had clapped her thin hands, and taken a

and the supernatural. Indebted to true-crime accounts published in newspapers and cheap dime-novels in the 1820s and 1830s, sensational fiction flourished in the United States from the 1840s to the 1860s. Walt Whitman referred to this type of literature as "blood and thunder romances with alliterative titles and plots of startling interest" (*The Uncollected Poetry and Prose of Walt Whitman*, ed. Emory Holloway [Gloucester, MA: Peter Smith, 1972], p. 201). One of the most famous sensational works of the nineteenth century was *The Quaker City; or, The Monks of Monk Hall: A Romance of Philadelphia Life, Mystery, and Crime* by George Lippard, a friend of Edgar Allan Poe's. Published in ten paper issues in 1844–1845, the novel focused on the decadent upper class of Philadelphia and was filled with sex and violence. Newspapers such as the *New York Ledger*, the *New York Herald*, *The Flag of Our Union*, and *Frank Leslie's Illustrated Newspaper* were among the largest purveyors of sensation stories in the United States. These papers were sometimes referred to as pictorial sheets because large graphic illustrations accompanied the fiction in order to grab attention and interest.

15. Lisbon, Portugal, experienced a catastrophic earthquake on November 1, 1855. Estimated by modern seismologists to be 8.5 to 9.0 in magnitude, the earthquake destroyed approximately 85 percent of the capital city's buildings and killed tens of thousands of people.

16. LMA's sensational tale "Pauline's Passion and Punishment" won a $100 prize offered by the publisher Frank Leslie and appeared in the January 3 and January 10, 1863, issues of *Frank Leslie's Illustrated Newspaper*. LMA noted: "Paid debts & was glad that my winter bore visible fruit" (*Journals* 118). Unlike Jo's attempt, LMA's prize-winning story was not her first sensational tale. From approximately 1858 to 1870, LMA penned over thirty sensational tales or novellas either anonymously or under the pseudonym A. M. Barnard. Among the themes she explored in her blood and thunder tales were power struggles between males and females (with the female most often winning), mind control, insanity, and hypnotism. Today, scholars agree that the discovery of previously unknown works such as "V. V.; or, Plots and Counterplots" (1865), "A Marble Woman; or, The Mysterious Model" (1865), and "Behind a Mask: or, A Woman's Power" (1866), have dramatically altered our understanding of LMA.

17. LMA often shared her literary work with Bronson, and there appears to have been only encouragement for her success. On April 30, 1869, after the publication of Part II of *Little Women*, Bronson observed: "She takes her growing repute modestly, being unwilling to believe her books have all the merit ascribed to them by the public. . . . She has various literary works in thought—among others a novel embodying our family adventures which she entitles *The Cost*

of an Idea. If written out with the dramatic genius with which she is gifted, the story will be a taking piece of family biography, as attractive as any fiction and having the merit of being purely American" (*Journals of BA* 396). LMA would never write the family story intended to demonstrate the high cost of Bronson's philosophical ideas. Her relationship with her father was a complicated one. She admired him greatly but also recognized the shortcomings of an equally impractical man and philosophy, which had forced hardships on her mother and sisters. In a revealing letter written to Bronson on the eve of their shared birthday—November 29—in 1855, she wrote: "I know *you* were a serene & placid baby when you began your wise meditations in the quiet Spindle hill farm house (I believe thats where you decended from on high) looking philosophically out of your cradle at the big world about you . . . Fifty six years have passed since then, & that peaceful babys golden head is silver now but the man looks as serenely at the big foolish world . . . & nothing but the lines on his face where troubles have been & four tall women at his side, show that years & trials have changed the wise little child into a wiser old man. Surely dear father some good angel or elf dropped a talisman in your cradle that gave you force to walk thro life in quiet sunshine while others groped the dark. I wish you could teach me its magic." Unlike the serene philosopher/father, LMA noted: "*I* was a crass crying brown baby, bawling at the disagreeable old world . . . I scrambled up to childhood, out of which after often losing my small self & wondering forlornly thro years of infant troubles & cares, I fell with a crash into girlhood & continued falling over fences, out of trees, up hill & down stairs tumbling from one year to another till strengthened by such violent exercise the topsey turvey girl shot up into a topsy turvey woman who now . . . sits big brown & brave, crying . . . because its such hard work to keep sunshiney & cheerful when life looks gloomy & full of troubles, but as the brown baby fought through its small trials so the brown woman will fight thro her big ones & come out I hope queen of herself tho not of the world" (*Selected Letters* 13–14).

18. In August 1857, LMA wrote: "A sad, anxious month. Betty [Lizzie] worse; Mother takes her to the seashore" (*Journals* 85).

19. By the time LMA began to write *Little Women*, she was the principal breadwinner in the Alcott household. Abigail, in her mid-sixties and in declining health, was no longer capable of sustained work, while Bronson's lectures brought in little money. LMA confessed in January 1868: "For many years we have not been so comfortable. May and I both earning. Annie with her good John to lean on, and the old people in a cosey home of their own" (*Journals* 162). A year later, she wrote to her friend Alfred Whitman: "I am such a

long breath, as if pining for fresh ocean breezes; then stopped herself, and motioned away the check which her sister waved before her.

"Ah, but you shall go, I've set my heart on it; that's what I tried for, and that's why I succeeded. I never get on when I think of myself alone, so it will help me to work for you, don't you see. Besides, Marmee needs the change, and she won't leave you, so you *must* go. Won't it be fun to see you come home plump and rosy again? Hurrah for Dr. Jo, who always cures her patients!"

To the sea-side they went,[18] after much discussion; and though Beth didn't come home as plump and rosy as could be desired, she was much better, while Mrs. March declared she felt ten years younger; so Jo was satisfied with the investment of her prize-money, and fell to work with a cheery spirit, bent on earning more of those delightful checks. She did earn several that year, and began to feel herself a power in the house;[19] for by the magic of a pen, her "rubbish" turned into comforts for them all. "The Duke's Daughter" paid the butcher's bill, "A Phantom Hand" put down a new carpet, and "The Curse of the Coventrys" proved the blessing of the Marches in the way of groceries and gowns.[20]

Wealth is certainly a most desirable thing, but poverty has its sunny side, and one of the sweet uses of adversity, is the genuine satisfaction which comes from hearty work of head or hand; and to the inspiration of necessity, we owe half the wise, beautiful, and useful blessings of the world. Jo enjoyed a taste of this satisfaction, and ceased to envy richer girls, taking great comfort in the knowledge that she could supply her own wants, and need ask no one for a penny.

Little notice was taken of her stories, but they found a market; and, encouraged by this fact, she resolved to make a bold stroke for fame and fortune. Having copied her novel for the fourth time, read it to all her confidential friends, and submitted it with fear and trembling to three publishers, she at last disposed of it, on condition that she would cut it down one-third, and omit all the parts which she particularly admired.[21]

"Now I must either bundle it back into my tin-kitchen, to mould, pay for printing it myself, or chop it up to suit purchasers, and get what I can for it. Fame is a very good thing to have in the house, but cash is more convenient; so I wish to take the sense of the meeting on this important subject," said Jo, calling a family council.

"Don't spoil your book, my girl, for there is more in it than you know, and the idea is well worked out. Let it wait and ripen," was her father's advice; and he practised as he preached, having waited patiently thirty years for fruit of his own to ripen, and being in no haste to gather it, even now, when it was sweet and mellow.[22]

"It seems to me that Jo will profit more by making the trial than by waiting," said Mrs. March. "Criticism is the best test of such work, for it will show her both unsuspected merits and faults, and help her to do better next time. We are too partial; but the praise and blame of outsiders will prove useful, even if she gets but little money."[23]

"Yes," said Jo, knitting her brows, "that's just it; I've been fussing over the thing so long, I really don't know whether it's good, bad, or indifferent. It will be a great help to have cool, impartial persons take a look at it, and tell me what they think of it."

"I wouldn't leave a word out of it; you'll spoil it if you do, for the interest of the story is more in the minds than in the actions of the people, and it will be all a muddle if you don't explain as you go on," said Meg, who firmly believed that this book was the most remarkable novel ever written.

"But Mr. Allen says, 'Leave out the explanations, make it brief and dramatic, and let the characters tell the story,'" interrupted Jo, turning to the publisher's note.[24]

"Do as he tells you; he knows what will sell, and we don't. Make a good, popular book, and get as much money as you can. By and by, when you've got a name, you can afford to digress, and have philosophical and metaphysical people in your novels," said Amy, who took a strictly practical view of the subject.

"Well," said Jo, laughing, "if my people *are* 'philosophical and metaphysical,' it isn't my fault, for I know nothing about such things, except what I hear father say, sometimes. If I've got some of his wise ideas jumbled up with my romance, so much the better for me. Now, Beth, what do you say?"

busy old bee I find no time for pleasure not even for writing letters . . . But publishers come roaring after me if I dont do my work, & money tempts my mercenary mind, so I scratch away hoping a time of rest will come in the course of ages" (*Selected Letters* 120). Several years later, in June 1872, after the success of *Little Women* and *Little Men*, LMA observed: "Twenty years ago I resolved to make the family independent if I could. At forty that is done. Debts all paid, even the outlawed ones, and we have enough to be comfortable. It has cost me my health, perhaps, but as I still live, there is more for me to do, I suppose" (*Journals* 182–183).

20. LMA, in her 1859 "Notes and Memoranda," records payment of $10 for a tale called "A Phantom Face." The story has not been located. "The Curse of the Coventrys" is an allusion to "Behind a Mask: or, A Woman's Power," the thriller LMA serialized in *The Flag of Our Union* in October and November 1866. Published under the pseudonym A. M. Barnard, the story tells of the divorced actress Jean Muir (whose initials are the same as Jo March), who poses as a much younger governess on the Coventrys' English estate and sets out to marry Sir John Coventry. Early in her literary career, LMA, like Jo, wrote for money. She humorously noted in September 1861: "Ticknor sent $50. Wrote a story for C[lapp]., as Plato needs new shirts, and Minerva a pair of boots, and Hebe a fall hat" (*Journals* 106).

21. LMA's first published novel, *Moods,* had been simmering for years when in August 1860 she was "possessed by my work" for a month (*Journals* 99). James Redpath, who had published LMA's *Hospital Sketches* (1863), refused *Moods* in February 1864 after LMA said she would not agree to shorten the book (see *Journals* 128). After being turned down by Ticknor and Fields in April 1864, *Moods* was then offered to the Boston publisher A. K. Loring that September. According to LMA, Loring "liked it exceedingly & asked me to shorten it if I could, else it would be too large to sell well. Was much disappointed, said I'd never touch it again & tossed it into the spidery little cupboard where it had so often returned after fruitless trips" (*Journals* 131–132). However, by October LMA wrote that "a way to shorten & arrange 'Moods' came into my head. The whole plan laid itself smoothly out before me & I slept no more that night but worked on it as busily as if mind & body had nothing to do with one another. Up early & began to write it all over again. The fit was on strong & for a fortnight I hardly slept or stirred but wrote, wrote like a thinking machine in full operation. When it was all rewritten, without copying, I found it much improved though I'd taken out ten chapters & sacrificed many of my favorite things, but being resolved to make it simple, strong & short I let every thing else go & hoped the book would be better for it" (*Journals* 132). The

much-revised *Moods*, published in December 1864 (though it carries an 1865 copyright date), was a flawed but ambitious first novel, one that depicts the struggles of the young Sylvia Yule, a forerunner of Jo March, as she grows from age seventeen into womanhood. In the book, LMA illustrates the particular problems young women face as they mature in the often-limited sphere afforded them in the mid-nineteenth century. Tackling issues such as an unhappy marriage and possible divorce, *Moods* was a serious novel, one that continued to be close to LMA's heart. In 1882, Roberts Brothers purchased *Moods'* copyright from A. K. Loring, and LMA drastically revised the book for re-publication.

22. Bronson Alcott never experienced the literary acclaim of LMA, though he enjoyed some reputation as a lecturer (really, a talker). And later in life he basked in his reputation as "the Sage of Concord." But his published early writings were mostly failures. His *Conversations with Children on the Gospels* (1836–1837), an attempt to explain his pedagogical theories, came in for particularly harsh treatment by the mainstream press and the religious establishment, and his "Orphic Sayings" (1840), published by Margaret Fuller in the *Dial,* was parodied in New York's *Knickerbocker* as "Gastric Sayings." Bronson, however, was aware of his own shortcomings as a writer. When Ralph Waldo Emerson confessed to Bronson in the spring of 1838 that Bronson should abandon hopes of publishing "Psyche," his study on the divinity of childhood, based on observations of his third daughter, Elizabeth, Alcott admitted in his journal: "But I am no scholar. My might is not in my pen. This is feeble. I do no justice to myself in literary composition. My organ is action and voice, rather. I am an actor and a sayer, rather than a writer" (*Journals of BA* 128). When Bronson planned to visit England in 1842, Emerson wrote to Rev. John Sterling: "[W]e shall send you a large piece of spiritual New England in the Shape of A. Bronson Alcott . . . A man who cannot write but whose conversation is unrivalled in its way; such insight, such discernment of spirits, such revolutionary impulses of thought; whilst he speaks he has no peer" (*The Letters of Ralph Waldo Emerson*, vol. 7, ed. Eleanor M. Tilton [New York: Columbia University Press, 1990–1995], p. 496). James Russell Lowell, an acquaintance of Bronson Alcott's, wrote about Alcott in his satiric piece "A Fable for Critics" (1848): "While he talks he is great, but goes out like a taper, / If you shut him up closely with pen, ink, and paper" (lines 650–651).

23. Abigail Alcott, like Bronson, encouraged and supported LMA's literary aspirations. On LMA's tenth birthday, Abigail wrote: "'I give you the pencil-case I promised, for I have observed that you are fond of writing, and wish to encourage the habit'" (quoted in Sandford Salyer, *Marmee: The Mother of Little Women* [Norman: University of Oklahoma Press, 1949], p. 71).

24. In 1864, A. K. Loring wrote LMA a seven-page letter, encouraging her to aim high and telling the author what he thought made a successful novel. Claiming he was "no scholar," Loring judged a book "by the impressions" it made, by "the *feelings* solely." If the story touched him, he could "make others read and believe in [it]." Preferring "conciseness in introducing the characters, getting them upon the stage and into action as quickly as possible," he wanted "a story of constant action, bustle and motion." He insisted that she appeal to the readers' emotions, not their intellect, telling her that the "one thing" that he had noticed when she had depicted "the deepest feelings" of a character was that she appealed "to the *head*" but failed to "touch the *heart* of the reader." The reader "sees it, but does not *feel it*" (Manuscript letter, Barrett Collection, University of Virginia Library).

25. The people of the ancient Greek city-state of Sparta were known for their bravery, endurance, and simple lifestyles.

26. LMA refers to an Aesop fable: A man and his son lead a donkey to town. People ridicule them for not riding the donkey. The father then has the son mount the animal, but the boy is soon shamed for riding while his poor father walks. Once they change places, the father is attacked for having his young child walk while the strong man rides. Finally, they decide to carry the donkey, so they tie his legs together and carry the animal on a pole. As they cross a bridge, the donkey frees one of its legs and causes the father and son to drop the donkey in the water, whereupon it drowns. The moral of the tale is that if you try to suit everyone, you will suit no one.

27. LMA, in February 1861, completed a draft of *Moods:* "Read all I had done to my family; and Father said: 'Emerson must see this. Where did you get your metaphysics?' Mother pronounced it wonderful, and Anna laughed and cried, as she always does, over my works, saying, 'My dear, I'm proud of you'" (*Journals* 104).

28. The *OED* defines *picked* as being "made bare or bald by picking, scratching, probing, etc." LMA is comparing her revision of her first novel to that of a bird picked clean of its feathers.

29. In her "Notes and Memoranda" for 1865, LMA lists two payments for *Moods,* totaling $250 (*Journals* 146). In 1866, she lists another $25 payment (*Journals* 155).

30. *Moods* did indeed receive mixed reviews. The January 21, 1865, edition of *Harper's Weekly* claimed the novel possessed "great power and absorbing interest" (35). However, Henry James, Jr., whom LMA knew, reviewed it in the July 1865 *North American Review:* "The two most striking facts with regard to 'Moods' are the author's ignorance of human nature, and her self-confidence in spite of this ignorance . . . [T]here is no reason why Miss Alcott should not write a very good novel, provided she will be satisfied to describe only that which she has seen" (280–281).

"I should so like to see it printed *soon*," was all Beth said, and smiled in saying it; but there was an unconscious emphasis on the last word, and a wistful look in the eyes that never lost their child-like candor, which chilled Jo's heart, for a minute, with a foreboding fear, and decided her to make her little venture "soon."

So, with Spartan firmness,[25] the young authoress laid her first-born on her table, and chopped it up as ruthlessly as any ogre. In the hope of pleasing every one, she took every one's advice; and, like the old man and his donkey in the fable, suited nobody.[26]

Her father liked the metaphysical streak which had unconsciously got into it,[27] so that was allowed to remain, though she had her doubts about it. Her mother thought that there *was* a trifle too much description; out, therefore, it came, and with it many necessary links in the story. Meg admired the tragedy; so Jo piled up the agony to suit her, while Amy objected to the fun, and, with the best intentions in life, Jo quenched the sprightly scenes which relieved the somber character of the story. Then, to complete the ruin, she cut it down one-third, and confidingly sent the poor little romance, like a picked[28] robin, out into the big, busy world to try its fate.

Well, it was printed, and she got three hundred dollars for it;[29] likewise plenty of praise and blame, both so much greater than she expected, that she was thrown into a state of bewilderment, from which it took her some time to recover.[30]

"You said, mother, that criticism would help me; but how can it, when it's so contradictory that I don't know whether I have written a promising book, or broken all the ten commandments," cried poor Jo, turning over a heap of notices, the perusal of which filled her with pride and joy one minute—wrath and dire dismay the next. "This man says, 'An exquisite book, full of truth, beauty, and earnestness; all is sweet, pure, and healthy,'" continued the perplexed authoress. "The next, 'The theory of the book is bad,—full of morbid fancies, spiritualistic ideas, and unnatural characters.' Now, as I had no theory of any kind, don't believe in spiritualism, and copied my characters from life, I don't see how this critic *can* be right. Another says, 'It's one of the best American novels which has appeared for years'[31] (I know better than that);

31. The 1869 edition of Part II of *Little Women* prints this passage as follows: "Another says, 'It's one of the best American novels which has appeared for years': (I know better than that); "and the next asserts that 'though it is original, and written with great force and feeling, it is a dangerous book.'" The use of double quotation marks before and after the interjected aside would make this comment one of the narrator's, not Jo's. LMA surely meant for these to be Jo's words. Anne K. Phillips and Gregory Eiselein were the first to point out and correct this error in their Norton Critical Edition of *Little Women* (New York: W. W. Norton, 2004), p. 385.

32. LMA wrote to Moncure Daniel Conway, co-editor of the Boston *Commonwealth,* on February 18, 1865: "'Moods' is not what I meant to have it, for I followed bad advice & took out many things which explained my idea & made the characters more natural & consistent. I see my mistake now for I find myself accused of Spiritualism, Free Love, Affinities & all sorts of horrors that I know very little about & dont believe in" (*Selected Letters* 108). Never satisfied with the novel, LMA revised it again in 1882 for Roberts Brothers.

33. John Keats (1795–1821), the British Romantic poet, died in Rome of tuberculosis. Percy Shelley, a champion of the poet, claims in the preface to *Adonais* (1821), his elegy for Keats, that the *Quarterly Review*'s harsh attack of Keats' poem *Endymion* hastened the poet's death. Lord Byron writes in his epic *Don Juan* (1819–1824): "Tis strange the mind, that very fiery particle / Should let itself be snuffed out by an article" (canto 2, stanza 60).

and the next asserts that 'though it is original, and written with great force and feeling, it is a dangerous book.' 'Tisn't! Some make fun of it, some over-praise, and nearly all insist that I had a deep theory to expound, when I only wrote it for the pleasure and the money. I wish I'd printed it whole, or not at all, for I do hate to be so horridly[b] misjudged."[32]

Her family and friends administered comfort and commendation liberally; yet it was a hard time for sensitive, high-spirited Jo, who meant so well, and had apparently done so ill. But it did her good, for those whose opinion had real value, gave her the criticism which is an author's best education; and when the first soreness was over, she could laugh at her poor little book, yet believe in it still, and feel herself the wiser and stronger for the buffeting she had received.

"Not being a genius, like Keats, it won't kill me,"[33] she said stoutly, "and I've got the joke on my side, after all; for the parts that were taken straight out of real life, are denounced as impossible and absurd, and the scenes that I made up out of my own silly head, are pronounced 'charmingly natural, tender, and true.' So I'll comfort myself with that; and, when I'm ready, I'll up again and take another."

Chapter 5

Domestic Experiences

IKE MOST other young matrons, Meg began her married life with the determination to be a model housekeeper. John should find home a paradise; he should always see a smiling face, should fare sumptuously every day, and never know the loss of a button. She brought so much love, energy, and cheerfulness to the work, that she could not but succeed, in spite of some obstacles. Her paradise was not a tranquil one; for the little woman fussed, was over-anxious to please, and bustled about like a true Martha,[1] cumbered with many cares. She was too tired, sometimes, even to smile; John grew dyspeptic after a course of dainty dishes, and ungratefully demanded plain fare. As for buttons, she soon learned to wonder where they went, to shake her head over the carelessness of men, and to threaten to make him sew them on himself, and then see if *his* work would stand impatient tugs and clumsy fingers any better than hers.

They were very happy, even after they discovered that they couldn't live on love alone. John did not find Meg's beauty diminished, though she beamed at him from behind the family coffee-pot; nor did Meg miss any of the romance from the daily parting, when her husband followed up his kiss with the tender inquiry, "Shall I send some veal or mutton[2] for dinner, darling?" The little house ceased to be a glorified bower,[3] but it became a home, and the young couple soon felt that it was a change for the better. At first they played keep-house,[4] and frolicked over it like children; then John took steadily to business, feeling the cares of the head of a family upon his shoulders; and Meg laid by her cambric[5] wrappers, put on a big apron, and fell to work, as before said, with more energy than discretion.

1. A woman who is busy with domestic work. The term originates from the New Testament (Luke 10:38–42), where Mary and Martha, sisters of Lazarus, meet Jesus when he visits their home after raising their brother from the dead. Mary stays with Jesus while Martha performs domestic work.

2. Calf's meat; an adult sheep's meat.

3. The *OED* defines *bower* as "a poetical word for 'abode.'"

4. A children's game of playing at being a family and managing a household.

5. Cambric cloth (also called batiste), originally from Cambrai, France, was, by the mid-nineteenth century a fine plain weave with a glossy appearance.

6. Mary Hooker Cornelius's *The Young Housekeeper's Friend; or, A Guide to Domestic Economy and Comfort* (Boston: Tappan, Whittemore, and Mason, ca. 1845). Eliza Farrar, wife of Harvard Professor John Farrar and author of the popular *Young Lady's Friend* (1837), wrote a prefatory letter for the book, praising the work: "A person, wholly ignorant of household affairs, may, by a diligent perusal of this book, become an accomplished housekeeper, and provide the most wholesome and palatable food, upon the most economical principles."

7. The *OED* defines *golden mean* as "the avoidance of excess in either direction."

8. Currants are a species of ribes berry popular in the nineteenth century for making pies and jellies. However, when the black currant was discovered to transmit the infectious white pine blister rust, currant farming was banned in the United States for fear it would destroy the logging industry. In 1966, the ban was left up to the jurisdiction of individual states.

9. Until the end of the nineteenth century, making jam, jelly, or preserves was still a domestic endeavor performed mostly by women. The cookbook that Meg consults, Mary Hooker Cornelius, *The Young Housekeeper's Friend; or, A Guide to Domestic Economy and Comfort*, provides the following recipe for currant jelly: "A pound of sugar to a pint of juice. Pound and sift the sugar, and heat it as hot as possible without dissolving or burning; boil the juice five minutes very fast, and while boiling add the hot sugar, stir it well, and when it has boiled again one minute, set it off. The time must be strictly observed" (pp. 58–59). For jam to jell, the mixture must heat to 104°C so that the acid and natural pectin in the fruit will react with the sugar. The jam will then set during cooling. Meg most likely did not heat the fruit-and-sugar mixture to a high enough temperature.

While the cooking mania lasted she went through Mrs. Cornelius's Receipt Book[6] as if it was a mathematical exercise, working out the problems with patience and care. Sometimes her family were invited in to help eat up a too bounteous feast of successes, or Lotty would be privately despatched with a batch of failures which were to be concealed from all eyes, in the convenient stomachs of the little Hummels. An evening with John over the account books usually produced a temporary lull in the culinary enthusiasm, and a frugal fit would ensue, during which the poor man was put through a course of bread pudding, hash, and warmed-over coffee, which tried his soul, although he bore it with praiseworthy fortitude. Before the golden mean[7] was found, however, Meg added to her domestic possessions what young couples seldom get on long without,—a family jar.

Fired with a housewifely wish to see her store-room stocked with home-made preserves, she undertook to put up her own currant[8] jelly. John was requested to order home a dozen or so of little pots, and an extra quantity of sugar, for their own currants were ripe, and were to be attended to at once. As John firmly believed that "my wife" was equal to anything, and took a natural pride in her skill, he resolved that she should be gratified, and their only crop of fruit laid by in a most pleasing form for winter use. Home came four dozen delightful little pots, half a barrel of sugar, and a small boy to pick the currants for her. With her pretty hair tucked into a little cap, arms bared to the elbow, and a checked apron which had a coquettish look in spite of the bib, the young housewife fell to work, feeling no doubts about her success; for hadn't she seen Hannah do it hundreds of times? The array of pots rather amazed her at first, but John was so fond of jelly, and the nice little jars would look so well on the top shelf, that Meg resolved to fill them all, and spend a long day picking, boiling, straining, and fussing over her jelly.[9] She did her best; she asked advice of Mrs. Cornelius; she racked her brain to remember what Hannah did that she had left undone; she reboiled, resugared, and restrained, but that dreadful stuff wouldn't *"jell."*

She longed to run home, bib and all, and ask mother to lend a hand, but John and she had agreed that they would never annoy any one with their private worries, experiments, or quarrels. They had laughed over that last word as if the idea it suggested was a most preposterous one; but they had held to their resolve, and whenever they could get on without help they did so, and no one interfered,—for Mrs. March had advised the plan. So Meg wrestled alone with the refractory[10] sweetmeats[11] all that hot summer day, and at five o'clock sat down in her topsy-turvey kitchen, wrung her bedaubed[12] hands, lifted up her voice, and wept.

Now in the first flush of the new life, she had often said,—

"My husband shall always feel free to bring a friend home whenever he likes. I shall always be prepared; there shall be no flurry, no scolding, no discomfort, but a neat house, a cheerful wife, and a good dinner. John, dear, never stop to ask my leave, invite whom you please, and be sure of a welcome from me."

How charming that was, to be sure! John quite glowed with pride to hear her say it, and felt what a blessed thing it was to have a superior wife. But, although they had had company from time to time, it never happened to be unexpected, and Meg had never had an opportunity to distinguish herself, till now. It always happens so in this vale of tears;[13] there is an inevitability about such things which we can only wonder at, deplore, and bear as we best can.

If John had not forgotten all about the jelly, it really would have been unpardonable in him to choose that day, of all the days in the year, to bring a friend home to dinner unexpectedly. Congratulating himself that a handsome repast had been ordered that morning, feeling sure that it would be ready to the minute, and indulging in pleasant anticipations of the charming effect it would produce, when his pretty wife came running out to meet him, he escorted his friend to his mansion, with the irrepressible satisfaction of a young host and husband.

It is a world of disappointments, as John discovered when he reached the Dove-cote. The front door usually stood hospitably open; now it was not only shut, but locked, and yesterday's mud still adorned the steps. The parlor windows were closed and curtained, no picture of the pretty wife sewing on the piazza,[14] in white, with a distracting little bow in her hair, or a bright-eyed

10. Stubborn.
11. Preserved fruit.
12. Splattered with the currants.
13. The *OED* defines this phrase as meaning "the world regarded as a place of trouble, sorrow, misery, or weeping."
14. The verandah; the front porch.

15. Bloody-looking. The boy is stained from picking the currant berries.

16. In the nineteenth century, it was the custom for a man or woman to address their spouse as *Mr.* or *Mrs.* in the presence of friends or acquaintances who were not immediate family.

17. Calmness that LMA believed was characteristic of Germans.

18. Bessie Holyoke, in her letter of August 8, 1878, describes visiting Anna Alcott Pratt, who told her that the episode about the currants actually happened, "only the currants were tomatoes" (quoted in *Her Own Time* 25).

hostess, smiling a shy welcome as she greeted her guest. Nothing of the sort—for not a soul appeared, but a sanguinary-looking[15] boy asleep under the currant bushes.

"I'm afraid something has happened; step into the garden, Scott, while I look up Mrs. Brooke,"[16] said John, alarmed at the silence and solitude.

Round the house he hurried, led by a pungent smell of burnt sugar, and Mr. Scott strolled after him, with a queer look on his face. He paused discreetly at a distance when Brooke disappeared; but he could both see and hear, and, being a bachelor, enjoyed the prospect mightily.

In the kitchen reigned confusion and despair; one edition of jelly was trickled from pot to pot, another lay upon the floor, and a third was burning gaily on the stove. Lotty, with Teutonic phlegm,[17] was calmly eating bread and currant wine, for the jelly was still in a hopelessly liquid state, while Mrs. Brooke, with her apron over her head, sat sobbing dismally.

"My dearest girl, what is the matter?" cried John, rushing in with awful visions of scalded hands, sudden news of affliction, and secret consternation at the thought of the guest in the garden.

"Oh, John, I *am* so tired, and hot, and cross, and worried! I've been at it till I'm all worn out. Do come and help me, or I *shall* die;" and the exhausted housewife cast herself upon his breast, giving him a sweet welcome in every sense of the word, for her pinafore had been baptized at the same time as the floor.[18]

"What worries you, dear? Has anything dreadful happened?" asked the anxious John, tenderly kissing the crown of the little cap, which was all askew.

"Yes," sobbed Meg, despairingly.

"Tell me quick, then; don't cry, I can bear anything better than that. Out with it, love."

"The—the jelly won't jell—and I don't know what to do!"

John Brooke laughed then as he never dared to laugh afterward; and the derisive Scott smiled involuntarily as he heard the hearty peal, which put the finishing stroke to poor Meg's woe.

"Is that all? Fling it out of the window, and don't bother any more about it. I'll buy you quarts if you want it; but for heaven's sake don't have hysterics, for I've brought Jack Scott home to dinner, and—"

John got no further, for Meg cast him off, and clasped her hands with a tragic gesture as she fell into a chair, exclaiming in a tone of mingled indignation, reproach, and dismay,—

"A man to dinner, and everything in a mess! John Brooke, how *could* you do such a thing?"

"Hush, he's in the garden; I forgot the confounded jelly, but it can't be helped now," said John, surveying the prospect with an anxious eye.

"You ought to have sent word, or told me this morning, and you ought to have remembered how busy I was," continued Meg, petulantly; for even turtle-doves will peck when ruffled.

"I didn't know it this morning, and there was no time to send word, for I met him on the way out. I never thought of asking leave, when you have always told me to do as I liked. I never tried it before, and hang me if I ever do again!" added John, with an aggrieved air.

"I should hope not! Take him away at once; I can't see him, and there isn't any dinner."

"Well, I like that! Where's the beef and vegetables I sent home, and the pudding you promised?" cried John, rushing to the larder.

"I hadn't time to cook anything; I meant to dine at mother's. I'm sorry, but I was *so* busy,"—and Meg's tears began again.

John was a mild man, but he was human; and after a long day's work, to come home tired, hungry and hopeful, to find a chaotic house, an empty table, and a cross wife, was not exactly conducive to repose of mind or manner. He restrained himself, however, and the little squall would have blown over but for one unlucky word.

"It's a scrape, I acknowledge; but if you will lend a hand, we'll pull through, and have a good time yet. Don't cry, dear, but just exert yourself a bit, and knock us up something to eat. We're both as hungry as hunters, so we shan't mind what it is. Give us the cold meat, and bread and cheese; we won't ask for jelly."

19. The field of battle. LMA means Meg left the argument.

20. A lunch of assorted items. The two men ate whatever they could find in the kitchen rather than any type of planned lunch.

21. The *OED* defines this phrase as "a mild oath," or "a mere exclamation" and notes its first usage in print as Ben Jonson in 1616. According to *Brewer's Dictionary of Phrase and Fable,* 15th ed. (New York: Harper Collins, 1995), "'St George' was the battle cry of English soldiers, and from this arose such expressions as 'before George', 'fore George'" and this expression (165).

He meant it to be a good-natured joke, but that one word sealed his fate. Meg thought it was *too* cruel to hint about her sad failure, and the last atom of patience vanished as he spoke.

"You must get yourself out of the scrape as you can; I'm too used up to 'exert' myself for any one. It's like a man, to propose a bone and vulgar bread and cheese for company. I won't have anything of the sort in my house. Take that Scott up to mother's, and tell him I'm away—sick, dead, anything. I won't see him, and you two can laugh at me and my jelly as much as you like; you won't have anything else here;" and having delivered her defiance all in one breath, Meg cast away her pinafore, and precipitately left the field[19] to bemoan herself in her own room.

What those two creatures did in her absence, she never knew; but Mr. Scott was not taken "up to mother's," and when Meg descended, after they had strolled away together, she found traces of a promiscuous lunch[20] which filled her with horror. Lotty reported that they had eaten "a much, and greatly laughed; and the master bid her throw away all the sweet stuff, and hide the pots."

Meg longed to go and tell mother; but a sense of shame at her own short-comings, of loyalty to John, "who might be cruel, but nobody should know it," restrained her; and after a summary clearing up, she dressed herself prettily, and sat down to wait for John to come and be forgiven.

Unfortunately, John didn't come, not seeing the matter in that light. He had carried it off as a good joke with Scott, excused his little wife as well as he could, and played the host so hospitably, that his friend enjoyed the impromptu dinner, and promised to come again. But John was angry, though he did not show it; he felt that Meg had got him into a scrape, and then deserted him in his hour of need. "It wasn't fair to tell a man to bring folks home any time, with perfect freedom, and when he took you at your word, to flare up and blame him, and leave him in the lurch, to be laughed at or pitied. No, by George,[21] it wasn't! and Meg must know it." He had fumed inwardly during the feast, but when the flurry was over, and he strolled home, after seeing Scott off, a milder mood came over him. "Poor little thing! it was hard upon her when she tried so heartily to please me. She was wrong, of course, but then she was young. I must be patient, and teach her." He hoped she had not gone home—he hated gossip and interference. For a minute he was ruffled again at the mere thought of it; and then the fear that Meg would cry herself sick, softened his heart, and sent him on at a quicker pace, resolving to be calm and kind, but firm, quite firm, and show her where she had failed in her duty to her spouse.

Meg likewise resolved to be "calm and kind, but firm," and show *him* his duty. She longed to run to meet him, and beg pardon, and be kissed and comforted, as she was sure of being; but, of course, she did nothing of the sort; and when she saw John coming, began to hum quite naturally, as she rocked and sewed like a lady of leisure in her best parlor.

John was a little disappointed not to find a tender Niobe;[22] but, feeling that his dignity demanded the first apology, he made none: only came leisurely in, and laid himself upon the sofa, with the singularly relevant remark,—

"We are going to have a new moon,[23] my dear."

"I've no objection," was Meg's equally soothing remark.

A few other topics of general interest were introduced by Mr. Brooke, and wet-blanketed by Mrs. Brooke, and conversation languished. John went to one window, unfolded his paper, and wrapt himself in it, figuratively speaking. Meg went to the other window, and sewed as if new rosettes[24] for her slippers were among the necessaries of life. Neither spoke—both looked quite "calm and firm," and both felt desperately uncomfortable.

"Oh, dear," thought Meg, "married life is very trying, and does need infinite patience, as well as love, as mother says." The word "mother" suggested other maternal counsels given long ago, and received with unbelieving protests.

"John is a good man, but he has his faults, and you must learn to see and bear with them, remembering your own. He is very decided, but never will be obstinate, if you reason kindly, not oppose impatiently. He is very accurate, and particular about the truth—a good trait, though you call him 'fussy.' Never deceive him by look or word, Meg, and he will give you the confidence you deserve, the support you need. He has a temper, not like ours,

22. In Greek mythology, Niobe boasts of her fourteen children (the number varies in other versions) to Leto, who had only two: the twins Apollo and Artemis. The two sons kill Niobe's children with bows and arrows. Devastated, Niobe goes to Mount Sipylus, where Zeus turns her to stone that weeps forever.

23. The *OED* notes that the original meaning of *new moon* is "the moon when it appears as a slender crescent shortly after its conjunction with the sun." In astronomical terms, a new moon occurs when the moon is not visible from the earth because it is in conjunction with the sun; this phase was called a *dark moon*.

24. Small flower designs.

—one flash, and then all over—but the white, still anger that is seldom stirred, but once kindled, is hard to quench. Be careful, very careful, not to wake his anger against yourself, for peace and happiness depend on keeping his respect. Watch yourself, be the first to ask pardon if you both err, and guard against the little piques,[25] misunderstandings, and hasty words that often pave the way for bitter sorrow and regret."

These words came back to Meg, as she sat sewing in the sunset, —especially the last. This was the first serious disagreement; her own hasty speeches sounded both silly and unkind, as she recalled them, her own anger looked childish now, and thoughts of poor John, coming home to such a scene quite melted her heart. She glanced at him with tears in her eyes, but he did not see them; she put down her work and got up, thinking, "I *will* be the first to say, 'forgive me,'" but he did not seem to hear her; she went very slowly across the room, for pride was hard to swallow, and stood by him, but he did not turn his head. For a minute, she felt as if she really couldn't do it; then came the thought, "This is the beginning, I'll do my part, and have nothing to reproach myself with," and stooping down she softly kissed her husband on the forehead. Of course that settled it; the penitent kiss was better than a world of words, and John had her on his knee in a minute, saying tenderly,—

"It was too bad to laugh at the poor little jelly-pots; forgive me, dear, I never will again!"

But he did, oh, bless you, yes, hundreds of times, and so did Meg, both declaring that it was the sweetest jelly they ever made; for family peace was preserved in that little family jar.

After this, Meg had Mr. Scott to dinner by special invitation, and served him up a pleasant feast without a cooked wife for the first course; on which occasion she was so gay and gracious, and made everything go off so charmingly, that Mr. Scott told John he was a happy fellow, and shook his head over the hardships of bachelor-hood all the way home.

In the autumn, new trials and experiences came to Meg. Sallie Moffat renewed her friendship, was always running out for a dish of gossip at the little house, or inviting "that poor dear" to come in and spend the day at the big house. It was pleasant, for in dull weather Meg often felt lonely;—all were busy at home, John absent till night, and nothing to do but sew, or read, or potter about. So it naturally fell out that Meg got into the way of gadding[26] and gossiping with her friend. Seeing Sallie's pretty things made her long for such, and pity herself because she had not got them. Sally was very kind, and often offered her the coveted trifles; but Meg declined them, knowing that John wouldn't like it; and then this foolish little woman went and did what John disliked infinitely worse.

She knew her husband's income, and she loved to feel that he trusted her, not only with his happiness, but what some men seem to value more, his money. She knew where it was, was free to take what she liked, and all he asked was that she should keep account of every penny, pay bills once a month, and remember that she was a poor man's wife. Till now she had done well, been prudent and exact, kept her little account-books neatly, and showed them to him monthly, without fear. But that autumn the serpent got into Meg's paradise, and tempted her, like many a modern Eve, not with apples, but with dress. Meg didn't like to be pitied and made to feel poor; it irritated her; but she was ashamed to confess it, and now and then she tried to console herself by buying something pretty, so that Sally needn't think she had to scrimp. She always felt wicked after it, for the pretty things were seldom necessaries; but then they cost so little, it wasn't worth worrying about; so the trifles increased unconsciously, and in the shopping excursions she was no longer a passive looker-on.

But the trifles cost more than one would imagine; and when she cast up her accounts at the end of the month, the sum total rather scared her. John was busy that month, and left the bills to her; the next month he was absent; but the third he had a grand quarterly settling up, and Meg never forgot it. A few days before she had done a dreadful thing, and it weighed upon her conscience. Sallie had been buying silks, and Meg ached for a new one—just a handsome light one for parties—her black silk was so common, and thin things for evening wear were only proper for girls. Aunt March usually gave the sisters a present of twenty-five

26. Going places without any real purpose.

27. The edging for a dress.

28. The *OED* defines *hug-me-tight* as a "woman's short close-fitting jacket" and cites *Godey's Lady's Book* of 1860 as its first usage. LMA's passage here is cited as the second usage.

dollars apiece, at New Year; that was only a month to wait, and here was a lovely violet silk going at a bargain, and she had the money, if she only dared to take it. John always said what was his was hers; but would he think it right to spend not only the prospective five-and-twenty, but another five-and-twenty out of the household fund? That was the question. Sallie had urged her to do it, had offered to loan the money, and with the best intentions in life, had tempted Meg beyond her strength. In an evil moment the shopman held up the lovely, shimmering folds, and said, "A bargain, I assure you, ma'am." She answered, "I'll take it"; and it was cut off and paid for, and Sallie had exulted, and she had laughed as if it was a thing of no consequence, and driven away feeling as if she had stolen something, and the police were after her.

When she got home, she tried to assuage the pangs of remorse by spreading forth the lovely silk; but it looked less silvery now, didn't become her, after all, and the words "fifty dollars" seemed stamped like a pattern down each breadth. She put it away; but it haunted her, not delightfully, as a new dress should, but dreadfully, like the ghost of a folly that was not easily laid. When John got out his books that night, Meg's heart sank; and, for the first time in her married life, she was afraid of her husband. The kind, brown eyes looked as if they could be stern; and though he was unusually merry, she fancied he had found her out, but didn't mean to let her know it. The house bills were all paid, the books all in order. John had praised her, and was undoing the old pocket-book which they called the "bank," when Meg, knowing that it was quite empty, stopped his hand, saying nervously,—

"You haven't seen my private expense book, yet."

John never asked to see it; but she always insisted on his doing so, and used to enjoy his masculine amazement at the queer things women wanted, and make him guess what "piping"[27] was, demand fiercely the meaning of a "hug-me-tight,"[28] or wonder how a little thing composed of three rosebuds, a bit of velvet and a pair of strings, could possibly be a bonnet, and cost five or six dollars. That night he looked as if he would like the fun of quizzing her figures, and pretending to be horrified at her extravagance, as he often did, being particularly proud of his prudent wife.

The little book was brought slowly out, and laid down before him. Meg got behind his chair, under pretence of smoothing the wrinkles out of his tired forehead, and standing there, she said, with her panic increasing with every word,—

"John, dear, I'm ashamed to show you my book, for I've really been dreadfully extravagant lately. I go about so much I must have things, you know, and Sallie advised my getting it, so I did; and my New-Year's money will partly pay for it; but I was sorry after I'd done it, for I knew you'd think it wrong in me."

John laughed, and drew her round beside him, saying good-humoredly, "Don't go and hide, I won't beat you if you *have* got a pair of killing[29] boots; I'm rather proud of my wife's feet, and don't mind if she does pay eight or nine dollars for her boots, if they are good ones."

That had been one of her last "trifles," and John's eye had fallen on it as he spoke. "Oh, what *will* he say when he comes to that awful fifty dollars!" thought Meg, with a shiver.

"It's worse than boots, it's a silk dress," she said, with the calmness of desperation, for she wanted the worst over.

"Well, dear, what is 'the dem'd total?' as Mr. Mantalini says."[30] That didn't sound like John, and she knew he was looking up at her with the straightforward look that she had always been ready to meet and answer with one as frank, till now. She turned the page and her head at the same time, pointing to the sum which would have been bad enough without the fifty, but which was appalling to her with that added. For a minute the room was very still; then John said, slowly—but she could feel it cost him an effort to express no displeasure,—

"Well, I don't know that fifty is much for a dress, with all the furbelows and quinny-dingles[31] you have to have to finish it off these days."

"It isn't made or trimmed," sighed Meg faintly, for a sudden recollection of the cost still to be incurred quite overwhelmed her.

"Twenty[a] yards of silk seems a good deal to cover one small woman, but I've no doubt my wife will look as fine as Ned Moffat's when she gets it on," said John dryly.

"I know you are angry, John, but I can't help it; I don't mean to

29. Devastatingly attractive.

30. Mr. Mantalini, a character from Dickens's *Nicholas Nickleby* (1838–1839), uses *damned* almost every time he speaks. John's allusion here is ironic since Mr. Mantalini steals money from his wife and eventually is placed in a debtor's prison.

31. A *furbelow* is a flounce on a woman's dress, a decorative boarder that is sewn by its upper edge to the dress while the bottom is left hanging. *Quinny-dingle* is an obscure word. The 1880–1881 edition replaces it with *notions,* which were cheap but often useful items related to clothes, such as ribbons or buttons.

waste your money, and I didn't think those little things would count up so. I can't resist them when I see Sallie buying all she wants, and pitying me because I don't; I try to be contented, but it is hard, and I'm tired of being poor."

The last words were spoken so low she thought he did not hear them, but he did, and they wounded him deeply, for he had denied himself many pleasures for Meg's sake. She could have bitten her tongue out the minute she had said it, for John pushed the books away and got up, saying, with a little quiver in his voice, "I was afraid of this; I do my best, Meg." If he had scolded her, or even shaken her, it would not have broken her heart like those few words. She ran to him and held him close, crying, with repentant tears, "Oh, John! my dear, kind, hard-working boy, I didn't mean it! It was so wicked, so untrue and ungrateful, how could I say it! Oh, how could I say it!"

He was very kind, forgave her readily, and did not utter one reproach; but Meg knew that she had done and said a thing which would not be forgotten soon, although he might never allude to it again. She had promised to love him for better for worse; and then she, his wife, had reproached him with his poverty, after spending his earnings recklessly. It was dreadful; and the worst of it was John went on so quietly afterward, just as if nothing had happened, except that he stayed in town later, and worked at night when she had gone to cry herself to sleep. A week of remorse nearly made Meg sick; and the discovery that John had countermanded the order for his new great-coat,[32] reduced her to a state of despair which was pathetic to behold. He had simply said, in answer to her surprised inquiries as to the change, "I can't afford it, my dear."

Meg said no more, but a few minutes after he found her in the hall with her face buried in the old great-coat, crying as if her heart would break.

They had a long talk that night, and Meg learned to love her husband better for his poverty, because it seemed to have made a man of him—giving him the strength and courage to fight his own way—and taught him a tender patience with which to bear and comfort the natural longings and failures of those he loved.

Next day she put her pride in her pocket, went to Sallie, told the truth, and asked her to buy the silk as a favor. The good-natured Mrs. Moffat willingly did so, and had the delicacy not to make her a present of it immediately afterward. Then Meg ordered home the great-coat, and, when John arrived, she put it on, and asked him how he liked her new silk gown. One can imagine what answer he made, how he received his present, and what a blissful state of things ensued.[33] John came home early, Meg gadded no more; and that great-coat was put on in the morning by a very happy husband, and taken off at night by a most devoted little wife. So the year rolled round, and at midsummer there came to Meg a new experience,—the deepest and tenderest of a woman's life.

Laurie came creeping[b] into the kitchen of the Dove-cote one Saturday, with an excited face, and was received with the clash of cymbals; for Hannah clapped her hands with a saucepan in one, and the cover in the other.

"How's the little Ma? Where is everybody? Why didn't you tell me before I came home?" began Laurie, in a loud whisper.

"Happy as a queen, the dear! Every soul of 'em is upstairs a worshipin'; we didn't want no hurrycanes round. Now you go into the parlor, and I'll send 'em down to you," with which somewhat involved reply Hannah vanished, chuckling ecstatically.

Presently Jo appeared, proudly bearing a flannel bundle laid forth upon a large pillow. Jo's face was very sober, but her eyes twinkled, and there was an odd sound in her voice of repressed emotion of some sort.

"Shut your eyes and hold out your arms," she said invitingly.

Laurie backed precipitately into a corner, and put his hands behind him with an imploring gesture,—"No, thank you; I'd rather not. I shall drop it, or smash it, as sure as fate."

"Then you shan't see your nevvy,"[34] said Jo, decidedly, turning as if to go.

"I will, I will! only you must be responsible for damages;" and, obeying orders, Laurie heroically shut his eyes while something was put into his arms. A peal of laughter from Jo, Amy, Mrs. March, Hannah and John, caused him to open them the next minute, to find himself invested with two babies instead of one.[35]

33. The episode of the overcoat is an important incident in Meg and John's marriage. Meg realizes that John's overcoat is a necessity in the cold Massachusetts winter; the silk for her dress is a luxury. Meg's actions here help make the marriage more equal and rational.

34. Nephew.

35. Anna Alcott and John Bridge Pratt had two sons, Frederick Alcott Pratt (1863–1910) and John Sewall Pratt Alcott (1865–1923). John was legally adopted by LMA in June 1887 to ensure an heir for her literary copyrights. LMA never mentions that Meg is pregnant but suddenly introduces the births. Most likely LMA, who invented the nicknames, chose twins so she could write both children into the novel at once.

36. The *OED* defines *well-sweep* as "an apparatus for drawing water from a well, consisting of a long pole attached to an upright which serves as a fulcrum."

No wonder they laughed, for the expression of his face was droll enough to convulse a Quaker, as he stood and stared wildly from the unconscious innocents to the hilarious spectators, with such dismay that Jo sat down on the floor and screamed.

"Twins, by Jupiter!" was all he said for a minute; then turning to the women with an appealing look that was comically piteous, he added, "Take 'em quick, somebody! I'm going to laugh, and I shall drop 'em."

John rescued his babies, and marched up and down, with one on each arm, as if already initiated into the mysteries of baby-tending, while Laurie laughed till the tears ran down his cheeks.

"It's the best joke of the season, isn't it? I wouldn't have told you, for I set my heart on surprising you, and I flatter myself I've done it," said Jo, when she got her breath.

"I never was more staggered in my life. Isn't it fun? Are they boys? What are you going to name them? Let's have another look. Hold me up, Jo; for upon my life it's one too many for me," returned Laurie, regarding the infants with the air of a big, benevolent Newfoundland looking at a pair of infantile kittens.

"Boy and girl. Aren't they beauties?" said the proud papa, beaming upon the little, red squirmers as if they were unfledged angels.

"Most remarkable children I ever saw. Which is which?" and Laurie bent like a well-sweep[36] to examine the prodigies.

"Amy put a blue ribbon on the boy and a pink on the girl, French fashion, so you can always tell. Besides, one has blue eyes and one brown. Kiss them, Uncle Teddy," said wicked Jo.

"I'm afraid they mightn't like it," began Laurie, with unusual timidity in such matters.

"Of course they will; they are used to it now; do it this minute, sir," commanded Jo, fearing he might propose a proxy.

Laurie screwed up his face, and obeyed with a gingerly peck at each little cheek that produced another laugh, and made the babies squeal.

"There, I knew they didn't like it! That's the boy; see him kick! he hits out with his fists like a good one. Now then, young Brooke, pitch into a man of your own size, will you?" cried Laurie, delighted with a poke in the face from a tiny fist, flapping aimlessly about.

"He's to be named John Laurence, and the girl Margaret, after mother and grandmother. We shall call her Daisy, so as not to have two Megs, and I suppose the mannie will be Jack, unless we find a better name," said Amy, with aunt-like interest.

"Name him Demijohn, and call him 'Demi'[37] for short," said Laurie.

"Daisy and Demi,—just the thing! I *knew* Teddy would do it," cried Jo, clapping her hands.

Teddy certainly had done it that time, for the babies were "Daisy" and "Demi" to the end of the chapter.

37. *Demi* is literally defined as "half-sized," so Laurie is implying "little John."

Early daguerreotype of Louisa May Alcott, circa late 1850s. In *Louisa May Alcott: Her Life, Letters and Journals* (1889), Ednah Dow Cheney, a friend of the Alcott family, recalls: "Miss Alcott's appearance was striking and impressive rather than beautiful. Her figure was tall and well-proportioned, indicating strength and activity, and she walked with freedom and majesty. Her head was large, and her rich brown hair was long and luxuriant, giving a sense of fulness and richness of life to her massive features" (388).

Southside of Concord (circa 1865).

LITTLE WOMEN

Chapter 6

Calls

1. Jo alludes to Shakespeare's tragedy *Merchant of Venice* (ca. 1596) in which Shylock, the Jewish merchant, strictly follows the "letter" of the law. After borrowing money from Shylock, Antonio loses his ships and is unable to pay his debt to the merchant. The security, or bond, for the loan is a pound of flesh, which Shylock now demands since the debt cannot be repaid: "I'll have my bond. Speak not against my bond" (3.3.4).

2. Originally a mantua-maker was one who made a mantua, a type of loose gown fashionable in the late seventeenth and early eighteenth centuries. By the nineteenth century, it came to mean dressmaker.

"Come, Jo, it's time."

"For what?"

"You don't mean to say you have forgotten that you promised to make half a dozen calls with me to-day?"

"I've done a good many rash and foolish things in my life, but I don't think I ever was mad enough to say I'd make six calls in one day, when a single one upsets me for a week."

"Yes you did; it was a bargain between us. I was to finish the crayon of Beth for you, and you were to go properly with me, and return our neighbor's visits."

"If it was fair—that was in the bond; and I stand to the letter of my bond, Shylock.[1] There is a pile of clouds in the east; it's *not* fair, and I don't go."

"Now that's shirking. It's a lovely day, no prospect of rain, and you pride yourself on keeping promises; so be honorable; come and do your duty, and then be at peace for another six months."

At that minute Jo was particularly absorbed in dressmaking; for she was mantua-maker[2] general to the family, and took especial credit to herself because she could use a needle as well as a pen. It was very provoking to be arrested in the act of a first trying-on, and ordered out to make calls in her best array, on a warm July day. She hated calls of the formal sort, and never made any till Amy cornered[a] her with a bargain, bribe, or promise. In the present instance, there was no escape; and having clashed her scissors rebelliously, while protesting that she smelt thunder, she gave in, put away her work, and taking up her hat and gloves with an air of resignation, told Amy the victim was ready.

3. A colloquial phrase that means to do the civil or proper thing.
4. Umbrella or parasol.
5. A dress made with a stiff, translucent muslin.

"Jo March, you are perverse enough to provoke a saint! You don't intend to make calls in that state, I hope," cried Amy, surveying her with amazement.

"Why not? I'm neat, and cool, and comfortable; quite proper for a dusty walk on a warm day. If people care more for my clothes than they do for me, I don't wish to see them. You can dress for both, and be as elegant as you please; it pays for you to be fine; it doesn't for me, and furbelows only worry me."

"Oh, dear!" sighed Amy; "now she's in a contrary fit, and will drive me distracted before I can get her properly ready. I'm sure it's no pleasure to me to go to-day, but it's a debt we owe society, and there's no one to pay it but you and me. I'll do anything for you, Jo, if you'll only dress yourself nicely, and come and help me do the civil.³ You can talk so well, look so aristocratic in your best things, and behave so beautifully, if you try, that I'm proud of you. I'm afraid to go alone; do come and take care of me."

"You're an artful little puss to flatter and wheedle your cross old sister in that way. The idea of my being aristocratic and well-bred, and your being afraid to go anywhere alone! I don't know which is the most absurd. Well, I'll go if I must, and do my best; you shall be commander of the expedition, and I'll obey blindly; will that satisfy you?" said Jo, with a sudden change from perversity to lamb-like submission.

"You're a perfect cherub! Now put on all your best things, and I'll tell you how to behave at each place, so that you will make a good impression. I want people to like you, and they would if you'd only try to be a little more agreeable. Do your hair the pretty way, and put the pink rose in your bonnet; it's becoming, and you look too sober in your plain suit. Take your light kids[b] and the embroidered handkerchief. We'll stop at Meg's, and borrow her white sun-shade,⁴ and then you can have my dove-colored one."

While Amy dressed, she issued her orders, and Jo obeyed them; not without entering her protest, however, for she sighed as she rustled into her new organdie,⁵ frowned darkly at herself as she tied her bonnet strings in an irreproachable bow, wrestled viciously with pins as she put on her collar, wrinkled up her features generally as she shook out the handkerchief, whose embroidery

LITTLE WOMEN

was as irritating to her nose as the present mission was to her feelings; and when she had squeezed her hands into tight gloves with two[c] buttons and a tassel, as the last touch of elegance, she turned to Amy with an imbecile expression of countenance, saying meekly,—

"I'm perfectly miserable; but if you consider me presentable, I die happy."

"You are highly satisfactory; turn slowly round, and let me get a careful view." Jo revolved, and Amy gave a touch here and there, then fell back with her head on one side, observing graciously, "Yes, you'll do, your head is all I could ask, for that white bonnet *with* the rose is quite ravishing. Hold back your shoulders, and carry your hands easily, no matter if your gloves do pinch. There's one thing you can do well, Jo, that is wear a shawl—I can't; but it's very nice to see you, and I'm so glad Aunt March gave you that lovely one; it's simple, but handsome, and those folds over the arm are really artistic. Is the point of my mantle[6] in the middle, and have I looped my dress evenly? I like to show my boots, for my feet *are* pretty, though my nose isn't."

"You are a thing of beauty, and a joy forever,"[7] said Jo, looking through her hand with the air of a connoisseur at the blue feather against the gold hair. "Am I to drag my best dress through the dust, or loop it up, please ma'am?"

"Hold it up when you walk, but drop it in the house; the sweeping style suits you best, and you must learn to trail your skirts gracefully. You haven't half buttoned one cuff; do it at once. You'll never look finished if you are not careful about the little details, for they make up the pleasing whole."

Jo sighed, and proceeded to burst the buttons off her glove, in doing up her cuff; but at last both were ready, and sailed away, looking as "pretty as picters," Hannah said, as she hung out of the upper window to watch them.

"Now, Jo dear, the Chesters are very elegant people,[d] so I want you to put on your best deportment. Don't make any of your abrupt remarks, or do anything odd, will you? Just be calm, cool and quiet,—that's safe and lady-like; and you can easily do it for fifteen minutes," said Amy, as they approached the first place,

6. The point of a mantle, a long loose sleeveless cloak worn as an outer garment, is where it fastens at the neck with either a cord or a brooch.

7. Jo paraphrases the famous first line of John Keats's poem *Endymion* (1818): "A thing of beauty is a joy forever."

8. A reference to Alfred, Lord Tennyson's poem "Maud" (1855): "she has neither savour nor salt, / But a cold and clear-cut face, as I found when her carriage past, / Perfectly beautiful: let it be granted her: where is the fault? / All that I saw (for her eyes were downcast, not to be seen) / Faultily faultless, icily regular, splendidly null" (ll: 78–82).

9. The *OED* defines *stock and stone* as a phrase that is "applied contemptuously to an idol or a sacred image."

having borrowed the white parasol and been inspected by Meg, with a baby on each arm.

"Let me see; 'Calm, cool and quiet'! yes, I think I can promise that. I've played the part of a prim young lady on the stage, and I'll try it off. My powers are great, as you shall see; so be easy in your mind, my child."

Amy looked relieved, but naughty Jo took her at her word; for, during the first call, she sat with every limb gracefully composed, every fold correctly draped, calm as a summer sea, cool as a snow-bank, and as silent as a sphinx. In vain Mrs. Chester alluded to her "charming novel," and the Misses Chester introduced parties, picnics, the Opera and the fashions; each and all were answered by a smile, a bow, and a demure "Yes" or "No," with the chill on. In vain Amy telegraphed the word "Talk," tried to draw her out, and administered covert pokes with her foot; Jo sat as if blandly unconscious of it all, with deportment like "Maud's" face, "Icily regular, splendidly null."[8]

"What a haughty, uninteresting creature that oldest Miss March is!" was the unfortunately audible remark of one of the ladies, as the door closed upon their guests. Jo laughed noiselessly all through the hall, but Amy looked disgusted at the failure of her instructions, and very naturally laid the blame upon Jo.

"How could you mistake me so? I merely meant you to be properly dignified and composed, and you made yourself a perfect stock and stone.[9] Try to be sociable at the Lambs; gossip as other girls do, and be interested in dress, and flirtations, and whatever nonsense comes up. They move in the best society, are valuable persons for us to know, and I wouldn't fail to make a good impression there for anything."

"I'll be agreeable; I'll gossip and giggle, and have horrors and raptures over any trifle you like. I rather enjoy this, and now I'll imitate what is called 'a charming girl'; I can do it, for I have May Chester as a model, and I'll improve upon her. See if the Lambs don't say, 'What a lively, nice creature that Jo March is!'"

Amy felt anxious, as well she might, for when Jo turned freak-ish there was no knowing where she would stop. Amy's face was a study when she saw her sister skim into the next drawing-room,

LITTLE WOMEN

kiss all the young ladies with effusion, beam graciously upon the young gentlemen, and join in the chat with a spirit which amazed the beholder. Amy was taken possession of by Mrs. Lamb, with whom she was a favorite, and forced to hear a long account of Lucretia's last attack, while three delightful young gentlemen hovered near, waiting for a pause when they might rush in and rescue her. So situated she was powerless to check Jo, who seemed possessed by a spirit of mischief, and talked away as volubly as the old lady. A knot of heads gathered about her, and Amy strained her ears to hear what was going on; for broken sentences filled her with alarm, round eyes and uplifted hands tormented her with curiosity, and frequent peals of laughter made her wild to share the fun. One may imagine her suffering on overhearing fragments of this sort of conversation:—

"She rides splendidly,—who taught her?"

"No one; she used to practise mounting, holding the reins, and sitting straight on an old saddle in a tree. Now she rides anything, for she don't know what fear is, and the stable-man lets her have horses cheap, because she trains them to carry ladies so well. She has such a passion for it, I often tell her if everything else fails she can be a pretty horse-breaker,ᵉ and get her living so."[10]

At this awful speech Amy contained herself with difficulty, for the impression was being given that she was rather a fast young lady, which was her especial aversion. But what could she do? for the old lady was in the middle of her story, and long before it was done Jo was off again, making more droll revelations, and committing still more fearful blunders.

"Yes, Amy was in despair that day, for all the good beasts were gone, and of three left, one was lame, one blind, and the other so balky that you had to put dirt in his mouth before he would start. Nice animal for a pleasure party, wasn't it?"

"Which did she choose?" asked one of the laughing gentlemen, who enjoyed the subject.

"None of them; she heard of a young horse at the farm-house over the river, and, though a lady had never ridden him, she resolved to try, because he was handsome and spirited. Her struggles were really pathetic; there was no one to bring the horse to the saddle, so she took the saddle to the horse. My dear creature, she

10. May Alcott, who loved horseback riding, noted in her journal for October 31, 1862: "Just returned from a most delightful ride on horseback with Edith Emerson [Ralph Waldo Emerson's daughter]. We are going with a party of six on Saturday again as its fine weather for riding & I am so fond of it. My idea of perfect happiness is to own a horse, that I can order when I like & use every day." Two days later, on November 2, she wrote: "I have riden horseback regularly once a week ever since my birthday in July & know I am a great deal better for it. I have tried all the horses in town, many of them never having had a lady or saddle on them before" (Manuscript journal, Houghton Library, Harvard University, bMS Am 1817 [56]).

11. Brave.

12. A yellowish brown or pale brown.

13. A small case, usually made of metal, for carrying calling cards.

actually rowed it over the river, put it on her head, and marched up to the barn, to the utter amazement of the old man!"

"Did she ride the horse?"

"Of course she did, and had a capital time. I expected to see her brought home in fragments, but she managed him perfectly, and was the life of the party."

"Well, I call that plucky!"[11] and young Mr. Lamb turned an approving glance upon Amy, wondering what his mother could be saying to make the girl look so red and uncomfortable.

She was still redder and more uncomfortable a moment after, when a sudden turn in the conversation introduced the subject of dress. One of the young ladies asked Jo where she got the pretty drab[12] hat she wore to the picnic; and stupid Jo, instead of mentioning the place where it was bought two years ago, must needs answer, with unnecessary frankness, "Oh, Amy painted it; you can't buy those soft shades, so we paint ours any color we like. It's a great comfort to have an artistic sister."

"Isn't that an original idea?" cried Miss Lamb, who found Jo great fun.

"That's nothing compared to some of her brilliant performances. There's nothing the child can't do. Why, she wanted a pair of blue boots for Sallie's party, so she just painted her soiled white ones the loveliest shade of sky-blue you ever saw, and they looked exactly like satin," added Jo, with an air of pride in her sister's accomplishments that exasperated Amy till she felt that it would be a relief to throw her card-case[13] at her.

"We read a story of yours the other day, and enjoyed it very much," observed the elder Miss Lamb, wishing to compliment the literary lady, who did not look the character just then, it must be confessed. Any mention of her "works" always had a bad effect upon Jo, who either grew rigid and looked offended, or changed the subject with a *brusque* remark, as now. "Sorry you could find nothing better to read. I write that rubbish because it sells, and ordinary people like it. Are you going to New York this winter?"

As Miss Lamb had "enjoyed" the story, this speech was not exactly grateful or complimentary. The minute it was made Jo saw her mistake; but, fearing to make the matter worse, suddenly remembered that it was for her to make the first move toward departure, and did so with an abruptness that left three people with half-finished sentences in their mouths.

"Amy, we *must* go. *Good*-by, dear; *do* come and see us; we are *pining* for a visit. I don't dare to ask *you,* Mr. Lamb; but if you *should* come, I don't think I shall have the heart to send you away."

Jo said this with such a droll imitation of May Chester's gushing[14] style, that Amy got out of the room as rapidly as possible, feeling a strong desire to laugh and cry at the same time.

"Didn't I do that well?" asked Jo, with a satisfied air, as they walked away.

"Nothing could have been worse," was Amy's crushing[15] reply. "What possessed you to tell those stories about my saddle, and the hats and boots, and all the rest of it?"

"Why, it's funny, and amuses people. They know we are poor, so it's no use pretending that we have grooms, buy three or four hats a season, and have things as easy and fine as they do."

"You needn't go and tell them all our little shifts,[16] and expose our poverty in that perfectly unnecessary way. You haven't a bit of proper pride, and never will learn when to hold your tongue, and when to speak," said Amy despairingly.

Poor Jo looked abashed, and silently chafed the end of her nose with the stiff handkerchief, as if performing a penance for her misdemeanors.

"How shall I behave here?" she asked, as they approached the third mansion.

"Just as you please; I wash my hands of you," was Amy's short answer.

"Then I'll enjoy myself. The boys are at home, and we'll have a comfortable time. Goodness knows I need a little change, for elegance has a bad effect upon my constitution," returned Jo, gruffly, being disturbed by her failures to suit.

An enthusiastic welcome from three big boys and several pretty children, speedily soothed her ruffled feelings; and, leaving Amy to entertain the hostess and Mr. Tudor, who happened to be calling likewise, Jo devoted herself to the young folks, and found the change refreshing. She listened to college stories with deep in-

14. The *OED* notes that this colloquial expression means "to give verbal expression to feelings or opinions in an over-effusive, exaggerated, or sentimental fashion." Jo's imitative skills no doubt serve her well as a writer of stories, but this cruel performance, which comes at the expense of her sister's friend, also suggests Jo's immaturity.

15. Disappointing.

16. The *OED* defines this usage of *shift* as "an expedient necessitated by stress of circumstances; a forced measure." Amy insists that Jo does not need to reveal all the frugal ways she makes her things look better.

17. Jo's slang means that she thought Tom Brown, the protagonist of Thomas Hughes's *Tom Brown's School Days* (1857), was a good fellow. The book, which was extremely popular in both England and America, details Tom's time at Rugby, a British boarding school, in the 1830s.

18. Edward Albert (1841–1910), Prince of Wales and the future Edward VII, was the son of Queen Victoria and Prince Albert. He visited America in 1860, the first heir to the British throne to do so. In Boston, LMA "saw the Prince of Wales trot over the Common with his train at a review. A yellow-haired laddie very like his mother. Fanny W. and I nodded and waved as he passed, and he openly winked his boyish eye at us; for Fanny, with her yellow curls and wild waving, looked rather rowdy, and the poor little prince wanted some fun. We laughed and thought that we had been more distinguished by the saucy wink than by a stately bow. Boys are always jolly,—even princes" (*Journals* 100).

terest, caressed pointers and poodles without a murmur, agreed heartily that "Tom Brown was a brick,"[17] regardless of the improper form of praise; and when one lad proposed a visit to his turtle-tank, she went with an alacrity which caused mamma to smile upon her, as that motherly lady settled the cap, which was left in a ruinous condition by filial hugs,—bear-like but affectionate,—and dearer to her than the most faultless *coiffure* from the hands of an inspired Frenchwoman.

Leaving her sister to her own devices, Amy proceeded to enjoy herself to her heart's content. Mr. Tudor's uncle had married an English lady who was third cousin to a living lord, and Amy regarded the whole family with great respect. For, in spite of her American birth and breeding, she possessed that reverence for tides which haunts the best of us,—that unacknowledged loyalty to the early faith in kings which set the most democratic nation under the sun in a ferment at the coming of a royal yellow-haired laddie,[18] some years ago, and which still has something to do with the love the young country bears the old,—like that of a big son for an imperious little mother, who held him while she could, and let him go with a farewell scolding when he rebelled. But even the satisfaction of talking with a distant connection of the British nobility did not render Amy forgetful of time; and, when the proper number of minutes had passed, she reluctantly tore herself from this aristocratic society, and looked about for Jo,—fervently hoping that her incorrigible sister would not be found in any position which should bring disgrace upon the name of March.

It might have been worse; but Amy considered it bad, for Jo sat on the grass with an encampment of boys about her, and a dirty-footed dog reposing on the skirt of her state and festival dress, as she related one of Laurie's pranks to her admiring audience. One small child was poking turtles with Amy's cherished parasol, a second was eating gingerbread over Jo's best bonnet, and a third playing ball with her gloves. But all were enjoying themselves; and when Jo collected her damaged property to go, her escort accompanied her, begging her to come again, "it was such fun to hear about Laurie's larks."

"Capital boys, aren't they? I feel quite young and brisk again after that," said Jo, strolling along with her hands behind her, partly from habit, partly to conceal the bespattered parasol.

"Why do you always avoid Mr. Tudor?" asked Amy, wisely refraining from any comment upon Jo's dilapidated appearance.

"Don't like him; he puts on airs, snubs his sisters, worries his father, and don't speak respectfully of his mother. Laurie says he is fast,[19] and *I* don't consider him a desirable acquaintance; so I let him alone."

"You might treat him civilly, at least. You gave him a cool nod; and just now you bowed and smiled in the politest way to Tommy Chamberlain, whose father keeps a grocery store. If you had just reversed the nod and the bow, it would have been right," said Amy, reprovingly.

"No it wouldn't," returned perverse Jo; "I neither like, respect, nor admire Tudor, though his grandfather's uncle's nephew's niece *was* third cousin to a lord. Tommy is poor, and bashful, and good, and very clever; I think well of him, and like to show that I do, for he *is* a gentleman in spite of the brown paper parcels."

"It's no use trying to argue with you," began Amy.

"Not the least, my dear," cut in Jo, "so let us look amiable, and drop a card here,[20] as the Kings are evidently out, for which I'm deeply grateful."

The family card-case having done its duty, the girls walked on, and Jo uttered another thanksgiving on reaching the fifth house, and being told that the young ladies were engaged.

"Now let us go home, and never mind Aunt March to-day. We can run down there any time, and it's really a pity to trail through the dust in our best bibs and tuckers,[21] when we are tired and cross."

"Speak for yourself, if you please; aunt likes to have us pay her the compliment of coming in style, and making a formal call; it's a little thing to do, but it gives her pleasure, and I don't believe it will hurt your things half so much as letting dirty dogs and clumping boys spoil them. Stoop down, and let me take the crumbs off of your bonnet."

"What a good girl you are, Amy," said Jo, with a repentant glance from her own damaged costume to that of her sister, which was fresh and spotless still.

19. Has a disregard for morals or propriety.

20. In Alcott's day it was proper etiquette to leave a calling card at a home whose occupants were away so they would know who had stopped by while they were out. Typically, calling cards were colorfully illustrated with artwork.

21. The phrase is a colloquial expression for "best clothes."

Henry David Thoreau (1817–1862) was a long-time friend of the Alcott family. While serving as a nurse in Georgetown in winter 1863, LMA recalled Thoreau's death that previous spring and composed "Thoreau's Flute," a poem later published in the *Atlantic Monthly Magazine* in September 1863: "We sighing said, 'Our Pan is dead; / His pipe hangs mute beside the river . . . / Spring mourns as for untimely frost . . . / The Genius of the wood is lost.'"

22. Beautiful women.

23. Puritans treated people who were sinners or non-church members differently than they did people of their own faith.

24. LMA, in 1879, closed a letter to the *Woman's Journal:* "Yours for reforms of all kinds" (*Selected Letters* 238). In the nineteenth century, Massachusetts stood at the center of radical reform movements that worked to create a more equal and just society, and the Alcotts were participants in all the major causes: abolition, women's rights, education reform, and assistance to the poor and needy. Among their close friends were some of New England's most prominent liberals and reformers, including William Lloyd Garrison, Abigail's brother Rev. Samuel Joseph May, Ralph Waldo Emerson, Henry David Thoreau, Margaret Fuller, Elizabeth Palmer Peabody, Theodore Parker, Frank Sanborn, and Thomas Wentworth Higginson. When Lucy Stone, the feminist activist and editor of the *Woman's Journal,* wrote to LMA in 1873, asking for her help in the suffrage movement, LMA responded: "I read your note aloud to the family, asking 'What shall I say to Mrs Stone?' my honored father instantly replied: 'Tell her you are ready to follow your leader, sure that you could not have a better one.' My brave old mother, with the ardor of many unquenchable Mays shining in her face, cried out: 'Tell her I am seventy-three, but I mean to go to the polls before I die, even if my three daughters have to carry me'" (*Selected Letters* 178).

"I wish it was as easy for me to do little things to please people, as it is for you. I think of them, but it takes too much time to do them; so I wait for a chance to confer a big favor, and let the small ones slip; but they tell best in the end, I guess."

Amy smiled, and was mollified at once, saying with a maternal air,—

"Women should learn to be agreeable, particularly poor ones; for they have no other way of repaying the kindnesses they receive. If you'd remember that, and practise it, you'd be better liked than I am, because there is more of you."

"I'm a crotchety old thing, and always shall be; but I'm willing to own that you are right; only it's easier for me to risk my life for a person than to be pleasant to them when I don't feel like it. It's a great misfortune to have such strong likes and dislikes, isn't it?"

"It's a greater not to be able to hide them. I don't mind saying that I don't approve of Tudor any more than you do; but I'm not called upon to tell him so; neither are you, and there is no use in making yourself disagreeable because he is."

"But I think girls ought to show when they disapprove of young men; and how can they do it except by their manners? Preaching don't do any good, as I know to my sorrow, since I've had Teddy to manage; but there are many little ways in which I can influence him without a word, and I say we *ought* to do it to others if we can."

"Teddy is a remarkable boy, and can't be taken as a sample of other boys," said Amy, in a tone of solemn conviction, which would have convulsed the "remarkable boy," if he had heard it. "If we were belles,[22] or women of wealth and position, we might do something, perhaps; but for us to frown at one set of young gentlemen, because we don't approve of them, and smile upon another set, because we do, wouldn't have a particle of effect, and we should only be considered odd and Puritanical."[23]

"So we are to countenance things and people which we detest, merely because we are not belles and millionaires, are we? That's a nice sort of morality."

"I can't argue about it, I only know that it's the way of the world; and people who set themselves against it, only get laughed at for their pains. I don't like reformers, and I hope you will never try to be one."

"I do like them, and I shall be one if I can; for in spite of the laughing, the world would never get on without them.[24] We can't agree about that, for you belong to the old set, and I to the new; you will get on the best, but I shall have the liveliest time of it. I should rather enjoy the brickbats[25] and hooting, I think."

"Well, compose yourself now, and don't worry aunt with your new ideas."

"I'll try not to, but I'm always possessed to burst out with some particularly blunt speech or revolutionary sentiment before her; it's my doom, and I can't help it."

They found Aunt Carrol with the old lady, both absorbed in some very interesting subject; but they dropped it as the girls came in, with a conscious look which betrayed that they had been talking about their nieces. Jo was not in a good humor, and the perverse fit returned; but Amy, who had virtuously done her duty, kept her temper, and pleased everybody, was in a most angelic frame of mind. This amiable spirit was felt at once, and both aunts "my dear'd" her affectionately, looking what they afterwards said emphatically,—"That child improves every day."

"Are you going to help about the fair, dear?" asked Mrs. Carrol, as Amy sat down beside her with the confiding air elderly people like so well in the young.

"Yes, aunt, Mrs. Chester asked me if I would, and I offered to tend a table, as I have nothing but my time to give."

"I'm not," put in Jo, decidedly; "I hate to be patronized, and the Chesters think it's a great favor to allow us to help with their highly connected fair. I wonder you consented, Amy—they only want you to work."[26]

"I am willing to work,—it's for the Freedmen[27] as well as the Chesters, and I think it very kind of them to let me share the

Ralph Waldo Emerson (1803–1882), poet, essayist, and lecturer, was seen by his neighbors as one of Concord's leading citizens. When Emerson died on April 27, 1882, LMA wrote: "Our best & greatest American gone. The nearest & dearest friend father has ever had, & the man who has helped me most by his life, his books, his society" (*Journals* 234).

For more on LMA and reform see Madeleine B. Stern, ed., *L. M. Alcott: Signature of Reform* (Boston: Northeastern University Press, 2002), and Roberta Seelinger Trites, *Twain, Alcott, and the Birth of the Adolescent Reform Novel* (Iowa City: University of Iowa Press, 2007).

25. A piece of a brick used as a projectile.

26. Mary Peabody Mann, widow of the educator Horace Mann and sister to Sophia Hawthorne, wife of Nathaniel Hawthorne, held fairs in Concord to help her older sister Elizabeth Palmer Peabody raise money to build an orphanage for black children in Washington, D.C. In February 1864, LMA noted: "Mrs. Mann got up a Fair for Colored Orphans at Georgetown. We helped & the thing made $500" (*Journals* 135n11). She later cancelled this passage. In June 1864, LMA wrote: "Mrs. Mann had a sequel to her Fair & we took part. May had the flower table & made $80, I the refreshments & made $75. The H[awthorne?]'s, P[eabody?]'s & M[ann?]'s very cross & mad" (*Journals* 130).

27. Freedmen were the southern slaves freed by Abraham Lincoln's

Emancipation Proclamation on January 1, 1863, and by the Union's victory in the Civil War. Thousands of former slaves faced severe problems: lack of food, no health care, inadequate housing, no education. President Lincoln foresaw that the needs of former slaves would be great after the war, and he created the Freedmen's Bureau to help fill these needs. On March 3, 1865, Congress passed a bill authorizing the creation of the Freedmen's Bureau. George Luther Stearns of Medford, MA, abolitionist and longtime friend of the Alcott family, helped found the bureau. The first readers of *Little Women,* especially the socially conscious constituents in the Northeast, would have been keenly sensitive to the plight of former slaves and would have applauded Mrs. Chester's fair. Even as the Civil War was raging, LMA had wanted to go to the South to help the freed slaves, or "contraband," as they were called. In October 1863, less than nine months after her Civil War nursing experience at Georgetown, D.C., LMA wrote: "Thought much about going to Port Royal to teach contrabands" (*Journals* 120). According to Bronson, LMA was thinking of a new work, along the lines of *Hospital Sketches:* "[James T.] Fields speaks admiringly of Louisa's book. He will like to print 'Plantation Sketches' in the *Atlantic* if she goes to Carolina to write them as she now thinks she may, teaching the freedman on the plantations meanwhile" (*Journals of BA* 359–360). But plans did not work out. LMA, on November 12, 1863, wrote to Thomas Wentworth Higginson, colonel of the First South Carolina Volunteers, the first Negro regiment in the Union army, then encamped in Beaufort, SC: "I should like of all things to go South & help the blacks as I am no longer allowed to nurse the whites. The former seems the greater work, & would be most interesting to me. I offered to go as a teacher on one of the Islands but Mr. Philbrey objected because I had no natural protector to go with me, so I was obliged to give that up" (*Selected Letters* 96).

labor and the fun. Patronage don't trouble me when it is well meant."

"Quite right and proper; I like your grateful spirit, my dear; it's a pleasure to help people who appreciate our efforts; some don't, and that is trying," observed Aunt March, looking over her spectacles at Jo, who sat apart rocking herself with a somewhat morose expression.

If Jo had only known what a great happiness was wavering in the balance for one of them, she would have turned dove-like in a minute; but, unfortunately, we don't have windows in our breasts, and cannot see what goes on in the minds of our friends; better for us that we cannot as a general thing, but now and then it would be such a comfort—such a saving of time and temper. By her next speech, Jo deprived herself of several years of pleasure, and received a timely lesson in the art of holding her tongue.

"I don't like favors; they oppress and make me feel like a slave; I'd rather do everything for myself, and be perfectly independent."

"Ahem!" coughed Aunt Carrol, softly, with a look at Aunt March.

"I told you so," said Aunt March, with a decided nod to Aunt Carrol.

Mercifully unconscious of what she had done, Jo sat with her nose in the air, and a revolutionary aspect, which was anything but inviting.

"Do you speak French, dear?" asked Mrs. Carrol, laying her hand on Amy's.

"Pretty well, thanks to Aunt March, who lets Esther talk to me as often as I like," replied Amy, with a grateful look, which caused the old lady to smile affably.

"How are you about languages?" asked Mrs. Carrol of Jo.

"Don't know a word; I'm very stupid about studying anything; can't bear French, it's such a slippery, silly sort of language," was the *brusque* reply.

Another look passed between the ladies, and Aunt March said to Amy, "You are quite strong and well, now dear, I believe? Eyes don't trouble you any more, do they?"

Interior of a freedmen's school.

"Not at all, thank you, ma'am; I'm very well, and mean to do great things next winter, so that I may be ready for Rome, whenever that joyful time arrives."

"Good girl! you deserve to go, and I'm sure you will some day," said Aunt March, with an approving pat on the head, as Amy picked up her ball for her.

> "Cross patch, draw the latch,
> Sit by the fire and spin,"[28]

squalled Polly, bending down from his perch on the back of her chair, to peep into Jo's face, with such a comical air of impertinent inquiry, that it was impossible to help laughing.

"Most observing bird," said the old lady.

"Come and take a walk, my dear?" cried Polly, hopping toward the china-closet, with a look suggestive of lump-sugar.

28. First two lines of a nursery rhyme originally published in John Newbery's *Mother Goose's Melody; or, Sonnets for the Cradle* (ca. 1760). A cross patch is an ill-tempered person. The last two lines are: "Take a cup and drink it up, / Then call your neighbors in."

"Thank you, I will—come Amy," and Jo brought the visit to an end, feeling, more strongly than ever, that calls did have a bad effect upon her constitution. She shook hands in a gentlemanly manner, but Amy kissed both the aunts, and the girls departed, leaving behind them the impression of shadow and sunshine; which impression caused Aunt March to say, as they vanished,—

"You'd better do it, Mary; I'll supply the money," and Aunt Carrol to reply decidedly, "I certainly will, if her father and mother consent."

Chapter 7

Consequences

RS. CHESTER'S fair was so very elegant and select, that it was considered a great honor by the young ladies of the neighborhood to be invited to take a table, and every one was much interested in the matter. Amy was asked, but Jo was not, which was fortunate for all parties, as her elbows were decidedly akimbo[1] at this period of her life, and it took a good many hard knocks to teach her how to get on easily. The "haughty, uninteresting creature" was let severely alone; but Amy's talent and taste were duly complimented by the offer of the Art table, and she exerted herself to prepare and secure appropriate and valuable contributions to it.

Everything went on smoothly till the day before the fair opened; then there occurred one of the little skirmishes which it is almost impossible to avoid, when some five-and-twenty women, old and young, with all their private piques and prejudices, try to work together.

May Chester was rather jealous of Amy because the latter was a greater favorite than herself; and, just at this time, several trifling circumstances occurred to increase the feeling. Amy's dainty pen-and-ink work entirely eclipsed May's painted vases; that was one thorn; then the all-conquering Tudor had danced four times with Amy, at a late party, and only once with May; that was thorn number two; but the chief grievance that rankled in her soul, and gave her an excuse for her unfriendly conduct, was a rumor which some obliging gossip had whispered to her, that the March girls had made fun of her at the Lambs. All the blame of this should have fallen upon Jo, for her naughty imitation had been too life-like to escape detection, and the frolicksome Lambs had permitted the joke to escape. No hint of this had reached the culprits, however, and Amy's dismay can be imagined, when, the very evening before the fair, as she was putting her last touches to her pretty table, Mrs. Chester, who, of course, resented the supposed ridicule of her daughter, said in a bland tone, but with a cold look,—

"I find, dear, that there is some feeling among the young ladies about my giving this table to any one but my girls. As this is the most prominent, and some say the most attractive table of all—and they are the chief getters-up of the fair—it is thought best for them to take this place. I'm sorry, but I know you are too sincerely interested in the cause to mind a little personal disappointment, and you shall have another table if you like."

Mrs. Chester fancied beforehand that it would be easy to deliver this little speech; but when the time came, she found it rather difficult to utter it naturally, with Amy's unsuspicious eyes looking straight at her, full of surprise and trouble.

Amy felt that there was something behind this, but could not guess what, and said quietly—feeling hurt, and showing that she did,—

"Perhaps you had rather I took no table at all?"

"Now, my dear, don't have any ill feeling, I beg; it's merely a matter of expediency, you see; my girls will naturally take the lead, and this table is considered their proper place. *I* think it very appropriate to you, and feel very grateful for your efforts to make it so pretty; but we must give up our private wishes, of course, and I will see that you have a good place elsewhere. Wouldn't you like the flower-table? The little girls undertook it, but they are discouraged. You could make a charming thing of it, and the flower-table is always attractive, you know."

"Especially to gentlemen," added May, with a look which enlightened Amy as to one cause of her sudden fall from favor. She colored angrily, but took no other notice of that girlish sarcasm, and answered with unexpected amiability,—

"It shall be as you please, Mrs. Chester; I'll give up my place here at once, and attend to the flowers, if you like."

"You can put your own things on your own table, if you pre-fer," began May, feeling a little conscience-stricken, as she looked at the pretty racks, the painted shells, and quaint illumina-tions Amy had so carefully made and so gracefully arranged. She meant it kindly, but Amy mistook her meaning, and said quickly,—

"Oh, certainly, if they are in your way"; and sweeping her con-tributions into her apron, pell-mell, she walked off, feeling that herself and her works of art had been insulted past forgiveness.

"Now she's mad; Oh, dear, I wish I hadn't asked you to speak, mamma," said May, looking disconsolately at the empty spaces on her table.

"Girls' quarrels are soon over," returned her mother, feeling a trifle ashamed of her own part in this one, as well she might.

The little girls hailed Amy and her treasures with delight, which cordial reception somewhat soothed her perturbed spirit, and she fell to work, determined to succeed florally, if she could not artis-tically. But everything seemed against her; it was late, and she was tired; every one was too busy with their own affairs to help her, and the little girls were only hindrances, for the dears fussed and chattered like so many magpies, making a great deal of confusion in their artless efforts to preserve the most perfect order. The ever-green arch wouldn't stay firm after she got it up, but wiggled and threatened to tumble down on her head when the hanging bas-kets were filled; her best tile got a splash of water, which left a se-pia tear on the cupid's cheek; she bruised her hands with ham-mering, and got cold working in a draught, which last affliction filled her with apprehensions for the morrow. Any girl-reader who has suffered like afflictions, will sympathize with poor Amy, and wish her well through her task.[2]

There was great indignation at home when she told her story that evening. Her mother said it was a shame, but told her she had done right. Beth declared she wouldn't go to the old fair at all, and Jo demanded why she didn't take all her pretty things and leave those mean people to get on without her.

"Because they are mean is no reason why I should be. I hate such things; and though I think I've a right to be hurt, I don't in-

2. In June 1864, Mary Mann, widow of Horace Mann, with the assistance of her sister Sophia Hawthorne, held a fair in Concord in order to help their older sister Elizabeth Palmer Peabody raise money to construct an orphanage for black children in Washington, D.C. Mary Mann wrote to her son, Horace Mann, Jr., from Concord on June 19, 1864: "It was very pleasant and I think we shall have 300.00 clear of expenses . . . Abby [May Alcott] had the table in front of the platform for flowers and took 70 dollars. She had an arch over the table thus to which were suspended shell flower baskets and the hat birds perched all about, and the table was covered with vases of flow-ers and her pictures on shells and stones. They were very much ad-mired and she received innumerable orders for more. She had the old manse on one [Hawthorne's first home in Concord near the Old North Bridge], Mr. Emerson's arbor [constructed by Bronson Alcott and Thoreau] and other Concord scenes" (Manuscript Collection, Antioch College).

3. A type of parchment made from calves' or lambs' skins.

4. "Thou shalt not avenge, nor bear any grudge against the children of thy people, but thou shalt love thy neighbor as thyself: I am the Lord" (Leviticus 19:18).

tend to show it. They will feel that more than angry speeches or huffy actions, won't they, Marmee?"

"That's the right spirit, my dear; a kiss for a blow is always best, though it's not very easy to give it, sometimes," said her mother, with the air of one who had learned the difference between preaching and practising.

In spite of various very natural temptations to resent and retaliate, Amy adhered to her resolution all the next day, bent on conquering her enemy by kindness. She began well, thanks to a silent reminder that came to her unexpectedly, but most opportunely. As she arranged her table that morning, while the little girls were in an ante-room filling the baskets, she took up her pet production, a little book, the antique cover of which her father had found among his treasures, and in which, on leaves of vellum,[3] she had beautifully illuminated different texts. As she turned the pages, rich in dainty devices, with very pardonable pride, her eye fell upon one verse that made her stop and think. Framed in a brilliant scroll-work of scarlet, blue and gold, with little spirits of good-will helping one another up and down among the thorns and flowers, were the words, "Thou shalt love thy neighbor as thyself."[4]

"I ought, but I don't," thought Amy, as her eye went from the bright page to May's discontented face behind the big vases, that could not hide the vacancies her pretty work had once filled. Amy stood a minute, turning the leaves in her hand, reading on each some sweet rebuke for all heart-burnings and uncharitableness of spirit. Many wise and true sermons are preached us every day by unconscious ministers in street, school, office, or home; even a fair-table may become a pulpit, if it can offer the good and helpful words which are never out of season. Amy's conscience preached her a little sermon from that text, then and there; and she did what many of us don't always do—took the sermon to heart, and straightway put it in practice.

A group of girls were standing about May's table, admiring the pretty things, and talking over the change of saleswomen. They dropped their voices, but Amy knew they were speaking of her, hearing one side of the story, and judging accordingly. It was not pleasant, but a better spirit had come over her, and, presently, a chance offered for proving it. She heard May say, sorrow-fully,—

"It's too bad, for there is no time to make other things, and I don't want to fill up with odds and ends. The table was just complete then—now it's spoilt."

"I dare say she'd put them back if you asked her," suggested some one.

"How could I after all the fuss;" began May, but she did not finish, for Amy's voice came across the hall, saying pleasantly,—

"You may have them, and welcome, without asking, if you want them. I was just thinking I'd offer to put them back, for they belong to your table rather than mine. Here they are; please take them, and forgive me if I was hasty in carrying them away last night."

As she spoke, Amy returned her contribution with a nod and a smile, and hurried away again, feeling that it was easier to do a friendly thing than it was to stay and be thanked for it.

"Now, I call that lovely of her, don't you?" cried one girl.

May's answer was inaudible; but another young lady, whose temper was evidently a little soured by making lemonade, added, with a disagreeable laugh, "Very lovely; for she knew she wouldn't sell them at her own table."

Now that was hard; when we make little sacrifices we like to have them appreciated, at least; and for a minute Amy was sorry she had done it, feeling that virtue was not always its own reward. But it is,—as she presently discovered; for her spirits began to rise, and her table to blossom under her skilful hands; the girls were very kind, and that one little act seemed to have cleared the atmo-sphere amazingly.

It was a very long day, and a hard one to Amy, as she sat behind her table often quite alone, for the little girls deserted very soon; few cared to buy flowers in summer, and her bouquets began to droop long before night.

The Art table *was* the most attractive in the room; there was a crowd about it all day long, and the tenders were constantly flying to and fro with important faces and rattling money-boxes. Amy often looked wistfully across, longing to be there, where she felt at home and happy, instead of in a corner with nothing to do.

It might seem no hardship to some of us; but to a pretty, blithe young girl, it was not only tedious, but very trying; and the thought of being found there in the evening by her family, and Laurie and his friends, made it a real martyrdom.

She did not go home till night, and then she looked so pale and quiet that they knew the day had been a hard one, though she made no complaint, and did not even tell what she had done. Her mother gave her an extra cordial cup of tea, Beth helped her dress, and made a charming little wreath for her hair, while Jo astonished her family by getting herself up with unusual care, and hinting, darkly, that the tables were about to be turned.

"Don't do anything rude, pray, Jo; I won't have any fuss made, so let it all pass, and behave yourself," begged Amy, as she departed early, hoping to find a reinforcement of flowers to refresh her poor little table.

"I merely intend to make myself entrancingly agreeable to every one I know, and to keep them in your corner as long as possible. Teddy and his boys will lend a hand, and we'll have a good time yet," returned Jo, leaning over the gate to watch for Laurie. Presently the familiar tramp was heard in the dusk, and she ran out to meet him.

"Is that my boy?"

"As sure as this is my girl!" and Laurie tucked her hand under his arm with the air of a man whose every wish was gratified.

"Oh, Teddy, such doings!" and Jo told Amy's wrongs with sisterly zeal.

"A flock of our fellows are going to drive over by and by, and I'll be hanged if I don't make them buy every flower she's got, and camp down before her table afterward," said Laurie, espousing her cause with warmth.

"The flowers are not at all nice, Amy says, and the fresh ones may not arrive in time. I don't wish to be unjust or suspicious, but I shouldn't wonder if they never came at all. When people do one mean thing they are very likely to do another," observed Jo, in a disgusted tone.

"Didn't Hayes give you the best out of our gardens? I told him to."

"I didn't know that; he forgot, I suppose; and, as your grandpa was poorly, I didn't like to worry him by asking, though I did want some."

"Now, Jo, how could you think there was any need of asking! They are just as much yours as mine; don't we always go halves in everything?" began Laurie, in the tone that always made Jo turn thorny.

"Gracious! I hope not! half of some of your things wouldn't suit me at all. But we mustn't stand philandering here; I've got to help Amy, so you go and make yourself splendid; and if you'll be so very kind as to let Hayes take a few nice flowers up to the Hall, I'll bless you forever."

"Couldn't you do it now?" asked Laurie, so suggestively that Jo shut the gate in his face with inhospitable haste, and called through the bars, "Go away, Teddy; I'm busy."

Thanks to the conspirators, the tables *were* turned that night, for Hayes sent up a wilderness of flowers, with a lovely basket arranged in his best manner for a centre-piece; then the March family turned out *en masse,* and Jo exerted herself to some purpose, for people not only came, but stayed, laughing at her nonsense, admiring Amy's taste, and apparently enjoying themselves very much. Laurie and his friends gallantly threw themselves into the breach, bought up the bouquets, encamped before the table, and made that corner the liveliest spot in the room. Amy was in her element now, and, out of gratitude, if nothing more, was as sprightly and gracious as possible,—coming to the conclusion, about that time, that virtue *was* its own reward, after all.

Jo behaved herself with exemplary propriety; and when Amy was happily surrounded by her guard of honor, Jo circulated about the hall, picking up various bits of gossip, which enlightened her upon the subject of the Chester change of base. She reproached herself for her share of the ill-feeling, and resolved to exonerate Amy as soon as possible; she also discovered what Amy had done about the things in the morning, and considered her a model of magnanimity. As she passed the Art table, she glanced over it for her sister's things, but saw no signs of them. "Tucked away out of sight, I dare say," thought Jo, who could forgive her own wrongs, but hotly resented any insult offered her family.

"Good evening, Miss Jo; how does Amy get on?" asked May,

5. A united group, usually referring to military troops. LMA uses an extended military metaphor here as Jo instructs the boys to take "the field," charging together as a "phalanx," or infantry unit. Laurie and his male friends are coming to the aid of Amy, but they are also supporting a cause worth fighting for—the freedmen.

with a conciliatory air,—for she wanted to show that she also could be generous.

"She has sold everything she had that was worth selling, and now she is enjoying herself. The flower-table is always attractive, you know, 'especially to gentlemen.'"

Jo *couldn't* resist giving that little slap, but May took it so meekly she regretted it a minute after, and fell to praising the great vases, which still remained unsold.

"Is Amy's illumination anywhere about? I took a fancy to buy that for father;" said Jo, very anxious to learn the fate of her sister's work.

"Everything of Amy's sold long ago; I took care that the right people saw them, and they made a nice little sum of money for us," returned May, who had overcome sundry small temptations as well as Amy that day.

Much gratified, Jo rushed back to tell the good news; and Amy looked both touched and surprised by the report of May's words and manner.

"Now, gentlemen, I want you to go and do your duty by the other tables as generously as you have by mine—especially the Art-table," she said, ordering out "Teddy's Own," as the girls called the college friends.

"'Charge, Chester, charge!' is the motto for that table; but do your duty like men, and you'll get your money's worth of *art* in every sense of the word," said the irrepressible Jo, as the devoted phalanx[5] prepared to take the field.

"To hear is to obey, but March is fairer far than May," said little Parker, making a frantic effort to be both witty and tender, and getting promptly quenched by Laurie, who said: "Very well, my son, for a small boy!" and walked him off with a paternal pat on the head.

"Buy the vases," whispered Amy to Laurie, as a final heaping of coals of fire on her enemy's head.

To May's great delight, Mr. Laurence not only bought the vases, but pervaded the hall with one under each arm. The other gentlemen speculated with equal rashness in all sorts of frail trifles, and wandered helplessly about afterward, burdened with wax flowers,

LITTLE WOMEN

Amy's table at the fair. Frank Merrill, *Little Women: Illustrated* (1880).

painted fans, filagree portfolios,[6] and other useful and appropriate purchases.

Aunt Carrol was there, heard the story, looked pleased, and said something to Mrs. March in a corner, which made the latter lady beam with satisfaction, and watch Amy with a face full of mingled pride and anxiety, though she did not betray the cause of her pleasure till several days later.

The fair was pronounced a success; and when May bade Amy "good-night," she did not "gush," as usual, but gave her an affectionate kiss, and a look which said, "Forgive and forget." That satisfied Amy; and when she got home she found the vases paraded on the parlor chimney-piece,[7] with a great bouquet in each. "The reward of merit for a magnanimous March," as Laurie announced with a flourish.

"You've a deal more principle, and generosity, and nobleness of character than I ever gave you credit for, Amy. You've behaved sweetly, and I respect you with all my heart," said Jo, warmly, as they brushed their hair together late that night.

"Yes, we all do, and love her for being so ready to forgive. It

6. Portfolios decorated with a delicate jewel work crafted with thread and beads.

7. Mantlepiece.

8. LMA accompanied the invalid Anna Weld and her half brother George, the children of William Fletcher Weld, a Boston shipping merchant, to Europe. The journey lasted from July 19, 1865, to July 19, 1866, and LMA visited England, Germany, Belgium, France, and Switzerland.

9. Echoing this passage is an entry from LMA's journal. In November 1860, a family friend sent May $30 to study art in Boston with David Claypoole Johnston. LMA claimed that May "is one of the fortunate ones, and gets what she wants easily. I have to grub for my help, or go without it. Good for me, doubtless, or it would n't be so; so cheer up, Louisa, and grind away!" (*Journals* 100).

must have been dreadfully hard, after working so long, and setting your heart on selling your own pretty things. I don't believe I could have done it as kindly as you did," added Beth, from her pillow.

"Why, girls, you needn't praise me so; I only did as I'd be done by. You laugh at me when I say I want to be a lady, but I mean a true gentlewoman in mind and manners, and I try to do it as far as I know how. I can't explain exactly, but I want to be above the little meannesses, and follies, and faults that spoil so many women. I'm far from it now, but I do my best, and hope in time to be what mother is."

Amy spoke earnestly, and Jo said, with a cordial hug,—

"I understand now what you mean, and I'll never laugh at you again. You are getting on faster than you think, and I'll take lessons of you in true politeness, for you've learned the secret, I believe. Try away, deary, you'll get your reward some day, and no one will be more delighted than I shall."

A week later Amy did get her reward, and poor Jo found it hard to be delighted. A letter came from Aunt Carrol, and Mrs. March's face was illuminated to such a degree when she read it, that Jo and Beth, who were with her, demanded what the glad tidings were.

"Aunt Carrol is going abroad next month, and wants—"

"Me to go with her!" burst in Jo, flying out of her chair in an uncontrollable rapture.

"No, dear, not you, it's Amy."

"Oh, mother! she's too young; it's my turn first; I've wanted it so long—it would do me so much good, and be so altogether splendid—I *must* go."[8]

"I'm afraid it's impossible, Jo; aunt says Amy, decidedly, and it is not for us to dictate when she offers such a favor."

"It's always so; Amy has all the fun, and I have all the work. It isn't fair, oh, it isn't fair!" cried Jo, passionately.[9]

"I'm afraid it is partly your own fault, dear. When aunt spoke to me the other day, she regretted your blunt manners and too independent spirit; and here she writes as if quoting something you had said,—'I planned at first to ask Jo; but as "favors burden her," and she "hates French," I think I won't venture to invite her. Amy is more docile, will make a good companion for Flo, and receive gratefully any help the trip may give her.'"

"Oh, my tongue, my abominable tongue! why can't I learn to keep it quiet?" groaned Jo, remembering words which had been her undoing. When she had heard the explanation of the quoted phrases, Mrs. March said, sorrowfully,—

"I wish you could have gone, but there is no hope of it this time; so try to bear it cheerfully, and don't sadden Amy's pleasure by reproaches or regrets."

"I'll try," said Jo, winking hard,[10] as she knelt down to pick up the basket she had joyfully upset. "I'll take a leaf out of her book, and try not only to seem glad, but to be so, and not grudge her one minute of happiness; but it won't be easy, for it is a dreadful disappointment;" and poor Jo bedewed the little fat pincushion she held, with several very bitter tears.

"Jo, dear, I'm very selfish, but I couldn't spare you, and I'm glad you ain't going quite yet," whispered Beth, embracing her, basket and all, with such a clinging touch and loving face, that Jo felt comforted in spite of the sharp regret that made her want to box her own ears, and humbly beg Aunt Carrol to burden her with this favor, and see how gratefully she would bear it.

By the time Amy came in, Jo was able to take her part in the family jubilation; not quite as heartily as usual, perhaps, but without repinings at Amy's good fortune. The young lady herself received the news as tidings of great joy,[11] went about in a solemn sort of rapture, and began to sort her colors[12] and pack her pencils that evening, leaving such trifles as clothes, money, and passports[13] to those less absorbed in visions of art than herself.

"It isn't a mere pleasure trip to me, girls," she said impressively, as she scraped her best palette. "It will decide my career; for if I have any genius, I shall find it out in Rome, and will do something to prove it."

"Suppose you haven't?" said Jo, sewing away, with red eyes, at the new collars which were to be handed over to Amy.

"Then I shall come home and teach drawing for my living," replied the aspirant for fame, with philosophic composure; but she made a wry face at the prospect, and scratched away at her palette as if bent on vigorous measures before she gave up her hopes.

"No you won't; you hate hard work, and you'll marry some rich

10. Blinking her eyes to hold back her tears.

11. The phrase comes from the New Testament's nativity story, when an angel appeared to the shepherds in the fields: "And the angel said unto them, Fear not: for, behold, I bring you good tidings of great joy, which shall be to all people" (Luke 2:10).

12. Watercolors.

13. In the nineteenth century (indeed until 1941) it was not a statutory requirement that U.S. citizens have passports to travel to foreign countries, except briefly during the Civil War; however, some travelers procured them for the safety they afforded.

14. Lady Bountiful is a wealthy widow who is well liked for her charitable deeds and her skill as a healer in the comedy *The Beaux' Stratagem* (1707) by the Irish playwright George Farquhar (1677–1707). The name later came to mean a kind, generous woman.

15. LMA and May Alcott did indeed go to Rome together in November 1870 and stayed until March 15, 1871. Unfortunately, while there they learned of John Bridge Pratt's unexpected death on November 27. Soon thereafter, while still in Rome, LMA wrote *Little Men,* which she dedicated to her two nephews, John and Fred Pratt.

man, and come home to sit in the lap of luxury all your days," said Jo.

"Your predictions sometimes come to pass, but I don't believe that one will. I'm sure I wish it would, for if I can't be an artist myself, I should like to be able to help those who are," said Amy, smiling, as if the part of Lady Bountiful[14] would suit her better than that of a poor drawing teacher.

"Hum!" said Jo, with a sigh; "if you wish it you'll have it, for your wishes are always granted—mine never."

"Would you like to go?" asked Amy, thoughtfully flattening[a] her nose with her knife.

"Rather!"

"Well, in a year or two I'll send for you, and we'll dig in the Forum for relics, and carry out all the plans we've made so many times."[15]

"Thank you; I'll remind you of your promise when that joyful day comes, if it ever does," returned Jo, accepting the vague but magnificent offer as gratefully as she could.

There was not much time for preparation, and the house was in a ferment till Amy was off. Jo bore up very well till the last flutter of blue ribbon vanished, when she retired to her refuge, the garret, and cried till she couldn't cry any more. Amy likewise bore up stoutly till the steamer sailed; then, just as the gangway was about to be withdrawn, it suddenly came over her, that a whole ocean was soon to roll between her and those who loved her best, and she clung to Laurie, the last lingerer, saying with a sob,—

"Oh, take care of them for me; and if anything should happen—"

"I will, dear, I will; and if anything happens, I'll come and comfort you," whispered Laurie, little dreaming how soon he would be called upon[b] to keep his word.

So Amy sailed away to find the old world, which is always new and beautiful to young eyes, while her father and friend watched her from the shore, fervently hoping that none but gentle fortunes would befall the happy-hearted girl, who waved her hand to them till they could see nothing but the summer sunshine dazzling on the sea.

Chapter 8

Our Foreign Correspondent

"LONDON.[1]

DEAREST PEOPLE[2]

"Here I really sit at a front window of the Bath Hotel, Piccadilly.[3] It's not a fashionable place, but uncle stopped here years ago, and won't go anywhere else; however, we don't mean to stay long, so it's no great matter. Oh, I can't begin to tell you how I enjoy it all! I never can, so I'll only give you bits out of my note-book, for I've done nothing but sketch and scribble since I started.

"I sent a line from Halifax[4] when I felt pretty miserable, but after that I got on delightfully, seldom ill, on deck all day, with plenty of pleasant people to amuse me. Every one was very kind to me, especially the officers. Don't laugh, Jo, gentlemen really are very necessary aboard ship, to hold on to, or to wait upon one; and as they have nothing to do, it's a mercy to make them useful, otherwise they would smoke themselves to death, I'm afraid.

"Aunt and Flo were poorly all the way, and liked to be let alone, so when I had done what I could for them, I went and enjoyed myself. Such walks on deck, such sunsets, such splendid air and waves! It was almost as exciting as riding a fast horse, when we went rushing on so grandly. I wish Beth could have come, it would have done her so much good; as for Jo, she would have gone up and sat on the main-top jib, or whatever the high thing is called, made friends with the engineers, and tooted on the Captain's speaking trumpet,[5] she'd have been in such a state of rapture.

"It was all heavenly, but I was glad to see the Irish coast, and found it very lovely, so green and sunny, with brown cabins here and there, ruins on some of the hills, and gentlemen's country-

1. LMA traveled to Europe for the first time just prior to the writing of *Little Women*, accompanying Anna Weld, an invalid, and her half-brother George on an extended tour that lasted from July 19, 1865, to July 19, 1866. William Fletcher Weld, their father, was a wealthy Boston shipping merchant, whose fleet, known as the "Black Horse Flag," eventually comprised over sixty ships and steamers. With the Welds, LMA visited England, Germany, Belgium, Switzerland, and France. She arrived in Liverpool, England, on July 29, 1865, and spent the first four days of August in London: "Went to Parks, Westminster Abbey & some of the famous streets. I felt as if I'd got into a novel while going about in the places I'd read so much of" (*Journals* 141). Near the end of her trip, she would spend more time in London, from May 18 to July 7, 1866.

2. In the nineteenth century it was understood that letters—except those of an expressly private nature—would be read aloud or passed from one family member to another. LMA's own letters home were intended to be read by the entire family and close friends. On May 19, 1870, Ellen Emerson, the oldest child of Ralph Waldo Emerson, wrote her sister, Edith, that she and her mother, Lidian, "went in the carryall to see Mrs Alcott and hear the letters [sent by LMA and May from their trip abroad in 1870–1871]" (*The Letters of Ellen Tucker Emerson*, vol. 2, ed. Edith E. W. Gregg. [Kent, OH: Kent State University Press, 1982], p. 555).

3. Piccadilly, a major street in central London, runs from Hyde Park Corner in the west to Piccadilly Circus in the east. The Bath Hotel, probably named after the nearby Bath House, residence of Alexander Barring, Lord Ashburton, was located at 25 Arlington Street. According to her journals, LMA did not stay at the Bath Hotel while in London.

4. Halifax, Nova Scotia, a major Canadian seaport and often a stop on transatlantic shipping routes.

5. A megaphone.

Chap VII.
"Our Foreign Correspondent."

—

London Aug

Dearest People.

Here I sit at the front window
of the Bath Hotel Piccadilly. Its not a
fashionable place but Uncle stopped here
years ago & wont go any where else; however
we dont mean to stay here long so its no
great matter. Oh, if I could begin to tell
you how I enjoy it all! I never can, so
ill give you bits out of my journal, for
i've done nothing but stare, sketch &
scribble since I started.

I sent you a line from Halifax when
I felt pretty miserable, but after that
I got on delightfully, seldom ill, on deck
all day, with plenty of pleasant people to
amuse me. Every one was very kind, especially the gentlemen. Dont laugh, Jo,
I didn't flirt, & one really does need
gentlemen to hold on by, or to wait upon
one, & they have nothing else to do, so its
a mercy to make them useful, otherwise they
would smoke themselves to death.

Aunt & Flo were poorly all the way

LMA's manuscript for "Our Foreign Correspondent." Only two chapters of the manuscript of *Little Women* are known to exist. Both are slightly different from the final printed version.

seats in the valleys, with deer feeding in the parks. It was early in the morning, but I didn't regret getting up to see it, for the bay was full of little boats, the shore *so* picturesque, and a rosy sky over head; I never shall forget it.

"At Queenstown[6] one of my new acquaintances left us,—Mr. Lennox,—and when I said something about the Lakes of Killarney,[7] he sighed, and sung, with a look at me,—

> 'Oh, have you e'er heard of Kate Kearney,
> She lives on the banks of Killarney;
> From the glance of her eye,
> Shun danger and fly,
> For fatal's the glance of Kate Kearney.'[8]

Wasn't that nonsensical?

"We only stopped at Liverpool[9] a few hours. It's a dirty, noisy place, and I was glad to leave it. Uncle rushed out and bought a pair of dog-skin gloves,[10] some ugly, thick shoes, and an umbrella, and got shaved *à la* mutton-chop,[11] the first thing. Then he flattered himself that he looked like a true Briton; but the first time he had the mud cleaned off his shoes, the little boot-black knew that an American stood in them, and said, with a grin, 'There yer har, sir, I've give 'em the latest Yankee shine.' It amused uncle immensely. Oh, I *must* tell you what that absurd Lennox did! He got his friend Ward, who came on with us, to order a bouquet for me, and the first thing I saw in my room, was a lovely one, with 'Robert Lennox's compliments,' on the card. Wasn't that fun, girls? I like travelling.

"I never *shall* get to London if I don't hurry. The trip was like riding through a long picture-gallery, full of lovely landscapes. The farm-houses were my delight; with thatched roofs, ivy up to the eaves, latticed windows, and stout women with rosy children at the doors. The very cattle looked more tranquil than ours, as they stood knee-deep in clover, and the hens had a contented cluck, as if they never got nervous, like Yankee biddies.[12] Such perfect color I never saw—the grass so green, sky so blue, grain so yellow, woods so

May Alcott by Rose Peckham (1842–1822). Completed in Paris in 1877 by May's friend and former roommate, the portrait hangs today in Orchard House. May wrote to her mother that "'it is a likeness which I should wish to be remembered by; as it idealizes my bad points, and it rather exaggerates my good ones'" (quoted in Caroline Ticknor, *May Alcott: A Memoir* [Boston: Little, Brown, 1928], p. 178).

6. Cobh, Ireland, an important transatlantic port, located on the south coast of County Cork. It was renamed Queenstown in honor of Queen Victoria's 1849 visit to Ireland.

7. Located near the town of Killarney in County Kerry, Ireland, and surrounded by mountains, the three lakes include the largest one, Lough Leane (Irish for "Lake of Learning"), Muckross Lake (also called Middle Lake), and Upper Lake.

8. The ballad "Kate Kearney" was written by Sidney Owenson Morgan (1781?–1859). Lady Morgan, a successful and popular novelist, was well known for her novel *The Wild Irish Girl* (1806). The ballad's tune has been attributed to the composer Alexander Lee (1802–1851), but it is also said to be a traditional Irish tune. Mr. Lennox sings the first verse.

9. Liverpool, on the west coast of England, was a major seaport and industrial city. On her first voyage to Europe in July 1865, LMA arrived at the port and noted: "Rested & looked about a little & took a drive about the dirty city. I never saw so many beggars nor such desperate looking ones" (*Journals* 141).

10. Dog-skin gloves were made of dog skin, which was extremely flexible; however, the term was also used for a type of sheepskin leather.

11. Popular during the mid-nineteenth century, mutton-chops are sideburns that widen as they reach the lower jaw. Bronson Alcott, Henry David Thoreau, and Ralph Waldo Emerson all sported mutton-chops at some point in their lives.

12. Chickens.

13. Originally constructed around a Norman tower, Kenilworth Castle, in Warwickshire, England, was enlarged in the twelfth century by King John. After the success of Sir Walter Scott's novel *Kenilworth* (1821), the castle became a popular tourist stop.

14. What Flo mistakes for a gallows is the headframe or winding tower above a colliery or coal mine, used to convey workers up and down within a vertical main shaft. The Industrial Revolution of the mid-nineteenth century, which started in Britain, was dependent on coal to power steam engines.

15. "The Flirtations of Capt. Cavendish" appeared in the July 1865 edition of *London Society* (8.43:1–15), a British illustrated monthly. In the tale, Cavendish meets the two Brooks sisters, Americans traveling in Europe. He is attracted to Cotilda Brooks, whom he finds intelligent and worthy of being his wife. Throughout the tale, he consults Mr. Harmon, a baronet's son, over his choices for a bride. After meeting Maria Jane Bodger, daughter of Sir Bodger, a baronet, and heir to an immense fortune, Cavendish decides to propose to her. She refuses him, telling him that she has just been engaged to Mr. Harmon. Spurned, Cavendish proposes to Cotilda but discovers that she has just accepted Sir Bodger's proposal. LMA likely read this tale since she arrived in London in July 1865 with Anna Weld. The story of wanting to marry for wealth parallels Amy's desire.

16. Regent Street was designed by the British architect John Nash (1752–1835) after being commissioned by the Prince Regent (later to be King George IV) in 1811. The original purpose was to offer easy transportation from Carlton House, the prince's home, to Regent Park. Built between 1814 and 1825, it became one of London's most fashionable streets.

17. The Hansom cab (short for cabriolet), patented in York, England, by Joseph Hansom in 1834, was a low two-wheeled vehicle pulled by one horse. Designed to be fast, the vehicle held two people, with the driver seated outside on an elevated rear seat and the reins stretching over the top. A folding wooden door in the front, the "wooden apron" Amy refers to, kept the passengers dry and safe. A trap door in the roof allowed the passenger to communicate with and pay the driver. The cab soon became the choice vehicle for hire, and its use quickly spread across Europe.

18. Hyde Park, one of the large Royal Parks in London, comprises 350 acres. Henry VIII obtained the Manor of Hyde, part of the Westminster Abbey property, in 1536 and enclosed the land for private use as a deer park. In 1637, Charles I opened the park to the general public, and it soon became a popular gathering place.

dark—I was in a rapture all the way. So was Flo; and we kept bouncing from one side to the other, trying to see everything while we were whisking along at the rate of sixty miles an hour. Aunt was tired, and went to sleep, but uncle read his guide-book, and wouldn't be astonished at anything. This is the way we went on: Amy flying up,—'Oh, that must be Kenilworth,[13] that gray place among the trees!' Flo darting to my window,—'How sweet; we must go there some time, won't we, pa?' Uncle calmly admiring his boots,—'No my dear, not unless you want beer; that's a brewery.'

"A pause,—then Flo cried out, 'Bless me, there's a gallows and a man going up.' 'Where, where!' shrieks Amy, staring out at two tall posts with a cross-beam, and some dangling chains. 'A colliery,'[14] remarks uncle, with a twinkle of the eye. 'Here's a lovely flock of lambs all lying down,' says Amy. 'See, pa, aren't they pretty!' added Flo, sentimentally. 'Geese, young ladies,' returns uncle, in a tone that keeps us quiet till Flo settles down to enjoy 'The Flirtations of Capt. Cavendish,'[15] and I have the scenery all to myself.

"Of course it rained when we got to London, and there was nothing to be seen but fog and umbrellas. We rested, unpacked, and shopped a little between the showers. Aunt Mary got me some new things, for I came off in such a hurry I wasn't half ready. A sweet white hat and blue feather, a distracting muslin[a] to match, and the loveliest mantle you ever saw. Shopping in Regent Street[16] is perfectly splendid; things seem so cheap—nice ribbons only sixpence a yard. I laid in a stock, but shall get my gloves in Paris. Don't that sound sort of elegant and rich?

"Flo and I, for the fun of it, ordered a Hansom cab,[17] while aunt and uncle were out, and went for a drive, though we learned afterward that it wasn't the thing for young ladies to ride in them alone. It was so droll! for when we were shut in by the wooden apron, the man drove so fast that Flo was frightened, and told me to stop him. But he was up outside behind somewhere, and I couldn't get at him. He didn't hear me call, nor see me flap my parasol in front, and there we were, quite helpless, rattling away, and whirling around corners, at a break-neck pace. At last, in my despair, I saw a little door in the roof, and on poking it open, a red eye appeared, and a beery voice said,—

400

LITTLE WOMEN

"'Now then, mum?'

"I gave my order as soberly as I could, and slamming down the door, with a 'Aye, aye, mum,' the old thing made his horse walk,[b] as if going to a funeral. I poked again, and said, 'A little faster;' then off he went, helter-skelter, as before, and we resigned ourselves to our fate.

"To-day was fair, and we went to Hyde Park,[18] close by, for we are more aristocratic than we look. The Duke of Devonshire[19] lives near. I often see his footmen lounging at the back gate; and the Duke of Wellington's house[20] is not far off. Such sights as I saw, my dear! It was as good as Punch,[21] for there were fat dowagers,[22] rolling about in their red and yellow coaches, with gorgeous Jeameses[23] in silk stockings and velvet coats, up behind, and powdered coachmen in front. Smart maids, with the rosiest children I ever saw; handsome girls, looking half asleep; dandies, in queer English hats and lavender kids, lounging about, and tall soldiers, in short red jackets and muffin caps[24] stuck on one side, looking so funny, I longed to sketch them.

"Rotten Row means '*Route de Roi,*' or the king's way; but now it's more like a riding-school than anything else. The horses are splendid, and the men, especially the grooms, ride well, but the women are stiff, and bounce, which isn't according to our rules. I longed to show them a tearing American gallop, for they trotted solemnly up and down in their scant habits[25] and high hats, looking like the women in a toy Noah's Ark. Every one rides—old men, stout ladies, little children, and the young folks do a deal of flirting here; I saw a pair exchange rose-buds, for it's the thing to wear one in the button-hole, and I thought it rather a nice little idea.

"In the P.M. to Westminster Abbey;[26] but don't expect me to describe it, that's impossible—so I'll only say it was sublime! This evening we are going to see Fechter,[27] which will be an appropriate end to the happiest day of my life.

"*Midnight.*

"It's very late, but I can't let my letter go in the morning without telling you what happened last evening. Who do you think came in, as we were at tea? Laurie's English friends, Fred and

19. William Cavendish, the Seventh Duke of Devonshire (1808–1891), succeeded his cousin as duke in 1858 and resided at Devonshire House, located on Piccadilly Street between Berkeley Street and Stratton Street.

20. Arthur Richard Wellesley, the Second Duke of Wellington (1807–1884), was a soldier and politician before succeeding his father as duke in 1852 and entering the House of Lords. The duke resided at Apsley House, known as Number One, London, located at the southeastern corner of Hyde Park.

21. *Punch, or the London Charivari* was a popular nineteenth-century illustrated British weekly noted for its humor and satire.

22. Dignified elderly ladies.

23. Jeames, a humorous name for a liveried footman, derives from the main character in *The Diary of C. Jeames de la Pluche, Esq.* (1859) by William Makepiece Thackery (1811–1863).

24. A muffin cap is a loose-fitting hat, similar to a beret, but with a brim going all the way around the band.

25. British and European women usually rode sidesaddle when horseback riding. Riding habits of the 1860s generally consisted of a tailored coat or high buttoned-down bodice with a matching long full skirt. A starched petticoat under the skirt would make it appear fuller. Wool breeches were often worn under the petticoats. Top hats were formal riding wear, most often worn when hunting. Riding hats normally followed the fashion of the day and were often secured with ribbons that tied under ladies' chins. Because the skirt was long and full, it often got caught in one of the saddle horns, causing an accident. Such a hazard led to the introduction of the safety apron late in the nineteenth century. By calling the habits *scant,* Amy means that such full dresses were inadequate to the purpose of riding.

26. Westminster Abbey, officially known as the Collegiate Church of St. Peter at Westminster, was constructed between 1042 and 1052 on the old site of St. Peter's Abbey under the orders of King Edward the Confessor, the first of many royals to be interred there. Many of England's greatest writers are also buried or commemorated there (in Poets' Corner), including Jane Austen, Geoffrey Chaucer, William Shakespeare, and William Wordsworth. LMA visited Westminster Abbey in August 1865. LMA's beloved Charles Dickens would be buried there on June 14, 1870, two years after the publication of *Little Women.*

27. The British actor Charles Albert Fetcher (1824–1879) was known, first in France and then in England, for his portrayal of Shakespeare's Iago, Hamlet, and Othello. He first performed in America in 1870. LMA saw him act in *Camille* on December 9, 1875,

but was disappointed, as she wrote to her father: "This was in French & F. did the lover well but has grown fat & I never ca[re] to see him again" (*Selected Letters* 206).

28. Frank Vaughn, Fred's twin, befriended Beth in Part I's Chapter 12, "Camp Laurence." On crutches when the March sisters first met him, Frank had injured his leg while leaping a fence on his horse during a foxhunt.

29. Frank alludes to the large leghorn bonnet Jo wore to the Camp Laurence outing.

30. Lacking concentration; scattered.

31. Hampton Court, located in Richmond upon Thames, a neighborhood of London, was originally the residence of Cardinal Wolsey (1473–1530). Constructed around 1514, it was presented as a gift to Henry VIII (1491–1547) when Wolsey failed to secure an annulment for the king's marriage to Catherine of Aragon. Henry VIII enlarged it, as did William III (1650–1702). The last monarch to reside there was George II (1683–1760). The palace was restored and opened to the public in 1838 by Queen Victoria.

32. South Kensington Museum was opened by Queen Victoria in June 1857 and housed art works from the Royal Collection. The following year gas lights were installed and the museum also opened in the evenings. In 1899, its name changed to the Victoria and Albert Museum.

33. Pope Leo X commissioned the Italian Renaissance painter Raphael to complete ten cartoons (preparatory drawings), for tapestries to be hung in the Sistine Chapel. Of these cartoons, painted between 1515 and 1516, seven survive, depicting events in the life of Peter and Paul. The ten tapestries were hung in 1619. In 1623, the future Charles I bought the cartoons from an Italian collection. Sir Christopher Wren and William Talman designed a special gallery for the large cartoons in 1699.

34. J. M. W. Turner (1775–1851), British landscape painter (during the late 1870s, May Alcott would earn a reputation as an excellent copier of Turner; some of these copies are on display today at Orchard House); Sir Thomas Lawrence (1769–1830), British portrait painter and president of the Royal Academy; Sir Joshua Reynolds (1723–1792), British portrait painter and one of the founders and first president of the Royal Academy; William Hogarth (1697–1764), British painter, printmaker, and cartoonist.

Frank Vaughn! I was *so* surprised, for I shouldn't have known them, but for the cards. Both are tall fellows, with whiskers; Fred handsome in the English style, and Frank much better, for he only limps slightly, and uses no crutches.[28] They had heard from Laurie where we were to be, and came to ask us to their house, but uncle won't go, so we shall return the call, and see them as we can. They went to the theater with us, and we did have *such* a good time, for Frank devoted himself to Flo, and Fred and I talked over past, present, and future fun as if we had know each other all our days. Tell Beth Frank asked for her, and was sorry to hear of her ill health. Fred laughed when I spoke of Jo, and sent his 'respectful compliments to the big hat.'[29] Neither of them had forgotten Camp Laurence, or the fun we had there. What ages ago it seems, don't it?

"Aunt is tapping on the wall for the third time, so I *must* stop. I really feel like a dissipated[30] London fine lady, writing here so late, with my room full of pretty things, and my head a jumble of parks, theaters, new gowns and gallant creatures who say 'Ah,' and twirl their blond mustaches, with the true English lordliness. I long to see you all, and in spite of my nonsense am, as ever, your loving
AMY."

"PARIS.

"DEAR GIRLS:

"In my last I told you about our London visit,—how kind the Vaughns were, and what pleasant parties they made for us. I enjoyed the trips to Hampton Court[31] and the Kensington Museum,[32] more than anything else,—for at Hampton I saw Raphael's Cartoons,[33] and, at the Museum, rooms full of pictures by Turner, Lawrence, Reynolds, Hogarth,[34] and the other great creatures. The day in Richmond Park[35] was charming,—for we had a regular English picnic,—and I had more splendid oaks and groups of deer than I could copy; also heard a nightingale, and saw larks go up. We 'did' London to our hearts' content,—thanks to Fred and Frank,—and were sorry to go away; for, though English people are slow to take you in, when they once make up their minds to do it they cannot be outdone in hospitality,

LITTLE WOMEN

May Alcott's painting of Westminster Abbey, watercolor, 1879.

35. Richmond Park, once known as the Manor of Sheen during the reign of King Edward (1272–1307), is the largest Royal Park in London (today comprising 2,360 acres). Henry VII (1457–1509), formerly the Earl of Richmond, constructed Richmond Palace in the vicinity around 1501, giving the area its new name. In 1637, Charles I, whose court occupied Richmond Palace, enclosed the park for his herds of red and fallow deer, whose descendants still inhabit the park today. LMA noted seeing the deer at Richmond Park when she visited it in May 1866 (*Journals* 151).

36. The Louvre Museum, located on the right bank of the Seine River in Paris, opened to the public in 1793.

37. Napoleon Bonaparte (1769–1821), military general, became the leader of France in 1799. He assumed the title emperor of France in 1804 but abdicated in 1814. Amy refers to the Cradle of the King of Rome, which was made of wood, bronze, and silver, and presented to Napoleon and his wife by the city of Paris upon the birth of their son, Napoleon II, in 1811, who from birth assumed the title king of Rome. Marie Antoinette (1755–1793), queen consort of Louis XVI, was beheaded by guillotine in 1793. Charlemagne (742–814), king of the Franks from 768 and emperor of Rome from 800 until his death, expanded the Frankish empire throughout western and central Europe. St. Denis, third-century bishop of Paris, was martyred around 275 AD. The pontifical ring of St. Denis is gold with a large sapphire in the center surrounded by pearls and gems.

38. The gardens and buildings that surround the Palais-Royal (completed in 1639) opened to the public in 1784 as a shopping and entertainment center. It quickly became popular with the citizens and tourists as a marketplace.

39. Jewelry or trinkets.

40. Comprising approximately 2,090 acres, Bois de Boulogne, on the western edge of Paris, was formed from the "Boulogne Woods" and established as a park by Napoleon III in 1852.

41. Charles Louis Napoleon Bonaparte, Napoleon III, emperor of France (1808–1873). He was elected the first president of the French Second Republic in 1848. Near the end of his third year in office, he seized control of the government, and a year later, in 1852, he established the Second French Empire and declared himself emperor.

42. Empress Eugénie de Montijo (1826–1920), of Spanish nobility, married Napoleon III in 1853 (after he was rejected by two other royal princesses).

43. Napoleon Eugène Louis Jean Joseph, Napoleon IV, Prince Imperial (1856–1879), was the only child of Napoleon III and Empress Eugénie.

44. Riders on carriage horses who attend a royal carriage in the absence of a coachman.

I think. The Vaughns hope to meet us in Rome next winter, and I shall be dreadfully disappointed if they don't, for Grace and I are great friends, and the boys very nice fellows,—especially Fred.

"Well, we were hardly settled here when he turned up again, saying he had come for a holiday, and was going to Switzerland. Aunt looked sober at first, but he was so cool about it she couldn't say a word; and now we get on nicely, and are very glad he came, for he speaks French like a native, and I don't know what we should do without him. Uncle don't know ten words, and insists on talking English very loud, as if it would make people understand him. Aunt's pronunciation is old-fashioned, and Flo and I, though we flattered ourselves that we knew a good deal, find we don't, and are very grateful to have Fred do the 'parley-vooing' as uncle calls it.

"Such delightful times as we are having! sight-seeing from morning till night! stopping for nice lunches in the gay *cafés,* and meeting with all sorts of droll adventures. Rainy days I spend in the Louvre,[36] revelling in pictures. Jo would turn up her naughty nose at some of the finest, because she has no soul for art; but *I* have, and I'm cultivating eye and taste as fast as I can. She would like the relics of great people better, for I've seen her Napoleon's cocked hat and gray coat, his baby's cradle and his old toothbrush; also Marie Antoinette's little shoe, the ring of Saint Denis, Charlemagne's sword,[37] and many other interesting things. I'll talk for hours about them when I come, but haven't time to write.

"The Palais Royale[38] is a heavenly place,—so full of *bijouterie*[39] and lovely things that I'm nearly distracted because I can't buy them. Fred wanted to get me some, but of course I didn't allow it. Then the Bois[40] and Champs Elysées are *tres magnifique.* I've seen the imperial family several times,—the Emperor[41] an ugly, hard-looking man, the Empress[42] pale and pretty, but dressed in horrid taste, *I* thought,—purple dress, green hat, and yellow gloves. Little Nap.[43] is a handsome boy, who sits chatting to his tutor, and kisses his hand to the people as he passes in his four-horse barouche, with postilions[44] in red satin jackets, and a mounted guard before and behind.

"We often walk in the Tuileries gardens,[45] for they are lovely, though the antique Luxembourg gardens[46] suit me better. Pere la Chaise[47] is very curious,—for many of the tombs are like small rooms, and, looking in, one sees a table, with images or pictures of the dead, and chairs for the mourners to sit in when they come to lament. That is so Frenchy—*n'est ce pas?*[48]

"Our rooms are on the Rue de Rivoli,[49] and, sitting in the balcony, we look up and down the long, brilliant[50] street. It is so pleasant that we spend our evenings talking there,—when too tired with our day's work to go out. Fred is very entertaining, and is altogether the most agreeable young man I ever knew,—except Laurie,—whose manners are more charming. I wish Fred was dark, for I don't fancy light men;[51] however, the Vaughns are very rich, and come of an excellent family, so I won't find fault with their yellow hair, as my own is yellower.

"Next week we are off to Germany and Switzerland; and, as we shall travel fast, I shall only be able to give you hasty letters. I keep my diary, and try to 'remember correctly and describe clearly all that I see and admire,' as father advised. It is good practice for me, and, with my sketch-book, will give you a better idea of my tour than these scribbles.

"Adieu; I embrace you tenderly.

"Votre Amie."[52]

"HEIDELBERG.

"MY DEAR MAMMA:

"Having a quiet hour before we leave for Berne,[53] I'll try to tell you what has happened, for some of it is very important, as you will see.

"The sail up the Rhine[54] was perfect, and I just sat and enjoyed it with all my might. Get father's old guide-books, and read about it; I haven't words beautiful enough to describe it. At Coblenz[55] we had a lovely time, for some students from Bonn, with whom Fred got acquainted on the boat, gave us a serenade. It was a moonlight night, and, about one o'clock, Flo and I were waked by the most delicious music under our windows. We flew up, and hid behind the curtains; but sly peeps showed us Fred and the stu-

45. Established in 1564 by Catherine de Medicis (1519–1589), wife of King Henry II of France, as the gardens of Tuileries Palace, the gardens, located between the Louvre and the Place de Concorde, were opened to the public in 1667.

46. Luxembourg Gardens, well known for their statuary, were the gardens of the French Senate, which was housed in Luxembourg Palace.

47. Established by Napoleon in 1805, Pére la Chaise, noted for its landscaping, is the largest cemetery in Paris and the burial place of numerous notable people.

48. French for "Isn't it?"

49. Constructed between 1802 and 1865, the Rue de Rivoli passes the Louvre and the Tuileries gardens; under the arcades on the north side of the street are cafés and numerous fashionable commercial shops.

50. Amy describes the street as *brilliant* because of the shiny, glittering gaslights of the street and buildings at night.

51. Here LMA gives the first hint that Amy will find love elsewhere. In Part I, Chapter 3, "The Laurence Boy," Jo describes Laurie, whose mother was Italian, as having "[c]urly black hair, brown skin, big black eyes."

52. French for "Your Amy" or "Your Friend."

53. Bern ("Berne" in French) is located just west of central Switzerland and has, since 1848, served as the seat of the Swiss government.

54. The Rhine River, 766 miles in length, begins in the eastern Swiss Alps and flows to the North Sea coast in the Netherlands.

55. Koblenz, located on both banks of the Rhine at the confluence of the Moselle River, became a part of France in 1801, but then a Prussian city by the act of the Congress of Vienna in 1815. In August 1865, LMA wrote: "On the 12th began a lovely voyage up the Rhine. It was too beautiful to describe so I shall not try, but I feel richer & better for that memorable day. We reached Coblentz at sunset & I was up half the night enjoying the splendid view of the fortress opposite the town, the moonlight river with its bridge of boats & troops crossing at midnight" (*Journals* 142).

56. High on the east bank of the Rhine, Ehrenbreitstein Fortress was built by Prussia from 1817 to 1832.

57. Located in the Rhineland, Nassau, noted for its medicinal hot springs, lies in the Lahn River Valley of Germany.

58. Baden-Baden, Germany, is situated on the bank of the Oos River in the western foothills of the Black Forest. Noted for its hot springs (*baden* is German for *bath*), the town, which also had a casino, was at the height of its popularity during the middle of the nineteenth century. LMA visited Baden-Baden in October 1865, calling it "a very fashionable place" (*Journals* 143).

59. Amy alludes to Fred's gambling at the casino.

60. In September 1865, LMA visited Frankfurt: "Here I saw & enjoyed a good deal. The statues of Goethe, Schiller, Faust, Gutenburg & Schaeffer in the Squares. Goethe's house, a tall plain building with each story projecting over the lower & a Dutch roof. A marble slab over the front door recording the date of Goethe's birth. I took a look at it & wanted to go in as it was empty, but there was no time" (*Journals* 143).

dents singing away down below. It was the most romantic thing I ever saw; the river, the bridge of boats, the great fortress[56] opposite, moonlight everywhere, and music fit to melt a heart of stone.

"When they were done we threw down some flowers, and saw them scramble for them, kiss their hands to the invisible ladies, and go laughing away,—to smoke, and drink beer, I suppose. Next morning Fred showed me one of the crumpled flowers in his vest pocket, and looked very sentimental. I laughed at him, and said I didn't throw it, but Flo,—which seemed to disgust him, for he tossed it out of the window, and turned sensible again. I'm afraid I'm going to have trouble with that boy,—it begins to look like it.

"The baths at Nassau[57] were very gay, so was Baden-Baden,[58] where Fred lost some money,[59] and I scolded him. He needs some one to look after him when Frank is not with him. Kate said once she hoped he'd marry soon, and I quite agree with her that it would be well for him. Frankfurt was delightful; I saw Goethe's house, Schiller's statue, and Dannecker's famous 'Ariadne.'[60] It was very lovely, but I should have enjoyed it more if I had known the story better. I didn't like to ask, as every one knew it, or pretended they did. I wish Jo would tell me all about it; I ought to have read more, for I find I don't know anything, and it mortifies me.

"Now comes the serious part,—for it happened here, and Fred is just gone. He has been so kind and jolly that we all got quite fond of him; I never thought of anything but a travelling friendship, till the serenade night. Since then I've begun to feel that the moonlight walks, balcony talks, and daily adventures were something more to him than fun. I haven't flirted, mother, truly,—but remembered what you said to me, and have done my very best. I can't help it if people like me; I don't try to make them, and it worries me if I don't care for them, though Jo says I haven't got any heart. Now I know mother will shake her head, and the girls say, 'Oh, the mercenary little wretch!' but I've made up my mind, and if Fred asks me, I shall accept him, though I'm not madly in love. I like him, and we get on comfortably together. He is handsome, young, clever enough, and very rich,—ever so much richer than the Laurences. I don't think his family would object, and I should be very happy, for they are all kind, well-bred, generous people, and they like me. Fred, as the eldest twin, will have the estate, I suppose,—and such a splendid one as it is! A city house, in a fashionable street,—not so showy as our big houses, but twice as comfortable, and full of solid luxury, such as English people believe in. I like it, for it's genuine; I've seen the plate,[61] the family jewels, the old servants, and pictures of the country place with its park, great house, lovely grounds, and fine horses. Oh, it would be all I should ask! and I'd rather have it than any title such as girls snap up so readily, and find nothing behind. I may be mercenary, but I hate poverty, and don't mean to bear it a minute longer than I can help. One of us *must* marry well; Meg didn't, Jo won't, Beth can't, yet,—so I shall, and make everything cosy all round. I wouldn't marry a man I hated or despised. You may be sure of that; and, though Fred is not my model hero, he does very well, and, in time, I should get fond enough of him if he was very fond of me, and let me do just as I liked. So I've been turning the matter over in my mind the last week,—for it was impossible to help seeing that Fred liked me. He said nothing, but little things showed it; he never goes with Flo, always gets on my side of the carriage, table, or promenade, looks sentimental when we are alone, and frowns at any one else who ventures to speak to me. Yesterday, at dinner, when an Austrian officer stared at us, and then said something to his friend,—a rakish-looking Baron,— about *'ein wonderschönes Blöndchen,*[62] Fred looked as fierce as a lion, and cut his meat so savagely, it nearly flew off his plate. He isn't one of the cool, stiff Englishmen, but is rather peppery, for he has Scotch blood in him, as one might guess from his bonnie blue eyes.

"Well, last evening we went up to the castle[63] about sunset,—at least all of us but Fred, who was to meet us there after going to the Poste Restante[64] for letters. We had a charming time poking about the ruins, the vaults where the monster tun is, and the beautiful gardens made by the Elector, long ago, for his English wife.[65] I liked the great terrace best, for the view was divine; so, while the rest went to see the rooms inside, I sat there trying to sketch the gray-stone lion's head on the wall, with scarlet woodbine sprays

61. Gold or silver vessels.

62. German for "a pretty little blonde thing."

63. Located on a hillside above the town, the Heidelberg Castle is one of the most prominent European ruins. The French count Charles de Graimberg (1774–1864) lived at the castle for a time during the first two decades of the nineteenth century, protecting it from vandals and looters; he did much to promote the castle to tourists and to convince the town to preserve the ruins.

64. Poste Restante (French for *post remaining*) is a service whereby one's mail is held at a post office until the recipient asks for it. In the United States, it is called general delivery.

65. Frederick V, Elector Palatine (1596–1632) from 1610 to 1623, married the eldest daughter of James I of England, Elizabeth Stuart (1596–1662), in 1613, and they resided at Heidelberg Castle. The elector commissioned the French engineer Salomon de Caus (1576–1626) to design the Hortus Palatinus (Garden of the Palatinate), often called the eighth wonder of the world because large terraces had to be constructed and leveled on the steep hillside. The tun, a large wine vat, was constructed of wood in 1751 and could hold 58,100 gallons.

66. The Neckar River, a tributary of the Rhine, begins in the Black Forest and flows into the Rhine 228 miles later at Mannheim, Germany.

67. LMA accompanied Anna Weld to Heidelberg in October 1865, calling it "a charming place surrounded by Mts. We went to the Castle & had a fine time roving about the ruins, looking at the view from the great terrace, admiring the quaint stone images of knights, saints, monsters & angels, & visiting the big tun in the cellar by torchlight. The moon rose while we were there & completed the enchantment of the scene" (*Journals* 143).

68. Flushed with a red color and shaky.

69. To declare his love for her and propose marriage.

hanging round it. I felt as if I'd got into a romance, sitting there watching the Neckar[66] rolling through the valley, listening to the music of the Austrian band below, and waiting for my lover,—like a real story-book girl.[67] I had a feeling that something was going to happen, and I was ready for it. I didn't feel blushy or quakey,[68] but quite cool, and only a little excited.

"By and by I heard Fred's voice, and then he came hurrying through the great arch to find me. He looked so troubled that I forgot all about myself, and asked what the matter was. He said he'd just got a letter begging him to come home, for Frank was very ill; so he was going at once, in the night train, and only had time to say 'good-by.' I was very sorry for him, and disappointed for myself,—but only for a minute,—because he said, as he shook hands,—and said it in a way that I could not mistake,—'I shall soon come back,—you won't forget me, Amy?'

"I didn't promise, but I looked at him and he seemed satisfied, —and there was no time for anything but messages and goodbyes, for he was off in an hour, and we all miss him very much. I know he wanted to speak,[69] but I think, from something he once hinted, that he had promised his father not to do anything of the sort yet awhile,—for he is a rash boy, and the old gentleman dreads a foreign daughter-in-law. We shall soon meet in Rome; and then, if I don't change my mind, I'll say 'Yes, thank you,' when he says, 'Will you, please?'

"Of course this is all *very private,* but I wished you to know what was going on. Don't be anxious about me; remember I am your 'prudent Amy,' and be sure I will do nothing rashly. Send me as much advice as you like; I'll use it if I can. I wish I could see you for a good talk, Marmee. Love and trust me.

Ever your   AMY."

LITTLE WOMEN

Chapter 9

Tender Troubles

J O, I'M ANXIOUS about Beth."

"Why, mother, she has seemed unusually well since the babies came."

"It's not her health that troubles me now; it's her spirits. I'm sure there is something on her mind, and I want you to discover what it is."

"What makes you think so, mother?"

"She sits alone a good deal, and doesn't talk to her father as much as she used. I found her crying over the babies the other day. When she sings, the songs are always sad ones, and now and then I see a look in her face that I don't understand. This isn't like Beth, and it worries me."

"Have you asked her about it?"

"I have tried once or twice; but she either evaded my questions, or looked so distressed, that I stopped. I never force my children's confidence, and I seldom have to wait for it long."

Mrs. March glanced at Jo as she spoke, but the face opposite seemed quite unconscious of any secret disquietude[1] but Beth's; and, after sewing thoughtfully for a minute, Jo said,—

"I think she is growing up, and so begins to dream dreams, and have hopes, and fears, and fidgets, without knowing why, or being able to explain them. Why, mother, Beth's eighteen; but we don't realize it, and treat her like a child, forgetting she's a woman."

"So she is; dear heart, how fast you do grow up," returned her mother, with a sigh and a smile.

"Can't be helped, Marmee; so you must resign yourself to all sorts of worries, and let your birds hop out of the nest, one by one. I promise never to hop very far, if that is any comfort to you."

"It is a great comfort, Jo; I always feel strong when you are at home, now Meg is gone. Beth is too feeble, and Amy too young to depend upon; but when the tug comes, you are always ready."

"Why, you know I don't mind hard jobs much, and there must always be one scrub in a family. Amy is splendid in fine works, and I'm not; but I feel in my element when all the carpets are to be taken up, or half the family fall sick at once. Amy is distinguishing herself abroad; but if anything is amiss at home, I'm your man."

"I leave Beth to your hands then, for she will open her tender little heart to her Jo sooner than to any one else. Be very kind, and don't let her think any one watches or talks about her. If she only would get quite strong and cheerful again, I shouldn't have a wish in the world."

"Happy woman! I've got heaps."

"My dear, what are they?"

"I'll settle Bethy's troubles, and then I'll tell you mine. They are not very wearing, so they'll keep;" and Jo stitched away with a wise nod, which set her mother's heart at rest about her, for the present at least.

While apparently absorbed in her own affairs, Jo watched Beth; and, after many conflicting conjectures, finally settled upon one which seemed to explain the change in her. A slight incident gave Jo the clue to the mystery, she thought, and lively fancy, loving heart did the rest. She was affecting to write busily one Saturday afternoon, when she and Beth were alone together; yet, as she scribbled, she kept her eye on her sister, who seemed unusually quiet. Sitting at the window, Beth's work often dropped into her lap, and she leaned her head upon her hand, in a dejected attitude, while her eyes rested on the dull, autumnal landscape. Suddenly some one passed below, whistling like an operatic blackbird, and a voice called out,—

"All serene! Coming in to-night."

Beth started, leaned forward, smiled and nodded, watched the passer-by till his quick tramp died away, then said softly, as if to herself,—

"How strong, and well, and happy that dear boy looks."

"Hum!" said Jo, still intent upon her sister's face; for the bright color faded as quickly as it came, the smile vanished, and presently a tear lay shining on the window-ledge. Beth whisked it off, and glanced apprehensively at Jo; but she was scratching away at a tremendous rate, apparently engrossed in "Olympia's Oath."[2] The instant Beth turned, Jo began her watch again, saw Beth's hand go quietly to her eyes more than once, and, in her half-averted face, read a tender sorrow that made her own eyes fill. Fearing to betray herself, she slipped away, murmuring something about needing more paper.

"Mercy on me, Beth loves Laurie!" she said, sitting down in her own room, pale with the shock of the discovery which she believed she had just made.[3] "I never dreamt of such a thing! What *will* mother say? I wonder if he—" there Jo stopped, and turned scarlet with a sudden thought. "If he shouldn't love back again, how dreadful it would be. He must; I'll make him!" and she shook her head threateningly at the picture of the mischievous looking boy laughing at her from the wall. "Oh dear, we *are* growing up with a vengeance. Here's Meg married, and a ma, Amy flourishing away at Paris, and Beth in love. I'm the only one that has sense enough to keep out of mischief." Jo thought intently for a minute, with her eyes fixed on the picture; then she smoothed out her wrinkled forehead, and said, with a decided nod at the face opposite,—"No, thank you sir! you're very charming, but you've no more stability than a weather-cock; so you needn't write touching notes, and smile in that insinuating way, for it won't do a bit of good, and I won't have it."

Then she sighed, and fell into a reverie, from which she did not wake till the early twilight sent her down to take new observations, which only confirmed her suspicion. Though Laurie flirted with Amy, and joked with Jo, his manner to Beth had always been peculiarly kind and gentle, but so was everybody's; therefore, no one thought of imagining that he cared more for her than for the others. Indeed, a general impression had prevailed in the family,

2. In her "Notes and Memoranda" for 1859, LMA writes that she received $10 for "Ottilla's Oath" (*Journals* 96). Possibly written for the *American Union,* the story has not come to light because a full run of the newspaper has not been located.

3. As Jo will later discover, she is not yet such an astute reader of other people as she fancies herself.

4. Flirting.

5. Here LMA indirectly reports Jo's thoughts. Either unable or unwilling to recognize the true object of Laurie's "one all-absorbing passion," Jo can nonetheless put her finger on exactly the right literary diagnosis for her friend's condition: he is Byronic. The Byronic hero is a character type named after the British Romantic poet Lord Byron (1788–1824) and exemplified by the poet's life and work. In a book review of 1831, Lord Macaulay memorably describes the charming but flawed Byronic hero as "'a man proud, moody, cynical, with defiance on his brow, and misery in his heart, a scorner of his kind, implacable in revenge, yet capable of deep and strong affection'" (quoted in Rupert Christiansen, *Romantic Affinities: Portraits from an Age, 1780–1830* [New York: Putnam, 1988], p. 201).

6. The *OED* defines *dig* as American slang that means "to study hard and closely." Chapter 12 in Part II of *Little Women* is given as an example of usage.

of late, that "our boy" was getting fonder than ever of Jo, who, however, wouldn't hear a word upon the subject, and scolded violently if any one dared to suggest it. If they had known the various tender passages of the past year, or rather attempts at tender passages, which had been nipped in the bud, they would have had the immense satisfaction of saying, "I told you so." But Jo hated "philandering,"[4] and wouldn't allow it, always having a joke or a frown[a] ready at the least sign of impending danger.

When Laurie first went to college, he fell in love about once a month; but these small flames were as brief as ardent, did no damage, and much amused Jo, who took great interest in the alternations of hope, despair, and resignation, which were confided to her in their weekly conferences. But there came a time when Laurie ceased to worship at many shrines, hinted darkly at one all-absorbing passion, and indulged occasionally in Byronic fits of gloom.[5] Then he avoided the tender subject altogether, wrote philosophical notes to Jo, turned studious, and gave out that he was going to "dig,"[6] intending to graduate in a blaze of glory. This suited the young lady better than twilight confidences, tender pressures of the hand, and eloquent glances of the eye; for with Jo, brain developed earlier than heart, and she preferred imaginary heroes to real ones, because, when tired of them, the former could be shut up in the tin-kitchen till called for, and the latter were less manageable.

Things were in this state when the grand discovery was made, and Jo watched Laurie that night as she had never done before. If she had not got the new idea into her head, she would have seen nothing unusual in the fact, that Beth was very quiet, and Laurie very kind to her. But having given the rein to her lively fancy, it galloped away with her at a great pace; and common sense, being rather weakened by a long course of romance writing, did not come to the rescue. As usual, Beth lay on the sofa, and Laurie sat in a low chair close by, amusing her with all sorts of gossip; for she depended on her weekly "spin," and he never disappointed her. But that evening, Jo fancied that Beth's eyes rested on the lively, dark face beside her with peculiar pleasure, and that she listened with intense interest to an account of some exciting cricket match,

Jo's "mood" pillow. Barbara Cooney, *Little Women* (1955).

though the phrases, "caught off a tice," "stumped off his ground," and "the leg hit for three,"[7] were as intelligible to her as Sanscrit.[8] She also fancied, having set her heart upon seeing it, that she saw a certain increase of gentleness in Laurie's manner, that he dropped his voice now and then, laughed less than usual, was a little absent-minded, and settled the afghan over Beth's feet with an assiduity[9] that was really almost tender.

"Who knows! stranger things have happened," thought Jo, as she fussed about the room. "She will make quite an angel of him, and he will make life delightfully easy and pleasant for the dear, if they only love each other. I don't see how he can help it; and I do believe he would if the rest of us were out of the way."

As every one *was* out of the way but herself, Jo began to feel that she ought to dispose of herself with all speed. But where should she go? and burning to lay herself upon the shrine of sisterly devotion, she sat down to settle that point.

7. In *Sketches from Concord and Appleton* (1895), Frank Preston Stearns, a student at Frank Sanborn's academy in Concord during the 1860s, writes: "I remember meeting [Louisa] at the Radical club in Boston in January 1868, and her drawing me into a corner where she told me that she was writing a book for young people and would like to know about the game of cricket" (quoted in *Her Own Time* 86). A *tice* is an older name for a yorker, a fast ball that is thrown at the feet of the batter. Laurie means that the ball was caught after it was hit by the batter following this type of delivery. "Stumped off his ground" is an out made by the wicket-keeper, or catcher, who has caught the batter out of his ground (which is similar to a batter's box in baseball) in an attempt to hit the ball. The batter can hit the ball close to his leg. Such a hit is called a leg hit. "The leg hit for three" refers to a hit close to the batter's leg that results in three runs.

8. The oldest Indo-European language, Sanskrit is considered the sacred language of India.

9. Close attention.

10. LMA's "mood" pillow is displayed on the parlor couch at Orchard House today. Approximately twenty inches long, the oval pillow was originally covered in crimson but was recovered in 1975 in a rust-colored velvet. When the pillow was placed flat on the couch, LMA was in no mood to entertain company or family.

11. Laurie means that he has enough to be satisfied.

12. Indulging.

Now the old sofa was a regular patriarch of a sofa—long, broad, well-cushioned and low. A trifle shabby, as well it might be, for the girls had slept and sprawled on it as babies, fished over the back, rode on the arms, and had menageries under it as children, and rested tired heads, dreamed dreams, and listened to tender talk on it as young women. They all loved it, for it was a family refuge, and one corner had always been Jo's favorite lounging place. Among the many pillows that adorned the venerable couch was one, hard, round, covered with prickly horse-hair, and furnished with a knobby button at each end; this repulsive pillow was her especial property, being used as a weapon of defence, a barricade, or a stern preventive of too much slumber.[10]

Laurie knew this pillow well, and had cause to regard it with deep aversion; having been unmercifully pummelled with it in former days, when romping was allowed, and now frequently debarred by it from taking the seat he most coveted, next to Jo in the sofa corner. If "the sausage," as they called it, stood on end, it was a sign that he might approach and repose; but if it laid flat across the sofa, woe to the man, woman or child who dared disturb it. That evening Jo forgot to barricade her corner, and had not been in her seat five minutes, before a massive form appeared beside her, and with both arms spread over the sofa-back, both long legs stretched out before him, Laurie exclaimed with a sigh of satisfaction,—

"Now *this* is filling at the price!"[11]

"No slang," snapped Jo, slamming down the pillow. But it was too late—there was no room for it; and coasting on to the floor, it disappeared in a most mysterious manner.

"Come, Jo, don't be thorny. After studying himself to a skeleton all the week, a fellow deserves petting,[12] and ought to get it."

"Beth will pet you, I'm busy."

"No, she's not to be bothered with me; but you like that sort of thing, unless you've suddenly lost your taste for it. Have you? Do you hate your boy, and want to fire pillows at him?"

Anything more wheedlesome than that touching appeal was seldom seen,[b] but Jo quenched "her boy" by turning on him with the stern query,—

"How many bouquets have you sent Miss Randal this week?"

Parlor of Orchard House today, with the dining room in the background. LMA's "mood pillow" is on the couch.

"Not one, upon my word! She's engaged. Now then."

"I'm glad of it; that's one of your foolish extravagances, sending flowers and things to girls, for whom you don't care two pins," continued Jo, reprovingly.

"Sensible girls, for whom I do care whole papers of pins,[13] won't let me send them 'flowers and things,' so what can I do? my feelings must have a *went*."[14]

"Mother doesn't approve of flirting, even in fun; and you do flirt desperately, Teddy."

"I'd give anything if I could answer, 'So do you.' As I can't, I'll merely say that I don't see any harm in that pleasant little game, if all parties understand that it's only play."

"Well, it does look pleasant, but I can't learn how it's done. I've tried, because one feels awkward in company, not to do as everybody else is doing; but I don't seem to get on," said Jo, forgetting to play Mentor.

13. Straight pins used for sewing were sold stuck in rows on paper.

14. Laurie imitates Sam Weller in *Pickwick Papers,* who confuses his *v*'s and *w*'s. LMA often used Wellerisms in her own personal writing. For example, in February 1866, she noted: "Wrote a little on three stories which would come into my head & worry me till I gave them a 'went'" (*Journals* 150).

15. On August 23, 1863, May Alcott, after noting LMA's literary talent, confessed in her journal: "I wish *I* had any real talent for anything but flirting, it certainly is an art in its way & as I never am wicked & malicious about it I have no prickings of conscience after an interesting season of this harmless occupation" (Manuscript journal, Houghton Library, Harvard University bMS Am 1817 [57]).

16. Laurie quotes from the last stanza of the nursery rhyme "Little Jenny Wren"; however, he is incorrect about Cock Robin. In the four-stanza poem, it is Robin Redbreast who helps cure Jenny Wren. She promises to be his afterward, but once well she disavows her love:

> Robin being angry,
> Hoped upon a twig,
> Saying, "Out upon you!
> Fie upon you! Bold-faced jig!"

This rhyme is a short and different version of the eleven-stanza poem "The Happy Courtship, Merry Marriage and Pic-nic Dinner, of Cock Robin and Jenny Wren. To which is added, Alas! The Doleful Death of the Bridegroom," published by John Harris, the British publisher, in 1806. LMA perhaps confused the two poems.

17. A man who, because of his wealth and social standing, would make a good husband.

18. One who is conceited and foolish.

"Take lessons of Amy; she has a regular talent for it."[15]

"Yes, she does it very prettily, and never seems to go too far. I suppose it's natural to some people to please without trying, and others to always say and do the wrong thing in the wrong place."

"I'm glad you can't flirt; it's really refreshing to see a sensible, straightforward girl, who can be jolly and kind without making a fool of herself. Between ourselves, Jo, some of the girls I know really do go on at such a rate I'm ashamed of them. They don't mean any harm, I'm sure; but if they knew how we fellows talked about them afterward, they'd mend their ways, I fancy."

"They do the same; and, as their tongues are the sharpest, you fellows get the worst of it, for you are as silly as they, every bit. If you behaved properly, they would; but, knowing you like their nonsense, they keep it up, and then you blame them."

"Much you know about it, ma'am!" said Laurie, in a superior tone. "We don't like romps and flirts, though we may act as if we did sometimes. The pretty, modest girls are never talked about, except respectfully, among gentlemen. Bless your innocent soul, if you could be in my place for a month you'd see things that would astonish you a trifle. Upon my word, when I see one of those harem-scarem girls, I always want to say with our friend Cock Robin,—

> "'Out upon you, fie upon you,
> Bold-faced jig!'"[16]

It was impossible to help laughing at the funny conflict between Laurie's chivalrous reluctance to speak ill of womankind, and his very natural dislike of the unfeminine folly of which fashionable society showed him many samples. Jo knew that "young Laurence" was regarded as a most eligible *parti*[17] by worldly mammas, was much smiled upon by their daughters, and flattered enough by ladies of all ages to make a cockscomb[18] of him; so she watched him rather jealously, fearing he would be spoilt, and rejoiced more than she confessed to find that he still believed in modest girls. Returning suddenly to her admonitory tone, she said, dropping her voice, "If you *must* have a 'went,' Teddy, go and devote yourself to one of the 'pretty modest girls' whom you do respect, and not waste your time with the silly ones."

"You really advise it?" and Laurie looked at her with an odd mixture of anxiety and merriment in his face.

"Yes, I do; but you'd better wait till you are through college, on the whole, and be fitting yourself for the place meantime. You're not half good enough for—well, whoever the modest girl may be;" and Jo looked a little queer likewise, for a name had almost escaped her.

"That I'm not!" acquiesced Laurie, with an expression of humility quite new to him, as he dropped his eyes, and absently wound Jo's apron tassel round his finger.

"Mercy on us, this will never do," thought Jo; adding aloud, "Go and sing to me. I'm dying for some music, and always like yours."

"I'd rather stay here, thank you."

"Well, you can't; there isn't room. Go and make yourself useful, since you are too big to be ornamental. I thought you hated to be tied to a woman's apron-string," retorted Jo, quoting certain rebellious words of his own.

"Ah, that depends on who wears the apron!" and Laurie gave an audacious tweak at the tassel.

"Are you going?" demanded Jo, diving for the pillow.

He fled at once, and the minute it was well "Up with the bonnets of bonnie Dundee,"[19] she slipped away, to return no more till the young gentleman had departed in high dudgeon.[20]

Jo lay long awake that night, and was just dropping off when the sound of a stifled sob made her fly to Beth's bedside, with the anxious inquiry, "What is it, dear?"

"I thought you were asleep," sobbed Beth.

"Is it the old pain, my precious?"

"No; it's a new one; but I can bear it," and Beth tried to check her tears.

"Tell me all about it, and let me cure it as I often did the other."

"You can't; there is no cure." There Beth's voice gave way, and, clinging to her sister, she cried so despairingly that Jo was frightened.

19. The last line of a song by Sir Walter Scott celebrating John Graham, the Laird of Claverhouse and First Viscount of Dundee (1648–1689). A Jacobite, Graham was one of the few Scottish nobles who championed James VII of Scotland. He died in victory, defeating the British army in battle at Killiecrankie. Scott's eleven-stanza song was composed for his unperformed play *The Doom of Devorgoil* (1830).

20. Anger.

"Where is it? Shall I call mother?"

Beth did not answer the first question; but in the dark one hand went involuntarily to her heart, as if the pain was there; with the other she held Jo fast, whispering eagerly, "No, no, don't call her; don't tell her! I shall be better soon. Lie down here and 'poor' my head. I'll be quiet, and go to sleep; indeed I will."

Jo obeyed; but as her hand went softly to and fro across Beth's hot forehead and wet eyelids, her heart was very full, and she longed to speak. But young as she was Jo had learned that hearts, like flowers, cannot be rudely handled, but must open naturally; so, though she believed she knew the cause of Beth's new pain, she only said, in her tenderest tone, "Does anything trouble you, deary?"

"Yes, Jo!" after a long pause.

"Wouldn't it comfort you to tell me what it is?"

"Not now, not yet."

"Then I won't ask; but remember, Bethy, that mother and Jo are always glad to hear and help you, if they can."

"I know it. I'll tell you by and by."

"Is the pain better now?"

"Oh, yes, much better; you are so comfortable, Jo!"

"Go to sleep, dear; I'll stay with you."

So cheek to cheek they fell asleep, and on the morrow Beth seemed quite herself again; for, at eighteen, neither heads nor hearts ache long, and a loving word can medicine most ills.

But Jo had made up her mind, and, after pondering over a project for some days, she confided it to her mother.

"You asked me the other day what my wishes were. I'll tell you one of them, Marmee," she began, as they sat alone together. "I want to go away somewhere this winter for a change."

"Why, Jo?" and her mother looked up quickly, as if the words suggested a double meaning.

With her eyes on her work, Jo answered soberly, "I want something new; I feel restless, and anxious to be seeing, doing, and learning more than I am. I brood too much over my own small affairs, and need stirring up, so, as I can be spared this winter I'd like to hop a little way and try my wings."

"Where will you hop?"

"To New York. I had a bright idea yesterday, and this is it. You know Mrs. Kirke wrote to you for some respectable young person to teach her children and sew. It's rather hard to find just the thing, but I think I should suit if I tried."

"My dear, go out to service in that great boarding-house!" and Mrs. March looked surprised, but not displeased.

"It's not exactly going out to service; for Mrs. Kirke is your friend,—the kindest soul that ever lived,—and would make things pleasant for me, I know. Her family is separate from the rest, and no one knows me there. Don't care if they do; it's honest work, and I'm not ashamed of it."

"Nor I; but your writing?"

"All the better for the change. I shall see and hear new things, get new ideas, and, even if I haven't much time there, I shall bring home quantities of material for my rubbish."

"I have no doubt of it; but are these your only reasons for this sudden fancy?"

"No, mother."

"May I know the others?"

Jo looked up and Jo looked down, then said slowly, with sudden color in her cheeks. "It may be vain and wrong to say it, but—I'm afraid—Laurie is getting too fond of me."

"Then you don't care for him in the way it is evident he begins to care for you?" and Mrs. March looked anxious as she put the question.

"Mercy, no! I love the dear boy as I always have, and am immensely proud of him; but as for anything more, it's out of the question."

"I'm glad of that, Jo!"

"Why, please?"

"Because, dear, I don't think you suited to one another. As friends, you are very happy, and your frequent quarrels soon blow over; but I fear you would both rebel if you were mated for life. You are too much alike, and too fond of freedom, not to mention hot tempers and strong wills, to get on happily together, in a relation which needs infinite patience and forbearance, as well as love."

21. In fact, Laurie has been dropping numerous, not-very-subtle hints, all of which Jo has ignored or not wished to understand.

22. Jo refers to Mrs. Moffat's comment, overheard by Meg three years earlier, that Mrs. March "has laid her plans . . . and will play her cards well," meaning that she intended to marry one of her daughters to the wealthy Laurie. Now, Jo says, Annie Moffat still has her chance to marry Laurie.

"That's just the feeling I had, though I couldn't express it. I'm glad you think he is only beginning to care for me. It would trouble me sadly to make him unhappy; for I couldn't fall in love with the dear old fellow merely out of gratitude, could I?"

"You are sure of his feeling for you?"

The color deepened in Jo's cheeks, as she answered with the look of mingled pleasure, pride, and pain which young girls wear when speaking of first lovers,—

"I'm afraid it is so, mother; he hasn't said anything, but he looks a great deal.[21] I think I had better go away before it comes to anything."

"I agree with you, and if it can be managed you shall go."

Jo looked relieved, and, after a pause, said,—smiling,—

"How Mrs. Moffat would wonder at your want of management, if she knew;[22] and how she will rejoice that Annie may still hope."

"Ah, Jo, mothers may differ in their management, but the hope is the same in all—the desire to see their children happy. Meg is so, and I am content with her success. You I leave to enjoy your liberty till you tire of it; for only then will you find that there is something sweeter. Amy is my chief care now, but her good sense will help her. For Beth, I indulge no hopes except that she may be well. By the way, she seems brighter this last day or two. Have you spoken to her?"

"Yes; she owned she had a trouble, and promised to tell me by and by. I said no more, for I think I know it"; and Jo told her little story.

Mrs. March shook her head, and did not take so romantic a view of the case, but looked grave, and repeated her opinion that, for Laurie's sake, Jo should go away for a time.

"Let us say nothing about it to him till the plan is settled; then I'll run away before he can collect his wits and be tragical. Beth must think I'm going to please myself, as I am, for I can't talk about Laurie to her; but she can pet and comfort him after I'm gone, and so cure him of this romantic notion. He's been through so many little trials of the sort, he's used to it, and will soon get over his love-lornity."

Jo spoke hopefully, but could not rid herself of the foreboding fear that this "little trial" would be harder than the others, and that Laurie would not get over his "love-lornity" as easily as heretofore.

The plan was talked over in a family council, and agreed upon; for Mrs. Kirke gladly accepted Jo, and promised to make a pleasant home for her. The teaching would render her independent; and such leisure as she got might be made profitable by writing, while the new scenes and society would be both useful and agreeable. Jo liked the prospect, and was eager to be gone, for the home-nest was growing too narrow for her restless nature and adventurous spirit.[23] When all was settled, with fear and trembling she told Laurie; but, to her surprise, he took it very quietly. He had been graver than usual of late, but very pleasant; and when jokingly accused of turning over a new leaf, he answered, soberly, "So I am; and I mean this one shall stay turned."

Jo was very much relieved that one of his virtuous fits should come on just then, and made her preparations with a lightened heart,—for Beth seemed more cheerful,—and hoped she was doing the best for all.

"One thing I leave to your especial care," she said, the night before she left.

"You mean your papers?" asked Beth.

"No—my boy; be very good to him, won't you?"

"Of course I will; but I can't fill your place, and he'll miss you sadly."

"It won't hurt him; so remember, I leave him in your charge, to plague, pet, and keep in order."

"I'll do my best, for your sake," promised Beth, wondering why Jo looked at her so queerly.

When Laurie said "Good-by," he whispered, significantly. "It won't do a bit of good, Jo. My eye is on you; so mind what you do, or I'll come and bring you home."

23. In October 1856, LMA left her family, who were then living in Walpole, N.H., and moved into Mrs. Mary Ann Reed's boardinghouse at 34 Chauncy Street in Boston, where she had "a skyparlor for $3 a week, with fire and board." David Reed, Mary's husband, published the *Christian Register*. LMA noted: "I don't often pray in words; but when I set out that day with all my worldly goods in the little old trunk, my own earnings ($25) in my pocket, and much hope and resolution in my soul, my heart was very full, and I said to the Lord, 'Help us all, and keep us for one another,' as I never said it before, while I looked back at the dear faces watching me, so full of love and hope and faith." Later, LMA inserted in brackets: "[Jo in N. Y.—L. M. A.]" (*Journals* 79). In November, she noted: "I find my little room up in the attic very cosey, and a house full of boarders very amusing to study. Mrs. Reed very kind" (*Journals* 79). While in Boston, LMA sewed for Mrs. Reed and wrote stories. In December, she began teaching Alice Lovering on Beacon Street for three hours a day (see *Journals* 81). LMA returned home in the spring of 1857.

1. A ginger biscuit or ginger snap.

2. An attic room.

3. LMA described her room at Mrs. Reed's to Anna in November 1856: "It is 'situate' at the top of the big house a queer pie shaped room, but nicely carpeted, with two bureau's (for which I gave praise) a dormer window with a table & rocking chair in it for my private benefit. A head bumping closet rich in shelves & pegs holds my reserved resources & just outside the door (there being no 'chimbly' inside) is a Tophet stove which warms all out doors & freezes me" (*Selected Letters* 18). She did have a view of a church tower, which inspired her story "The Cross on the Church Tower," published in 1857 in the January 24 edition of *Saturday Evening Gazette* (see *Journals* 81).

4. There is no story with this exact title. LMA may have confused "The Three Little Pigs" with "The Wolf and the Seven Little Goats," as the tales are similar. First published in Jacob and Wilhelm Grimm's 1812 *Children's and Household Tales*, "The Wolf and the Seven Little Goats" tells of a mother goat who leaves her seven kids at home alone while she goes in search of food, warning them to beware of the bad wolf. The wolf soon approaches, pretending to be their mother. The suspicious kids twice turn him away before he gains entrance to the house by disguising his voice and covering his dark feet with dough and flour. Once inside he devours all but the youngest kid, who has hidden in the clock case. After returning home to learn what has happened, the mother goes in search of the wolf. She finds him asleep after his heavy meal, cuts open his stomach with her scissors, and removes her six kids—who are still alive. She then gathers stones, places them in the wolf's belly, and sews him back up. The wolf wakes up thirsty and goes to drink water at the well, where he topples over from the weight of the stones and drowns.

5. In her letter to Anna on November 2, 1856, LMA noted her bashfulness: "They [the boarders] were just going to dinner so I said I'd warm my feet & wait till by & by, but Mrs Reed came up from the table & embraced me like a Ma, urged me to come & eat, & when I was afeared & said 'No', took me to my room" (*Selected Letters* 18).

6. Working or performing tasks. Similar to the modern expression "on the go."

Chapter 10

Jo's Journal

"NEW YORK, NOV.

DEAR MARMEE AND BETH:

"I'm going to write you a regular volume, for I've got lots to tell, though I'm not a fine young lady travelling on the continent. When I lost sight of father's dear old face, I felt a trifle blue, and might have shed a briny drop or two, if an Irish lady with four small children, all crying more or less, hadn't diverted my mind; for I amused myself by dropping gingerbread nuts[1] over the seat every time they opened their mouths to roar.

"Soon the sun came out; and taking it as a good omen, I cleared up likewise, and enjoyed my journey with all my heart.

"Mrs. Kirke welcomed me so kindly I felt at home at once, even in that big house full of strangers. She gave me a funny little sky-parlor—all she had;[2] but there is a stove in it, and a nice table in a sunny window, so I can sit here and write whenever I like. A fine view, and a church tower opposite, atone for the many stairs, and I took a fancy to my den on the spot.[3] The nursery, where I am to teach and sew, is a pleasant room next Mrs. Kirke's private parlor, and the two little girls are pretty children—rather spoilt, I guess, but they took to me after telling them 'The Seven Bad Pigs';[4] and I've no doubt I shall make a model governess.

"I am to have my meals with the children, if I prefer it to the great table, and for the present I do, for I *am* bashful, though no one will believe it.[5]

"'Now my dear, make yourself at home,' said Mrs. K. in her motherly way; 'I'm on the drive[6] from morning to night, as you may suppose, with such a family; but a great anxiety will be off my mind if I know the children are safe with you. My rooms are always open to you, and your own shall be as comfortable as I can make it. There are some pleasant people in the house, if you feel sociable, and your evenings are always free. Come to me if anything goes wrong, and be as happy as you can. There's the tea-bell; I must run and change my cap'; and off she bustled, leaving me to settle myself in my new nest.

"As I went down stairs, soon after, I saw something I liked. The flights are very long in this tall house, and as I stood waiting at the head of the third one for a little servant girl to lumber up, I saw a queer-looking man[a] come along behind her, take the heavy hod[7] of coal out of her hand, carry it all the way up, put it down at a door near by, and walk away, saying, with a kind nod and a foreign accent,—

"'It goes better so. The little back is too young to haf such heaviness.'

"Wasn't it good of him? I like such things; for, as father says, trifles show character. When I mentioned it to Mrs. K., that evening, she laughed, and said,—

"'That must have been Professor Bhaer; he's always doing things of that sort.'

"Mrs. K. told me he was from Berlin; very learned and good, but poor as a church mouse,[8] and gives lessons to support himself and two little orphan nephews whom he is educating here, according to the wishes of his sister, who married an American.[9] Not a very romantic story, but it interested me; and I was glad to hear that Mrs. K. lends him her parlor for some of his scholars. There is a glass door between it and the nursery, and I mean to peep at him, and then I'll tell you how he looks. He's most forty, so it's no harm, Marmee.

"After tea and a go-to-bed romp with the little girls, I attacked the big work-basket,[10] and had a quiet evening chatting with my new friend. I shall keep a journal-letter,[11] and send it once a week; so good-night, and more to-morrow."

"*Tuesday Eve.*

"Had a lively time in my seminary,[12] this morning, for the children acted like Sancho;[13] and at one time I really thought I should

7. A scuttle to carry coal.

8. *Brewer's Dictionary of Phrase & Fable* (15th ed.) notes the origin of the phrase: "In a church there is no cupboard or pantry where a mouse may take his food, and he thus has an extremely lean time" (New York: Harper Collins, 1995), 57.

9. LMA presents a vision of nineteenth-century America at once realistic and idealistic: a country of immigrants who wish to assimilate and who share an egalitarian dream. For LMA assimilation is a process of mutual influence. As Bhaer's sister married an American, so, too, will Bhaer himself.

10. Sewing basket.

11. LMA did compose long letters to Anna from Boston. She wrote in November 1856: "I *must* begin my letter or I shall never get it done I have so much to tell my lass about the jovial times I'm having in this Vanity Fair. To begin journal fashion" (*Selected Letters* 21). Subsequent letters she titled "The Boston Bulletin" (see *Selected Letters* 27).

12. A classroom.

13. Alluding to Sancho Panza in *Don Quixote,* Jo means that they acted either too comically or like illiterates.

14. Jo alludes to the poem "Mabel on Midsummer Day: A Story of the Olden Time" by Mary Botham Howitt (1799–1888), the prolific English poet (most famous for the poem "The Spider and the Fly"). The poem was first published in Howitt's *Marien's Pilgrimmage; A Fire-Side Story, and Other Poems* (1859). The poem concludes: "Tis good, like little Mabel, / To have a willing mind!" LMA would meet Howitt in Rome in January 1871 (see *Little Women Abroad* 267).

15. "Know'st thou the land" is part of the first line of Mignon's song in *Wilhelm Meister's Apprenticeship* (1796) by Johann Wolfgang von Goethe (book 3, chapter 1). LMA first encountered Goethe's works in October 1847 when she read *Goethe's Correspondence with a Child* (1835), first published in America in 1841, which were the letters between Bettina von Amim and the author (see *Journals* 60). In 1885, upon rereading her journal, she inserted: "First taste of Goethe. Three years later R. W. E. gave me 'Wilhelm Meister,' and from that day Goethe has been my chief idol" (*Journals* 60). In "Recollections of My Childhood" (1888), LMA wrote about the Goethe/Emerson connection: "Browsing over Mr. Emerson's library I found 'Goethe's Correspondence with a Child,' and was at once fired with the desire to be a second Bettine, making my father's friend my Goethe. So I wrote letters to him, but was wise enough never to send them, left wild flowers on the doorsteps of my 'Master,' sung Mignon's song in very bad German under his window, and was fond of wandering by moonlight, or sitting in a cherry-tree at midnight till the owls scared me to bed" (quoted in *Her Own Time* 36).

16. The *OED* defines *gabble* as "voluble, noisy, confused, unintelligible talk."

17. Worn; shabby.

18. Clever; intelligent.

19. Serious.

shake them all round. Some good angel inspired me to try gymnastics, and I kept it up till they were glad to sit down and keep still. After luncheon, the girl took them out for a walk, and I went to my needle-work, like little Mabel, 'with a willing mind.'[14] I was thanking my stars that I'd learned to make nice button-holes, when the parlor door opened and shut, and someone began to hum,—

'Kennst du das land,'[15]

like a big bumble-bee. It was dreadfully improper, I know, but I couldn't resist the temptation; and lifting one end of the curtain before the glass door, I peeped in. Professor Bhaer was there; and while he arranged his books, I took a good look at him. A regular German—rather stout, with brown hair tumbled all over his head, a bushy beard, droll[b] nose, the kindest eyes I ever saw, and a splendid big voice that does one's ears good, after our sharp or slipshod American gabble.[16] His clothes were rusty,[17] his hands were large, and he hadn't a handsome feature in his face, except his beautiful teeth; yet I liked him, for he had a fine[18] head; his linen was spandy[b] nice, and he looked like a gentleman, though two buttons were off his coat, and there was a patch on one shoe. He looked sober[19] in spite of his humming, till he went to the window to turn the hyacinth bulbs toward the sun, and stroke the cat, who received him like an old friend. Then he smiled; and when a tap came at the door, called out in a loud, brisk tone,—

"'Herein!'

"I was just going to run, when I caught sight of a morsel of a child carrying a big book, and stopped to see what was going on.

"'Me wants my Bhaer,' said the mite, slamming down her book, and running to meet him.

"'Thou shalt haf thy Bhaer; come, then, and take a goot hug from him, my Tina,' said the Professor, catching her up, with a laugh, and holding her so high over his head that she had to stoop her little face to kiss him.

"'Now me mus tuddy my lessin,' went on the funny little thing; so he put her up at the table, opened the great dictionary she had brought, and gave her a paper and pencil, and she scribbled away,

LITTLE WOMEN

THE PHILOSOPHER AND THE LITTLE GIRL AMONG THE BOOKS

Of course you know this is Ralph Waldo Emerson, and you can see that he is talking books with the young girl; but who do you suppose that girl is? She is Louisa May Alcott, author of "Little Women"! When she was a little girl, living in Concord, U.S.A., she used to be a regular visitor at the home of the Emersons, and she spent many happy hours with the great man, who used to go about with her among the books and help her pick out the ones he thought she would like best and that it would do her the most good to read. The scene is typical of the many happy gatherings in Emerson's home, for it was a favourite meeting-place for writers, philosophers, and other notable figures from all parts of the country.

Louisa May Alcott and Ralph Waldo Emerson. In "Reminiscences of Ralph Waldo Emerson" (1885), LMA wrote that Emerson "opened [to her] the riches of Shakespeare, Dante, Goethe and Carlyle." She noted that she would "venture into Mr. Emerson's library and ask what I should read, never conscious of the audacity of my demand, so genial was my welcome" (p. 285).

turning a leaf now and then, and passing her little fat finger down the page, as if finding a word, so soberly, that I nearly betrayed myself by a laugh, while Mr. Bhaer stood stroking her pretty hair, with a fatherly look, that made me think she must be his own, though she looked more French than German.

20. The *OED* defines *Prut!* as "an exclamation of contempt or disbelief."

"Another knock, and the appearance of two young ladies sent me back to my work, and there I virtuously remained through all the noise and gabbling that went on next door. One of the girls kept laughing affectedly, and saying, 'Now Professor,' in a coquettish tone, and the other pronounced her German with an accent that must have made it hard for him to keep sober.

"Both seemed to try his patience sorely; for more than once I heard him say, emphatically, 'No, no, it is *not* so, you haf not attend to what I say'; and once there was a loud rap, as if he struck the table with his book, followed by the despairing exclamation, 'Prut![20] it all goes bad this day.'

"Poor man, I pitied him; and when the girls were gone, took just one more peep, to see if he survived it. He seemed to have thrown himself back in his chair, tired out, and sat there with his eyes shut, till the clock struck two, when he jumped up, put his books in his pocket, as if ready for another lesson, and, taking little Tina, who had fallen asleep on the sofa, in his arms, he carried her quietly away. I guess he has a hard life of it.

"Mrs. Kirke asked me if I wouldn't go down to the five-o'clock dinner; and, feeling a little bit homesick, I thought I would, just to see what sort of people are under the same roof with me. So I made myself respectable, and tried to slip in behind Mrs. Kirke; but as she is short, and I'm tall, my efforts at concealment were rather a failure. She gave me a seat by her, and after my face cooled off, I plucked up courage, and looked about me. The long table was full, and every one intent on getting their dinner—the gentlemen especially, who seemed to be eating on time, for they *bolted* in every sense of the word, vanishing as soon as they were done. There was the usual assortment of young men, absorbed in themselves; young couples absorbed in each other; married ladies in their babies, and old gentlemen in politics. I don't think I shall care to have much to do with any of them, except one sweet-faced maiden lady, who looks as if she had something in her.

"Cast away at the very bottom of the table was the Professor, shouting answers to the questions of a very inquisitive, deaf old gentleman on one side, and talking philosophy with a Frenchman on the other. If Amy had been here, she'd have turned her back on him forever, because, sad to relate, he had a great appetite, and shovelled in his dinner in a manner which would have horrified 'her ladyship.' I didn't mind, for I like 'to see folks eat with a relish,' as Hannah says, and the poor man must have needed a deal of food, after teaching idiots all day.

"As I went upstairs after dinner, two of the young men were settling their beavers[21] before the hall mirror, and I heard one say low to the other, 'Who's the new party?'

"'Governess, or something of that sort.'

"'What the deuce is she at our table for?'

"'Friend of the old lady's.'

"'Handsome head, but no style.'

"'Not a bit of it. Give us a light and come on.'

"I felt angry at first, and then I didn't care, for a governess is as good as a clerk, and I've got sense, if I haven't style, which is more than some people have, judging from the remarks of the elegant beings who clattered away, smoking like bad chimneys. I hate ordinary people!"[22]

"Thursday.

"Yesterday was a quiet day, spent in teaching, sewing, and writing in my little room,—which is very cosy, with a light and fire. I picked up a few bits of news, and was introduced to the Professor. It seems that Tina is the child of the Frenchwoman who does the fine ironing[23] in the laundry here. The little thing has lost her heart to Mr. Bhaer, and follows him about the house like a dog whenever he is at home, which delights him,—as he is very fond of children, though a 'bacheldore.'[24] Kitty and Minnie Kirke likewise regard him with affection, and tell all sorts of stories about the plays he invents, the presents he brings, and the splendid tales he tells. The young men quiz him, it seems, call him Old Fritz, Lager Beer, Ursa Major, and make all manner of jokes on his name.[25] But he enjoys it like a boy, Mrs. K. says, and takes it so good-naturedly that they all like him, in spite of his odd ways.

"The maiden lady is a Miss Norton,—rich, cultivated, and kind. She spoke to me at dinner to-day (for I went to table again, it's such fun to watch people[26]), and asked me to come and see her at her room. She has fine books and pictures, knows interesting persons, and seems friendly; so I shall make myself agreeable, for I

21. A beaver is a hat, often a top hat, made from felted beaver's fur. The 1880–1881 edition changed *beavers* to *hats*.

22. Jo means that she dislikes those who judge others by social standing and outward trappings—their clothes, the shape of a head, and so on. Bhaer, of course, is anything but ordinary.

23. Ironing of delicate materials or ironing that needed special attention.

24. Bachelor.

25. The young men play off of Bhaer's name. Ursa Major, the Great Bear, is a major constellation in the northern hemisphere.

26. As a writer Jo keenly observes all around her, noting small details that define people's personalities. LMA was also an observer. Her personal letters, especially those written while abroad in 1865–1866 and 1870–1871, are filled with brief sketches of personal observations, mostly of people. In fact, it was the sketch form in which she first found her true style: *Hospital Sketches* (1863) presents short vignettes drawn from her letters to family and friends. She continued writing sketches throughout her career, combining autobiography and fiction, much as she does in *Little Women.* In his introduction to *The Sketches of Louisa May Alcott* (New York: Ironweed Press, 2001), Gregory Eiselein notes: "Alcott's lively style and democratic lack of pretension are well suited to the genre [the sketch], and her ironic self-awareness highlights the important role of the observer in the literary sketch" (p. 10).

27. Jo means she was more adult-like or proper than most girls her age.

28. The *OED* defines *enfant terrible* as "a child who embarrasses his elders by untimely remarks."

29. German embroidery has long been famous. In the mid-nineteenth century, a type of embroidery or needlepoint known as Berlin work became extremely popular. Printed charted patterns on canvas were embroidered with colored yarn, and the embroidery was used for slippers, furniture covers, and other decorative objects.

30. The rebellious archangel who fell from heaven as recounted in Milton's *Paradise Lost* (1667; rev. 1674). Lucifer is extremely prideful, as shown by his most famous line in the epic poem: "Better to reign in Hell, than serve in Heav'n" (Book 1, line 263).

do want to get into good society, only it isn't the same sort that Amy likes.

"I was in our parlor last evening, when Mr. Bhaer came in with some newspapers for Mrs. Kirke. She wasn't there, but Minnie, who is a little old woman,[27] introduced me very prettily: 'This is mamma's friend, Miss March.'

"'Yes; and she's jolly, and we like her lots,' added Kitty, who is an *'enfant terrible.'*[28]

"We both bowed, and then we laughed, for the prim introduction and the blunt addition were rather a comical contrast.

"'Ah, yes; I hear these naughty ones go to vex you, Mees Marsch. If so again, call at me and I come,' he said, with a threatening frown that delighted the little wretches.

"I promised I would, and he departed; but it seems as if I was doomed to see a good deal of him, for to-day, as I passed his door on my way out, by accident I knocked against it with my umbrella. It flew open, and there he stood in his dressing-gown, with a big blue sock on one hand and a darning-needle in the other; he didn't seem at all ashamed of it, for when I explained and hurried on, he waved his hand, sock and all, saying, in his loud, cheerful way,—

"'You haf a fine day to make your walk. *Bon voyage, mademoiselle.'*

"I laughed all the way down stairs; but it was a little pathetic, also, to think of the poor man having to mend his own clothes. The German gentlemen embroider,[29] I know,—but darning hose is another thing, and not so pretty."

"Saturday.

"Nothing has happened to write about, except a call on Miss Norton, who has a room full of lovely things, and who was very charming, for she showed me all her treasures, and asked me if I would sometimes go with her to lectures and concerts, as her escort,—if I enjoyed them. She put it as a favor; but I'm sure Mrs. Kirke has told her about us, and she does it out of kindness to me. I'm as proud as Lucifer,[30] but such favors from such people don't burden me, and I accepted gratefully.

"When I got back to the nursery there was such an uproar in the parlor that I looked in, and there was Mr. Bhaer down on his hands and knees, with Tina on his back, Kitty leading him with a jump-rope, and Minnie feeding two small boys with seed-cakes,[31] as they roared and ramped in cages built of chairs.

"'We are playing *nargerie*' explained Kitty.

"'Dis is mine effalunt!' added Tina, holding on by the Professor's hair.

"'Mamma always allows us to do what we like Saturday afternoon, when Franz and Emil come, don't she, Mr. Bhaer?' said Minnie.

"The 'effalunt' sat up, looking as much in earnest as any of them, and said, soberly, to me,—

"'I gif you my wort it is so. If we make too large a noise you shall say "hush!" to us, and we go more softly.'

"I promised to do so, but left the door open, and enjoyed the fun as much as they did,—for a more glorious frolic I never witnessed. They played tag, and soldiers, danced and sung, and when it began to grow dark they all piled on to the sofa about the Professor, while he told charming fairy stories of the storks on the chimney-tops, and the little 'Kobolds,' who ride the snow-flakes as they fall.[32] I wish Americans were as simple and natural as Germans, don't you?[33]

"I'm so fond of writing, I should go spinning on forever if motives of economy didn't stop me; for though I've used thin paper, and written fine, I tremble to think of the stamps this long letter will need. Pray forward Amy's as soon as you can spare them. My small news will sound very flat after her splendors, but you will like them, I know. Is Teddy studying so hard that he can't find time to write to his friends? Take good care of him for me, Beth, and tell me all about the babies, and give heaps of love to every one.

"From your faithful   JO.

"P.S. On reading over my letter, it strikes me as rather Bhaery; but I am always interested in odd people, and I really had nothing else to write about.[34] Bless you."

"DEC.

"MY PRECIOUS BETSEY:[35]

"As this is to be a scribble-scrabble[36] letter, I direct it to you, for it may amuse you, and give you some idea of my goings on; for,

31. A cake made with flour, butter, sugar, eggs, and caraway or other flavorful seeds. Seed cakes were extremely popular in England during the nineteenth century.

32. Storks often nest on chimney tops and return to the same one year after year. In German folklore, kobolds are trickster gnomes who live deep within mines; they can also be spirits that haunt houses but also perform deeds for those who live there.

33. Jo's comment provides the first real hint that she is romantically interested in Bhaer. Jo herself is "simple and natural" in many ways. LMA holds an optimistic view of life and its possibilities: she believes that people (and also society) are truly capable of improvement, but her view is complicated somewhat by her belief in *personality* (personality understood as something deep and abiding). It is LMA's belief in the perdurability of personality that makes Laurie and Jo ill suited for each other and explains why Bhaer and Jo make better partners. As she gets to know Bhaer well, Jo will understand how suited they are for each other.

34. Jo's letter is indeed rather "Bhaery," as even the casual reader will observe. But Jo's letters are also literary exercises, and they include deft sketches of other characters who inhabit Mrs. Kirke's boarding house. By way of contrast, Amy's letters in Chapter 8, "Our Foreign Correspondent," are quite different. Amy fills hers with the sights of Europe, almost as if they were a guidebook, revealing little of those she writes about—except herself, of course.

35. Jo writes to Meg here. LMA often addressed her older sister Anna as "Betsey." In their theatricals, LMA played Sairey Gamp to Anna's Betsey Prig, both of whom were nurses in Charles Dickens's *The Life and Adventures of Martin Chuzzlewit* (1843–1844).

36. Covered with scribble, often written quickly.

37. Amy means *Herculean* efforts," a reference to the labors or great feats of Hercules, the Roman demigod, son of Zeus and the mortal Alcmene.

38. High spirits or energy.

39. A pipe made of meerschaum, also called sepiolite, which is a soft mineral (white, gray, or yellowish) that looks like hardened clay.

40. Bhaer's lack of order or fuss has caught Jo's eye (she herself cares little for neatness), but so has his interest in children. Recall Jo's attraction to young people in Chapter 6 of Part II, "Calls," where at the third house she and Amy visited Jo "devoted herself to the young folks" while Amy engaged with the adults.

41. *Brewer's Dictionary of Phrase & Fable* (15th ed.) notes the meaning of the phrase: "To treat [people] without any consideration; to disregard their feelings and interests completely. The shoes of a horse that is roughshod for slippery weather are equipped with points or calks" (New York: Harper Collins, 1995), 910.

42. The *OED* defines this usage of *pass* as "(to arrive at) a bad or regrettable state of affairs."

though quiet, they are rather amusing, for which, oh, be joyful! After what Amy would call Herculaneum efforts,[37] in the way of mental and moral agriculture, my young ideas begin to shoot, and my little twigs to bend, as I could wish. They are not so interesting to me as Tina and the boys, but I do my duty by them, and they are fond of me. Franz and Emil are jolly little lads, quite after my own heart, for the mixture of German and American spirit in them produces a constant state of effervescence.[38] Saturday afternoons are riotous times, whether spent in the house or out; for on pleasant days they all go to walk, like a seminary, with the Professor and myself to keep order; and then such fun!

"We are very good friends now, and I've begun to take lessons. I really couldn't help it, and it all came about in such a funny[d] way, that I must tell you. To begin at the beginning. Mrs. Kirke called to me, one day, as I passed Mr. Bhaer's room, where she was rummaging.

"'Did you ever see such a den, my dear? Just come and help me put these books to rights, for I've turned everything upside down, trying to discover what he has done with the six new handkerchiefs I gave him, not long ago.'

"I went in, and while we worked I looked about me, for it was 'a den,' to be sure. Books and papers, everywhere; a broken meerschaum,[39] and an old flute over the mantle-piece, as if done with; a ragged bird, without any tail, chirped on one window-seat, and a box of white mice adorned the other; half-finished boats, and bits of string, lay among the manuscripts; dirty little boots stood drying before the fire, and traces of the dearly beloved boys, for whom he makes a slave of himself, were to be seen all over the room.[40] After a grand rummage three of the missing articles were found,—one over the bird-cage, one covered with ink, and a third burnt brown, having been used as a holder.

"'Such a man!' laughed good-natured Mrs. K., as she put the relics in the rag-bag. 'I suppose the others are torn up to rig ships, bandage cut fingers, or make kite tails. It's dreadful, but I can't scold him; he's so absent-minded and good-natured, he lets those boys ride over him rough-shod.[41] I agreed to do his washing and mending, but he forgets to give out his things, and I forget to look them over, so he comes to a sad pass[42] sometimes.'

43. Bungled; spoiled.
44. Professor Bhaer means *joking*.

"'Let me mend them,' said I; 'I don't mind it, and he needn't know. I'd like to,—he's so kind to me about bringing my letters, and lending books.'

"So I have got his things in order, and knit heels into two pairs of the socks,—for they were boggled[43] out of shape with his queer darns. Nothing was said, and I hoped he wouldn't find it out,—but one day last week he caught me at it. Hearing the lessons he gives to others has interested and amused me so much, that I took a fancy to learn; for Tina runs in and out, leaving the door open, and I can hear. I had been sitting near this door, finishing off the last sock, and trying to understand what he said to a new scholar, who is as stupid as I am; the girl had gone, and I thought he had also, it was so still, and I was busily gabbling over a verb, and rocking to and fro in a most absurd way, when a little crow made me look up, and there was Mr. Bhaer looking and laughing quietly, when he made signs to Tina not to betray him.

"'So,' he said, as I stopped and stared like a goose, 'you peep at me, I peep at you, and that is not bad; but see, I am not pleasanting[44] when I say, haf you a wish for German?'

"'Yes; but you are too busy; I am too stupid to learn,' I blundered out, as red as a beet.

"'Prut! we will make the time, and we fail not to find the sense. At efening I shall gif a little lesson with much gladness; for, look you, Mees Marsch, I haf this debt to pay,' and he pointed to my work. 'Yes! they say to one another, these so kind ladies, "he is a stupid old fellow; he will see not what we do; he will never opserve that his sock-heels go not in holes any more; he will think his buttons grow out new when they fall, and believe that strings make theirselves." Ah! but I haf an eye, and I see much. I haf a heart, and I feel the thanks for this. Come,—a little lesson then and now, or—no more good fairy works for me and mine.'

"Of course I couldn't say anything after that, and as it really is a splendid opportunity, I made the bargain, and we began. I took four lessons, and then I stuck fast in a grammatical bog. The Professor was very patient with me, but it must have been torment to him, and now and then he'd look at me with such an expression of mild despair, that it was a toss up with me whether to laugh or cry. I tried both ways; and when it came to a sniff of utter mortifi-

45. German for *fairy tales.*

46. Hans Christian Andersen (1805–1875), the Danish author of numerous fairy tales, including "The Little Match Girl," "The Ugly Duckling," and "The Little Mermaid."

47. Determined. *Brewer's Dictionary of Phrase & Fable* (15th ed.) notes the origin of the phrase: "Whatever the risk; at any cost. The term comes from racing. If you can't win by a neck you are nowhere" (New York: Harper Collins, 1995), 738.

48. Also known as "The Steadfast Tin Soldier," this Andersen fairy tale was published in *Fairy Tales, Told for Children. New Collection* (1838). It tells the story of a tin soldier who falls in love with a paper ballerina.

cation and woe, he just threw the grammar on to the floor, and marched out of the room. I felt myself disgraced and deserted forever, but didn't blame him a particle, and was scrambling my papers together, meaning to rush upstairs and shake myself hard, when in he came, as brisk and beaming as if I'd covered my name with glory:—[e]

"'Now we shall try a new way. You and I will read these pleasant little Märchen[45] together, and dig no more in that dry book, that goes in the corner for making us trouble.'

"He spoke so kindly, and opened Hans Andersen's fairy tales[46] so invitingly before me, that I was more ashamed than ever, and went at my lesson in a neck-or-nothing[47] style that seemed to amuse him immensely. I forgot my bashfulness, and pegged away (no other word will express it) with all my might, tumbling over long words, pronouncing according to the inspiration of the minute, and doing my very best. When I finished reading my first page, and stopped for breath, he clapped his hands and cried out, in his hearty way, 'Das ist gute! Now we go well! My turn. I do him in German; gif me your ear.' And away he went, rumbling out the words with his strong voice, and a relish which was good to see as well as hear. Fortunately, the story was the 'Constant Tin Soldier,'[48] which is droll, you know, so I could laugh,—and I did, —though I didn't understand half he read,—for I couldn't help it, he was so earnest, I so excited, and the whole thing so comical.

"After that we got on better, and now I read my lessons pretty well; for this way of studying suits me, and I can see that the grammar gets tucked into the tales and poetry, as one gives pills in jelly. I like it very much, and he don't seem tired of it yet,—which is very good of him, isn't it? I mean to give him something on Christmas, for I don't dare offer money. Tell me something nice, Marmee.

"I'm glad Laurie seems so happy and busy,—that he has given up smoking, and lets his hair grow. You see Beth manages him better than I did. I'm not jealous, dear; do your best, only don't make a saint of him. I'm afraid I couldn't like him without a spice of human naughtiness. Read him bits of my letters. I haven't time to write much, and that will do just as well. Thank heaven Beth continues so comfortable."

"A happy New-Year to you all, my dearest family, which of course includes Mr. L. and a young man by the name of Teddy. I can't tell you how much I enjoyed your Christmas bundle, for I didn't get it till night, and had given up hoping. Your letter came in the morning, but you said nothing about a parcel, meaning it for a surprise; so I was disappointed, for I'd had a 'kind of feeling' that you wouldn't forget me. I felt a little low in my mind, as I sat up in my room, after tea; and when the big, muddy, battered-looking bundle was brought to me, I just hugged it, and pranced. It was so *homey* and refreshing, that I sat down on the floor, and read, and looked, and eat, and laughed and cried, in my usual absurd way. The things were just what I wanted, and all the better for being made instead of bought. Beth's new 'ink-bib' was capital; and Hannah's box of hard gingerbread will be a treasure. I'll be sure and wear the nice flannels[49] you sent, Marmee, and read carefully the books father has marked. Thank you all, heaps and heaps![50]

"Speaking of books, reminds me that I'm getting rich in that line; for, on New-Year's day, Mr. Bhaer gave me a fine Shakespeare. It is one he values much, and I've often admired it, set up in the place of honor, with his German Bible, Plato, Homer, and Milton; so you may imagine how I felt when he brought it down, without its cover, and showed me my name in it, 'from my friend Friedrich Bhaer.'

"'You say often you wish a library; here I gif you one; for between these two lids (he meant covers) is many books in one. Read him well, and he will help you much; for the study of character in this book will help you to read it in the world, and paint it with your pen.'

"I thanked him as well as I could, and talk now about 'my library,' as if I had a hundred books. I never knew how much there was in Shakespeare before; but then I never had a Bhaer to explain it to me. Now *don't* laugh at his horrid name; it isn't pronounced either Bear or Beer, as people *will* say it, but something between the two, as only Germans can do[f] it. I'm glad you both like what I tell you about him, and hope you will know him some day.

49. Underclothes made from flannel cloth.

50. In her letter of December 28–31, 1856, to Anna, LMA wrote about receiving presents at Mrs. Reed's: "Got home cold, tired & low in my mind, & the first thing I saw was a box from home. I . . . ripped it open & plunged in, laughing, crying, munching the gingerbread, putting on the flannel cap, flapping the yellow butterfly holder & sprinkling salt water over letters & presents in a perfectly rapterous & imbecile manner" (*Selected Letters* 28).

51. Small bellows to help start a fire.

52. French for *handkerchiefs*.

53. A curio or art piece.

54. Jo could mean either an impertinent person or an insignificant one.

55. Mrs. Malaprop, the comic character who confuses or misuses words in *The Rivals* (1775), says both of these lines in Act 3, Scene 3, of the play. First, she tells Captain Jack Absolute: "Sure, if I reprehend any thing in this world, it is the use of my oracular tongue, and a nice derangement of epitaphs!" Later in the scene, she refers to Lydia Languish, telling Absolute: "Oh, there's nothing to be hoped for from her! she's as headstrong as an allegory on the banks of the Nile." In July 1855, LMA played Mrs. Malaprop in the Walpole Amateur Dramatic Company's performance (see *Journals* 75).

56. In Shakespeare's comedy *A Midsummer Night's Dream* (ca. 1595), Nick Bottom is the weaver who is part of the acting troupe the Mechanicals. His head is changed into an ass's head by the mischievous Puck. Titania, queen of the fairies and wife of Oberon, falls in love with Bottom after Puck enchants her.

Mother would admire his warm heart, father his wise head. I admire both, and feel rich in my new 'friend Friedrich Bhaer.'

"Not having much money, or knowing what he'd like, I got several little things, and put them about the room, where he would find them unexpectedly. They were useful, pretty, or funny—a new stand-dish on his table, a little vase for his flower—he always has one—or a bit of green in a glass, to keep him fresh, he says; and a holder for his blower,[51] so that he needn't burn up what Amy calls 'mouchoirs.'[52] I made it like those Beth invented—a big butterfly with a fat body, and black and yellow wings, worsted feelers, and bead eyes. It took his fancy immensely, and he put it on his mantle-piece as an article of *virtu*;[53] so it was rather a failure after all. Poor as he is, he didn't forget a servant or a child in the house; and not a soul here, from the French laundry-woman to Miss Norton, forgot him. I was so glad of that.

"They got up a masquerade, and had a gay time, New-Year's eve. I didn't mean to go down, having no dress; but, at the last minute, Mrs. Kirke remembered some old brocades, and Miss Norton lent me lace and feathers; so I rigged[g] up as Mrs. Malaprop, and sailed in with a mask on. No one knew me, for I disguised my voice, and no one dreamed of the silent, haughty Miss March (for they think I am very stiff and cool, most of them; and so I am to whipper-snappers[54]) could dance, and dress, and burst out into a 'nice derangement of epitaphs, like an allegory on the banks of the Nile.'[55] I enjoyed it very much; and when we unmasked it was fun to see them stare at me. I heard one of the young men tell another that he knew I'd been an actress; in fact, he thought he remembered seeing me at one of the minor theatres. Meg will relish that joke. Mr. Bhaer was Nick Bottom, and Tina was Titania—a perfect little fairy in his arms.[56] To see them dance was 'quite a landscape,' to use a Teddyism.

"I had a very happy New-Year, after all; and when I thought it over in my room, I felt as if I was getting on a little in spite of my many failures; for I'm cheerful all the time now, work with a will, and take more interest in other people than I used to, which is satisfactory. Bless you all. Ever your loving

JO."

LITTLE WOMEN

Chapter II

A Friend

THOUGH very happy in the social atmosphere about her, and very busy with the daily work that earned her bread, and made it sweeter for the effort, Jo still found time for literary labors. The purpose which now took possession of her was a natural one to a poor and ambitious girl; but the means she took to gain her end were not the best. She saw that money conferred power; money and power, therefore, she resolved to have; not to be used for herself alone, but for those whom she loved more than self. The dream of filling home with comforts, giving Beth everything she wanted, from strawberries in winter to an organ in her bedroom; going abroad herself, and always having *more* than enough, so that she might indulge in the luxury of charity, had been for years Jo's most cherished castle in the air.[1]

The prize-story experience had seemed to open a way which might, after long travelling, and much up-hill work, lead to this delightful *chateau en Espagne*.[2] But the novel disaster quenched her courage for a time, for public opinion is a giant which has frightened stouter-hearted Jacks on bigger beanstalks than hers.[3] Like that immortal hero, she reposed a while after the first attempt, which resulted in a tumble, and the least lovely of the giant's treasures, if I remember rightly.[4] But the "up again and take another" spirit was as strong in Jo as in Jack; so she scrambled up on the shady side, this time, and got more booty, but nearly left behind her what was far more precious than the money-bags.

She took to writing sensation stories—for in those dark ages, even all-perfect America read rubbish. She told no one, but concocted a "thrilling tale," and boldly carried it herself to Mr. Dash-

1. In October 1863, after the success of *Hospital Sketches*, LMA reported in her journal: "Fifteen years of hard grubbing may be coming to something after all, & I may yet 'pay all the debts, fix the house, send May to Italy & keep the old folks cosy,' as I've said I would so long yet so hopelessly" (*Journals* 121).

2. French for "Castle in Spain," commonly known as Castle in the Air, or a daydream.

3. *Moods* (1864), LMA's first novel, met with many negative reviews. Boston's *Independent* for February 16, 1865, wrote: "Novelists can win applause just so long as they 'hold the mirror up to nature;' but a *made* story—a case manufactured to meet a point—no matter how ingenious it may be, always fails to appeal to the popular heart. The plot of 'Moods' is open to the suspicion of having come to maturity under a bell-glass . . . Our lady-writers especially seem to revel in the portrayal of all sorts of mental misery, just as some of the old artists delighted to paint a man roasting on a grid-iron, or breaking on the rack. *Cui bono?*" (quoted in Beverly Lyon Clark, ed., *Louisa May Alcott: The Contemporary Reviews* [Cambridge: Cambridge University Press, 2004], pp. 31–32). On January 26, 1865, the *Providence Daily Journal* wrote: "One of the foolish novels. A story about married life, written evidently by one who knows nothing about it" (quoted in Clark, p. 31). In May 1865, LMA confessed: "My next book shall have no *ideas* in it, only facts, & the people shall be as ordinary as possible, then critics will say its all right" (*Journals* 140).

4. First issued by the publisher Benjamin Tabart as a sixpenny booklet *The History of Jack and the Bean-Stalk. Printed from the Original Manuscript. Never Before Published. 1807*, the English folktale "Jack and the Beanstalk" most likely derives from an oral tradition. On Jack's first climb up the beanstalk, he steals the hen that lays golden eggs from the giant. Upon leaving, he has some trouble finding his way out of the castle, but encounters no problems in climbing down the beanstalk.

Norman Rockwell, *Jo Concocted a Thrilling Tale* (1938).

wood, editor of the "Weekly Volcano."[5] She had never read Sartor Resartus,[6] but she had a womanly instinct that clothes possess an influence more powerful over many than the worth of character or the magic of manners. So she dressed herself in her best, and, trying to persuade herself that she was neither excited nor nervous, bravely climbed two pairs of dark and dirty stairs to find herself in a disorderly room, a cloud of cigar smoke, and the presence of three gentlemen sitting with their heels rather higher than their hats, which articles of dress none of them took the trouble to remove on her appearance.[7] Somewhat daunted by this reception, Jo hesitated on the threshold, murmuring in much embarrassment,—

"Excuse me; I was looking for the 'Weekly Volcano office'; I wished to see Mr. Dashwood."

Down went the highest pair of heels, up rose the smokiest gentleman, and, carefully cherishing his cigar between his fingers, he advanced with a nod, and a countenance expressive of nothing but sleep. Feeling that she must get through with the matter somehow, Jo produced her manuscript, and, blushing redder and redder with each sentence, blundered out fragments of the little speech carefully prepared for the occasion.

"A friend of mine desired me to offer—a story—just as an experiment—would like your opinion—be glad to write more if this suits."

While she blushed and blundered, Mr. Dashwood had taken the manuscript, and was turning over the leaves with a pair of rather dirty fingers, and casting critical glances up and down the neat pages.

"Not a first attempt, I take it?" observing that the pages were numbered, covered only on one side, and *not* tied up with a ribbon—sure sign of a novice.

"No, sir; she has had some experience, and got a prize for a tale in the 'Blarneystone Banner.'"

"Oh, did she?" and Mr. Dashwood gave Jo a quick look, which seemed to take note of everything she had on, from the bow in her bonnet to the buttons on her boots. "Well, you can leave it, if you like; we've more of this sort of thing on hand than we know

5. For her creation of *The Weekly Volcano*, LMA draws upon her experience with several newspapers that published sensational fiction. As early as 1858, she was writing for the *American Union*, in which the thriller "Marion Earle" was published. On June 22, 1862, LMA wrote to Alf Whitman: "I intend to illuminate the Ledger with a blood & thunder tale as they are easy to 'compoze' & are better paid than moral & elaborate works of Shakespeare, so dont be shocked if I send you a paper containing a picture of Indians, pirates wolves, bears & distressed damsels in a grand tableau over a title like this 'The Maniac Bride' or 'The Bath of Blood. A thrilling tale of passion, &c.'" (*Selected Letters* 79). While no thriller has been found in the pages of the *New York Ledger*, LMA, between 1863 to 1870, contributed at least twenty-six thrillers to three Frank Leslie publications: *Frank Leslie's Illustrated Newspaper, Frank Leslie's Lady's Magazine*, and *Frank Leslie's Chimney Corner*. Paid $25 to $100 per tale, LMA found the genre a profitable market. However, at the same time, she was also publishing for other periodicals such as *The Atlantic Monthly;* to preserve her reputation, the thrillers appeared anonymously. After her first successes with the New York firm of Leslie, she turned to the Boston-based publisher Eliot, Thomes & Talbot in 1865, where she published under the pseudonym "A. M. Barnard" in *The Flag of Our Union*. Although Ednah Dow Cheney hinted at the thrillers in her biography *Louisa May Alcott: Her Life, Letters and Journals* (1889), the existence of LMA's thrillers remained unknown until 1943, when Leona Rostenberg examined the correspondence between LMA and her publishers. Finally, in 1975, Madeleine B. Stern republished the first of LMA's sensational stories in *Behind a Mask*. Today over thirty thrillers have been uncovered, forming an important part of LMA's literary canon. See Madeleine B. Stern, ed., *Louisa May Alcott Unmasked: Collected Thrillers* (Boston: Northeastern University Press, 1995).

6. *Sartor Resartus* (1833–1834), translated as *The Tailor Retailored,* by the Scottish author Thomas Carlyle (1795–1881). Part autobiography and part satire, the work was purported to be commentary on a German philosopher, the author of *Clothes: their Origin and Influences.* Influential in the development of New England Transcendentalism, Carlyle became friends and established a lengthy correspondence with Ralph Waldo Emerson, who wrote the preface to the first book publication of *Sartor Resartus* (Boston, 1836). Bronson Alcott also met Carlyle when he traveled to England in 1841. At the age of twenty, LMA listed Carlyle's *French Revolution: A History* (1837) and *Critical and Miscellaneous Essays* (1839) at the top of a list of books she liked best (*Journals* 67).

7. This is one of the more memorable descriptive sentences in

Little Women: it conjures quite an unflattering image of a boorish, clubby, and slightly seedy male-dominated American publishing culture. American publishing would not become more diversified until the twentieth century, which saw the publication of experimental fiction and poetry as well as works by feminist, black, Hispanic, and European authors.

8. With winking self-regard the author ridicules one aesthetic while embracing another of far greater value and importance. The reader will recall that Part I of *Little Women* has already been successful when LMA pens these words. In other words, "Not quite correct" means consider the example of the book in your hands, reader. Many millions of copies later, LMA has been vindicated. Ten years after *Little Women* was published, LMA wrote to an aspiring author: "'Little Women' was written when I was ill & to prove that I could *not* write books for girls. The publisher thought it *flat,* so did I, & neither hoped much for or from it. We found out our mistake, & since then, though I do not enjoy writing 'moral tales' for the young, I do it because it pays well (*Selected Letters* 232).

what to do with, at present; but I'll run my eye over it, and give you an answer next week."

Now, Jo did *not* like to leave it, for Mr. Dashwood didn't suit her at all; but, under the circumstances, there was nothing for her to do but bow and walk away, looking particularly tall and dignified, as she was apt to do, when nettled or abashed. Just then she was both; for it was perfectly evident from the knowing glances exchanged among the gentlemen, that her little fiction of "my friend" was considered a good joke; and a laugh produced by some inaudible remark of the editor, as he closed the door, completed her discomfiture. Half resolving never to return, she went home, and worked off her irritation by stitching pinafores vigorously; and in an hour or two was cool enough to laugh over the scene, and long for next week.

When she went again, Mr. Dashwood was alone, whereat she rejoiced. Mr. Dashwood was much wider awake than before,—which was agreeable,—and Mr. Dashwood was not too deeply absorbed in a cigar to remember his manners,—so the second interview was much more comfortable than the first.

"We'll take this" (editors never say "I"), "if you don't object to a few alterations. It's too long,—but omitting the passages I've marked will make it just the right length," he said, in a business-like tone.

Jo hardly knew her own MS. again, so crumpled and underscored were its pages and paragraphs; but, feeling as a tender parent might on being asked to cut off her baby's legs in order that it might fit into a new cradle, she looked at the marked passages, and was surprised to find that all the moral reflections,—which she had carefully put in as ballast for much romance,—had all been stricken out.

"But, sir, I thought every story should have some sort of a moral, so I took care to have a few of my sinners repent."

Mr. Dashwood's editorial gravity relaxed into a smile, for Jo had forgotten her "friend," and spoken as only an author could.

"People want to be amused, not preached at, you know. Morals don't sell nowadays;" which was not quite a correct statement, by the way.[8]

"You think it would do with these alterations, then?"

"Yes; it's a new plot, and pretty well worked up—language good, and so on," was Mr. Dashwood's affable reply.

"What do you—that is, what compensation—" began Jo, not exactly knowing how to express herself.

"Oh, yes,—well, we give from twenty-five to thirty for things of this sort. Pay when it comes out," returned Mr. Dashwood, as if that point had escaped him; such trifles do escape the editorial mind, it is said.

"Very well; you can have it," said Jo, handing back the story, with a satisfied air; for, after the dollar-a-column work, even twenty-five seemed good pay.

"Shall I tell my friend you will take another if she has one better than this?" asked Jo, unconscious of her little slip of the tongue, and emboldened by her success.

"Well, we'll look at it; can't promise to take it; tell her to make it short and spicy, and never mind the moral. What name would your friend like to put on it?" in a careless tone.

"None at all, if you please; she doesn't wish her name to appear, and has no *nom de plume*,"[9] said Jo, blushing in spite of herself.

"Just as she likes, of course. The tale will be out next week; will you call for the money, or shall I send it?" asked Mr. Dashwood, who felt a natural desire to know who his new contributor might be.

"I'll call; good morning, sir."

As she departed, Mr. Dashwood put up his feet, with the graceful remark, "Poor and proud, as usual, but she'll do."

Following Mr. Dashwood's directions, and making Mrs. Northbury her model, Jo rashly took a plunge into the frothy sea of sensational literature; but, thanks to the life-preserver thrown her by a friend, she came up again, not much the worse for her ducking.

Like most young scribblers, she went abroad for her characters and scenery, and banditti,[10] counts, gypsies, nuns, and duchesses appeared upon her stage, and played their parts with as much accuracy and spirit as could be expected. Her readers were not particular about such trifles as grammar, punctuation, and probability,

9. French for "name of pen," or pen name, a pseudonym.
10. Robbers or bandits.

and Mr. Dashwood graciously permitted her to fill his columns at the lowest prices, not thinking it necessary to tell her that the real cause of his hospitality was the fact that one of his hacks, on being offered higher wages, had basely left him in the lurch.

She soon became interested in her work,—for her emaciated purse grew stout, and the little hoard she was making to take Beth to the mountains next summer, grew slowly but surely, as the weeks passed. One thing disturbed her satisfaction, and that was that she did not tell them at home. She had a feeling that father and mother would not approve,—and preferred to have her own way first, and beg pardon afterward. It was easy to keep her secret, for no name appeared with her stories; Mr. Dashwood had, of course, found it out very soon, but promised to be dumb; and, for a wonder, kept his word.

She thought it would do her no harm, for she sincerely meant to write nothing of which she should be ashamed, and quieted all pricks of conscience by anticipations of the happy minute when she should show her earnings and laugh over her well-kept secret.

But Mr. Dashwood rejected any but thrilling tales; and, as thrills could not be produced except by harrowing up the souls of the readers, history and romance, land and sea, science and art, police records and lunatic asylums, had to be ransacked for the purpose. Jo soon found that her innocent experience had given her but few glimpses of the tragic world which underlies society; so, regarding it in a business light, she set about supplying her deficiencies with characteristic energy. Eager to find material for stories, and bent on making them original in plot, if not masterly in execution, she searched newspapers for accidents, incidents, and crimes; she excited the suspicions of public librarians by asking for works on poisons; she studied faces in the street,—and characters good, bad, and indifferent, all about her; she delved in the dust of ancient times, for facts or fictions so old that they were as good as new, and introduced herself to folly, sin, and misery, as well as her limited opportunities allowed. She thought she was prospering finely; but, unconsciously, she was beginning to desecrate some of the womanliest attributes of a woman's character. She was living in bad society; and, imaginary though it was, its influence affected her, for she was feeding heart and fancy on dangerous and unsubstantial food, and was fast brushing the innocent bloom from her nature by a premature acquaintance with the darker side of life, which comes soon enough to all of us.

She was beginning to feel rather than see this, for much describing of other people's passions and feelings set her to studying and speculating about her own,—a morbid amusement, in which healthy young minds do not voluntarily indulge. Wrong-doing always brings its own punishment; and, when Jo most needed hers, she got it.

I don't know whether the study of Shakespeare helped her to read character, or the natural instinct of a woman for what was honest, brave and strong; but while endowing her imaginary heroes with every perfection under the sun, Jo was discovering a live hero, who interested her in spite of many human imperfections. Mr. Bhaer, in one of their conversations, had advised her to study simple, true, and lovely characters, wherever she found them, as good training for a writer; Jo took him at his word,—for she coolly turned round and studied him,—a proceeding which would have much surprised him, had he known it,—for the worthy Professor was very humble in his own conceit.[11]

Why everybody liked him was what puzzled Jo, at first. He was neither rich nor great, young nor handsome,—in no respect what is called fascinating, imposing, or brilliant; and yet he was as attractive as a genial fire, and people seemed to gather about him as naturally as about a warm hearth. He was poor, yet always appeared to be giving something away,—a stranger, yet every one was his friend; no longer young,—but as happy-hearted as a boy; plain and odd,—yet his face looked beautiful to many, and his oddities were freely forgiven for his sake. Jo often watched him, trying to discover the charm, and, at last, decided that it was benevolence which worked the miracle. If he had any sorrow "it sat with its head under its wing,"[12] and he turned only his sunny side to the world. There were lines upon his forehead, but Time seemed to have touched him gently, remembering how kind he was to others. The pleasant curves about his mouth were the memorials of many friendly words and cheery laughs; his eyes were

11. His own opinion of himself.

12. LMA quotes from the song "Bang Begger" by Joseph Mather (1737–1804). In the song, a bird witnesses a young apprentice, Will, receive a brutal flogging, at which the bird "wept for a while with head under its wing" before eventually singing about the injustice (Song 45, line 7, in *The Songs of Joseph Mather* [Sheffield: Pawson and Brailsford, 1862], 67).

13. Scratchy.

14. Robert Browning's "Evelyn Hope" from *Men and Women* (1855). This dramatic monologue explores Browning's idea of romantic love as the narrator, three times the age of the deceased sixteen-year-old Hope, is alone with her corpse: "Is it too late then, Evelyn Hope? / What, your soul was pure and true, / The good stars met in your horoscope, / Made you of spirit, fire and dew" (lines 17–20).

15. Anne Louise Germaine de Staël-Holstein (1766–1817), Swiss author, wrote the semi-autobiographical *Corinne, or Italy* (1807), the story of the Scottish peer Lord Nevil who is torn between loving the Italian poetess Corinne and the English woman Lucile. One of the book's themes explores how women of great genius are held back by society. In 1852, LMA includes Madame de Staël in her list of favorite writers and books (*Journals* 67).

16. In James Boswell's *Life of Samuel Johnson, LL.D.*, 3rd ed. vol. 1 (London: H. Baldwin and Son for Charles Dilly, 1799), the biographer writes: "I suppose no person ever enjoyed with more relish the infusion of that fragrant [tea] leaf than Johnson. The quantities which he drank of it at all hours were so great, that his nerves must have been uncommonly strong, not to have been extremely relaxed by such intemperate use of it. He assured me, that he never felt the least inconvenience from it; which is a proof that the fault of his constitution was rather a too great tension of fibres, than the contrary" (209).

17. Talkativeness.

18. An allusion to Louis Agassiz (1807–1873), the Swiss paleontologist, glaciologist, and geologist. Agassiz was one of the most important scientists studying the natural history of the earth in the nineteenth century, and he was the first to argue scientifically that the planet had undergone an ice age. He became a professor of zoology and geology at Harvard in 1847 and was a member, along with Emerson, Longfellow, Lowell, and Holmes, of the famous Saturday Club, which met in Boston.

19. In Greek mythology, Orpheus was a musician, poet, and inspired singer, perhaps most famous for attempting unsuccessfully to lead his wife, Eurydice, from Hades. He also helped Jason and the Argonauts get safely past the Sirens by playing his lute so loudly that it drowned out their singing.

never cold or hard, and his big hand had a warm, strong grasp that was more expressive than words.

His very clothes seemed to partake of the hospitable nature of the wearer. They looked as if they were at ease, and liked to make him comfortable; his capacious waistcoat was suggestive of a large heart underneath; his rusty coat had a social air, and the baggy pockets plainly proved that little hands often went in empty and came out full; his very boots were benevolent, and his collars never stiff and raspy[13] like other people's.

"That's it!" said Jo to herself, when she at length discovered that genuine good-will toward one's fellow-men could beautify and dignify even a stout German teacher, who shovelled in his dinner, darned his own socks, and was burdened with the name of Bhaer.

Jo valued goodness highly, but she also possessed a most feminine respect for intellect, and a little discovery which she made about the Professor added much to her regard for him. He never spoke of himself, and no one ever knew that in his native city he had been a man much honored and esteemed for learning and integrity, till a countryman came to see him, and, in a conversation with Miss Norton, divulged the pleasing fact. From her Jo learned it,—and liked it all the better because Mr. Bhaer had never told it. She felt proud to know that he was an honored Professor in Berlin, though only a poor language-master in America, and his homely, hard-working life, was much beautified by the spice of romance which this discovery gave it.

Another and a better gift than intellect was shown her in a most unexpected manner. Miss Norton had the *entrée* into literary society, which Jo would have had no chance of seeing but for her. The solitary woman felt an interest in the ambitious girl, and kindly conferred many favors of this sort both on Jo and the Professor. She took them with her, one night, to a select symposium, held in honor of several celebrities.

Jo went prepared to bow down and adore the mighty ones whom she had worshipped with youthful enthusiasm afar off. But her reverence for genius received a severe shock that night, and it took her some time to recover from the discovery that the great creatures were only men and women, after all. Imagine her dismay,

LITTLE WOMEN

on stealing a glance of timid admiration at the poet whose lines suggested an ethereal being fed on "spirit, fire, and dew,"[14] to behold him devouring his supper with an ardor which flushed his intellectual countenance. Turning as from a fallen idol, she made other discoveries which rapidly dispelled her romantic illusions. The great novelist vibrated between two decanters with the regularity of a pendulum; the famous divine flirted openly with one of the Madame de Staëls of the age, who looked daggers at another Corinne,[15] who was amiably satirizing her, after out-manœuvring her in efforts to absorb the profound philosopher, who imbibed tea Johnsonianly[16] and appeared to slumber,—the loquacity[17] of the lady rendering speech impossible. The scientific celebrities, forgetting their mollusks and Glacial Periods,[18] gossiped about art, while devoting themselves to oysters and ices with characteristic energy; the young musician, who was charming the city like a second Orpheus,[19] talked horses; and the specimen of the British nobility present happened to be the most ordinary man of the party.

Before the evening was half over, Jo felt so completely *désillusionnée*,[20] that she sat down in a corner, to recover herself. Mr. Bhaer soon joined her, looking rather out of his element, and presently several of the philosophers, each mounted on his hobby,[21] came ambling up to hold an intellectual tournament in the recess.[22] The conversation was miles beyond Jo's comprehension, but she enjoyed it, though Kant and Hegel were unknown gods, the Subjective and Objective unintelligible terms;[23] and the only thing "evolved from her inner consciousness," was a bad headache after it was all over. It dawned upon her gradually, that the world was being picked to pieces, and put together on new, and, according to the talkers, on infinitely better principles than before; that religion was in a fair way to be reasoned into nothingness, and intellect was to be the only God. Jo knew nothing about philosophy or metaphysics of any sort, but a curious excitement, half pleasurable, half painful, came over her, as she listened with a sense of being turned adrift into time and space, like a young balloon out on a holiday.[24]

She looked round to see how the Professor liked it, and found him looking at her with the grimmest expression she had ever

20. Disillusioned.

21. A hobby horse is a play horse, most often a stick attached to a form of horse's head. The phrase "to ride one's hobby horse" means to follow one's love for something, and it became the basis for the word *hobby*. Here LMA means that each held forth on their favorite ideas.

22. LMA here satirizes the Boston literary scene—and more particularly the Radical Club, formed by Transcendentalists and prominent Unitarian thinkers. Begun in 1867, "the club," as LMA referred to it, lasted until 1880. LMA often attended, with and without her father, since women, such as Julia Ward Howe, were an active part of the organization. In January 1868, just several months before she started writing *Little Women*, LMA noted: "To the club with Father. A good paper on the 'Historical View of Jesus.' Father spoke finely . . . The talk lasted until two, and then the hungry philosophers remembered they had bodies and rushed away, still talking" (*Journals* 164). A month later, she recorded that she again attended the Radical Club with Bronson: "A curious jumble of fools and philosophers" (*Journals* 165).

23. Immanuel Kant (1724–1804) and Georg Wilhelm Friedrich Hegel (1770–1831) were German philosophers of Idealism, who greatly influenced the New England Transcendentalist movement. Hegel distinguished the Subjective spirit from the Objective realm.

24. In *Alcott Memoirs* (1915), Frederick L. H. Willis recalled: "Once when asked a definition of a philosopher [LMA] instantly replied, 'A man up in a balloon with his family at the strings tugging to pull him down'" (quoted in *Her Own Time* 180). LMA often poked fun at her father and other Transcendentalists. In an undated poem, recorded in Maria S. Porter's "Recollections of Louisa May Alcott" (1892), LMA writes: "Philosophers sit in their sylvan hall / And talk of the duties of man, / Of Chaos and Cosmos, Hegel and Kant, / With the Oversoul well in the van; / All on their hobbies they amble away, / And a terrible dust they make; / Disciples devout both gaze and adore, / As daily they listen, and bake!" (quoted in *Her Own Time* 70).

25. A metaphysical philosophy that pursued the ultimate nature of being and thought, which was not the physical world. Bronson Alcott's friend (and later his biographer) William Torrey Harris (1835–1909) published and edited the *Journal of Speculative Philosophy* from 1867 to 1893.

26. Like a soldier, Bhaer stood by his colors—his flag; that is, he stood by his beliefs.

27. The phrase appears in Ralph Waldo Emerson's "Greatness," which was delivered as a lecture in 1868–1869 and later published in *Letters and Social Aims* (1876), "What are these but the promise and the preparation of a day when the air of the world shall be purified by nobler society, when the measure of greatness shall be usefulness in the highest sense, greatness consisting in truth, reverence and good will?" (*Letters and Social Aims: The Concord Edition of the Complete Works of Ralph Waldo Emerson* [Boston and New York: Houghton, Mifflin, 1904], p. 319). While LMA does not record hearing this lecture in her journals or letters, it is possible that she did or that she read an account of it.

28. In "Friendship" (1841), Ralph Waldo Emerson writes: "I hate the prostitution of the name of friendship to signify modish and worldly alliances . . . The end of friendship is a commerce the most strict and homely that can be joined; more strict than any of which we have experience. It is for aid and comfort through all the relations and passages of life and death. It is fit for serene days, and graceful gifts and country rambles, but also for rough roads and hard fare, shipwreck, poverty, and persecution. It keeps company with the sallies of the wit and the trances of religion. We are to dignify to each other the daily needs and offices of man's life, and embellish it by courage, wisdom and unity. It should never fall into something usual and settled, but should be alert and inventive and add rhyme and reason to what was drudgery" (pp. 205–206). Emerson concludes, "The essence of friendship is entireness, a total magnanimity and trust. It must not surmise or provide for infirmity. It treats its object as a god, that it may deify both." (*Essays First Series, The Concord Edition of The Complete Works of Ralph Waldo Emerson* [Boston and New York: Houghton, Mifflin, 1904], p. 217). If Jo and Friedrich Bhaer are to enjoy the benefits and pleasures of real friendship, Jo realizes, then they must engage as equals.

29. The cocked-hat, or bicorne (two-cornered) hat, was popular during the 1790s as part of military dress and remained in vogue until WWI. It is often associated with Napoleon Bonaparte.

seen him wear. He shook his head, and beckoned her to come away, but she was fascinated, just then, by the freedom of Speculative Philosophy,[25] and kept her seat, trying to find out what the wise gentlemen intended to rely upon after they annihilated all the old beliefs.

Now Mr. Bhaer was a diffident man, and slow to offer his own opinions, not because they were unsettled, but too sincere and earnest to be lightly spoken. As he glanced from Jo to several other young people attracted by the brilliancy of the philosophic pyrotechnics, he knit his brows, and longed to speak, fearing that some inflammable young soul would be led astray by the rockets, to find, when the display was over, that they had only an empty stick, or a scorched hand.

He bore it as long as he could; but when he was appealed to for an opinion, he blazed up with honest indignation, and defended religion with all the eloquence of truth—an eloquence which made his broken English musical, and his plain face beautiful. He had a hard fight, for the wise men argued well; but he didn't know when he was beaten, and stood to his colors[26] like a man. Somehow, as he talked, the world got right again to Jo; the old beliefs that had lasted so long, seemed better than the new. God was not a blind force, and immortality was not a pretty fable, but a blessed fact. She felt as if she had solid ground under her feet again; and when Mr. Bhaer paused, out-talked, but not one whit convinced, Jo wanted to clap her hands and thank him.

She did neither; but she remembered this scene, and gave the Professor her heartiest respect, for she knew it cost him an effort to speak out then and there, because his conscience would not let him be silent. She began to see that character is a better possession than money, rank, intellect, or beauty; and to feel that if greatness is what a wise man has defined it to be,—"truth, reverence, and good will,"[27]—then her friend Friedrich Bhaer was not only good, but great.

This belief strengthened daily. She valued his esteem, she coveted his respect, she wanted to be worthy of his friendship;[28] and, just when the wish was sincerest, she came near to losing everything. It all grew out of a cocked-hat;[29] for one evening the Profes-

Professor Bhaer's cockade hat. Frank Merrill, *Little Women: Illustrated* (1880).

30. *Wallenstein's Death* (1799) was the third in the Wallenstein trilogy, by Johann Christoph Friedrich Schiller (1759–1805), the German playwright and poet. The drama tells the story of the decline and eventual assassination of General Albrecht von Wallenstein during the Thirty Years' War (1618–1648). LMA includes Schiller's plays in her 1852 list of favorite works (*Journals* 67).

sor came in to give Jo her lesson, with a paper soldier-cap on his head, which Tina had put there, and he had forgotten to take off.

"It's evident he doesn't prink at[a] his glass before coming down," thought Jo, with a smile, as he said "Goot efening," and sat soberly down, quite unconscious of the ludicrous contrast between his subject and his head-gear, for he was going to read her the "Death of Wallenstein."[30]

She said nothing at first, for she liked to hear him laugh out his big, hearty laugh, when anything funny happened, so she left him to discover it for himself, and presently forgot all about it; for to hear a German read Schiller is rather an absorbing occupation. After the reading came the lesson, which was a lively one, for Jo was in a gay mood that night, and the cocked-hat kept her eyes dancing with merriment. The Professor didn't know what to make of her, and stopped, at last, to ask with an air of mild surprise that was irresistible,—

Developed in the fifteenth century, a bass-viol, or viola da gamba, is a stringed instrument of the viol family. Played with a bow, it sounds similar to a cello.

"Mees Marsch, for what do you laugh in your master's face? Haf you no respect for me, that you go on so bad?"

"How can I be respectful, sir, when you forget to take your hat off?" said Jo.

Lifting his hand to his head, the absent-minded Professor gravely felt and removed the little cocked-hat, looked at it a minute, and then threw back his head, and laughed like a merry bass-viol.[31]

"Ah! I see him now; it is that imp Tina who makes me a fool with my cap. Well, it is nothing; but see you, if this lesson goes not well, you too shall wear him."

But the lesson did not go at all, for a few minutes, because Mr. Bhaer caught sight of a picture on the hat; and, unfolding it, said with an air of great disgust,—

"I wish these papers did not come in the house; they are not for children to see, nor young people to read. It is not well; and I haf no patience with those who make this harm."

Jo glanced at the sheet, and saw a pleasing illustration composed of a lunatic, a corpse, a villain, and a viper. She did not like it; but the impulse that made her turn it over was not one of displeasure, but fear, because, for a minute she fancied the paper was the "Volcano." It was not, however, and her panic subsided as she remembered that, even if it had been, and one of her own tales in it, there would have been no name to betray her. She had betrayed herself, however, by a look and a blush; for, though an absent man, the Professor saw a good deal more than people fancied. He knew that Jo wrote, and had met her down among the newspaper offices more than once; but as she never spoke of it, he asked no questions, in spite of a strong desire to see her work. Now it occurred to him that she was doing what she was ashamed to own, and it troubled him. He did not say to himself, "It is none of my business; I've no right to say anything," as many people would have done; he only remembered that she was young and poor, a girl far away from mother's love and father's care; and he was moved to help her with an impulse as quick and natural as that which would prompt him to put out his hand to save a baby from a puddle. All this flashed through his mind in a minute, but not a trace of it appeared in his face; and by the time the paper was turned, and Jo's needle threaded, he was ready to say quite naturally, but very gravely,—

"Yes, you are right to put it from you. I do not think that good young girls should see such things. They are made pleasant to some, but I would more rather give my boys gunpowder to play with than this bad trash."

"All may not be bad—only silly, you know; and if there is a demand for it, I don't see any harm in supplying it. Many very respectable people make an honest living out of what are called sensation stories," said Jo, scratching gathers[32] so energetically that a row of little slits followed her pin.

"There is a demand for whisky, but I think you and I do not care to sell it. If the respectable people knew what harm they did, they would not feel that the living *was* honest. They haf no right to put poison in the sugar-plum,[33] and let the small ones eat it. No; they should think a little, and sweep mud in the street before they do this thing!"

Mr. Bhaer spoke warmly, and walked to the fire, crumpling the paper in his hands. Jo sat still, looking as if the fire had come to her; for her cheeks burned long after the cocked-hat had turned to smoke, and gone harmlessly up the chimney.

"I should like much to send all the rest after him," muttered the Professor, coming back with a relieved air.

Jo thought what a blaze her pile of papers, upstairs, would make, and her hard-earned money lay rather heavily on her conscience at that minute. Then she thought consolingly to herself, "Mine are not like that; they are only silly, never bad; so I won't be worried;" and, taking up her book, she said, with a studious face,—

"Shall we go on, sir? I'll be very good and proper now."

"I shall hope so," was all he said, but he meant more than she imagined; and the grave, kind look he gave her, made her feel as if the words "Weekly Volcano" were printed in large type, on her forehead.

As soon as she went to her room, she got out her papers, and carefully re-read every one of her stories. Being a little short-

32. The *OED* defines *gathers* as "that part of a dress which is gathered or drawn in." Jo is so disconcerted and embarrassed by the conversation that she is actually cutting the material with her needle.

33. The *OED* defines a *sugar-plum* as "a small round or oval sweetmeat, made of boiled sugar and variously flavoured and coloured; a comfit."

34. In LaSalle Corbell Picket's *Across My Path: Memories of People I Have Known* (1916), the author recalls a conversation she had with LMA in Boston, where LMA denied that *Little Women* was her true style: "I think my natural ambition is for the lurid style." When asked why she did not write what she pleased, LMA answered: "How should I dare to interfere with the proper grayness of old Concord? The dear old town has never known a startling hue since the redcoats were there. . . . And my favorite characters! Suppose they went to cavorting at their own sweet will, to the infinite horror of dear Mr. Emerson, who never imagined a Concord person as walking off a plumb line stretched between two pearly clouds in the empyrean. To have had Mr. Emerson for an intellectual god all one's life is to be invested with a chain armor of propriety. . . . And what would my own good father think of me . . . if I set folks to doing the things that I have a longing to see my people do? No, my dear, I shall always be a wretched victim to the respectable traditions of Concord" (quoted in *Her Own Time* 184–185). Unlike Jo, LMA did not stop writing sensational fiction until 1870, by which time *Little Women* had ensured her fame and financial security.

sighted, Mr. Bhaer sometimes used eye-glasses, and Jo had tried them once, smiling to see how they magnified the fine print of her book; now she seemed to have got on the Professor's mental or moral spectacles also, for the faults of these poor stories glared at her dreadfully, and filled her with dismay.

"They *are* trash, and will soon be worse than trash if I go on; for each is more sensational than the last. I've gone blindly on, hurting myself and other people, for the sake of money;—I know it's so—for I can't read this stuff in sober earnest without being horribly ashamed of it; and *what should* I do if they were seen at home, or Mr. Bhaer got hold of them?"[34]

Jo turned hot at the bare idea, and stuffed the whole bundle into her stove, nearly setting the chimney afire with the blaze.

"Yes, that's the best place for such inflammable nonsense; I'd better burn the house down, I suppose, than let other people blow themselves up with my gunpowder," she thought, as she watched the "Demon of the Jura" whisk away, a little black cinder with fiery eyes.

But when nothing remained of all her three months' work, except a heap of ashes, and the money in her lap, Jo looked sober, as she sat on the floor, wondering what she ought to do about her wages.

"I think I haven't done much harm *yet,* and may keep this to pay for my time," she said, after a long meditation, adding, impatiently, "I almost wish I hadn't any conscience, it's so inconvenient. If I didn't care about doing right, and didn't feel uncomfortable when doing wrong, I should get on capitally. I can't help wishing, sometimes, that father and mother hadn't been so dreadfully particular about such things."

Ah, Jo, instead of wishing that, thank God that "father and mother *were* particular," and pity from your heart those who have no such guardians to hedge them round with principles which may seem like prison walls to impatient youth, but which will prove sure foundations to build character upon in womanhood.

Jo wrote no more sensational stories, deciding that the money did not pay for her share of the sensation; but, going to the other extreme, as is the way with people of her stamp, she took a course

LITTLE WOMEN

of Mrs. Sherwood, Miss Edgeworth, and Hannah More;[35] and then produced a tale which might have been more properly called an essay or a sermon, so intensely moral was it. She had her doubts about it from the beginning; for her lively fancy and girlish romance felt as ill at ease in the new style as she would have done masquerading in the stiff and cumbrous costume of the last century. She sent this didactic gem to several markets, but it found no purchaser; and she was inclined to agree with Mr. Dashwood, that morals didn't sell.

Then she tried a child's story, which she could easily have disposed of if she had not been mercenary enough to demand filthy lucre for it. The only person who offered enough to make it worth her while to try juvenile literature, was a worthy gentleman who felt it his mission to convert all the world to his particular belief. But much as she liked to write for children, Jo could not consent to depict all her naughty boys as being eaten by bears, or tossed by mad bulls, because they did not go to a particular Sabbath-school, nor all the good infants who did go, of course,[b] as rewarded by every kind of bliss, from gilded gingerbread to escorts of angels, when they departed this life, with psalms or sermons on their lisping tongues. So nothing came of these trials; and Jo corked up her inkstand, and said, in a fit of very wholesome humility,—

"I don't know anything; I'll wait till I do before I try again, and, meantime, 'sweep mud in the street,' if I can't do better—that's honest, any way;" which decision proved that her second tumble down the bean-stalk had done her some good.

While these internal revolutions were going on, her external life had been as busy and uneventful as usual; and if she sometimes looked serious, or a little sad, no one observed it but Professor Bhaer. He did it so quietly, that Jo never knew he was watching to see if she would accept and profit by his reproof; but she stood the test, and he was satisfied; for, though no words passed between them, he knew that she had given up writing. Not only did he guess it by the fact that the second finger of her right hand was no longer inky, but she spent her evenings down stairs, now, was met no more among newspaper offices, and studied with a dogged patience, which assured him that she was bent on occupying her mind with something useful, if not pleasant.

35. Mary Martha Sherwood (1775–1851) was a prolific English writer of didactic or evangelical works for children. One of her more popular books was *The History of the Fairchild Family* (1818) and its two sequels (1842; 1847), which depict the Fairchild parents teaching their three children religious and moral lessons from the events in their life. Hannah More (1745–1833), English playwright, poet, and social reformer, was active in the moral and religious education of children through Sunday Schools and was the author of *Strictures on the Modern System of Female Education* (1799).

He helped her in many ways, proving himself a true friend, and Jo was happy; for while her pen lay idle, she was learning other lessons besides German, and laying a foundation for the sensation story of her own life.

It was a pleasant winter and a long one, for she did not leave Mrs. Kirke till June. Every one seemed sorry when the time came; the children were inconsolable, and Mr. Bhaer's hair stuck straight up all over his head—for he always rumpled it wildly when disturbed in mind.

"Going home! Ah, you are happy that you haf a home to go in," he said, when she told him, and sat silently pulling his beard, in the corner, while she held a little levee[36] on that last evening.

She was going early, so she bade them all good-by over night; and when his turn came, she said, warmly,—

"Now, sir, you won't forget to come and see us, if you ever travel our way, will you? I'll never forgive you, if you do, for I want them all to know my friend."

"Do you? Shall I come?" he asked, looking down at her with an eager expression, which she did not see.

"Yes, come next month; Laurie graduates then, and you'd enjoy Commencement as something new."

"That is your best friend, of whom you speak?" he said, in an altered tone.

"Yes, my boy Teddy; I'm very proud of him, and should like you to see him."

Jo looked up, then, quite unconscious of anything but her own pleasure, in the prospect of showing them to one another. Something in Mr. Bhaer's face suddenly recalled the fact that she might find Laurie more than a best friend, and simply because she particularly wished not to look as if anything was the matter, she involuntarily began to blush; and the more she tried not to, the redder she grew. If it had not been for Tina on her knee, she didn't know what would have become of her. Fortunately, the child was moved to hug her; so she managed to hide her face an instant, hoping the Professor did not see it. But he did, and his own changed again from that momentary anxiety to its usual expression, as he said, cordially,—

"I fear I shall not make the time for that, but I wish the friend much success, and you all happiness; Gott bless you!" and with that, he shook hands warmly, shouldered Tina, and went away.

But after the boys were abed, he sat long before his fire, with the tired look on his face, and the *"heimweh,"* or homesickness lying heavy at his heart. Once when he remembered Jo, as she sat with the little child in her lap, and that new softness in her face, he leaned his head on his hands a minute, and then roamed about the room, as if in search of something that he could not find.

"It is not for me; I must not hope it now," he said to himself, with a sigh that was almost a groan; then, as if reproaching himself for the longing that he could not repress, he went and kissed the two towzled heads upon the pillow, took down his seldom-used meerschaum, and opened his Plato.

He did his best, and did it manfully; but I don't think he found that a pair of rampant boys, a pipe, or even the divine Plato, were very satisfactory substitutes for wife and child, and home.

Early as it was, he was at the station, next morning, to see Jo off; and, thanks to him, she began her solitary journey with the pleasant memory of a familiar face smiling its farewell, a bunch of violets to keep her company, and, best of all, the happy thought,—

"Well, the winter's gone, and I've written no books—earned no fortune; but I've made a friend worth having, and I'll try to keep him all my life."

1. While the college Laurie attends is never named, it is likely, given the novel's setting near Boston and Mr. Laurence's great wealth and social standing, Harvard. Since the class of 1642, Harvard has had a Latin Oration every year, where the top scholar of the graduating class gives an address in Latin during the graduation ceremony.

2. Wendell Phillips (1811–1884), Boston-born antislavery leader. At Harvard, Edward T. Channing, Boylston Professor of Rhetoric and Oratory, who taught Phillips, disliked flowery language, emphasizing instead plain speaking. As an orator, Phillips followed this advice and became known as abolition's Golden Trumpet. It was Phillips who declared in 1861, "This is the Negro's hour." He would go on to become an activist for the rights of Native Americans, the woman's rights movement, and temperance reform. Active in the radical reform movements, the Alcott family moved within the same circles as Phillips and heard him speak on numerous occasions.

3. Demosthenes (ca. 384–322 B.C.E.) was a Greek orator and statesman. Even though the Athenian suffered from a speech impediment as a youth, he became one of the most famous orators in history.

4. Jo is incorrect about the title. George Frederic Handel's "See, the conqu'ring hero comes" was composed in 1747 for his oratorio *Joshua,* first performed in Covent Garden, London, in 1748. Beethoven, in 1796, would compose twelve variations of the tune for the piano cello. "See, the conqu'ring hero comes" became a popular tune for brass bands in the nineteenth century.

Chapter 12

Heartache

WHATEVER his motive might have been, Laurie "dug"[a] to some purpose that year, for he graduated with honor, and gave the Latin Oration[1] with the grace of a Phillips,[2] and the eloquence of a Demosthenes,[3]—so his friends said. They were all there—his grandfather, oh, so proud! Mr. and Mrs. March, John and Meg, Jo and Beth, and all exulted over him with the sincere admiration which boys make light of at the time, but fail to win from the world by any after-triumphs.

"I've got to stay for this confounded supper,—but I shall be home early to-morrow; you'll come and meet me as usual, girls?" Laurie said, as he put the sisters into the carriage after the joys of the day were over. He said "girls," but he meant Jo,—for she was the only one who kept up the old custom; she had not the heart to refuse her splendid, successful boy anything, and answered, warmly,—

"I'll come, Teddy, rain or shine, and march before you, playing *'Hail the conquering hero comes,'*[4] on a jews-harp."

Laurie thanked her with a look that made her think, in a sudden panic, "Oh, deary me! I know he'll say something, and then what shall I do?"

Evening meditation and morning work somewhat allayed her fears, and, having decided that she wouldn't be vain enough to think people were going to propose when she had given them every reason to know what her answer would be, she set forth at the appointed time, hoping Teddy wouldn't go and make her hurt his poor little feelings. A call at Meg's, and a refreshing sniff and sip at the Daisy and Demijohn, still further fortified her for the *tête-*

a-tête, but when she saw a stalwart figure looming in the distance, she had a strong desire to turn about and run away.

"Where's the jews-harp, Jo?" cried Laurie, as soon as he was within speaking distance.

"I forgot it"; and Jo took heart again, for that salutation could not be called lover-like.

She always used to take his arm on these occasions; now she did not, and he made no complaint,—which was a bad sign,—but talked on rapidly about all sorts of far-away subjects, till they turned from the road into the little path that led homeward through the grove. Then he walked more slowly, suddenly lost his fine flow of language, and, now and then, a dreadful pause occurred. To rescue the conversation from one of the wells of silence into which it kept falling, Jo said, hastily,—

"Now you must have a good, long holiday!"

"I intend to."

Something in his resolute tone made Jo look up quickly, to find him looking down at her with an expression that assured her the dreaded moment had come, and made her put out her hand with an imploring,—

"No, Teddy,—please don't!"

"I will; and you *must* hear me. It's no use, Jo; we've got to have it out, and the sooner the better for both of us," he answered, getting flushed and excited all at once.

"Say what you like, then; I'll listen," said Jo, with a desperate sort of patience.

Laurie was a young lover, but he was in earnest, and meant to "have it out," if he died in the attempt; so he plunged into the subject with characteristic impetuosity, saying, in a voice that *would* get choky now and then, in spite of manful efforts to keep it steady,—

"I've loved you ever since I've known you, Jo,—couldn't help it, you've been so good to me,—I've tried to show it, but you wouldn't let me; now I'm going to make you hear, and give me an answer, for I *can't* go on so any longer."

"I wanted to save you this; I thought you'd understand—" began Jo, finding it a great deal harder than she expected.

"I know you did; but girls are so queer you never know what they mean. They say No, when they mean Yes; and drive a man out of his wits just for the fun of it," returned Laurie, entrenching himself behind an undeniable fact.

"*I* don't. I never wanted to make you care for me so, and I went away to keep you from it if I could."

"I thought so; it was like you, but it was no use. I only loved you all the more, and I worked hard to please you, and I gave up billiards and everything you didn't like, and waited and never complained, for I hoped you'd love me, though I'm not half good enough—" here there was a choke that couldn't be controlled, so he decapitated butter-cups while he cleared his "confounded throat."

"You, you are; you're a great deal too good for me, and I'm so grateful to you, and so proud and fond of you, I don't see why I can't love you as you want me to. I've tried, but I can't change the feeling, and it would be a lie to say I do when I don't."

"Really, truly, Jo?"

He stopped short, and caught both her hands as he put his question with a look that she did not soon forget.

"Really, truly, dear!"

They were in the grove now,—close by the stile;[5] and when the last words fell reluctantly from Jo's lips, Laurie dropped her hands and turned as if to go on, but for once in his life that fence was too much for him; so he just laid his head down on the mossy post, and stood so still that Jo was frightened.

"Oh, Teddy, I'm so sorry, so desperately sorry, I could kill myself if it would do any good! I wish you wouldn't take it so hard; I can't help it; you know it's impossible for people to make themselves love other people if they don't," cried Jo, inelegantly but remorsefully, as she softly patted his shoulder, remembering the time when he had comforted her so long ago.

"They do sometimes," said a muffled voice from the post.

"I don't believe it's the right sort of love, and I'd rather not try it," was the decided answer.

There was a long pause, while a blackbird sung blithely on the willow by the river, and the tall grass rustled in the wind. Presently Jo said, very soberly, as she sat down on the step of the stile,—

"Laurie, I want to tell you something."

He started as if he had been shot, threw up his head, and cried out, in a fierce tone,—

"*Don't* tell me that, Jo; I can't bear it now!"

"Tell what?" she asked, wondering at his violence.

"That you love that old man."

"What old man?" demanded Jo, thinking he must mean his grandfather.

"That devilish Professor you were always writing about. If you say you love him I know I shall do something desperate"—and he looked as if he would keep his word, as he clenched his hands with a wrathful spark in his eyes.

Jo wanted to laugh, but restrained herself, and said, warmly, for she, too, was getting excited with all this,—

"Don't swear, Teddy! He isn't old, nor anything bad, but good and kind, and the best friend I've got—next to you. Pray don't fly into a passion; I want to be kind, but I know I shall get angry if you abuse my Professor. I haven't the least idea of loving him, or anybody else."

"But you will after a while, and then what will become of me?"

"You'll love some one else, too, like a sensible boy, and forget all this trouble."

"I *can't* love any one else; and I'll never forget you, Jo, never! never!" with a stamp to emphasize his passionate words.

"What *shall* I do with him?" sighed Jo, finding that emotions were more unmanageable than she expected. "You haven't heard what I wanted to tell you. Sit down and listen; for indeed I want to do right, and make you happy," she said, hoping to soothe him with a little reason,—which proved that she knew nothing about love.

Seeing a ray of hope in that last speech, Laurie threw himself down on the grass at her feet, leaned his arm on the lower step of the stile, and looked up at her with an expectant face. Now that arrangement was not conducive to calm speech or clear thought on Jo's part; for how *could* she say hard things to her boy while he watched her with eyes full of love and longing, and lashes still wet with the bitter drop or two her hardness of heart had wrung from him? She gently turned his head away, saying, as she stroked the wavy hair which had been allowed to grow for her sake,—how touching that was to be sure!—

"I agree with mother, that you and I are not suited to each other, because our quick tempers and strong wills would probably make us very miserable, if we were so foolish as to—" Jo paused a little over the last word, but Laurie uttered it with a rapturous expression,—

"Marry,—no we shouldn't! If you loved me, Jo, I should be a perfect saint,—for you could make me anything you like!"

"No I can't. I've tried and failed, and I won't risk our happiness by such a serious experiment. We don't agree, and we never shall; so we'll be good friends all our lives, but we won't go and do anything rash."

"Yes, we will if we get the chance," muttered Laurie, rebelliously.

"Now do be reasonable, and take a sensible view of the case," implored Jo, almost at her wit's end.

"I won't be reasonable; I don't want to take what you call 'a sensible view'; it won't help me, and it only makes it harder. I don't believe you've got any heart."

"I wish I hadn't!"

There was a little quiver in Jo's voice, and, thinking it a good omen, Laurie turned round, bringing all his persuasive powers to bear as he said, in the wheedlesome tone that had never been so dangerously wheedlesome before,—

"Don't disappoint us, dear! every one expects it. Grandpa has set his heart upon it,—your people like it,—and I can't get on without you. Say you will, and let's be happy! do, do!"

Not until months afterward did Jo understand how she had the strength of mind to hold fast to the resolution she had made when she decided that she did not love her boy, and never could. It was very hard to do, but she did it, knowing that delay was both useless and cruel.

Laurie (Christian Bale) proposes to Jo (Winona Ryder) in 1994's *Little Women*.

"I can't say 'Yes' truly, so I won't say it at all. You'll see that I'm right, by and by, and thank me for it"—she began, solemnly.

"I'll be hanged if I do!" and Laurie bounced up off the grass, burning with indignation at the bare idea.

"Yes you will!" persisted Jo; "you'll get over this after a while, and find some lovely, accomplished girl, who will adore you, and make a fine mistress for your fine house. I shouldn't. I'm homely, and awkward, and odd, and old, and you'd be ashamed of me, and we should quarrel,—we can't help it even now, you see,—and I shouldn't like elegant society and you would, and you'd hate my scribbling, and I couldn't get on without it, and we should be unhappy, and wish we hadn't done it,—and everything would be horrid!"[6]

"Anything more?" asked Laurie, finding it hard to listen patiently to this prophetic burst.

"Nothing more,—except that I don't believe I shall ever marry; I'm happy as I am, and love my liberty too well to be in any hurry to give it up for any mortal man."[7]

"I know better!" broke in Laurie, "you think so now; but there'll come a time when you *will* care for somebody, and you'll love him tremendously, and live and die for him. I know you

6. Sarah Elbert, in *Hunger for Home*, observes: "Jo does not want to be an adoring adornment to a fashionable man's home. Nor will she give up her writing to satisfy Laurie, and his proposal reveals just how much 'scribbling' really means to her. If merely saving her 'pathetic family' [words LMA often used to describe the Alcotts] from poverty were her only motivation, she might marry Laurie and enrich them all. She might even produce leisured, graceful literature under his patronage. But she won't be patronized and she won't concede . . . In the nineteenth-century world of *Little Women*, there are only two alternatives following the relative sexual equality of childhood: romantic love or rational affection . . . Jo's decision, as Alcott knew, presents the reader with a bitter pill, for nearly everyone wants Laurie to win Jo . . . [Jo] enjoys being Laurie's chum, plays at being his mother, but is never tempted to be his domestic companion; once wed they will cease to be equals" (p. 208).

7. In June 1860, after visiting her newlywed sister Anna and her husband, LMA declared: "Very sweet and pretty, but I'd rather be a free spinster and paddle my own canoe" (*Journals* 99).

will,—it's your way,—and I shall have to stand by and see it"— and the despairing lover cast his hat upon the ground with a gesture that would have seemed comical, if his face had not been so tragical.

"Yes, I *will* live and die for him, if he ever comes and makes me love him in spite of myself, and you must do the best you can," cried Jo, losing patience with poor Teddy. "I've done my best, but you *won't* be reasonable, and it's selfish of you to keep teasing for what I can't give. I shall always be fond of you,—very fond indeed, as a friend,—but I'll never marry you; and the sooner you believe it the better for both of us,—so now."

That speech was like fire to gunpowder. Laurie looked at her a minute, as if he did not quite know what to do with himself, then turned sharply away, saying, in a desperate sort of tone,—

"You'll be sorry some day, Jo."

"Oh, where are you going?" she cried, for his face frightened her.

"To the devil!" was the consoling answer.

For a minute Jo's heart stood still, as he swung himself down the bank, toward the river; but it takes much folly, sin, or misery to send a young man to a violent death, and Laurie was not one of the weak sort, who are conquered by a single failure. He had no thought of a melodramatic plunge, but some blind instinct led him to fling hat and coat into his boat, and row away with all his might, making better time up the river than he had done in many a race. Jo drew a long breath, and unclasped her hands as she watched the poor fellow trying to outstrip the trouble which he carried in his heart.

"That will do him good, and he'll come home in such a tender, penitent state of mind, that I shan't dare to see him," she said; adding, as she went slowly home, feeling as if she had murdered some innocent thing, and buried it under the leaves,—

"Now I must go and prepare Mr. Laurence to be very kind to my poor boy. I wish he'd love Beth; perhaps he may, in time, but I begin to think I was mistaken about her. Oh dear! how can girls like to have lovers, and refuse them? I think it's dreadful."

Being sure that no one could do it so well as herself, she went straight to Mr. Laurence, told the hard story bravely through, and then broke down, crying so dismally over her own insensibility, that the kind old gentleman, though sorely disappointed, did not utter a reproach. He found it difficult to understand how any girl could help loving Laurie, and hoped she would change her mind, but he knew even better than Jo, that love cannot be forced, so he shook his head sadly, and resolved to carry his boy out of harm's way; for Young Impetuosity's[8] parting words to Jo disturbed him more than he would confess.

When Laurie came home, dead tired, but quite composed, his grandfather met him as if he knew nothing, and kept up the delusion very successfully, for an hour or two. But when they sat together in the twilight, the time they used to enjoy so much, it was hard work for the old man to ramble on as usual, and harder still for the young one to listen to praises of the last year's success, which to him now seemed like love's labor lost. He bore it as long as he could, then went to his piano, and began to play. The windows were open; and Jo, walking in the garden with Beth, for once understood music better than her sister, for he played the "Sonata Pathetique,"[9] and played it as he never did before.

"That's very fine, I dare say, but it's sad enough to make one cry; give us something gayer, lad," said Mr. Laurence, whose kind old heart was full of sympathy, which he longed to show, but knew not how.

Laurie dashed into a livelier strain, played stormily for several minutes, and would have got through bravely, if, in a momentary lull, Mrs. March's voice had not been heard calling,—

"Jo, dear, come in; I want you."

Just what Laurie longed to say, with a different meaning! As he listened, he lost his place; the music ended with a broken chord, and the musician sat silent in the dark.

"I can't stand this," muttered the old gentleman—up he got, groped his way to the piano, laid a kind hand on either of the broad shoulders, and said, as gently as a woman,—

"I know, my boy, I know."

No answer for an instant; then Laurie asked, sharply,—

"Who told you?"

8. *Impetuosity,* which is rash or impulsive behavior, is often said to be a trait of immature youth.

9. Ludwig van Beethoven's Piano Sonata No. 8 in C Minor, Op. 13, known as the *Sonata Pathétique,* was composed in 1798 and published in 1799. It is often described as one of the composer's most tragic, haunting, and beautiful works.

"Jo herself."

"Then there's an end of it!" and he shook off his grandfather's hands with an impatient motion; for, though grateful for the sympathy, his man's pride could not bear a man's pity.

"Not quite; I want to say one thing, and then there shall be an end of it," returned Mr. Laurence, with unusual mildness. "You won't care to stay at home, just now, perhaps?"

"I don't intend to run away from a girl. Jo can't prevent my seeing her, and I shall stay and do it as long as I like," interrupted Laurie, in a defiant tone.

"Not if you are the gentleman I think you. I'm disappointed, but the girl can't help it; and the only thing left for you to do, is to go away for a time. Where will you go?"

"Anywhere; I don't care what becomes of me;" and Laurie got up, with a reckless laugh, that grated on his grandfather's ear.

"Take it like a man, and don't do anything rash, for God's sake. Why not go abroad, as you planned, and forget it?"

"I can't."

"But you've been wild to go, and I promised you should, when you got through college."

"Ah, but I didn't mean to go alone!" and Laurie walked fast through the room, with an expression which it was well his grandfather did not see.

"I don't ask you to go alone; there's some one ready and glad to go with you, anywhere in the world."

"Who, sir?" stopping to listen.

"Myself."

Laurie came back as quickly as he went, and put out his hand, saying huskily,—

"I'm a selfish brute; but—you know—grandfather—"

"Lord help me, yes, I do know, for I've been through it all before, once in my own young days, and then with your father. Now, my dear boy, just sit quietly down, and hear my plan. It's all settled, and can be carried out at once," said Mr. Laurence, keeping hold of the young man, as if fearful that he would break away, as his father had done before him.

"Well, sir, what is it?" and Laurie sat down without a sign of interest in face or voice.

"There is business in London that needs looking after; I meant you should attend to it; but I can do it better myself, and things here will get on very well with Brooke to manage them. My partners do almost everything; I'm merely holding on till you take my place, and can be off at any time."

"But you hate travelling, sir; I can't ask it of you at your age," began Laurie, who was grateful for the sacrifice, but much preferred to go alone, if he went at all.

The old gentleman knew that perfectly well, and particularly desired to prevent it; for the mood in which he found his grandson, assured him that it would not be wise to leave him to his own devices. So, stifling a natural regret at the thought of the home comforts he would leave behind him, he said, stoutly,—[10]

"Bless your soul, I'm not superannuated yet. I quite enjoy the idea; it will do me good, and my old bones won't suffer, for travelling nowadays is almost as easy as sitting in a chair."

A restless movement from Laurie suggested that *his* chair was not easy, or that he did not like the plan, and made the old man add, hastily,—

"I don't mean to be a marplot[11] or a burden; I go because I think you'd feel happier than if I were left behind. I don't intend to gad about with you, but leave you free to go where you like, while I amuse myself in my own way. I've friends in London and Paris, and should like to visit them; meantime, you can go to Italy, Germany, Switzerland, where you will, and enjoy pictures, music, scenery and adventures, to your heart's content."

Now, Laurie felt just then that his heart was entirely broken, and the world a howling wilderness; but, at the sound of certain words which the old gentleman artfully introduced into his closing sentence, the broken heart gave an unexpected leap, and a green oasis or two suddenly appeared in the howling wilderness. He sighed, and then said, in a spiritless tone,—

"Just as you like, sir; it doesn't matter where I go, or what I do."

10. Assertively; firmly.

11. One who stops the successful completion of an undertaking. The word comes from the character Marplot in *The Busie Body* (1709), a play by Susanna Centlivre (ca. 1667–1723), one of the most successful British female playwrights of the eighteenth century. In the drama Marplot prevents couples from wooing each other.

12. While most readers know the meaning of the phrase (to act at the opportune time), modern readers may no longer be aware of its etymology. *Brewer's Dictionary of Phrase & Fable* (15th ed.) notes the origin of the phrase: "A metaphor from the blacksmith's shop, since iron cannot be bent or turned once it has cooled" ([New York: Harper Collins, 1995], p. 1035).

"It does to me—remember that, my lad; I give you entire liberty, but I trust you to make an honest use of it. Promise me that, Laurie."

"Anything you like, sir."

"Good!" thought the old gentleman; "you don't care now, but there'll come a time when that promise will keep you out of mischief, or I'm much mistaken."

Being an energetic individual, Mr. Laurence struck while the iron was hot;[12] and before the blighted being recovered spirit enough to rebel, they were off. During the time necessary for preparation, Laurie bore himself as young gentleman usually do in such cases. He was moody, irritable, and pensive by turns; lost his appetite, neglected his dress, and devoted much time to playing tempestuously on his piano; avoided Jo, but consoled himself by staring at her from his window, with a tragical face that haunted her dreams by night, and oppressed her with a heavy sense of guilt by day. Unlike some sufferers, he never spoke of his unrequited passion, and would allow no one, not even Mrs. March, to attempt consolation, or offer sympathy. On some accounts, this was a relief to his friends; but the weeks before his departure were very uncomfortable, and every one rejoiced that the "poor, dear fellow was going away to forget his trouble, and come home happy." Of course he smiled darkly at their delusion, but passed it by, with the sad superiority of one who knew that his fidelity, like his love, was unalterable.

When the parting came he affected high spirits, to conceal certain inconvenient emotions which seemed inclined to assert themselves. This gayety did not impose upon anybody, but they tried to look as if it did, for his sake, and he got on very well till Mrs. March kissed him, with a whisper full of motherly solicitude; then, feeling that he was going very fast, he hastily embraced them all round, not forgetting the afflicted Hannah, and ran down stairs as if for his life. Jo followed a minute after to wave her hand to him if he looked round. He did look round, came back, put his arms about her, as she stood on the step above him, and looked up at her with a face that made his short appeal eloquent and pathetic.

"Oh, Jo, can't you?"

"Teddy, dear, I wish I could!"

That was all, except a little pause; then Laurie straightened himself up, said "It's all right, never mind," and went away without another word. Ah, but it wasn't all right, and Jo *did* mind; for while the curly head lay on her arm a minute after her hard answer, she felt as if she had stabbed her dearest friend; and when he left her, without a look behind him, she knew that the boy Laurie never would come again.

Chapter 13

Beth's Secret

When Jo came home that spring, she had been struck with the change in Beth. No one spoke of it, or seemed aware of it, for it had come too gradually to startle those who saw her daily; but to eyes sharpened by absence it was very plain, and a heavy weight fell on Jo's heart as she saw her sister's face. It was no paler, and but littler thinner than in the autumn; yet there was a strange, transparent look about it, as if the mortal was being slowly refined away, and the immortal shining through the frail flesh with an indescribably pathetic beauty. Jo saw and felt it, but said nothing at the time, and soon the first impression lost much of its power, for Beth seemed happy,—no one appeared to doubt that she was better; and, presently, in other cares, Jo for a time forgot her fear.

But when Laurie was gone, and peace prevailed again, the vague anxiety returned and haunted her. She had confessed her sins and been forgiven; but when she showed her savings and proposed the mountain trip, Beth had thanked her heartily, but begged not to go so far away from home. Another little visit to the seashore would suit her better, and, as grandma could not be prevailed upon to leave the babies, Jo took Beth down to the quiet place, where she could live much in the open air, and let the fresh sea-breezes blow a little color into her pale cheeks.

It was not a fashionable place, but, even among the pleasant people there, the girls made few friends, preferring to live for one another. Beth was too shy to enjoy society, and Jo too wrapt up in her to care for any one else; so they were all in all to each other, and came and went, quite unconscious of the interest they excited in those about them,—who watched with sympathetic eyes the strong sister and the feeble one, always together, as if they felt instinctively that a long separation was not far away.

They did feel it, yet neither spoke of it; for often between ourselves and those nearest and dearest to us there exists a reserve which it is very hard to overcome. Jo felt as if a veil had fallen between her heart and Beth's; but when she put out her hand to lift it up there seemed something sacred in the silence, and she waited for Beth to speak. She wondered, and was thankful also, that her parents did not seem to see what she saw; and, during the quiet weeks, when the shadow grew so plain to her, she said nothing of it to those at home, believing that it would tell itself when Beth came back no better. She wondered still more if her sister really guessed the hard truth, and what thoughts were passing through her mind during the long hours when she lay on the warm rocks with her head in Jo's lap, while the winds blew healthfully over her, and the sea made music at her feet.

One day Beth told her. Jo thought she was asleep, she lay so still; and, putting down her book, sat looking at her with wistful eyes,—trying to see signs of hope in the faint color on Beth's cheeks. But she could not find enough to satisfy her,—for the cheeks were very thin, and the hands seemed too feeble to hold even the rosy little shells they had been gathering. It came to her then more bitterly than ever that Beth was slowly drifting away from her, and her arms instinctively tightened their hold upon the dearest treasure she possessed. For a minute her eyes were too dim for seeing, and, when they cleared, Beth was looking up at her so tenderly, that there was hardly any need for her to say,—

"Jo, dear, I'm glad you know it. I've tried to tell you, but I couldn't."

There was no answer except her sister's cheek against her own, —not even tears,—for when most deeply moved Jo did not cry. She was the weaker then, and Beth tried to comfort and sustain her with her arms about her, and the soothing words she whispered in her ear.

"I've known it for a good while, dear, and now I'm used to it, it

1. Bronson Alcott recorded "a sweet and tender interview" with his daughter Lizzie—reminiscent of the one between Jo and Beth —in which his daughter spoke "resignedly of the change, desiring the passage rather than remaining longer with us":

> I asked, "Have you thoughts of your not recovering sometimes?"
>
> "Yes; nor have I believed otherwise for a long while past. It will be something new in our family, and I can best be spared of the four."
>
> I said, "I shall see Dr. Geist and hear what he says of your prospects, Elizabeth."
>
> "'Twill be as well one way as the other; with me as with the rest of you."
>
> I inquired, "Have you some notions of your state after the change?"
>
> "Not so clear as I could wish, but you will have me none the less, and I prefer going as soon as may be."— She seems to have anticipated the possibilities, and has busied herself lately . . . in disposing of her little things as gifts to friends. (*Journals of BA* 303–304)

Jo and Beth at the shore. Hammatt Billings, Part II of *Little Women* (1869).

isn't hard to think of or to bear. Try to see it so, and don't be troubled about me, because it's best; indeed it is."[1]

"Is this what made you so unhappy in the autumn, Beth? You did not feel it then, and keep it to yourself so long, did you?" asked Jo, refusing to see or say that it *was* best, but glad to know that Laurie had no part in Beth's trouble.

"Yes; I gave up hoping then, but I didn't like to own it;[2] I tried to think it was a sick fancy,[3] and would not let it trouble any one. But when I saw you all so well, and strong, and full of happy plans, it was hard to feel that I could never be like you,—and then I was miserable, Jo."

"Oh, Beth, and you didn't tell me,—didn't let me comfort and help you! How could you shut me out, and bear it all alone?"

Jo's voice was full of tender reproach, and her heart ached to think of the solitary struggle that must have gone on while Beth learned to say good-by to health, love, and life, and take up her cross so cheerfully.

"Perhaps it was wrong, but I tried to do right; I wasn't sure, no one said anything, and I hoped I was mistaken. It would have been selfish to frighten you all when Marmee was so anxious about Meg, and Amy away, and you so happy with Laurie,—at least I thought so then."

"And I thought you loved him, Beth, and I went away because I couldn't," cried Jo,—glad to say all the truth.

Beth looked so amazed at the idea, that Jo smiled in spite of her pain, and added, softly,—

"Then you didn't, deary? I was afraid it was so, and imagined your poor little heart full of love-lornity all that while."

"Why, Jo! how could I, when he was so fond of you?" asked Beth, as innocently as a child. "I do love him dearly; he is so good to me, how can I help it? But he could never be anything to me but my brother. I hope he truly will be, some time."

"Not through me," said Jo, decidedly. "Amy is left for him, and they would suit excellently,—but I have no heart for such things now. I don't care what becomes of anybody but you, Beth. You *must* get well."

"I want to,—oh, so much! I try, but every day I lose a little, and feel more sure that I shall never gain it back. It's like the tide, Jo, when it turns,—it goes slowly, but it can't be stopped."

"It *shall* be stopped,—your tide must not turn so soon,—nineteen is too young. Beth, I can't let you go. I'll work, and pray, and fight against it. I'll keep you in spite of everything; there must be ways,—it can't be too late. God won't be so cruel as to take you from me," cried poor Jo, rebelliously,—for her spirit was far less piously submissive than Beth's.

Simple, sincere people seldom speak much of their piety; it shows itself in acts, rather than in words, and has more influence than homilies or protestations. Beth could not reason upon or explain the faith that gave her courage and patience to give up life, and cheerfully wait for death. Like a confiding child, she asked no questions, but left everything to God and nature, Father and mother of us all, feeling sure that they, and they only, could teach and strengthen heart and spirit for this life and the life to come. She did not rebuke Jo with saintly speeches, only loved her better for her passionate affection, and clung more closely to the dear human love, from which our Father never means us to be weaned, but through which He draws us closer to Himself. She could not say, "I'm glad to go," for life was very sweet to her; she could only sob out, "I'll try to be willing," while she held fast to Jo, as the first bitter wave of this great sorrow broke over them together.

By and by Beth said, with recovered serenity,—

"You'll tell them this, when we go home?"

"I think they will see it without words," sighed Jo; for now it seemed to her that Beth changed every day.

"Perhaps not; I've heard that the people who love best are often blindest to such things. If they don't see it, you will tell them for me. I don't want any secrets, and it's kinder to prepare them. Meg has John and the babies to comfort her, but you must stand by father and mother, won't you, Jo?"

"If I can, but, Beth, I don't give up yet; I'm going to believe that it *is* a sick fancy, and not let you think it's true." said Jo, trying to speak cheerfully.

Beth lay a minute thinking, and then said in her quiet way,—

"I don't know how to express myself, and shouldn't try to any one but you, because I can't speak out, except to my old Jo.ᵃ I only mean to say, that I have a feeling that it never was intended I should live long. I'm not like the rest of you; I never made any plans about what I'd do when I grew up; I never thought of being married, as you all did. I couldn't seem to imagine myself anything but stupid little Beth, trotting about at home, of no use anywhere but there.[4] I never wanted to go away, and the hard part now is the leaving you all. I'm not afraid, but it seems as if I should be homesick for you even in heaven."

Jo could not speak; and for several minutes there was no sound but the sigh of the wind, and the lapping of the tide. A white-winged gull flew by, with the flash of sunshine on its silvery breast; Beth watched it till it vanished, and her eyes were full of sadness. A little gray-coated sand-bird came tripping over the beach, "peeping" softly to itself, as if enjoying the sun and sea; it came quite close to Beth, looked at her with a friendly eye, and sat upon a warm stone dressing its wet feathers, quite at home. Beth smiled, and felt comforted, for the tiny thing seemed to offer its small friendship, and remind her that a pleasant world was still to be enjoyed.

"Dear little bird! See, Jo, how tame it is. I like peeps better than the gulls, they are not so wild and handsome, but they seem happy, confiding little things. I used to call them my birds, last summer; and mother said they reminded her of me—busy, quaker-colored[5] creatures, always near the shore, and always chirping that contented little song of theirs. You are the gull, Jo, strong and wild, fond of the storm and the wind, flying far out to sea, and happy all alone. Meg is the turtle-dove, and Amy is like the lark she writes about, trying to get up among the clouds, but always dropping down into its nest again. Dear little girl! she's so ambitious, but her heart is good and tender, and no matter how high she flies, she never will forget home. I hope I shall see her again, but she seems *so* far away."

"She is coming in the spring, and I mean that you shall be all ready to see and enjoy her. I'm going to have you well and rosy, by that time," began Jo, feeling that of all the changes in Beth, the talking change was the greatest, for it seemed to cost no effort now, and she thought aloud in a way quite unlike bashful Beth.

"Jo, dear, don't hope any more; it won't do any good, I'm sure of that. We won't be miserable, but enjoy being together while we wait. We'll have happy times, for I don't suffer much, and I think the tide will go out easily, if you help me."

4. In real life, LMA worried that Lizzie, or Betty, as she was sometimes called, would die young because her sister never seemed to make plans for an adult life. LMA confessed in her journal in June 1857: "Betty was feeble, but seemed to cheer up for a time. The long, cold, lonely winter has been too hard for the frail creature, and we are all anxious about her. I fear she may slip away; for she never seemed to care much for this world beyond home" (*Journals* 85).

5. Drab or gray colors. The word derives from the plain dress worn by early Quakers.

6. From late 1857 until Elizabeth Alcott's death on March 14, 1858, LMA did spend most of her time caring for her younger sister. While Anna took over household duties, LMA helped Mrs. Alcott nurse Lizzie.

7. By November 1857, LMA recorded Elizabeth Alcott's turn for the worse: "Twenty-five this month. I feel my quarter of a century rather heavy on my shoulders just now. I lead two lives. One seems gay with plays, etc., the other very sad,—in Betty's room; for though she wishes us to act, and loves to see us get ready, the shadow is there, and Mother and I see it. Betty loves to have me with her; and I am with her at night, for Mother needs rest. Betty says she feels 'strong' when I am near. So glad to be of use" (*Journals* 86). Bronson Alcott, who had been absent since mid-November, holding conversations in upstate New York and Ohio, returned to Concord in January after receiving news of Elizabeth Alcott's failing health. He wrote in his journal on January 23, 1858: "I find my family well, save my child Elizabeth, who is wasted to the mere shadow of what she was, and feeble exceedingly . . . All are anxious, very, and doubting sometimes her final recovery from this extreme debility and emaciation of body" (*Journals of BA* 303).

Jo leaned down to kiss the tranquil face; and with that silent kiss, she dedicated herself soul and body to Beth.[6]

She was right—there was no need of any words when they got home, for father and mother saw plainly, now, what they had prayed to be saved from seeing. Tired with her short journey, Beth went at once to bed, saying how glad she was to be home; and when Jo went down, she found that she would be spared the hard task of telling Beth's secret.[7] Her father stood leaning his head on the mantel-piece, and did not turn as she came in; but her mother stretched out her arms as if for help, and Jo went to comfort her without a word.

Chapter 14

New Impressions

AT THREE O'CLOCK in the afternoon, all the fashionable world at Nice may be seen on the Promenade des Anglais[1]—a charming place; for the wide walk, bordered with palms, flowers, and tropical shrubs, is bounded on one side by the sea, on the other by the grand drive, lined with hotels and villas, while beyond lie orange orchards and the hills. Many nations are represented, many languages spoken, many costumes worn; and, on a sunny day, the spectacle is as gay and brilliant as a carnival. Haughty English, lively French, sober Germans, handsome Spaniards, ugly Russians, meek Jews, free-and-easy Americans,—all drive, sit, or saunter here, chatting over the news, and criticising the latest celebrity who has arrived—Ristori[2] or Dickens, Victor Emanuel or the Queen of the Sandwich Islands.[3] The equipages[4] are as varied as the company, and attract as much attention, especially the low basket barouches in which ladies drive themselves, with a pair of dashing ponies, gay nets to keep their voluminous flounces from overflowing the diminutive vehicles, and little grooms on the perch behind.[5]

Along this walk, on Christmas day, a tall young man walked slowly, with his hands behind him, and a somewhat absent expression of countenance. He looked like an Italian, was dressed like an Englishman, and had the independent air of an American—a combination which caused sundry pairs of feminine eyes to look approvingly after him, and sundry dandies in black velvet suits, with rose-colored neckties, buff gloves,[6] and orange flowers in their button-holes, to shrug their shoulders, and then envy him his inches. There were plenty of pretty faces to admire, but the young man took little notice of them, except to glance now and

1. First called Camin deis Anglés (the English Way), the Promenade des Anglais, a pathway along the beach in Nice, was funded by wealthy Englishmen who wintered there in 1822–1824. LMA, who stayed in Nice with Anna Weld from December 1865 to the first of May 1866, noted: "I soon tired of the fashionable Promenade for every one was on exhibition. Sometimes before or after the fashionable hour I walked there & enjoyed the sea & sky" (*Journals* 149).

2. Adelaide Ristori (1822–1906), the Italian actress known as the Marquise, was one of the most famous tragedians of the nineteenth century. Among her roles were Maria Antoinette, Medea, Mary Stuart, and Lady Macbeth. In 1866, she made the first of four tours to the United States and retired to Rome in 1885. While in Nice in April 1866, LMA had the opportunity to see the performer: "Saw Ristori twice, once in Medea & once in Elizabeth. Never saw such acting; especially in Queen Bess, it was splendid, & the changes from the young, violent, coquettish woman to the peevish old crone dying with her crown on, vain, ambitious & remorseful" (*Journals* 150–151). In November 1867, LMA, in Boston, again saw Ristori and claimed she "admired her even more than I did in Nice" (*Journals* 159).

3. Victor Emmanuel II (1820–1878) was king of Sardinia from 1849 to 1861, and on March 17, 1861, he became the first king of a unified Italy. LMA and her sister May saw the king when he arrived in Rome in January 1871, his first visit to the city after the Italian army had taken the Papal State on September 20, 1870 (see *Little Women Abroad* 258–262). Queen Consort Emma Kalanikaumakaamano Kaleleonālani Na'ea Rooke of Hawai'i (1836–1885), wife of King Kamehameha IV (1834–1863), visited the French Riviera in December 1865, staying in France until spring 1866. The Hawaiian Islands were named the Sandwich Islands by the explorer James Cook during his voyages of the 1770s. John Montagu, the Fourth Earl of Sandwich, was a major financial supporter of Cook's expeditions. While in Nice in 1866, LMA encountered the people she writes about here: "A ball was given at our Pension & we went. A queer set, Russians, Spaniards, French English Americans Italians Jews & Sandwich Islanders. They danced wildly, dressed gaily & sounded as if the 'confusion of tongues' was come again" (*Journals* 149).

4. The carriages and horses.

5. LMA seems to be describing a chaise or chay rather than the larger barouche. A chaise was a lightweight, two-wheeled carriage with a stand for a groom in the rear.

6. Light brownish-yellow gloves.

7. One of the main gathering spots in Nice, the Public Garden, filled with palms, pepper trees, laurel, aloes, and myrtles, is located between the sea and the Place Masséna.

8. Castle Hill, located in southeast Nice, is the site of La Colline du Château, which was built in the thirteenth century by the Savoy dynasty and destroyed by the French army, led by the Duke of Berwick, in 1706. The Parc du Chateau, consisting of large gardens and pathways, was constructed atop the hill between 1828 and 1858.

9. A phrase possibly originating from the epithet the "mad King," in reference to George III (1738–1820). King of England from 1760 until his death, George III suffered from mental illness, now thought to be porphyria, a blood disease that results in neurological complications.

10. Guidebooks for the period do not list a hotel named *Chauvain;* however, it was the name of a major street in Nice.

11. A lady's parasol with a leather whip at its tip.

12. Castle Hill offers beautiful views in all directions. To the west are the coastline, the promontory of the resort town of Antibes, the mouth of the Var River, and the town of Nice spread out just below. To the north are the Alps and the castle of St. André. To the east are the ancient Fort du Mont Alban and Mont Boron, which separate Nice from Villefranche-sur-Mer. To the south, Castle Hill slopes precipitously to the Mediterranean Sea.

then at some blonde girl or lady in blue. Presently he strolled out of the promenade, and stood a moment at the crossing, as if undecided whether to go and listen to the band in the Jardin Publique,[7] or to wander along the beach toward Castle Hill.[8] The quick trot of ponies' feet made him look up, as one of the little carriages, containing a single lady, came rapidly down the street. The lady was young, blonde, and dressed in blue. He stared a minute, then his whole face woke up, and, waving his hat like a boy, he hurried forward to meet her.

"Oh, Laurie! is it really you? I thought you'd never come!" cried Amy, dropping the reins, and holding out both hands, to the great scandalization of a French mamma, who hastened her daughter's steps, lest she should be demoralized by beholding the free manners of these "mad English."[9]

"I was detained by the way, but I promised to spend Christmas with you, and here I am."

"How is your grandfather? When did you come? Where are you staying?"

"Very well—last night—at the Chauvain.[10] I called at your hotel, but you were all out."

"Mon Dieu! I have so much to say, and don't know where to begin.[a] Get in, and we can talk at our ease; I was going for a drive, and longing for company. Flo's saving up for to-night."

"What happens, then—a ball?"

"A Christmas party at our hotel. There are many Americans there, and they give it in honor of the day. You'll go with us, of course? aunt will be charmed."

"Thank you! where now?" asked Laurie, leaning back and folding his arms, a proceeding which suited Amy, who preferred to drive; for her parasol-whip[11] and blue reins, over the white ponies' backs, afforded her infinite satisfaction.

"I'm going to the banker's first, for letters, and then to Castle Hill; the view is so lovely,[12] and I like to feed the peacocks. Have you ever been there?"

"Often, years ago; but I don't mind having a look at it."

"Now tell me all about yourself. The last I heard of you, your grandfather wrote that he expected you from Berlin."

"Yes, I spent a month there, and then joined him in Paris, where he has settled for the winter. He has friends there, and finds plenty to amuse him; so I go and come, and we get on capitally."

"That's a sociable arrangement," said Amy, missing something in Laurie's manner, though she couldn't tell what.

"Why, you see he hates to travel, and I hate to keep still; so we each suit ourselves, and there is no trouble. I am often with him, and he enjoys my adventures, while I like to feel that some one is glad to see me when I get back from my wanderings. Dirty old hole, isn't it?" he added, with a sniff of disgust,[b] as they drove along the boulevard to the Place Napoleon,[13] in the old city.

"The dirt is picturesque, so I don't mind. The river and the hills are delicious, and these glimpses of the narrow cross streets are my delight. Now we shall have to wait for that procession to pass; it's going to the Church of St. John."[14]

While Laurie listlessly watched the procession of priests under their canopies, white-veiled nuns bearing lighted tapers, and some brotherhood in blue, chanting as they walked, Amy watched him, and felt a new sort of shyness steal over her, for he was changed, and she couldn't find the merry-faced boy she left, in the moody-looking man beside her. He was handsomer than ever, and greatly improved, she thought; but now that the flush of pleasure at meeting her was over, he looked tired and spiritless—not sick, nor exactly unhappy, but older and graver than a year or two of prosperous life should have made him. She couldn't understand it, and did not venture to ask questions; so she shook her head, and touched up her ponies, as the procession wound away across the arches of the Paglioni bridge,[15] and vanished in the church.

"Que pensez vous?"[16] she said, airing her French, which had improved in quantity, if not in quality, since she came abroad.

"That mademoiselle has made good use of her time, and the result is charming," replied Laurie, bowing, with his hand on his heart, and an admiring look.

She blushed with pleasure, but, somehow, the compliment did not satisfy her like the blunt praises he used to give her at home, when he promenaded round her on festival occasions, and told her she was "altogether jolly," with a hearty smile and an approv-

13. Place Napoleon would later be renamed Place Garibaldi, for Giuseppe Garibaldi (1807–1882), the hero of the Italian unification who was born in Nice. This plaza at the northern end of the old city served as an entry gate into the town.

14. One of the ten chapels located in the Nice Cathedral is dedicated to Saint John the Baptist.

15. The Paglioni River runs down the mountain near the western walls of Nice and into the Mediterranean Sea. Visitors coming from Provence enter the city over this stone bridge with three arches.

16. French for "What do you think?"

17. Guidebooks of the period do not list a hotel or pension with this name.

ing pat on the head. She didn't like the new tone; for though not *blasé,* it sounded indifferent in spite of the look.

"If that's the way he's going to grow up, I wish he'd stay a boy," she thought, with a curious sense of disappointment and discomfort; trying, meantime, to seem quite easy and gay.

At Avigdor's[17] she found the precious home-letters, and, giving the reins to Laurie, read them luxuriously as they wound up the shady road between green hedges, where tea-roses bloomed as freshly as in June.

"Beth is very poorly, mother says. I often think I ought to go home, but they all say 'stay'; so I do, for I shall never have another chance like this," said Amy, looking sober over one page.

"I think you are right, there; you could do nothing at home, and it is a great comfort to them to know that you are well and happy, and enjoying so much, my dear."

He drew a little nearer, and looked more like his old self, as he said that; and the fear that sometimes weighed on Amy's heart was lightened,—for the look, the act, the brotherly "my dear," seemed to assure her that if any trouble did come, she would not be alone in a strange land. Presently she laughed, and showed him a small sketch of Jo in her scribbling suit, with the bow rampantly erect upon her cap, and issuing from her mouth the words, "Genius burns!"

Laurie smiled, took it, put it in his vest pocket "to keep it from blowing away," and listened with interest to the lively letter Amy read him.

"This will be a regularly merry Christmas to me, with presents in the morning, you and letters in the afternoon, and a party at night," said Amy, as they alighted among the ruins of the old fort, and a flock of splendid peacocks came trooping about them, tamely waiting to be fed. While Amy stood laughing on the bank above him as she scattered crumbs to the brilliant birds, Laurie looked at her as she had looked at him, with a natural curiosity to see what changes time and absence had wrought. He found nothing to perplex or disappoint, much to admire and approve; for, overlooking a few little affectations of speech and manner, she was as sprightly and graceful as ever, with the addition of that inde-

Amy (Samantha Mathis)
and Laurie (Christian Bale)
in Europe in Armstrong's
Little Women (1994).

scribable something in dress and bearing which we call elegance. Always mature for her age, she had gained a certain *aplomb*[18] in both carriage and conversation, which made her seem more of a woman of the world than she was; but her old petulance now and then showed itself, her strong will still held its own, and her native frankness was unspoiled by foreign polish.

Laurie did not read all this while he watched her feed the peacocks, but he saw enough to satisfy and interest him, and carried away a pretty little picture of a bright-faced girl standing in the sunshine, which brought out the soft hue of her dress, the fresh color of her cheeks, the golden gloss of her hair, and made her a prominent figure in the pleasant scene.

As they came up on to the stone plateau that crowns the hill, Amy waved her hand as if welcoming him to her favorite haunt, and said, pointing here and there,—

"Do you remember the Cathedral and the Corso,[19] the fishermen dragging their nets in the bay, and the lovely road to Villa Franca, Schubert's Tower,[20] just below, and, best of all, that speck far out to sea which they say is Corsica?"[21]

"I remember; it's not much changed," he answered, without enthusiasm.

18. Poise, self-confidence.

19. The Nice Cathedral, constructed from 1650 to 1699, was dedicated to the Virgin Mary and Saint Reparata. The Corso Illuminé, a nighttime parade during Nice's Carnival when revelers carry moccoletti, small lighted candles, and try to extinguish others' candles. LMA attended Carnival in Nice in 1866: "Funny but not so fine a sight as I expected" (*Journals* 150).

20. Villefranche-sur-Mer, a small port town just east of Nice along Mont Boron and 6.2 miles southwest of Monaco. LMA—or Amy—may be confusing Franz Schubert with Hector Berlioz (1803–1869), the French Romantic composer who wrote his overture *Le roi Lear (King Lear),* Opus 4, while staying in the Bellanda Tower (what he called the Tower of Ponchettes) in 1831.

21. Corsica, southeast of the French mainland, is an island in the Mediterranean Sea. Separated from Europe by the Ligurian Sea, this French island is actually closer to Italy.

22. Napoleon Bonaparte was born in Ajaccio, the capital city of Corsica, in 1769. The usurper Laurie is thinking of is Jo, who has stolen his heart.

23. Of all the Alcott sisters, May, like Amy, loved society—the parties, the dresses, the flirting. In October 1861, May wrote to her friend Alfred Whitman: "You hint . . . sarcastically at my having lovers, all of which I can deny as I don't think there is a single young man of my acquaintance that cares a pin for me really, only they sort of like to flirt and have a good time, and so do I, but I don't think I have a real lover in the world and find myself blooming and happy without them so don't worry myself" (Manuscript letter, Houghton Library, Harvard University, bMS Am 1130 [31]).

24. Often used to make ball dresses, tarlatan is a thin, lightweight cotton fabric. Tulle is a silk net.

25. Illusion, originally called zephyr, is thin, transparent tulle.

"What Jo would give for a sight of that famous speck!" said Amy, feeling in good spirits, and anxious to see him so also.

"Yes," was all he said, but he turned and strained his eyes to see the island which a greater usurper than even Napoleon[22] now made interesting in his sight.

"Take a good look at it for her sake, and then come and tell me what you have been doing with yourself all this while," said Amy, seating herself, ready for a good talk.

But she did not get it; for, though he joined her, and answered all her questions freely, she could only learn that he had roved about the Continent and been to Greece. So, after idling away an hour, they drove home again; and, having paid his respects to Mrs. Carrol, Laurie left them, promising to return in the evening.

It must be recorded of Amy, that she deliberately "prinked" that night. Time and absence had done its work on both the young people; she had seen her old friend in a new light,—not as "our boy," but as a handsome and agreeable man, and she was conscious of a very natural desire to find favor in his sight. Amy knew her good points, and made the most of them, with the taste and skill which is a fortune to a poor and pretty woman.[23]

Tarlatan and tulle[24] were cheap at Nice, so she enveloped herself in them on such occasions, and, following the sensible English fashion of simple dress for young girls, got up charming little toilettes with fresh flowers, a few trinkets, and all manner of dainty devices, which were both inexpensive and effective. It must be confessed that the artist sometimes got possession of the woman, and indulged in antique *coiffures,* statuesque attitudes, and classic draperies. But, dear heart, we all have our little weaknesses, and find it easy to pardon such in the young, who satisfy our eyes with their comeliness, and keep our hearts merry with their artless vanities.

"I do want him to think I look well, and tell them so at home," said Amy to herself, as she put on Flo's old white silk ball dress, and covered it with a cloud of fresh illusion,[25] out of which her white shoulders and golden head emerged with a most artistic effect. Her hair she had the sense to let alone, after gathering up the

LITTLE WOMEN

thick waves and curls into a Hebe-like knot at the back of her head.[26]

"It's not the fashion, but it's becoming, and I can't afford to make a fright of myself," she used to say, when advised to frizzle, puff, or braid as the latest style commanded.

Having no ornaments fine enough for this important occasion, Amy looped her fleecy skirts with rosy clusters of azalea, and framed the white shoulders in delicate green vines. Remembering the painted boots, she surveyed her white satin slippers with girlish satisfaction, and *chasséed* down the room, admiring her aristocratic feet all by herself.

"My new fan just matches my flowers, my gloves fit to a charm, and the real lace on aunt's *mouchoir* gives an air to my whole dress. If I only had a classical nose and mouth I should be perfectly happy," she said, surveying herself with a critical eye, and a candle in each hand.

In spite of this affliction, she looked unusually gay and graceful as she glided away; she seldom ran,—it did not suit her style, she thought,—for, being tall, the stately and Junoesque[27] was more appropriate than the sportive or piquante.[28] She walked up and down the long saloon[29] while waiting for Laurie, and once arranged herself under the chandelier, which had a good effect upon her hair; then she thought better of it, and went away to the other end of the room,—as if ashamed of the girlish desire to have the first view a propitious one. It so happened that she could not have done a better thing, for Laurie came in so quietly she did not hear him; and, as she stood at the distant window with her head half turned, and one hand gathering up her dress, the slender, white figure against the red curtains was as effective as a well-placed statue.

"Good evening, Diana!"[30] said Laurie, with the look of satisfaction she liked to see in his eyes when they rested on her.

"Good evening, Apollo!"[31] she answered, smiling back at him, —for he, too, looked unusually *débonnaire,*[32]—and the thought of entering the ball-room on the arm of such a personable man, caused Amy to pity the four plain Misses Davis from the bottom of her heart.

26. The figure of Hebe, the Greek goddess of youth, daughter of Zeus and Hera, was a popular garden or fountain statue in the nineteenth century. Her hair is tied in a small knot at the back of her head.

27. A tall, dignified beauty as typified by Juno, the wife of Zeus in Roman mythology.

28. Charming.

29. A large room or hall in the hotel used for dances.

30. The twin sister of Apollo, Diana (known as Artemis by the Greeks) was the Roman goddess of the hunt, the moon, and birth. She was one of the three Roman goddesses who promised never to marry. In December 1878, LMA began *Diana and Persis,* a novel inspired by May Alcott's romance and marriage to Ernest Nieriker. After May's death in December 1879, LMA, having completed four chapters, abandoned the work. One of the novel's major themes is the question of whether a female artist can have professional success and marriage at the same time. See *Diana and Persis,* ed. Sarah Elbert (New York: Arnno Press, 1978).

31. Apollo, Greek god of the sun and light, was the ideal of athletic youth. As leader of the Muses, he was the patron god of music and poetry.

32. Possessing a sophisticated charm.

33. The holder, usually silver, that Laurie gives Amy is in the form of a bracelet so she can wear the small bunch of flowers on her wrist.

34. Guidebooks of the period do not indicate a shop in Nice, France, by this name. LMA may have taken it from *cardiglia,* a fine Italian lace, popular in the nineteenth century.

35. Dining hall.

36. In Shakespeare's *Hamlet,* Gertrude, Hamlet's mother, does not wear black because she is already remarried to Claudius when the action of the play begins. In fact, in one of the most famous scenes of *Hamlet* (Act I, Scene 2), Gertrude admonishes her son for still wearing black: "'Good, Hamlet, cast they nighted color off.'" LMA perhaps got the idea that Gertrude wears "black velvet" from a performance she saw or from an illustration.

37. Serene Highness was a title used by German noble families until the end of WWI.

38. In 1822, the five sons of Mayer Amschel Rothschild (1744–1812), all heads of banks across Europe and England, were granted the title of baron by Austria's Francis I. In 1847, Queen Victoria honored one of his grandsons, a British financier, with the title Sir Anthony Nathan de Rothschild, First Baronet.

"Here are your flowers! I arranged them myself, remembering that you didn't like what Hannah calls a 'sot-bookay,'" said Laurie, handing her a delicate nosegay, in a holder[33] that she had long coveted as she daily passed it in Cardiglia's[34] window.

"How kind you are!" she exclaimed, gratefully; "if I'd known you were coming I'd have had something ready for you to-day,—though not as pretty as this, I'm afraid."

"Thank you; it isn't what it should be, but you have improved it," he added, as she snapped the silver bracelet on her wrist.

"Please don't!"

"I thought you liked that sort of thing!"

"Not from you; it doesn't sound natural, and I like your old bluntness better."

"I'm glad of it!" he answered, with a look of relief; then buttoned her gloves for her, and asked if his tie was straight, just as he used to do when they went to parties together, at home.

The company assembled in the long *salle a manger,*[35] that evening, was such as one sees nowhere but on the continent. The hospitable Americans had invited every acquaintance they had in Nice, and, having no prejudice against titles, secured a few to add luster to their Christmas ball.

A Russian prince condescended to sit in a corner for an hour, and talk with a massive lady, dressed like Hamlet's mother,[36] in black velvet, with a pearl bridle under her chin. A Polish count, aged eighteen, devoted himself to the ladies, who pronounced him "a fascinating dear," and a German Serene Something,[37] having come for the supper alone, roamed vaguely about, seeking what he might devour. Baron Rothschild's[38] private secretary, a large-nosed Jew, in tight boots, affably beamed upon the world, as if his master's name crowned him with a golden halo; a stout Frenchman, who knew the Emperor, came to indulge his mania for dancing, and Lady de Jones, a British matron, adorned the scene with her little family of eight. Of course, there were many light-footed, shrill-voiced American girls, handsome, lifeless looking English ditto, and a few plain but piquante French demoiselles. Likewise the usual set of travelling young gentlemen, who disported themselves gaily, while mammas of all nations lined the

LITTLE WOMEN

walls, and smiled upon them benignly when they danced with their daughters.

Any young girl can imagine Amy's state of mind when she "took the stage" that night, leaning on Laurie's arm. She knew she looked well, she loved to dance, she felt that her foot was on her native heath in a ball-room, and enjoyed the delightful sense of power which comes when young girls first discover the new and lovely kingdom they are born to rule by virtue of beauty, youth, and womanhood. She did pity the Davis girls, who were awkward, plain, and destitute of escort—except a grim papa and three grimmer maiden aunts—and she bowed to them in her friendliest manner, as she passed; which was good of her, as it permitted them to see her dress, and burn with curiosity to know who her distinguished-looking friend might be. With the first burst of the band, Amy's color rose, her eyes began to sparkle, and her feet to tap the floor impatiently; for she danced well, and wanted Laurie to know it; therefore, the shock she received can better be imagined than described, when he said, in a perfectly tranquil tone,—

"Do you care to dance?"

"One usually does at a ball!"

Her amazed look and quick answer caused Laurie to repair his error as fast as possible.

"I meant the first dance. May I have the honor?"

"I can give you one if I put off the Count. He dances divinely; but he will excuse me, as you are an old friend," said Amy, hoping that the name would have a good effect, and show Laurie that she was not to be trifled with.

"Nice little boy, but rather a short Pole to support the steps of

'A daughter of the gods
Divinely tall, and most divinely fair,'"[39]

was all the satisfaction she got, however.

The set in which they found themselves was composed of English, and Amy was compelled to walk decorously through a cotillion,[40] feeling all the while as if she could dance the Tarantula[41] with relish. Laurie resigned her to the "nice little boy," and went to do his duty to Flo, without securing Amy for the joys to come,

39. The lines are from Alfred, Lord Tennyson, *A Dream of Fair Women* (lines 87–88). Inspired by Chaucer's "Legends of Good Women" (ca. 1384), the poem was originally published in 1833, but was greatly revised upon republication in 1842. The lines Laurie quotes actually refer to Helen of Troy, the daughter of Zeus and Leda in Greek mythology.

40. A cotillion, usually a quadrille to Americans, was a formal dance that involved a number of elaborate steps.

41. Amy, ridiculed for her malapropisms in Part I of *Little Women,* makes a joke here at her own expense. The dance is actually the Tarantella, a fast, whirling dance that originated with southern Italian peasants in the fifteenth century. Amy's ability to laugh at herself demonstrates how she has grown up.

42. At formal balls, gentlemen requested in advance to dance with a lady, and she wrote down their names in her dance book, often called a dance card. The dance book, actually more like a booklet, listed the ball's dances in order on one side of the page, with space on the other side for the gentlemen's names. Covers were usually decorative, often giving the host's name. A small cord was generally threaded in the spine so the lady could attach the dance book to her wrist or gown.

43. The polka-redowa, often called the original polka of Bohemia, is a ballroom dance that originated from a Bohemian folk-dance. Popular during the mid-nineteenth century, it is more like a waltz than a polka as it is danced in 3/4 or 3/8 time rather than 2/4 time like a true polka.

44. Amy is fixing her hair with a hairpin to keep it in place.

45. India rubber, also called caoutchouc, is the milky resin of numerous plants in Africa, India, or South America, which becomes a highly elastic natural rubber.

which reprehensible want of forethought was properly punished, for she immediately engaged herself till supper,[42] meaning to relent if he then gave any sign of penitence. She showed him her ball-book with demure satisfaction when he strolled, instead of rushing, up to claim her for the next, a glorious polka-redowa;[43] but his polite regrets didn't impose upon her, and when she galloped away with the Count, she saw Laurie sit down by her aunt, with an actual expression of relief.

That was unpardonable; and Amy took no more notice of him for a long while, except a word now and then, when she came to her chaperon, between the dances, for a necessary pin[44] or a moment's rest. Her anger had a good effect, however, for she hid it under a smiling face, and seemed unusually blithe and brilliant. Laurie's eyes followed her with pleasure, for she neither romped nor sauntered, but danced with spirit and grace, making the delightsome pastime what it should be. He very naturally fell to studying her from this new point of view; and before the evening was half over, had decided that "little Amy was going to make a very charming woman."

It was a lively scene, for soon the spirit of the social season took possession of every one, and Christmas merriment made all faces shine, hearts happy, and heels light. The musicians fiddled, tooted, and banged as if they enjoyed it; everybody danced who could, and those who couldn't admired their neighbors with uncommon warmth. The air was dark with Davises, and many Joneses gambolled like a flock of young giraffes. The golden secretary darted through the room like a meteor with a dashing Frenchwoman, who carpeted the floor with her pink satin train. The Serene Teuton found the supper-table, and was happy, eating steadily through the bill of fare, and dismaying the garcons by the ravages he committed. But the Emperor's friend covered himself with glory, for he danced *everything,* whether he knew it or not, and introduced impromptu pirouettes when the figures bewildered him. The boyish abandon of that stout man was charming to behold; for though he "carried weight," he danced like an india-rubber[45] ball. He ran, he flew, he pranced; his face glowed, his bald head shown, his coat tails waved wildly, his pumps actually

LITTLE WOMEN

twinkled in the air, and when the music stopped, he wiped the drops from his brow, and beamed upon his fellow-men like a French Pickwick without glasses.

Amy and her Pole distinguished themselves by equal enthusiasm, but more graceful agility; and Laurie found himself involuntarily keeping time to the rhythmic rise and fall of the white slippers, as they flew by, as indefatigably as if winged. When little Vladimir finally relinquished her, with assurances that he was "desolated to leave so early," she was ready to rest, and see how her recreant[46] knight had borne his punishment.

It had been successful; for, at three-and-twenty, blighted affections find a balm in friendly society, and young nerves will thrill, young blood dance, and healthy young spirits rise, when subjected to the enchantment of beauty, light, music, and motion. Laurie had a waked-up look as he rose to give her his seat; and when he hurried away to bring her some supper, she said to herself, with a satisfied smile,—

"Ah, I thought that would do him good!"

"You look like Balzac's 'Femme piente par elle même,'"[47] he said, as he fanned her with one hand, and held her coffee-cup in the other.

"My rouge won't come off;" and Amy rubbed her brilliant cheek, and showed him her white glove, with a sober simplicity that made him laugh outright.

"What do you call this stuff?" he asked, touching a fold of her dress that had blown over his knee.

"Illusion."

"Good name for it; it's very pretty—new thing, isn't it?"

"It's as old as the hills; you have seen it on dozens of girls, and you never found out that it was pretty till now—*stupide!*"

"I never saw it on you, before, which accounts for the mistake, you see."

"None of that, it is forbidden; I'd rather take coffee than compliments, just now. No, don't lounge,[48] it makes me nervous."

Laurie sat bolt upright, and meekly took her empty plate, feeling an odd sort of pleasure in having "little Amy" order him about; for she had lost her shyness now, and felt an irresistible

46. Negligent in allegiance or duty.

47. Laurie refers to "La Femme comme il faut" ("The Proper Woman") by Honoré de Balzac (1799–1850), first published in 1839 and revised as "Autre etude de femme" ("Another Study of Woman") in his most famous work, *La Comédie humaine (The Human Comedy)*, published in 1842. The 1880–1881 edition of *Little Women* corrects the French spelling: "Femme peinte par elle-même."

48. To slouch or to lean on something.

desire to trample on him, as girls have a delightful way of doing when lords of creation show any signs of subjection.

"Where did you learn all this sort of thing?" he asked, with a quizzical look.

"As 'this sort of thing' is rather a vague expression, would you kindly explain?" returned Amy, knowing perfectly well what he meant, but wickedly leaving him to describe what is indescribable.

"Well—the general air, the style, the self-possession, the—the—illusion—you know," laughed Laurie, breaking down, and helping himself out of his quandary with the new word.

Amy was gratified, but, of course, didn't show it, and demurely answered,—

"Foreign life polishes one in spite of one's self; I study as well as play; and as for this"—with a little gesture toward her dress—"why, tulle is cheap; posies to be had for nothing, and I am used to making the most of my poor little things."

Amy rather regretted that last sentence, fearing it wasn't in good taste; but Laurie liked her the better for it, and found himself both admiring and respecting the brave patience that made the most of opportunity, and the cheerful spirit that covered poverty with flowers. Amy did not know why he looked at her so kindly, nor why he filled up her book[49] with his own name, and devoted himself to her for the rest of the evening, in the most delightful manner; but the impulse that wrought this agreeable change was the result of one of the new impressions which both of them were unconsciously giving and receiving.

Chapter 15

On the Shelf

N FRANCE the young girls have a dull time of it till they are married, when *"Vive la liberté"*[1] becomes their motto. In America, as every one knows, girls early sign the declaration of independence, and enjoy their freedom with republican zest; but the young matrons usually abdicate with the first heir to the throne, and go into a seclusion almost as close as a French nunnery, though by no means as quiet. Whether they like it or not, they are virtually put upon the shelf as soon as the wedding excitement is over, and most of them might exclaim, as did a very pretty woman the other day, "I'm as handsome as ever, but no one takes any notice of me because I'm married."[2]

Not being a belle, or even a fashionable lady, Meg did not experience this affliction till her babies were a year old,—for in her little world primitive customs prevailed, and she found herself more admired and beloved than ever.

As she was a womanly little woman, the maternal instinct was very strong, and she was entirely absorbed in her children, to the utter exclusion of everything and everybody else. Day and night she brooded over them with tireless devotion and anxiety, leaving John to the tender mercies of the help,—for an Irish lady now presided over the kitchen department.[3] Being a domestic man, John decidedly missed the wifely attentions he had been accustomed to receive; but, as he adored his babies, he cheerfully relinquished his comfort for a time, supposing, with masculine ignorance, that peace would soon be restored. But three months passed, and there was no return of repose; Meg looked worn and nervous,—the babies absorbed every minute of her time,—the

1. "Vive la liberté" (long live liberty) was a rallying cry during the French Revolution (1789–1799). LMA suggests that French women are more free after marriage.

2. LMA suggests that most American women are married to produce children (or rather a *male* heir) and then quickly put aside ("put upon the shelf"). John Brooke appears the exception to a depressing rule in his abiding devotions to his wife.

3. Irish immigrants were often hired as domestic help in the nineteenth century. Ralph Waldo Emerson's family employed both an Irish maid and an Irish cook. LMA, like many New Englanders of her time, held stereotypical prejudices about the Irish. Writing to her cousin Elizabeth Wells on October 9, 1883, LMA complains about her nursemaid for Lulu, her niece whom she is raising: "Changing nurses is bad, but they seem to have no strength, these Yankee girls, though the brains & conscience are there. The Pats [Irish] are strong but have no principle, & so we rastle along as well as we can with em" (*Selected Letters* 273).

4. A small allocation of food.

5. A shipping list gives information on current prices of staple commodities and other commercial intelligence.

house was neglected,—and Kitty, the cook, who took life "aisy," kept him on short commons.[4] When he went out in the morning he was bewildered by small commissions for the captive mamma; if he came gaily in at night, eager to embrace his family, he was quenched by a "Hush! they are just asleep after worrying all day." If he proposed a little amusement at home, "No, it would disturb the babies." If he hinted at a lecture or a concert, he was answered with a reproachful look, and a decided—"Leave my children for pleasure, never!" His sleep was broken by infant wails and visions of a phantom figure pacing noiselessly to and fro, in the watches of the night; his meals were interrupted by the frequent flight of the presiding genius, who deserted him, half-helped, if a muffled chirp sounded from the nest above; and, when he read his paper of an evening, Demi's colic got into the shipping-list,[5] and Daisy's fall affected the price of stocks,—for Mrs. Brooke was only interested in domestic news.

The poor man was very uncomfortable, for the children had bereft him of his wife; home was merely a nursery, and the perpetual "hushing" made him feel like a brutal intruder whenever he entered the sacred precincts of Babydom. He bore it very patiently for six months, and, when no signs of amendment appeared, he did what other paternal exiles do,—tried to get a little comfort elsewhere. Scott had married and gone to housekeeping not far off, and John fell into the way of running over for an hour or two of an evening, when his own parlor was empty, and his own wife singing lullabies that seemed to have no end. Mrs. Scott was a lively, pretty girl, with nothing to do but be agreeable,—and she performed her mission most successfully. The parlor was always bright and attractive, the chess-board ready, the piano in tune, plenty of gay gossip, and a nice little supper set forth in tempting style.

John would have preferred his own fireside if it had not been so lonely; but as it was, he gratefully took the next best thing, and enjoyed his neighbor's society.

Meg rather approved of the new arrangement at first, and found it a relief to know that John was having a good time instead of dozing in the parlor, or tramping about the house and waking the children. But by and by, when the teething worry was over, and the idols went to sleep at proper hours, leaving mamma time to rest, she began to miss John, and find her work-basket dull company, when he was not sitting opposite in his old dressing-gown, comfortably scorching his slippers on the fender.[6] She would not ask him to stay at home, but felt injured because he did not know that she wanted him without being told,—entirely forgetting the many evenings he had waited for her in vain. She was nervous and worn out with watching and worry, and in that unreasonable frame of mind which the best of mothers occasionally experience when domestic cares oppress them, want of exercise robs them of cheerfulness, and too much devotion to that idol of American women,—the teapot,—makes them feel as if they were all nerve and no muscle.

"Yes," she would say, looking in the glass, "I'm getting old and ugly; John don't find me interesting any longer, so he leaves his faded wife and goes to see his pretty neighbor, who has no incumbrances. Well, the babies love me; they don't care if I am thin and pale, and haven't time to crimp my hair; they are my comfort, and some day John will see what I've gladly sacrificed for them,—won't he, my precious?"

To which pathetic appeal Daisy would answer with a coo, or Demi with a crow, and Meg would put by her lamentations for a maternal revel, which soothed her solitude for the time being. But the pain increased as politics absorbed John, who was always running over to discuss interesting points with Scott, quite unconscious that Meg missed him. Not a word did she say, however, till her mother found her in tears one day, and insisted on knowing what the matter was,—for Meg's drooping spirits had not escaped her observation.

"I wouldn't tell any one except you, mother; but I really do need advice, for if John goes on much longer I might as well be a widow," replied Mrs. Brooke, drying her tears on Daisy's bib, with an injured air.

"Goes on how, my dear?" asked her mother, anxiously.

"He's away all day, and at night, when I want to see him, he is continually going over to the Scotts'. It isn't fair that I should have

6. A metal fireguard before a fireplace to keep the wood or coal from falling onto the floor.

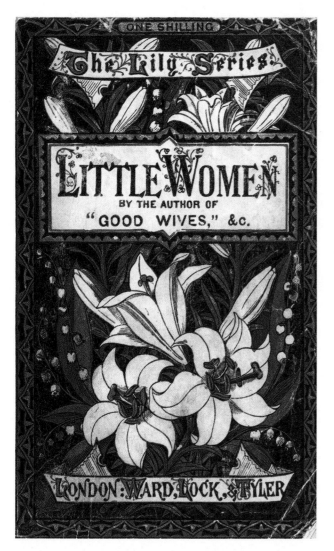

British edition of Part I of *Little Women* (1878) "by the author of *Good Wives*," the common name given to most British editions of Part II.

the hardest work, and never any amusement. Men are very selfish, even the best of them."

"So are women; don't blame John till you see where you are wrong yourself."

"But it can't be right for him to neglect me."

"Don't you neglect him?"

"Why, mother; I thought you'd take my part!"

"So I do as far as sympathizing goes; but I think the fault is yours, Meg."

"I don't see how."

"Let me show you. Did John ever neglect you, as you call it, while you made it a point to give him your society of an evening, —his only leisure time?"

"No; but I can't do it now, with two babies to tend."

"I think you could, dear; and I think you ought. May I speak quite freely, and will you remember that it's mother who blames as well as mother who sympathizes?"

"Indeed I will! speak to me as if I was little Meg again. I often feel as if I needed teaching more than ever, since these babies look to me for everything."

Meg drew her low chair beside her mother's, and, with a little interruption in either lap, the two women rocked and talked lovingly together, feeling that the tie of motherhood made them more one than ever.

"You have only made the mistake that most young wives make, —forgotten your duty to your husband in your love for your children. A very natural and forgivable mistake, Meg, but one that had better be remedied before you take to different ways; for children should draw you nearer than ever, not separate you,—as if they were all yours, and John had nothing to do but support them. I've seen it for some weeks, but have not spoken, feeling sure it would come right, in time."

"I'm afraid it won't. If I ask him to stay he'll think I'm jealous; and I wouldn't insult him by such an idea. He don't see that I want him, and I don't know how to tell him without words."

"Make it so pleasant he won't want to go away. My dear, he's longing for his little home; but it isn't home without you, and you are always in the nursery."

"Oughtn't I to be there?"

"Not all the time; too much confinement makes you nervous, and then you are unfitted for everything. Besides, you owe something to John as well as to the babies; don't neglect husband for children,—don't shut him out of the nursery, but teach him how to help in it. His place is there as well as yours, and the children need him; let him feel that he has his part to do, and he will do it gladly and faithfully, and it will be better for you all."[7]

"You really think so, mother?"

"I know it, Meg, for I've tried it; and I seldom give advice unless I've proved its practicability. When you and Jo were little, I went on just as you do,[a] feeling as if I didn't do my duty unless I devoted myself wholly to you. Poor father took to his books, after I had refused all offers of help, and left me to try my experiment alone. I struggled along as well as I could, but Jo was too much for me. I nearly spoilt her by indulgence. You were poorly, and I worried about you till I fell sick myself. Then father came to the rescue, quietly managed everything, and made himself so helpful that I saw my mistake, and never have been able to get on without him since. That is the secret of our home happiness; he does not let business wean him from the little cares and duties that affect us all, and I try not to let domestic worries destroy my interest in his pursuits. Each do our part alone in many things, but at home we work together, always."

"It is so, mother; and my great wish is to be to my husband and children what you have been to yours. Show me how; I'll do anything you say."

"You always were my docile[8] daughter. Well, dear, if I were you I'd let John have more to do with the management of Demi,—for the boy needs training, and it's none too soon to begin. Then I'd do what I have often proposed,—let Hannah come and help you; she is a capital nurse, and you may trust the precious babies to her while you do more housework. You need the exercise, Hannah would enjoy the rest, and John would find his wife again. Go out more; keep cheerful as well as busy,—for you are the sunshine-

7. Bronson Alcott did not shut himself out of the nursery. Instead, he engaged fully in the nurturing and disciplining of his daughters. As Abigail Alcott wrote to her brother Samuel J. May on March 27, 1831, just after the birth of their first daughter, Anna, Bronson was a father who was "'for domestic and parental excellence—inferior to none'" (quoted in Madelon Bedell, *The Alcotts: Biography of a Family* [New York: Clarkson N. Potter, 1980], p. 56). In Chapter 1 of *The American Woman's Home* (1869), an advice book on domesticity published the same year as Part II of *Little Women,* Catherine E. Beecher and her sister Harriet Beecher Stowe suggested: "The useless, troublesome infant is served in the humblest offices; while both parents unite in training it to an equality with themselves in every advantage."

8. Teachable.

9. LMA encourages married women to extend their sphere beyond the home. It is not enough to be concerned, as Meg was earlier, with "domestic news" alone. Women must participate in the world's work. LMA wrote a public letter to the *Woman's Journal,* a feminist periodical, on February 4, 1882: "To those who see what brave and noble parts women elsewhere are taking in the larger and more vital questions of the time, the thought very naturally comes: 'What a pity that so much good sense, energy, time, and money could not be used for more pressing needs than church-fairs, tea-parties, or clubs for the study of pottery, Faust, and philosophy!'" (*Selected Letters* 256).

10. Mrs. March alludes to the New Testament: "And above all things have fervent charity among yourselves; for charity shall cover the multitude of sins" (1 Peter 4:8). The original Greek New Testament uses the word *agape,* which the Catholic Vulgate and the King James Bible translated as *charity.* Most other English editions of the Bible translate it as *love.*

11. Sermon.

maker of the family, and if you get dismal there is no fair weather. Then I'd try to take an interest in whatever John likes, talk with him, let him read to you, exchange ideas, and help each other in that way. Don't shut yourself up in a bandbox because you are a woman, but understand what is going on, and educate yourself to take your part in the world's work, for it all affects you and yours."[9]

"John is so sensible, I'm afraid he will think I'm stupid if I ask questions about politics and things."

"I don't believe he would; love covers a multitude of sins,[10] and of whom could you ask more freely than of him? Try it, and see if he doesn't find your society far more agreeable than Mrs. Scott's suppers."

"I will. Poor John! I'm afraid I *have* neglected him sadly, but I thought I was right, and he never said anything."

"He tried not to be selfish, but he *has* felt rather forlorn, I fancy. This is just the time, Meg, when young married people are apt to grow apart, and the very time when they ought to be most together; for the first tenderness soon wears off, unless care is taken to preserve it; and no time is so beautiful and precious to parents, as the first years of the little lives given to them to train. Don't let John be a stranger to the babies, for they will do more to keep him safe and happy in this world of trial and temptation, than anything else, and through them you will learn to know and love one another as you should. Now, dear, good-by; think over mother's preachment,[11] act upon it if it seems good, and God bless you all!"

Meg did think it over, found it good, and acted upon it, though the first attempt was not made exactly as she planned to have it. Of course, the children tyrannized over her, and ruled the house as soon as they found out that kicking and squalling brought them whatever they wanted. Mamma was an abject slave to their caprices, but papa was not so easily subjugated, and occasionally afflicted his tender spouse, by an attempt at paternal discipline with his obstreperous son. For Demi inherited a trifle of his sire's firmness of character—we won't call it obstinacy—and when he made up his little mind to have or to do anything, all the king's horses and all the king's men could not change that pertinacious little mind. Mamma thought the dear too young to be taught to

Demi refuses to go to sleep. Tasha Tudor, *Little Women* (1969).

conquer his prejudices, but papa believed that it never was too soon to learn obedience; so Master Demi early discovered, that when he undertook to "wrastle" with "parpar," he always got the worst of it; yet, like the Englishman, Baby respected the man who conquered him, and loved the father, whose grave "No, no," was more impressive than all of the mother's love pats.

A few days after the talk with her mother, Meg resolved to try a social evening with John; so she ordered a nice supper,[12] set the parlor in order, dressed herself prettily, and put the children to

12. That is, Meg told the Irish cook what to prepare.

bed early, that nothing should interfere with her experiment. But, unfortunately, Demi's most unconquerable prejudice was against going to bed, and that night he decided to go on a rampage; so poor Meg sung and rocked, told stories, and tried every sleep-provoking wile she could devise, but all in vain—the big eyes wouldn't shut; and long after Daisy had gone to byelow,[13] like the chubby little bunch of good nature she was, naughty Demi lay staring at the light, with the most discouragingly wide-awake expression of countenance.

"Will Demi lie still, like a good boy, while mamma runs down and gives poor papa his tea?" asked Meg, as the hall door softly closed, and the well-known step went tip-toeing into the dining-room.

"Me has tea!" said Demi, preparing to join in the revel.

"No; but I'll save you some little cakies for breakfast, if you'll go bye-bye, like Daisy. Will you, lovey?"

"Iss!" and Demi shut his eyes tight, as if to catch sleep, and hurry the desired day.

Taking advantage of the propitious moment, Meg slipped away, and ran down to greet her husband with a smiling face, and the little blue bow in her hair, which was his especial admiration. He saw it at once, and said, with pleased surprise,—

"Why, little mother, how gay we are to-night. Do you expect company?"

"Only you, dear."

"Is it a birthday, anniversary, or anything?"

"No; I'm tired of being a dowdy, so I dressed up as a change. You always make yourself nice for table, no matter how tired you are; so, why shouldn't I, when I have the time?"

"I do it out of respect to you, my dear," said old-fashioned John.

"Ditto, ditto, Mr. Brooke," laughed Meg, looking young and pretty again, as she nodded to him over the teapot.

"Well, it's altogether delightful, and like old times. This tastes right; I drink your health, dear!" and John sipped his tea with an air of reposeful rapture, which was of very short duration, however; for, as he put down his cup, the door-handle rattled mysteriously, and a little voice was heard, saying, impatiently,—

"Opy doy; me's tummin!"

"It's that naughty boy; I told him to go to sleep alone, and here he is, down stairs, getting his death a-cold pattering over that canvas," said Meg, answering the call.

"Mornin' now," announced Demi, in a joyful tone, as he entered, with his long night-gown gracefully festooned over his arm, and every curl bobbing gaily, as he pranced about the table, eyeing the "cakies" with loving glances.

"No, it isn't morning yet; you must go to bed, and not trouble poor mamma; then you can have the little cake with sugar on it."

"Me loves parpar," said the artful one, preparing to climb the paternal knee, and revel in forbidden joys. But John shook his head, and said to Meg,—

"If you told him to stay up there, and go to sleep alone, make him do it, or he will never learn to mind you."

"Yes, of course; come, Demi!" and Meg led her son away, feeling a strong desire to spank the little marplot who hopped beside her, laboring under the delusion that the bribe was to be administered as soon as they reached the nursery.

Nor was he disappointed; for that short-sighted woman actually gave him a lump of sugar, tucked him into his bed, and forbade any more promenades till morning.

"Iss!" said Demi the perjured, blissfully sucking his sugar, and regarding his first attempt as eminently successful.

Meg returned to her place, and supper was progressing pleasantly, when the little ghost walked again, and exposed the maternal delinquencies, by boldly demanding,—

"More sudar, marmar."

"Now this won't do," said John, hardening his heart against the engaging little sinner. "We shall never know any peace till that child learns to go to bed properly. You have made a slave of yourself long enough; give him one lesson, and then there will be an end of it. Put him in his bed, and leave him, Meg."

"He won't stay there; he never does, unless I sit by him."

"I'll manage him. Demi, go upstairs, and get into your bed, as mamma bids you."

14. A female slave.

15. One who has authority or control.

"S'ant!" replied the young rebel, helping himself to the coveted "cakie," and beginning to eat the same with calm audacity.

"You must never say that to papa; I shall carry you if you don't go yourself."

"Go 'way; me don't love parpar;" and Demi retired to his mother's skirts for protection.

But even that refuge proved unavailing, for he was delivered over to the enemy, with a "Be gentle with him, John," which struck the culprit with dismay; for when mamma deserted him, then the judgment-day was at hand. Bereft of his cake, defrauded of his frolic, and borne away by a strong hand to that detested bed, poor Demi could not restrain his wrath; but openly defied papa, and kicked and screamed lustily all the way upstairs. The minute he was put into bed on one side, he rolled out at the other, and made for the door, only to be ignominiously caught up by the tail of his little toga, and put back again, which lively performance was kept up till the young man's strength gave out, when he devoted himself to roaring at the top of his voice. This vocal exercise usually conquered Meg; but John sat as unmoved as the post, which is popularly believed to be deaf. No coaxing, no sugar, no lullaby, no story—even the light was put out and only the red glow of the fire enlivened the "big dark" which Demi regarded with curiosity rather than fear. This new order of things disgusted him, and he howled dismally for "marmar," as his angry passions subsided, and recollections of his tender bond-woman[14] returned to the captive autocrat.[15] The plaintive wail which succeeded the passionate roar went to Meg's heart, and she ran up to say, beseechingly,—

"Let me stay with him; he'll be good, now, John."

"No, my dear, I've told him he must go to sleep, as you bid him; and he must, if I stay here all night."

"But he'll cry himself sick," pleaded Meg, reproaching herself for deserting her boy.

"No he won't, he's so tired he will soon drop off, and then the matter is settled; for he will understand that he has got to mind. Don't interfere; I'll manage him."

"He's my child, and I can't have his spirit broken by harshness."

"He's my child, and I won't have his temper spoilt by indulgence. Go down, my dear, and leave the boy to me."

When John spoke in that masterful tone, Meg always obeyed, and never regretted her docility.

"Please let me kiss him, once, John?"

"Certainly; Demi, say 'good-night' to mamma, and let her go and rest, for she is very tired with taking care of you all day."

Meg always insisted upon it, that the kiss won the victory; for, after it was given, Demi sobbed more quietly, and lay quite still at the bottom of the bed, whither he had wriggled in his anguish of mind.

"Poor little man! he's worn out with sleep and crying; I'll cover him up, and then go and set Meg's heart at rest," thought John, creeping to the bedside, hoping to find his rebellious heir asleep.

But he wasn't; for the moment his father peeped at him, Demi's eyes opened, his little chin began to quiver, and he put up his arms, saying, with a penitent hiccough, "Me's dood, now."

Sitting on the stairs, outside, Meg wondered at the long silence which followed the uproar; and, after imagining all sorts of impossible accidents, she slipped into the room, to set her fears at rest. Demi lay fast asleep; not in his usual spread-eagle attitude, but in a subdued bunch, cuddled close in the circle of his father's arm, and holding his father's finger, as if he felt that justice was tempered with mercy, and had gone to sleep a sadder and wiser baby. So held, John had waited with womanly patience till the little hand relaxed its hold; and, while waiting, had fallen asleep, more tired by that tussle with his little son than with his whole day's work.

As Meg stood watching the two faces on the pillow, she smiled to herself, and then slipped away again, saying, in a satisfied tone,—

"I never need fear that John will be too harsh with my babies, he *does* know how to manage them, and will be a great help, for Demi *is* getting too much for me."

When John came down at last, expecting to find a pensive or reproachful wife, he was agreeably surprised to find Meg placidly trimming a bonnet, and to be greeted with the request to read

17. During the mid-nineteenth century women often wore an informal cap indoors. The breakfast cap, also known as a morning cap or day cap, could be simple or lavishly decorated with ribbons, frills, or lace.

something about the election, if he was not too tired. John saw in a minute that a revolution of some kind was going on, but wisely asked no questions, knowing that Meg was such a transparent little person, she couldn't keep a secret to save her life, and therefore the clue would soon appear. He read a long debate with the most amiable readiness, and then explained it in his most lucid manner, while Meg tried to look deeply interested, to ask intelligent questions, and keep her thoughts from wandering from the state of the nation to the state of her bonnet. In her secret soul, however, she decided that politics were as bad as mathematics, and the mission of politicians seemed to be calling each other names; but she kept these feminine ideas to herself, and when John paused, shook her head, and said with what she thought diplomatic ambiguity,—

"Well, I really don't see what we are coming to."

John laughed, and watched her for a minute, as she poised a pretty little preparation of tulle[b] and flowers on her hand, and regarded it with the genuine interest which his harangue had failed to waken.

"She is trying to like politics for my sake, so I'll try and like millinery[16] for hers—that's only fair," thought John the just, adding aloud,—

"That's very pretty; is it what you call a breakfast cap?"[17]

"My dear man, it's a bonnet—my very best go-to-concert and theater bonnet!"

"I beg your pardon; it was so small, I naturally mistook it for one of the fly-away things you sometimes wear. How do you keep it on?"

"These bits of lace are fastened under the chin, with a rose-bud, so"—and Meg illustrated by putting on the bonnet, and regarding him with an air of calm satisfaction, that was irresistible.

"It's a love of a bonnet, but I prefer the face inside, for it looks young and happy again," and John kissed the smiling face, to the great detriment of the rose-bud under the chin.

"I'm glad you like it, for I want you to take me to one of the new concerts some night; I really need some music to put me in tune. Will you, please?"

"Of course I will, with all my heart, or anywhere else you like. You have been shut up so long, it will do you no end of good, and I shall enjoy it, of all things. What put it into your head, little mother?"

"Well, I had a talk with Marmee the other day, and told her how nervous, and cross, and out of sorts I felt, and she said I needed change, and less care; so Hannah is to help me with the children, and I'm to see to things about the house more, and now and then have a little fun, just to keep me from getting to be a fidgety, broken-down old woman before my time. It's only an experiment, John, and I want to try it for your sake, as much as for mine, because I've neglected you shamefully lately, and I'm going to make home what it used to be, if I can. You don't object, I hope?"

Never mind what John said, or what a very narrow escape the little bonnet had from utter ruin; all that we have any business to know, is that John did *not* appear to object, judging from the changes which gradually took place in the house and its inmates. It was not all Paradise by any means, but every one was better for the division of labor system; the children throve under the paternal rule, for accurate, steadfast John brought order and obedience into Babydom, while Meg recovered her spirits, and composed her nerves, by plenty of wholesome exercise, a little pleasure, and much confidential conversation with her sensible husband. Home grew home-like again, and John had no wish to leave it, unless he took Meg with him. The Scotts came to the Brookes now, and every one found the little house a cheerful place, full of happiness, content, and family love; even gay Sallie Moffat liked to go there. "It is always so quiet and pleasant here; it does me good, Meg," she used to say, looking about her with wistful eyes, as if trying to discover the charm, that she might use it in her great house, full of splendid loneliness, for there were no riotous, sunny-faced babies there, and Ned lived in a world of his own, where there was no place for her.

This household happiness did not come all at once, but John and Meg had found the key to it, and each year of married life taught them how to use it, unlocking the treasuries of real home-

18. The word *husband,* according to the *OED,* comes from the Old English *húsbonda,* meaning "master of a house; the male head of household."

19. Here the narrator offers a clear prescription for what married life should be: the house is filled with home-love and mutual helpfulness. Husband and wife walk side by side as equals. This is the egalitarian marriage that LMA champions, both in her fiction and in her nonfiction. In the September 1887 edition of the *Ladies Home Journal,* LMA, in her article "Early Marriages," once again, just six months before her death, stresses her vision for marriage by citing the example of a couple she knew: The man and woman "waited two years to know one another thoroughly, and to be ready in all ways for the union which binds for better or worse . . . Then they married on an income of six hundred dollars, and, contenting themselves with two pleasant rooms, lived like a pair of turtle doves; or better still, a busy, loving man and wife, each doing his or her part toward increasing the income; glad to work up hand in hand, growing nearer and dearer as they bore their sorrows and earned their successes together" (p. 3).

love and mutual helpfulness, which the poorest may possess, and the richest cannot buy. This is the sort of shelf on which young wives and mothers may consent to be laid, safe from the restless fret and fever of the world, finding loyal lovers in the little sons and daughters who cling to them, undaunted by sorrow, poverty or age; walking side by side, through fair and stormy weather, with a faithful friend, who is, in the true sense of the good old Saxon word, the "house-band,"[18] and learning, as Meg learned, that a woman's happiest kingdom is home, her highest honor the art of ruling it—not as a queen, but a wise wife and mother.[19]

1. *Muching* derives from the phrase "to make much of." In the 1880–1881 edition, it was changed to *petting*.

2. LMA believes in the perfectibility of the individual, but she recognizes important differences in temperament and personality. Here is one of the first strong indications we receive that Laurie and Amy make "natural" companions. In the end it is not that Laurie is unworthy of Jo's affections but rather that the two are not well suited to each other.

Chapter 16

Lazy Laurence

LAURIE went to Nice intending to stay a week, and remained a month. He was tired of wandering about alone, and Amy's familiar presence seemed to give a home-like charm to the foreign scenes in which she bore a part. He rather missed the "muching"[1] he used to receive, and enjoyed a taste of it again,—for no attentions, however flattering, from strangers, were half so pleasant as the sisterly adoration of the girls at home. Amy never would pet him like the others, but she was very glad to see him now, and quite clung to him,—feeling that he was the representative of the dear family for whom she longed more than she would confess. They naturally took comfort in each other's society,[2] and were much together,—riding, walking, dancing, or dawdling,—for, at Nice, no one can be very industrious during the gay season. But, while apparently amusing themselves in the most careless fashion, they were half-consciously making discoveries and forming opinions about each other. Amy rose daily in the estimation of her friend, but he sunk in hers, and each felt the truth before a word was spoken. Amy tried to please, and succeeded,—for she was grateful for the many pleasures he gave her, and repaid him with the little services to which womanly women know how to lend an indescribable charm. Laurie made no effort of any kind, but just let himself drift along as comfortably as possible, trying to forget, and feeling that all women owed him a kind word because one had been cold to him. It cost him no effort to be generous, and he would have given Amy all the trinkets in Nice if she would have taken them,—but, at the same time, he felt that he could not change the opinion she was forming of him,

3. Less than ten miles from Nice, France, the country of Monaco, on the Mediterranean Sea, was by the mid-nineteenth century a tourist destination.

4. According to LMA, Valrosa, a site she visited often when in Nice in spring 1866, was "a lovely villa buried in roses" (*Journals* 150).

5. Walked in a lazy manner.

6. A drawing room.

7. Kid gloves, made of goat or lamb skin, were fashionable for men in the 1860s and were made in a variety of colors.

8. A pannier is a pair of baskets that hung on each side of the donkey.

9. Probably LMA means the French word *capeline,* a loose hood of wool or a wide-brimmed hat usually made of straw.

10. The *OED* defines *distaff* as a "cleft staff about 3 feet long, on which, in the ancient mode of spinning, wool or flax was wound. It was held under the left arm, and the fibres of the material were drawn from it through the fingers of the left hand, and twisted spirally by the forefinger and thumb of the right, with the aid of the suspended spindle, round which the thread, as it was twisted or spun, was wound."

and he rather dreaded the keen blue eyes that seemed to watch him with such half-sorrowful, half-scornful surprise.

"All the rest have gone to Monaco[3] for the day; I preferred to stay at home and write letters. They are done now, and I am going to Valrosa[4] to sketch; will you come?" said Amy, as she joined Laurie one lovely day when he lounged[5] in as usual, about noon.

"Well, yes; but isn't it rather warm for such a long walk?" he answered slowly,—for the shaded *salon*[6] looked inviting, after the glare without.

"I'm going to have the little carriage, and Baptiste can drive,—so you'll have nothing to do but hold your umbrella and keep your gloves nice," returned Amy, with a sarcastic glance at the immaculate kids,[7] which were a weak point with Laurie.

"Then I'll go with pleasure," and he put out his hand for her sketch-book. But she tucked it under her arm with a sharp—

"Don't trouble yourself; it's no exertion to me, but *you* don't look equal to it."

Laurie lifted his eyebrows, and followed at a leisurely pace as she ran down stairs; but when they got into the carriage he took the reins himself, and left little Baptiste nothing to do but fold his arms and fall asleep on his perch.

The two never quarrelled; Amy was too well-bred, and just now Laurie was too lazy; so, in a minute he peeped under her hat-brim with an inquiring air; she answered him with a smile, and they went on together in the most amicable manner.

It was a lovely drive, along winding roads rich in the picturesque scenes that delight beauty-loving eyes. Here an ancient monastery, whence the solemn chanting of the monks came down to them. There a bare-legged shepherd, in wooden shoes, pointed hat, and rough jacket over one shoulder, sat piping on a stone, while his goats skipped among the rocks or lay at his feet. Meek, mouse-colored donkeys, laden with panniers[8] of freshly-cut grass, passed by, with a pretty girl in a *capaline*[9] sitting between the green piles, or an old woman spinning with a distaff[10] as she went. Brown, soft-eyed children ran out from the quaint stone hovels to offer nosegays, or bunches of oranges still on the bough. Gnarled olive-trees covered the hills with their dusky foliage, fruit hung golden in the orchard, and great scarlet anemonies[11] fringed the roadside; while beyond green slopes and craggy heights, the Maritime Alps[12] rose sharp and white against the blue Italian sky.

Valrosa well deserved its name,—for in that climate of perpetual summer roses blossomed everywhere. They overhung the archway, thrust themselves between the bars of the great gate with a sweet welcome to passers-by, and lined the avenue, winding through lemon-trees and feathery palms up to the villa on the hill. Every shadowy nook, where seats invited one to stop and rest, was a mass of bloom; every cool grotto had its marble nymph smiling from a veil of flowers; and every fountain reflected crimson, white, or pale pink roses, leaning down to smile at their own beauty. Roses covered the walls of the house, draped the cornices, climbed the pillars, and ran riot over the balustrade of the wide terrace, whence one looked down on the sunny Mediterranean and the white-walled city on its shore.

"This is a regular honey-moon Paradise, isn't it? Did you ever see such roses?" asked Amy, pausing on the terrace to enjoy the view, and a luxurious whiff of perfume that came wandering by.

"No, nor felt such thorns," returned Laurie, with his thumb in his mouth, after a vain attempt to capture a solitary scarlet flower that grew just beyond his reach.[13]

"Try lower down, and pick those that have no thorns," said Amy, deftly gathering three of the tiny cream-colored ones that starred the wall behind her. She put them in his button-hole, as a peace offering, and he stood a minute looking down at them with a curious expression, for in the Italian part of his nature there was a touch of superstition, and he was just then in that state of half-sweet, half-bitter melancholy, when imaginative young men find significance in trifles, and food for romance everywhere. He had thought of Jo in reaching after the thorny red rose,—for vivid flowers became her,—and she had often worn ones like that, from the green-house at home. The pale roses[14] Amy gave him were the sort that the Italians lay in dead hands,—never in bridal wreaths, —and, for a moment, he wondered if the omen was for Jo or for himself. But the next instant his American common-sense got the

11. Anemonies is a common perennial from the buttercup family, *Ranunculaceae,* with about 120 species with colorful flowers.

12. Bordering France and Italy, the Maritime Alps, reaching a height of 10,817 feet, are the southwestern range of the Alps near the Mediterranean Sea.

13. Laurie is not the only one who reads this episode symbolically, as Amy's freighted response—a double entendre—makes entirely clear. Whether or not she is prepared to admit it, Amy has already guessed what's wrong with Laurie. The solitary scarlet flower that wounds Laurie and is beyond his reach is, of course, the chestnut-haired Jo.

14. In the nineteenth-century language of flowers, red roses symbolize love, passion, and respect, while pale roses signify friendship.

15. Natural depravity is the idea that all people are born evil or depraved because of Adam and Eve's fall. The French theologian John Calvin (1509–1564) stressed this idea, and it became one of the basic tenets of the Puritan church.

16. *Cigarette* is French for a small cigar, which is what Laurie means. Modern cigarettes did not become popular until the twentieth century.

17. An Italian phrase that literally means "sweet doing nothing." Delicious idleness.

better of sentimentality, and he laughed a heartier laugh than Amy had heard since he came.

"It's good advice,—you'd better take it and save your fingers," she said, thinking her speech amused him.

"Thank you, I will!" he answered in jest,—and a few months later he did it in earnest.

"Laurie, when are you going to your grandfather?" she asked, presently, as she settled herself on a rustic seat.

"Very soon."

"You have said that a dozen times within the last three weeks."

"I dare say; short answers save trouble."

"He expects you, and you really ought to go."

"Hospitable creature! I know it."

"Then why don't you do it?"

"Natural depravity,[15] I suppose."

"Natural indolence, you mean. It's really dreadful!" and Amy looked severe.

"Not so bad as it seems, for I should only plague him if I went, so I might as well stay, and plague you a little longer—you can bear it better; in fact, I think it agrees with you excellently!" and Laurie composed himself for a lounge on the broad ledge of the balustrade.

Amy shook her head, and opened her sketch-book with an air of resignation, but she had made up her mind to lecture "that boy," and in a minute she began again.

"What are you doing just now?"

"Watching lizards."

"No, no! I mean what do you intend, and wish to do?"

"Smoke a cigarette,[16] if you'll allow me."

"How provoking you are! I don't approve of cigars, and I will only allow it on condition that you let me put you into my sketch; I need a figure."

"With all the pleasure in life. How will you have me? full-length, or three-quarters; on my head or my heels? I should respectfully suggest a recumbent posture, then put yourself in also, and call it *'Dolce far niente.'*"[17]

"Stay as you are, and go to sleep if you like. *I* intend to work hard," said Amy in her most energetic tone.

"What delightful enthusiasm!" and he leaned against a tall urn, with an air of entire satisfaction.

"What would Jo say if she saw you now?" asked Amy impatiently, hoping to stir him up by the mention of her still more energetic sister's name.

"As usual: 'Go away, Teddy. I'm busy'!" He laughed as he spoke, but the laugh was not natural, and a shade passed over his face, for the utterance of the familiar name touched the wound that was not healed yet. Both tone and shadow struck Amy, for she had seen and heard them before, and now she looked up in time to catch a new expression on Laurie's face—a hard, bitter look, full of pain, dissatisfaction and regret. It was gone before she could study it, and the listless expression back again. She watched him for a moment with artistic pleasure, thinking how like an Italian he looked, as he lay basking in the sun, with uncovered head, and eyes full of Southern[18] dreaminess; for he seemed to have forgotten her, and fallen into a reverie.

"You look like the effigy of a young knight asleep on his tomb," she said, carefully tracing the well-cut profile defined against the dark stone.

"Wish I was!"

"That's a foolish wish, unless you have spoilt your life. You are so changed, I sometimes think—" there Amy stopped with a half-timid, half-wistful look, more significant than her unfinished speech.

Laurie saw and understood the affectionate anxiety which she hesitated to express, and looking straight into her eyes, said, just as he used to say it to her mother,—

"It's all right, ma'am!"

That satisfied her, and set at rest the doubts that had began to worry her lately. It also touched her, and she showed that it did, by the cordial tone in which she said,—

"I'm glad of that! I didn't think you'd been a very bad boy, but I fancied you might have wasted money at that wicked Baden-Baden, lost your heart to some charming Frenchwoman with a

18. The dreaminess or indolence inspired by being in the South of France.

19. A female variant of Raphael.

20. Laurie wonders if Amy knows that Jo had rejected him as a possible husband.

21. Writing about his friend Margaret Fuller, Ralph Waldo Emerson noted the difficulties faced by a nineteenth-century woman who desired a professional career: a woman "congratulates herself when she is not called to the market, to the courts, to the polls, to the stage, to the orchestra. Only the most extraordinary genius can make the career of an artist secure and agreeable to her" (Ralph Waldo Emerson, Henry Channing, and James Freeman Clarke, eds., *Memoirs of Margaret Fuller Ossoli* [Boston: Phillips, Sampson, 1852], pp. 321–322). Amy realizes that she lacks the genius required to succeed in an extremely competitive, male-dominated field. May Alcott, however, persisted in following her own muse. Writing to her mother from Paris on March 19, 1877, May noted that she had just viewed paintings by Frederick Arthur Bridgman (1847–1928) and others in her American set of friends, almost all male: "Just wait till the women have studied 8 or 9 years as most of these artists have & we will beat them with their own weapons. I felt much encouraged by seeing this collection & begin already to feel my power in art grow within me" (Manuscript letter, Concord Free Public Library, Alcott-Nieriker-Pratt Family Correspondence, [1856]–1912, Folder 3).

22. An untalented painter.

husband, or got into some of the scrapes that young men seem to consider a necessary part of a foreign tour. Don't stay out there in the sun, come and lie on the grass here, and 'let us be friendly,' as Jo used to say when we got in the sofa-corner and told secrets."

Laurie obediently threw himself down on the turf, and began to amuse himself by sticking daisies into the ribbons of Amy's hat, that lay there.

"I'm all ready for the secrets," and he glanced up with a decided expression of interest in his eyes.

"I've none to tell; you may begin."

"Haven't one to bless myself with. I thought perhaps you'd had some news from home."

"You have heard all that has come lately. Don't you hear often? I fancied Jo would send you volumes."

"She's very busy; I'm roving about so, it's impossible to be regular, you know. When do you begin your great work of art, Raphaella?"[19] he asked, changing the subject abruptly after another pause, in which he had been wondering if Amy knew his secret,[20] and wanted to talk about it.

"Never!" she answered, with a despondent, but decided air. "Rome took all the vanity out of me, for after seeing the wonders there, I felt too insignificant to live, and gave up all my foolish hopes in despair."

"Why should you, with so much energy and talent?"

"That's just why, because talent isn't genius, and no amount of energy can make it so. I want to be great, or nothing.[21] I won't be a common-place dauber,[22] so I don't intend to try any more."

"And what are you going to do with yourself now, if I may ask?"

"Polish up my other talents, and be an ornament to society, if I get the chance."

It was a characteristic speech, and sounded daring; but audacity becomes young people, and Amy's ambition had a good foundation. Laurie smiled, but he liked the spirit with which she took up a new purpose, when a long cherished one died, and spent no time lamenting.

LITTLE WOMEN

"Good! and here is where Fred Vaughn comes in, I fancy."

Amy preserved a discreet silence, but there was a conscious look in her downcast face, that made Laurie sit up and say gravely,—

"Now I'm going to play brother, and ask questions. May I?"

"I don't promise to answer."

"Your face will, if your tongue don't.[a] You aren't woman of the world enough yet to hide your feelings, my dear. I've heard rumors about Fred and you last year, and it's my private opinion, that if he had not been called home so suddenly, and detained so long, that something would have come of it—hey?"

"That's not for me to say," was Amy's prim reply; but her lips would smile, and there was a traitorous sparkle of the eye, which betrayed that she knew her power and enjoyed the knowledge.

"You are not engaged, I hope?" and Laurie looked very elder-brotherly and grave all of a sudden.

"No."

"But you will be, if he comes back and goes properly down upon his knees, won't you?"

"Very likely."

"Then you are fond of old Fred?"

"I could be if I tried."

"But you don't intend to try till the proper moment? Bless my soul, what unearthly prudence! He's a good fellow, Amy, but not the man I fancied you'd like."

"He is rich, a gentleman, and has delightful manners,"—began Amy, trying to be quite cool and dignified, but feeling a little ashamed of herself, in spite of the sincerity of her intentions.[23]

"I understand—queens of society can't get on without money, so you mean to make a good match and start in that way? Quite right and proper as the world goes, but it sounds odd from the lips of one of your mother's girls."

"True, nevertheless!"

A short speech, but the quiet decision with which it was uttered, contrasted curiously with the young speaker. Laurie felt this instinctively, and laid himself down again, with a sense of disap-

23. May Alcott, at age twenty-three, confessed in her journal of August 23, 1863: "I dont say I should'nt prefer a true *male* friend but as Platonic attachments are treacherous & no one cares to marry a girl without beauty or wealth, I seem to be left rather to myself which is perhaps the safest way after all & if I have any talent to develope perhaps if left to myself I may work out something that will prove I have'nt entirely wasted my time & youth" (Manuscript journal, Harvard University, Houghton Library, bMS Am 1817 [57]).

24. Lazy Lawrence is a symbol of laziness in a number of proverbial folk sayings. *The History of Lawrence Lazy,* an anonymous chapbook published about 1670, was popular even in the nineteenth century. Maria Edgeworth, one of LMA's favorite childhood authors, published the story "Lazy Lawrence" in her second book, *The Parent's Assistant; or Stories for Children* (1796), which also included her famous story "The Purple Jar."

pointment which he could not explain. His look and silence, as well as a certain inward self-disapproval, ruffled Amy—and made her resolve to deliver her lecture without delay.

"I wish you'd do me the favor to rouse yourself a little," she said sharply.

"Do it for me, there's a dear girl!"

"I could if I tried," and she looked as if she would like doing it in the most summary style.

"Try then, I give you leave," returned Laurie, who enjoyed having some one to tease, after his long abstinence from his favorite pastime.

"You'd be angry in five minutes."

"I'm never angry with you. It takes two flints to make a fire; you are as cool and soft as snow."

"You don't know what I can do—snow produces a glow and a tingle, if applied rightly. Your indifference is half affectation, and a good stirring up would prove it."

"Stir away, it won't hurt me, and it may amuse you, as the big man said when his little wife beat him. Regard me in the light of a husband or a carpet, and beat till you are tired, if that sort of exercise agrees with you."

Being decidedly nettled herself, and longing to see him shake off the apathy that so altered him, Amy sharpened both tongue and pencil, and began,—

"Flo and I have got a new name for you; it's 'Lazy Laurence';[24] how do you like it?"

She thought it would annoy him, but he only folded his arms under his head, with an imperturbable—"That's not bad! thank you, ladies."

"Do you want to know what I honestly think of you?"

"Pining to be told."

"Well, I despise you."

If she had even said "I hate you," in a petulant or coquettish tone, he would have laughed, and rather liked it; but the grave, almost sad accent in her voice, made him open his eyes, and ask quickly,—

"Why, if you please?"

"Because with every chance for being good, useful and happy, you are faulty, lazy and miserable."

"Strong language, mademoiselle."

"If you like it, I'll go on."

"Pray do, it's quite interesting."

"I thought you'd find it so; selfish people always like to talk about themselves."

"Am *I* selfish?" the question slipped out involuntarily, and in a tone of surprise, for the one virtue on which he prided himself was generosity.

"Yes, very selfish," continued Amy, in a calm, cool voice, twice as effective, just then, as an angry one. "I'll show you how, for I've studied you while we have been frolicking, and I'm not at all satisfied with you. Here you have been abroad nearly six months, and done nothing but waste time and money, and disappoint your friends."

"Isn't a fellow to have any pleasure after a four-years' grind?"

"You don't look as if you'd had much; at any rate you are none the better for it, as far as I can see. I said when we first met, that you had improved; now I take it all back, for I don't think you half so nice as when I left you at home. You have grown abominably lazy, you like gossip, and waste time on frivolous things; you are contented to be petted and admired by silly people, instead of being loved and respected by wise ones. With money, talent, position, health, and beauty,—ah, you like that, old vanity! but it's the truth, so I can't help saying it,—with all these splendid things to use and enjoy, you can find nothing to do but dawdle, and instead of being the man you might and ought to be, you are only—" there she stopped, with a look that had both pain and pity in it.

"Saint Laurence on a gridiron,"[25] added Laurie, blandly finishing the sentence. But the lecture began to take effect, for there was a wide-awake sparkle in his eyes now, and a half-angry, half-injured expression replaced the former indifference.

"I supposed you'd take it so. You men tell us we are angels, and say we can make you what we will; but the instant we honestly try to do you good, you laugh at us, and won't listen, which proves

25. Saint Lawrence (ca. 225–258), a Christian deacon under Pope St. Sixtus, was the keeper of the treasures of the Catholic Church, including the holy grail. According to legend, when the prefect of Rome martyred the pope, he demanded that Lawrence bring him the church's treasures. Lawrence asked for several days to gather them, and when granted the time, he distributed the treasures among the poor. On August 10, the prefect had Lawrence burnt alive on a girdiron or griddle. According to some versions of the legend, St. Lawrence is the patron saint of lazy people because he humorously called out to the Romans as he was on the girdiron: "Turn me. I'm done on this side." Some accounts identify St. Lawrence as the figure behind Lazy Lawrence in proverbial sayings. Laurie seems aware of this part of the legend as he appears to link St. Lawrence with laziness.

26. An allusion to the martyred St. Lawrence.

27. Xavier Jouvin (1801–1844), a glover from Grenoble, France, who in 1834 invented the cutting die that gave a constant shape to the leather or cloth and ensured a more precise fit.

28. A seal ring had a symbol or emblem that was used to press into hot wax when sealing a letter or envelope.

how much your flattery is worth." Amy spoke bitterly, and turned her back on the exasperating martyr[26] at her feet.

In a minute a hand came down over the page, so that she could not draw, and Laurie's voice said, with a droll imitation of a penitent child,—

"I will be good! oh, I will be good!"

But Amy did not laugh, for she was in earnest; and, tapping on the outspread hand with her pencil, said soberly,—

"Aren't you ashamed of a hand like that? It's as soft and white as a woman's, and looks as if it never did anything but wear Jouvin's best gloves,[27] and pick flowers for ladies. You are not a dandy, thank heaven! so I'm glad to see there are no diamonds or big seal rings[28] on it, only the little old one Jo gave you so long ago. Dear soul! I wish she was here to help me!"

"So do I!"

The hand vanished as suddenly as it came, and there was energy enough in the echo of her wish to suit even Amy. She glanced down at him with a new thought in her mind,—but he was lying with his hat half over his face, as if for shade, and his mustache hid his mouth. She only saw his chest rise and fall, with a long breath that might have been a sigh, and the hand that wore the ring nestle down into the grass, as if to hide something too precious or too tender to be spoken of. All in a minute various hints and trifles assumed shape and significance in Amy's mind, and told her what her sister never had confided to her. She remembered that Laurie never spoke voluntarily of Jo; she recalled the shadow on his face just now, the change in his character, and the wearing of the little old ring, which was no ornament to a handsome hand. Girls are quick to read such signs, and feel their eloquence; Amy had fancied that perhaps a love-trouble was at the bottom of the alteration, and now she was sure of it; her keen eyes filled, and, when she spoke again, it was in a voice that could be beautifully soft and kind when she chose to make it so.

"I know I have no right to talk so to you, Laurie; and if you weren't the sweetest-tempered fellow in the world, you'd be very angry with me. But we are all so fond and proud of you, I couldn't bear to think they should be disappointed in you at home as I

LITTLE WOMEN

have been,—though perhaps they would understand the change better than I do."

"I think they would," came from under the hat, in a grim tone, quite as touching as a broken one.

"They ought to have told me, and not let me go blundering and scolding, when I should have been more kind and patient than ever. I never did like that Miss Randal, and now I hate her!" said artful Amy,—wishing to be sure of her facts this time.[29]

"Hang Miss Randal!" and Laurie knocked the hat off his face with a look that left no doubt of his sentiments toward that young lady.

"I beg pardon; I thought—" and there she paused diplomatically.

"No, you didn't; you knew perfectly well I never cared for any one but Jo." Laurie said that in his old, impetuous tone, and turned his face away as he spoke.

"I did think so; but as they never said anything about it, and you came away, I supposed I was mistaken. And Jo wouldn't be kind to you? Why, I was sure she loved you dearly."

"She *was* kind, but not in the right way; and it's lucky for her she didn't love me, if I'm the good-for-nothing fellow you think me. It's her fault, though, and you may tell her so."

The hard, bitter look came back again as he said that, and it troubled Amy, for she did not know what balm to apply.

"I was wrong; I didn't know; I'm very sorry I was so cross, but I can't help wishing you'd bear it better, Teddy, dear."

"Don't! that's her name for me!" and Laurie put up his hand with a quick gesture to stop the words spoken in Jo's half-kind, half-reproachful tone. "Wait till you've tried it yourself," he added, in a low voice, as he pulled up the grass by the handful.

"I'd take it manfully, and be respected if I couldn't be loved," cried[b] Amy, with the decision of one who knew nothing about it.

Now Laurie flattered himself that he *had* borne it remarkably well,—making no moan, asking no sympathy, and taking his trouble away to live it down alone. Amy's lecture put the matter in a new light, and for the first time it did look weak and selfish to lose heart at the first failure, and shut himself up in moody indif-

29. Amy wants to be certain that it is Jo and not another woman who is making Laurie lovelorn; the subject of Miss Randall is a canard, as Laurie well understands.

ference. He felt as if suddenly shaken out of a pensive dream, and found it impossible to go to sleep again. Presently he sat up, and asked, slowly,—

"Do you think Jo would despise me as you do?"

"Yes, if she saw you now. She hates lazy people. Why don't you do something splendid, and *make* her love you?"

"I did my best, but it was no use."

"Graduating well, you mean? That was no more than you ought to have done, for your grandfather's sake. It would have been shameful to fail after spending so much time and money, when every one knew you *could* do well."

"I did fail, say what you will, for Jo wouldn't love me," began Laurie, leaning his head on his hand in a despondent attitude.

"No you didn't, and you'll say so in the end,—for it did you good, and proved that you could do something if you tried. If you'd only set about another task of some sort, you'd soon be your hearty, happy self again, and forget your trouble."

"That's impossible!"

"Try it and see. You needn't shrug your shoulders, and think 'Much she knows about such things.' I don't pretend to be wise, but I *am* observing, and I see a great deal more than you'd imagine. I'm interested in other people's experiences and inconsistencies; and, though I can't explain, I remember and use them for my own benefit. Love Jo all your days, if you choose,—but don't let it spoil you,—for it's wicked to throw away so many good gifts because you can't have the one you want.[30] There,—I won't lecture any more, for I know you'll wake up, and be a man in spite of that hard-hearted girl."

Neither spoke for several minutes. Laurie sat turning the little ring on his finger, and Amy put the last touches to the hasty sketch she had been working at while she talked. Presently she put it on his knee, merely saying,—

"How do you like that?"

He looked and then he smiled,—as he could not well help doing, for it was capitally done. The long, lazy figure on the grass, with listless face, half-shut eyes, and one hand holding a cigar, from which came the little wreath of smoke that encircled the dreamer's head.

"How well you draw!" he said, with a genuine surprise and pleasure at her skill, adding, with a half-laugh,—

"Yes, that's me."

"As you are,—this is as you were," and Amy laid another sketch beside the one he held.

It was not nearly so well done, but there was a life and spirit in it which atoned for many faults, and it recalled the past so vividly that a sudden change swept over the young man's face as he looked. Only a rough sketch of Laurie taming a horse; hat and coat were off, and every line of the active figure, resolute face, and commanding attitude, was full of energy and meaning. The handsome brute, just subdued, stood arching his neck under the tightly-drawn rein, with one foot impatiently pawing the ground, and ears pricked up as if listening for the voice that had mastered him. In the ruffled mane, the rider's breezy hair and erect attitude, there was a suggestion of suddenly arrested motion, of strength, courage, and youthful buoyancy that contrasted sharply with the supine grace of the *"Dolce far niente"* sketch. Laurie said nothing; but, as his eye went from one to the other, Amy saw him flush up and fold his lips together as if he read and accepted the little lesson she had given him. That satisfied her; and, without waiting for him to speak, she said, in her sprightly way,—

"Don't you remember the day you played 'Rarey'[31] with Puck, and we all looked on? Meg and Beth were frightened, but Jo clapped and pranced, and I sat on the fence and drew you. I found that sketch in my portfolio the other day, touched it up, and kept it to show you."

"Much obliged! You've improved immensely since then, and I congratulate you. May I venture to suggest in 'a honeymoon Paradise' that five o'clock is the dinner hour at your hotel?"

Laurie rose as he spoke, returned the pictures with a smile and a bow, and looked at his watch, as if to remind her that even moral lectures should have an end. He tried to resume his former easy, indifferent air, but it *was* an affectation now,—for the rousing had been more efficacious than he would confess. Amy felt the shade of coldness in his manner, and said to herself,—

"Now I've offended him. Well, if it does him good, I'm glad,—if

31. John Solomon Rarey (1827–1866), the horse whisperer from Ohio who developed a method for calming horses. By tying up one of the horse's legs, Rarey would get the animal to lie down, and he would then stroke it until it felt comfortable in his company. In 1858, he traveled to London to calm one of Queen Victoria's horses, and in 1861 he gave public demonstrations of his method in New York City.

32. Someone who incites a person to do things.

33. When Odysseus, king of Ithaca, sails off to fight the Trojans in Homer's *Odyssey*, it is the wise Mentor he entrusts as instructor and overseer of his son, Telemachus.

it makes him hate me, I'm sorry; but it's true, and I can't take back a word of it."

They laughed and chatted all the way home; and little Baptiste, up behind, thought that Monsieur and Mademoiselle were in charming spirits. But both felt ill at ease; the friendly frankness was disturbed, the sunshine had a shadow over it, and, despite their apparent gayety, there was a secret discontent in the heart of each.

"Shall we see you this evening, *mon frere?*" asked Amy, as they parted at her aunt's door.

"Unfortunately I have an engagement. *Au revoir, Mademoiselle,*" and Laurie bent as if to kiss her hand, in the foreign fashion, which became him better than many men. Something in his face made Amy say, quickly and warmly,—

"No; be yourself with me, Laurie, and part in the good old way. I'd rather have a hearty English handshake than all the sentimental salutations in France."

"Good-by, dear," and, with these words, uttered in the tone she liked, Laurie left her, after a hand-shake almost painful in its heartiness.

Next morning, instead of the usual call, Amy received a note which made her smile at the beginning, and sigh at the end:—

"MY DEAR MENTOR:

"Please make my adieux to your aunt, and exult within yourself, for 'Lazy Laurence' has gone to his grandpa, like the best of boys. A pleasant winter to you, and may the gods grant you a blissful honeymoon at Valrosa. I think Fred would be benefited by a rouser.[32] Tell him so, with my congratulations.

> "Yours gratefully,
> TELEMACHUS."[33]

"Good boy! I'm glad he's gone," said Amy, with an approving smile; the next minute her face fell as she glanced about the empty room, adding, with an involuntary sigh,—

"Yes, I *am* glad,—but how I shall miss him."

Chapter 17

The Valley of the Shadow

WHEN THE FIRST BITTERNESS was over, the family accepted the inevitable, and tried to bear it cheerfully, helping one another by the increased affection which comes to bind households tenderly together in times of trouble. They put away their grief, and each did their part toward making that last year a happy one.[1]

The pleasantest room in the house was set apart for Beth,[2] and in it was gathered everything that she most loved—flowers, pictures, her piano, the little work-table, and the beloved pussies. Father's best books found their way there, mother's easy chair, Jo's desk, Amy's loveliest[a] sketches; and every day Meg brought her babies on a loving pilgrimage, to make sunshine for Aunty Beth. John quietly set apart a little sum, that he might enjoy the pleasure of keeping the invalid supplied with the fruit she loved and longed for; old Hannah never wearied of concocting dainty dishes to tempt a capricious appetite, dropping tears as she worked; and, from across the sea, came little gifts and cheerful letters, seeming to bring breaths of warmth and fragrance from lands that know no winter.

Here, cherished like a household saint in its shrine, sat Beth, tranquil and busy as ever; for nothing could change the sweet, unselfish nature; and even while preparing to leave life, she tried to make it happier for those who should remain behind. The feeble fingers were never idle, and one of her pleasures was to make little things for the school children daily passing to and fro. To drop a pair of mittens from her window for a pair of purple hands, a needle-book[3] for some small mother of many dolls, pen-wipers

1. LMA recorded Elizabeth Alcott's decline in her January 1858 journal: "Lizzie much worse; Dr. G. says there is no hope. [After this line, LMA later inserted: "Jo and Beth"] A hard thing to bear; but if she is only to suffer, I pray she may go soon. She was glad to know she was to 'get well,' as she called it, and we tried to bear it bravely for her sake. We gave up plays; Father came home; and Anna took the housekeeping, so that Mother and I could devote ourselves to her. Sad quiet days in her room, and strange nights keeping up the fire and watching the dear little shadow try to wile away the long sleepless hours without troubling me" (*Journals* 88).

2. Although the Alcotts purchased Orchard House in September 1857, they did not move into the home until July 1858, because Bronson was completing extensive repairs. Instead, they lived in half of a house on Bedford Street in Concord center, behind the town hall. It was here that Elizabeth Alcott died. The house is no longer standing.

3. A cloth booklet with sewing needles stuck in it.

4. The *OED* defines *pot-hook* as a "curved or hooked stroke made with a pen . . . when learning to write." The term derives from the iron hook from which a kettle or pot hung in the fireplace.

5. In February 1858, LMA wrote: "A mild month, Betty very comfortable, and we hope a little. Dear Betty is slipping away, and every hour is too precious to waste . . . Lizzie makes little things, and drops them out of the windows to the school-children, smiling to see their surprise . . . Dear little saint! I shall be better all my life for these sad hours with you" (*Journals* 88). Lydia Hosmer Wood recollected in "Beth Alcott's Playmate: A Glimpse of Concord Town in the Days of *Little Women*" (1913) that the dying girl did indeed make gifts for friends: "After Beth had been laid away, they found among her treasures a number of little keepsakes which she had made for her family and friends as a last remembrance. She must have known that her end was near, because for months before she died she was always busy sewing, but she would never say what she was sewing for, and it wasn't until she was silenced forever that any one knew. Each little thing, so perfectly made, was carefully wrapped and labeled with the name of the person to whom it was to go. For my brother Henry she had made a penwiper of two leather disks with twelve little leaves of black taffeta between, all tied together with cerise ribbon; for Cyrus a pin-block covered with green checked silk on one side and a purplish brown on the other; for my sister Sarah, a blue needle-book lined with white silk; and for me one of purple silk with a yellow lining. These I count among my most prized possessions" (quoted in *Her Own Time* 168).

6. Anna Alcott wrote to her father on January 6, 1858: "[Lizzie] is very cheerful, & knows the truth, the whole, which she says she has known herself a long time and is glad it is to be so as she is ready & willing to go any time, & I think she is[.] She has for a month been nervous, cross, & pretty disliked us all, & been wholly unlike herself. Still we had 'nt realized she was worse til Sat. . . . Lizzy's memory & mind seem weakened & her body is a perfect skeleton. She sat & sewed today in bed as usual & does 'nt seem at all affected by the almost certainty of her not recovering. She doesn't care for any of us, & doesn't want mother near her, thinks I am horrid, & only wants to be let alone to do her sewing" (Manuscript letter, Houghton Library, Harvard University, bMS Am 1130.9).

7. In *The Pilgrim's Progress,* the Shining Ones are servants of the "Lord of the Hill," or literally angels of God. After crossing the River of Death, Christian is at Mt. Zion, where the Celestial City is located. LMA means that angels are ready to meet Beth once she has died and gone to Heaven.

for young penmen toiling through forests of pot-hooks,[4] scrap-books for picture-loving eyes, and all manner of pleasant devices, till the reluctant climbers up the ladder of learning found their way strewn with flowers, as it were, and came to regard the gentle giver as a sort of fairy god-mother, who sat above there, and showered down gifts miraculously suited to their tastes and needs. If Beth had wanted any reward, she found it in the bright little faces always turned up to her window, with nods and smiles, and the droll little letters which came to her, full of blots and gratitude.[5]

The first few months were very happy ones, and Beth often used to look round, and say "How beautiful this is," as they all sat together in her sunny room, the babies kicking and crowing on the floor, mother and sisters working near, and father reading in his pleasant voice, from the wise old books, which seemed rich in good and comfortable words, as applicable now as when written centuries ago—a little chapel, where a paternal priest taught his flock the hard lessons all must learn, trying to show them that hope can comfort love, and faith make resignation possible. Simple sermons, that went straight to the souls of those who listened; for the father's heart was in the minister's religion, and the frequent falter in the voice gave a double eloquence to the words he spoke or read.

It was well for all that this peaceful time was given them as preparation for the sad hours to come; for, by and by, Beth said the needle was "so heavy," and put it down forever; talking wearied her, faces troubled her, pain claimed her for its own, and her tranquil spirit was sorrowfully perturbed by the ills that vexed her feeble flesh.[6] Ah me! such heavy days, such long, long nights, such aching hearts and imploring prayers, when those who loved her best were forced to see the thin hands stretched out to them beseechingly, to hear the bitter cry, "Help me, help me!" and to feel that there was no help. A sad eclipse of the serene soul, a sharp struggle of the young life with death; but both were mercifully brief, and then, the natural rebellion over, the old peace returned more beautiful than ever. With the wreck of her frail body, Beth's soul grew strong; and, though she said little, those about her felt that she was ready, saw that the first pilgrim called was likewise the fittest, and waited with her on the shore, trying to see the Shining Ones coming to receive her when she crossed the river.[7]

Jo never left her for an hour since Beth had said, "I feel stronger when you are here." She slept on a couch in the room, waking often to renew the fire, to feed, lift, or wait upon the patient creature who seldom asked for anything, and "tried not to be a trouble." All day she haunted the room, jealous of any other nurse, and prouder of being chosen then than of any honor her life ever brought her. Precious and helpful hours to Jo, for now her heart received the teaching that it needed; lessons in patience were so sweetly taught her, that she could not fail to learn them; charity for all, the lovely spirit that can forgive and truly forget unkindness, the loyalty to duty that makes the hardest easy, and the sincere faith that fears nothing, but trusts undoubtingly.

Often when she woke, Jo found Beth reading in her well-worn little book,[8] heard her singing softly, to beguile the sleepless night, or saw her lean her face upon her hands, while slow tears dropped through the transparent fingers; and Jo would lie watching her, with thoughts too deep for tears, feeling that Beth, in her simple, unselfish way, was trying to wean herself from the dear old life, and fit herself for the life to come, by sacred words of comfort, quiet prayers, and the music she loved so well.

Seeing this did more for Jo than the wisest sermons, the saintliest hymns, the most fervent prayers that any voice could utter; for, with eyes made clear by many tears, and a heart softened by the tenderest sorrow, she recognized the beauty of her sister's life —uneventful, unambitious, yet full of the genuine virtues which "smell sweet, and blossom in the dust";[9] the self-forgetfulness that makes the humblest on earth remembered soonest in heaven, the true success which is possible to all.

One night, when Beth looked among the books upon her table, to find something to make her forget the mortal weariness that was almost as hard to bear as pain, as she turned the leaves of her old favorite Pilgrim's Progress, she found a little paper scribbled over, in Jo's hand. The name caught her eye, and the blurred look of the lines made her sure that tears had fallen on it.

"Poor Jo! she's fast asleep, so I won't wake her to ask leave; she

Jo and Beth. Jessie Willcox Smith, *Little Women* (1915).

8. Her New Testament.

9. The line comes from *The Contention of Ajax and Ulysses for the Armour of Achilles* (1659), a drama by the British playwright James Shirley (1596–1666). Alcott quotes the final line of the last stanza of a funeral dirge presented in scene three of the play: "All heads must come, / To the cold Tomb. / Only the Actions of the Just, / Smell sweet and blossom in the dust." The poem, Shirley's most well-known lines, was often excerpted and included in collections under various titles. It was also set to music by Henry Lawes (1595–1662) under the title "The Triumph of Death" and included in *The Treasury of Musick* (1669). LMA may also have remembered the lines from Thoreau's lecture "The Martydom of John Brown," delivered in Concord on October 30, 1859, just two weeks after Brown's raid at Harpers Ferry and later published as the essay "A Plea for Capt. John Brown" in *Echoes of Harpers Ferry* (1860), edited by James Redpath, who had published LMA's *Hospital Sketches* in 1863.

10. LMA wrote in January 1858: "[Lizzie] sews, reads, sings softly, and lies looking at the fire,—so sweet and patient and so worn, my heart is broken to see the change. I wrote some lines one night on 'Our Angel in the House'" (*Journals* 88). In *Louisa May Alcott: Her Life, Letters and Journals* (Boston: Roberts Brothers, 1889), Ednah Dow Cheney reprints "My Beth" from *Little Women,* retitling it "Our Angel in the House," (pp. 75–76). LMA's manuscript for "Our Angel in the House" has not been located.

shows me all her things, and I don't think she'll mind if I look at this," thought Beth, with a glance at her sister, who lay on the rug, with the tongs beside her, ready to wake up the minute the log fell apart.

"MY BETH.[10]

"Sitting patient in the shadow
　　Till the blessed light shall come,
A serene and saintly presence
　　Sanctifies our troubled home.
Earthly joys, and hopes, and sorrows.
　　Break like ripples on the strand
Of the deep and solemn river
　　Where her willing feet now stand.

"Oh, my sister, passing from me,
　　Out of human care and strife,
Leave me, as a gift, those virtues
　　Which have beautified your life.
Dear, bequeath me that great patience
　　Which has power to sustain
A cheerful, uncomplaining spirit
　　In its prison-house of pain.

"Give me, for I need it sorely,
　　Of that courage, wise and sweet,
Which has made the path of duty
　　Green beneath your willing feet.
Give me that unselfish nature,
　　That with charity divine
Can pardon wrong for love's dear sake—
　　Meek heart, forgive me mine!

"Thus our parting daily loseth
　　Something of its bitter pain,
And while learning this hard lesson,
　　My great loss becomes my gain.

For the touch of grief will render
    My wild nature more serene,
Give to life new aspirations—
    A new trust in the unseen.

"Henceforth, safe across the river,
    I shall see forever more
A beloved, household spirit
    Waiting for me on the shore.
Hope and faith, born of my sorrow,
    Guardian angels shall become,
And the sister gone before me,
    By their hands shall lead me home."

Blurred and blotted, faulty and feeble as the lines were, they brought a look of inexpressible comfort to Beth's face, for her one regret had been that she had done so little; and this seemed to assure her that her life had not been useless—that her death would not bring the despair she feared. As she sat with the paper folded between her hands, the charred log fell asunder. Jo started up, revived the blaze, and crept to the bedside, hoping Beth slept.

"Not asleep, but so happy, dear. See, I found this and read it; I knew you wouldn't care. Have I been all that to you, Jo?" she asked, with wistful, humble earnestness.

"Oh, Beth, so much, so much!" and Jo's head went down upon the pillow, beside her sister's.

"Then I don't feel as if I'd wasted my life. I'm not so good as you make me, but I *have* tried to do right; and now, when it's too late to begin even to do better, it's such a comfort to know that some one loves me so much, and feels as if I'd helped them."[b]

"More than any one in the world, Beth. I used to think I couldn't let you go; but I'm learning to feel that I don't lose you; that you'll be more to me than ever, and death can't part us, though it seems to."

"I know it cannot, and I don't fear it any longer, for I'm sure I shall be your Beth still, to love and help you more than ever. You must take my place, Jo, and be everything to father and mother when I'm gone. They will turn to you—don't fail them; and if it's

Elizabeth Stuart Phelps Ward (1844–1911), author of *The Gates Ajar* (1868).

hard to work alone, remember that I don't forget you, and that you'll be happier in doing that, than writing splendid books, or seeing all the world; for love is the only thing that we can carry with us when we go, and it makes the end so easy."

"I'll try, Beth;" and then and there Jo renounced her old ambition, pledged herself to a new and better one, acknowledging the poverty of other desires, and feeling the blessed solace of a belief in the immortality of love.

So the spring days came and went, the sky grew clearer, the earth greener, the flowers were up fair and early, and the birds came back in time to say good-by to Beth, who, like a tired but trustful child, clung to the hands that had led her all her life, as father and mother guided her tenderly through the valley of the shadow,[11] and gave her up to God.[12]

Seldom, except in books, do the dying utter memorable words, see visions, or depart with beatified countenances; and those who have sped many parting souls know, that to most the end comes as naturally and simply as sleep.[13] As Beth had hoped, the "tide went out easily"; and in the dark hour before the dawn, on the bosom where she had drawn her first breath, she quietly drew her last, with no farewell but one loving look and a little sigh.[14]

With tears, and prayers, and tender hands, mother and sisters made her ready for the long sleep that pain would never mar again—seeing with grateful eyes the beautiful serenity that soon replaced the pathetic patience that had wrung their hearts so long, and feeling with reverent joy, that to their darling death was a benignant angel—not a phantom full of dread.[15]

When morning came, for the first time in many months the fire was out, Jo's place was empty, and the room was very still. But a bird sang blithely on a budding bough, close by, the snow-drops blossomed freshly at the window, and the spring sunshine streamed in like a benediction over the placid face upon the pillow—a face so full of painless peace, that those who loved it best smiled through their tears, and thanked God that Beth was well at last.[16]

11. An allusion to the New Testament: "Yea, though I walk through the valley of the shadow of death, I will fear no evil: for thou art with me; thy rod and thy staff they comfort me (Psalm 23:4).

12. Beth's death would have resonated powerfully with *Little Women*'s first American readers—the nation was still grieving in the aftermath of the most costly war in U.S. history. Every community suffered terrible losses. How does a nation come to terms with

death, spirit, and afterlife? In *This Republic of Suffering: Death and the American Civil War* (New York: Alfred A. Knopf, 2008), Drew Gilpin Faust writes: "Where had all those young men gone? Friends and relatives who rushed to battlefields in an effort to locate their bodies undertook what was in some sense just the first step in the search for the missing. Even if their material remains could be retrieved and decently buried, the fate of the self and the soul, as well as the meaning of the departed life remained unknown. Survivors . . . asked with new war-born urgency what happened when life on earth ceased" (pp. 171–172). The question also became an obsession in popular fiction. Published the same year as *Little Women,* Elizabeth Stuart Phelps Ward's *The Gates Ajar* (1868) epitomizes post–Civil War consolation literature. The book was hugely popular in nineteenth-century America, second only to *Uncle Tom's Cabin* (1851–1852) in terms of sales. In the novel, the young Mary Cabot, whose brother has recently been killed during the war, comes to an understanding of life after death with the help of her aunt Winifred. Phelps's view of heaven is a kind of domestic afterlife, replete with Victorian furniture, in which family members are reunited. In *Little Women,* LMA does not envision a domestic afterlife, but she does offer the consolation that the March family will not really be parted from Beth. Interestingly, Phelps serialized a story entitled "Our Little Woman" in the November and December 1872 issues of *Our Young Folks.*

13. Undoubtedly LMA has in mind the death of the angelic Nell in Charles Dickens's *The Old Curiosity Shop* (1840–1841), perhaps the most famous—*and* infamous—deathbed scene in all of English literature. Many of the novel's first readers were overcome with grief at Little Nell's death, while later readers have seen it as ridiculously sentimental. LMA may also have had in mind the death of Little Eva in *Uncle Tom's Cabin* (1851–1852). Eva's last words recapitulate those of numerous innocents who die in nineteenth-century sentimental fiction: "O! love,—joy,—peace!" Beth's death was not LMA's first attempt at depicting such an emotional scene. In *Hospital Sketches* (1863), she describes the death of John Suhre, a Virginia blacksmith, who bravely dies holding LMA's hand.

14. Elizabeth Alcott died on March 14, 1858, two days before Anna's birthday, and LMA noted the event: "My dear Beth died at three this morning, after two years of patient pain. Last week she put her work away, saying the needle was 'too heavy,' and having given us her few possessions, made ready for the parting in her own simple, quiet way. For two days she suffered much, begging for ether, though its effect was gone. Tuesday she lay in Father's arms, and called us round her, smiling contentedly as she

said, 'All here!' I think she bid us good by then, as she held our hands and kissed us tenderly. Saturday she slept, and at midnight became unconscious, quietly breathing her life away till three; then, with one last look of the beautiful eyes, she was gone.

"A curious thing happened, and I will tell it here, for Dr. G. said it was a fact. A few moments after the last breath came, as Mother and I sat silently watching the shadow fall on the dear little face, I saw a light mist rise from the body, and float up and vanish in the air. Mother's eyes followed mine, and when I said, 'What did you see?' she described the same light mist. Dr. G. said it was the life departing visibly.

"For the last time we dressed her in her usual cap and gown, and laid her on the bed,—at rest at last. What she had suffered was seen in the face, for at twenty-three she looked like a woman of forty, so worn was she, and all her pretty hair gone . . . So the first break comes, and I know what death means,—a liberator for her, a teacher for us" (*Journals* 88–89).

15. In *Communities of Women: An Idea in Fiction* (Cambridge: Harvard University Press, 1978), Nina Auerbach makes an interesting argument: "Beth's long wasting is the waning of childhood and the collective death of the sisters; in a sense, she dies so that the others can marry. Beth is usually recalled as a tranquil domestic angel, but the intensity of her yearning for home recalls that of Emily Brontë's heretical Catherine Linton [in *Wuthering Heights* (1847)]" (p. 65). Whether or not we agree with this assessment, certainly Beth's memory will come to represent for the surviving sisters the spirit of their childhood home.

16. Bronson Alcott noted on March 14: "This morning is clear and calm, and so our daughter Elizabeth ascends with transfigured features to the heavenly airs she had sought so long. She died at 3, passing beyond our mortal grasp. She lived a short, innocent, and diligent life with us, and has an early translation" (*Journals of BA* 307). Elizabeth Alcott was buried in Concord's Sleepy Hollow Cemetery. Ralph Waldo Emerson, Henry D. Thoreau, Frank Sanborn, and John Bridge Pratt were the pallbearers. LMA wrote to her cousin Eliza Wells on March 19, 1858: "We asked no one to the funeral & sent no word to Boston for we wished to be alone, & fathers friends did all we needed more beautifully & acceptably than any we could have asked & everything was simple & quiet as she would have liked it" (*Selected Letters* 33). LMA, her parents, and Anna Alcott Pratt and her family would also be buried in Sleepy Hollow Cemetery. (May Alcott Neiriker is buried outside Paris, although a memorial stone erected by LMA may be seen by visitors to Sleepy Hollow.)

1. LMA alludes to Maria Weston Chapman's satirical poem "These Are the Times That Try Men's Souls," written in response to the famous pastoral letter published by conservative clergy that admonished female abolitionists who moved beyond traditional "spheres." In 1837, the South Carolina abolitionists Angelina and Sarah Grimke were touring New England, speaking out loudly against the evils of slavery. On June 28, 1837, outraged conservative Massachusetts clergymen issued "The Pastoral Letter of the General Association of Congregational Ministers of Massachusetts," chastising female abolitionists who spoke in public instead of confining themselves to the domestic sphere: "But when she a [woman] assumes the place and tone of a man as a public reformer, our care and protection of her seem unnecessary, we put ourselves in self defence against her, she yields the power which God has given her for protection, and her character becomes unnatural . . . We cannot, therefore, but regret the mistaken conduct of those who encourage females to bear an obtrusive and ostentatious part in measures of reform, and countenance any of that sex who so far forget themselves as to itinerate in the character of public lecturers and teachers." Maria Weston Chapman responded with "The Times That Try Men's Souls" (1837), attributing it to "The Lords of Creation." The poem reads in part: "Confusion has seized us, and all things go wrong, / The women have leaped from 'their spheres,' / And instead of fixed stars, shoot as comets along, /And are setting the world by the ears! / . . . So freely they move in their chosen ellipse, / The 'Lords of Creation' / do fear an eclipse . . . They've taken a notion to speak for themselves, / And are wielding the tongue and the pen; / They've mounted the rostrum; the termagant elves, / And—oh horrid—are talking to men." Maria Weston Chapman, three of her sisters (Caroline, Anne, and Deborah), William Lloyd Garrison, Edmund Quincy, Wendell Phillips, and Rev. Samuel J. May (LMA's uncle) belonged to the abolitionist group known as the Boston Clique. Chapman was also founder of the Boston Female Anti-Slavery Society in 1833 (Abigail Alcott was a member) and editor of *The Liberty Bell,* the most popular anti-slavery annual, which published contributions by Henry Wadsworth Longfellow, Lydia Maria Child, Thomas Wentworth Higginson, and Ralph Waldo Emerson, among others. Chapman was also friends with Mary Brooks, who, in October 1837, helped found the Concord Female Anti-Slavery Society, partially inspired by the Grimke sisters, who had spoken in Concord three nights in September 1837.

Chapter 18

Learning to Forget

AMY'S LECTURE did Laurie good, though, of course, he did not own it till long afterward; men seldom do,—for when women are the advisers, the lords of creation[1] don't take the advice till they have persuaded themselves that it is just what they intended to do; then they act upon it, and, if it succeeds, they give the weaker vessel half the credit of it; if it fails, they generously give her the whole. Laurie went back to his grandfather, and was so dutifully devoted for several weeks that the old gentleman declared the climate of Nice had improved him wonderfully, and he had better try it again. There was nothing the young gentleman would have liked better,—but elephants could not have dragged him back after the scolding he had received; pride forbid,—and whenever the longing grew very strong, he fortified his resolution by repeating the words that had made the deepest impression,—"I despise you;" "Go and do something splendid that will *make* her love you."

Laurie turned the matter over in his mind so often that he soon brought himself to confess that he *had* been selfish and lazy; but then when a man has a great sorrow, he should be indulged in all sorts of vagaries till he has lived it down. He felt that his blighted affections were quite dead now; and, though he should never cease to be a faithful mourner, there was no occasion to wear his weeds[2] ostentatiously. Jo *wouldn't* love him, but he might *make* her respect and admire him by doing something which should prove that a girl's "No" had not spoilt his life. He had always meant to do something, and Amy's advice was quite unnecessary. He had only been waiting till the aforesaid blighted affections were decently interred; that being done, he felt that he was ready to "hide his stricken heart, and still toil on."[3]

Sarah Grimke (1792–1873) and Angelina Grimke (1805–1879) were Charleston-born sisters who became active in the antislavery movement in the mid-1830s. Among the first females to enter the public arena as speakers for reform, the two also championed woman's rights. Their meetings in Massachusetts helped spark the organization of the Concord Female Anti-Slavery Society in 1837.

As Goethe, when he had a joy or a grief, put it into a song, so Laurie resolved to embalm his love-sorrow in music, and to compose a Requiem which should harrow up Jo's soul and melt the heart of every hearer. So the next time the old gentleman found him getting restless and moody, and ordered him off, he went to Vienna, where he had musical friends, and fell to work with the firm determination to distinguish himself. But, whether the sorrow was too vast to be embodied in music, or music too ethereal to uplift a mortal woe, he soon discovered that the Requiem was beyond him, just at present. It was evident that his mind was not in working order yet, and his ideas needed clarifying; for often, in

2. A black mourning suit.

3. An exact quotation that matches this one has not been located. However, the next paragraph starts with a reference to Goethe, which brings to mind two important works by the German author: *The Sorrows of Young Werther* (1774; rev. 1787) and *The Appenticeship of Wilhelm Meister* (1796), both popular works that focus on unrequited love.

the middle of a plaintive strain, he would find himself humming a dancing tune that vividly recalled the Christmas ball at Nice,—especially the stout Frenchman,—and put an effectual stop to tragic composition for the time being.

Then he tried an Opera,—for nothing seemed impossible in the beginning,—but here, again, unforeseen difficulties beset him. He wanted Jo for his heroine, and called upon his memory to supply him with tender recollections and romantic visions of his love. But memory turned traitor; and, as if possessed by the perverse spirit of the girl, would only recall Jo's oddities, faults, and freaks, would only show her in the most unsentimental aspects,—beating mats with her head tied up in a bandanna, barricading herself with the sofa-pillow, or throwing cold water over his passion *à la* Gummidge,—and an irresistible laugh spoilt the pensive picture he was endeavoring to paint. Jo wouldn't be put into the Opera at any price, and he had to give her up with a "Bless that girl, what a torment she is!" and a clutch at his hair, as became a distracted composer.

When he looked about him for another and a less intractable damsel to immortalize in melody, memory produced one with the most obliging readiness. This phantom wore many faces, but it always had golden hair, was enveloped in a diaphanous cloud, and floated airily before his mind's eye in a pleasing chaos of roses, peacocks, white ponies and blue ribbons. He did not give the complaisant wraith any name, but he took her for his heroine, and grew quite fond of her, as well he might,—for he gifted her with every gift and grace under the sun, and escorted her, unscathed, through trials which would have annihilated any mortal woman.

Thanks to this inspiration, he got on swimmingly for a time, but gradually the work lost its charm, and he forgot to compose, while he sat musing, pen in hand, or roamed about the gay city to get new ideas and refresh his mind, which seemed to be in a somewhat unsettled state that winter. He did not do much, but he thought a great deal, and was conscious of a change of some sort going on in spite of himself. "It's genius simmering, perhaps,—I'll let it simmer, and see what comes of it," he said, with a secret suspicion, all the while, that it wasn't genius, but something far more common. Whatever it was, it simmered to some purpose, for he grew more and more discontented with his desultory life, began to long for some real and earnest work to go at, soul and body, and finally came to the wise conclusion that every one who loved music was not a composer. Returning from one of Mozart's grand Operas, splendidly performed at the Royal Theatre,[4] he looked over his own, played a few of the best parts, sat staring up at the busts of Mendelssohn, Beethoven, and Bach, who stared benignly back again; then suddenly he tore up his music-sheets, one by one, and, as the last fluttered out of his hand, he said soberly, to himself,—

"She is right! talent isn't genius, and you can't make it so. That music has taken the vanity out of me as Rome took it out of her, and I won't be a humbug any longer. Now what shall I do?"

That seemed a hard question to answer, and Laurie began to wish he had to work for his daily bread.[5] Now, if ever, occurred an eligible opportunity for "going to the devil," as he once forcibly expressed it,—for he had plenty of money and nothing to do,—and Satan is proverbially fond of providing employment for full and idle hands. The poor fellow had temptations enough from without and from within, but he withstood them pretty well,—for much as he valued liberty he valued good faith and confidence more,—so his promise to his grandfather, and his desire to be able to look honestly into the eyes of the women who loved him, and say "All's well," kept him safe and steady.

Very likely some Mrs. Grundy[6] will observe, "I don't believe it; boys will be boys, young men must sow their wild oats, and women must not expect miracles." I dare say *you* don't, Mrs. Grundy, but it's true, nevertheless. Women work a good many miracles, and I have a persuasion that they may perform even that of raising the standard of manhood by refusing to echo such sayings. Let the boys be boys,—the longer the better,—and let the young men sow their wild oats if they must,—but mothers, sisters, and friends may help to make the crop a small one, and keep many tares[7] from spoiling the harvest, by believing,—and showing that they believe,—in the possibility of loyalty to the virtues which make men manliest in good women's eyes. If it *is* a feminine delusion, leave us to enjoy it while we may,—for without it

4. The second oldest theater in Europe, the Burgtheater opened for performances in 1748. In 1794, it was named the Imperial Royal Court Theater. The theater hosted its last performance in 1888—the year of LMA's death.

5. An allusion to the Lord's Prayer: "Give us this day our daily bread" (Matthew 6:10).

6. Mrs. Grundy, a bastion of respectability in Thomas Morton's play *Speed of the Plough* (1798). Dame Ashfield, her neighbor, often wonders how Mrs. Grundy (who never appears on stage) would react to certain events or situations.

7. Originally an undesirable weed in grain fields, a *tare* is defined as an unwanted element.

8. The attitude that young men cannot control their sexual urges and should therefore be allowed to "sow their wild oats" infuriated LMA. In "Early Marriages," published in the *Ladies Home Journal* for September 1887, LMA writes: "Who so well as [a mother] can guard the eager boy against his own passions and appetites, teaching him the hard lesson of self-control before the world, the flesh, and the devil begin to tempt him as a man? . . . Fathers should do their part as faithfully, first by trying to set an example of true manhood for their sons to follow . . . Boys, for such I love to call you . . . set up a high standard of manhood and never tire of trying to reach it. Don't begin your day with a cigar and end it in a theatre, billiard-saloon or club-room . . . Never believe the pernicious saying that 'young men *must* sow wild oats.' All men may sow good seed if they will, and reap honor, happiness and peace instead of the bitter crop so many mourn over when the harvest comes. Keep a clean mind, a brave spirit, and a tender heart, then you will have the right to ask some sweet woman to cast her lot with yours and make life rich and happy" (p. 3).

9. The saying is attributed to Mozart. In Mannheim, Germany, in 1777, the Austrian composer met Aloysia Weber (ca. 1760–1839), a soprano, who refused his marriage proposal. Mozart, however, remained friends with Aloysia and her family. The Webers, following their daughter's professional musical career, moved to Vienna in 1779, where Aloysia married Joseph Lange, an actor and painter, on October 31, 1780. When Mozart arrived in Vienna in 1781, he boarded with the Weber family and eventually married Aloysia's younger sister Constanze (1762–1842) on August 4, 1782.

half the beauty and the romance of life is lost, and sorrowful forebodings would embitter all our hopes of the brave, tender-hearted little lads, who still love their mothers better than themselves, and are not ashamed to own it.[8]

Laurie thought that the task of forgetting his love for Jo would absorb all his powers for years; but, to his great surprise, he discovered it grew easier every day. He refused to believe it at first,—got angry with himself, and couldn't understand it; but these hearts of ours are curious and contrary things, and time and nature work their will in spite of us. Laurie's heart *wouldn't* ache; the wound persisted in healing with a rapidity that astonished him, and, instead of trying to forget, he found himself trying to remember. He had not foreseen this turn of affairs, and was not prepared for it. He was disgusted with himself, surprised at his own fickleness, and full of a queer mixture of disappointment and relief that he could recover from such a tremendous blow so soon. He carefully stirred up the embers of his lost love, but they refused to burst into a blaze; there was only a comfortable glow that warmed and did him good without putting him into a fever, and he was reluctantly obliged to confess that the boyish passion was slowly subsiding into a more tranquil sentiment,—very tender, a little sad and resentful still,—but that was sure to pass away in time, leaving a brotherly affection which would last unbroken to the end.

As the word "brotherly" passed through his mind in one of these reveries, he smiled, and glanced up at the picture of Mozart that was before him,—

"Well, he was a great man; and when he couldn't have one sister he took the other, and was happy."[9]

Laurie did not utter the words, but he thought them; and the next instant kissed the little old ring, saying to himself,—

"No I won't! I haven't forgotten, I never can. I'll try again, and if that fails, why then—"

Leaving his sentence unfinished, he seized pen and paper and wrote to Jo, telling her that he could not settle to anything while there was the least hope of her changing her mind. Couldn't she, wouldn't she,—and let him come home and be happy? While waiting for an answer he did nothing,—but he did it energetically, for he was in a fever of impatience. It came at last, and settled his mind effectually on one point,—for Jo decidedly couldn't and wouldn't. She was wrapped up in Beth, and never wished to hear the word "love" again. Then she begged him to be happy with somebody else, but always to keep a little corner of his heart for his loving sister Jo. In a post-script she desired him not to tell Amy that Beth was worse; she was coming home in the spring, and there was no need of saddening the remainder of her stay. That would be time enough, please God, but Laurie must write to her often, and not let her feel lonely, homesick, or anxious.

"So I will, at once. Poor little girl; it will be a sad going home for her, I'm afraid;" and Laurie opened his desk, as if writing to Amy had been the proper conclusion of the sentence left unfinished some weeks before.

But he did not write the letter that day; for, as he rummaged out his best paper, he came across something which changed his purpose. Tumbling about in one part of the desk, among bills, passports, and business documents of various kinds, were several of Jo's letters, and in another compartment were three notes from Amy, carefully tied up with one of her blue ribbons, and sweetly suggestive of the little dead roses put away inside. With a half-repentant, half-amused expression, Laurie gathered up all Jo's letters, smoothed, folded, and put them neatly into a small drawer of the desk, stood a minute turning the ring thoughtfully on his finger, then slowly drew it off, laid it with the letters, locked the drawer, and went out to hear High Mass at Saint Stefan's,[10] feeling as if there had been a funeral; and, though not overwhelmed with affliction, this seemed a more proper way to spend the rest of the day, than in writing letters to charming young ladies.

The letter went very soon, however, and was promptly answered, for Amy *was* homesick, and confessed it in the most delightfully confiding manner. The correspondence flourished famously, and letters flew to and fro, with unfailing regularity, all through the early spring. Laurie sold his busts, made allumettes[11] of his opera, and went back to Paris, hoping somebody would arrive before long. He wanted desperately to go to Nice, but would not till he was asked; and Amy would not ask him, for just then

10. St. Stephan's Cathedral, a grand Romanesque and Gothic structure and the seat of the archbishop of Vienna.

11. A match used for lighting candles or lamps. The word derives from the French *allumer,* meaning "to light."

12. If this is Amy's moment of triumph in her moral growth, it is also a moment of triumph for LMA: certainly one of the great achievements of *Little Women* is the convincing mutual and mutually dependent growth of Amy and Laurie.

she was having little experiences of her own, which made her rather wish to avoid the quizzical eyes of "our boy."

Fred Vaughn had returned, and put the question to which she had once decided to answer, "Yes, thank you"; but now she said, "No, thank you," kindly but steadily; for when the time came, her courage failed her, and she found that something more than money and position was needed to satisfy the new longing that filled her heart so full of tender hopes and fears.[12] The words, "Fred is a good fellow, but not at all the man I fancied you would ever like," and Laurie's face, when he uttered them, kept returning to her as pertinaciously as her own did, when she said in look, if not in words, "I shall marry for money." It troubled her to remember that now, she wished she could take it back, it sounded so unwomanly. She didn't want Laurie to think her a heartless, worldly creature; she didn't care to be a queen of society now half so much as she did to be a lovable woman; she was so glad he didn't hate her for the dreadful things she said, but took them so beautifully, and was kinder than ever. His letters were such a comfort—for the home letters were very irregular and not half so satisfactory as his when they did come. It was not only a pleasure, but a duty to answer them, for the poor fellow was forlorn, and needed petting, since Jo persisted in being stony-hearted. She ought to have made an effort, and tried to love him—it couldn't be very hard—many people would be proud and glad to have such a dear boy care for them; but Jo never would act like other girls, so there was nothing to do but be very kind, and treat him like a brother.

If all brothers were treated as well as Laurie was at this period, they would be a much happier race of beings than they are. Amy never lectured now; she asked his opinion on all subjects; she was interested in everything he did, made charming little presents for him, and sent him two letters a week, full of lively gossip, sisterly confidences, and captivating sketches of the lovely scenes about her. As few brothers are complimented by having their letters carried about in their sisters' pockets, read and re-read diligently, cried over when short, kissed when long, and treasured carefully, we will not hint that Amy did any of these fond and foolish things. But she certainly did grow a little pale and pensive that spring, lost much of her relish for society, and went out sketching alone a good deal. She never had much to show when she came home, but was studying nature, I dare say, while she sat for hours with her hands folded, on the terrace at Valrosa, or absently sketched any fancy that occurred to her—a stalwart knight carved on a tomb, a young man asleep in the grass, with his hat over his eyes, or a curly-haired girl in gorgeous array, promenading down a ball-room, on the arm of a tall gentleman, both faces being left a blur, according to the last fashion in art, which was safe, but not altogether satisfactory.

Her aunt thought that she regretted her answer to Fred; and, finding denials useless, and explanations impossible, Amy left her to think what she liked, taking care that Laurie should know that Fred had gone to Egypt. That was all, but he understood it, and looked relieved, as he said to himself, with a venerable air,—

"I was sure she would think better of it. Poor old fellow, I've been through it all, and I can sympathize."

With that he heaved a great sigh, and then, as if he had discharged his duty to the past, put his feet up on the sofa, and enjoyed Amy's letter luxuriously.

While these changes were going on abroad, trouble had come at home; but the letter telling that Beth was failing, never reached Amy; and when the next found her, the grass was green above her sister. The sad news met her at Vevay, for the heat had driven them from Nice in May, and they had travelled slowly to Switzerland, by way of Genoa and the Italian lakes.[13] She bore it very well, and quietly submitted to the family decree, that she should not shorten her visit, for, since it was too late to say good-by to Beth, she had better stay, and let absence soften her sorrow. But her heart was very heavy—she longed to be at home; and every day looked wistfully across the lake, waiting for Laurie to come and comfort her.

He did come very soon; for the same mail brought letters to them both, but he was in Germany, and it took some days to reach him. The moment he read it, he packed his knapsack, bade adieu to his fellow-pedestrians, and was off to keep his promise, with a heart full of joy and sorrow, hope and suspense.

He knew Vevay well; and as soon as the boat touched the little quay, he hurried along the shore to La Tour,[14] where the Carrols

13. Genoa, an ancient port city in northwest Italy. With their mild Mediterranean climate and beautiful gardens, the Italian lakes were among the most fashionable resort areas during the nineteenth century. LMA and her sister May would visit them in 1870 (see *Little Women Abroad* 233–243).

14. La Tour-de-Peilz, Switzerland, a small town in the district of Vevey, is located on Lake Geneva between Montreux and Vevey.

were living *en pension*.[15] The garcon was in despair that the whole family had gone to take a promenade on the lake—but no, the blonde mademoiselle might be in the chateau garden. If *monsieur* would give himself the pain of sitting down, a flash of time should present her. But monsieur could not wait even "a flash of time," and in the middle of the speech, departed to find mademoiselle himself.

A pleasant old garden on the borders of the lovely lake, with chestnuts rustling overhead, ivy climbing everywhere, and the black shadow of the tower[16] falling far across the sunny water. At one corner of the wide, low wall, was a seat, and here Amy often came to read or work, or console herself with the beauty all about her. She was sitting here that day, leaning her head on her hand, with a homesick heart and heavy eyes, thinking of Beth, and wondering why Laurie did not come. She did not hear him cross the court-yard beyond, nor see him pause in the archway that led from the subterranean path into the garden. He stood a minute, looking at her with new eyes, seeing what no one had ever seen before—the tender side of Amy's character. Everything about her mutely suggested love and sorrow; the blotted letters in her lap, the black ribbon that tied up her hair, the womanly pain and patience in her face; even the little ebony cross at her throat seemed pathetic to Laurie, for he had given it to her, and she wore it as her only ornament. If he had any doubts about the reception she would give him, they were set at rest the minute she looked up and saw him; for, dropping everything, she ran to him, exclaiming in a tone of unmistakable love and longing,—

"Oh, Laurie, Laurie! I knew you'd come to me!"

I think everything was said and settled then; for, as they stood together quite silent for a moment, with the dark head bent down protectingly over the light one, Amy felt that no one could comfort and sustain her so well as Laurie, and Laurie decided that Amy was the only woman in the world who could fill Jo's place, and make him happy. He did not tell her so; but she was not disappointed, for both felt the truth, were satisfied, and gladly left the rest to silence.

In a minute Amy went back to her place; and while she dried

her tears, Laurie gathered up the scattered papers, finding in the sight of sundry well-worn letters and suggestive sketches, good omens for the future. As he sat down beside her, Amy felt shy again, and turned rosy red at the recollection of her impulsive greeting.

"I couldn't help it; I felt so lonely and sad, and was so very glad to see you. It was such a surprise to look up and find you, just as I was beginning to fear you wouldn't come," she said, trying in vain to speak quite naturally.

"I came the minute I heard. I wish I could say something to comfort you for the loss of dear little Beth, but I can only feel, and—" he could not get any farther, for he, too, turned bashful all of a sudden, and did not quite know what to say. He longed to lay Amy's head down on his shoulder and tell her to have a good cry, but he did not dare, so took her hand instead, and gave it a sympathetic squeeze that was better than words.

"You needn't say anything,—this comforts me," she said, softly. "Beth is well and happy, and I mustn't wish her back,—but I dread the going home, much as I long to see them all. We won't talk about it now, for it makes me cry, and I want to enjoy you while you stay. You needn't go right back, need you?"

"Not if you want me, dear."

"I do, so much! Aunt and Flo are very kind, but you seem like one of the family, and it would be so comfortable to have you for a little while."

Amy spoke and looked so like a homesick child whose heart was full, that Laurie forgot his bashfulness all at once, and gave her just what she wanted,—the petting she was used to, and the cheerful conversation she needed.

"Poor little soul! you look as if you'd grieved yourself half sick. I'm going to take care of you, so don't cry any more, but come and walk about with me,—the wind is too chilly for you to sit still," he said, in the half-caressing, half-commanding way that Amy liked, as he tied on her hat, drew her arm through his, and began to pace up and down the sunny walk, under the new-leaved chestnuts. He felt more at ease upon his legs, and Amy found it very pleasant to have a strong arm to lean upon, a famil-

17. Laurie is not so eager to give credit where credit is due; however, that Amy does not correct Laurie, when such an observation might only make him recalcitrant, is further evidence of her own growth.

18. "The blessings of thy father have prevailed above the blessings of my progenitors unto the utmost bound of the everlasting hills: they shall be on the head of Joseph, and on the crown of the head of him that was separate from his brethren" (Genesis 49:26).

19. LMA paraphrases the New Testament: "A new commandment I give unto you, That ye love one another; as I have loved you, that ye also love one another. By this shall all men know that ye are my disciples, if ye have love one to another" (John 13:34–35).

iar face to smile at her, and a kind voice to talk delightfully for her alone.

The quaint old garden had sheltered many pairs of lovers, and seemed expressly made for them, so sunny and secluded was it, with nothing but the tower to overlook them, and the wide lake to carry away the echo of their words, as it rippled by below. For an hour this new pair walked and talked, or rested on the wall, enjoying the sweet influences which gave such a charm to time and place; and when an unromantic dinner bell warned them away, Amy felt as if she left her burden of loneliness and sorrow behind her in the Chateau garden.

The moment Mrs. Carrol saw the girl's altered face she was illuminated with a new idea, and exclaimed to herself, "Now I understand it all,—the child has been pining for young Laurence. Bless my heart! I never thought of such a thing!"

With praiseworthy discretion, the good lady said nothing, and betrayed no sign of enlightenment, but cordially urged Laurie to stay, and begged Amy to enjoy his society, for it would do her more good than so much solitude. Amy was a model of docility; and, as her aunt was a good deal occupied with Flo, she was left to entertain her friend, and did it with more than her usual success.

At Nice, Laurie had lounged and Amy had scolded; at Vevay, Laurie was never idle, but always walking, riding, boating, or studying, in the most energetic manner; while Amy admired everything he did, and followed his example as far and as fast as she could. He said the change was owing to the climate, and she did not contradict him, being glad of a like excuse for her own recovered health and spirits.[17]

The invigorating air did them both good, and much exercise worked wholesome changes in minds as well as bodies. They seemed to get clearer views of life and duty up there among the everlasting hills;[18] the fresh winds blew away desponding doubts, delusive fancies and moody mists; the warm spring sunshine brought out all sorts of aspiring ideas, tender hopes and happy thoughts,—the lake seemed to wash away the troubles of the past, and the grand old mountains to look benignly down upon them, saying, "Little children, love one another."[19]

In spite of the new sorrow it was a very happy time,—so happy that Laurie could not bear to disturb it by a word. It took him a little while to recover from his surprise at the rapid cure of his first, and, as he had firmly believed, his last and only love. He consoled himself for the seeming disloyalty by the thought that Jo's sister was almost the same as Jo's self, and the conviction that it would have been impossible to love any other woman but Amy so soon and so well. His first wooing had been of the tempestuous order, and he looked back upon it as if through a long vista of years, with a feeling of compassion blended with regret. He was not ashamed of it, but put it away as one of the bitter-sweet experiences of his life, for which he could be grateful when the pain was over. His second wooing he resolved should be as calm and simple as possible; there was no need of having a scene,—hardly any need of telling Amy that he loved her; she knew it without words, and had given him his answer long ago. It all came about so naturally that no one could complain, and he knew that everybody would be pleased,—even Jo. But when our first little passion has been crushed, we are apt to be wary and slow in making a second trial; so Laurie let the days pass, enjoying every hour, and leaving to chance the utterance of the word that would put an end to the first and sweetest part of his new romance.

He had rather imagined that the *denouément* would take place in the chateau garden by moonlight, and in the most graceful and decorous manner; but it turned out exactly the reverse,—for the matter was settled on the lake, at noonday, in a few blunt words. They had been floating about all the morning, from gloomy St. Gingolf to sunny Montreux,[20] with the Alps of Savoy on one side, Mont St. Bernard and the Dent du Midi[21] on the other, pretty Vevay in the valley, and Lausanne[22] upon the hill beyond, a cloudless blue sky overhead, and the bluer lake below, dotted with the picturesque boats that look like white-winged gulls.

They had been talking of Bonnivard as they glided past Chillon,[23] and of Rousseau as they looked up at Clarens, where he wrote his Heloise.[24] Neither had read it, but they knew it was a love story, and each privately wondered if it was half as interesting as their own. Amy had been dabbling her hand in the water dur-

20. Located on the border of France and Switzerland, Saint-Gingolph, a small town on the south bank of Lake Geneva. Montreux, Switzerland, is located on the north shore of Lake Geneva.

21. Part of the western range of the Alps, the Savoy Alps are located in southeast France. The Pass of St. Bernard, the oldest Alpine pass, has been used since the Bronze Age. With seven major "dents" visible, Dents du Midi (Teeth of the Moon) are the mountains prominently seen from the south shore of Lake Geneva.

22. Lausanne, Switzerland, the capital of the canton of Vaud, sits on the shore of Lake Geneva on the southern slope of the Swiss plateau, approximately thirty-nine miles northeast of Geneva. LMA passed through the town in October 1865: "The view of the lake was lovely with rocky Mts opposite, little towns at their feet, vineyards along the hillsides & pretty boats on the lake the water of which was the loveliest blue" (*Journals* 144).

23. The Castle of Chillon, located on Lake Geneva near Montreux, seems to rise out of the water with a wooden bridge connecting the castle to the mainland. A champion of the Reformation, the Swiss patriot Francois Bonnivard (ca. 1493–1570) opposed Charles III, the Duke of Savoy, and was eventually imprisoned in the castle's dungeon from 1530 to 1536, inspiring Lord Bryon's famous poem "The Prisoner of Chillon" (1816). LMA visited Chillon while staying in Vevey in fall 1865.

24. Jean-Jacques Rousseau (1712–1778), Swiss author and philosopher, published the extremely popular epistolary novel *Julie, ou la nouvelle Héloïse (Julie, or the New Héloïse)* in 1761, a story of forbidden love and redemption. The narrator is incorrect. While Rousseau's novel was set in Clarens, Switzerland, it was actually written in Paris.

25. The *OED* defines *trim* as "distribut[ing] the load of (a ship or boat) so that she floats on an even keel."

26. LMA's metaphor illustrates at once the suitability of Amy and Laurie for each other and shows how a modern marriage based on equality, dignity, and love should function. Amy and Laurie will work together to make their way through life.

ing the little pause that fell between them, and, when she looked up, Laurie was leaning on his oars, with an expression in his eyes that made her say, hastily,—merely for the sake of saying something,—

"You must be tired,—rest a little, and let me row; it will do me good, for since you came I have been altogether lazy and luxurious."

"I'm not tired, but you may take an oar if you like. There's room enough, though I have to sit nearly in the middle, else the boat won't trim,"[25] returned Laurie, as if he rather liked the arrangement.

Feeling that she had not mended matters much, Amy took the offered third of a seat, shook her hair over her face, and accepted an oar. She rowed as well as she did many other things; and, though she used both hands, and Laurie but one, the oars kept time, and the boat went smoothly through the water.[26]

"How well we pull together, don't we?" said Amy, who objected to silence just then.

"So well, that I wish we might always pull in the same boat. Will you, Amy?" very tenderly.

"Yes, Laurie!" very low.

Then they both stopped rowing, and unconsciously added a pretty little *tableau* of human love and happiness to the dissolving views reflected in the lake.

Chapter 19

All Alone

T WAS EASY TO promise self-abnegation when self was wrapt up in another, and heart and soul were purified by a sweet example; but when the helpful voice was silent, the daily lesson over, the beloved presence gone, and nothing remained but loneliness and grief, then Jo found her promise very hard to keep. How could she "comfort father and mother," when her own heart ached with a ceaseless longing for her sister; how could she "make the house cheerful," when all its light, and warmth, and beauty, seemed to have deserted it when Beth left the old home for the new; and where, in all the world, could she "find some useful, happy work to do," that would take the place of the loving service which had been its own reward? She tried in a blind, hopeless way to do her duty, secretly rebelling against it all the while, for it seemed unjust that her few joys should be lessened, her burdens made heavier, and life get harder and harder as she toiled along. Some people seemed to get all sunshine, and some all shadow; it was not fair, for she tried more than Amy to be good, but never got any reward,—only disappointment, trouble, and hard work.

Poor Jo! these were dark days to her, for something like despair came over her when she thought of spending all her life in that quiet house, devoted to humdrum cares, a few poor little[a] pleasures, and the duty that never seemed to grow any easier. "I can't do it. I wasn't meant for a life like this, and I know I shall break away and do something desperate if somebody don't come and help me," she said to herself, when her first efforts failed, and she fell into the moody, miserable state of mind which often comes when strong wills have to yield to the inevitable.

1. Bronson Alcott seems never to have resented the fame of his more successful daughter. If called upon in his conversations or talks —and he was often called upon—he spoke of LMA. On December 1, 1870, he confessed in his journal after speaking in Cleveland, Ohio: "As to Louisa, I find I have a pretty dramatic story to tell of her childhood and youth, gaining in interest as she comes up into womanhood and literary note. Yesterday in the schools I was called upon to tell her story, most of the scholars being familiar with her book and curious to learn what I might tell them about her history. I am introduced as the father of Little Women, and am riding in the Chariot of Glory wherever I go" (*Journals of BA* 404). In Sonnet 16 of his *Sonnets and Canzonets* (1882), Bronson characterized LMA as "Duty's faithful child." After Bronson suffered a stroke in October 1882, from which he never fully recovered (he was never able to write again), LMA assumed care of him. On his eighty-sixth birthday, LMA wrote "To My Father," in which she cast him as the pilgrim in his favorite book, *The Pilgrim's Progress,* ending the four-stanza poem: "The staff set by, the sandals off, / Still pondering the precious scroll, / Serene and strong, he waits the call / That frees and wings a happy soul" (*Selected Letters* 295). The father and daughter, who shared a joint birthday of November 29, would die within two days of each other in 1888.

2. On September 25, 1856, Bronson Alcott confessed: "I being taken as a heretic and seceder from the primitive faith. But, taught two catechisms—the Westminster and Episcopal—in my youth, I chanced to like neither as I could wish, and have belonged to the Church of One Member, a creed of one subscriber, till now; and now free to secede from that if once better informed and feeling the duty incumbent upon conscience and faith" (*Journals of BA* 285–286). Also Bronson, lecturing on New England authors in the early 1870s, once said: "Emerson's church consists of one member—himself." See Hubert Hoeltje, "Some Iowa Lectures and Conversations of Amos Bronson Alcott," *Iowa Journal of History and Politics* 29 (July 1931), pp. 375–401.

But some one did come and help her, though Jo did not recognize her good angels at once, because they wore familiar shapes, and used the simple spells best fitted to poor humanity. Often she started up at night, thinking Beth called her; and when the sight of the little empty bed made her cry with the bitter cry of an unsubmissive sorrow, "Oh, Beth! come back! come back!" she did not stretch out her yearning arms in vain; for, as quick to hear her sobbing as she had been to hear her sister's faintest whisper, her mother came to comfort her. Not with words only, but the patient tenderness that soothes by a touch, tears that were mute reminders of a greater grief than Jo's, and broken whispers, more eloquent than prayers, because hopeful resignation went hand-in-hand with natural sorrow. Sacred moments! when heart talked to heart in the silence of the night, turning affliction to a blessing, which chastened grief and strengthened love. Feeling this, Jo's burden seemed easier to bear, duty grew sweeter, and life looked more endurable, seen from the safe shelter of her mother's arms.

When aching heart was a little comforted, troubled mind likewise found help; for one day she went to the study, and, leaning over the good gray head lifted to welcome her with a tranquil smile, she said, very humbly,—

"Father, talk to me as you did to Beth. I need it more than she did, for I'm all wrong."

"My dear, nothing can comfort me like this," he answered, with a falter in his voice, and both arms round her, as if he, too, needed help, and did not fear to ask it.

Then, sitting in Beth's little chair close beside him, Jo told her troubles, the resentful sorrow for her loss, the fruitless efforts that discouraged her, the want of faith that made life look so dark, and all the sad bewilderment which we call despair. She gave him entire confidence,—he gave her the help she needed, and both found consolation in the act; for the time had come when they could talk together not only as father and daughter, but as man and woman, able and glad to serve each other with mutual sympathy as well as mutual love.[1] Happy, thoughtful times there in the old study which Jo called "the church of one member,"[2] and from which she came with fresh courage, recovered cheerfulness, and a more submissive spirit,—for the parents who had taught one child to meet death without fear, were trying now to teach another to accept life without despondency or distrust, and to use its beautiful opportunities with gratitude and power.

Other helps had Jo, humble, wholesome duties and delights, that would not be denied their part in serving her, and which she slowly learned to see and value. Brooms and dishcloths never could be as distasteful as they once had been, for Beth had presided over both; and something of her housewifely spirit seemed to linger round the little mop and the old brush, that was never thrown away. As she used them, Jo found herself humming the songs Beth used to hum, imitating Beth's orderly ways, and giving the little touches here and there that kept everything fresh and cozy, which was the first step toward making home happy, though she didn't know it, till Hannah said with an approving squeeze of the hand,—

"You thoughtful creter, you're determined we shan't miss that dear lamb ef you can help it. We don't say much, but we see it, and the Lord will bless you for't, see ef He don't."

As they sat sewing together, Jo discovered how much improved her sister Meg was; how well she could talk, how much she knew about good, womanly impulses, thoughts and feelings, how happy she was in husband and children, and how much they were all doing for each other.

"Marriage is an excellent thing after all. I wonder if I should blossom out, half as well as you have, if I tried it, always *'perwisin'* I could,"[3] said Jo,[b] as she constructed a kite for Demi, in the topsy-turvy nursery.

"It's just what you need to bring out the tender, womanly half of your nature, Jo. You are like a chestnut burr,[4] prickly outside, but silky-soft within, and a sweet kernel, if one can only get at it. Love will make you show your heart some day, and then the rough burr will fall off."

"Frost opens chestnut burrs, ma'am, and it takes a good shake to bring them down. Boys go nutting, and I don't care to be bagged by them," returned Jo, pasting away at the kite, which no

3. LMA quotes one of her favorite Dickens characters, Sairey Gamp from *Martin Chuzzlewit* (1843–1844). In Chapter 25, Gamp, in a conversation with the undertaker Mr. Mould, says: "'Mrs. Harris,' I says to her, 'none on us knows what we can do till we tries; and wunst, when me and Gamp kept ouse, I thought so too. But now,' I says, 'my half a pint of porter fully satisfies; perwisin', Mrs. Harris, that it is brought reg'lar, and draw'd mild.'"

4. Jo has chestnut-colored hair.

5. The weight on the kite's tail, usually a ribbon tied in a knot or bow.

6. The *OED* defines *mortified* as "dead to sin or worldly desires; having the appetites and passions in subjection; prompted by a spirit of religious self-mortification." LMA means that the bonnet is plain, displaying no "worldly desires."

7. Pamphlets espousing a religious, political, or reform viewpoint.

wind that blows would ever carry up, for Daisy had tied herself on as a bob.[5]

Meg laughed, for she was glad to see a glimmer of Jo's old spirit, but she felt it her duty to enforce her opinion by every argument in her power; and the sisterly chats were not wasted, especially as two of Meg's most effective arguments were the babies, whom Jo loved tenderly. Grief is the best opener for some hearts, and Jo's was nearly ready for the bag; a little more sunshine to ripen the nut, then, not a boy's impatient shake, but a man's hand reached up to pick it gently from the burr, and find the kernal sound and sweet. If she suspected this, she would have shut up tight, and been more prickly than ever; fortunately she wasn't thinking about herself, so, when the time came, down she dropped.

Now, if she had been the heroine of a moral story-book, she ought at this period of her life to have become quite saintly, renounced the world, and gone about doing good in a mortified[6] bonnet, with tracts[7] in her pocket. But you see Jo wasn't a heroine; she was only a struggling human girl, like hundreds of others, and she just acted out her nature, being sad, cross, listless or energetic, as the mood suggested. It's highly virtuous to say we'll be good, but we can't do it all at once, and it takes a long pull, a strong pull, and a pull all together, before some of us even get our feet set in the right way. Jo had got so far, she was learning to do her duty, and to feel unhappy if she did not; but to do it cheerfully—ah, that was another thing! She had often said she wanted to do something splendid, no matter how hard; and now she had her wish,—for what could be more beautiful than to devote her life to father and mother, trying to make home as happy to them as they had to her? And, if difficulties were necessary to increase the splendor of the effort, what could be harder for a restless, ambitious girl, than to give up her own hopes, plans and desires, and cheerfully live for others?

Providence had taken her at her word; here was the task,—not what she had expected, but better, because self had no part in it; now could she do it? She decided that she would try; and, in her first attempt, she found the helps I have suggested. Still another was given her, and she took it,—not as a reward, but as a comfort,

Jo's literary efforts. Frank Merrill, original artwork for *Little Women: Illustrated* (1880).

as Christian took the refreshment afforded by the little arbor where he rested, as he climbed the hill called Difficulty.[8]

"Why don't you write? that always used to make you happy," said her mother, once, when the desponding fit overshadowed Jo.

"I've no heart to write, and if I had, nobody cares for my things."

"We do; write something for us, and never mind the rest of the world. Try it, dear; I'm sure it would do you good, and please us very much."

"Don't believe I can;" but Jo got out her desk, and began to overhaul her half-finished manuscripts.

An hour afterward her mother peeped in, and there she was scratching away, with her black pinafore on, and an absorbed expression, which caused Mrs. March to smile, and slip away, well pleased with the success of her suggestion. Jo never knew how it happened, but something got into that story that went straight to

8. In Book One of *The Pilgrim's Progress,* Christian climbs the Hill of Difficulty on his journey to the Palace Beautiful. Midway up the hill, he stops in an arbor made by the Lord of the Hill for tired travelers. In Book Two, Christiana, along with her sons and Mercy, takes the same strenuous path up the hill, but like Christian, her party must rest at the Lord of the Hill's arbor before completing their journey.

9. While many readers believe LMA is writing about the reception of Part I of *Little Women*, she may be referring to her autobiographical book *Hospital Sketches*, an account of her nursing experience during the Civil War, which was serialized in four installments of the *Boston Commonwealth* between May 22 and June 26, 1863, and published in book form in August 1863 by James Redpath of Boston. Moncure Daniel Conway, reformer and co-editor of the *Boston Commonwealth* with Franklin Sanborn, wrote: "The series . . . showed every variety of ability, and excited much attention" (*Autobiography, Memories, and Experiences,* 2 vols. [Boston: Houghton, Mifflin, 1904], 1:369). LMA recorded the event in April 1863: "I made three 'Hospital Sketches.' Much to my surprise they made a great hit, & people bought the papers faster than they could be supplied" (*Journals* 118). In her "Notes and Memoranda" for 1863, she confessed: "Hospital Sketches come out & I find I've done a good thing without knowing it" (*Journals* 122). In November 1863, LMA wrote to a friend: "'Hospital Sketches' still continues a great joke to me, & a sort of perpetual surprise-party, for to this day I cannot see why people like a few extracts from topsey turvey letters written on inverted tin kettles, in my pantry, while waiting for gruel to warm or poultices to cool, for boys to wake and be tormented, on stairs, in window seats & other sequestered spots favorable to literary inspiration. People are very kind & very easily pleased as I'm much obliged, but I dont understand it at all & probably never shall" (*Selected Letters* 95). In 1879, upon re-reading her 1863 journal, LMA inserted the following: "the Sketches never made much money, but showed me '*my style*', & taking the hint I went where glory waited me" (*Journals* 124n24). She also wrote later, after the success of *Little Women*, to a young woman writer asking for advice: "[W]hen I wrote Hospital Sketches by the beds of my soldier boys in the shape of letters home I had no idea that I was taking the first step toward what is called fame . . . but I discovered the secret of winning the ear & touching the heart of the public by simply telling the comic & pathetic incidents of life" (*Selected Letters* 232).

10. In "*Little Women:* Alcott's Civil War" (*Feminist Studies* 5:2 [Summer 1979], pp. 369–383), Judith Fetterly notes: "Good writing for women is not the product of ambition or even enthusiasm, nor does it seek worldly recognition. Rather it is the product of a mind seeking solace for private pain, that scarcely knows what it is doing and that seeks only to please others and, more specifically, those few others who constitute the immediate family. Jo has gone from burning genius to a state where what she writes isn't even hers" (p. 374).

the hearts of those who read it; for, when her family had laughed and cried over it, her father sent it, much against her will, to one of the popular magazines, and, to her utter surprise, it was not only paid for, but others requested. Letters from several persons, whose praise was honor, followed the appearance of the little story, newspapers copied it, and strangers as well as friends admired it. For a small thing, it was a great success; and Jo was more astonished than when her novel was commended and condemned all at once.

"I don't understand it; what *can* there be in a simple little story like that, to make people praise it so?" she said, quite bewildered.

"There is truth in it, Jo—that's the secret; humor and pathos make it alive, and you have found your style at last. You wrote with no thought of fame or money, and put your heart into it, my daughter; you have had the bitter, now comes the sweet; do your best, and grow as happy as we are in your success."[9]

"If there *is* anything good or true in what I write, it isn't mine; I owe it all to you and mother, and to Beth," said Jo, more touched by her father's words than by any amount of praise from the world.

So, taught by love and sorrow, Jo wrote her little stories, and sent them away to make friends for themselves and her, finding it a very charitable world to such humble wanderers, for they were kindly welcomed, and sent home comfortable tokens to their mother, like dutiful children, whom good fortune overtakes.[10]

When Amy and Laurie wrote of their engagement, Mrs. March feared that Jo would find it difficult to rejoice over it, but her fears were soon set at rest; for, though Jo looked grave at first, she took it very quietly, and was full of hopes and plans for "the children," before she read the letter twice. It was a sort of written duet, wherein each glorified the other in lover-like fashion, very pleasant to read, and satisfactory to think of, for no one had any objection to make.

"You like it, mother?" said Jo, as they laid down the closely-written sheets, and looked at one another.

"Yes, I hoped it would be so, ever since Amy wrote that she had refused Fred. I felt sure then that something better than what you call 'the mercenary spirit' had come over her, and a hint here and there in her letters made me suspect that love and Laurie would win the day."

"How sharp you are, Marmee, and how silent; you never said a word to me."

"Mothers have need of sharp eyes and discreet tongues, when they have girls to manage. I was half afraid to put the idea into your head, lest you should write, and congratulate them before the thing was settled."

"I'm not the scatter-brain I was; you may trust me, I'm sober and sensible enough for any one's *confidante* now."

"So you are, dear, and I should have made you mine, only I fancied it might pain you to learn that your Teddy loved any one else."

"Now, mother, did you really think I could be so silly and selfish, after I'd refused his love, when it was freshest, if not best?"

"I knew you were sincere then, Jo, but lately I have thought that if he came back, and asked again, you might, perhaps, feel like giving another answer. Forgive me, dear, I can't help seeing that you are very lonely, and sometimes there is a hungry look in your eyes that goes to my heart; so I fancied that your boy might fill the empty place, if he tried now."

"No, mother, it is better as it is, and I'm glad Amy has learned to love him. But you are right in one thing; I *am* lonely, and perhaps if Teddy had tried again, I might have said 'Yes,' not because I love him any more, but because I care more to be loved, than when he went away."[11]

"I'm glad of that, Jo, for it shows that you are getting on. There are plenty to love you, so try to be satisfied with father and mother, sisters and brothers, friends and babies, till the best lover of all comes to give you your reward."

"Mothers are the *best* lovers in the world; but, I don't mind whispering to Marmee, that I'd like to try all kinds. It's very curious, but the more I try to satisfy myself with all sorts of natural affections, the more I seem to want. I'd no idea hearts could take in so many—mine is so elastic, it never seems full now, and I used to be quite contented with my family; I don't understand it."

"I do," and Mrs. March, smiled her wise smile, as Jo turned back the leaves to read what Amy said of Laurie.

11. This is a startling and frank admission, and the reader feels the truth of it; LMA is too good an artist to refuse to allow her characters to doubt and second-guess themselves—or to suggest that only a single outcome is possible when life presents numerous opportunities. Jo might easily have married Teddy, if the romance between Amy and Laurie hadn't blossomed, although it's true that Amy and Laurie are better suited for each other. As LMA anticipated as she was writing Part II of *Little Women* in 1868, many young readers would protest that they wanted Jo to marry Laurie. Once the sequel was published, she received many letters like the one she used for an 1871 advertisement for the novel. "We have all been reading 'Little Women,' and we liked it so much I could not help wanting to write you . . . We were all so disappointed about your not marrying Laurie; I cried over that part,—for I could not help it" (See illustration p. viii.)

12. Weight placed in a ship's hold so it will not capsize when at sea.

13. A schoolbook with a set form of exercises, such as grammar or mathematics. Jo is looking at her old German exercise books.

"It is so beautiful to be loved as Laurie loves me; he isn't sentimental; doesn't say much about it, but I see and feel it in all he says and does, and it makes me so happy and so humble, that I don't seem to be the same girl I was. I never knew how good, and generous, and tender he was till now, for he lets me read his heart, and I find it full of noble impulses, and hopes, and purposes, and am so proud to know it's mine. He says he feels as if he 'could make a prosperous voyage now with me aboard as mate, and lots of love for ballast.'[12] I pray he may, and try to be all he believes me, for I love my gallant captain with all my heart, and soul, and might, and never will desert him, while God lets us be together. Oh, mother, I never knew how much like heaven this world could be, when two people love and live for one another!"

"And that's our cool, reserved, and worldly Amy! Truly love does work miracles. How very, very happy they must be!" and Jo laid the rustling sheets together with a careful hand, as one might shut the covers of a lovely romance, which holds the reader fast till the end comes, and he finds himself alone in the work-a-day world again.

By and by Jo roamed away upstairs, for it was rainy, and she could not walk. A restless spirit possessed her, and the old feeling came again, not bitter as it once was, but a sorrowfully patient wonder why one sister should have all she asked, the other nothing. It was not true; she knew that, and tried to put it away, but the natural craving for affection was strong, and Amy's happiness woke the hungry longing for some one to "love with heart and soul, and cling to, while God let them be together."

Up in the garret, where Jo's unquiet wanderings ended, stood four little wooden chests in a row, each marked with its owner's name, and each filled with relics of the childhood and girlhood ended now for all. Jo glanced into them, and when she came to her own, leaned her chin on the edge, and stared absently at the chaotic collection, till a bundle of old exercise-books[13] caught her eye. She drew them out, turned them over, and re-lived that pleasant winter at kind Mrs. Kirke's. She had smiled at first, then she looked thoughtful, next sad, and when she came to a little message written in the Professor's hand, her lips began to tremble, the books slid out of her lap, and she sat looking at the friendly words, as they took a new meaning, and touched a tender spot in her heart.

"Wait for me, my friend, I may be a little late, but I shall surely come."

"Oh, if he only would! So kind, so good, so patient with me always; my dear old Fritz, I didn't value him half enough when I had him, but now how I should love to see him, for every one seems going away from me, and I'm all alone."

And holding the little paper fast, as if it were a promise yet to be fulfilled, Jo laid her head down on a comfortable rag-bag, and cried, as if in opposition to the rain pattering on the roof.

Was it all self-pity, loneliness, or low spirits? or was it the waking up of a sentiment which had bided its time as patiently as its inspirer? Who shall say.[14]

14. LMA leaves the question unanswered. Her readers will answer it differently.

1. Almost six months before she began *Little Women,* LMA confessed: "[Anna] is a happy woman! I sell *my* children; and though they feed me, they don't love me as hers do" (*Journals* 163).

2. In a letter of February 7, 1755, an indignant Samuel Johnson famously admonished Philip Dormer, Earl of Chesterfield, whom he believed claimed too much credit for the production of his *Dictionary of the English Language:* "Is not a Patron, My Lord, one who looks with unconcern on a Man struggling for Life in the Water and when he has reached ground encumbers him with help. The notice which you have been pleased to take of my Labours, had it been early, had been kind; but it has been delayed till I am indifferent and cannot enjoy it, till I am solitary and cannot impart it, till I am known and do not want it" (*The Letters of Samuel Johnson,* 5 vols., ed. Bruce Redford [Princeton: Princeton University Press, 1992–1994], vol. 1:56).

3. Did LMA, a literary spinster at thirty-six when she penned these words, think "the prospect was not inviting"? It is interesting to note LMA's reflection on the occasion of her thirtieth birthday. She confessed: "Thirty years old. Decided to go to Washington as a nurse . . . I want new experiences" (*Journals* 110).

4. In the April 11, 1868, edition of the *New York Ledger,* LMA published "Happy Women," an article of advice to female readers: "One of the trials of woman-kind is the fear of being an old maid. To escape this dreadful doom, young girls rush into matrimony with a recklessness which astonishes the beholder; never pausing to remember that the loss of liberty, happiness, and self-respect is poorly repaid by the barren honor of being called 'Mrs.' instead of 'Miss.' Fortunately, the foolish prejudice is fast disappearing, conquered by the success of a certain class belonging to the sisterhood" (reprinted in Elaine Showalter, ed., *Alternative Alcott* [New Brunswick, NJ: Rutgers University Press, 1988], pp. 203–206).

Chapter 20

Surprises

JO WAS ALONE in the twilight, lying on the old sofa, looking at the fire, and thinking. It was her favorite way of spending the hour of dusk; no one disturbed her, and she used to lie there on Beth's little red pillow, planning stories, dreaming dreams, or thinking tender thoughts of the sister who never seemed far away. Her face looked tired, grave, and rather sad, for to-morrow was her birthday, and she was thinking how fast the years went by, how old she was getting, and how little she seemed to have accomplished. Almost twenty-five, and nothing to show for it,—Jo was mistaken in that; there was a good deal to show, and by and by she saw, and was grateful for it.

"An old maid—that's what I'm to be. A literary spinster, with a pen for a spouse, a family of stories for children,[1] and twenty years hence a morsel of fame, perhaps; when, like poor Johnson, I'm old and can't enjoy it—solitary, and can't share it, independent, and don't need it.[2] Well, I needn't be a sour saint nor a selfish sinner; and, I dare say, old maids are very comfortable when they get used to it; but—" and there Jo sighed, as if the prospect was not inviting.

It seldom is, at first, and thirty seems the end of all things to five-and-twenty; but it's not as bad as it looks, and one can get on quite happily if one has something in one's self to fall back upon. At twenty-five, girls begin to talk about being old maids, but secretly resolve that they never will; at thirty, they say nothing about it, but quietly accept the fact[3]; and, if sensible, console themselves by remembering that they have twenty more useful, happy years, in which they may be learning to grow old gracefully.[4] Don't laugh at the spinsters, dear girls, for often very tender, tragical romances are hidden away in the hearts that beat so quietly under the sober gowns, and many silent sacrifices of youth, health, ambition, love itself, make the faded faces beautiful in God's sight. Even the sad, sour sisters should be kindly dealt with, because they have missed the sweetest part of life if for no other reason; and, looking at them with compassion, not contempt, girls in their bloom should remember that they too may miss the blossom time—that rosy cheeks don't last forever, that silver threads will come in the bonnie brown hair, and, that by and by, kindness and respect will be as sweet as love and admiration now.

Gentlemen, which means boys,[5] be courteous to the old maids, no matter how poor and plain and prim, for the only chivalry worth having is that which is the readiest to pay deference to the old, protect the feeble, and serve womankind, regardless of rank, age, or color. Just recollect the good aunts who have not only lectured and fussed, but nursed and petted, too often without thanks —the scrapes they have helped you out of, the "tips" they have given you from their small store, the stitches the patient old fingers have set for you, the steps the willing old feet have taken, and gratefully pay the dear old ladies the little attentions that women love to receive as long as they live. The bright-eyed girls are quick to see such traits, and will like you all the better for them; and, if death, almost the only power that can part mother and son, should rob you of yours, you will be sure to find a tender, welcome, and maternal cherishing from some Aunt Priscilla, who has kept the warmest corner of her lonely old heart for "the best nevvy in the world."

Jo must have fallen asleep (as I dare say my reader has during this little homily), for, suddenly, Laurie's ghost seemed to stand before her. A substantial, life-like ghost leaning over her, with the very look he used to wear when he felt a good deal, and didn't like to show it. But, like Jenny in the ballad,—

"She could not think it he,"[6]

and lay staring up at him, in startled silence, till he stooped and kissed her. Then she knew him, and flew up, crying joyfully,—

5. Here the narrator directly addresses "the lords of creation."

6. LMA refers to the popular ballad "Auld Robin Gray" (1783) by the Scottish writer Lady Anne Lindsay Barnard (1750–1825). The ballad tells of the romance between the young lovers Jennie and Jamie. While Jamie goes to sea to earn money to support a wife, Jennie's father breaks his arm, her mother falls ill, and the cow is stolen. Hearing that Jamie's ship has been wrecked at sea, Jennie no sooner consents to marry Old Robin Gray than she is surprised by an approaching figure: "I hadna been a wife a week but only four, / When mournfu' as I sat on the stane at the door, / I saw my Jamie's wraith, for I couldna think it he— / Till he said, I'm come hame to marry thee" (lines 25–28). Faithful Jennie, however, keeps her vow to Old Robin Gray.

7. While most readers will know the meaning of the phrase (to reveal a secret or surprise), few may know its etymological origins. *Brewer's Dictionary of Phrase & Fable* (15th ed.) notes that the phrase comes from "*a pig in a poke*": "The reference is to a former common trick of trying to palm off a cat as a suckling pig . . . Opening the poke or sack [*let the cat out of the bag*], and the trick was disclosed" (New York: Harper Collins, 1995), p. 829.

"Oh my Teddy! Oh my Teddy!"

"Dear Jo, you are glad to see me, then?"

"Glad! my blessed boy, words can't express my gladness. Where's Amy?"

"Your mother has got her, down at Meg's. We stopped there by the way, and there was no getting my wife out of their clutches."

"Your what?" cried Jo—for Laurie uttered those two words with an unconscious pride and satisfaction, which betrayed him.

"Oh, the dickens! now I've done it"; and he looked so guilty that Jo was down upon him like a flash.

"You've gone and got married?"

"Yes, please, but I never will again;" and he went down upon his knees with a penitent clasping of hands, and a face full of mischief, mirth, and triumph.

"Actually married?"

"Very much so, thank you."

"Mercy on us; what dreadful thing will you do next?" and Jo fell into her seat, with a gasp.

"A characteristic, but not exactly complimentary congratulation," returned Laurie, still in an abject attitude, but beaming with satisfaction.

"What can you expect, when you take one's breath away, creeping in like a burglar, and letting cats out of bags[7] like that? Get up, you ridiculous boy, and tell me all about it."

"Not a word, unless you let me come in my old place, and promise not to barricade."

Jo laughed at that as she had not done for many a long day, and patted the sofa invitingly, as she said, in a cordial tone,—

"The old pillow is up garret, and we don't need it now: so, come and 'fess, Teddy."

"How good it sounds to hear you say 'Teddy'; no one ever calls me that but you;" and Laurie sat down with an air of great content.

"What does Amy call you?"

"My lord."

"That's like her—well, you look it"; and Jo's eye plainly betrayed that she found her boy comelier than ever.

The pillow was gone, but there *was* a barricade, nevertheless; a natural one raised by time, absence, and change of heart. Both felt it, and for a minute looked at one another as if that invisible barrier cast a little shadow over them. It was gone directly, however, for Laurie said, with a vain attempt at dignity,—

"Don't I look like a married man and the head of a family?"

"Not a bit, and you never will. You've grown bigger and bonnier, but you are the same scapegrace[8] as ever."

"Now, really, Jo, you ought to treat me with more respect," began Laurie, who enjoyed it all immensely.

"How can I, when the mere idea of you, married and settled, is so irresistibly funny that I can't keep sober," answered Jo, smiling all over her face, so infectiously, that they had another laugh, and then settled down for a good talk, quite in the pleasant old fashion.

"It's no use your going out in the cold to get Amy, for they are all coming up, presently; I couldn't wait; I wanted to be the one to tell you the grand surprise, and have 'first skim,' as we used to say, when we squabbled about the cream."[9]

"Of course you did, and spoilt your story by beginning at the wrong end. Now, start right, and tell me how it all happened; I'm pining to know."

"Well, I did it to please Amy," began Laurie, with a twinkle, that made Jo exclaim,—

"Fib number one; Amy did it to please you. Go on, and tell the truth, if you can, sir."

"Now she's beginning to marm it, isn't it jolly to hear her?" said Laurie to the fire, and the fire glowed and sparkled as if it quite agreed. "It's all the same, you know, she and I being one. We planned to come home with the Carrols, a month or more ago, but they suddenly changed their minds, and decided to pass another winter in Paris. But grandpa wanted to come home; he went to please me, and I couldn't let him go alone, neither could I leave Amy; and Mrs. Carrol had got English notions about chaperons, and such nonsense, and wouldn't let Amy come with us. So I just settled the difficulty, by saying, 'Let's be married, and then we can do as we like.'"

8. The *OED* defines *scapegrace* as a "man or boy of reckless and disorderly habits; an incorrigible scamp. Often used playfully." It is derived from "One who escapes the grace of God."

9. After a cow was milked, a cream settled at the top. The thicker the cream, the better the milk tasted. Even milk in bottles could be judged by the layer of cream. Laurie means that he wanted to be the one to tell Jo about his marriage to Amy.

"Of course you did; you always have things to suit you."

"Not always;" and something in Laurie's voice made Jo say, hastily,—

"How did you ever get aunt to agree?"

"It was hard work; but, between us, we talked her over, for we had heaps of good reasons on our side. There wasn't time to write and ask leave, but you all liked it, had consented to it by and by— and it was only 'taking time by the fetlock,' as my wife says."

"Aren't we proud of those two words, and don't we like to say them?" interrupted Jo, addressing the fire in her turn, and watching with delight the happy light it seemed to kindle in the eyes that had been so tragically gloomy when she saw them last.

"A trifle, perhaps; she's such a captivating little woman I can't help being proud of her. Well, then, uncle and aunt were there to play propriety; we were so absorbed in one another we were of no mortal use apart, and that charming arrangement would make everything easy all round; so we did it."

"When, where, how?" asked Jo, in a fever of feminine interest and curiosity, for she could not realize it a particle.

"Six weeks ago, at the American consul's, in Paris—a very quiet wedding, of course; for even in our happiness we didn't forget dear little Beth."

Jo put her hand in his as he said that, and Laurie gently smoothed the little red pillow, which he remembered well.

"Why didn't you let us know afterward?" asked Jo, in a quieter tone, when they had sat quite still a minute.

"We wanted to surprise you; we thought we were coming directly home, at first, but the dear old gentleman, as soon as we were married, found he couldn't be ready under a month, at least, and sent us off to spend our honey-moon wherever we liked. Amy had once called Valrosa a regular honey-moon home, so we went there, and were as happy as people are but once in their lives. My faith, wasn't it love among the roses!"

Laurie seemed to forget Jo, for a minute, and Jo was glad of it; for the fact that he told her these things so freely and naturally, assured her that he had quite forgiven and forgotten. She tried to draw away her hand; but, as if he guessed the thought that prompted the half-involuntary impulse, Laurie held it fast, and said, with a manly gravity she had never seen in him before,—

"Jo, dear, I want to say one thing, and then we'll put it by forever. As I told you, in my letter, when I wrote that Amy had been so kind to me, I never shall stop loving you; but the love is altered, and I have learned to see that it is better as it is. Amy and you change places in my heart, that's all. I think it was meant to be so, and would have come about naturally, if I had waited, as you tried to make me; but I never could be patient, and so I got a heartache. I was a boy then—headstrong and violent; and it took a hard lesson to show me my mistake. For it *was* one, Jo, as you said, and I found it out, after making a fool of myself. Upon my word, I was so tumbled up in my mind, at one time, that I didn't know which I loved best—you or Amy, and tried to love both alike; but I couldn't; and when I saw her in Switzerland, everything seemed to clear up all at once. You both got into your right places, and I felt sure that it was well off with the old love, before it was on with the new; that I could honestly share my heart between sister Jo and wife Amy, and love them dearly. Will you believe it, and go back to the happy old times, when we first knew one another?"

"I'll believe it, with all my heart; but, Teddy, we never can be boy and girl again—the happy old times can't come back, and we mustn't expect it. We are man and woman now, with sober work to do, for play-time is over, and we must give up frolicking.[10] I'm sure you feel this; I see the change in you, and you'll find it in me; I shall miss my boy, but I shall love the man as much, and admire him more, because he means to be what I hoped he would. We can't be little playmates any longer, but we will be brother and sister, to love and help one another all our lives, won't we, Laurie?"

He did not say a word, but took the hand she offered him, and laid his face down on it for a minute, feeling that out of the grave of a boyish passion, there had risen a beautiful, strong friendship to bless them both. Presently Jo said cheerfully, for she didn't want the coming home to be a sad one,—

"I can't make it true that you children are really married, and

10. In *Twain, Alcott, and the Birth of the Adolescent Reform Novel* (Iowa City: University of Iowa Press, 2007), Roberta Seelinger Trites notes that Jo "serves as a metaphor for her culture's need to change. Alcott depicts negatively those characters who are haughty, dogmatic, lazy, or—worst of all—intolerant, while she values strength and courage and honesty and independence and the opportunity that the need for hard work provides the individual." In this exchange between Jo and Laurie, LMA indicates "that the most significant difference between childhood and adulthood is concern for others" (50).

11. In chapter 21 of Dickens's *David Copperfield* (1849–1850), Daniel Peggoty, a fisherman and brother to Clara Peggoty, David's former nurse, greets David and his friend James Steerforth when they arrive at his home: "'Why, that you two gent'lmen—gent'lmen growed—should come to here roof tonight, of all nights.'"

12. Wrinkles in her face.

going to set up housekeeping. Why, it seems only yesterday that I was buttoning Amy's pinafore, and pulling your hair when you teased. Mercy me, how time does fly!"

"As one of the children is older than yourself, you needn't talk so like a grandma. I flatter myself I'm a 'gentleman growed,' as Peggotty said of David,[11] and when you see Amy, you'll find her rather a precocious infant," said Laurie, looking amused at her maternal air.

"You may be a little older in years, but I'm ever so much older in feeling, Teddy. Women always are; and this last year has been such a hard one, that I feel forty."

"Poor Jo! we left you to bear it alone, while we went pleasuring. You *are* older; here's a line, and there's another;[12] unless you smile, your eyes look sad, and when I touched the cushion, just now, I found a tear on it. You've had a great deal to bear, and had to bear it all alone; what a selfish beast I've been!" and Laurie pulled his own hair, with a remorseful look.

But Jo only turned over the traitorous pillow, and answered in a tone which she tried to make quite cheerful,—

"No, I had father and mother to help me, the dear babies to comfort me, and the thought that you and Amy were safe and happy, to make the troubles here easier to bear. I *am* lonely, sometimes, but I dare say it's good for me, and—"

"You never shall be again," broke in Laurie, putting his arm about her, as if to fence out every human ill. "Amy and I can't get on without you, so you must come and teach the children to keep house, and go halves in everything, just as we used to do, and let us pet you, and all be blissfully happy and friendly together."

"If I shouldn't be in the way, it would be very pleasant. I begin to feel quite young already; for, somehow, all my troubles seemed to fly away when you came. You always were a comfort, Teddy;" and Jo leaned her head on his shoulder, just as she did years ago, when Beth lay ill, and Laurie told her to hold on to him.

He looked down at her, wondering if she remembered the time, but Jo was smiling to herself, as if, in truth, her troubles *had* all vanished at his coming.

"You are the same Jo still, dropping tears about one minute, and laughing the next. You look a little wicked now; what is it, grandma?"

"I was wondering how you and Amy get on together."

"Like angels!"

"Yes, of course, at first—but which rules?"

"I don't mind telling you that she does, now; at least I let her think so,—it pleases her, you know. By and by we shall take turns, for marriage, they say, halves one's rights and doubles one's duties."[13]

"You'll go on as you begin, and Amy will rule you all the days of your life."

"Well, she does it so imperceptibly that I don't think I shall mind much. She is the sort of woman who knows how to rule well; in fact, I rather like it, for she winds one round her finger as softly and prettily as a skein of silk, and makes you feel as if she was doing you a favor all the while."

"That ever I should live to see you a henpecked husband and enjoying it!" cried Jo, with uplifted hands.

It was good to see Laurie square his shoulders, and smile with masculine scorn at that insinuation, as he replied, with his "high and mighty" air,—

"Amy is too well-bred for that, and I am not the sort of man to submit to it. My wife and I respect ourselves and one another too much ever to tyrannize or quarrel."

Jo liked that, and thought the new dignity very becoming, but the boy seemed changing very fast into the man, and regret mingled with her pleasure.

"I am sure of that; Amy and you never did quarrel as we used to. She is the sun, and I the wind, in the fable, and the sun managed the man best, you remember."[14]

"She can blow him up as well as shine on him," laughed Laurie. "Such a lecture as I got at Nice! I give you my word it was a deal worse than any of your scoldings. A regular rouser; I'll tell you all about it some time,—*she* never will, because, after telling me that she despised and was ashamed of me, she lost her heart to the despicable party, and married the good-for-nothing."

"What baseness! Well, if she abuses you come to me, and I'll defend you!"

13. In his 1851 essay "Über die Weiber" ("Of Women"), the German philosopher Arthur Schopenhauer (1788–1860), who held a low opinion of both women and matrimony, famously wrote that marriage "means to halve one's rights and double one's duties." He would not have shared Laurie's progressive views.

14. Jo refers to Aesop's fable, often called "The North Wind and the Sun," where the two argue who is the most powerful. Spotting a traveler on the road, they agree to see who can make the man remove his cloak. The wind tries first and blows as hard as he can, but the traveler only wraps the cloak tighter. When the wind relents, the sun shines as hot as it can, forcing the man finally to remove his cloak. Jo means that Amy's persuasion managed Laurie better than Jo's forceful nature.

"I look as if I needed it, don't I?" said Laurie, getting up and striking an attitude which suddenly changed from the imposing to the rapturous, as Amy's voice was heard calling,—

"Where is she? where's my dear old Jo?"

In trooped the whole family, and every one was hugged and kissed all over again, and, after several vain attempts, the three wanderers were set down to be looked at and exulted over. Mr. Laurence, hale and hearty as ever, was quite as much improved as the others by his foreign tour,—for the crustiness seemed to be nearly gone, and the old-fashioned courtliness had received a polish which made it kindlier than ever. It was good to see him beam at "my children," as he called the young pair; it was better still to see Amy pay him the daughterly duty and affection which completely won his old heart; and, best of all, to watch Laurie revolve about the two as if never tired of enjoying the pretty picture they made.

The minute she put her eyes upon Amy, Meg became conscious that her own dress hadn't a Parisian air,—that young Mrs. Moffat would be entirely eclipsed by young Mrs. Laurence, and that "her ladyship" was altogether a most elegant and graceful woman. Jo thought, as she watched the pair, "How well they look together! I was right, and Laurie has found the beautiful, accomplished girl who will become his home better than clumsy old Jo, and be a pride, not a torment to him." Mrs. March and her husband smiled and nodded at each other with happy faces,—for they saw that their youngest had done well, not only in worldly things, but the better wealth of love, confidence, and happiness.

For Amy's face was full of the soft brightness which betokens a peaceful heart, her voice had a new tenderness in it, and the cool, prim carriage was changed to a gentle dignity, both womanly and winning. No little affectations marred it, and the cordial sweetness of her manner was more charming than the new beauty or the old grace, for it stamped her at once with the unmistakable sign of the true gentlewoman she had hoped to become.

"Love has done much for our little girl," said her mother, softly.

"She has had a good example before her all her life, my dear," Mr. March whispered back, with a loving look at the worn face and gray head beside him.

Daisy found it impossible to keep her eyes off her "pitty aunty," but attached herself like a lap-dog to the wonderful châtelaine[15] full of delightful charms. Demi paused to consider the new relationship before he compromised himself by the rash acceptance of a bribe, which took the tempting form of a family of wooden bears, from Berne.[16] A flank movement[17] produced an unconditional surrender, however, for Laurie knew where to have him:—

"Young man, when I first had the honor of making your acquaintance you hit me in the face; now I demand the satisfaction of a gentleman!" and with that the tall uncle proceeded to toss and tousle the small nephew in a way that damaged his philosophical dignity as much as it delighted his boyish soul.

"Blest if she ain't in silk from head to foot; ain't it a relishin' sight to see her settin' there as fine as a fiddle, and hear folks calling little Amy 'Mis. Laurence!'" muttered old Hannah, who could not resist frequent "peeks" through the slide[18] as she set the table in a most decidedly promiscuous[19] manner.

Mercy on us, how they did talk! first one, then the other, then all burst out together,—trying to tell the history of three years in half an hour. It was fortunate that tea was at hand, to produce a lull and provide refreshment,—for they would have been hoarse and faint if they had gone on much longer. Such a happy procession as filed away into the little dining-room! Mr. March proudly escorted "Mrs. Laurence"; Mrs. March as proudly leaned on the arm of "my son"; the old gentleman took Jo with a whispered "You must be my girl now," and a glance at the empty corner by the fire, that made Jo whisper back, with trembling lips, "I'll try to fill her place, sir."

The twins pranced behind, feeling that the millennium[20] was at hand,—for every one was so busy with the new comers that they were left to revel at their own sweet will, and you may be sure they made the most of the opportunity. Didn't they steal sips of tea, stuff gingerbread *ad libitum,*[21] get a hot biscuit apiece, and, as a crowning trespass, didn't they each whisk a captivating little tart into their tiny pockets, there to stick and crumble treacherously,— teaching them that both human nature and pastry are frail! Burdened with the guilty consciousness of the sequestered tarts, and

15. A decorative belt hook worn at the waist with ornamental chains holding useful household objects such as scissors, keys; often a watch chain with charms.

16. Bears are the heraldic emblems of Bern, Switzerland. Its old clock tower features a procession of wooden bears across the dial when it tolls.

17. The *OED* defines this military expression as "the extreme left or right side of an army or body of men in military formation; a wing."

18. A sliding panel that allows someone from the kitchen to look into the dining room or another portion of the house.

19. Careless or disorderly.

20. A time of peace and happiness. The Bible refers to the millennium as the one thousand years Jesus will reign over earth (Rev. 20:1–5).

21. According to the *OED*, the Latin phrase means, "at one's pleasure or discretion; at will, as one pleases."

22. A childish version of Jo or JoJo.

23. Originally the wool from the Spanish merino sheep, the term came to mean any fine wool.

24. The expression *to drive six white horses* indicates wealth and status as one would have to be wealthy to afford a carriage pulled by six horses.

25. A fine-quality lace, often made with a needle.

26. In *Songs of Affection* (1830), the British poet Felicia Hemans (1793–1835) published "Bernardo Del Carpio," an extremely popular poem, even in America. The tenth stanza begins: "Then covering with his steel-gloved hands his darkly / mournful brow, / 'No more, there is no more,' he said, 'to lift the / sword for now.'"

27. Hash was made from meat (usually roast beef or corned beef), potatoes, and spices mixed together. Fish balls were made of minced fish that was rolled into a ball and fried.

fearing that Dodo's[22] sharp eyes would pierce the thin disguise of cambric and merino[23] which hid their booty, the little sinners attached themselves to "Dranpa," who hadn't his spectacles on. Amy, who was handed about like refreshments, returned to the parlor on Father Laurence's arm; the others paired off as before, and this arrangement left Jo companionless. She did not mind it at the minute, for she lingered to answer Hannah's eager inquiry,—

"Will Miss Amy ride in her coop *(coupé),* and use all them lovely silver dishes that's stored away over yander?"

"Shouldn't wonder if she drove six white horses,[24] ate off gold plate, and wore diamonds and point-lace[25] every day. Teddy thinks nothing too good for her," returned Jo, with infinite satisfaction.

"No more there is![26] Will you have hash or fish-balls[27] for breakfast?" asked Hannah, who wisely mingled poetry and prose.

"I don't care," and Jo shut the door, feeling that food was an uncongenial topic just then. She stood a minute looking at the party vanishing above, and, as Demi's short plaid legs toiled up the last stair, a sudden sense of loneliness came over her, so strongly that she looked about her with dim eyes, as if to find something to lean upon,—for even Teddy had deserted her. If she had known what birthday gift was coming every minute nearer and nearer, she would not have said to herself "I'll weep a little weep when I go to bed; it won't do to be dismal now." Then she drew her hand over her eyes,—for one of her boyish habits was never to know where her handkerchief was,—and had just managed to call up a smile, when there came a knock at the porch door.

She opened with hospitable haste, and started as if another ghost had come to surprise her,—for there stood a stout,[a] bearded gentleman, beaming on her from the darkness like a midnight sun.

"Oh, Mr. Bhaer, I *am* so glad to see you!" cried Jo, with a clutch, as if she feared the night would swallow him up before she could get him in.

"And I to see Miss Marsch,—but no, you haf a party—" and the Professor paused as the sound of voices and the tap of dancing feet came down to them.

"No, we haven't,—only the family. My brother[b] and sister have just come home, and we are all very happy. Come in, and make one of us."[28]

Though a very social man, I think Mr. Bhaer would have gone decorously away, and come again another day; but how could he when Jo shut the door behind him, and bereft him of his hat? Perhaps her face had something to do with it, for she forgot to hide her joy at seeing him, and showed it with a frankness that proved irresistible to the solitary man, whose welcome far exceeded his boldest hopes.

"If I shall not be Monsieur De Trop[29] I will so gladly see them all. You haf been ill, my friend?"

He put the question abruptly, for, as Jo hung up his coat, the light fell on her face, and he saw a change in it.

"Not ill, but tired and sorrowful; we have had trouble since I saw you last."

"Ah, yes, I know! my heart was sore for you when I heard that;" and he shook hands again with such a sympathetic face, that Jo felt as if no comfort could equal the look of the kind eyes, the grasp of the big, warm hand.

"Father, mother, this is my friend, Professor Bhaer," she said, with a face and tone of such irrepressible pride and pleasure, that she might as well have blown a trumpet and opened the door with a flourish.

If the stranger had had any doubts about his reception, they were set at rest in a minute by the cordial welcome he received. Every one greeted him kindly, for Jo's sake, at first, but very soon they liked him for his own. They could not help it, for he carried the talisman that opens all hearts, and these simple people warmed to him at once, feeling even the more friendly because he was poor,—for poverty enriches those who live above it, and is a sure passport to truly hospitable spirits. Mr. Bhaer sat looking about him with the air of a traveller who knocks at a strange door, and, when it opens, finds himself at home. The children went to him like bees to a honey-pot; and, establishing themselves on each knee, proceeded to captivate him by rifling his pockets, pulling his beard, and investigating his watch, with juvenile audacity. The women telegraphed their approval to one another, and Mr. March,

Professor Bhaer surprises Jo. Clara M. Burd, *Little Women* (1926).

28. The *OED* defines *make one of* as meaning "to assimilate oneself to the company one joins."

29. *De trop* is French for "too much." Bhaer means Mr. Not Wanted or Mr. In the Way.

31. Like Jupiter, the king of the Gods in Roman mythology; when Bhaer's hair stands on end his apparently forceful forehead looks thoughtful and dignified.

feeling that he had got a kindred spirit, opened his choicest stores for his guest's benefit, while silent John listened and enjoyed the talk, but said not a word, and Mr. Laurence found it impossible to go to sleep.

If Jo had not been otherwise engaged, Laurie's behavior would have amused her; for a faint twinge, not of jealousy, but something like suspicion, caused that gentleman to stand aloof at first, and observe the new comer with brotherly circumspection. But it did not last long; he got interested in spite of himself, and, before he knew it, was drawn into the circle, for Mr. Bhaer talked well in this genial atmosphere, and did himself justice. He seldom spoke to Laurie, but he looked at him often, and a shadow would pass across his face, as if regretting his own lost youth, as he watched the young man in his prime. Then his eye would turn to Jo so wistfully, that she would have surely answered the mute inquiry if she had seen it; but Jo had her own eyes to take care of, and, feeling that they could not be trusted, she prudently kept them on the little sock she was knitting, like a model maiden aunt.

A stealthy glance now and then refreshed her like sips of fresh water after a dusty walk, for the sidelong peeps showed her several propitious omens. Mr. Bhaer's face had lost the absent-minded expression, and looked all alive with interest in the present moment—actually young and handsome, she thought, forgetting to compare him with Laurie, as she usually did strange men, to their great detriment. Then he seemed quite inspired; though the burial customs of the ancients, to which the conversation had strayed, might not be considered an exhilarating topic. Jo quite glowed with triumph when Teddy got quenched[30] in an argument, and thought to herself, as she watched her father's absorbed face, "How he would enjoy having such a man as my Professor to talk with every day!" Lastly, Mr. Bhaer was dressed in a spandy-new[c] suit of black, which made him look more like a gentleman than ever. His bushy hair had been cut, and smoothly brushed, but didn't stay in order long, for, in exciting moments, he rumpled it up in the droll way he used to do, and Jo liked it rampantly erect, better than flat, because she thought it gave his fine forehead a Jove-like[31] aspect. Poor Jo! how she did glorify that plain man, as she sat knitting away so quietly, yet letting nothing escape her—not even the fact that Mr. Bhaer actually had gold sleeve-buttons in his immaculate wristbands.[32]

"Dear old fellow; he couldn't have got himself up with more care, if he'd been going a-wooing,"[33] said Jo to herself; and then a sudden thought, born of the words, made her blush so dreadfully, that she had to drop her ball, and go down after it, to hide her face.

The manœuvre did not succeed as well as she expected, however; for, though just in the act of setting fire to a funeral pile, the Professor dropped his torch, metaphorically speaking, and made a dive after the little blue ball. Of course they bumped their heads smartly together, saw stars, and both came up flushed and laughing, without the ball, to resume their seats, wishing they had not left them.

Nobody knew where the evening went to, for Hannah skilfully abstracted[34] the babies at an early hour, nodding like two rosy poppies, and Mr. Laurence went home to rest. The others sat round the fire, talking away, utterly regardless of the lapse of time, till Meg, whose maternal mind was impressed with a firm conviction that Daisy had tumbled out of bed, and Demi set his night-gown afire, studying the structure of matches, made a move to go.

"We must have our sing in the good old way, for we are all together again, once more," said Jo, feeling that a good shout would be a safe and pleasant vent for the jubilant emotions of her soul.

They were not *all* there, but no one found the words thoughtless or untrue; for Beth still seemed among them—a peaceful presence—invisible, but dearer than ever; since death could not break the household league that love made indissoluble. The little chair stood in its old place; the tidy basket, with the bit of work she left unfinished when the needle grew so heavy, was still on its accustomed shelf; the beloved instrument, seldom touched now, had not been moved; and above it, Beth's face, serene and smiling, as in the early days, looked down upon them, seeming to say, "Be happy! I am here."

"Play something, Amy; let them hear how much you have im-

32. Wristbands were detachable cuffs. In the mid-nineteenth century, shirts were not washed after every use, but detachable cuffs and collars were cleaned frequently. In most public or social settings, a man wore a waistcoat (vest) and a coat, so the cuffs and collar were the most noticeable part of a dress shirt.

33. Courting.

34. Removed.

35. The Irish poet Thomas Moore (1779–1852) published "Come, Ye Disconsolate" in *Sacred Songs* (1816). Amy sings the first stanza: "Come, ye disconsolate, where'er ye languish, / Come to the shrine of God fervently kneel; / Here bring your wounded hearts, here tell your anguish; / Earth has no sorrow that heav'n cannot heal."

36. A grasshopper chirps by rubbing its hind leg against its forewing.

37. A translation of the last line of stanza one of Goethe's "Mignon's Song."

proved," said Laurie, with pardonable pride in his promising pupil.

But Amy whispered, with full eyes, as she twirled the faded stool,—

"Not to-night, dear; I can't show off to-night."

But she did show something better than brilliancy or skill, for she sung Beth's songs, with a tender music in her voice which the best master could not have taught, and touched the listeners' hearts with a sweeter power than any other inspiration could have given her. The room was very still when the clear voice failed suddenly, at the last line of Beth's favorite hymn. It was hard to say,—

"Earth hath no sorrow that heaven cannot heal";[35]

and Amy leaned against her husband, who stood behind her, feeling that her welcome home was not quite perfect without Beth's kiss.

"Now we must finish with Mignon's song, for Mr. Bhaer sings that," said Jo, before the pause grew painful; and Mr. Bhaer cleared his throat with a gratified "hem," as he stepped into the corner where Jo stood, saying,—

"You will sing with me; we go excellently well together."

A pleasing fiction, by the way, for Jo had no more idea of music than a grasshopper;[36] but she would have consented, if he had proposed to sing a whole opera, and warbled away, blissfully regardless of time and tune. It didn't much matter, for Mr. Bhaer sang like a true German, heartily and well; and Jo soon subsided into a subdued hum, that she might listen to the mellow voice that seemed to sing for her alone.

"Know'st thou the land where the citron blooms,"

used to be the Professor's favorite line; for "das land" meant Germany to him; but now he seemed to dwell, with peculiar warmth and melody, upon the words,—

"There, oh there, might I with thee,
Oh my beloved, go";[37]

and one listener was so thrilled by the tender invitation, that she longed to say she did know the land, and would joyfully depart thither, whenever he liked.

The song was considered a great success, and the singer bashfully retired,[d] covered with laurels. But a few minutes afterward, he forgot his manners entirely, and stared at Amy putting on her bonnet—for she had been introduced simply as "my sister," and no one had called her by her new name since he came. He forgot himself still farther, when Laurie said, in his most gracious manner, at parting,—

"My wife and I are very glad to meet you, sir; please remember that there is always a welcome waiting for you, over the way."

Then the Professor thanked him so heartily, and looked so suddenly illuminated with satisfaction, that Laurie thought him the most delightfully-demonstrative old fellow he ever met.

"I too shall go; but I shall gladly come again, if you will gif me leave, dear madame, for a little business in the city will keep me here some days."

He spoke to Mrs. March, but he looked at Jo; and the mother's voice gave as cordial an assent as did the daughter's eyes; for Mrs. March was not so blind to her children's interest as Mrs. Moffat supposed.

"I suspect that is a wise man," remarked Mr. March, with placid satisfaction, from the hearth-rug, after the last guest had gone.

"I know he is a good one," added Mrs. March, with decided approval, as she wound up the clock.

"I thought you'd like him," was all Jo said, as she slipped away to her bed.

She wondered what the business was that brought Mr. Bhaer to the city, and finally decided that he had been appointed to some great honor, somewhere, but had been too modest to mention the fact. If she had seen his face when, safe in his own room, he looked at the picture of a severe and rigid young lady, with a good deal of hair, who appeared to be gazing darkly into futurity, it might have thrown some light upon the subject, especially when he turned off the gas, and kissed the picture in the dark.

1. *Brewer's Dictionary of Phrase & Fable* (15th ed.) notes the origin of the phrase: "To cause confusion. Before the days of the hay baler, hay was tossed about with a pitchfork before being gathered in" (New York: Harper Collins, 1995), 503.

2. A bootjack is a tool that helps pull off boots easily. It usually has a u-shaped mouth in which the boot heel is placed. One then places the other foot on the opposite end of the tool, using one's weight to pull off the boot.

Chapter 21

My Lord and Lady

PLEASE, Madam Mother, could you lend me my wife for half an hour? The luggage has come, and I've been making hay[1] of Amy's Paris finery, trying to find some things I want," said Laurie, coming in the next day to find Mrs. Laurence sitting in her mother's lap, as if being made "the baby" again.

"Certainly; go dear; I forgot that you have any home but this," and Mrs. March pressed the white hand that wore the wedding-ring, as if asking pardon for her maternal covetousness.

"I shouldn't have come over if I could have helped it; but I can't get on without my little woman any more than a—"

"Weathercock can without wind," suggested Jo, as he paused for a simile; Jo had grown quite her own saucy self again since Teddy came home.

"Exactly; for Amy keeps me pointing due west most of the time, with only an occasional whiffle round to the south, and I haven't had an easterly spell since I was married; don't know anything about the north, but am altogether salubrious and balmy,—hey, my lady?"

"Lovely weather so far; I don't know how long it will last, but I'm not afraid of storms, for I'm learning how to sail my ship. Come home, dear, and I'll find your bootjack;[2] I suppose that's what you are rummaging after among my things. Men are *so* helpless, mother," said Amy, with a matronly air, which delighted her husband.

"What are you going to do with yourselves after you get settled?" asked Jo, buttoning Amy's cloak as she used to button her pinafores.

"We have our plans; we don't mean to say much about them yet, because we are such very new brooms,[3] but we don't intend to be idle. I'm going into business with a devotion that shall delight grandpa, and prove to him that I'm not spoilt. I need something of the sort to keep me steady. I'm tired of dawdling, and mean to work like a man."

"And Amy, what is she going to do?" asked Mrs. March, well pleased at Laurie's decision, and the energy with which he spoke.

"After doing the civil all round, and airing our best bonnet, we shall astonish you by the elegant hospitalities of our mansion, the brilliant society we shall draw about us, and the beneficial influence we shall exert over the world at large. That's about it, isn't it, Madame Recamier?"[4] asked Laurie, with a quizzical look at Amy.

"Time will show. Come away, Impertinence, and don't shock my family by calling me names before their faces," answered Amy, resolving that there should be a home with a good wife in it before she set up a *salon* as a queen of society.

"How happy those children seem together!" observed Mr. March, finding it difficult to become absorbed in his Aristotle after the young couple had gone.

"Yes, and I think it will last," added Mrs. March, with the restful expression of a pilot who has brought a ship safely into port.

"I know it will. Happy Amy!" and Jo sighed, then smiled brightly as Professor Bhaer opened the gate with an impatient push.

Later in the evening, when his mind had been set at rest about the bootjack, Laurie said suddenly to his wife, who was flitting about, arranging her new art treasures,—

"Mrs. Laurence."

"My lord!"

"That man intends to marry our Jo!"

"I hope so; don't you, dear?"

"Well, my love, I consider him a trump, in the fullest sense of that expressive word, but I do wish he was a little younger and a good deal richer."

"Now, Laurie, don't be too fastidious and worldly-minded. If they love one another it doesn't matter a particle how old they are,

3. A person who is enthusiastic about taking charge and making changes.

4. Known for her beauty, Jeanne-Françoise Julie Adélaïde Bernard Récamier (1777–1849) was an influential member of French society who established a fashionable salon in Paris for literary and political elites in the late eighteenth and early nineteenth centuries.

5. In Part I's Chapter 9, "Meg Goes to Vanity Fair," Marmee tells Jo and Meg: "My dear girls, I *am* ambitious for you, but not to have you make a dash in the world,—marry rich men merely because they are rich, or have splendid houses, which are not homes, because love is wanting. Money is a needful and precious thing,—and, when well used, a noble thing,—but I never want you to think it is the first or only prize to strive for. I'd rather see you poor men's wives, if you were happy, beloved, contented, than queens on thrones, without self-respect and peace."

nor how poor. Women *never* should marry for money—" Amy caught herself up short as the words escaped her, and looked at her husband, who replied, with malicious gravity,—

"Certainly not, though you do hear charming girls say that they intend to do it sometimes. If my memory serves me, you once thought it your duty to make a rich match; that accounts, perhaps, for your marrying a good-for-nothing like me."

"Oh, my dearest boy, don't, don't say that! I forgot you were rich when I said 'Yes.' I'd have married you if you hadn't a penny, and I sometimes wish you *were* poor that I might show how much I love you;" and Amy, who was very dignified in public and very fond in private, gave convincing proofs of the truth of her words.

"You don't really think I am such a mercenary creature as I tried to be once, do you? It would break my heart, if you didn't believe that I'd gladly pull in the same boat with you, even if you had to get your living by rowing on the lake."

"Am I an idiot and a brute? How could I think so, when you refused a richer man for me, and won't let me give you half I want to now, when I have the right? Girls do it every day, poor things, and are taught to think it is their only salvation; but you had better lessons, and, though I trembled for you at one time, I was not disappointed,—for the daughter was true to the mother's teaching.[5] I told mamma so yesterday, and she looked as glad and grateful as if I'd given her a check for a million, to be spent in charity. You are not listening to my moral remarks, Mrs. Laurence,"—and Laurie paused, for Amy's eyes had an absent look, though fixed upon his face.

"Yes I am, and admiring the dimple in your chin at the same time. I don't wish to make you vain, but I must confess that I'm prouder of my handsome husband than of all his money. Don't laugh,—but your nose is *such* a comfort to me," and Amy softly caressed the well-cut feature with artistic satisfaction.

Laurie had received many compliments in his life, but never one that suited him better, as he plainly showed, though he did laugh at his wife's peculiar taste, while she said slowly,—

"May I ask you a question, dear?"

"Of course you may."

LITTLE WOMEN

"Shall you care if Jo does marry Mr. Bhaer?"

"Oh, that's the trouble, is it? I thought there was something in the dimple that didn't suit you. Not being a dog in the manger,[6] but the happiest fellow alive, I assure you I can dance at Jo's wedding with a heart as light as my heels. Do you doubt it, *ma amie?*"[a]

Amy looked up at him, and was satisfied; her last little jealous fear vanished forever, and she thanked him, with a face full of love and confidence.

"I wish we could do something for that capital old Professor. Couldn't we invent a rich relation, who shall obligingly die out there in Germany, and leave him a tidy little fortune?" said Laurie, when they began to pace up and down the long drawing-room, arm-in-arm, as they were fond of doing, in memory of the chateau garden.

"Jo would find us out, and spoil it all; she is very proud of him, just as he is, and said yesterday that she thought poverty was a beautiful thing."

"Bless her dear heart, she won't think so when she has a literary husband, and a dozen little professors and professorins[7] to support. We won't interfere now, but watch our chance, and do them a good turn in spite of themselves. I owe Jo for a part of my education, and she believes in people's paying their honest debts, so I'll get round her in that way."

"How delightful it is to be able to help others, isn't it? That was always one of my dreams, to have the power of giving freely; and, thanks to you, the dream has come true."

"Ah, we'll do lots of good, won't we? There's one sort of poverty that I particularly like to help. Out-and-out beggars get taken care of, but poor gentlefolks fare badly, because they won't ask, and people don't dare to offer charity; yet there are a thousand ways of helping them, if one only knows how to do it so delicately that it don't offend. I must say, I like to serve a decayed gentleman better than a blarneying beggar; I suppose it's wrong, but I do, though it is harder."

"Because it takes a gentleman to do it," added the other member of the domestic admiration society.

"Thank you, I'm afraid I don't deserve that pretty compliment.

6. Laurie alludes to the fable, often attributed to Aesop, of the dog who would not allow the ox or horse to eat the hay in the manger. The expression refers to a person who begrudges someone else what he or she does not really want.

7. German for "female professors."

8. In his 1870 essay "Rousseau and the Sentimentalists," James Russell Lowell, poet and former editor of *The Atlantic,* writes: "Talent is that which is in a man's power; genius is that in whose power a man is." For the Transcendentalists the main characteristic of genius was originality. As Emerson observes in "Self-Reliance" (1841): "To believe your own thought, to believe that what is true for you in your private heart is true for all men—that is genius." Both Amy and Laurie give up aspirations of becoming an artist and a musician respectively because they feel that while they have talent, they do not possess genius. However, here we learn that those with education, talent, and means find noble and ennobling employment in helping others who possess true genius and ambition. Laurie, for instance, plans to pay back Jo for her efforts in encouraging his education.

9. Amy refers to the legend of King Cophetua and the beggar girl Penelophon. According to the story, the African king instantly falls in love with the beggar girl when he sees her. In some versions, he throws gold coins in the road, and when she picks one up, he informs her of his love and tells her that he wants her for his wife. She agrees and as a queen loses all the qualities of a beggar. The legend appears in a number of versions dating back to medieval times. Shakespeare refers to it in *Romeo and Juliet, Richard II,* and *Love's Labor's Lost.* Alfred, Lord Tennyson, also used it as the basis for his poem "The Beggar Maid" (1842).

10. In the New Testament, Dorcas, also called Tabitha, lived at Joppa, where she "was full of good works and almsdeeds which she did." She grew ill and died. Hearing that the apostle Peter was nearby, two men went for him. When they arrived back at Joppa, Peter entered the room where Dorcas was laid out, "and all the widows stood by him weeping, and shewing the coats and garments which Dorcas made, while she was with them." Peter knelt, prayed, and commanded her to rise, which she did (Acts 9:36–41).

11. St. Martin (ca. 316–397), Tour's third appointed bishop, is a patron of France and soldiers. According to legend, as a soldier he gave half of his cloak to a poor man. Later, he told of a vision in which he saw Jesus wearing the torn cloak.

But I was going to say, that while I was dawdling about abroad, I saw a good many talented young fellows making all sorts of sacrifices, and enduring real hardships, that they might realize their dreams. Splendid fellows, some of them, working like heroes, poor and friendless, but so full of courage, patience and ambition, that I was ashamed of myself, and longed to give them a right good lift. Those are people whom it's a satisfaction to help, for if they've got genius, it's an honor to be allowed to serve them, and not let it be lost or delayed for want of fuel to keep the pot boiling; if they haven't, it's a pleasure to comfort the poor souls, and keep them from despair, when they find it out."[8]

"Yes indeed; and there's another class who can't ask, and who suffer in silence; I know something of it, for I belonged to it, before you made a princess of me, as the king does the beggar-maid in the old story.[9] Ambitious girls have a hard time, Laurie, and often have to see youth, health, and precious opportunities go by, just for want of a little help at the right minute. People have been very kind to me, and whenever I see girls struggling along, as we used to do, I want to put out my hand and help them, as I was helped."

"And so you shall, like an angel as you are!" cried Laurie, resolving, with a glow of philanthropic zeal, to found and endow an institution, for the express benefit of young women with artistic tendencies. "Rich people have no right to sit down and enjoy themselves, or let their money accumulate for others to waste. It's not half so sensible to leave a lot of legacies when one dies, as it is to use the money wisely while alive, and enjoy making one's fellow-creatures happy with it. We'll have a good time ourselves, and add an extra relish to our own pleasure, by giving other people a generous taste. Will you be a little Dorcas,[10] going about emptying a big basket of comforts, and filling it up with good deeds?"

"With all my heart, if you will be a brave St. Martin, stopping, as you ride gallantry through the world, to share your cloak with the beggar."[11]

"It's a bargain, and we shall get the best of it!"

So the young pair shook hands upon it, and then paced hap-

Bronson Alcott seated in front of Orchard House with one of his grandsons, circa late 1860s. Bronson constructed the rustic fence around the yard in 1865.

pily on again, feeling that their pleasant home was more home-like, because they hoped to brighten other homes, believing that their own feet would walk more uprightly along the flowery path before them, if they smoothed rough ways for other feet, and feeling that their hearts were more closely knit together by a love which could tenderly remember those less blest than they.

1. The *OED* defines *years of discretion* as "the time of life at which a person is presumed to be capable of exercising discretion or prudence."

2. Baby talk for *needle*.

3. John S. Pratt Alcott (Daisy), LMA's nephew, in "The 'Little Women' of Long Ago" (1913), recalled Bronson teaching him the alphabet in this manner: "Instead of using a book alphabet he invented one of his own, which he illustrated with anything he happened to have on hand,—even if it was only himself, as, when, lying on his back, with his legs straddled in the air, he personified a 'Y,' to our intense enjoyment and edification—for I have never forgotten how a 'Y' looks from that day to this" (quoted in *Her Own Time* 159).

4. Aided at different times by Elizabeth Palmer Peabody, her youngest sister, Sophia Peabody (the future wife of Nathaniel Hawthorne), and Margaret Fuller, Bronson Alcott was progressive in his teaching methods and philosophy in the 1830s. Having as instructors three intellectual women who were, in many ways, more educated than he, especially in classical subjects such as Greek and Latin, and who were important feminists in their own right, greatly helped Alcott's educational goals. In *Bronson Alcott, Teacher* (New York: Macmillan, 1940), Dorothy McCuskey offers this characterization of Alcott's teaching aims: "Alcott tried to make the school as much like the desirable circumstances of everyday life as possible. There were no formal precepts, but rather a living together as happily as possible . . . He thought of the intellectual faculties of the child in terms of association, attention, taste, memory, judgment, reflection, reason, and imagination. In all his schools for young children Alcott paid particular attention to the development of the imagination, partly because he felt it was neglected elsewhere, and partly because he considered the child to be dependent upon it before reason and judgment develop. For this reason he used stories, pictures, and imaginative poetry.

"For the cultivation of the other 'intellectual faculties' there were simple exercises in adding and subtracting by means of fingers, cubes, and other tangible objects. The children looked at books, spelled a little and marked on slates, for Alcott felt it good that their hands should be busy. Singing and instrumental music he valued as a means of cultivating the ear and voice, and he liked marching and dancing to music" (pp. 47–48).

Chapter 22

Daisy and Demi

I CANNOT FEEL that I have done my duty as humble historian of the March family, without devoting at least one chapter to the two most precious and important members of it. Daisy and Demi had now arrived at years of discretion;[1] for in this fast age babies of three or four assert their rights, and get them, too, which is more than many of their elders do. If there ever were a pair of twins in danger of being utterly spoilt by adoration, it was these prattling Brookes. Of course they were the most remarkable children ever born; as will be shown when I mention that they walked at eight months, talked fluently at twelve months, and at two years they took their places at table, and behaved with a propriety which charmed all beholders. At three Daisy demanded a "needler,"[2] and actually made a bag with four stitches in it; she likewise set up housekeeping in the side-board, and managed a microscopic cooking-stove with a skill that brought tears of pride to Hannah's eyes, while Demi learned his letters with his grandfather, who invented a new mode of teaching the alphabet by forming letters with his arms and legs,—thus uniting gymnastics for head and heels.[3] The boy early developed a mechanical genius which delighted his father, and distracted his mother, for he tried to imitate every machine he saw, and kept the nursery in a chaotic condition, with his "sewing-sheen,"—a mysterious structure of string, chairs, clothes-pins and spools, for wheels to go "wound and wound"; also a basket hung over the back of a chair, in which he vainly tried to hoist his too confiding sister, who, with feminine devotion, allowed her little head to be bumped till rescued, when the young inventor indignantly remarked, "Why, marmar, dat's my lellywaiter, and me's trying to pull her up."[4]

Though utterly unlike in character, the twins got on remarkably well together, and seldom quarrelled more than thrice a day. Of course, Demi tyrannized over Daisy, and gallantly defended her from every other aggressor; while Daisy made a galley-slave[5] of herself, and adored her brother, as the one perfect being in the world. A rosy, chubby, sunshiny little soul was Daisy, who found her way to everybody's heart, and nestled there. One of the captivating children, who seem made to be kissed and cuddled, adorned and adored like little goddesses, and produced for general approval on all festive occasions. Her small virtues were so sweet, that she would have been quite angelic, if a few small naughtinesses had not kept her delightfully human. It was all fair weather in her world, and every morning she scrambled up to the window in her little nightgown to look out, and say, no matter whether it rained or shone, "Oh, pitty day, oh, pitty day!" Every one was a friend, and she offered kisses to a stranger so confidingly, that the most inveterate bachelor relented and baby-lovers became faithful worshippers.

"Me loves evvybody," she once said, opening her arms, with her spoon in one hand, and her mug in the other, as if eager to embrace and nourish the whole world.

As she grew, her mother began to feel that the Dove-cote would be blest by the presence of an inmate as serene and loving as that

5. A *galley-slave* was a person who was forced to row the oars on a galley, a boat propelled by both sails and oars.

Frederick and John (seated) Pratt, LMA's nephews, who served as the models for Demi and Daisy.

6. In his classroom, Bronson employed the Socratic method of asking opposing questions to stimulate critical thinking. In his 1874 journal, he wrote: "Method is everything, in reform as in teaching in the schools; and for this reason the great reformers and teachers of the past have been practical if not theoretical Methodists. Pythagoras, Plato (whose method was Socrates' idealized), Aristotle—all taught methodically, and disciplined the minds of their pupils in dialectic and logic, as the crown of their efforts . . . We teach only by obeying the mind's processes. To prompt thought by thinking in accordance with its own laws—in this lies the art of teaching . . . The true logic, the ideal dialectic, walks abreast of the mind as a friend and prompter, a guide not as an antagonist." (*The Journals of BA* 444). Evidence of Bronson's use of Socratic dialogue can be seen in Elizabeth Palmer Peabody's *Record of a School: Exemplifying the General Principles of Spiritual Culture* (1835), an account of Alcott's teaching at the Temple School in Boston, and in Bronson's own controversial *Conversations with Children on the Gospels* (1836–1837).

7. Bronson Alcott, like many Transcendentalists, believed that children understand far more than people give them credit for. The Romantic notion that the child is wiser and closer to divine vision finds its quintessential expression in William Wordsworth's poem "Ode: Intimations of Immortality" (1807): "But trailing clouds of glory do we come / From God, who is our home: / Heaven lies about us in our infancy! / . . . At length the Man perceives it will die away, / And fade into the light of common day" (lines 65–77). Upon visiting Alcott's Temple School in mid-June 1836, Ralph Waldo Emerson wrote in his journal: "Yesterday I went to Mr Alcott's school & heard a conversation upon the Gospel of John. I thought the experiment of engaging young children upon questions of taste & truth successful. A few striking things were said by them. I felt strongly . . . as I watched the gradual dawn of thought upon the minds of all, that to truth is no age or season. It appears or it does not appear, & when the child perceives it, he is no more a child . . .

which had helped to make the old house home, and to pray that she might be spared a loss like that which had lately taught them how long they had entertained an angel unawares. Her grandfather often called her "Beth," and her grandmother watched over her with untiring devotion, as if trying to atone for some past mistake, which no eye but her own could see.

Demi, like a true Yankee, was of an inquiring turn, wanting to know everything, and often getting much disturbed, because he could not get satisfactory answers to his perpetual "What for?"

He also possessed a philosophic bent, to the great delight of his grandfather, who used to hold Socratic conversations with him,[6]

LITTLE WOMEN

in which the precocious pupil occasionally posed his teacher to the undisguised satisfaction of the women folk.

"What makes my legs go, Dranpa?" asked the young philosopher, surveying those active portions of his frame with a meditative air, while resting after a go-to-bed frolic one night.

"It's your little mind, Demi," replied the sage, stroking the yellow head respectfully.

"What is a little mine?"

"It is something which makes your body move, as the spring made the wheels go in my watch when I showed it to you."

"Open me; I want to see it go wound."

"I can't do that any more than you could open the watch. God winds you up, and you go till He stops you."

"Does I?" and Demi's brown eyes grew big and bright as he took in the new thought. "Is I wounded up like the watch?"

"Yes; but I can't show you how; for it is done when we don't see."

Demi felt of his back, as if expecting to find it like that of the watch, and then gravely remarked,—

"I dess Dod does it when I's asleep."

A careful explanation followed, to which he listened so attentively that his anxious grandmother said,—

"My dear, do you think it wise to talk about such things to that baby? He's getting great bumps over his eyes, and learning to ask the most unanswerable questions."

"If he is old enough to ask the questions he is old enough to receive true answers. I am not putting the thoughts into his head, but helping him unfold those already there. These children are wiser than we are, and I have no doubt the boy understands every word I have said to him.[7] Now, Demi, tell me where you keep your mind."

If the boy had replied like Alcibiades, "By the gods, Socrates, I cannot tell,"[8] his grandfather would not have been surprised; but when, after standing a moment on one leg, like a meditative young stork, he answered, in a tone of calm conviction, "In my little belly," the old gentleman could only join in grandma's laugh, and dismiss the class in metaphysics.

There might have been cause for maternal anxiety, if Demi had

Typical nineteenth-century children's fashion.

age, sex are nothing: we are alike before the great Whole. Little Josiah Quincy [grandson of then-President Josiah Quincy of Harvard College] now six years, six months old, is a child having something wonderful & divine in him" (*The Journals and Miscellaneous Notebooks of Ralph Waldo Emerson,* ed. Merton M. Sealts, Jr. [Cambridge, MA: The Belknap Press of Harvard University Press, 1965], vol. 5:175).

8. Alcibiades was an Athenian general, statesman, and orator (450–404 B.C.E.). He appears in three Socratic dialogues: Plato's *Symposium, Protagoras,* and *Alcibiades I* and *II.* In *Alcibiades I,* he is engaged in dialogue with Socrates on the just and unjust. He responds to the question about how he can tell the difference, saying: "But by the gods Socrates, I do not know at all what I am saying, but it is really like feeling strange."

9. In Charles Dickens's *Oliver Twist; or, The Parish Boy's Progress* (1837–1839), Jack Dawkins, the Artful Dodger, is a talented pickpocket in Fagin's gang of young criminals.

10. Small pastries. The patty cake is best remembered from the children's rhyme: "Pat-a-cake, pat-a-cake, baker's man, / Bake me a cake as fast as you can; / Pat it and prick it, and mark it with a B, / Put it in the oven for baby and me." The rhyme, according to Iona and Peter Opie, first appeared in Tom D'Urfey, *The Campaigners* (1698). It was also included in *Mother Goose's Melody; or, Sonnets for the Cradle* (c. 1765). A game of claps and hand motions often accompanied the rhyme (*The Oxford Dictionary of Nursery Rhymes*, eds. Iona and Peter Opie [Oxford University Press, 1951], p. 341).

11. Demi's head is powdered from the flour used in making patty cakes.

12. The nursery rhyme "The Three Little Kittens," who lost their mittens, is attributed to Eliza Lee Cabot Follen (1787–1860), a Boston author and abolitionist. It first appeared in the United States in *New Nursery Songs for All Good Children* (1843). "To Market, To Market," a knee rhyme (the child is bounced on the adult's knee as the rhyme is recited), appeared in *Songs for the Nursery collected from the Works of the Most Renowned Poets* (London: Tabart and Company, 1805): "To market, to market, to buy a penny bun, Home again, home again, market is done." See Iona and Peter Opie, eds., *The Oxford Dictionary of Nursery Rhymes* (Oxford University Press, 1951), pp. 257, 299.

not given convincing proofs that he was a true boy, as well as a budding philosopher; for, often, after a discussion which caused Hannah to prophecy, with ominous nods, "that child ain't long for this world," he would turn about and set her fears at rest by some of the pranks with which dear, dirty, naughty little rascals distract and delight their parents' souls.

Meg made many moral rules, and tried to keep them; but what mother was ever proof against the winning wiles, the ingenious evasions, or the tranquil audacity of the miniature men and women who so early show themselves accomplished Artful Dodgers?[9]

"No more raisins, Demi, they'll make you sick," says mamma to the young person who offers his services in the kitchen with unfailing regularity on plum-pudding day.

"Me likes to be sick."

"I don't want to have you,—so run away and help Daisy make patty-cakes."[10]

He reluctantly departs, but his wrongs weigh upon his spirit; and, by and by, when an opportunity comes to redress them, he outwits mamma by a shrewd bargain.

"Now you have been good children, and I'll play anything you like," says Meg, as she leads her assistant cooks upstairs, when the pudding is safely bouncing in the pot.

"Truly, marmar?" asks Demi, with a brilliant idea in his well-powdered head.[11]

"Yes, truly; anything you say," replies the short-sighted parent, preparing herself to sing "The Three Little Kittens" half a dozen times over, or to take her family to "Buy a penny bun," regardless of wind or limb.[12] But Demi corners her by the cool reply,—

"Then we'll go and eat up all the raisins."

Aunt Dodo was chief playmate and *confidante* of both children, and the trio turned the little house topsy-turvy. Aunt Amy was as yet only a name to them, Aunt Beth soon faded into a pleasantly vague memory, but Aunt Dodo was a living reality, and they made the most of her,—for which compliment she was deeply grateful. But when Mr. Bhaer came, Jo neglected her playfellows, and dismay and desolation fell upon their little souls. Daisy, who was fond of going about peddling kisses, lost her best customer and became bankrupt; Demi, with infantile penetration, soon discovered that Dodo like to play with "the bear-man" better than she did with him; but, though hurt, he concealed his anguish, for he hadn't the heart to insult a rival who kept a mine[13] of chocolate drops in his waistcoat pocket, and a watch that could be taken out of its case and freely shaken by ardent admirers.

Some persons might have considered these pleasing liberties as bribes; but Demi didn't see it in that light, and continued to patronize the "the bear-man" with pensive affability, while Daisy bestowed her small affections upon him at the third call, and considered his shoulder her throne, his arm her refuge, his gifts treasures of surpassing worth.

Gentlemen are sometimes seized with sudden fits of admiration for the young relatives of ladies whom they honor with their regard; but this counterfeit philoprogenitiveness[14] sits uneasily upon them, and does not deceive anybody a particle. Mr. Bhaer's devotion was sincere, however, likewise effective,—for honesty is the best policy in love as in law; he was one of the men who are at home with children, and looked particularly well when little faces made a pleasant contrast with his manly one. His business, whatever it was, detained him from day to day, but evening seldom failed to bring him out to see—well, he always asked for Mr. March, so I suppose *he* was the attraction. The excellent papa labored under the delusion that he was, and revelled in long discussions with the kindred spirit, till a chance remark of his more observing grandson suddenly enlightened him.

Mr. Bhaer came in one evening to pause on the threshold of the study, astonished by the spectacle that met his eye. Prone upon the floor lay Mr. March, with his respectable legs in the air, and beside him, likewise prone, was Demi, trying to imitate the attitude with his own short, scarlet-stockinged legs, both grovellers so seriously absorbed that they were unconscious of spectators, till Mr. Bhaer laughed his sonorous laugh, and Jo cried out, with a scandalized face,—

"Father, father! here's the Professor!"

13. The *OED* defines *mine* as "an abundant or constant source of supply."

14. Love of children.

15. Jo alludes to Sam Weller's reversal of his *v*'s and *w*'s in Dickens's *Pickwick Papers*.

16. German for "little boy."

17. The American author Mason Locke Weems (1759–1825), known as Parson Weems, originated the myth of young George Washington and the cherry tree in his bestselling book *A History of the Life and Death, Virtues and Exploits, of General George Washington* (1800). In the book, Washington admits to his father: "I can't tell a lie, Pa; you know I can't tell a lie. I did cut it with my hatchet." LMA also may have been familiar with a visual representation of the episode. John C. McRae, well known in the nineteenth century for his historical scenes, created an engraving circa 1855 based on a painting of G. G. White, which depicted Washington holding the hatchet and talking with his father before the tree.

Down went the black legs and up came the gray head, as the preceptor said, with undisturbed dignity,—

"Good evening, Mr. Bhaer. Excuse me for a moment,—we are just finishing our lesson. Now, Demi, make the letter and tell its name."

"I knows him," and, after a few convulsive efforts, the red legs took the shape of a pair of compasses, and the intelligent pupil triumphantly shouted "It's a We, Dranpa, it's a We!"

"He's a born Weller,"[15] laughed Jo, as her parent gathered himself up, and her nephew tried to stand on his head, as the only mode of expressing his satisfaction that school was over.

"What have you been at to-day, bübchen?"[16] asked Mr. Bhaer, picking up the gymnast.

"Me went to see little Mary."

"And what did you there?"

"I kissed her," began Demi, with artless frankness.

"Prut! thou beginnest early. What did the little Mary say to that?" asked Mr. Bhaer, continuing to confess the young sinner, who stood upon the knee, exploring the waistcoat pocket.

"Oh, she liked it, and she kissed me, and I liked it. *Don't* little boys like little girls?" asked Demi, with his mouth full, and an air of bland satisfaction.

"You precocious chick,—who put that into your head?" said Jo, enjoying the innocent revelations as much as the Professor.

"Tisn't in mine head, it's in mine mouf," answered literal Demi, putting out his tongue, with a chocolate-drop on it,—thinking she alluded to confectionery, not ideas.

"Thou shouldst save some for the little friend; sweets to the sweet, mannling," and Mr. Bhaer offered Jo some with a look that made her wonder if chocolate was not the nectar drunk by the gods. Demi also saw the smile, was impressed by it, and artlessly inquired,—

"Do great boys like great girls, too, 'Fessor?"

Like young Washington, Mr. Bhaer "couldn't tell a lie";[17] so he gave the somewhat vague reply, that he believed they did, sometimes, in a tone that made Mr. March put down his clothes-brush, glance at Jo's retiring face, and then sink into his chair, looking as if the "precocious chick" had put an idea into *his* head that was both sweet and sour.

Why Dodo, when she caught him in the china-closet half an hour afterward, nearly squeezed the breath out of his little body with a tender embrace, instead of shaking him for being there, and why she followed up this novel performance by the unexpected gift of a big slice of bread and jelly, remained one of the problems over which Demi puzzled his small wits, and was forced to leave unsolved forever.

Chapter 23

Under the Umbrella

WHILE LAURIE AND AMY were taking conjugal strolls over velvet carpets, as they set their house in order, and planned a blissful future, Mr. Bhaer and Jo were enjoying promenades of a different sort, along muddy roads and sodden fields.

"I always do take a walk toward evening, and I don't know why I should give it up, just because I happen to meet the Professor on his way out," said Jo to herself, after two or three encounters; for, though there were two paths to Meg's, whichever one she took she was sure to meet him, either going or returning. He was always walking rapidly, and never seemed to see her till quite close, when he would look as if his short-sighted eyes had failed to recognize the approaching lady till that moment. Then, if she was going to Meg's, he always had something for the babies; if her face was turned homeward, he had merely strolled down to see the river, and was just about returning, unless they were tired of his frequent calls.

Under the circumstances, what could Jo do but greet him civilly, and invite him in? If she *was* tired of his visits, she concealed her weariness with perfect skill, and took care that there should be coffee for supper, "as Friedrich—I mean Mr. Bhaer—don't like tea."

By the second week, every one knew perfectly well what was going on, yet every one tried to look as if they were stone-blind to the changes in Jo's face—never asked why she sang about her work, did up her hair three times a day, and got so blooming¹ with her evening exercise; and no one seemed to have the slightest suspicion that Professor Bhaer, while talking philosophy with the father, was giving the daughter lessons in love.

Jo couldn't even lose her heart in a decorous manner, but sternly tried to quench her feelings; and, failing to do so, led a somewhat agitated life. She was mortally afraid of being laughed at for surrendering, after her many and vehement declarations of independence. Laurie was her especial dread; but, thanks to the new manager,[2] he behaved with praiseworthy propriety, never called Mr. Bhaer "a capital old fellow" in public, never alluded, in the remotest manner, to Jo's improved appearance, or expressed the least surprise at seeing the Professor's hat on the Marches hall-table, nearly every evening. But he exulted in private, and longed for the time to come when he could give Jo a piece of plate, with a bear and a ragged staff on it as an appropriate coat of arms.

For a fortnight, the Professor came and went with lover-like regularity; then he stayed away for three whole days, and made no sign—a proceeding which caused everybody to look sober, and Jo to become pensive, at first, and then,—alas for romance,—very cross.

"Disgusted, I dare say, and gone home as suddenly as he came. It's nothing to me, of course; but I *should* think he would have come and bid us good-by, like a gentleman," she said to herself, with a despairing look at the gate, as she put on her things for the customary walk, one dull afternoon.

"You'd better take the little umbrella, dear; it looks like rain," said her mother, observing that she had on her new bonnet, but not alluding to the fact.

"Yes, Marmee; do you want anything in town? I've got to run in and get some paper," returned Jo, pulling out the bow under her chin, before the glass, as an excuse for not looking at her mother.

"Yes; I want some twilled silesia, a paper of number nine needles,[3] and two yards of narrow lavender ribbon. Have you got your thick boots on, and something warm under your cloak?"

"I believe so," answered Jo, absently.

"If you happen to meet Mr. Bhaer, bring him home to tea; I quite long to see the dear man," added Mrs. March.

Jo heard *that,* but made no answer, except to kiss her mother,

2. His wife, Amy.

3. A cotton fabric with diagonal parallel ribs. Needle numbers refer to the diameter of the needle. In knitting, the size of the needles affects the size of the stitches. A number nine American needle is 5.50 millimeters.

and walk rapidly away, thinking with a glow of gratitude, in spite of her heartache,—

"How good she is to me! What *do* girls do who haven't any mothers to help them through their troubles?"

The dry-goods stores were not down among the counting-houses,[4] banks, and wholesale warerooms, where gentlemen most do congregate; but Jo found herself in that part of the city before she did a single errand, loitering along as if waiting for some one, examining engineering instruments in one window, and samples of wool in another, with most unfeminine interest; tumbling over barrels, being half-smothered by descending bales, and hustled unceremoniously by busy men, who looked as if they wondered "how the deuce she got there." A drop of rain on her cheek recalled her thoughts from baffled hopes[5] to ruined ribbons; for the drops continued to fall, and, being a woman as well as a lover, she felt that, though it was too late to save her heart, she might her bonnet. Now she remembered the little umbrella, which she had forgotten to take in her hurry to be off; but regret was unavailing, and nothing could be done but borrow one, or submit to a drenching. She looked up at the lowering sky, down at the crimson bow, already flecked with black, forward along the muddy street, then one long, lingering look behind, at a certain grimy warehouse, with "Hoffmann, Swartz & Co." over the door, and said to herself, with a sternly-reproachful air,—

"It serves me right! What business had I to put on all my best things, and come philandering down here, hoping to see the Professor? Jo, I'm ashamed of you! No, you shall *not* go there to borrow an umbrella, or find out where he is, from his friends. You shall slop[6] away, and do your errands in the rain; and if you catch your death, and ruin your bonnet, it's no more than you deserve. Now then!"

With that she rushed across the street so impetuously, that she narrowly escaped annihilation from a passing truck,[7] and precipitated herself into the arms of a stately old gentleman, who said, "I beg pardon, ma'am," and looked mortally offended. Somewhat daunted, Jo righted herself, spread her handkerchief over the devoted ribbons, and putting temptation behind her, hurried on, with increasing dampness about the ankles, and much clashing of umbrellas overhead. The fact that a somewhat dilapidated blue one remained stationary above the unprotected bonnet, attracted her attention; and, looking up, she saw Mr. Bhaer looking down.

"I feel to know the strong-minded lady who goes so bravely under many horse-noses, and so fast through much mud. What do you down here, my friend?"

"I'm shopping."

Mr. Bhaer smiled, as he glanced from the pickle-factory on one side, to the wholesale hide and leather concern on the other; but he only said, politely,—

"You haf no umbrella; may I go also, and take for you the bundles?"

"Yes, thank you."

Jo's cheeks were as red as her ribbon, and she wondered what he thought of her; but she didn't care, for in a minute she found herself walking away, arm-in-arm with her Professor, feeling as if the sun had suddenly burst out with uncommon brilliancy, that the world was all right again, and that one thoroughly happy woman was paddling through the wet that day.

"We thought you had gone," said Jo, hastily, for she knew he was looking at her,—her bonnet wasn't big enough to hide her face, and she feared he might think the joy it betrayed unmaidenly.

"Did you believe that I should go with no farewell to those who haf been so heavenly kind to me?" he asked, so reproachfully, that she felt as if she had insulted him by the suggestion, and answered, heartily,—

"No, *I* didn't; I knew you were busy about your own affairs, but we rather missed you,—father and mother especially."

"And you?"

"I'm always glad to see you, sir."

In her anxiety to keep her voice quite calm, Jo made it rather cool, and the frosty little monosyllable at the end seemed to chill the Professor, for his smile vanished, as he said, gravely,—

"I thank you, and come one more time before I go."

"You *are* going, then?"

"I haf no longer any business here; it is done."

"Successfully, I hope?" said Jo, for the bitterness of disappointment was in that short reply of his.

"I ought to think so, for I haf a way opened to me by which I can make my bread and gif my Jünglings[8] much help."

"Tell me, please! I like to know all about the—the boys," said Jo eagerly.

"That is so kind, I gladly tell you. My friends find for me a place in a college, where I teach as at home, and earn enough to make the way smooth for Franz and Emil. For this I should be grateful, should I not?"

"Indeed you should! How splendid it will be to have you doing what you like, and be able to see you often, and the boys—" cried Jo, clinging to the lads as an excuse for the satisfaction she could not help betraying.

"Ah! But we shall not meet often, I fear; this place is at the West."

"So far away!" and Jo left her skirts to their fate, as if it didn't matter now what became of her clothes or herself.

Mr. Bhaer could read several languages, but he had not learned to read women yet. He flattered himself that he knew Jo pretty well, and was, therefore, much amazed by the contradictions of voice, face, and manner, which she showed him in rapid succession that day,—for she was in half a dozen different moods in the course of half an hour. When she met him she looked surprised, though it was impossible to help suspecting that she had come for that express purpose. When he offered her his arm, she took it with a look that filled him with delight; but when he asked if she missed him, she gave such a chilly, formal reply, that despair fell upon him. On learning his good fortune she almost clapped her hands,— was the joy all for the boys? Then, on hearing his destination, she said, "So far away!" in a tone of despair that lifted him on to a pinnacle of hope; but the next minute she tumbled him down again by observing, like one entirely absorbed in the matter,—

"Here's the place for my errands; will you come in? It won't take long."

Jo rather prided herself upon her shopping capabilities, and particularly wished to impress her escort with the neatness and despatch with which she would accomplish the business. But, owing to the flutter she was in, everything went amiss; she upset the tray of needles, forgot the silesia was to be "twilled" till it was cut off, gave the wrong change, and covered herself with confusion by asking for lavender ribbon at the calico counter. Mr. Bhaer stood by, watching her blush and blunder; and, as he watched, his own bewilderment seemed to subside, for he was beginning to see that on some occasions women, like dreams, go by contraries.

When they came out, he put the parcel under his arm with a more cheerful aspect, and splashed through the puddles as if he rather enjoyed it, on the whole.

"Should we not do a little what you call shopping for the babies, and haf a farewell feast to-night if I go for my last call at your so pleasant home?" he asked, stopping before a window full of fruit and flowers.

"What will we buy?" asked Jo, ignoring the latter part of his speech, and sniffing the mingled odors with an affectation of delight, as they went in.

"May they haf oranges and figs?" asked Mr. Bhaer, with a paternal air.

"They eat them when they can get them."

"Do you care for nuts?"

"Like a squirrel."

"Hamburg grapes;[9] yes, we shall drink to the Fatherland in those?"

Jo frowned upon that piece of extravagance, and asked why he didn't buy a frail[10] of dates, a cask of raisins, and a bag of almonds, and done with it? Whereat Mr. Bhaer confiscated her purse, produced his own, and finished the marketing by buying several pounds of grapes, a pot of rosy daisies, and a pretty jar of honey, to be regarded in the light of a demijohn. Then, distorting his pockets with the knobby bundles, and giving her the flowers to hold, he put up the old umbrella, and they travelled on again.

"Miss Marsch, I haf a great favor to ask of you," began the Professor, after a moist promenade of half a block.

9. Black grapes from Germany, often grown in greenhouses, used in table wine.

10. A basket made of rushes used for fruit such as figs and raisins.

"Yes, sir," and Jo's heart began to beat so hard she was afraid he would hear it.

"I am bold to say it in spite of the rain, because so short a time remains to me."

"Yes, sir," and Jo nearly smashed the small flower-pot with the sudden squeeze she gave it.

"I wish to get a little dress for my Tina, and I am too stupid to go alone. Will you kindly gif me a word of taste and help?"

"Yes, sir," and Jo felt as calm and cool all of a sudden, as if she had stepped into a refrigerator.

"Perhaps also a shawl for Tina's mother, she is so poor and sick, and the husband is such a care,—yes, yes, a thick, warm shawl would be a friendly thing to take the little mother."

"I'll do it with pleasure, Mr. Bhaer. I'm going very fast, and he's getting dearer every minute," added Jo to herself; then, with a mental shake, she entered into the business with an energy which was pleasant to behold.

Mr. Bhaer left it all to her, so she chose a pretty gown for Tina, and then ordered out the shawls. The clerk, being a married man, condescended to take an interest in the couple, who appeared to be shopping for their family.

"Your lady may prefer this; it's a superior article, a most desirable color, quite chaste and genteel," he said, shaking out a comfortable gray shawl, and throwing it over Jo's shoulders.

"Does this suit you, Mr. Bhaer?" she asked, turning her back to him, and feeling deeply grateful for the chance of hiding her face.

"Excellently well, we will haf it," answered the Professor, smiling to himself, as he paid for it, while Jo continued to rummage the counters, like a confirmed bargain-hunter.

"Now shall we go home?" he asked, as if the words were very pleasant to him.

"Yes, it's late, and I'm *so* tired." Jo's voice was more pathetic than she knew, for now the sun seemed to have gone in as suddenly as it came out, the world grew muddy and miserable again, and for the first time she discovered that her feet were cold, her head ached, and that her heart was colder than the former, fuller of pain than the latter. Mr. Bhaer was going away; he only cared

Professor Bhaer proposes to Jo under the umbrella.
Norman Rockwell, *Heart's Dearest* (1938).

for her as a friend, it was all a mistake, and the sooner it was over the better. With this idea in her head, she hailed an approaching omnibus with such a hasty gesture that the daisies flew out of the pot, and were badly damaged.

"That is not our omniboos," said the Professor, waving the loaded vehicle away, and stopping to pick up the poor little posies.

"I beg your pardon, I didn't see the name distinctly. Never mind, I can walk, I'm used to plodding in the mud," returned Jo, winking hard, because she would have died rather than openly wipe her eyes.

Mr. Bhaer saw the drops on her cheeks, though she turned her head away; the sight seemed to touch him very much, for suddenly stooping down, he asked in a tone that meant a great deal,—

"Heart's dearest, why do you cry?"

Now if Jo had not been new to this sort of thing she would have said she wasn't crying, had a cold in her head, or told any other feminine fib proper to the occasion; instead of which that undignified creature answered, with an irrepressible sob,—

"Because you are going away."

"Ah, my Gott,ª that is *so* good!" cried Mr. Bhaer, managing to clasp his hands in spite of the umbrella and the bundles. "Jo, I haf nothing but much love to gif you; I came to see if you could care for it, and I waited to be sure that I was something more than a friend. Am I? Can you make a little place in your heart for old Fritz?" he added, all in one breath.

"Oh, yes!" said Jo, and he was quite satisfied, for she folded both hands over his arm, and looked up at him with an expression that plainly showed how happy she would be to walk through life beside him, even though she had no better shelter than the old umbrella, if he carried it.

It was certainly proposing under difficulties, for even if he had desired to do so, Mr. Bhaer could not go down upon his knees, on account of the mud, neither could he offer Jo his hand, except figuratively, for both were full; much less could he indulge in tender demonstrations in the open street, though he was near it; so the only way in which he could express his rapture was to look at her, with an expression which glorified his face to such a degree that there actually seemed to be little rainbows in the drops that sparkled on his beard. If he had not loved Jo very much, I don't think he could have done it *then*, for she looked far from lovely, with her skirts in a deplorable state, her rubber boots splashed to the ankle, and her bonnet a ruin. Fortunately, Mr. Bhaer considered her the most beautiful woman living, and she found him more "Jove-like" than ever, though his hat-brim was quite limp with the little rills trickling thence upon his shoulders (for he held the umbrella all over Jo), and every finger of his gloves needed mending.[11]

Passers-by probably thought them a pair of harmless lunatics, for they entirely forgot to hail a 'bus, and strolled leisurely along, oblivious of deepening dusk and fog. Little they cared what anybody thought, for they were enjoying the happy hour that seldom comes but once in any life—the magical moment which bestows youth on the old, beauty on the plain, wealth on the poor, and gives human hearts a foretaste of heaven. The Professor looked as if he had conquered a kingdom, and the world had nothing more to offer him in the way of bliss, while Jo trudged beside him, feeling as if her place had always been there, and wondering how she ever could have chosen any other lot. Of course, she was the first to speak—intelligibly, I mean, for the emotional remarks which followed her impetuous "Oh, yes!" were not of a coherent or reportable character.

"Friedrich, why didn't you—"

"Ah, heaven! she gifs me the name that no one speaks since Minna died!" cried the Professor, pausing in a puddle to regard her with grateful delight.

"I always call you so to myself—I forgot; but I won't, unless you like it."

"Like it! it is more sweet to me than I can tell. Say 'thou,' also, and I shall say your language is almost as beautiful as mine."

"Isn't 'thou' a little sentimental?" asked Jo, privately thinking it a lovely monosyllable.

"Sentimental? yes; thank Gott, we Germans believe in sentiment, and keep ourselves young mit it. Your English 'you' is so cold—say 'thou,' heart's dearest, it means so much to me," pleaded Mr. Bhaer, more like a romantic student than a grave professor.

"Well, then, why didn't thou tell me all this sooner?" asked Jo, bashfully.

"Now I shall haf to show thee all my heart, and I so gladly will, because thou must take care of it hereafter. See, then, my Jo—ah, the dear, funny little name!—I had a wish to tell something the day I said good-by in New York; but I thought the handsome friend was betrothed to thee, and so I spoke not. Would'st thou have said 'Yes,' then, if I *had* spoken?"

11. Bhaer's proposal is in marked contrast to that of Laurie a few chapters earlier. Instead of the intimate boat on tranquil Lake Geneva, with the Castle of Chillon and Vevey as its backdrop, Professor Bhaer's proposal occurs on a muddy, rainy public street. LMA takes pains to remind the reader what Bhaer cannot do: he cannot drop to his knees because of the mud; he cannot offer her his hands, occupied as they are with the bundles and his umbrella; he cannot show affection in public. LMA nonetheless presents an intimate scene that possesses great tenderness, one that has often been depicted by *Little Women*'s illustrators over the years.

12. Bhaer alludes to the German folktale "Briar Rose," which was published in 1812 in Jacob and Wilhelm Grimm's *Kinder-und-Hausmärchen (Children's and Household Tales).* Some scholars believe the tale is not original to Germany but is borrowed from Charles Perrault's 1697 "Sleeping Beauty," published in *Histoires ou Contes du Temps passé (Tales of Stories of the Past with Morals).* In both tales, the prince makes his way through the woods and the briars that have grown up around the castle before he awakens the sleeping maiden.

13. A German maxim: "The first love is the best."

14. LMA originally published "In the Garret" in *The Flag of Our Union* 20:1 (March 18, 1865). Here the sisters were named Nan, Lu, Bess, and Amy.

"I don't know; I'm afraid not, for I didn't have any heart, just then."

"Prut! that I do not believe. It was asleep till the fairy prince came through the wood, and waked it up.[12] Ah, well, 'Die erste Liebe ist die beste';[13] but that I should not expect."

"Yes, the first love *is* the best; so be contented, for I never had another. Teddy was only a boy, and soon got over his little fancy," said Jo, anxious to correct the Professor's mistake.

"Good! then I shall rest happy, and be sure that thou givest me all. I haf waited so long, I am grown selfish, as thou wilt find, Professorin."

"I like that," cried Jo, delighted with her new name. "Now tell me what brought you, at last, just when I most wanted you?"

"This,"—and Mr. Bhaer took a little worn paper out of his waistcoat pocket.

Jo unfolded it, and looked much abashed, for it was one of her own contributions to a paper that paid for poetry, which accounted for her sending it an occasional attempt.

"How could that bring you?" she asked, wondering what he meant.

"I found it by chance; I knew it by the names and the initials, and in it there was one little verse that seemed to call me. Read and find him; I will see that you go not in the wet."

Jo obeyed, and hastily skimmed through the lines which she had christened—

"IN THE GARRET.[14]

"Four little chests all in a row,
      Dim with dust, and worn by time,
All fashioned and filled, long ago,
      By children now in their prime.
Four little keys hung side by side,
      With faded ribbons, brave and gay,
When fastened there with childish pride,
      Long ago, on a rainy day.
Four little names, one on each lid,
      Carved out by a boyish hand,

LITTLE WOMEN

And underneath, there lieth hid
    Histories of the happy band
Once playing here, and pausing oft
    To hear the sweet refrain,
That came and went on the roof aloft,
    In the falling summer rain.

"'Meg' on the first lid, smooth and fair,
    I look in with loving eyes,
For folded here, with well-known care,
    A goodly gathering lies—
The record of a peaceful life,
    Gifts to gentle child and girl,
A bridal gown, lines to a wife,
    A tiny shoe, a baby curl.
No toys in this first chest remain,
    For all are carried away,
In their old age, to join again
    In another small Meg's play.
Ah, happy mother! well I know
    You hear like a sweet refrain,
Lullabies ever soft and low,
    In the falling summer rain.

"'Jo' on the next lid, scratched and worn,
    And within a motley store
Of headless dolls, of school-books torn,
    Birds and beasts that speak no more.
Spoils brought home from the fairy ground
    Only trod by youthful feet,
Dreams of a future never found,
    Memories of a past still sweet;
Half-writ poems, stories wild,
    April letters, warm and cold,
Diaries of a wilful child,
    Hints of a woman early old,
A woman in a lonely home,
    Hearing like a sad refrain,—

15. Saint Catherine of Siena (1347–1380), born in Siena, Italy, was, like Beth, the second youngest child in a large family. As a young girl she saw visions and devoted herself to Christ. At age sixteen, she became a Dominican tertiary, a lay member of the Dominican order, and tended to the sick and poor. Saint Catherine was canonized in 1461.

16. A ribbon, band, or hairnet (often worn at the back of the neck) to hold back the hair.

'Be worthy love, and love will come,'
    In the falling summer rain.

"My 'Beth!' the dust is always swept
    From the lid that bears your name,
As if by loving eyes that wept,
    By careful hands that often came.
Death canonized for us one saint,
    Ever less human than divine,
And still we lay, with tender plaint,
    Relics in this household shrine.
The silver bell, so seldom rung,
    The little cap which last she wore,
The fair, dead Catherine[15] that hung
    By angels borne above her door;
The songs she sang, without lament,
    In her prison-house of pain,
Forever are they sweetly blent
    With the falling summer rain.

"Upon the last lid's polished field—
    Legend now both fair and true—
A gallant knight bears on his shield,
    'Amy' in letters gold and blue.
Within the snoods[16] that bound her hair,[b]
    Slippers that have danced their last,
Faded flowers laid by with care,
    Fans whose airy toils are past—
Gay valentines all ardent flames,
    Trifles that have borne their part
In girlish hopes, and fears, and shames.
    The record of a maiden heart,
Now learning fairer, truer spells,
    Hearing, like a blithe refrain,
The silver sound of bridal bells
    In the falling summer rain.

"Four little chests all in a row,
    Dim with dust, and worn by time,

Four women, taught by weal[17] and woe,
    To love and labor in their prime.
Four sisters, parted for an hour,—
    None lost, one only gone before,
Made by love's immortal power,
    Nearest and dearest evermore.
Oh, when these hidden stores of ours
    Lie open to the Father's sight,
May they be rich in golden hours,—
    Deeds that show fairer for the light.
Lives whose brave music long shall ring
    Like a spirit-stirring strain,
Souls that shall gladly soar and sing
    In the long sunshine, after rain.

"J. M."

17. Happiness or prosperity.
18. A horse that is ridden in battle.

"It's very bad poetry, but I felt it when I wrote it one day when I was very lonely, and had a good cry on a rag-bag. I never thought it would go where it could tell tales," said Jo, tearing up the verses the Professor had treasured so long.

"Let it go,—it has done its duty,—and I will haf a fresh one when I read all the brown book in which she keeps her little secrets," said Mr. Bhaer with a smile, as he watched the fragments fly away on the wind. "Yes," he added earnestly, "I read that, and I think to myself, 'She has a sorrow, she is lonely, she would find comfort in true love.' I haf a heart full, full for her; shall I not go and say, 'If this is not too poor a thing to gif for what I shall hope to receive, take it in Gott's name.'"

"And so you came to find that it was not too poor, but the one precious thing I needed," whispered Jo.

"I had no courage to think that at first, heavenly kind as was your welcome to me. But soon I began to hope, and then I said, 'I will haf her if I die for it,' and so I will!" cried Mr. Bhaer, with a defiant nod, as if the walls of mist closing round them were barriers which he was to surmount or valiantly knock down.

Jo thought that was splendid, and resolved to be worthy of her knight, though he did not come prancing on a charger[18] in gorgeous array.

19. LMA's insistence on establishing egalitarian marriage in *Little Women* comes to its most complete realization in the union between Jo and Friedrich Bhaer. As Anne Dalke observes in "'The House-Band': The Education of Men in *Little Women* (*College English* 47 [1985]): "Marmee's plea for the equal involvement of both partners in the demands of family life is put into increasingly successful practice by each of her sons-in-law in turn. Meg is house-bound while John goes out to work. Laurie and Amy have a more equitable arrangement: both stay at home. But it is Jo's marriage which is most explicitly made over on the matriarchal pattern. She chooses the life work for herself and her partner, and provides the setting for their new school. She and her professor enlarge the family beyond the ties of blood, putting women's traditional strengths to work in an arena wider than that of the immediate household" (p. 77).

20. Jo's marriage to Professor Bhaer annoys many readers, who complain that he is too old, more of a father figure than a husband, and that Jo should have remained a literary spinster. However, it is a pairing that evidently pleased LMA, even though she thought it a "funny" match. Elaine Showalter, in *Sister's Choice: Tradition and Change in American Women's Writing* (Oxford: Clarendon Press, 1991), argues: "As a couple, Jo and Bhaer have both values and feelings in common; they share an interest in educational reform, in new ideas, and in practical philanthropy. Most important, he understands her need to work" (62). In *A Hunger for Home: Louisa May Alcott's Place in American Culture* (New Brunswick: Rutgers University Press, 1987), Sarah Elbert notes: "Bhaer has all the qualities Bronson Alcott lacked: warmth, intimacy, and a tender capacity for expressing his affection—the feminine attributes Alcott admired and hoped men could acquire in a rational, feminist world . . . He touches everyone, hugs and carries children about on his back. Bronson, despite all his genuine idealism and devotion to humanity, was emotionally reserved and distant. Fritz Bhaer loves material reality, is eminently approachable, and values all the things that Bronson Alcott rejects, such as good food, warm rooms, and appealing domestic disorder" (210).

"What made you stay away so long?" she asked presently, finding it so pleasant to ask confidential questions, and get delightful answers, that she could not keep silent.

"It was not easy, but I could not find the heart to take you from that so happy home until I could haf a prospect of one to gif you, after much time perhaps, and hard work. How could I ask you to gif up so much for a poor old fellow, who has no fortune but a little learning?"

"I'm glad you *are* poor; I couldn't bear a rich husband!" said Jo, decidedly, adding, in a softer tone, "Don't fear poverty; I've known it long enough to lose my dread, and be happy working for those I love; and don't call yourself old,—I never think of it, —I couldn't help loving you^c if you were seventy!"

The Professor found that so touching that he would have been glad of his handkerchief if he could have got at it; as he couldn't, Jo wiped his eyes for him, and said, laughing, as she took away a bundle or two,—

"I may be strong-minded, but no one can say I'm out of my sphere now,—for woman's special mission is supposed to be drying tears and bearing burdens. I'm to carry my share, Friedrich, and help to earn the home. Make up your mind to that, or I'll never go," she added, resolutely, as he tried to reclaim his load.[19]

"We shall see. Haf you patience to wait a long time, Jo? I must go away and do my work alone; I must help my boys first, because even for you I may not break my word to Minna. Can you forgif that, and be happy, while we hope and wait?"

"Yes, I know I can; for we love one another, and that makes all the rest easy to bear. I have my duty also, and my work. I couldn't enjoy myself if I neglected them even for you,—so there's no need of hurry or impatience. You can do your part out West,—I can do mine here,—and both be happy, hoping for the best, and leaving the future to be as God wills."[20]

"Ah! thou gifest me such hope and courage, and I haf nothing to gif back but a full heart and these empty hands," cried the Professor, quite overcome.

Jo never, never would learn to be proper; for when he said that as they stood upon the steps, she just put both hands into his, whispering tenderly, "Not empty now"; and, stooping down, kissed her Friedrich under the umbrella. It was dreadful, but she would have done it if the flock of draggle-tailed[21] sparrows on the hedge had been human beings,—for she was very far gone indeed, and quite regardless of everything but her own happiness. Though it came in such a very simple guise, that was the crowning moment of both their lives, when, turning from the night, and storm, and loneliness, to the household light, and warmth, and peace, waiting to receive them with a glad "Welcome home," Jo led her lover in, and shut the door.

21. Tail feathers that have been dragged through water and mud.

Chapter 24

Harvest Time

FOR A YEAR Jo and her Professor worked and waited, hoped and loved; met occasionally, and wrote such voluminous letters, that the rise in the price of paper was accounted for, Laurie said. The second year began rather soberly, for their prospects did not brighten, and Aunt March died suddenly. But when their first sorrow was over,—for they loved the old lady in spite of her sharp tongue,—they found they had cause for rejoicing, for she had left Plumfield to Jo, which made all sorts of joyful things possible.

"It's a fine old place, and will bring a handsome sum, for of course you intend to sell it?" said Laurie, as they were all talking the matter over, some weeks later.

"No, I don't," was Jo's decided answer, as she petted the fat poodle, whom she had adopted, out of respect to his former mistress.

"You don't mean to live there?"

"Yes, I do."

"But, my dear girl, it's an immense house, and will take a power[1] of money to keep it in order. The garden and orchard alone need two or three men, and farming isn't in Bhaer's line, I take it."

"He'll try his hand at it there, if I propose it."

"And you expect to live on the produce of the place? Well, that sounds Paradisiacal, but you'll find it desperate hard work."

"The crop we are going to raise is a profitable one;" and Jo laughed.

"Of what is this fine crop to consist, ma'am?"

"Boys! I want to open a school for little lads—a good, happy, homelike school, with me to take care of them, and Fritz to teach them."[2]

"There's a truly Joian plan for you! Isn't that just like her?" cried Laurie, appealing to the family, who looked as much surprised as he.

"I like it," said Mrs. March, decidedly.

"So do I," added her husband, who welcomed the thought of a chance for trying the Socratic method of education on modern youth.

"It will be an immense care for Jo," said Meg, stroking the head of her one all-absorbing son.

"Jo can do it, and be happy in it. It's a splendid idea—tell us all about it," cried Mr. Laurence, who had been longing to lend the lovers a hand, but knew that they would refuse his help.

"I knew you'd stand by me, sir. Amy does too—I see it in her eyes, though she prudently waits to turn it over in her mind before she speaks. Now, my dear people," continued Jo, earnestly, "just understand that this isn't a new idea of mine, but a long-cherished plan. Before my Fritz came, I used to think how, when I'd made my fortune, and no one needed me at home, I'd hire a big house, and pick up some poor, forlorn little lads, who hadn't any mothers, and take care of them, and make life jolly for them before it was too late. I see so many going to ruin for want of help, at the right minute; I love so to do anything for them; I seem to feel their wants, and sympathize with their troubles; and, oh, I should *so* like to be a mother to them!"

Mrs. March held out her hand to Jo, who took it smiling, with tears in her eyes, and went on in the old enthusiastic way, which they had not seen for a long while.

"I told my plan to Fritz once, and he said it was just what he would like, and agreed to try it when we got rich. Bless his dear heart, he's been doing it all his life,—helping poor boys, I mean, —not getting rich; that he'll never be—money don't stay in his pocket long enough to lay up any. But now, thanks to my good old aunt, who loved me better than I ever deserved, *I'm* rich—at least I feel so, and we can live at Plumfield, perfectly well, if we have a flourishing school. It's just the place for boys—the house is

2. Although LMA taught school a number of times in the 1850s and early 1860s, she never operated an all-boys school like Plumfield. However, LMA always identified more with boys than with girls—just as Jo does in *Little Women.* Alf Whitman, who served as partial inspiration for Laurie, writes in "Miss Alcott's Letters to Her Laurie" (1901) that "justice has never been done to the sweetest and most attractive side of her nature—her real love for boys, which sprang from the boy nature that was hers in so marked a degree . . . She always said she ought to have been a boy, and that she could not be one was one of the many crosses she had to bear" (quoted in *Her Own Time* 102). In her essay "My Boys" in volume I of *Aunt Jo's Scrap-Bag* (Boston: Roberts Brothers, 1872), LMA observes that as soon as boys "outgrow their babyhood their trials begin, and they are regarded as nuisances till they are twenty-one . . . Yet that very time of neglect is the period when they most need all manner of helps, and ought to have them. I like boys and oysters raw; so, though good manners are always pleasing, I don't mind the rough outside burr which repels most people, and perhaps that is why the burrs open and let me see the soft lining and taste the sweet nut hidden inside" (pp. 1–2).

3. Ragged, poor boys.
4. Shy.
5. An awkward youth.

big, and the furniture strong and plain. There's plenty of room for dozens inside, and splendid grounds outside. They could help in the garden and orchard—such work is healthy, isn't it, sir? Then Fritz can train and teach in his own way, and father will help him. I can feed, and nurse, and pet, and scold them; and mother will be my stand-by. I've always longed for lots of boys, and never had enough; now I can fill the house full, and revel in the little dears to my heart's content. Think what luxury; Plumfield my own, and a wilderness of boys to enjoy it with me!"

As Jo waved her hands; and gave a sigh of rapture, the family went off into a gale of merriment, and Mr. Laurence laughed till they thought he'd have an apoplectic fit.

"I don't see anything funny," she said, gravely, when she could be heard. "Nothing could be more natural and proper than for my Professor to open a school, and for me to prefer to reside on my own estate."

"She is putting on airs already," said Laurie, who regarded the idea in the light of a capital joke. "But may I inquire how you intend to support the establishment? If all the pupils are little ragamuffins,[3] I'm afraid your crop won't be profitable, in a worldly sense, Mrs. Bhaer."

"Now don't be a wet-blanket, Teddy. Of course, I shall have rich pupils, also,—perhaps begin with such altogether; then, when I've got a start, I can take in a ragamuffin or two, just for a relish. Rich people's children often need care and comfort, as well as poor. I've seen unfortunate little creatures left to servants, or backward[4] ones pushed forward, when it's real cruelty. Some are naughty through mismanagement or neglect, and some lose their mothers. Besides, the best have to get through the hobbledehoy[5] age, and that's the very time they need most patience and kindness. People laugh at them, and hustle them about, try to keep them out of sight, and expect them to turn, all at once, from pretty children into fine young men. They don't complain much, —plucky little souls,—but they feel it. I've been through something of it, and I know all about it. I've a special interest in such young bears, and like to show them that I see the warm, honest, well-meaning boy-hearts, in spite of the clumsy arms and legs,

LITTLE WOMEN

and the topsy-turvy heads. I've had experience, too, for haven't I brought up one boy to be a pride and honor to his family?"

"I'll testify that you tried to do it," said Laurie, with a grateful look.

"And I've succeeded beyond my hopes; for here you are, a steady, sensible, business man, doing lots of good with your money, and laying up the blessings of the poor, instead of dollars. But you aren't merely a business man,—you love good and beautiful things, enjoy them yourself, and let others go halves, as you always did in the old times. I *am* proud of you, Teddy, for you get better every year, and every one feels it, though you won't let them say so. Yes, and when I have my flock, I'll just point to you, and say, 'There's your model, my lads.'"

Poor Laurie didn't know where to look, for, man though he was, something of the old bashfulness came over him, as this burst of praise made all faces turn approvingly upon him.

"I say, Jo, that's rather too much," he began, just in his old boyish way. "You have all done more for me than I can ever thank you for, except by doing my best not to disappoint you. You have rather cast me off lately, Jo, but I've had the best of help, nevertheless; so, if I've got on at all, you may thank these two for it,"—and he laid one hand gently on his grandfather's white head, the other on Amy's golden one, for the three were never far apart.

"I do think that families are the most beautiful things in all the world!" burst out Jo, who was in an unusually uplifted frame of mind, just then. "When I have one of my own, I hope it will be as happy as the three I know and love the best. If John and my Fritz were only here, it would be quite a little heaven on earth," she added more quietly. And that night, when she went to her room, after a blissful evening of family counsels, hopes and plans, her heart was so full of happiness, that she could only calm it by kneeling beside the empty bed always near her own, and thinking tender thoughts of Beth.

It was a very astonishing year, altogether, for things seemed to happen in an unusually rapid and delightful manner. Almost before she knew where she was, Jo found herself married and settled at Plumfield. Then a family of six or seven boys sprung up like

6. *Brewer's Dictionary of Phrase & Fable* (15th ed.) notes the origin of the phrase: "A Victorian term for the MAN IN THE STREET, more particularly people of no note or people unworthy of notice" (New York: Harper Collins, 1995), p. 1084. The phrase is much older, however, than the nineteenth century. John Owen (1616–1693), the British Nonconformist minister, chaplain to Oliver Cromwell, and Dean of Christ Church at Oxford University, spoke out in 1657 against public talk about the university's decline: "[O]ur critical situation and our common interests were discussed out of journals and newspapers by every Tom, Dick and Harry" (*The Oxford Orations of John Owen,* ed. Peter Toon [Callington, Cornwall: Gospel Communication, 1971], p. 41).

7. Alcott alludes to the cow in the nursery rhyme "This is the House that Jack Built," which was first published by John Newbery in *Nurse Truelove's New-Year's-Gift: or, the Book of Books for Children* (1755): "This is the cow with the crumpled horn, / That tossed the dog, That worried the cat. . . ." See *The Oxford Book of Nursery Rhymes,* ed. Iona and Peter Opie (Oxford University Press, 1951), pp. 229–232.

8. Laurie puns on Professor Bhaer's name, comparing Plumfield to the bear garden, a round structure with a high fence in mid-sixteenth-century London where bear baiting occurred, a blood sport in which the animals were cruelly tormented by dogs or people for entertainment.

mushrooms, and flourished surprisingly. Poor boys, as well as rich,—for Mr. Laurence was continually finding some touching case of destitution, and begging the Bhaers to take pity on the child, and he would gladly pay a trifle for its support. In this way the sly old gentleman got round proud Jo, and furnished her with the style of boy in which she most delighted.

Of course it was up-hill work at first, and Jo made queer mistakes; but the wise Professor steered her safely into calmer waters, and the most rampant ragamuffin was conquered in the end. How Jo did enjoy her "wilderness of boys," and how poor, dear Aunt March would have lamented had she been there to see the sacred precincts of prim, well-ordered Plumfield overrun with Toms, Dicks, and Harrys.[6] There was a sort of poetic justice about it after all,—for the old lady had been the terror of all the boys for miles round; and now the exiles feasted freely on forbidden plums, kicked up the gravel with profane boots unreproved, and played cricket in the big field where the irritable "cow with a crumpled horn"[7] used to invite rash youths to come and be tossed. It became a sort of boys' paradise, and Laurie suggested that it should be called the "Bhaer-garten,"[8] as a compliment to its master, and appropriate to its inhabitants.

It never was a fashionable school, and the Professor did not lay up a fortune, but it *was* just what Jo intended it to be, "a happy, home-like place for boys who needed teaching, care, and kindness." Every room in the big house was soon full, every little plot in the garden soon had its owner, a regular menagerie appeared in barn and shed,—for pet animals were allowed,—and, three times a day, Jo smiled at her Fritz from the head of a long table lined on either side with rows of happy young faces, which all turned to her with affectionate eyes, confiding words, and grateful hearts full of love for "Mother Bhaer." She had boys enough now, and did not tire of them, though they were not angels by any means, and some of them caused both Professor and Professorin much trouble and anxiety. But her faith in the good spot which exists in the heart of the naughtiest, sauciest, most tantalizing little ragamuffin gave her patience, skill, and, in time, success,—for no mortal boy could hold out long with Father Bhaer shining on him as benevolently as the sun, and Mother Bhaer forgiving him seventy times seven.[9] Very precious to Jo was the friendship of the lads, their penitent sniffs and whispers after wrong-doing, their droll or touching little confidences, their pleasant enthusiasms, hopes, and plans; even their misfortunes,—for they only endeared them to her all the more. There were slow boys and bashful boys, feeble boys and riotous boys, boys that lisped and boys that stuttered, one or two lame ones, and a merry little quadroon, who could not be taken in elsewhere, but who was welcome to the "Bhaer-garten," though some people predicted that his admission would ruin the school.[10]

Yes, Jo was a very happy woman there, in spite of hard work, much anxiety, and a perpetual racket. She enjoyed it heartily, and found the applause of her boys more satisfying than any praise of the world,—for now she told no stories except to her flock of enthusiastic believers and admirers. As the years went on, two little lads of her own came to increase her happiness. Rob, named for grandpa, and Teddy,—a happy-go-lucky baby, who seemed to have inherited his papa's sunshiny temper as well as his mother's lively spirit. How they ever grew up alive in that whirlpool of boys, was a mystery to their grandma and aunts; but they flourished like dandelions in spring, and their rough nurses loved and served them well.

There were a great many holidays at Plumfield, and one of the most delightful was the yearly apple-picking,—for then the Marches, Laurences, Brookeses, and Bhaers turned out in full force, and made a day of it. Five years after Jo's wedding one of these fruitful festivals occurred. A mellow October day, when the air was full of an exhilarating freshness which made the spirits rise, and the blood dance healthily in the veins. The old orchard wore its holiday attire; golden-rod and asters fringed the mossy walls; grasshoppers skipped briskly in the sere grass,[11] and crickets chirped like fairy pipers at a feast. Squirrels were busy with their small harvesting, birds twittered their adieux from the alders in the lane, and every tree stood ready to send down its shower of red or yellow apples at the first shake. Everybody was there,—everybody laughed and sang, climbed up and tumbled down; everybody declared that there never had been such a perfect day or

9. LMA alludes to the New Testament: "Then came Peter to him, and said, Lord, how oft shall my brother sin against me, and I forgive him? till seven times? Jesus saith unto him, I say not unto thee, Until seven times: but, Until seventy times seven" (Matthew 18:21–22).

10. A quadroon was a person who was one-fourth black. With no explanation, the quadroon at Plumfield does not reappear in the sequels *Little Men* (1871) and *Jo's Boys* (1886). Surely, LMA was thinking of her father's stand on integration when she included the boy here. After the collapse of the Temple School in June 1838, Bronson Alcott enrolled an African-American student named Susan Robinson in the small school conducted in his house on Beach Street, Boston, in 1839. Parents withdrew their white children after Alcott refused to dismiss the student, leaving the school with only five pupils, three of whom were his daughters, and Alcott deeply in debt. The school closed in June 1839 and effectively ended Bronson's career as an educator. See Odel Shepard, *Pedlar's Progress: The Life of Bronson Alcott* (Boston: Little, Brown, 1937), p. 210.

11. Dried grass.

12. Thomas Tusser (1524–1580) was an English poet and farmer, most known for his works on agriculture, including *Five Hundred Points of Good Husbandry* (1557). Abraham Cowley (1618–1667) was an English poet and essayist, who late in his life dedicated more of his study to botany and experimental science. In 1650, he published the essay "Of Agriculture." Lucius Junius Moderatus Columella (4 A.D.–ca 70 A.D.) served in the Roman army before devoting himself to farming. His twelve-volume *De Re Rustica*, written as a book of advice, made him an influential Roman author on agriculture. Frederick C. Dahlstrand writes: "A major theme of [Bronson] Alcott's later writings was the cultivation of the land. *Tablets* [1868], *Concord Days* [1872], *Table Talk* [1877] and his essays in the *Commonwealth* were filled with quotations from and references to the pastoral poets and essayists: Virgil, Columella, Varro, Cowley. It was the garden and the orchard, he told his readers, that distinguished civilized human beings from the forester and hunter" (*Amos Bronson Alcott: An Intellectual Biography* [East Brunswick, N.J.: Fairleigh Dickinson University Press, 1982], p. 333).

13. Mr. March quotes from Abraham Cowley's 1666 poem "The Garden. To J. Evelyn, Esquire": "He bids th' ill-natur'd Crab produce / The gentle Apple's winey Juice" (stanza 10, lines 200–201).

14. Germanic. The word derives from the Teutons, an ancient Germanic tribe who inhabited Jutland (present-day Denmark) and in 113–101 B.C.E. defeated the Gauls and threatened the Romans.

15. A company of firemen. Hooks were used to pull down burning structures.

16. Pomona was a wood nymph who was believed to protect fruit trees. With her pruning knife, she cultivated them and guarded the gardens and orchards. Her name derives from the Latin *pomum,* meaning fruit.

17. Tears or rips in their clothing.

such a jolly set to enjoy it,—and every one gave themselves up to the simple pleasures of the hour as freely as if there were no such things as care or sorrow in the world.

Mr. March strolled placidly about, quoting Tusser, Cowley, and Columella[12] to Mr. Laurence, while enjoying—

"The gentle apple's winey juice."[13]

The Professor charged up and down the green aisles like a stout Teutonic[14] knight, with a pole for a lance, leading on the boys, who made a hook and ladder company[15] of themselves, and performed wonders in the way of ground and lofty tumbling. Laurie devoted himself to the little ones, rode his small daughter in a bushel basket, took Daisy up among the birds' nests, and kept adventurous Rob from breaking his neck. Mrs. March and Meg sat among the apple piles like a pair of Pomonas,[16] sorting the contributions that kept pouring in; while Amy, with a beautiful motherly expression in her face, sketched the various groups, and watched over one pale lad who sat adoring her with his little crutch beside him.

Jo was in her element that day, and rushed about with her gown pinned up, her hat anywhere but on her head, and her baby tucked under her arm, ready for any lively adventure which might turn up. Little Teddy bore a charmed life, for nothing ever happened to him, and Jo never felt any anxiety when he was whisked up into a tree by one lad, galloped off on the back of another, or supplied with sour russets by his indulgent papa, who labored under the Germanic delusion that babies could digest anything, from pickled cabbage to buttons, nails, and their own small shoes. She knew that little Ted would turn up again in time, safe and rosy, dirty and serene, and she always received him back with a hearty welcome,—for Jo loved her babies tenderly.

At four o'clock a lull took place, and baskets remained empty, while the apple-pickers rested, and compared rents[17] and bruises. Then Jo and Meg, with a detachment of the bigger boys, set forth the supper on the grass,—for an out-of-door tea was always the crowning joy of the day. The land literally flowed with milk and honey on such occasions,—for the lads were not required to sit at table, but allowed to partake of refreshment as they liked,—freedom being the sauce best beloved by the boyish soul. They availed themselves of the rare privilege to the fullest extent, for some tried the pleasing experiment of drinking milk while standing on their heads, others lent a charm to leap-frog by eating pie in the pauses of the game, cookies were sown broadcast[18] over the field, and apple turnovers roosted in the trees like a new style of bird. The little girls had a private tea-party, and Ted roved among the edibles at his own sweet will.

When no one could eat any more, the Professor proposed the first regular toast, which was always drunk at such times,—"Aunt March, God bless her!" A toast heartily given by the good man, who never forgot how much he owed her, and quietly drunk by the boys, who had been taught to keep her memory green.

"Now, grandma's sixtieth birthday! Long life to her, with three times three!"[19]

That was given with a will,[20] as you may well believe; and the cheering once begun, it was hard to stop it. Everybody's health was proposed, from Mr. Laurence, who was considered their special patron, to the astonished guinea-pig, who had strayed from its proper sphere in search of its young master. Demi, as the oldest grandchild, then presented the queen of the day with various gifts, so numerous that they were transported to the festive scene in a wheelbarrow. Funny presents, some of them, but what would have been defects to other eyes were ornaments to grandma's,— for the children's gifts were all their own. Every stitch Daisy's patient little fingers had put into the handkerchiefs she hemmed, was better than embroidery to Mrs. March; Demi's shoe-box was a miracle of mechanical skill, though the cover wouldn't shut; Rob's footstool had a wiggle in its uneven legs, that she declared was very soothing; and no page of the costly book Amy's child gave her, was so fair as that on which appeared, in tipsy capitals, the words,—"To dear Grandma, from her little Beth."

During this ceremony the boys had mysteriously disappeared; and, when Mrs. March had tried to thank her children, and broken down, while Teddy wiped her eyes on his pinafore, the Professor suddenly began to sing. Then, from above him, voice after voice took up the words, and from tree to tree echoed the music

18. Scattered widely.

19. The phrase "three times three" appears often in nineteenth-century toasts. In more modern times, it has transformed into "three cheers for . . ."

20. A delight.

Apple harvest. Frank Merrill, *Little Women: Illustrated* (1880).

21. In "Music as Leitmotif in Louisa May Alcott's *Little Women*" (*Children's Literature* 24 [1996], pp. 74–85), Colleen Reardon notes that this scene parallels the scene at the end of Chapter 1, Part I, where Marmee and the four sisters sing, emphasizing community in the family: "It is not until the last chapter of the book, when the living March sisters, their husbands, and their children gather to celebrate Marmee's sixtieth birthday, that choral singing signals the establishment of a new, larger clan with Jo as its matriarch. Here, Friedrich Bhaer and Jo's boys serenade the extended family with a song for which Jo herself provided the words and Laurie the music" (75).

of the unseen choir, as the boys sung, with all their hearts, the little song Jo had written, Laurie set to music, and the Professor trained his lads to give with the best effect.[21] This was something altogether new, and it proved a grand success, for Mrs. March couldn't get over her surprise, and insisted on shaking hands with every one of the featherless birds, from tall Franz and Emil to the little quadroon, who had the sweetest voice of all.

After this, the boys dispersed for a final lark, leaving Mrs. March and her daughters under the festival tree.

"I don't think I ever ought to call myself 'Unlucky Jo' again, when my greatest wish has been so beautifully gratified," said Mrs. Bhaer, taking Teddy's little fist out of the milk pitcher, in which he was rapturously churning.

"And yet your life is very different from the one you pictured so long ago. Do you remember our castles in the air?" asked Amy, smiling as she watched Laurie and John playing cricket with the boys.

"Dear fellows! It does my heart good to see them forget business, and frolic for a day," answered Jo, who now spoke in a maternal way of all mankind. "Yes, I remember; but the life I wanted then seems selfish, lonely and cold to me now. I haven't given up the hope that I may write a good book yet,[22] but I can wait, and I'm sure it will be all the better for such experiences and illustrations as these;" and Jo pointed from the lively lads in the distance to her father, leaning on the Professor's arm, as they walked to and fro in the sunshine, deep in one of the conversations which both enjoyed so much, and then to her mother, sitting enthroned among her daughters, with their children in her lap and at her feet, as if all found help and happiness in the face which never could grow old to them.

"My castle was the most nearly realized of all. I asked for splendid things, to be sure, but in my heart I knew I should be satisfied, if I had a little home, and John, and some dear children like these. I've got them all, thank God, and am the happiest woman in the world;" and Meg laid her hand on her tall boy's head, with a face full of tender and devout content.

"My castle is very different from what I planned, but I would not alter it, though, like Jo, I don't relinquish all my artistic hopes, or confine myself to helping others fulfil their dreams of beauty. I've begun to model a figure of baby, and Laurie says it is the best thing I've ever done. I think so myself, and mean to do it in marble, so that whatever happens, I may at least keep the image of my little angel."

As Amy spoke, a great tear dropped on the golden hair of the sleeping child in her arms; for her one well-beloved daughter was a frail little creature, and the dread of losing her was the shadow over Amy's sunshine.[23] This cross was doing much for both father and mother, for one love and sorrow bound them closely together. Amy's nature was growing sweeter, deeper and more tender; Laurie was growing more serious, strong and firm, and both

22. LMA, at least in the few years after the publication of *Little Women,* never really understood what a wonderful book she had written in the story of Meg, Jo, Beth, and Amy. On December 2, 1870, Bronson Alcott, while in Ohio giving Conversations, observed: "Write to Louisa, telling her of the enthusiasm with which her book is here received, and the admiration felt for the author— all of which she will be slow to accept, cannot even comprehend" (*Journals of BA* 404). LMA had always envisioned that the great book she might one day write would be a much different kind of book than *Little Women.* As late as April 1887, less than a year before her death, LMA confessed to a reporter: "I yet hope to write a few of the novels which have been simmering in my brain while necessity & unexpected success have confined me to juvenile literature" (*Selected Letters* 307–308). As Sarah Elbert observes in *A Hunger for Home* (Brunswick, NJ: Rutgers University Press, 1987): "Louisa May Alcott found it almost impossible to include *Little Women* in the canon of good literature as she knew it. Contemptuous of an audience that loved 'Mrs. S. L. A. N. G. Northbury,' perfectly cognizant of the commercial basis for the growing genre of juvenile fiction, and brought up on Concord's canon of 'splendid' works, it is no wonder that *Little Women*'s author was skeptical of her own achievements" (p. 214).

23. In actual life, it would be May Alcott who would die at age thirty-nine in Paris in December 1879, ten years after the publication of Part II of *Little Women.* Her daughter, Louisa May Neiriker, nicknamed Lulu, would come to America in September 1880 to be raised by her Aunt Louisa. After LMA's death in 1888, she returned to live with her father, Ernest Neiriker, a businessman. She spent most of her life in Switzerland, dying there in 1975 at the age of ninety-six. Although she returned to Concord only a few times, she remembered the Alcotts well. When writing *The Alcotts: Biography of a Family* (New York: Clarkson N. Potter, 1980), Madelon Bedell visited Lulu in Switzerland: "I thought of Lulu and I remembered her amazing voice and the clue she had given me to the truth behind the Alcott legend. 'The Alcotts were *large,*' she said, raising her head skyward in the intensity of her recollection. She used the word in the French sense, *l-ar-rge;* expansive, wide, heedless of small cautions and little safeties" (p. xv).

24. LMA quotes from the final lines of Henry Wadsworth Long-fellow's three-stanza poem "The Rainy Day," which appeared in *Ballads and Other Poems* (1842).

25. Sweet fern, *Comptonia,* is actually a deciduous shrub, not a fern. When dried, crushed, and burned, its leaves gave off an aromatic odor and were used as a cheap substitute for tobacco.

were learning that beauty, youth, good fortune, even love itself, cannot keep care and pain, loss and sorrow, from the most blest; for—

> "Into each life some rain must fall,
> Some days must be dark, and sad, and dreary."[24]

"She is growing better, I am sure of it, my dear; don't despond, but hope, and keep happy," said Mrs. March, as tender-hearted Daisy stooped from her knee, to lay her rosy cheek against her little cousin's pale one.

"I never ought to, while I have you to cheer me up, Marmee, and Laurie to take more than half of every burden," replied Amy, warmly. "He never lets me see his anxiety, but is so sweet and patient with me, so devoted to Beth, and such a stay and comfort to me always, that I can't love him enough. So, in spite of my one cross, I can say with Meg, 'Thank God, I'm a happy woman.'"

"There's no need for me to say it, for every one can see that I'm far happier than I deserve," added Jo, glancing from her good husband to her chubby children, tumbling on the grass beside her. "Fritz is getting gray and stout, I'm growing as thin as a shadow, and am over thirty;[a] we never shall be rich, and Plumfield may burn up any night, for that incorrigible Tommy Bangs *will* smoke sweet-fern[25] cigars under the bed-clothes, though he's set himself afire three times already. But in spite of these unromantic facts, I have nothing to complain of, and never was so jolly in my life. Excuse the remark, but living among boys, I can't help using their expressions now and then."

"Yes, Jo, I think your harvest will be a good one," began Mrs. March, frightening away a big black cricket, that was staring Teddy out of countenance.

"Not half so good as yours, mother. Here it is, and we never can thank you enough for the patient sowing and reaping you have done," cried Jo, with the loving impetuosity which she never would outgrow.

"I hope there will be more wheat and fewer tares every year," said Amy softly.

"A large sheaf, but I know there's room in your heart for it, Marmee dear," added Meg's tender voice.

LITTLE WOMEN

Touched to the heart, Mrs. March could only stretch out her arms, as if to gather children and grandchildren to herself, and say, with face and voice full of motherly love, gratitude, and humility—

"Oh, my girls, however long you may live, I never can wish you a greater happiness than this!"[26]

26. The saga of the March family continues in two later novels: *Little Men* and *Jo's Boys*. While both books sold well, they never matched the extraordinary success of *Little Women*. In 1871, LMA published *Little Men, or Life at Plumfield with Jo's Boys,* a novel that follows the adventures of Plumfield's students, including Nan, who becomes the school's first female student (excluding Meg's daughter, Daisy Brooke). The work allowed LMA to explore Bronson Alcott's educational ideas and reforms. At the urging of Thomas Niles at Roberts Brothers, LMA returned to the Marches in *Jo's Boys, and How They Turned Out* (1886), a novel that finds the original Plumfield students now young adults. With students of different genders, races, and classes, Plumfield has become the educational dream that Bronson Alcott envisioned in his Temple School. Nan, reminiscent of the young Jo March, grows up to become a physician—and remains unmarried. As *Jo's Boys* (Boston: Roberts Brothers, 1886) concludes, the narrator writes: "It is a strong temptation to the weary historian to close the present tale with an earthquake which should engulf Plumfield and its environs so deeply in the bowels of the earth that no youthful Schliemann could ever find a vestige of it. But as that somewhat melodramatic conclusion might shock my gentle readers, I will refrain . . ." (pp. 364–365). Instead, LMA sums up the lives of the book's characters and ends by observing, "[L]et the music stop, the lights die out, and the curtain fall forever on the March family" (p. 365).

Textual Variants

First Edition	1880–1881 Edition
Part I	
Chapter 1	
a those dreadful children	those tiresome children
b. fly out of the window or box her ears?"	fly out of the window or cry?"
c. in her apron pockets,	in her pockets,
d. by the hero of the piece.	by the villain of the piece.
e. if the audience shout,	if the audience laugh,
f. a stout, motherly lady,	a tall, motherly lady,
g. She wasn't a particularly handsome person, but mothers are always lovely to their children,	She was not elegantly dressed, but a noble-looking woman,
h. prink over your plate,	simper over your plate,
i. "I *am* a selfish pig!	"I *am* a selfish girl!
Chapter 2	
a. do your cakes,	fry your cakes,
b. the funny party.	the queer party.
c. cried the poor woman,	said the poor woman,
d. her own shawl.	her own cloak.
e. study dreadful hard.	study very hard.
f. sniffing at the half dead posy	smelling the half-dead posy
Chapter 3	
a. shows horridly,	shows badly,
b. I'll be as prim as a dish,	I'll be as prim as I can,
c. the proper quirks?	the proper ways?
d. let Meg do the pretty.	let Meg sail about.

First Edition	1880–1881 Edition
e. haven't been about enough	haven't been into company
f. long nose, nice teeth, little hands and feet, tall as I am;	handsome nose; fine teeth; small hands and feet; taller than I am;
g. "Not for two or three years yet;	"Not for a year or two;
h. a queer little French bow.	a gallant little bow.
i. a horrid wrench.	a sad wrench.
j. those silly things.	those silly shoes.
k. it's past ten	It's past nine,
l. Making a dive	Making a dart
m. from my party in my carriage,	from the party in a carriage,

Chapter 4

a. and drive home in a carriage	and drive home
b. who had swarmed	which had scrambled
c. who bounced in,	who stalked in,
d. and bounced out again.	and stalked out again.
e. before three.	before two.
f. the slushy road	the snowy walk
g. nor a minx,	nor a wretch,
h. the girls shout	the girls laugh

Chapter 5

a. clumping through the hall,	tramping through the hall,
b. "You know me,"	"You know us,"
c. you'd shout at them,	you'd laugh at them,
d. the things stood straight	the things made straight
e. Her brown face	Her face

Chapter 6

a. the shiny pedals.	the bright pedals.

Chapter 7

a. twelve mortal times;	six dreadful times;
b. that pathetic little figure	that pathetic figure
c. the reproachful look	the reproachful glance
d. altogether too conceited and important,	be rather conceited,

TEXTUAL VARIANTS

First Edition	1880–1881 Edition

Chapter 8

a. is fussing over her dolls,

b. "Has any one taken my story?"

c. you'll never get your silly old story again,"

is fussing over her piano,	
"Has any one taken my book?"	
you'll never see your silly old book again,"	

Chapter 9

a. a winter of hard work,

b. Sallie offered to do her hair,

c. chattered, prinked, and flew about

d. I shall ask that Laurence,

e. "Just say I looked nice,

a winter of irksome work

Sallie offered to dress her hair

chattered, and flew about

I shall ask young Laurence

"Just say I looked pretty well

Chapter 10

a. Up bounced Snodgrass,

Up rose Snodgrass,

Chapter 11

a. about as festive

b. "Hum!" said Jo;

c. fixing up

d. but be clever

e. in the grave;

f. one or two bits of sewing were necessary, but neglected till the last minute.

g. laughing audibly

about as gay

"No," said Jo;

fitting up

but be civil

in the garden;

one or two necessary bits of sewing neglected till the last minute.

laughing inaudibly

Chapter 12

a. but very good-natured and merry

b. as long as they please,

c. a commanding gesture,

d. Of course the British beat—they always do; and, having taken the pirate captain prisoner,

e. for he is nearly ready, and as soon as he is off I shall turn soldier."

f. so I put the saddle on it,

but very good-natured

as long as he pleases,

a commanding air,

Of course the British beat; they always do," "No, they don't!" cried Jo, aside, "Having taken the pirate captain prisoner,

for he is ready; and soon as he is off, I shall turn soldier, I am needed."

so Jo put the saddle on it,

First Edition	1880–1881 Edition
Chapter 13	
a. a dipper,	a basket,
b. moved a brake before her face,	waved a brake before her face,
c. "Only what your grandpa told mother about him;	"Only what your grandpa told us about him,—
Chapter 14	
a. Jo bent over her work	Jo bent over the leaves
Chapter 15	
a. I could fix things	I could manage things
b. pegging away at mathematics	working away at mathematics
c. the penny postman	the postman
d. one black tail, longer, but not so thick as mine,	one black tail, not so thick as mine,
e. "Be comforted, dear heart! there is always light behind the clouds."	"Be comforted, dear soul! There is always light behind the clouds."
Chapter 16	
a. had come, showing them how rich in sunshine their lives had been. The little books	had come, the little books
b. "Three cheers for dear old father!"	"Three cheers for dear father!"
c. we busily wield a broom	we bravely wield a broom
Chapter 17	
a. "I thought it was most well."	"I thought it was almost well."
b. finish my story."	finish my writing."
c. in her lap	in her arms
d. as clever as possible	as sweet as possible
Chapter 18	
a. she don't love Bethy	she can't love Bethy
Chapter 19	
a. to take a deal of comfort	to take a great deal of comfort

TEXTUAL VARIANTS

First Edition	1880–1881 Edition

Chapter 20

a. petting pa and truckling to you,

b. Oh, deary me! why weren't we all boys?

petting papa and helping you,

Oh, dear me! why weren't we all boys,

Chapter 21

a. I caught her singing that song about 'the silver-voiced brook,' and once she said

b. Laurie folded his hands together, with such an imploring gesture, and rolled up his eyes in such a meekly repentant way

c. pounded again;

d what the row's about."

I caught her singing that song he gave her, and once she said

Laurie folded his hands together with such an imploring gesture

knocked again;

what the fuss's about.

Chapter 22

a. Hannah "felt in her bones that it was going to be an uncommonly plummy day."

b. nor prink at the glass,

Hannah "felt in her bones" that it was going to be an unusually fine day,

nor look in the glass,

Part 2
Chapter 1

a. as earnest and as young at heart as they;

b. "Such as old fellows

c. "Me! don't be alarmed;

as young at heart as they;

"Such as fellows

"Don't be alarmed;

Chapter 2

a. a decided underlip.

b. galloping down the path

a decided chin.

promenading down the path

Chapter 3

a. did *not* suggest Murillo;

b. the fourth time

suggested Murillo;

the second time

Chapter 4

a. a black pinafore

b. to be so horridly misjudged."

a black woollen pinafore

to be so misjudged."

First Edition	1880–1881 Edition
Chapter 5	
a. "Twenty yards of silk	"Twenty-five yards of silk
b. came creeping	came sneaking
Chapter 6	
a. cornered her	compelled her
b. light kids	light gloves
c. with two buttons	with three buttons
d. the Chesters are very elegant people	the Chesters consider themselves very elegant people
e. she can be a pretty horse-breaker,	she can be a horse-breaker,
Chapter 7	
a. flattening her nose	patting her nose
b. little dreaming how soon he would be called upon	little dreaming that he would be called upon
Chapter 8	
a. A sweet white hat and blue feather, a distracting muslin to match,	A white hat and blue feather, a muslin dress to match,
b. with a 'Aye, aye, mum,' the old thing made his horse walk,	with an 'Aye, aye, mum,' the man made his horse walk,
Chapter 9	
a. or a frown ready	or a smile ready
b. seldom seen,	seldom heard
Chapter 10	
a. queer-looking man	gentleman
b. droll nose	good nose
c. was spandy nice,	was very nice,
d. a funny way	a droll way
e. as if I'd covered my name with glory:—	as if I'd covered myself with glory,
f. Germans can do it.	Germans can give it.
g. rigged up	dressed up
Chapter 11	
a. prink at his glass	look in his glass
b. who did go, of course, as rewarded	who did go, as rewarded

First Edition	1880–1881 Edition

Chapter 12

a. Laurie "dug" to some purpose | Laurie studied to some purpose

Chapter 13

a. to my old Jo. | to my Jo.

Chapter 14

a. "Mon Dieu! I have so much to say, and don't know where to begin. | "I have so much to say, I don't know where to begin!
b. Dirty old hole, isn't it?" he added, with a sniff of disgust, | Dirty old hole, is n't it?" he added, with a look of disgust,

Chapter 15

a. as you do | as you are
b. of tulle and flowers | of lace and flowers

Chapter 16

a. if your tongue don't | if your tongue won't
b. cried Amy | said Amy,

Chapter 17

a. loveliest sketches; | finest sketches;
b. helped them," | helped her."

Chapter 19

a. poor little pleasures | small pleasures
b. if I tried it, always 'perwisin' I could," said Jo, | if I tried it ?" said Jo

Chapter 20

a. a stout, bearded gentleman | a tall, bearded gentleman,
b. My brother and sister | My sister and friends
c. a spandy-new suit of black, | a new suit of black.
d. the singer bashfully retired | the singer retired

First Edition	1880–1881 Edition

Chapter 21

a. *ma amie?"*   my darling?

Chapter 23

a. "Ah, my Gott,   "Ach, mein Gott,

b. Within the snoods that bound her hair,   Within lie snoods that bound her hair,

c. don't call yourself old,—I never think of it,—I couldn't help loving you   don't call yourself old,—forty is the prime of life. I couldn't help loving you

Chapter 24

a. and am over thirty;   and am thirty;

Further Reading

The following list of critical and biographical works about Louisa May Alcott, her family, and *Little Women* contains only books. A number of critical articles are cited in the notes and annotations to this volume. Readers are encouraged to examine the excellent bibliography of articles related to *Little Women* found in *"Little Women" and the Feminist Imagination: Criticism, Controversy, Personal Essays,* ed. Beverly Lyon Clark and Janice M. Alberghene (New York: Garland, 1999). Although now over a decade old, it remains one of the most comprehensive bibliographies to date.

Alcott, A. Bronson. *The Journals of Bronson Alcott.* Ed. Odell Shepard. Boston: Little, Brown, 1938.

———. *The Letters of A. Bronson Alcott.* Ed. Richard Herrnstadt. Ames: Iowa State University Press, 1969.

Alcott, Abigail May. *My Heart Is Boundless: Writings of Abigail May Alcott, Louisa's Mother.* Ed. Eve LaPlante. New York: The Free Press, 2012.

Alcott, Louisa May. *The Journals of Louisa May Alcott.* Ed. Joel Myerson and Daniel Shealy, assoc. ed. Madeleine B. Stern. Boston: Little, Brown, 1989; Athens: University of Georgia Press, 1997.

———. *The Selected Letters of Louisa May Alcott.* Ed. Joel Myerson and Daniel Shealy, assoc. ed. Madeleine B. Stern. Boston: Little, Brown, 1987; Athens: University of Georgia Press, 1995.

Alcott, Louisa May, and May Alcott. *Little Women Abroad: The Alcott Sisters' Letters from Europe, 1870–1871.* Ed. Daniel Shealy. Athens: University of Georgia Press, 2008.

Barton, Cynthia H. *Transcendental Wife: The Life of Abigail May Alcott.* Lanham, N.Y.: University Press of America, 1996.

Bedell, Madelon. *The Alcotts: Biography of a Family.* New York: Charles N. Potter, 1980.

Cheever, Susan, *Louisa May Alcott: A Personal Biography.* New York: Simon & Schuster, 2010.

Cheney, Ednah Dow. *Louisa May Alcott: Her Life, Letters and Journals.* Boston: Roberts Brothers, 1889.

Clark, Beverly Lyon, ed. *Louisa May Alcott: The Contemporary Reviews.* Cambridge, England: Cambridge University Press, 2004.

Clark, Beverly Lyon, and Janice M. Alberghene, eds. *"Little Women" and the Feminist Imagination: Criticism, Controversy, Personal Essays.* New York: Garland, 1999.

Dahlstrand, Frederick C. *Amos Bronson Alcott: An Intellectual Biography.* Madison, N.J.: Farleigh Dickinson University Press, 1982.

Delamar, Gloria T. *Louisa May Alcott and "Little Women": Biography, Critique, Publications, Poems, Songs and Contemporary Relevance.* Jefferson, N.C.: McFarland and Company, 1990.

Doyle, Christine. *Louisa May Alcott & Charlotte Brontë: Transatlantic Translations.* Knoxville: University of Tennessee Press, 2000.

Eiselein, Gregory, and Anne K. Phillips, eds. *The Louisa May Alcott Encyclopedia.* Foreword by Madeleine B. Stern. Westport, Conn.: Greenwood Press, 2001.

Elbert, Sarah. *A Hunger for Home: Louisa May Alcott's Place in American Culture.* New Brunswick, N.J.: Rutgers University Press, 1987.

Keyser, Elizabeth Lennox. *"Little Women": A Family Romance.* Twayne's Masterwork Studies, no. 170. New York: Twayne, 1999; rpt. University of Georgia Press, 2000.

———. *Whispers in the Dark: The Fiction of Louisa May Alcott.* Knoxville: University of Tennessee Press, 1993.

LaPlante, Eve. *Marmee amd Louisa: The Untold Story of Louisa May Alcott and Her Mother.* New York: The Free Press, 2012.

MacDonald, Ruth K. *Louisa May Alcott.* Twayne United States Authors Series, no. 457. Boston: Twayne, 1983.

Marsella, Joy A. *The Promise of Destiny: Children and Women in the Short Stories of Louisa May Alcott.* Westport, Conn.: Greenwood Press, 1983.

Matteson, John. *Eden's Outcasts: The Story of Louisa May Alcott and Her Father.* New York: W. W. Norton, 2007.

Meigs, Cornelia. *Invincible Louisa: The Story of the Author of "Little Women."* Boston: Little, Brown, 1933.

Payne, Alma J. *Louisa May Alcott: A Reference Guide.* Boston: G. K. Hall, 1980.

Reisen, Harriet. *Louisa May Alcott: The Woman Behind "Little Women."* New York: Henry Holt, 2009.

Saxton, Martha. *Louisa May: A Modern Biography of Louisa May Alcott.* New York: Avon, 1978.

Shealy, Daniel, ed. *Alcott in Her Own Time: A Biographical Chronicle of Her Life, Drawn from Recollections, Interviews, and Memoirs by Family, Friends, and Associates.* Iowa City: University of Iowa Press, 2005.

Shepard, Odell. *Pedlar's Progress: The Life of Bronson Alcott.* Boston: Little, Brown, 1937.

Stern, Madeleine B. *Louisa May Alcott.* Norman: University of Oklahoma Press, 1950; 1978; revised *Louisa May Alcott: A Biography.* New York: Random House, 1996.

———. *Louisa May Alcott: From Blood & Thunder to Hearth and Home.* Boston: Northeastern University Press, 1999.

———, ed. *Critical Essays on Louisa May Alcott.* Boston: G. K. Hall, 1984.

———, ed. *L. M. Alcott: Signature of Reform.* Boston: Northeastern University Press, 2002.

Strickland, Charles. *Victorian Domesticity: Families in the Art and Life of Louisa May Alcott.* Tuscaloosa: University of Alabama Press, 1983.

Ticknor, Caroline. *May Alcott: A Memoir.* Boston: Little, Brown, 1928.

Trites, Roberta Seelinger. *Twain, Alcott, and the Birth of the Adolescent Reform Novel.* Iowa City: University of Iowa Press, 2007.

FURTHER READING

Illustration Credits

ILLUSTRATION CREDITS

ILLUSTRATION CREDITS

ILLUSTRATION CREDITS

Acknowledgments

In preparing this volume, I have incurred many debts of gratitude. The help and generosity of a number of individuals and institutions have made this edition possible.

John Gregory Kulka, my editor at Harvard University Press, first proposed this edition and offered knowledge, encouragement, and support throughout the project. His intellectual engagement with the edition and his exceptional editorial advice made this a better book. Heather M. Hughes, editorial assistant at the press, provided help all along the way, always answering numerous queries promptly and cheerfully. Her work obtaining a number of images for the art program at a crucial point in the project was invaluable. I am also grateful to Christine Thorsteinsson at Harvard University Press for her exemplary copyediting. Her questions and eye for detail helped improve the work. Annamarie Why made the book a visual delight. Eric Mulder brought out the very best in the illustrations.

I am grateful to the following institutions for permission to publish material from their collections: Boston Public Library (Rare Books and Manuscript Department); Concord Free Public Library (Special Collections); Houghton Library, Harvard University; Fales Library, New York University; Orchard House, home of the Alcotts; and the University of South Carolina (Irvin Department of Rare Books and Special Collections).

Among the number of people who helped me, I especially would like to thank Ronald A. Bosco, Larry Carlson, Paula Connolly, Helen Deese, Christine Doyle, Karen English, Sandy Petrulionis, Nancy Porter, Harriet Reisen, Mary Shelden, Roberta Seelinger Trites, and Mark West. Catherine Rivard generously shared her knowledge of May Alcott. Megan Marshall provided valuable information on the Hawthorne and Peabody families. Joel Myerson, my colleague on a number of Alcott projects, as always provided good counsel in textual editing matters. Scott Villemagne offered expert technical support in screen captures. Research assistants Kathleen Keady and Savannah Kemmerling worked tirelessly in helping to enter the text and in obtaining digital images. I am also grateful to the editors of previous editions of *Little Women*, most notably the work of Anne K. Phillips, Gregory Eiselein, and Elaine Showalter.

Jan Turnquist, executive director of Orchard House, home of the Alcotts, generously allowed me to use archival material from the Louisa May Alcott Memorial Association collection and answered numerous questions about the Alcotts. Maria Powers, executive assistant, helped secure digital images for the volume. As they have always done, everyone at Orchard House cheerfully answered queries and supported my research. For more information about Orchard House and the Alcotts, please visit their website at www.louisamayalcott.org.

Leslie Wilson, head of Special Collections at the Concord Free Public Library, shared her knowledge of Concord history and families. Her assistance, as always, has proved invaluable.

Leslie Morris, curator of modern books and manuscripts at the Houghton Library at Harvard University, provided me access to the Alcott-Pratt collection and generously allowed me to quote from material in the archives. The staff of the Houghton Library, especially Susan Halpert, offered their usual friendly expert help in tracking down material.

This work was supported in part by funds from the Foundation of the University of North Carolina at Charlotte and from the State of North Carolina. I would like to acknowledge the support of the Department of English and Nancy A. Gutierrez, dean of the college of Liberal Arts and Sciences at UNC-Charlotte.

Little Women: An Annotated Edition is dedicated to my children, Luke and Hannah, whose love makes all the work worthwhile. A special thanks goes to them for inviting the March sisters into our home over the last two years.